THE CAVE DREAMERS

JEANNE WILLIAMS

 AVON
PUBLISHERS OF BARD, CAMELOT, DISCUS AND FLARE BOOKS

THE CAVE DREAMERS is an original publication of Avon Books. This work has never before appeared in book form.

AVON BOOKS
A division of
The Hearst Corporation
959 Eighth Avenue
New York, New York 10019

Front and back cover illustrations by Mark English
Book design by Sheldon Winicour

Library of Congress Cataloging in Publication Data
  Williams, Jeanne.
  The cave dreamers.

  1. Basques—Fiction. I. Title.
PS3573.I44933C3   1983   813'.54   82-90554
ISBN 0-380-83501-0

First Avon Printing, June, 1983

This book is for every woman who has
loved a daughter or needed a mother; and
for Gretchen Holbert and Begoña Zubieta Yandiola,
one of Nevada, one of Vizcaya, but both of
the ancient blood.

She came to you, a dream,
in between
asleep and awake.
Dark and archaic,
she laid her red hand
upon you
and showed you
a cave of always summer
where blue
birds ever hover.
You listened,
you questioned
and rose crying, "Mother."
    —Settle Madden
        used by permission

READERS INTERESTED in the Basques will enjoy *A Book of the Basques* by Rodney Gallop (1970) and *Amerikanuak* by William A. Douglass and Jon Bilbao (1975). Both are published by the University of Nevada Press, Reno, Nevada, as are the following: *Basque Nationalism* by Stanley Payne (1975); *The Witches' Advocate* by Gustav Henningsen (1980); *Beltran: Basque Sheepman of the American Southwest* by Beltran Paris as told to William A. Douglass (1979); and *Gold Camp Drifter 1906–1910* by Emmett L. Arnold (1973). I was also helped by *Essays in Honor of Jon Bilbao*, edited by William A. Douglass, Richard W. Etulain, and William H. Jacobsen Jr., published by Desert Research Institute Publications on the Social Sciences, No. 13, Reno, Nevada (1977). Roslyn M. Frank's essay, ''The Religious Role of the Woman in Basque Culture,'' shed light on the priestess-like role of the mistress of a household and the role of a *serora*.

A Shepherd Watches, a Shepherd Sings by Louis Irigaray and Theodore Taylor, Doubleday (1977), is a warm and fascinating biography. Otis E. Young Jr.'s two excellent books helped with the mining sections: *Western Mining* (1970) and *Black Powder and Hand Steel* (1975), both from the University of Oklahoma Press, Norman, Oklahoma. *Death in Murélaga* by William A. Douglass, University of Washington Press, Seattle (1969), depicts persistence and change in funeral customs. Violet Alford's classic *Pyrenean Festivals*, Chatto and Windus, London (1937), traces the old Basque dances in rich detail. Also useful were Ann Rogers' *A Basque Story Cookbook*, Scribner's (1968); Wentworth Webster's *Basque Legends*, Griffith and Farran, London (1877); W. S. Merwin's translation of *Poem of the Cid*, New American Library (1962); Will Durant's *The Age of Faith* (1950) and *The Reformation* (1957), Simon and Schuster; *The Illustrated History of Ships*, edited by E. L. Cornwell, Crescent Books, New York (1979);

and *The Armada* by Garrett Mattingly, Houghton Mifflin (1959).

Of the many unpublished manuscripts I read in the Basque Studies Library, Richard Harris Lane's "The Cultural Ecology of Sheep Nomadism: Northeastern Nevada 1870–1972," Ph.D. dissertation, Yale University, 1974, was particularly relevant and full of interesting anecdotes.

Ever since Roberta Cheney introduced me to May Arkwright Hutton, that amazing woman has intrigued me. Her life is told in *Liberated Woman* by James Montgomery, Gingko House Publishers, Spokane, 1974.

Other useful books were *In Search of Adam* by Herbert Wendt, Houghton-Mifflin, New York (1956); and *Food in History* by Reay Tannahill, Stein and Day, New York (1973).

I am indebted to Linda White and Jill Berner of the Basque Studies Program at the University of Nevada in Reno. From my first phone call, they have been unfailingly helpful and made the time I spent in that magnificent collection the most fruitful and enjoyable library research I have ever done.

Gretchen Holbert, of Elko and Reno, gave me her excellent article, "Elko's Overland Hotel," published in *The Northeastern Nevada Historical Society Quarterly*, No. 3. Winter 1975, which tells about her grandparents, the Sabalas, in *The Scattered Fire*. Gretchen's kind introduction to her kinfolk in Bilbao opened a different world. Victoria Zubieta Escudero walked with me through the Seven Streets and graciously invited me to her beautiful home. She and her sister, Divina Zubieta, located many useful and entrancing books which they insisted on giving me, among them the indispensable *Mitos y Leyendas Del Pais Vasco*, edited by Jose Berruezo, Induban, San Sebastián, Spain, 1973. Begoña Zubieta Yandiola very kindly took me around, translated, and shared her knowledge. Her company made my time in the Basque Country a unique experience, whether we were enjoying *churros* and chocolate or climbing a hill above Gernika with Cathy Clarkson of Boise, Idaho. Dr. Narciso Zubieta took a day from his busy schedule and arranged a journey through three of the Basque provinces, from the seacoast to below Amboto, Mari's mountain. His explanations of everything from ancient tombs to modern shipping were most enlightening and added greatly to a trip that would have been enchanting in any case. I would also like to thank Angel Zelaieta of Bilbao for answering questions and recommending sources. My appreciation goes to Sandra and Colin Creasey for exploring the French Basque country with me; and special thanks to Jane, Duncan, and Ben for patiently enduring our searches for festivals, caves, and museums.

Closer to home, I am grateful to Dr. Richard Etulain of the University of New Mexico for his criticism of the manuscript; to Joseba Zulaika for talking with me about Mari and the Basques; to Myrtle Kraft and the Cochise County Library Staff for helping me get books; to my husband, Bob, and daughter, Kristin, for reading and suggestions; to Settle Madden for permission to use her poem; to my beloved friend and typist of many years, Leila Madeheim, for beginning the ms; and to Beulah Fleming of Santa Fe for finishing it.

Meg Blackstone deserves special thanks for making some inspiring suggestions for the last part of the book. My editor, Page Cuddy, has been a marvel of sensitivity and practical advice. And loving thanks to Claire Smith, who believed in the book from the beginning.

Jeanne Williams, Portal, Arizona, August 1982

CONTENTS

I

The Cave Dreamer

ONLY MEN could paint the magic animals: aurochs with mighty chests and tapering flanks, horses, reindeer, ibexes, musk oxen, stags, wooly rhinoceroses and long-haired mammoths with fierce tusks. There were cave bears, too, the great beasts that provided meat during the cruel winters when they slept back in caverns where they were easily killed. Deep in the caves, working by torches, hunters painted animals on the walls to make sure there would be enough of them to feed and clothe their people.

Ezda, as she gathered big radishes, turnips and onions, tanned hides or made them into garments with her bone needle, thought often of those painted creatures, their spirits dwelling awesomely in the hidden darkness. She wished that she could have made them, not only for insuring plentiful food but for joy in their grace or wonder at their fearsomeness. In the lengthening winters when days were short and dark, Ezda longed most of all to paint birds—lovely, flashing bright ones and those of quieter hue. At such times, she also besought her mother's spirit to hasten the coming of the birds, the time of sun and plenty when no one starved and young were born.

Five summers ago, Bara, the ablest hunter of the band, had won Ezda for his wife by promising to hunt for her aging parents. There were no children even though Bara had given the shaman many good furs for a huge-breasted, massive-hipped stone image. Ezda didn't like the almost-headless figure but Bara insisted that it be placed in a niche by their bed pelts. He wanted sons to help hunt and fight off strangers who might covet their sheltering caves.

At last, Bara brought a new wife home, Ola, plump and always giggling. Hearing them at night as she lay alone, Ezda felt herself thrown away like a rind or a broken tool, though when

3

she looked at her reflection in a pool, she saw that she was prettier and shapelier than her rival. At least Ola was good-natured, even though she preened herself on being Bara's bed-mate. Ezda did most of the food-gathering and collecting of wood. She preferred to do the cooking for she had learned which plants gave good flavors and how to use an animal paunch for stewing tasty meals as a change from spitted meat. Often, amiably enough, she and Ola sewed and chatted together. It was when Ola's belly began to swell with the fruit denied Ezda that the discarded wife began to wail inside herself and think she could not bear her lot.

She began to stay away from the cave as much as she could without slacking her work. Out of her shamed grief, she at last dared to attempt what she had only dreamed. Finding a cave the men had never used, she entered a tunnel that narrowed till she had to crawl. It was dark and she was frightened but she kept going until she could stand up, knowing that she had reached an inner cavern.

Returning next day with a torch, she crept through the entrance corridor and stood in a beautiful chamber with rounded sides where sparkling bits of mineral shone in the soft brilliance.

Ezda caught in a breath of delight.

This was her place!

Here she would make her birds, keep them through the winter, magic their return in the spring. Here she would paint the baby she wanted and could not have, her mother who had died three hard winters ago and whom she still missed. This was a cave for dreams.

She scarcely envied Ola now. Each morning after the work was done, Ezda went to her secret. Gradually, she accumulated charcoal and red, brown, gray and yellow clays, rocks with streaks of green or azure. Mixed with fat, these filled in with color the outlines that she drew with pointed bits of charcoal. She practiced on the rougher walls till she could make birds and figures that were recognizable. Then she picked the largest, smoothest surface and began the work she had thirsted to do.

For many days, by the burning of many pine knots, Ezda moved dreams and wishes from the depths of her heart and mind to the wall of the secret chamber. Birds of summer—

yellow, red, orange, brown and black—and a pair of nesting doves. She painted her mother with a red so dark it was almost brown, and in her arms, placed a baby, rounding his cheeks and hands, raising his chubby fingers to reach for the bird that Ezda loved best of all, one of blue made from ground rock for which she had hunted a long time.

"Give me the baby if you can," she told her mother, feeling that the older woman was really there. "Otherwise, keep him for me till I come."

The joy of her work transformed Ezda's bearing. She no longer made herself apologetically small, walking with shoulders hunched to hide her milkless breasts. She could even smile at Bara for now she had something he had not brought her, something of her own. In her cave were birds of summer, the presence of her mother and a child she would hold someplace, sometime, if not now.

Puzzling, intrigued, Bara said huskily, "There is a shine on you." That night he came to her bed.

Ola's daughter was born in the cold time and was a scrawny little mite but Ezda's son was as lusty as the springtime in which he came. He delighted his parents with his quickness and strength but a sickness took him in his fourth winter, just as he was learning to throw the small spear that Bara had made for him. Ezda had another son and a small daughter by then but she greatly lamented her first-born, child of the secret created from her despair.

They painted his little body with red ochre and buried him with his spear, scraper and toys. Only in the cave could Ezda believe that he wasn't truly gone but merely sleeping in the warm safety of his grandmother's arms.

Drawing strength from her refuge, Ezda did not retreat from daily life. She learned that seeds accidentally dropped on refuse might sprout into plants the next spring and she learned to sow the seeds and care for them. She noticed that frozen meat stayed fresh and that the sun could dry strips of flesh or extra fish taken with the bone gorges that Bara had invented. It was she who had suggested to him that reindeer seemed drawn to places where people urinated and that perhaps a concentration of the fluid would act as a lure for the animals and make them easy to kill. Urine evidently had salt like that brought from the sea and this drew the reindeer.

Ezda lived long after Bara died, consulted by the sick for her brews and ointments, loved by children for her stories. Her teeth were few but still her smile was wise and kind, showing a rare pride that set her apart. Only once was she angry enough with her family to leave them for a time and go they knew not where. It was when they killed the last cave bear.

Her feeling that winters were growing longer than they had been in her youth was confirmed by the deterioration of the huge beasts. The plants they lived on existed for only a few moons of the year. Since bears did not eat meat, they spent most of their lives in the blackness of their caves. Their seldom-used teeth grew inflamed; some developed teeth so large that they could not chew and starved to death. The creatures had the disease that people suffered when they had no fresh greens for too long and seemed crippled with the same miseries that afflicted Ezda in cold, wet weather.

These protracted winters caused hunters to rely heavily on the drowsing bear. Why brave the bitter cold in search of elusive quarry when far back in one's own dwelling a massive feast lay all but helpless?

Ezda had been warning her grandsons and others that no amount of magic pictures would bring back the bears were they slaughtered at such a rate. No one listened. One autumn day, a sore-jawed old bear seeking his rest was driven with shouting and prodding into a narrow recess. To Ezda his roars were as pitiful as his limp.

"We have seen no others this autumn," she told the exultant hunters. "He may be the last of all those who have shared the caves with us and fed us in the snow times."

Again no one listened. A dozen spears drove into the abscessed body. The bear's great arms spread. The sound coming from his splayed jaws was that of a woman weeping. He seemed to melt, shuddering, into a heap of mangy fur but his claws scratched a last mark on the cave wall. From such marks men had learned to paint. Ezda ate none of that bear, who proved indeed to be the last. Leaving the revelers, she went to her cave where she remained until the thought of her grandchildren—especially her favorite, little Ala—drew her back.

It was the cruelest winter that Ezda had seen. Snow was too deep for hunters to venture far. Stored seeds, roots, dried berries, fish and meat were gone. Hunters probed to the back of every cave big enough to admit a bear but found none alive. When a rabbit was snared, hunters and pregnant women got meat. The others sipped broth and gnawed marrow.

By the stick on which she marked moons, Ezda saw that it was a long time till spring. The food she was eating might keep Ala alive. One morning she took this favorite granddaughter to the secret cave, allowing her to marvel at the painting of her ancestress, the baby and the many birds.

"This is a place for you and your daughter," Ezda told the little girl, whose dark eyes shone in the torchlight. "This cave is for women. Wait until one of our blood is ready, then show her. We will leave a power that will last after all the animals men paint are gone from the earth." She smiled at Ala. "In our cave, it is always summer."

Placing her palm in the mixed tallow and red earth she had brought, Ezda printed her hand on the wall. Then the child, standing on tiptoe, made her mark, too. They started home but when they were close enough for Ala to find her way alone, Ezda gave her a hug and told her to run on.

"I'll be with you in a little while," she promised. "But first I must do something."

When Ala was out of sight, the old woman moved down the valley. Near a stand of trees, she left her garments where they would be found and used. Naked, she plunged into the drifted forest.

At first, cold pierced like thorns. She hobbled like the sad old cave bear, sobbing, a tight pain in her chest. As the pain muted, Ezda grew warm and sleepy. It was hard to keep her footing. At last she stumbled and did not get up.

So good to rest. . . .

Something soft and living stirred in her arms. She opened her eyes to see her little son. He smiled and laughed, touching her face as her own mother gathered them close. Then the sun was bright, the leaves were green, and the sky was full of birds.

II

The Sun
Captive

THE CAPTIVE'S HAIR was the color of the sun and his eyes were the gray-blue of the sky before a thunderstorm. His sinewy arms and shoulders were as dark as any Vascones' but where his woolen garment fell away from his chest, Katli had glimpsed skin as white as the milk of her goats. He would go to the sun god in the midsummer rites. Katli thought of him as she sat on a rock watching her sheep and goats and twisting goat hair into boots.

She was a slender, honey-skinned girl with a heavy mass of long black hair, slender hands and feet. Her nose was short and straight and she had a full, rather long mouth. Dark, wide-spaced eyebrows winging upward at the outer edges gave her thin face a wistful, questioning look, puzzled now as she considered her strange feelings toward the Roman.

She should have hated him for her father's death. Romans needed slaves for digging out the iron ore that lay deep in the sides of the mountains. Katli's folk had learned long ago from the Carthaginians how to smelt and work the metal and they had good weapons but they didn't use so much of the ore that anyone had to spend a lot of time in hacking for it.

Although a Roman chief named something that sounded like Pompey had set up headquarters at a place he called Pompaelo and the Vascones called Iruna, "the city," the Romans had decided generations ago that it was impossible to subdue the Vascones and contented themselves with extracting ore from the jagged ranges that gentled into foothills running down to the sea. They didn't often raid the Vascones to take slaves. Such forays usually resulted in numerous dead Romans.

Rising from bushes or springing out of the rocks, the Vascones made swift, ferocious onslaughts with iron lances and swords before they faded into the countryside with wild cries of shrieking laughter that imitated a horse's whinny.

Five years earlier an overwhelming Roman force had taken Katli's father, Irun, and four companions as prisoners. Preferring death to laboring under scourges, the Vascones had mocked their captors, trying to provoke them into slaughter. When the Romans marched them to the mines and penned them up, Irun and his comrades killed each other with stones. Robbed of laborers, the angry Romans had bound the last Vascone to a tree and let him die of thirst.

A war party of Vascones came too late to save him but they did surprise and kill the Romans, bringing Irun's body and those of the other tribesmen back for burial. Wrapped in his finest wool mantle and wearing his massive bronze armbands, Irun was buried with his weapons, Celtic gold collar, food and beer.

Eight lances were thrust into his mound, one for each enemy he had killed. It was the time of the full moon and after the burials, the people of Katli's valley had danced all night to induce the gods to grant happy honor to Irun and his friends in the after-life.

Since then, in summer hut or winter cave, Katli and her mother, Inya, had no man. They made good boots and wove rain-turning mantles of goat hair that they exchanged for meat, and occasionally they traded off one of their handsome earthenware bowls or jars. In this way they were quite self-sufficient.

Most families grew wheat, turnips and the garlic brought into the country by the Romans but Katli and Inya also grew radishes, leeks and carrots, spinach and cabbage. In spring, of course, all the women gathered tender shoots of nettles, thistles and cresses and in the fall they collected wild bounties of chestnuts and great supplies of acorns to be roasted and ground into meal for bread and porridge.

For several summers now, Katli, with other young herders, had taken sheep and goats up into the mountains for pasture, bringing them down again in the autumn. Farther east the sheep walks had made routes that were followed by Hannibal and Hasdrubal when the Carthaginians marched against Rome and after Rome colonized the regions south of the Vascones, the Romans had often built roads along north-south trails marked by the yearly sheep migration.

Katli's people had always lived in these valleys and mountains. She was certain of this for the secret of the Cave of Always Summer had been handed down through countless generations of women. After Katli's first bleeding, the year that Irun had died, Inya had taken her to that inner chamber and repeated the words that her mother had told her were from the forgotten one, she who had painted mother and child among the flying birds: "This is a place forever for the women of our blood. It is a place for dreams, for power that will last after the strongest warriors are dead and forgotten. In our cave, it is always summer."

A hard, clear substance had formed over the paintings, leaving them fresh and bright. Imprints of innumerable red-brown hands, some so small they must have been made by children, others full-sized, were revealed in the dancing torchlight, seeming to motion and caress. Inya's torch played off a fallen shard on which a blue bird spread its wings. At this, Katli had dropped to her knees with a cry of delight and begged to take the bird home but Inya had shaken her head.

"The bird belongs here, my daughter. You can come and see it when you will but you must leave it for those who come after." A frown had drawn her straight black brows together in her strong, severely beautiful face as she struggled to explain. "It is the way that hunters do not kill all the game or we save some of our wheat for seed. We must leave enough for those who will be born."

Katli had accepted her mother's words for she had been in other caverns and seen the great mammoths and cave bears that no longer existed. There were still aurochs such as those painted in running herds on some of the rock ceilings but not as many as were told of in old stories. The stories also told of the Iberians, who had brought sheep and goats across a now-vanished land bridge between Africa and what the Romans called Iberia.

Next had come the fair-haired, blue-eyed Celts, swooping down from the north on swift horses after having sacked Rome and been bought off with gold and land. Occupying Gaul, they spilled over the rugged mountains. While the Celts battled the Iberians, eventually mingling with them, the Vascones had helped themselves to sheep and goats but remained free and wild in their mountain fastnesses—just as they would during the waves of Carthaginian and Roman colonization of the Mediterranean seacoast and the more fertile and accessible lands to the south.

It was an ancient joke among the Vascones, who were not given to ceremony in their wars, that the naked Celtic leaders never joined battle without first bragging loudly of their ancestors and their own fighting prowess. This custom had caused a fair number of golden collars, amulets, horned helmets and jeweled daggers to fall into Vascone hands. Irun had been buried wearing such a gold heirloom collar and the family's greatest treasure was one of those beautiful daggers. Even when they went without meat for months, neither Inya nor Katli would have dreamed of parting with it.

All the invaders had brought useful knowledge, plants or animals, though it was difficult to remember now what had come from whom. Soli, the wrinkled old Star Man who studied the heavens and told the people when it was time to celebrate the solstices and midsummer, had once told Katli that much of his lore had come from Phoenicians, who had learned it from Babylonians and Egyptians. It was even harder for Katli to imagine a time when her people had no sheep or goats. She laughed now to watch the lambs and kids lord it on a crag or hill and butt away any playmates who tried to ascend. Owhoo, wolfish-looking but gentle with Katli and the sheep, pricked his black ears at her laughter.

"It's all right," she told him, stroking his dark muzzle. Watching the herd was a lonely occupation and she often talked to the rangy dog as though he were human. "I was just wondering how lambs can jump and skip and have so much fun before they turn into ewes with runny noses and rams who want to butt everything. But I guess people are the same way. I used to like to play with Uriak but now that he's grown up. . . ."

Her voice trailed off. Even as a boy, Uriak had been savage in defending his place in games, especially Lord of the Hill. Now he was foremost among the young warriors and best of all the hunters. His hazel eyes watched Katli in a way that made her heart pound like that of a rabbit in a snare. She did not love him and could only fear his desire.

She was in no hurry to become a wife and swell with babies. Though most of her friends were now mothers, Katli loved the tranquillity of her mother's home. United by the need to provide for themselves, they were like sisters, Inya the older and wiser. Uriak wasn't the only man to try to draw Katli into the shadows at the festivals, where that was permissible. But until she had seen the captive, she had never dreamed of a man, of being held in his arms, lost in his strength.

Now she did. She watched as Uriak and the others who had captured the Roman hustled him through the village to the cave where he would be kept under guard until his death. Katli had been shouting her joy along with the rest, though she'd had to admire the way in which he walked proudly, meeting the people's hatred with amused insolence.

Those storm-blue eyes had locked with hers. The smile faded from his lips. Something passed between them, a bolt of quivering fire. The shout died on her lips. She was consumed. The force within him had marked her as irrevocably as lightning blasts a young tree. If she never saw him again, that surge of energies coursing between them would bear more consequence than anything that might ever happen to her with any other man.

But he must die. And though he was a Roman, he haunted her waking thoughts and night dreams. As if he could see her, as if she were pleading with him and taunting him, she rose now and tossed off her dark mantle, swaying in her brief underdress of fine reddish wool. She loved to dance and often did to beguile the lonesome vigil over the herd.

Picking up her tambourine, a circle of split willow lashed with sinew securing the skin stretched tautly across one end to reverberate the brass discs fixed loosely in the sides, Katli shook out a rattle of small, distant thunders. Then she moved slowly, sinuously, into a flowing of her whole body as she responded to the music and it to her.

When Katli danced, her most private and deepest feelings found their way into her movements, into the rising and falling of her arms, undulations powered from a center in her belly and loins, wildly spinning steps or languorous gliding.

It was one thing to dance to the moon god in a rapture that filled her bones with glowing heat so that she felt like embodied flame. Men's eyes followed her then, in awe that could not quench desire, but none dared touch her; her dance was to the god. Knowing this, some ancient female power within her exulted in their thwarted passion, was luminously manifest in a way that lingered after the dance was done.

But more, much more, than dancing in rites and festivals, Katli loved to dance alone, to offer herself to wind and sun, blend with *llurun*, the unseen energy pulsing through the earth. Each spring, to honor the Mothers at the season of her birth, she danced for them in the cave but the rest of her solitary dancing was done at times like this, when the spirit filled her and, with no eyes to watch, she could be utterly abandoned.

But on this day the blue of the sky evoked the Roman's eyes. Sun brilliance made her think of his hair. Radiant trembling coursed through her. Her body felt sweetly heavy as though thick, wild honey filled her veins. She cast off her single garment.

Legs arched, she swayed back, bud-like nipples of her firm young breasts shaped to points by the warm breeze, hair falling almost to the ground.

She moved with entreaty and pride and longing. *Why,* she demanded of the forces around her, *have you made my man an enemy, one who must die? Why have you cursed me?*

Though he could not see her entreaty, she danced to him in passion and defiance until she was exhausted but could not stop, tormented by a fever of need.

From these compulsive, futile movements she was suddenly, almost brutally, roused by Uriak's husky voice. "You are surely the sun god's own but he must share you with me."

Katli froze. Instinctively, she started to snatch up her dress but pride checked her. This man had intruded. It was he, not she, who should be abashed. She faced him in haughty nakedness.

Taller than most Vascones, with chestnut hair that hinted at a Celtic forebear, he had massive shoulders and moved with the careless ease of a man whose body was perfectly coordinated with a hunter's brain. A one-shouldered tunic of red wool was clasped around his waist by a splendid belt of gold medallions set with precious stones. As he stared at Katli, something flickered hotly in his hazel eyes and made his rather large mouth seem to turn redder and fleshier. He took a step forward, then halted at the sharpness of Katli's demand.

"Why are you here, Uriak? It is a long time since you have herded sheep."

"The best part of those days was in playing with you," he laughed. Huskiness thickened his voice. "But we're not children, Katli. The elders have chosen me for Horse God." One long stride and his hands were clasping her wrists, loosely yet with a leashed power that she feared to provoke. "You know the Horse chooses his consort. You will be mine."

It was the age-old custom of the people, necessary to please the sun and ensure the fertility of humans, animals and plants. Unless she were prepared to run off and live in solitude, Katli could not refuse. But when Uriak groaned and would have swept her into his arms, she used all her strength to wrench free. Putting a rock between them, she calmed Owhoo, who was growling as he bristled, and halted Uriak with her voice and eyes.

"The Horse Priestess must mate with him in the rites. She will do that for the people and wild things and the grass. But before and after, Uriak, I belong to myself."

His eyes dilated and his nostrils quivered as if scenting an elusive prey. After a duel of gazes, he shrugged and laughed. "Have your way now, girl. After the rites, you will beg to be my woman."

Turning, he sauntered away. Katli rubbed her wrists as though to erase his touch. She dressed quickly, furious in remembering the manner in which he had looked at her. At last he had found a way to have her. So be it. She would be priestess to his Horse, fulfill her obligation, but after the ceremony she would be free again.

There was one thing more, a duty that made her heart race with trepidation and guilty excitement. Long ago the Horse had been sacrificed after his mating. In recent times a captive took his place. As priestess, Katli must take the surrogate his food and drink. Thus she would see the Roman. But if one look from him had already captured her, how could she tend him, knowing that he must die?

Two guards were throwing dice outside the prison cave. They grinned at Katli as she approached with beer, a bowl of grain paste, rabbit stewed with leeks and small cakes of nuts and honey. During her time as priestess, Katli and her mother would eat well, for all the village brought food for the prisoner to the household of the Horse's consort.

Borug, a hulking, black-haired man with missing front teeth, winked slyly. "Be almost worth trading places with the Roman to get visited by you, Katli. Give us a nut cake?"

Foreseeing this, she had brought extra cakes and now she gave one to each man. "You wouldn't want to be in his place on the day of the rites, Borug," she admonished.

"No." He leered at her good-naturedly. "But I do envy our Horse!" He shambled to his feet. "Want me to go in with you?"

"I can manage."

Borug raised a warning finger. "You're a far cry from the scrawny old crone who has been feeding him."

"I'll call if I need you but thank you for your concern." Katli smiled at Borug and his companion, swarthy Erit. Both men had been comrades of her father and were, for all their joking, rather like uncles. As they settled back to their gaming, she took a deep breath and entered the cave.

The entrance allowed a person to stand but it was narrow, barely permitting a shaft of bright light to enter the rock chamber. Katli stood to one side while her eyes adjusted to the darkness. Then the Roman moved into the swath of sun and blinded her again.

Several weeks of confinement had lightened his skin. His hair blazed, thickly curling, seeming to have a life of its own, and his eyes—they took her as deep waters close over a swimmer beyond his depth.

He spoke in a language that she did not understand but the resonance of his deep voice, pitched softly in the cave, echoed within her and she felt as though she were drowning in his sound and gaze and beauty—but even more in that wild magic that flowed between them. He took the food from her, placed it on a rock and drew her into his arms, his body trembling as he sought her lips.

She felt that she must perish from the longing to be a part of him, a part of that strength and gentleness. When he carried her to a pile of furs spread over sweet, dry grass, she bared her body to receive him, welcoming him, the pain and the miracle he brought, the pulsing, quivering sheathing of his hardness within her, fevered striving for oneness . . . and then that engulfing, ever-spiraling marvel of self lost in the elemental and timeless, pulsing far beyond them, yet the home of their truest being.

Finally they rested in one another's arms in the greatest peace that Katli had ever known, greater than the blissful exhaustion after dancing to the gods. His hair had that sun sheen even in this dimness. Raising on one elbow, he stroked her face and throat, adored her breasts and body with his long, sure fingers.

Haltingly, in her own language, he told her then, "You bring me more than food. You bring life."

He knew the Vascone tongue because he had been aide to the governor at Pompaelo and was carrying a dispatch to one of the southern cities when his escort was killed and he was taken. He told her of life in Rome and she thought he teased her when he spoke of water that flowed in pipes, marble statues of gods and men, immense buildings with great pillars and feasts where slaves brought course after course of foods from all parts of the Empire while performers juggled and sang, wrestled and danced.

"You must have known many beautiful women," she whispered with a painful stabbing of jealousy.

He kissed her till she forgot everything and moaned in desire. "None as beautiful as you," he murmured, coming into her swollen with the urgency of his need, slowly and caressingly in order not to hurt her. "In all the Empire, in all of time, there was never anyone so beautiful as you."

"You stay a long time with that fellow," chided Borug a week after her first visit.

"He tells me about Rome. Wonderful stories, Borug." She smiled coaxingly and gave him a honey cake. "How else will I learn such things?"

He snorted. "When you have learned, what good will it do you? If ever you see Rome, my girl, it will be as a slave."

"I do not hope to see it but to hear—oh, I enjoy it, Borug, dear! Don't be an old bear."

His dark eyes studied her keenly. "Be careful, child. The man must die." At the stricken look on her face, he waved her on. "Oh, listen to his tall tales if it pleases you. But remember —he is the god's."

Marcus had already guessed the general nature of his fate from things he had heard and the good treatment he had received. One day when they lay in the patch of sun after sating themselves, he asked her to tell him more.

"No," she whispered.

Even though she knew what must happen, she usually succeeded in living in their joyous present, ignoring the threatening horror in the same way that all people laugh and love and work even though they know they must surely die. She kissed his navel, exploring it with her tongue, marveling at this evidence that once he had been linked to a woman's body, drawing nourishment from her.

"Is your mother alive?" she asked, suddenly feeling a terrible grief for her, for all women who bear sons to lose them to far-off wars and enterprises of man's devising.

"My mother lives," he said. "She is lovely still but never remarried after my father was killed in the fighting against Boudicca, the British soldier-queen. I have two sisters, one still playing with her dolls. The other should be married by now. She always said that she would name her first boy after me."

At least his women would never know exactly how he had died. He gripped her arms as though reading her mind and commanded, "Tell me."

She glanced away from him, looking to the darkest corner of the cave. "There is a dance," she muttered. "Uriak will be the Horse. I must entice him with grain and caresses until at last we mate." As Marcus froze, she touched him anxiously. "We are not ourselves," she insisted. "We are Horse and priestess."

Marcus covered her belly with his hand, rousing the latent heat that leaped at his touch. "It will be this body that he holds, his member that enters you!"

"No!"

His mouth closed over hers. For the first time he took her roughly but the act that was begun in frustrated rage was purified into cleansing flame that melded them together. When, calmed, he lay beside her, he murmured against her breast, "Tell me all of it."

"In the old times the Horse would have been gelded with a flint knife and torn apart by his worshipers, who would then devour him." Katli choked.

She had known, all the time, she had known, but making it into words brought it to terrible, imminent life.

"Now it is different," she said in a failing voice. "The Horse does not die. A captive takes his place."

A sigh went through him. "So that is how it is. I can die. It is worse to think of you with another man."

She shook her head. "That is Horse and priestess. What I cannot bear is your dying."

They held each other. The sacrilegious thought that had been forming at the back of her mind burst through as a shaped determination. "I must get you away from here."

"How? There are always guards."

"I usually give them some of your food. My mother knows herbs for sleeping. With plenty of beer—"

"But if you're caught—"

"All they can do is kill us. I would rather die than live without you." Once again they lost themselves in each other. In this rapture it seemed that they could never die and yet already inhabited eternity.

"It is the Roman," Inya said, tossing back graying hair secured by a woven fillet. "You want to drug the guards."

Katli stared at the ground of the hut. Her mother did not say, "Romans killed your father," but that bitter truth ached between them.

"Mother," she said desperately, "Marcus is my life."

Inya shuddered. "It is so?" she asked raggedly.

Katli nodded, lifting her face imploringly. Inya's stern, still-handsome face gradually softened into a faint smile. She stroked her daughter's hair and held her head against her heart.

"Do you know that this is the first time since you were a baby you asked for anything?" Then she said with abrupt decisiveness, "You shall have your herbs. And I will ask the Mothers to have a care for you."

A captive had never escaped before but Katli did not think that the guards would be punished beyond ridicule. Perhaps they might be ordered to produce an acceptable substitute. Borug was one of the village's best hunters. His skill would be needed during the long winter. Even so, Katli felt a pang of misgiving as she smiled at his jovial greeting and offered him and Erit a bowl of sprouted wheat sweetened with honey and a jug of beer.

Mixed into the wheat was a carefully estimated amount of nightshade, enough to cause drugged sleep but not enough to bring on convulsions and death.

"You're a good lass," Borug said, smacking his lips over the beer and producing his horn spoon. "Enjoy your Roman's stories. He won't be here to tell them much longer." His cheerful callousness hardened her resolve.

"I hope you like the food," she said and went into the cave.

She had thought that Marcus would be too anxious about their escape to want to make love but he drew her down to the furs piled in the sun. There they rediscovered each other's bodies—marveling, caressing and making soft little jokes until the waiting blaze leaped up and consumed them.

Later, holding her, he said, "Whatever happens, Katli, I have loved you and been blessed."

She gripped his arms. "We will get away!"

He smiled. "If the gods—yours and mine—are agreed upon it."

Gods! Whatever blood the sun and moon gods might require, she knew the Mothers in the cave would approve what she was doing. For the first time in her life, she wondered whether the Horse rites had anything to do with the course of the sun and the fertility of nature. Marcus had told her of many other lands where the sun shone on thriving crops and herds without the bribe of human sacrifice. If that were so, how many young men had died cruel deaths for nothing?

Sitting up, she said fiercely, "I would hate a god who took your life. But we must eat now. Mother says it won't take long for the nightshade to work."

When they had eaten, they packed the food they had been saving into an old mantle. Scarcely breathing, Katli went to the entrance and peered out.

Borug and Erit were slumped over their dice, the jug overturned. A narrow defile between the cave and the adjoining cliffs led into the mountains. Marcus would be exposed for the minute that it would take him to reach the rocky passage but if he covered his hair with a mantle and stooped over, a casual observer from the village would probably dismiss him as one of the guards going off to relieve himself.

She motioned to Marcus. He covered his head and picked up the bundle, following her. The shouts of playing children floated up from the village. It was difficult to move at a normal pace through the open space but after what seemed like a perilously long time, they reached the cliffs and started through the pass.

Dizzy with relief, Katli squeezed Marcus' hand. "No one saw us! We can be high in the mountains before the guards wake up."

Half a dozen men rose out of the rocks and bushes, seizing Marcus, wrestling him down as a pack fells a stag. Uriak gripped Katli with hands that bit into her flesh.

"It is well for the priestess to comfort the sun captive for he takes this pleasure to the god. But when you drugged the guards, Katli, that spoke of something more."

There was no use to beg for Marcus' life and she would not ask for her own. "Kill me," she said, "and find another consort."

"No." Uriak's hazel eyes burned over her. "You will expiate this folly by serving. If you will not do it in a fitting manner, I promise you that this captive will scream and plead for death before he finds it. He will be torn to bits in any case but there are slow ways and fast ways of doing that.''

Katli looked at Marcus. Bloodied and marked, he smiled at her.

"I will serve,'' she told Uriak.

The only thing she could do now for her love was give him a quick and easy death.

Now guards stood outside Katli's and Inya's hut. As a bit of refined torture, Uriak ordered that Katli continue to take Marcus his food, ordering also that the guards stay with them all the time. She lived for these moments of beholding him and hearing his voice but every day the rites drew nearer. She thought she must go mad from the horror of it.

She had been too distraught to notice herself but one day Inya frowned. "You have not had your flow this month.''

Katli glanced up. When she realized what it meant, she threw herself into Inya's arms and wept with mingled joy and grief. Her womb that had been all darkness felt lit with warmth and peace. She would have Marcus' child. In that way, he would live.

The next time the guards were chaffing each other, she whispered the news to Marcus. His eyes shone but then he closed his teeth on a groan. "My love, what will they do to you? And to the babe?''

Quickly, she brushed his hand. "Children born to a priestess belong to the god. Do not worry.''

He believed her and though he had always been brave, he now behaved in a way that baffled the guards and tore at Katli. "Aren't you afraid?'' she asked him one day.

"Of course. But I am a soldier. I think past what must happen and dream about our child.'' He paused and though before the guards they seldom touched, their eyes embraced. "How can I tell you, Katli? I have killed so many. It is a great thing to know that with you, I have made a life.''

"I will take good care of him,'' she promised.

"Him?" He laughed tenderly. "What if you have a pretty little girl?"

Katli shook her head. "No. We shall have a boy, with hair and eyes like yours. I shall never have another child or take another husband."

"Katli—"

She said adamantly, "Mother will help me." *And the spirits of the cave.* There was only one more thing she could do for her love. "I can give you enough of the drug I slipped the guards to make the rites seem like a dream. Or even enough to kill you if you would rather go that way."

He hesitated, then made a gesture of refusal. "They would guess who helped me cheat them. If I can see you until the end, the rest won't matter."

It would matter to her—all the rest of her life—but she must not make it harder for him. Still, it was he, not she, who spoke soft, comforting nonsense till the guards called a rough jest and it was time to leave.

Days wore on, the time between her visits to him seemingly endless, the moments with him pitifully brief. She could feel no evidence of the tiny life within her but knowledge that it was there glowed like a small, steady lamp in the blackness of her desolation.

Soli came to her one morning as she sat grinding grain for a paste to take to Marcus. The wrinkled old man wheezed with effort as he collapsed on a convenient log at the edge of the thatched shelter. He accepted the bowl of sprouted grain, honey and milk that Inya fetched, thanked her and then solemnly announced that he must speak privately with the Horse Priestess.

Inya disappeared with the water jars. The guards withdrew to a discreet distance. Soli gummed his food ruminatively, patted his belly and regarded Katli with shrewd, rheumy old eyes.

"Priestess, the day of the rites is near."

He knew, the whole village knew, that she had tried to escape with Marcus. Bent over the grinding stone, she said curtly, "Have you come to torment me with that, Star Man?"

He sighed and dropped formal address. "Katli, since my father taught me sky lore, I have set the times of five times the

number of my fingers. I have seen that many young men die.''
His voice sank to a whisper. ''And do you know something?
There have been good years and bad years. The captive's death
has nothing to do with it.''

Her heart stopped, then leaped. She dropped the pestle.
''Do you mean—''

He raised his finger to his lips. ''I do not think that we can
save your Roman. I do think, if you will it, that we can stop these
murders.''

''If he must die, what do I care about others?'' she cried.

''You care.''

Frustrated outrage struggled with new feelings that Marcus
had awakened in her—although she had felt presentiments of
them in the cave and when she danced. Deep inside she held a
compassion and sympathy for people, a concern that extended
beyond those whom she knew.

She sighed heavily. ''What must we do?''

Early on the morning of the rites, Uriak with his followers
came to her hut, where her entourage had gathered. Everyone
wore their ornaments and finest garments except for Katli and
Uriak. She wore a plain white robe girdled with a belt of woven
grain. A sort of scaffolding was fastened about Uriak's waist and
shoulders; it towered above him, holding upright the stuffed
head of a white horse. Its hide was tied around Uriak's waist so
that the tail moved jauntily when he walked.

The Horse and his companions made neighing sounds until
Katli emerged. Then he began to run ceremonially through the
village and the fields. Katli followed with her basket of wheat
cakes, leading the chant of women who danced behind and before her.

''Horse! Horse! Taste the grain of your mother. Do not run
away but come and dance with us!''

The chase lasted throughout the morning, the Horse sometimes lagging, trotting close to the priestess and snatching a cake
from her fingers but eluding her reach, while the celebrants
yelled lusty encouragement or ribald advice.

''Catch him by that big thing poking out of his kilt, priestess! That'll hold him!''

"Show him something besides a cake and he'll tame soon enough!"

"Don't wear yourself out, Horse. Save plenty of strength for the best part!"

Katli had seen the ceremony every year since she could remember, yet this one was so different. Marcus was still held in the prison cave and would be brought down later for the culmination of the rites. She glanced frequently toward the dazzling sun. Though Soli had warned her that the darkening he predicted would probably not come in time to save her lover, she could not help but hope for this.

"It may have been one of these coverings of the sun that led people to sacrifice," Soli had told her when he explained his plan. "Perhaps we can use this one, if my calculations are right, to end the slaughter."

"Why didn't you try long ago?" she asked bitterly.

"The sun never hid on the day of the rites. Anyway, you are the first priestess whom I could hope might be of help to me."

"Because I love the victim?"

His sad old eyes delved into her. "No. Because there is a power higher than the sun god's and you obey it."

As the sun rose higher and the climax neared, she prayed that Marcus might be spared.

The sun approached its zenith. Katli, with dragging feet, was swept along by her women to the threshing floor at the edge of the village, a large, slightly sunken rectangle paved with flat stones. At threshing time fires were built to heat the stones and then raked off. After that ears of grain were toasted until the outer chaff was brittle and could be separated from the grain by driving sheep and goats around the floor. But it was a long time till harvest. Today the stone platform had another use.

A couch of young wheat and flowers was heaped in the center. Marcus was at one end, surrounded by guards. He smiled at Katli. She tried to answer his silent greeting but her lips were painfully stiff. She went to him, though, and gave him a wheat cake, brushing his hand with hers to pass along some stems of nightshade.

"Take it," she whispered. "Oh, my love, take it."

Uriak, no longer elusive, sprang between them and spun her away. He scattered her basket of wheat cakes to the crowd, stripped off her robe so that she stood naked in the full blaze of the nooning sun. Then, still wearing the grotesque horse's head, he bore her down to the green couch.

She prayed that Marcus would not look. The villagers were silent now, their boisterousness hushed by the solemnity of the fateful mating. She was tight and unyielding to Uriak, who behaved with restraint until he gasped at the discovery that she was no longer virgin.

"Whore!" he breathed, piercing her.

Savagely, he wreaked his fury. When he rolled off her, he lay panting for a few minutes before he gathered strength to leap high in triumph, neigh and run into the fields.

Katli fumbled into her robe though the wheaten girdle was torn to uselessness. The sun throbbed down its golden rays until they seemed to enter her brain and pulse in liquid fire through her skull. The time had come. She could not meet it. She would die with Marcus. That was easy, all she wanted to do.

"Priestess!" Soli called from the edge of the threshing floor. He stepped forward and handed her the flint knife, ancient and stained with immemorial blood.

She took the weapon and moved toward Marcus, stopped, unable to go farther. But he came toward her. Bowing his bright head, he kissed her hands and knelt at her feet. His eyes were clear and very blue. He had not used the nightshade.

How could she watch those eyes? Yet how could she not? "I love you," she murmured and plunged the knife into his throat and across it.

The knife was for drawing first blood and later for gelding, not for death. The worshipers stared in amazement as the captive's blood spilled out and he fell across Katli's feet. Then a murmur of shock burst into frightened rage.

"The god is cheated!"

"That is not the proper death!"

"Sacrilege!"

"Kill the false priestess!"

In her numbed grief, Katli scarcely heard and had no will to run, not even for the sake of Marcus' child. But Soli stepped in front of her, holding up his thin old arms to still the crowd.

"The sun is not pleased with death," he cried, pointing to the heavens. "Watch! He will veil himself from this blood."

As he spoke, the sun was shadowed and though no one could look straight at it, within a few minutes, part of the fiery orb was obscured. There were cries of fear. Some fell to the ground. Others fled.

"The god is angry because of the priestess!" someone shouted. "Let's tear her apart as we should have torn the captive!" Those who were still on their feet surged forward.

Katli faced them before she dropped the flint knife to the stones and smashed it with the biggest rock she could find in her haste.

"The god has entered me," she called aloud, spreading her hands. "He commands that you celebrate as you have always done but without death. As a sign that he loves life and not blood, he will give me a child."

The villagers shifted uneasily. "She speaks the truth," Soli told them. "Look, the sun shines for her!"

Its dimming over, it blazed down in renewed splendor. Awed, the people drew back. Katli fell to her knees beside Marcus. If the sun had shrouded itself only a few moments sooner! If—

Inya's arms closed around her. Soli took off his best mantle and gently wrapped Marcus in it. "Let us bury him," he said. "Perhaps his spirit will enter your babe."

Uriak, when Katli would not be his woman, muttered throughout the valley that she swelled with a Roman's child, not that of a god's, but no one heeded. A priestess' child *was* the god's, whatever its mortal ancestry.

No more captives would die on the threshing floor and when Katli's son was born on a fine spring morning, his hair was a blaze of gold and his eyes were the color of the blue bird in the Cave of Always Summer.

III

The Cold Stone House

I

IN PRINCESS ZAHRA'S audience chamber, rose marble pillars supported ceilings of gold-inlaid cedarwood carved with intricate designs. The walls were of marble and gold and the doors were beautiful with ivory and glittering jewels. The princess sat gracefully on a low silk couch, surrounded by her musicians, poets, philosophers and guests. Scattered throughout the great room were groups of Cordova's most accomplished and powerful nobility—but these were mere constellations, with Zahra, the moon.

Will her beauty never fade? Lael wondered with despairing envy. Her heart contracted as the princess moved to display her slenderly opulent body that was enhanced rather than concealed by gossamer silks. Magnificent dark eyes laughed at a world Zahra had enjoyed as fully and sensuously as she now savored nougat from a golden tray of sweets on the ebony table before her while a serving maid replenished wine goblets.

Wine was forbidden by the Koran but such dour fundamentalism was still practiced only by the orthodox and fanatics such as the Almoravid king, Yusuf. He had crossed from Morocco seven years ago in 1084 to help the Spanish Moslem rulers defeat Alfonso IV of Castile, who had taken Moorish Toledo and was intent on reconquering lands the Moslems had ruled since the Berber Tariq gave his name to the rock near the place where his men had landed in 712—Gebel-al-Tariq, Gibralter.

Yusuf had returned to Africa but he had come back last year at the urging of the Moslem princes. They had hoped that he would crush Alfonso but though Yusuf had battled the Christians, his crusading faith had been affronted by the luxury and urbane religious tolerance of city states such as Seville, Granada and Cordova. Yusuf decided to make himself ruler of Moslem Spain. In March, 1091, he took Granada without opposition, sent its king to Africa in chains and delighted the people by revoking all taxes not authorized by the Koran. Now the ascetic and fervent warrior was expected to besiege Cordova and Seville.

This threat preoccupied Lael's father, Sayid ibn Omar, who stood with other older men in one corner of the hall. Even in this relaxed atmosphere, it would not have been seemly for Lael to join him. Besides, she had no wish to hear for the dozenth time of how Alfonso's Castilians had been terrified by the thunder of Yusuf's African drummers near Badajoz in 1085, the first time that drums had resounded in Europe, and how they had been decimated by disciplined, parallel lines of Turkish archers who shot flights of arrows on command. Still less did she care to hear how Yusuf had ordered the Christian dead beheaded and their heads heaped into great piles. From these grisly hillocks, muezzins the next morning had called the Faithful to prayer.

But it was quite unbearable to sit on a cushion near the princess, lute silent in her hands, and watch Zahra lazily entice Arslan, flattering the handsome, tawny-haired youth with questions pitched in a caressingly intimate voice and a provocative invitation in her intelligent, languorous eyes that few men had resisted, including Lael's father.

That passion had quickly mellowed to friendship; Omar was not one to share favors. But Zahra's wit, learning and brilliant poetic gifts still drew him often to her palace. Lael had been accompanying him for years, petted by Zahra and enjoying the lively gatherings, for Omar's palace, although austerely grand, was quiet.

She hadn't enjoyed this afternoon, though, as she watched Zahra spin the web in which Arslan seemed eager to be snared. At eighteen, he was two years older than Lael. She had worshiped him ever since their fathers, sworn companions, had taken them riding and hawking as children and trained them in archery and fencing.

A strange upbringing for a girl, be she Christian or Moslem, but Omar had no sons. When he brought Lael's mother, Lucira, home from a campaign in the north, he married his beautiful captive and dismissed his harem, dowering the women so that they could find new husbands or live independently. Lucira had died when Lael was too young to remember but her father had always been her companion, finding more comfort in rearing her than in filling his harem. He had told her that she looked like her mother, with changeable gray-green eyes, dark auburn hair and creamy skin.

Omar had raised Lael as a Christian, honoring Lucira's dying wish, but in reality her religion was permeated with Islamic beliefs and the teachings that she had absorbed from Abram, her wise old Jewish tutor, who had explored with her not only the Scriptures but Plato, Aristotle and Marcus Aurelius as well as the Talmud and the Koran.

"There is one God, father of all, and how our cruelties must grieve Him," Abram often said, to which Beltrana, Lael's Bascoli nurse, crossed herself and darkly muttered, "Heretic!"

Beltrana, as swarthy as a Moor, was the only free person in the palace who could not read and she clung to her ignorance proudly as though it were a shield against the heathens among whom she was compelled to live for Lael's sake.

Lael had been brought up then by a cultured Jew, an earthy, superstitious woman from a people even now not wholly converted to Christianity and a Moslem warrior-poet-lord who could improvise verses as easily as he rode or cast a spear. And whether hawking or bending an arched horn bow, it was Arslan whom she had tried to imitate, Arslan whose approval she had craved even beyond her father's.

She could not say when this childish adoration had changed. Three years ago, when his arrows outstripped hers so far that she had wept in chagrin and he had comforted her with gentle teasing? Two years ago, when she'd had a feverish illness and he came every day to read to her in his deepening voice that soothed her restlessness? Last summer, when he had caught her bolting horse and for a moment his body and arms had brushed against her?

However it had happened, she had known for months that he was the only man she would ever love, the only man for whom she would leave her father's palace and company. Reluctant to leave Omar, she had been content to wait—until today, when she had watched in mute, sick indignation as Zahra openly singled out Arslan and found excuses to touch him.

She—she's old enough to be his mother! Lael thought viciously, clenching her teeth. *No, his grandmother!*

Nibbling a pear-shaped marzipan, Zahra laid a graceful hand on the young man's broad shoulder. "You have inspired me to compose my first poem in over a year. Perhaps you would give me your opinion?"

Blushing, Arslan fidgeted. "Princess, I am no poet."

"But you are a man. It is that judgment I desire." Tilting her head at him, she made her voice playfully, yet boldly, caressing:

> "I will make love with you
> Only if you hold me so my earrings
> Tangle in the jewelry on my ankles."

Arslan blushed even more furiously. Titillated shock showed on some faces. There was a ripple of excited laughter. Each man was surely picturing Zahra in that position, which Lael could imagine all too clearly. Her father's house had no harem but there were plenty of servants who had not adopted Omar's asceticism, and Moorish Spain had inherited all the sensuous pleasures and perversions developed in thousands of harems.

Lael hadn't realized that she was staring furiously at the princess till Zahra lifted an eyebrow and smiled. "You do not like my verse, little one? Perhaps you will recite one of your own?"

"I have composed nothing worthy to be heard here, princess, but I will give you a poem of Rabi'a:

> 'O my Lord, if I worship you from fear of Hell,
> Burn me in Hell.
> If I worship you from hope of Paradise,
> exclude me from that place.
> But if I worship you for your own sake
> do not withhold from me your eternal beauty.' "

Rabi'a, dead now almost three hundred years, had lived celibate in the desert to better love her god. The pure passion of that sacred love cut like a flaming blade through the perfumed hedonism of Zahra's circle. Now the princess gave Lael a curious, measuring glance before she laughed merrily, spreading her jeweled hands in appeal.

"My friends, when women saints are quoted in this hall, what can one do? Lael, my treasure, you spoke with such fire that I fear you plan to emulate the mystic!"

"No," said Lael, rising and putting down the lute. Her barbarism would be whispered about, cited as an example of what happened when a girl was raised as a boy. Zahra's look indicated that a favored kitten had delivered a naughty scratch. Lael felt a pang. She had admired Zahra with small-child wholeheartedness but she could no longer be treated as a pet. She would not come here again.

Bowing, she said, "Thank you for your graciousness, princess. I must leave now, to exercise my horse."

"Listen to the child!" Zahra entreated her guests. "Mystics and horses! Allah be merciful!"

Face burning, Lael retreated. Her father was still in earnest discussion with other powerful men of the city. She often rode, accompanied by her groom, Hassan, and Omar wouldn't mind if she did so now. She simply had to leave this place where the very air was redolent of Zahra's perfume.

Beneath her silken over-robe Lael wore trousers for riding. As she left the hall, she gathered her voluminous white wool mantle about her, covering her hair. Even Zahra's stables were of marble, and fountains splashed melodiously in the courtyard where Hassan waited, idling with the other grooms. When he saw Lael, the middle-aged, nut-brown Moor sprang up and hurried forward, bowing profoundly.

"Let us go, Hassan. I wish to ride beyond the city."

"But, young mistress, your noble father—"

"My father is engaged." Hassan, as much as Omar, had taught her to ride and was more friend than servant. She abandoned her role of mistress. "Please, Hassan! I have to get away for a little while."

He eyed her keenly. His muscular hand moved to the curved dagger at his waist. "Has anyone—"

She smiled at his unquestioning devotion, knowing that had she said, "The Princess Zahra mocked me," he would have tried to avenge her, even at risk to his life. "Dear Hassan, it's not anyone who's my trouble but myself. Nothing that a long gallop on Al Zirr won't cure."

He shrugged his brawny shoulders and called to the boys lounging by the stable. In a few minutes they led out Al Zirr, the pure white of star ash, who pushed his velvet muzzle against Lael and sighed with bliss as she rubbed the spot between his ears. Sprung from a proud, sensitively intelligent line of horses that had shared tents with their Bedouin masters, Al Zirr had been chosen by Lael when he was a wobbly little colt. Now in his six-year-old prime, he had never felt spur or whip. A word or faint knee-pressure was all it took to guide him. Often Lael would have sworn that he obeyed her telepathically, though Hassan said that she must have given an unconscious cue. Hassan gave her a hand up into the light, padded saddle.

The silver stirrups were short so that her knees were bent and she seemed to be almost kneeling. This long-seated Moorish style of riding lent itself to racing, jumping and the lightning-fast cavalry charges that left Christian knights agape, if not dead, as they tried, legs dangling, to maneuver their chargers from heavy, high-cantled war saddles.

Hassan's mount was a Barb, longer coupled than Al Zirr, with a low-set tail growing from his slanting rump. The Berber conquerors had ridden such horses. Although they had great stamina, they lacked the aristocratic grace of the Arab and Hassan's Ma'ala seemed to know this, keeping a humble distance from Al Zirr's high-carried tail as they rode out of Zahra's richly carved gates.

Her palace was one of many, including Omar's, that stretched for miles along the banks of the Guadalquivir. Romans had bridged the river centuries before but Arab engineers had spanned it with a great stone bridge of seventeen arches. Lael rode over it, passing dark Moors and Berbers, fairer-skinned Arabs, Jews, and Andalusians who showed traces of the many bloods that had mingled in Cordova: Greek, Carthaginian, Roman, Visigoth and Celtiberian. There were also students and scholars from all of Europe and the Mediterranean regions for

Cordova was the most brilliant center of learning in the world, as well as the medical hub. Those who could afford it flocked there for surgery not yet dreamed of in other countries and the city's poor had unequaled medical care.

In addition to stations where minor ills could be treated, Cordova had close to fifty hospitals that were open to all, slave or free. Lepers and the insane had separate institutions. General hospitals housed divisions for surgery, orthopedics, internal medicine and eye diseases. Arab surgeons were even able to remove the cataracts that blinded the aging. Cleanliness and frequent baths were stressed, for Abd-er-Rahman I who in 756 declared Islamic Spain a Caliphate, independent of Damascus and ruled it as Caliph of Cordova, early built an aqueduct that brought quantities of fresh water for homes, gardens, myriad fountains and its many public baths.

Apart from culture and science, Cordova was renowned for its leather, ivory-carvers and shields. It was said that every family could afford a donkey and Lael automatically concluded that most foot travelers were beggars or foreign students.

But even beggars were lucky to live in Cordova! What city could rival it? Four hundred thousand books were in its library. There were two hundred thousand houses and and sixty thousand palaces. She was now passing the Great Mosque, most splendid of Cordova's hundreds, founded by the mighty Abd-er-Rahman I on the site of a Christian church that had earlier been a temple to the Roman god Janus. Its brick and stone battlements were crowned with irregular towers and the slender, lofty minaret rose high against the deep blue sky.

Many caliphs had added to or beautified the fabulous building, usually acknowledged to be the most splendid mosque in the world. Even had Lael been Moslem, as a woman she would not have been allowed inside. But she had heard of the fountains in the Court of Oranges, each hewn from a block of marble so immense that seventy oxen had strained to pull it from the quarry to the grounds; of vistas of arches springing from the gilded capitals of columns—over twelve hundred of them—in a dazzling mixture of purple-red porphyry, snowy alabaster and many hues of jasper and marble; mosaics sparkling with silver and gold on walls and floors; the gold-walled *mihrab*, the recess showing the *gibla*, or direction, of Mecca, ornamented with mosaics and gold inscriptions on a field of crimson and blue behind the pulpit. This gem-inlaid pulpit, or *minhar*, was made of small panels of ebony, citron, aloe, sandalwood and ivory. On it, in a jeweled box, lay a Koran copied by the Caliph Othman and stained with his dying blood.

It was incomparable, of course, but there were nearly twenty synagogues in Cordova, two renowned for their beauty, and as many Christian churches as well as a number of monasteries. Lael was proud of her city, proud of her mingled heritage, for Abram had taught her from the best of both traditions, leavening all with the sad-humorous wisdom of a Jew who, while he attended the synagogue out of loyalty to his people, was in his heart a Sufi, a mystic believing in an ineffable god who had no boundaries, a god who was perfect, all-encompassing love.

But Lael, though she thrilled to the rapture of Rabi'a and other mystics, had no comprehension of a love that could exclude the yearning she felt for Arslan. If it was wrong to love a fellow mortal so, she was guilty and could not even regret it. But as she left the city gates behind her, riding past fields made fertile by Moorish irrigation techniques, bitter, angry tears stung her eyes and she bent closer to Al Zirr's flowing mane, urging him into the easy, swinging lope that effortlessly devoured the road stretching across the plains to the mountains.

She had often hawked and hunted in the sierra with her father but Yusuf's victories had unsettled al-Andalus, or Andalusia, and these days no one ventured far beyond the city gates—which was what Hassan, she was sure, was about to tell her for she could hear hoofbeats behind, the heavy breathing of a striving horse.

It was wrong of her to endanger Hassan, perhaps call down her father's wrath upon him. She settled back, gave the sapphire-studded reins the slightest pressure along with a shift of her weight, slowing the stallion into a caracol that was checked by the horseman who had drawn abreast and now seized Al Zirr's reins.

Arslan's furious gray eyes burned into Lael's. "Little fool! What if I were a robber or a spy of Yusuf's or the infidel Alfonso's?"

"I would send you to Princess Zahra, who would appreciate the novelty!" Lael flamed.

His smooth, sun-browned skin reddened as his frown deepened. Hassan had stopped a discreet distance away, no doubt glad that she was being scolded.

"Is it your hope to make yourself as scandalous as the princess?" Arslan demanded. "It may have been all right for you to be her pet when you were small but your father should long since have stopped your visits!"

"What about yours?" she demanded fiercely. "Do you think you can satisfy a woman who has exhausted all the men of Cordova? You—you're just a boy!"

Dumfounded, Arslan stared at her in outrage before he burst out laughing. "If I'm a boy, you're a child."

"I'm not!" she stormed. "You great stupid! I—I know more about some things than you ever will."

His hold on the reins had relaxed. She tore them from his hands, crouched forward and gave Al Zirr his head. The stallion sprang forward like a loosed arrow. She lay close to his neck and breathed execrations at Arslan in Arabic and Spanish. He would never catch her. No horse could match Al Zirr when he carried only her light weight.

A coney sprang in front of them. Al Zirr shied. Lael shot over his head and instinctively rolled out of the path of his oncoming hoofs. The impact jarred every bone and vertebra, knocking her breathless.

Stunned, she lay in a heap at the side of the road. Then Arslan was lifting her, calling her name, shaking her so that her head lolled. "Lael! Are you all right? For the love of Allah, say something!"

"You—you're bruising my arms!" she spluttered. "And my head aches enough without your jerking it!"

He gave a final, exasperated shake before he caught her close. His heart pounded beneath her cheek. Dizzy with joy at the unimagined heaven of being in his arms, drawing in the faint smell of the rose water in which he had bathed and the stronger clean male scent, she had stopped struggling when his grim voice pierced through her happiness.

"If you were my wife, I'd have the eunuchs beat you—

through velvet so they wouldn't break your skin but soundly enough to teach you decent behavior!''

"Then isn't it lucky I'm not your wife?'' she flashed, arching away furiously, hands planted on his chest. "For if you had me beaten, I would surely kill you!''

For a moment they glared at each other. Hassan, who had caught Al Zirr, waited down the road—leaving her to be bullied, Lael thought indignantly. Suddenly Arslan muttered something under his breath, crushed her against him and—totally against Christian and Moslem teachings—found her lips.

After one convulsive struggle, she lay against him, overcome by the tumultuous sweet weakness spreading through her as much as by his strength. She offered herself like wine to be tasted, yielded utterly to his mouth, which lost its punishing hardness and kissed her eyes and hair before straying back to her lips like a deer coming to feed delicately on tender herbs.

She moaned and drew him close.

Hassan coughed. Rousing, Arslan raised his head. "You are beautiful, my heart's delight, but a fool for all your studies.''

"What do you mean?''

His voice filled with joyful wonder, rich masculinity in its first passion. "For two years I have waited for you to grow up. My father has addressed your father, who said you were too young.'' He laughed proudly, softly. "He cannot say that now. My father and I will speak with him this very night.''

It was too marvelous, too unexpected. Lael's head whirled. She groped for reality and studied him, trying to read his soul. Was it possible that he loved her as she loved him?

"But the princess?'' She lifted her chin. "I will not share you with her—or with any woman, Arslan. Don't ask for me unless you accept that.''

He drew her to her feet and smiled chidingly at her. "If one can drink from his own pure fountain, who will kneel at a common trough? Give me all your love, sweet, fierce Lael, and I'll have no strength for others.''

Sweeping her into his arms, he held her for a moment before he lifted her into the saddle. They rode back to the city with decorum but Lael's heart felt as though it must burst with happiness. In all the world there was no man so handsome and strong

as her love, no city so great as Cordova and no woman so
blessed.

Arslan's father and uncles would visit Omar as soon as possible to arrange the marriage. "It would please my family if you
converted to Islam," the young man ventured as they exchanged a few parting words in the courtyard.

Lael shook her head. "I was raised as a Christian by a
swearing of my father to my mother. To change my faith would
shame them both."

He did not argue though he must have known that her personal religion was broad, drawn from all that Abram had taught
her. And he knew that she and Beltrana heard Mass dutifully in
her mother's graceful little chapel, the service performed by the
same priest who had ministered to Lucira.

Hassan had led Al Zirr into the stables. No one was in sight
as Arslan pressed Lael's hands to his face. His warm breath
against her palms sent an exquisite tremor through her.

"Be Christian if you must but don't, I beg you, ride beyond
the gates in these troubled times."

"I'll promise if you'll keep away from the much more dangerous palace of Zahra!"

"What palace?" he laughed.

Bending quickly, he brushed her lips lightly with his before
he sprang into his saddle and rode through the arched gate.

II

AS ARSLAN disappeared, Beltrana emerged from a rose bower, resembling one of the goblin-like *Lamiñak* of her stories. Her dark skin was like wet leather crumpled and left in the sun to dry; her hooked chin reached only to Lael's shoulder; her clothing, from severe head covering to black Cordovan slippers, was black.

"Lord on High!" she wailed, wringing her root-brown hands. "I knew this is what would come of your being raised *birristi-barrasti!* Kissing a heathen!"

"He's no more a heathen than my father," Lael said hotly. "And I have not been raised carelessly!"

Beltrana shuddered. "What would you call it? Riding through the streets like a boy, frequenting the house of that scandalous princess, being taught by a Jew? And now I find an infidel *darga-darga* gulping from your lips!"

"To him we're the infidels," Lael retorted but she tried to be patient for Beltrana had miseries in her joints that the city's best physicians could not cure and she had remained in this foreign place while longing for her home in the northern mountains. Hugging her nurse, Lael checked further laments by spinning her about and proclaiming joyfully, "Arslan loves me, 'Trana dear! He's going to ask for me in marriage."

Beltrana groaned and pulled away, shaking her head as she studied Lael's face with sharp black eyes. "I am an old, sinful woman but I do think God might have granted my prayer that you would marry a Christian."

"I don't know any," Lael said practically.

Her nurse sniffed. "What are miracles for?"

"It's miracle enough that Arslan loves me," Lael laughed with irrepressible delight. "Cheer up, 'Trana dearest. Think of

44

how you'll enjoy singing lullabies to our babies and telling them all those terrifying stories about one-eyed, giant Tartaros or the Basa Jaun.''

"You never really believed those tales," grumbled Beltrana as they walked through the massive ebony doors of the palace. The Basa Jaun, or wild man, was an immense hairy creature whose stupidity was matched only by his ability to smell human flesh, which he found delectable.

"Of course I believed you," Lael shuddered. "I memorized the answers that the shepherd gave him when the Basa Jaun agreed to let him go if he could think of three absolutely indisputable facts."

Beltrana's tone softened. "Do you still remember?"

"The shepherd said it wasn't true when people called a moonlit night as clear as day or when they said that acorn bread was as good as wheaten. His third fact was to tell the Basa Jaun, 'If I had known you were here, I wouldn't have come.' That was true, certainly, and so the monster let the lad go."

Chuckling, Beltrana patted her hand. "You learned well. Perhaps I haven't spent my life for nought in this heathenish city." Then she gripped Lael's arm with sudden alarm. "Will Arslan let me stay with you?"

"He'll do anything I want," Lael answered with happy and perfect assurance.

They passed through an inner court, where fountains played and a great basin of quicksilver reflected the sun streaming through high windows, and went through arched marble columns to Lael's apartments. The largest room, where she embroidered, read, played her lute and studied, was also the room in which she took her meals, often joined by her father. It had its own small courtyard, green with orange and pomegranate trees, jasmine and roses, and here Beltrana and Abram maintained plantings for their special remedies.

Within, the chamber was rich simplicity. The ceiling, fragrant cedarwood, was carved in lotus and acanthus designs linked with palm tendrils. Alabaster walls were inscribed in gold with a border of Arabic script executed in flourishes with accent marks of gems. The arched doors were similarly adorned and the brilliant blue of the tiled floor was bordered by a mosaic of vines and spread with sumptuous Persian carpets that glowed like jewels in the patterned light filtering through ivory window grilles.

A dais running the length of the room was heaped with large cushions. An ebony stand held writing materials in its interior. A copper brazier, a large, low hexagonal brass table and several smaller ones holding lamps and vases completed the furnishings. There was a long wall niche to hold Lael's favorite books, bound in finest leathers. Moslems had learned the art of paper-making from the Chinese and had brought it to Spain, where it replaced parchment, the scraped skin of sheep and goats.

Lael's copy of *A Thousand Nights and a Night*, which had delighted people for five centuries, was written in ink made of powdered lapis lazuli, and liquid gold lettered a volume of quatrains, including some by Omar Khayyam, the greatest astronomer and mathematician of the age, who had reformed the calendar so that it required only a day's correction every three thousand, seven hundred and seventy years. Her father's library of over a thousand books contained one that had taken a skilled group of calligraphers, paper-makers, painters and bookbinders seventeen years to create and all of the brushes used in its production were made of the white neck-hair of kittens. His twenty volumes of the *Kitah al-Aghani*, a collection of Arabic verse, had purple-lacquer bindings designed in gold and silver.

A lyre was at one end of the dais, or *diwan*, several lutes of varying sizes and styles, a brass flute and Lucira's tambourine. Behind an ivory-inlaid screen was the sleeping alcove that Lael shared with Beltrana. The adjoining bath had a small toilet cubicle, equipped with a marble slab into which an oval hole had been cut. The sunken marble bath was almost large enough to swim in and the floors and walls were of enameled tile.

Many-colored glass ewers and vases held rose water and perfumed oils. Beneath a polished-steel mirror, alabaster jars of ointments, lip salve and eye cosmetics ranged on a marble-topped stand that held a bronze basin and water ewer. Concealed in the wall beyond the bath was a secret door leading to the stable courtyard. At one time it may have been used for escape—or to allow a lover to enter. Lael's servants had their own bath and rooms, while her father's entourage was housed in the other wing of the palace.

Raised in a Moslem household, Lael took cleanliness for granted. Every Moslem was required to pray five times daily and first had to wash at least face, hands and feet. Mohammed himself had said that Allah would not hear the prayers of the unclean. Once women had been allowed in the mosques, though not at the same time as the men. Now that their worship was restricted to the women's quarters, women tended to make a religion of pleasing their husbands and trying to gain more influence over them than that of competing wives and concubines. Such a life held no appeal for Lael. Arslan, her hunting and riding companion, would never expect her to conform to such a stifling tradition.

Hot and dusty from her gallop, she bathed in scented water, attended by matronly Zillah, who pumiced rough skin off her feet and briskly toweled her dry. Jealous of her nursling, Beltrana ordered the Moorish woman away and helped Lael slip into thin silken pantaloons, a tunic of sapphire blue and velvet slippers worked with pearls. After all the snarls were combed from her hair, Lael fastened it back with a flexible gold band.

Although disappointed that Omar did not join her, she enjoyed the slices of salted fish and cheese, olives, *makhfiya*— spiced, egg-dipped and filled kebabs—black truffles, *couscous* and roast kid flavored with tarragon, mint and lemon, served in a sauce thickened by ground walnuts and pistachios. Beltrana concentrated on *harisa*, a dish of vegetables and chicken flavored with powdered almonds. For dessert there was sherbet, date cakes frosted with marzipan, and nougat rolled in powdered sugar.

"I hope Arslan visits my father tonight," Lael fretted, washing her hands in the basin that Zillah proffered and drying them with a towel of finest Egyptian cotton.

"What's the hurry?" Beltrana muttered. She added with sly humor, "Perhaps the lad's father wants to meet you in broad day, before a betrothal. The Bascoli say that gold, women and linen should be chosen only by full light."

"Moslem men aren't supposed to see women's faces except for those of their harem and close relatives," Lael retorted.

"You'll soon be a close relative," Beltrana reminded her tartly. "Besides, how can a man avoid seeing you when you don't use a veil?"

Lael put her nurse in a good mood by letting her have the last word. Retiring to the *diwan*, she arranged some cushions close to a bronze lamp and tried to concentrate on one of her lessons for next day, a treatise by the great Persian physician, al-Razi, entitled "Why Ignorant Physicians, Laymen and Women Have More Success than Learned Medical Men." It was useless. She could not even lose herself in the sensuous poetry of Abu Nuwas:

> Accumulate as many sins as you are able;
> The Lord is ready to abate his ire. . . .

Putting aside her books with a sigh, she slipped out into the garden. Beltrana was immediately beside her, though she had seemed to be dozing. "Goodness, child, you're as restless as summer lightning. Your father won't come tonight. It's much too late now."

She put a coaxing hand on Lael's arm and addressed her by a pet Bascoli name that meant "little cat." "*Ttattu*, please play something on your lute. It eases the ache in my old bones to hear some of the tunes I've taught you from your mother's country."

Lael allowed herself to be persuaded. She took a cushion and sat in the cool air of the doorway, strumming idly as she tried to picture the valley between the mountains that had been Lucira's home. "My grandmother may still be alive," she said with a sudden rush of longing for the mother she had never known and a wish that she could talk to her about Arslan and her marriage. "I wish I could know her."

Beltrana crossed herself. "Better that you don't, my heart. Mistress Engrâce was a stern woman, very pious. She ransomed her house and herds from destruction by yielding her daughter to the Moslems but she counseled her to take her own life rather than become an infidel."

"Mother remained a Christian! I'm one, too."

Beltrana sighed, frowning as she studied her charge. "So you are, *Ttattu*, but you're also—oh, I don't know how to say it.

Mistress Engrâce would be shocked at how you live, the clothes you wear, the things you study and the books you read. She thinks such things are of the devil."

The nurse's words caused Lael a slight pang but since they concerned a woman whom she didn't know and wasn't likely to, she shrugged away the sense of rejection and played softly as she sang shepherd songs and other melodies.

> "Sadly sings the bird in the cage,
> Though it has plenty to eat and to drink. . . ."

That song always reminded her of a bit of Abram's lore. There was a plant known to Christians as the Herb of Mary that parent birds were said to bring to their caged young so that they might eat it and die rather than live imprisoned. Lael had possessed a number of beautiful birds when her tutor told her the story. After that she could no longer enjoy their plumage or singing and set them free, prevailing upon Omar to do the same with the birds in his courtyards.

Lael poured herself into her music. When her fingers tired, Beltrana smiled tenderly. "Come, my heart. It's time to rest. Let me brush your hair and sing to you as I did when you were little."

"I would like that," Lael said. On the threshold of becoming a wife, yearning with the futile wish to know her mother's people, she now had a sudden nostalgia for childhood. It was as though she wanted to savor its sweetness before it was forever lost.

As soon as she had cleaned her teeth, washed and put on a sleeping robe, she perched on the edge of her low bed, a thick mattress resting directly on the carpeted floor, and closed her eyes, relaxing as Beltrana's familiar, not-always-gentle fingers worked out the snarls and brushed till the auburn hair was vibrantly charged and clung to Lael's cheeks.

> "*Bonbolontena*, my darling,
> Do not go to sleep in the wood,
> For the wicked eagle would come and take you
> As though you were a little hare."

Lael had heard the nursery song countless times but now a sudden premonition made her shiver. "Sing something else, 'Trana. I don't like that one."

"You're nervous from all the excitement," Beltrana chided. "Lie down and let me rub your neck and shoulders."

"Won't that hurt your fingers?"

Beltrana's expression softened. "No, child. It makes them better." She spoke in Bascoli, as she often did when they were alone, for she wanted Lael to know her mother's tongue and besides, she was lonesome for the sound of it.

Face-down, Lael yielded to the kneading fingers and lullabies of her childhood.

> "*Binbili, bonbolo,* go to sleep.
> If we were in our valley,
> The ass would drum,
> The ox would dance
> And the goat would play
> The tambourine."

She smiled at the thought and then imagined that Arslan's arms were around her. Sweetly she relived his kisses and drifted into sleep.

Accompanied by Beltrana, scarcely able to contain her eagerness to know what her father would say to Arslan's suit, Lael met Abram for lessons in her father's library. It was a wonderland of rare and beautiful books, including many translations—Archimedes, Plato, Aristotle, Euclid, Galen, Hippocrates, Hero of Alexandria, and Ptolemy, works of science and mathematics and great epics such as the *Shahnamah*, the matchless story of Rustum and other Persian kings. Lael was especially proud of the Latin works of Martial, Juvenal and the Senecas for they had all come from Iberia, as had the Roman Emperors Trajan and Hadrian. Here was the inherited inventiveness, research, scholarship and literature of Greece, Rome, India, Persia and all the Arab world from the borders of Hind to Andalusia.

Lael had always been fascinated by the large globe that could be turned in its stand, showing great expanses of ocean around the known world, bounded by China and Kievan Russia on the east, Europe and Africa on the west. Even more wonderful was the celestial globe of brass, patterned after the one made ten years ago by Ibrahim al-Sahdi of Valencia. Engraved on it were forty-seven constellations, formed by more than a thousand stars.

Returning Lael's greeting, Abram turned from studying the globe and sat down on a straw mat while she and Beltrana occupied cushions. Where the nurse's skin was leather, Abram's was translucent parchment. His forked beard was streaked with white, as was his hair. All his life-force seemed concentrated in his eyes, dark and deep-set, as infinitely young as they were inestimably old.

"Even though the learned know that Ptolemy was wrong in thinking that this little earth is the center of the universe, most people go on thinking that the sun and all the stars revolve around us. A dangerous theory, child, the astronomical arrogance equivalent to believing that man is the crown and center of earthly creation."

Beltrana eyed him suspiciously. "I don't understand all that you are saying, Master Abram, but it sounds to me like heresy. You know well that it is the noble Sayid's command that his daughter be reared up a good Christian."

"Since you are the Christian, madam, that is your duty," Abram returned silkily. "The Sayid's charge to me has been to educate his daughter's mind. With your gracious consent, I will proceed with that."

Lael fought to keep her face straight. This sparring went on constantly between the two the most intimately concerned with her upbringing. Beltrana had never made her way through, around or behind Abram's urbane courtesy but she kept trying.

Subsiding with a baleful mutter, the old woman brought out her spindle and began to form and twist yarn made from the combed fleece of sheep from her native mountains. This fleece was not nearly as long and silky as that from the merinos brought into Iberia by the Moors but Beltrana insisted fervently upon its superiority and Omar went to considerable difficulty to keep her in good supply.

It was Abram's method to alternate subjects that were hard

for Lael with those that she acquired easily. After she had solved an intricate problem in trigonometry, he expatiated for a time on the difficulties of ruling.

"Abd-er-Rahman III, perhaps the greatest Caliph of Cordova, ruled for half a century. He unified Andalusia, repelled Christian invasions and was renowned for generosity, culture and justice. Yet what were the words he wrote before his death? Saying that he had always had more than his fill of riches, honors, powers and pleasures, he finished thus: 'I have diligently numbered the days of pure and genuine happiness which have fallen to my lot. They amount to fourteen . . .' "

Lael stirred uncomfortably. "Perhaps, honored teacher, he was never in love."

Abram recoiled. His beard jerked in shock. Lael thought she heard a smothered giggle from Beltrana, but when, mortified, she glanced at her, the nurse was blandly twirling her spindle.

"Perhaps you can name the caliph who kept ten thousand men and fifteen hundred beasts working for twenty-five years to build a palace of undreamed marvels for his favorite wife?"

Lael dropped her eyes. "Abd-er-Rahman III, honored teacher."

"And whence came the funds?

Cheeks burning, utterly confounded, Lael murmured. "A fortune was left to the caliph by one of his concubines."

Showing mercy, Abram asked no further sarcastic questions but regarded Lael sympathetically. "You have a woman's instincts in spite of your intelligence—a good thing surely, since you are not a man. But love has failed to solace some of those who pursued it most. There was probably never a man who enjoyed women more than did Harun al-Rashid, who was also a brave, able and just ruler. No wife or concubine could solace him, though, for the terrible thing he did to preserve the purity of his family's Arabian blood."

Lael frowned. "I do not know that story, my teacher."

"Harun's sister, Abbasa, loved his dearest friend, Jafar. The caliph at last let them marry after they had sworn never to meet except in his presence. As could be foreseen, they broke the promise and had two sons by the time the caliph learned the truth. Harun accompanied the executioner who killed Abbasa and saw her buried. Jafar's head was brought to him and so were the handsome little boys. He talked for a long time with his nephews, children of the two whom he had loved more than any others, and then he had them also killed. Tormented by grief and remorse, he died six years later. At such cost did Harun al-Rashid perform his duty.''

Flinching from the sorrowful tale, Lael said indignantly, ''He could have spared himself the trouble. During their conquests, Moslems have married or enslaved so many foreign women that no princely blood is pure Hashemite.''

Abram nodded. They passed on to geography and she tried to comprehend the manner in which Caliph al-Mamun's astronomers had measured terrestrial degrees and estimated the earth's circumference at twenty thousand miles.

''That leaves room for a lot of lands we don't know about,'' she pondered. ''Has anyone ever tried to sail west from here to China?''

''The Vikings probably weren't trying to reach China—they just like to rove and are crowded in their own lands—but they have made settlements ever farther west. Iceland, Greenland, then on part of a mainland. There may be a vast new country there, as important as Europe and Asia.''

''If there were, it seems we'd know about it,'' Lael said skeptically.

Abram smiled. ''If there is such a land mass and people inhabit it, that's what they're saying about us.''

She had her Greek lesson and then Abram began to question her about the treatise she was to have studied. ''I'm sorry, my teacher,'' she said, flushing and bowing her head. ''I tried to read it last night but the words ran away from me like scurrying mice.''

It was the first time she had ever had to make an excuse. When he recovered from his amazement, Abram scanned her keenly. ''Well, child, try to grasp those mice's tails.'' At his nod of dismissal, she rose to go but at the door his voice stopped her.

''Those fourteen happy days of Abd-er-Rahman III, Lael, I do not think were when he was destroying Pamplona in your mother's homeland, the capital of Sancho of Navarre; or when he brought Seville and Toledo firmly under his rule, or even when he assumed the title of Commander of the Faithful and Defender of the Faith.''

Frowning her perplexity, Lael asked, ''What were they, then?''

''Times he spent with his beloved,'' Abram replied and turned away.

When possible, Omar went to the Great Mosque for noon prayers. After that he often joined Lael. The men of Arslan's family also went frequently to the mosque. It was common practice to trade news and visit before and after prayers. Lael hoped with all her heart that Arslan's father and uncles would approach Omar that very morning. She didn't think she could stand the suspense of waiting for days. Or even till tomorrow.

Time passed. It began to seem that her father would not take the noon meal with her. Lael felt the sting of disappointed tears and had absolutely no appetite for the savory *maghmuma,* though the dish of layered mutton, onions and eggplant was one of her favorites. Beltrana scolded her into taking a portion but she was only picking at it when her father appeared in the doorway.

''Father!'' Springing up, she ran to meet him. He embraced her lovingly then laughed as he held her away.

''I have been on no journey, daughter, nor am I going on one. I wonder at your fervor, gratifying though it is.''

''Oh. Then you didn't . . . he didn't—''

She broke off in confusion. Omar was an indulgent father but he would not be pleased to hear of the escapade that had led Arslan to confess his love. The hint of a smile tugged at Omar's mouth as he surveyed his daughter.

Straight, tall, garbed in white silk, the Sayid had a lean, handsome face and black hair with no gray yet showing. In spite of his dedication to learning, he was an expert polo-player and a devout Moslem. He carried his shroud on journeys, rigorously kept the fast of Ramadan, had made pilgrimage to Mecca, and *hafiz* was among his titles, for as a youth, he had memorized the whole Koran. In one thing only did he ignore Mohammed's teachings: He gave half his revenues to charity instead of the limit of one-fifth. Almost ascetic since his wife's death, the somberness always left his face when he saw Lael and today there was a twinkle in his eyes.

"Yes, my treasure, he did and I did. That is, Arslan's father spoke to me in the mosque. I gather that you young people stole a few words together at Princess Zahra's yesterday."

"Father! Did you—"

Smiling, he took her in his arms and stroked her hair. "If you wish it, the wedding will be held at the time our astronomers deem most propitious." He sighed. "You are several years past the age when most girls are mothers but I have been reluctant to let you go."

"I won't be going far," she reminded him. "The palace of Arslan's family is less than a ten-minute ride."

Omar sighed again. "You will be Arslan's wife first, dear child, and my daughter second. But that is how it should be. I have been blessed to have you this long. Now shall we have a game of chess?"

Beltrana, Zillah and the other women began sewing bridal finery even before the astronomers considered Lael's and Arslan's birth dates, charted the time of her monthly flow and agreed on the best day for the marriage. The process took a week, time that dragged interminably for Lael though she continued her lessons, played chess and backgammon with her father and rode often with him.

She did not see Arslan. The families agreed that since the two young people were almost betrothed, it was no longer proper for them to behave like playmates, but they did write to each other every day. Lael read Arslan's missives repeatedly, pressing them to her heart and sleeping with them under her pillow.

It was another week till the betrothal, and the wedding feast was scheduled for ten days later. Lael did not know how she could endure so many days without seeing her beloved but hour by slow hour each day passed.

Meanwhile, she had reached a new basis of understanding with her father, who spoke of matters that he had never mentioned before. She learned that Abram had loved a granddaughter of Abd-er-Rahman III's wise and beloved Jewish doctor,

Hasdai ibn Shaprut, who had functioned almost as a vizier. The wealthy family had accepted Abram in spite of his poverty and because of his learning, and the couple had had one happy year together before the young wife died in delivering a stillborn child.

"He never married again," Omar said. "It has been a bond between us that he knew how I felt about your mother."

It was hard for Lael to imagine her wise and venerable teacher as possessed by such a passion but it made her understand his words about the great caliph's fourteen happy days. She hoped that Abram and his lovely bride had counted more than that.

Never before had Omar discussed religion with her. Now he did, preparing her to better fit into Arslan's household. "The Prophet never expected the impossible," Omar told her. "In dire hunger, unclean foods such as pork can be eaten, by exhausted travelers, the old, the sick, babies, pregnant women or those nursing a child." He slanted her a humorous glance. "Lying is permissible for these excellent reasons: to mend a quarrel, to save a life, to deceive the enemies of the faith during war and to please one's wife."

"I won't be pleased if Arslan lies to me," Lael protested.

"Then don't ask him too many questions," Omar advised. "It will be part of the marriage contract that you be allowed to retain your faith and any daughters may be reared as Christian, though sons must be Moslem."

Since the two men she loved best were Moslem, Lael could scarcely object to the proviso but as though to soothe any doubts, her father said gently, "It has been said that prayer lifts us halfway to God, fasting brings us to the door of His palace and almsgiving lets us in. Christian, Jew and Moslem share many beliefs and practices. But you will forgive me if I wonder why anyone would want to go to the Christian heaven. It is attractive only when compared to hell."

Lael's concept of heaven was a nebulous one of walking the golden streets of an opulent city, somehow mystically cured of all earthly desires by the shining presence of God. There was no doubt that the gardens of Paradise, where fruit trees bent to fill one's hand and there was continual feasting and joy, seemed more enticing but she couldn't resist a playful jab at her father.

"I know you will be relieved not to have to listen to long speeches at the banquets," she said soberly. "But what of the seventy-two beautiful houris, Father? Perhaps you will renounce them to recite the Koran?"

"Beholding Allah's face will be paradise enough," Omar said. "Beyond that I ask only one thing: to spend eternity with your mother." At Lael's startled glance, he smiled quietly and touched her hair. "Yes, it can be, my daughter. Moslems believe that true-believing Jews and Christians may also enter Paradise." He added softly, "Allah knows without her, I will have none."

III

AT THE BETROTHAL, Arslan pledged a princely dowry to Lael: a town house on the river, a country estate, jewels inherited from his grandmother, who had been the Frankish concubine of a caliph, and five hundred gold dinars. This would remain hers even should they be divorced, for Moslem law was that a woman's property never became her husband's but remained under her control.

Even Beltrana was impressed, and she was further impressed when Arslan, to honor Lael's beliefs, went through a Christian ceremony in her little chapel, the rite performed by a priest who winked at Arslan's faith in return for a generous gift to his church.

In the days between the betrothal and the wedding, Lael moved in a dream. She was busy selecting the personal belongings that she would take to Arslan's house and she stood patiently while the women measured hemlines and fretted over her garments. She caught snatches of frightened rumor among the servants—Yusuf was thought to be readying himself to march on the city—but such stories had hummed about ever since the fall of Granada.

"I don't understand it," she said once to her father as they shared the noon meal. "If Yusuf is Moslem, why does he attack Moslem cities?"

"Europe is Christian," observed Omar, "but that doesn't prevent countries from fighting each another. Yusuf's zeal, though, is not so much for territory as to restore the Faith. He abhors the luxurious ways into which Andalusia has fallen and he detests learning and non-Moslem influences. He is resolved to burn them out with a flaming sword."

"But Cordova has strong walls and brave men!"

"That may not be enough," said Omar somberly. "My child, if Yusuf wins, there'll be no place for you in this city. If neither Arslan nor I can take you away, I have instructed Beltrana to take you back to your grandmother. In the northern mountains you should be safe from Yusuf and his kind."

"But—" Staggered, refusing to contemplate a time when he and Arslan might not be with her, Lael picked on a lesser objection. "I—I don't know my grandmother. She may not like me!"

"Lael," Omar took her hands, "there will be no other place for you when Yusuf controls the whole south. Would you want to be a slave in some harem, be confined to a zenana for the rest of your life?"

It was as unthinkable as losing him and her love. She threw herself into his arms and hugged him fiercely. "Nothing will happen to you! You will see your grandchildren and teach them all to hunt and ride and make up poems."

"May Allah grant it," he said, caressing her hair. "Now go with Zillah, child. She is waiting to measure you for yet another garment."

So Lael knew the menace Yusuf posed, yet would not allow herself to think on it. The things Omar suggested were too terrible to admit into possibilities. Rich, powerful Cordova could surely withstand a maniacal raider from the desert! She wrote letters to Arslan, dreamed of him and burned for the days to pass.

For the first time in her life, Lael rode in a closed litter, escorted by her father, Abram and a train of servants. She wished that she could have ridden Al Zirr but she took comfort, in her great nervousness, in knowing that she was beautiful to behold in pale blue silk and cloth of gold. The unfamiliar veil tickled her nose but she wouldn't have to wear it after the wedding ceremony.

Though it was barely twilight, hundreds of lamps and lanterns lit the palace of the bridegroom and graced the street. As her father led her inside to be received by Arslan's family, musicians filled the air with sweet, plaintive music. Arslan's father, Hakam ibn Hussein, bowed deeply to Omar.

"Peace be with you."

Bowing even more profoundly, Omar replied, "On you be peace and the mercy and blessings of Allah."

Beyond them Lael saw Arslan, erect and handsome in white silk. Their eyes met with beautiful shock. It was as though their souls rushed to embrace while their bodies remained circumspectly in place.

Hakam ushered them into the great hall where many guests waited and where Lael was welcomed kindly by Arslan's mother, Zobeida, a plump but comely woman who obviously adored her son and wanted him to have whatever he desired, even this unusual bride.

The wedding required no official. Omar and Hakam conducted the prayers and ceremony that united their children, after which lavish gifts were presented and the musicians began to play again. Cymbals, horn, castanets, tambourine and drum accented lute, psaltery, pandore and lyre. Hakam was especially fond of music. Where most noble families might be content with four or five musicians, he had a dozen and their instruments were from Seville, famous for its artistry in the craft of producing fine-timbred instruments.

Seated on cushions beside low tables, guests chose from a profusion of sumptuous dishes, and wine flowed for the less strict Moslems. Next to Arslan, Lael wanted no food but he coaxed her with tender morsels and she nibbled fruit and sipped wine he poured for her.

When could they leave the feast? When would they be alone? Music, laughter, odors of richly spiced food and the unaccustomed wine combined to make Lael's head swim.

"Arslan," she whispered, "if I have to stay here much longer, I'm going to be sick or collapse!"

"You can't do that on our wedding night," he whispered back. "Bear up, sweetheart. You have been strong on even the most grueling rides and hunts."

He pressed her hand reassuringly but it was a relief to Lael when Arslan's mother and the women attendants of both households, including Beltrana and Zillah, who would be living in Lael's new home, took her to the bridal chamber and helped her bathe and anoint herself. They combed her hair and draped her in a diaphanous robe. As soon as the women withdrew, Arslan entered.

They stood apart for one moment, shyly. Then he took a long stride forward and she ran into his arms. He swept her up, trembling, and carried her to the perfumed bed.

"In the name of Allah the Compassionate, the Merciful," he breathed as he removed her veil and found her lips.

That was the end of ceremonies.

Ten perfect days. They did little but enjoy each other, making love in delightful ways Arslan had learned from the many women to whom a youth of his rank had early access. Just as fulfillingly, they read to each other, walked in the gardens, played their lutes and sang or challenged each other to backgammon or chess. Arslan prayed at the prescribed times, of course, and went to the mosque on Friday but the rest of the time he was with Lael.

Life would not go on this way. In a month or so they would move into the nearby house that was part of Lael's dowry, but for now they were lost in their own world and those about them smiled and were happy to see their bliss.

They were watching the fountains fall in showers of crystal light, intoxicated with each other and the scent of a thousand roses, when Hakam himself summoned Arslan, calling from the arched portico surrounding the garden.

Arslan put a rose in Lael's hand, smiled at her and went quickly to his father. He was back in a few minutes, pale about the lips.

"Lael, sweetheart, Yusuf is advancing on the city. All men able to fight must man the fortifications while the warriors go out to engage Yusuf's army."

He was a warrior, as were Omar and Hakam.

"We must leave as soon as we can," Arslan told her. "Your father has sent a messenger asking that you stay in his house while we're away. You will be under Abram's care. Perhaps you would be happier in your father's home until I come for you."

She would. Sleeping alone on the bed she had shared with Arslan would be a torment and she knew so few in the palace. "I will wait for you in my father's house," she said and tucked the rose into her girdle. "Let me help you make ready."

He was gone within the hour, along with Hakam and Omar, who had come to tell Lael good-bye. Abram had accompanied Omar in order to escort Lael home. She managed not to weep as father and husband embraced her and kissed her farewell but when they had ridden from the courtyard, scimitars and light mail flashing in the sun, she took the rose from her girdle and crushed the thorns in the palm of her hand.

During that day, the long lonely night and the next day, time seemed to stop. The city was in tumult and though Lael wanted to go to the city walls, Abram forbade it. "The governor is not loved by the populace. Should Yusuf overcome the warriors, it's likely that instead of defending the fortifications and enduring a long siege, the people will open the gates to Yusuf. They've heard of how he has cut taxes in the places that he's conquered and that though stern, he is just." He added cynically, "The poor always welcome a change of rulers, hoping things will improve."

He had instructed Beltrana to prepare saddlepacks of clothing and travel food and told Lael to select a few small things she most treasured. It was difficult to choose, even had she not been so frightened. At last Lael gave Beltrana her mother's crucifix to pack, Arslan's letters, a necklace he had given her, *A Thousand Nights and a Night* and a volume of Rabi'a's poetry.

She could not believe that they might actually have to leave the city, making off with only what they could carry. Even less could she bear to think that Arslan and Omar might not return. Beltrana brewed teas to help her rest but on both nights sleep was long in coming and she wept herself into exhaustion.

What was happening to Arslan and her father? She would have given anything to be with them, to share their fate. She had fallen into a restless slumber on the second night, reaching out in her sleep for Arslan and waking as she found he wasn't there, when she was roused by Beltrana, who was shaking her.

"Up, child! Dress quickly! We must leave the city."

Lael's heart plunged. "Arslan? My father?"

Beltrana pulled her to her feet. "Get into these clothes," she ordered.

Lael wrenched away. "Tell me! What has happened to them?"

"Dead," said Beltrana, the single word a flat blow. "Come now, do as your father bade you."

Lael's throat ached with the long, low cry of grief before she realized that the sound came from her. She seized Beltrana and shook her. "Are you sure? Are you lying just to make me leave?"

"Child, *Ttattu*, a groom of your father's saw them both die, along with Hakam. Unhorsed, they stood back-to-back and went down only after each was up to the armpits in slain enemies."

Numbly, still unable to believe, Lael asked, "Is the battle lost?"

"Lost," nodded Beltrana and though she had called the Cordovans heathens, tears spilled from her eyes. "Yusuf is advancing. He has sent word that he will be merciful to the people if they yield. All of the fighting men are either killed or captured. If there's a siege, it will be short." She almost tore off Lael's nightrobe. "*Ttattu*, hurry!"

Lael pressed her hands to her head. She felt as though pierced by the blades that had struck her loved ones. Had their heads been struck off, their bodies left for scavengers? And what if the groom was wrong?

"Maybe they're only wounded," she said. Hastily, she drew on the trousers and tunic Beltrana proffered, her fingers shaking so violently that she couldn't fasten the ties. "Where's the groom? He can take me to them!"

"He has gone to the walls. And he knows that your men are dead, my heart, for after Yusuf's host swept on, he dragged Arslan and your father from the piles of the dead and buried them in a small ravine. You can do nothing for them—except live."

"I don't want to! I'll go to the walls and fight! I'll—"

Beltrana gripped her shoulders. "Hush! You love Arslan. Perhaps you carry the seed of his child, the Lord Omar's grandchild. Will you destroy their only hope of living in flesh of their flesh?"

Her words checked Lael's frenzy but only for a moment. "I want Arslan!"

"So will you scream at death like a balked infant or will you give his seed a chance to grow within you?"

With a tremendous effort, using all her powers, Lael controlled her shuddering and forced back the unspeakable grief that threatened to engulf her.

"We will go," she said. "Back to my mother's country."

News of the defeat had spread with the return of fleeing survivors. Though it was still night, street lights showed people streaming along the raised sidewalks, some going to the mosques to pray, others the walls. From overheard arguments and shouts, it seemed evident that the common people had no wish to fight and provoke Yusuf.

"He is sent by Allah to purify the city," one old man cried. "He won't plunder the Faithful, only infidels and those who flout the Prophet's teachings."

His words were greeted by a roar of agreement. Sickened, Lael dragged her headcovering more firmly over her mouth to stifle the cry swelling to her lips. *So you will open the gates to the man whose muezzins call to prayer from hills of severed heads? Is it nothing to you that my husband and father died for all that has made Cordova great?*

The bulk of the population would prefer reduced taxes to any amount of culture, and stricter Moslems would rejoice in the fundamentalism that Yusuf would impose. Omar had been right. This beloved city had no place for her now.

At one of the small gates she turned to look back toward her home and the minaret of the Great Mosque, outlined in the glow of street lamps. She drew in one last breath. The air was heavy with the scent of roses. Then she reined Al Zirr after Abram.

Only her nurse and tutor rode with her. Zillah and the other servants naturally preferred accepting new masters and remaining in Cordova to a dangerous journey leading only to an alien mountain valley. Abram had distributed gold dinars throughout their baggage. At least they would not be beggars at Engrâce's door, though Omar's wealth and Lael's dowry were lost.

Omar, in providing for this extremity that he had died to prevent, had made a map for Abram and advised him on the safest route. "We are almost directly south of your mother's homeland," Abram told Lael the first time they stopped to rest. "We will avoid Toledo in case some of Yusuf's commanders are still hoping to take it, and cross the Tagus upriver from the city. After that we should be safe, though I fear we may meet more brigands in Castile than exist in all of Andalusia."

Sunk in despair, Lael scarcely heard him but Beltrana said fearfully, "I pray that we don't meet King Alfonso's armies, either. As I remember, it is a journey of about two weeks and when you aren't scorching on the plains or floundering in the rivers, you're freezing in the mountains." She ceased her lament to press several balls of *hais* into Lael's hand. "Eat, *Ttattu*. You must keep up your strength."

Dully, Lael obeyed but her throat ached as she chewed and swallowed the mixture of dates, almonds and breadcrumbs. *Hais* was a fine travel food and she had often enjoyed it while riding or hunting with her father and Arslan.

Would the rest of her life be an echo of the one she had shared with them? She thought it must. Her agony was so great that she wished she lay between them in their rocky grave.

Both to divert and instruct her, Abram pointed out the advantages that had been brought to the region by the Moors. Near Cordova, Moorish methods of irrigation grew spinach, asparagus, strawberries and flourishing fields of buckwheat, rice, sugar cane and cotton. Before the Moors, there had been no orchards of pomegranates, figs, cherries, oranges, lemons, peaches, grapefruit, quinces, bananas and dates. While the Romans had brought olives, it was Moslem techniques that had developed large groves.

Instead of the oxen used by the Visigoths, horses, mules and donkeys were now used for most plowing and carrying burdens, and humped cattle grazed contentedly in their adopted home. The Moslems knew how to practice stock-breeding to obtain splendid horses and beefy cattle.

Waving a hand at date palms bordering fertile cane fields, Abram said, ''Perhaps the Christian kings of Castile, Navarre, Leon and Aragon will one day drive the Moslems completely out of Spain and with them will go as much Eastern and classical culture as may escape Yusuf now. But the plants and animals they brought will remain, something of their music and architecture. And the mingling of their blood.''

To mix with Celtiberian, Phoenician, Roman and Visigoth. As centuries blended, the fall of Cordova would be but a single event among many, the passing of the golden age of Islamic Andalusia a mere ripple in the ocean that was history. But all that Lael loved and knew was in that world; Paradise was to her the rose gardens of her beloved. She turned her face northward with winter in her heart.

During the height of the Cordovan Caliphate, when the southern half of the peninsula had been governed from that city, laws had been more justly and evenly administered than they were under the capricious and often ineffective Visigothic kings and nobles who had oppressed the poor, persecuted Jews and survived on the crumbling ruins of Roman civilization. During the Caliphate it had been safe to travel but after its disintegration into sections controlled by various city states, robbers and cutthroats abounded.

Abram therefore wore a sword even though he had never used one. Lael, who would pass for a handsome stripling, had her arched bow and quiver of arrows, a javelin and sword. All three travelers carried daggers but Lael knew that should they be waylaid, it would be up to her to defend the little party.

Peasants, Moslem and Christian alike, were to be seen working their fields but from fear of Yusuf, there were few travelers. Near the Tagus they were overtaken by a group of Italian scholars fleeing Cordova to take up their studies in Toledo.

The populace had indeed opened the gates to Yusuf. On the whole he had behaved with magnanimity, though he had beheaded the governor and had at once issued decrees aimed not only at Jews and Christians but especially at Moslems who had lapsed into violation of the Koran.

''It is no place where one can ask questions,'' one of the students shrugged. ''And what kind of learning is obtained without questions?''

North of Toledo the travelers were always in sight of mountains or passing through them. Here they often stayed with shepherds, who kept their flocks high during the summer months and moved them to lower pastures in the fall, a custom from antiquity. Though Roman roads had since been built over some of them, sheepwalks hundreds of miles in length trailed whitely through the countryside. Some herds were common *churros*, with long, coarse wool, but many showed the fine, white, kinky wool of merinos brought from Africa.

Farmers resented the bi-yearly march of sheep through their lands but custom and law preserved the ancient privilege. It was even said that the northern kings were impelled to reconquer the south as much to regain their summer pastures as to vindicate their religion.

Shepherds were glad of company and news of the outside world. They refused pay for their simple and gladly offered food—clotted milk, dried acorns, hard white cheese and wine from skinbags, shared out in drinking horns. *Hais*, which the travelers were tired of by now, was to the herdsmen an exquisite delicacy.

''Your grandmother has many sheep,'' Beltrana said after they left one lonely camp and Lael wondered with dawning apprehension what her life would be like in the valley that she knew only from songs and stories. She had been too grief-stricken and dazed to think about the future and it had seemed that the journey would last forever, that she would spend eternity in traversing the way from Cordova to her mother's valley, but now the fierce Cantabrian Mountains rose to their west and as they neared Burgos, Abram and Beltrana agreed that they had only two or three more days of travel.

Burgos had been founded in the ninth century and for a time it had been the capital of old Castile. A summer villa of the kings was situated on the west and the city had been sacked by the Moslems but its chief fame lay in being the birthplace of El Cid Campeador, Rodrigo Diaz, though he was actually from Bivar, a little village slightly to the north. It was at the Church of Santa Gades in Burgos in 1072, that the young Rodrigo had compelled Alfonso to swear that he'd had no part in King Sancho's suspicious death before Rodrigo would become the new king's vassal. That union had begun a stormy series of ups and downs between a king jealous of power and his most famed knight. Alternately rewarded or humiliated by Alfonso, Rodrigo fought sometimes for him, sometimes against him. His title, El Cid, derived from the *sayid*, or lord, accorded him by Moslem armies he had led. Now he held Valencia for Alfonso, exacting tribute from the Moorish king, who had begged his help against the terrible Yusuf.

Beltrana insisted on stopping at the church to pray for the man who was becoming almost as mighty a legend as Santiago Matamoros—Saint James, the Moor Killer—whose bones had been found in the northwest and who was said to lead Christian armies from the sky while mounted on a great white horse.

Lael knew little about Saint James but El Cid plainly sold his military skills to whomever paid him best. She prayed instead for Arslan and her father, appealing to Mary to intercede in case God was not disposed to trouble himself with Moslems.

They had a dinner of fish at an inn but the rooms were so dirty that they decided to travel on a little way and sleep in the open. Next morning they crossed the Ebro River and came into a broad plain that stretched to blue mountains in all directions. From here to the sea and the kingdom of the Franks, it was Bascoli country.

IV

THE MOORS had penetrated this region only once, leaving no trace, but an old Roman road ran northward. Beltrana began to recognize landmarks—a familiar mountain, Roman ruins, strange-looking stone piles, stone and timber huts in the midst of fields still tilled by oxen. While not exactly villages, these scattered homes did usually share a small church. Each house possessed a garden, fruit trees and beehives but there seemed to be nothing grown for sheer love of beauty, though there were huge oak, beech and chestnut trees.

The valleys were beautiful, Lael could not deny that, but it was wild, untamed country. Nothing more different from Cordova could be imagined. Nodding toward a farmstead, she tried to keep alarm from her voice. "Beltrana, is my grandmother's house like that?"

"No, much finer," Beltrana beamed. Upon nearing her homeland, she had straightened and seemed years younger. "It's a real *dorrea,* a stone tower, with a courtyard." She prattled on happily as they entered a forest.

Lost in misgivings, Lael did not see or hear anything until a group of men swarmed out of the bushes. Two of them caught at Al Zirr's bridle. Lael made him rear, striking out with his forefeet. Unsheathing her sword, she skewered the closest man but not in time to save Abram, who was knocked from his donkey as he tried vainly to take out his sword.

Beltrana slid from her mule and ran to stand over Abram, waving her dagger and shrieking insults. Lael spun Al Zirr about in a circle, wounding another man. The brigands had not expected such strength of resistance. Armed with only knives and staves, they scrambled away from Al Zirr's hoofs and Lael's sword.

One of them cried, "They're Bascoli—at least the old crone is!"

Catching up their wounded, they vanished into the trees as swiftly as they had come. "Oh, the wicked ones!" Beltrana ranted. "There have ever been rogues and thieves in the mountains. They even prey on those making pilgrimage to Saint James Compostella, though they usually don't bother other Bascoli."

Lael scarcely heard. Kneeling by Abram, she was terrified at the seep of blood from his forehead. His lips were blue and his hands fluttered.

"Bring wine," she ordered.

As she tried to lift him, his eyes opened. She did not know whether it was a smile or a spasm of pain that moved his lips. "I—have had—more than fourteen days."

Breath struggled in his throat. A slight convulsion. Then he was limp and silent in her arms. "Abram!" Lael cried. When he did not respond, she shook him. "Abram! Here, drink some wine."

"He'll drink only in Paradise," Beltrana said and muttered a prayer. "God grant him grace even though he was an unbeliever."

Lael sat huddled with Abram in her arms. She had thought nothing else could hurt her—not ever—but this did. Were it not for her, he would have taken refuge in Toledo, found a patron and pursued his civilized, scholarly life. Only tenderness for her had brought him to this raw, wild country, and it had killed him.

"*Ttattu*, we must go on," Beltrana urged. "If we hurry, we can reach the andrea's house before true darkness."

It was natural for the nurse to slip back into thinking of Engrâce as the andrea, or mistress, yet it gave Lael a pang. Everything, everything, was going to be different. As she washed the blood from Abram, Beltrana said, "It might be easier if we buried him here."

"Why?"

Beltrana squirmed. "He can't be placed in the church or holy ground," she said defensively. "And it will upset the mistress. All she knows about Jews is that they killed Christ and helped the Moslems take over Spain.''

''Maybe we should go back to Burgos. Buy a little house with the gold—''

''Child, you aren't thinking!'' Beltrana cried in horror. ''Two unprotected women! And you so foreign, for all your Christian faith. How would we live when the gold was gone? No, you must do as your father wished and go to your grandmother.''

There seemed to be no choice but Lael wrapped Abram in his mantle. ''Help me get him on his donkey,'' she said defiantly. ''I will bury him close enough that I can pray sometimes at his grave.''

She didn't say that this solace was denied her for both Arslan and Omar but perhaps Beltrana thought of it. She argued no further but pantingly assisted Lael in hoisting Abram's gaunt body across his saddle. Covering him with a blanket, Lael secured the wrap to hold him in place but in a rush of anger she tossed his useless sword into the undergrowth.

Leading the donkey, she started on, blinded with tears. She prayed that in whatever hereafter Abram found himself, he would behold not only the glory of God but the sweet face of his bride. And now she realized how great had been her unconscious dependence on him. She loved Beltrana but the superstitious, uneducated old nurse could not keep her mind alive, discuss science and philosophy and share the beauty of books and verse.

She was indeed in her mother's country but she had a deep certainty that she would never belong here.

Mists hovering on the mountains dropped lower, shrouding the road ahead, turning the forests ghostly. Slow, steady, cold rain began to fall.

''It's not much farther,'' Beltrana called. ''See those caves? People lived there once. Maybe it was far back in the days when all animals and things could speak because some caves have animals painted in them, aurochs and others that we don't have anymore. Our *parrokia* is just down the valley.''

Soon they could see scattered houses and the small stone

church. Fog seemed to press down on everything. Cold, wet and exhausted with grief, Lael scanned the farmsteads hopefully but Beltrana pointed ahead.

"See? The *dorrea* on that slope? Hurry, child. Holy saints, won't your grandmother be surprised?"

Surprise was a pale word for the shock that congealed Engrâce's features, made harsher by the flickering light of the fire that burned in the middle of the room. The hair peaking in her seamed forehead formed a white streak amid black hair that was pulled straight back under a white coif. Her dark skin was weathered, her lips pressed together in a way that reminded Lael of the narrow, slit windows of the house. After a long scrutiny during which Lael tried not to shiver from cold and damp, her grandmother turned to Beltrana.

"This is Lucira's child?"

"Indeed, andrea." The nurse's first joyful confidence was slowly fading. She drew off Lael's headcovering. "See? The same hair, the same eyes."

Reluctant acknowledgment flickered in Engrâce's green eyes. "And her infidel father is dead?"

Lael's hands clenched. She took a step forward but Beltrana stopped her. "The Lord Omar sent her to you, andrea. She has been raised Christian. There is no place for her in Yusuf's kingdom."

"And you think there's a place here?" Engrâce's scant laughter was like the grating of a rusted chain. "Well, I suppose there's nothing for it. It's my punishment for letting a Moslem take my daughter. Perhaps the girl can be trained to be useful." Confronting Lael, she said loudly, speaking with exaggerated slowness as though to a deaf person, "Take off those wet things. Beltrana will show you to your room."

A gnarled, surly old man named Urta had taken their mounts in the courtyard, mumbling darkly when Beltrana explained about Abram. Lael did not like the thought of her teacher's body lying in the stable. Slowly, not wanting to make a mistake in her use of the language, she told Engrâce about the robbers and asked to bring Abram into the house.

"Is he Moslem?" Engrâce scowled.

"No, Grandmother. He is a Jew."

"A Jew?" Engrâce recoiled. "He shouldn't even be in the stable! Merciful God, what have I done to deserve this? A half-Moslem granddaughter arriving at my door with a dead Jew!"

Lael had been close to fainting with weariness but at this, anger revived her. Staring at her grandmother, she said firmly, "I will bury him now then."

Engrâce sucked in her breath. "Are you crazed? It's almost dark!"

"I will not leave him in the stable."

For a moment it seemed that Engrâce might strike her but then, considering, the older woman shrugged. "It must be done sometime. I will have Urta help you."

She stepped to the door and started to call just as the hunched-over servant lurched in with the saddlepacks. He grunted unhappily at Engrâce's orders. Beltrana hesitated for a moment before conquering her aching body and fear of Engrâce.

"I'll help," she said.

So Abram the scholar was buried beneath an oak tree, his fine hands crossed on his Talmud, while Lael asked his God not to blame him for her ignorance of the proper rites.

By then it was completely dark. Since Urta had shambled off the moment the grave was deep enough, Lael was able to throw her arms around Beltrana and cry, not only for Abram but for what lay before her.

"Grandmother hates me, 'Trana," she sobbed. "I can't stay here!"

"There, there," soothed her nurse, rocking her as she had when a childish grief had been overwhelming. "She'll come around. You're the only one who can keep the house going and bring offerings and candles to the family tomb after she's gone. It's just that we took her by surprise—and the andrea never liked that."

"Even if she were nice to me, I don't think I could stand it," Lael shuddered. "The house is like a jail."

"The better to keep out enemies," Beltrana argued. "*Ttattu*, your monthly flow should have started this week. Did it?"

Lael had not even thought about it. Now she counted back through the weeks and realized it was so. Her wedding date had been carefully gauged so as to provide the longest period of time possible between her flows. Ten days with her bridegroom, close to two weeks on the road. . . . It was past time.

Though she had wished to give Arslan many children and the chance to preserve his heritage had strengthened her will to live, the prospect, now that she had met her grandmother, frightened as much as thrilled her.

"Maybe the journey interfered."

Beltrana scoffed. "One could count the calendar by your seasons. No, if the journey did anything, it would have started your course. I feared it might. If your next time comes without anything happening, it will be certain. Think of how that would please your husband and father."

"Do you think they can know?"

Beltrana sighed, caressing Lael's cheek. "Child, only the good God could say."

"I hope they know about the baby," Lael said, "but not— not about Abram and my grandmother." Or the cold stone house.

They could smell the odor of scorching leather along with the friendlier aroma of soup even before they entered the big kitchen on the ground floor. Engrâce ladled bowls of thick stew from the cauldron suspended above the fire and put them on the table, where bread and cheese were already set out.

"Eat," she commanded. "I don't want anyone falling sick."

They had not eaten since noon. Lael sat on a bench across the table from Beltrana and hungrily devoured her portion. The walls of the large room were whitewashed. Niches held earthenware jars, a few wooden bowls, a pannikin and several wooden mugs. Strings of garlic and onions hung from the rafters as well as part of a ham.

Engrâce occupied the only chair, expertly twirling her spindle. Stealing a glance at her grandmother, Lael noticed for the first time that the curling leather at the edge of the hearth was not a scrap or bit of hide. It was one of her books.

Springing up with a cry, she ran forward and snatched the ruined volume from the flames. Only a bit of the cover and the bound section of the lapis-lazuli-lettered pages remained. And of the poems of Rabi'a, a small, glowing hull quivered at the center of the fire.

Lael dropped the smoldering leather on the hard earthen floor. "You wicked woman!" she gasped. "You—you—*why* have you burned my beautiful books?" For, reared to reverence books, the desecration was horrible to Lael, past understanding.

"They were heathen—of the devil." Engrâce was so amazed at this outburst that she had stopped spinning.

"They were not!" Possibly people like Engrâce and Yusuf would call *A Thousand Nights and a Night* improper but who could fault the lovely, fervent praises of Rabi'a for her God? Tears streamed down Lael's face. The death of the books was like the loss of dear and gracious friends. Her grandmother simply had not understood and had taken them for the Koran or books of magic. Swallowing, Lael said, "Grandmother, one book held the verse of a Moslem saint—"

"Saint? The Moslems have no saints." Engrâce put her head in her hands. "Holy Mother, pardon this girl's blasphemies! I cannot read but I have seen the priest's book. The words are nothing like those flowery dips and doodles in those devils' books." Rising, she loomed above Lael. "I suppose it's not your fault, the way you've been raised, and you are my daughter's child, the only one of my blood. God must have sent you here for your salvation. But I am *etcheko andrea*. You will obey me."

Turning to Beltrana, the woman gestured. "Take her to bed."

The nurse lit a rush lamp and took Lael's arm. "Come, *Ttattu*," she urged.

Lael scooped up the remains of her book. She and Beltrana had to go outside, where they reached the next floor by means of a wooden staircase. The flickering, odorous lamp lit their way down a narrow hall to a small chamber.

The floor, rubbed with beeswax, was warm from the fire below. In the room there was a big chest, a crucifix and a dark wooden bed with a blue-embroidered coverlet.

Someone had placed their packs in a corner. The gold dinars were gone but except for the books, nothing else was missing. There was even some precious paper, ink powder and quills in

Abram's pack. Beltrana rummaged until, next to a packet of the Herb of Mary and other remedies, she found a salve that she applied to Lael's blistered fingers.

"Don't ever talk to the andrea that way again," Beltrana warned. "I am surprised that she didn't beat you."

Lael, in all her life, had never received as much as a slap. Lifting her drooping head, she said fiercely, "That—that old peasant beat me? I would cut her throat!"

Beltrana clapped a hand across Lael's mouth. "She is your only kin! And the only relative your baby will have. Think of your child, *Ttattu*. Think of it and endure."

The nurse helped Lael out of her damp, mud-stained garments and tucked her into the big wooden bed with its straw mattress before she blew out the lamp and climbed in beside her. Beltrana's familiar body was the only comfort Lael had that first night in the *dorrea* but she clung to the thought of her child, picturing a boy who would look like Arslan, and weariness brought sleep almost at once.

Through the next days Lael called on the image of the child often. Apart from her resemblance to Lucira, there seemed to be nothing about her that pleased Engrâce, though the woman grudgingly allowed that the gold would at least pay for her granddaughter's keep. She wanted to sell Al Zirr, saying that he ate too much grain and was good for nothing, but at that Lael looked up as she cleaned out the stables.

"Grandmother, if you try to sell Al Zirr, I will take him and go away."

Engrâce's jaw dropped. "Go? Where would you go?"

"I don't know," Lael admitted. "But he carried me here, he is my friend and I must take care of him."

After a moment Engrâce muttered something about ingrates and turned to her work, for if she made a drudge of Lael, she did not spare herself and, with Urta, she did all of the work. She hired a boy from the neighborhood to tend her sheep, which were now in higher pastures, but said that the task would be a good one for Lael when the flock came down in the autumn. After all, though she'd admit that Lael tried hard, the girl was almost useless in the house, burning the bread, forgetting to stir the cauldron, clumsy at carding and spinning. She was best left to fetching water from the spring, carrying wood and mucking out the ox-byre and stable that occupied part of the ground floor of the *dorrea,* along with sections to store farm implements, hay and grain. These adjoined the kitchen, but had to be reached by an outside door.

Above this door, engraved in stone, was the motto of the house: *Ever Fruitful* and its name, Etchahoun, the Good House. Lael could spare a melancholy smile for being able to read Greek, Latin and Arabic but not her mother's language. There seemed to be no books written in it, anyway. The priest appeared to have memorized the services he read in Latin, making so many mistakes that Lael usually emerged from church with a chewed lip. Even if well-trained priests had wanted to penetrate the inhospitable region, the people of the community preferred a priest of their own. So an especially pious young man would be sent off to learn the rudiments of the priesthood and return to administer them in ways that deviated considerably from the stately rites and Masses to which Lael was accustomed.

One great difference in Lael's life lay in the position of her grandmother as *serora.* The *parrokia* had chosen her when she was a young woman but the selection had been a mere formality because the office had almost always been held by the mistress of Etchahoun, the Good House. The *serora* was closer to the heart of the neighborhood's religion than was the priest for her duties were simply a broadening of those of the *etcheko andrea* of every household: lighting and tending the fire, which still retained some of its sacred nature; watching over the souls and bodies of those of the household; overseeing the crops and animals, and making the proper offerings and prayers for the dead.

The priestesshood went back to the most remote times and so did the practice of choosing one woman to preside over the women's ceremonies and tend the sacred grotto where the church now stood. No one knew exactly who or what had been worshiped at the shrine and they were all good Christians now, and had been for two hundred years, but still it did no harm to dance in front of the church at midsummer and observe the ancient festivals that had merged into holy days.

Engrâce took Lael with her to help clean the church but only she took care of the altar cloths and adornments. She collected the offerings of candles, bread and other foods, sharing them with the priest and those in need, keeping only a little for herself. During services she lit and snuffed the candles and rang the church bell at the ritual times. When drought threatened, she rang the bell to summon rain.

An old man died a few weeks after Lael came to the valley. Each family had a *yarleku*, or sepulchral stone, on the church floor, beneath which people of that house were buried, though there were also graves in the little churchyard, some of them very ancient and marked with stones shaped roughly like people, the later ones resembling discs arising from a wedge-shaped base. After the priestly rites, when the dead man had been lowered into the tomb, the men left the church.

Solemnly, the women formed a procession led by Engrâce. As they approached the altar, she turned and took the bread and candles they carried and placed them on the shrine. After prayers, she lit the candles and then the women each took a taper and some of the bread, carrying them to the *yarleku*, where they were placed on the family stone.

As Engrâce led in the prayers, to Lael she seemed transformed, no longer a grim, aging woman but the embodiment of a power far older and deeper than Christianity. After the rituals, Engrâce went with the women to the old man's home.

The fire was gone from the hearth, the quenched brands scattered to the winds. The bees had been told that their master was dead and so had the cattle, who were said to have begun lowing at the moment of their master's death and had calmed only when the new *etcheko jaun* had visited them with the formal announcement.

In the kitchen, which was the heart of the house because of the fire, Engrâce said the *Requiescat in Pace*, first in Latin and then in Basque. After that she handed a funerary candle to the new *etcheko andrea*, who knelt to rekindle the household fire.

The simple but poignant ceremony touched Lael though she could not help but compare it to the hasty, unsolemnized burial given to Abram. She had done what she could to atone for the lack, heaping over his mound the most unusual and beautiful rocks that she could find, including a few heavy ones streaked with greenish-blue. Also she had buried the remnants of her lapis-lazuli-inscribed book with her teacher. Whenever she had a little time free of work, she went to sit by his grave and talked to him as though he were alive, pouring out her loneliness, her troubles with Engrâce and the everyday difficulties.

"No one bathes unless he falls in a stream or gets caught in a storm," she told him sadly. "There is not even a tub. But there's a place where the bushes grow close to the spring as it runs down the slope and I wash myself there. This winter I'll just have to sponge off with a cloth."

She brightened and a dreaming tone richened her voice as she spoke in Arabic, the tongue she did not use anymore, not even with Beltrana, for it infuriated Engrâce not to know what was being said. "Dear Abram, this winter I will have my baby, Arslan's baby. Can you tell him that for me? And my father, too? Oh, Abram, why did all of you die?"

But though she sometimes mourned and often complained by the side of Abram's tomb, she also talked much of her baby and resolving to educate him herself, she recited lessons at the grave so that she would not forget. Somehow she felt as though her teacher heard her. This was comforting, especially since she had never been able to feel any sort of contact with Arslan or Omar. Perhaps it was because she had never seen them dead and therefore had never really accepted their passing.

"It doesn't look right for you to spend so much time at the Jew's grave," Engrâce said.

"You pray for the souls of all the *parrokia* dead," Lael answered. "Abram has no one to pray for him but me."

"What good can prayers do an unbeliever who is surely in hell?"

"I don't think anyone can say who's in hell or heaven," Lael returned and Engrâce plagued her no longer on the matter, though she did seem to give her many more chores.

Only occasionally was there time to ride Al Zirr but every day Lael called him up from the field and fed him grain or an apple. Engrâce had confiscated her silken trousers and tunics. Lael dressed now in homespun linen and wool but she could kilt up her skirts and ride through a pass in the mountains, where she never encountered anyone. Engrâce did not forbid this.

"However you were raised and in spite of your father, you are the only blood of my blood," she said. "Perhaps if you learn our ways and attend church faithfully, you will find a husband for all your foreignness." Her straight black brows knit ferociously. "Etchahoun must go to you. There is no one else.

"I don't want a husband," Lael said. "I still love Arslan."

Engrâce made an impatient, clucking sound. "You cannot love a dead husband, girl. I should know, I've buried three." Her face softened as did her usually harsh voice. "One loves dead children."

Two of hers lay under the church floor where she burned candles for them every week, not waiting on the anniversary of their deaths. Knowing this made Lael's answer more gentle than it might have been.

"I am sure of that, Grandmother, but I also love my husband." She paused, wondering whether this were the right time to break the news. She had been reluctant to tell Engrâce but another month or two would make her condition obvious. "Anyway, I need not marry again to continue the family. I'm going to have a baby."

Engrâce dropped her spindle. "A baby! By that Moslem?"

"By my husband," Lael said, lifting her head proudly.

"Good God in heaven!" Engrâce picked up the spindle and jerkily straightened the fleece. "Is there no end to difficulties? Your child would be three-quarters Moslem. You must take a purge."

"Why?"

"So you can lose it, quickly, before anyone knows."

"But that's a sin."

Engrâce nodded in agitation. "Yes, but surely a lesser one than tainting our blood even further!"

Lael rose. She clenched her trembling hands. "I will go if that's the way you feel, Grandmother. This baby is the only reason I care at all to live."

She turned away as Beltrana cackled in alarm. Engrâce stepped in front of her, barring the way. "Perhaps if you married swiftly—"

"So it's what people think, not Moslem blood, that worries you!" Lael did not try to hide the contempt in her voice.

"Grandmother, I have nothing to be ashamed of. I was married by a priest in a Christian church."

"A priest married you?" Engrâce's voice rose.

"Indeed he did, mistress," put in Beltrana eagerly. "A proper service, all written down in the records." Her eyes shone at the memory. "Oh, what a church, andrea! If you could only see it."

"I do not know what sort of priests could live in a city where the holy bells of Saint James Compostella were carried on the backs of enslaved Christians to be melted into lamps for the mosque!" snorted Engrâce but the knowledge mollified her somewhat.

She might deplore the ways of her alien granddaughter but she needed her if the Good House was to remain in the family.

V

NO MORE was said about a purge though Engrâce did begin to teach Lael what herbs and treatments were good for animals and people. None of her remedies had helped Urta, though, who often grew breathless when engaged in heavy labor.

His symptoms, including pain shooting down the left arm, were so much like those for which Abram had successfully treated Hakam that Lael suggested they brew Urta a tea from the foxglove leaves that were among the herbs in Abram's pack.

Urta was suspicious at first but when the brew relieved him, he started carrying a small flask of it to the field in case he should start to feel sick. Engrâce was intrigued with Abram's medicines and reassured as to their efficacy since some of them were in her own pharmacopeia—the willow bark and the violets that she used for treating headaches, fever and arthritis.

News of Urta's dramatic improvement quickly spread. Soon people were coming not only to their *serora* for treatment but asking rather timidly if Lael might have a cure. They all hated and feared Moslems but tales of their healing skills had spread even to this remote valley.

One day when Lael and Beltrana were scrubbing clothes on flat rocks placed in the stream, Engrâce called from the house. Wringing out a coarse linen sheet, Lael spread it over some nearby bushes and hurried to the door.

A man was standing in the kitchen. He seemed much bigger than he actually was because of the bulk of his shoulders. He was dark-skinned but his hair was ruddy chestnut and his eyes were tawny gold. When Engrâce, flustered, said that he was Adam Otsoa from the next valley, Lael thought he suited his name, Wolf. There was something about him that frightened her even though he smiled.

More upsetting was that as soon as Engrâce had introduced them and mumbled that Otsoa had a trouble he thought Lael might treat, she bustled outside, though she did leave the door open and could be heard fussing at Urta in the courtyard.

"What is your problem, sir?" inquired Lael.

His eyes moved over her in a scalding way that seemed obscene, more so since she carried a baby in her womb. His full mouth curved as though anticipating the taste of something sweet.

"The sickness is here." Taking her hand, he carried it to his heart, pressing her palm against his chest so that she felt the deep, heavy beat.

Could he have Urta's disease and yet look so vigorous? "You look strong, sir," Lael puzzled. "Have you shortness of breath? A pain in your chest or arms?"

"Yes," he said and would not release her hand when she tried to draw it away.

A hot energy radiated from him, beating against her. Desperately trying to maintain a correct manner, Lael asked, "When did this affliction begin?"

His green eyes laughed down at her. "Last week it must have been. It happened suddenly."

"Yes?" How could a man look so merry in recounting the onset of an often-fatal ailment?

"I was hunting and came to the spring of your house for a drink. As I lifted my head, what should I see but one I took for Basa Andrea herself? She was bathing in the stream below." With a finger he brought Lael's chin up so that she had to face him. "That is when my pain began. Only you can cure it."

It took her a moment to understand. Flushing, she wrenched free. "Sir, you have no business spying on women!"

"I was only thirsty." His voice was as lazily caressing as were his eyes. "How could I guess that quenching one thirst would beget an even fiercer one? Come now, my pretty. Though you have bewitched me, you must know that few men will want to marry a Moor."

She did not bother to try to explain to him that her father

was not a Moor but descended from the princely Arabian Umayyads who had ruled the Moslem world until foes had killed all but one of the royal blood, Abd-er-Rahman I, who established the Caliphate of Cordova.

"Thank you for your favor but I still mourn my husband."

"You, a Christian?" His eyes widened. "No doubt you were forced to marry but—"

"I was not forced." Backing away, she put the fire between them, coals only, waiting to be built up that night. "I loved my husband. We were well-married in a church and—" she flung the words at him, foregoing modesty in order to send him on his way—"and I am going to bear his child!"

The tawny eyes seemed to capture the glow of the coals. His somewhat forethrust jaw hardened. "Then you need a husband worse than ever. I will let you keep your Moorish brat. After all, there will be plenty of time to get true heirs from you."

"I will not marry. Not you or anyone."

He made as though to move around the hearth. She picked up the cauldron ladle. "Well and well," he said with an unpleasant laugh. "Time will change your tune. You'd better hope I will still want you."

He loomed there, blocking the light from the door. Menace came from him so palpably that she would have cried out for her grandmother except that she didn't want him to know her fear. He sensed it anyway, nostrils swelling as his lips broke over his strong white teeth.

"I will see you again, Basa Andrea," he said. "I will see you often. When you bathe without shame as no Christian woman would, naked under the sky. When you sit by the Jew's grave. And—" his smile broadened—"when you ride that white horse into the mountains."

With a mocking nod, he swung out of the house. Lael's knees felt like water. She sank down on a bench as her grandmother hurried in.

"What did you say to turn him dark as a thunderstorm?"

"That I won't wed him."

Engrâce stared. "But he's the richest man in a dozen valleys! Handsome, a shrewd hunter, a fine ball-player and the best dancer. For three springs now he has danced the Horse in the celebrations before Lent. All the unmarried girls and several well-to-do widows have flirted with him for years.''

''I wish them joy of him.''

Honestly appalled, Engrâce spread her hands. ''Is it the child? Perhaps if I interceded—''

''He would take my 'brat,' '' Lael said wearily, ''but I will not take him.''

Engrâce sank into her chair. For once she looked helpless. ''You curl your lip at Adam Otsoa? In the name of God, whom will you have?''

''No one.''

Lael went back to the stream. But she shivered in spite of the sunlight; she felt as though the man's golden eyes dwelled on her. How hateful it was to never know when he was watching! She had loved bathing in the clear, sparkling water. Even though it was cold, the sun had kissed her flesh and she had toweled herself so briskly that she was soon warmed.

Reasoning that before long it would be too chilly for outdoor bathing did little to overcome her outrage but Urta, who could not do enough for her since she had eased his frightening ailment, made a small oaken tub for her that she used in her room, pouring in a jug of water that had been heated by placing it near the hearth.

She still visited Abram's grave, praying for her beloved dead and reciting the lessons she thought most important to pass on to her child. For several days she was afraid to go riding but it wouldn't be long before her pregnancy stopped those escapes and she yearned to ride in these last lovely days of summer, remembering how, in this season, Omar and Hakam had always taken her and Arslan into the mountains.

Her weapons were locked away in one of Engrâce's chests. Even to her grandmother's stern eye they had been too splendid for destruction, especially since some man of the family might use them one day. With them, Lael would have had little fear of Adam. As it was, she scabbarded a kitchen knife in layers of old cloth and fastened it at her waist before she took some radishes from the garden and went to call Al Zirr.

Scenting her before she whistled, he lifted his head and

loped across the green meadow. He came more to be petted and praised than he did for tidbits. When he had crunched the radishes as she crooned to him and stroked the muscled neck and shoulders, he followed her to the stable and accepted the bridle and saddle as though they were presents.

"Look at the great brute!" growled Urta, scratching his shaggy hair. "Sweet as Easter cakes with you but if I come near him, he's all teeth and hoofs." He shook his head in reluctant admiration. "He be a beauty, though. Fit for Santiago's charger. Or the Basa Andrea. They do say she rides a white steed in the midst of a golden whirlwind."

"And she sits in a mountain cave making golden pots and spinning golden thread when she's not combing her golden hair," Lael teased.

Mounting, she waved gaily at Urta as she rode off but his mention of the Basa Andrea, coupled with Adam's use of the name, made her uneasy. The queen of the witches was not feared in the way that her father, Basa Jaun, was for she often helped people escape him and was said to be kindly. All the same, on the Day of the Holy Cross people climbed to her cave and gave her a blessing, hoping that she was within for if she was, the rite would persuade her not to send storms for the rest of the year. Lael did not want to be linked to a witch, not even a benevolent one. She was already strange-seeming enough to her neighbors.

Instead of taking the usual pass into the mountains, she rode to a farther and narrower defile before leaving the broad valley. Adam Otsoa couldn't be everywhere even though he'd succeeded in making her feel that his hot eyes were always watching. He had fields and farms to oversee and was asked to dance in any neighborhood that was having a celebration. All the same, she felt safer in taking a different way.

It was slow. At times Al Zirr literally squeezed between rock faces but after a while the pass broadened, opening into a valley with a small stream running through it. Giving Al Zirr the pressure of her legs that signaled speed, she laughed and took off her headcovering, glorying in the wind as they loped through the flower-spangled grass. They covered the valley in both directions before, sighing, Lael caressed the smooth neck.

"We have to go home now, Al Zirr. And you know, we have to find a mare worthy of you. My son can learn to ride on you but, alas, old friend, by the time he is a man, you will be in the place where fleet horses go. So you must sire a mount for him."

Al Zirr whinnied softly. The few horse-owning members of the community had already asked whether Al Zirr could service their mares but Lael had refused so vehemently that Engrâce had not insisted. Though Engrâce derided the stallion's uselessness, she was secretly proud of him. Perhaps she could be prevailed on to let Urta take gold pieces to the autumn market fairs in hope of finding a suitable mare, or even hunt for one in Pamplona. Well-bred colts would soon pay back the mare's cost. Lael would wait for just the right one to train for her son.

If only Arslan could see him and teach him to ride! But she would do her best. She smiled, dreaming of a boy with Arslan's proud head, clear gray eyes and firm, gentle mouth. She loosened the reins as Al Zirr threaded his way back through the gorge.

With the speed of a springing cat, a man leaped from the boulders, catching Al Zirr's bridle. Laughing in triumph at her shock, Adam Otsoa mockingly hailed her.

"Basa Andrea! You have had a fine gallop. Now it is my turn."

He reached for her. Her hand groped for the knife. Even before she gave the signal, Al Zirr reared, lashing out.

Otsoa leaped back into the crevice from which he had come, scrambling out of the reach of the deadly hoofs. Lael called soothingly to her angry, startled horse and urged him forward. If she'd had her javelin or arrows, she might have tried to put an end to Otsoa's threatening but he would not come back within range of Al Zirr and to pursue him on foot with only a knife would be inviting disaster.

Freeing the knife, she kept watching behind as Al Zirr snorted but proceeded through the gap. Only after they were back in the home valley did she begin to tremble. There was no doubting what the man had intended. Except for Al Zirr, he would almost surely have accomplished it. She returned the knife to its wrappings and patted Al Zirr's shoulder.

"Well done, beauty. But I'll not ride you anymore till after the baby comes. By then that wolf should have found another woman. But I will still bring you good things to nibble and brush you until you shine."

Back in the courtyard she rubbed him well before leading him back to the pasture. With a pang of loss, she watched him trot down to the stream to drink before he lay down to roll in the grass. Giving up her rides meant that she dropped the last vestige of her old life. Much as she wanted Arslan's baby, there was sadness in saying farewell to her youth.

As if his behavior had not sufficiently curtailed her few pleasures, Adam began attending church in her *parrokia*.

He couldn't get close to her, thank goodness. The men occupied a loft above the back of the church, reached by a staircase, and kept to an outer aisle when approaching the altar. Only women sat in the main part of the church. But even with Beltrana close beside her and Engrâce lighting and snuffing the candles, Lael felt exposed, menaced by the man's determination that did not wane as she grew heavy with child. Each Sunday he was there.

When the sheep were brought down from the high pastures, she watched over them in the daytime though the real work was done by Briza, a big, brindled dog who had been raised with sheep and possibly thought he was one himself. He brought back any that ventured too far, frightened away wolves, who had a taste for mutton, and presided over the flock like a concerned and kindly tyrant.

Lael had feared that Adam might harrass her even though she was in sight of the house and she had asked both Urta and Beltrana to join her should they see him approaching. But he didn't bother her; it was as if he were waiting.

Lelo, a young shepherd who had been in the mountains that summer and now tended his flock in the next meadow, sometimes would leave his dogs in charge long enough that he could come visit. A simple-minded, good-natured lad, he asked Lael many questions about Cordova and the Moslems, listening to the answers as though they were fairy tales. He solemnly assured her that Basa Jaun had frequently stopped at his lonely camp and eaten prodigiously of cheese and milk.

"I always gave him his fill," shivered Lelo, hugging himself. "I didn't want him to decide to eat me. So he would sit there stuffing himself and making jokes. Hairy all over he was, with legs like a goat's, and hoofs. Sometimes he'd take my flute and play such music as you never heard."

"He sounds interesting," Lael smiled. "Does he ever come down here?"

"You'd better hope he doesn't," Lelo answered. He blushed and shot her a nervous glance. "You—you're not his daughter?"

Omar, to this peasant lad, must seem just as fantastic. Lael, in fact, sometimes wondered if she had dreamed it all: Cordova, her father, Arslan, the splendor of Princess Zahra. What had happened to that beautiful, lascivious woman? Lael hoped that she had escaped punishment and somehow continued to live in the manner that she had refined into an art.

Smiling playfully at the boy, Lael gave a merry laugh and thrust out feet, shod in tough leather sandals. "Now, Lelo, do I have goat legs and hoofs?"

"The Basa Andrea doesn't," he said stubbornly. "She is beautiful, like you, and often helps people."

"Then I don't see why anyone should be afraid of her."

The boy glanced about fearfully and crossed himself. "She is different," he muttered.

So am I, thought Lael. *And I shall always be. But my child will grow up here. I want him to belong, though he must know and be proud of his father and grandfather.* She realized, though, with a taste of ashes, that whatever she told her son of Cordova and Arslan and Omar would seem only bright, fanciful dreams, not quite as real as the Basa Jaun of these mountains.

"I am mortal, like you," she told Lelo carefully. "And I am in church each Sunday."

Her words seemed to convince him. But when he got a big splinter deep in his hand and she used aconite to numb the flesh while she removed the rotting wood, he looked at her worshipfully. "Maybe you're not Basa Andrea but you're not like other women."

"I come from another country. Now keep that hand out of the muck until it heals over. There seems to be something in dirt that can make small sores swell up and ruin an arm or leg."

With autumn, birds started flying south. Streams of doves flew down through the mountains. A huge oak tree between the house and church seemed to be in their line of flight and one day Lael was puzzled to see men climbing about in the tree while women and children fanned up the valley and stationed themselves as though in waiting. One man took a position on a ledge fairly close to the tree.

Shielding her eyes to see better, Lael asked Beltrana, "What's going on?"

"You'll see," promised the nurse. "Oh, look! Here come the doves!"

A great flock winged down the valley. The women and children shouted and waved at the birds if they started to swerve from the direction of the oak. Just as the doves neared it, the man on the ledge rose up and sent what looked like a hawk sailing up into the sky.

The frightened birds dived for the safety of the branches. There was a concerted shout of glee. A few minutes later the watchers in the tree scrambled down with filled nets and set off to the village with their victims.

"That—that's terrible!" cried Lael.

Beltrana squinted incredulously. "Why? It is as the old song says, 'The dove is beautiful in the air but even better in the dish.' Besides, you used to hunt."

"I never tricked my quarry," Lael retorted.

Beltrana shrugged. "I doubt that a dead bird cares much whether it strangles in a net or is killed by a costly falcon. It is dead meat all the same." Perhaps the old woman was right but that night Lael had a nightmare about birds flying free one moment and struggling in nets the next.

There was snow now on the peaks. While watching the sheep, Lael gathered chestnuts. She and Lelo roasted them and shared stories as they peeled and ate the meat. Engrâce had a long-handled iron cooker that could be filled with the nuts, placed in the coals and rotated. As the days shortened and the household no longer went to bed at nightfall, Urta, Beltrana and Lael sat around the hearth on benches while Engrâce, enthroned in the only chair, deftly spun and told stories.

One of her ancestors had helped to vanquish Charlemagne's rear guard at Roncevalles when Lord Roland was slain. Others had joined with the Goth, Pelayo, to defeat the Moors but had then battled the surrounding kings of Asturias and Navarre to retain their independence.

"Our first Jauna was Jaun Zuria, the White Lord," Engrâce said proudly. "He was the son of a serpent and a Scottish princess and ruled Vizcaya wisely and well."

"When was that?" queried Lael.

Engrâce's brow grooved into deeper lines. "Oh, it is many generations. Many. It must be over two hundred years since we chose our first Jauna." She crossed herself. "It is said that in the time of the Old Law, before we were Christians, we worshiped a divine princess whose consort was a serpent."

Perhaps through love of myth she liked to place ancestors in the armies under Charles Martel that checked the onsweeping Moslem thrust into Europe at Tours in 732. Of one thing there was no doubt. Invader after invader had tried to claim her country but they were all gone now, while the Bascoli, or vizcaínos, remained.

Though Engrâce was not interested in Moslem victories and glories, she was curious about the conquerors who had penetrated even beyond her mountains and into the Frankish kingdom.

"It is said that many Christian martyrs were beheaded in Cordova," she mused one evening.

"It's over a hundred years since there were any martyrs," Lael responded hotly.

"But blessed Saint Flora—"

Was a silly goose. Lael clamped her teeth on the thought and endeavored to speak calmly. "Flora almost demanded martyrdom. She kept appearing before the judge and denouncing Mohammed as an adulterer, imposter and villain. Can you imagine what would happen in a Christian court if someone spoke so of Jesus?"

Both Engrâce and Beltrana hastily muttered a prayer. "In

spite of her behaving like this on several occasions," Lael went on, "the judge would have released her had she recanted her harsh words. She would not and so he finally had her beheaded. The fanatical priest who had put her up to it kept calling for new martyrs. A number of people went to the judges and maligned Mohammed as a child of hell and a false prophet. They got exactly what they wanted, which was to lose their heads."

"They were defending the faith!"

"No. They were free to worship as Christians. It was only when they publicly blasphemed and refused to make retraction that they were killed. It was perfectly useless and I can only think it a shame that Eulogius, who egged them on, wasn't killed before he led others into such folly."

Engrâce's jaw dropped at this impiety. "How can Christians worship freely under Moslem rule?" she demanded.

"Multitudes do. It requires only that Christians don't slander Islam." She added drily, "That, in some cases, is too much to expect."

When Engrâce was tired, Beltrana told stories. The one that most delighted Urta was about the time when Our Lord promised Saint Peter a horse if he could recite a paternoster without thinking of the promised gift.

"That's easy," said Saint Peter. "Our Father, which art in heaven, hallowed be Thy name . . . Lord, will the horse have a saddle?"

The Lord shook his head. "Now, my friend, you shall get neither saddle nor horse."

Urta sometimes played his flute but when Lael asked him for a story, he rubbed his ear in embarrassment. "I know only one story, young mistress. Do you know what happened to the devil when he tried to learn our language?"

She shook her head. Stealing a sly glance at Engrâce, he said, "Well, the devil hid for seven years behind a door but the woman of the house had such a shrill voice that he couldn't understand her. So he learned only what the man said. Two words. *'Bai, andrea.'* Yes, lady."

Lael laughed but Beltrana said sourly, "That one is so old that the devil himself must be tired of it."

Urta grinned at her. *"Bai, andrea."*

* * *

November was announced when the men harvesting the fields were visited by a white mare—in reality two men draped in a sheet. The lofts and storerooms were filled with grain, hay, turnips, apples, onions and beans. Urta butchered a pig and the parts that were not made into sausage or eaten quickly were hung to smoke above the hearth.

On Christmas Eve after church services, which Adam Otsoa attended, Engrâce's household ate bread over which the sign of the cross had been made and Engrâce put up pieces of the crust in order to quell floods and violent storms. She also planted garlic that evening to make a cure for madness.

When the harvest was in, Urta watched the sheep but Lael carried water and wood up to the time of her eighth month, when Engrâce commanded her to stop. Still, every day till her confinement Lael went to the edge of the meadow and whistled for Al Zirr. She fed him treats and brushed him carefully, checking his hoofs to be sure they were free of hurtful objects or disease. Urta had found him no mate at the harvest fair but he would try again in the summer. Engrâce had seen the profit in breeding him and had consented to send Urta farther afield if no mare was found by autumn.

Also, in that season of her heaviness, Lael took out Abram's paper, ink powder and quills and wrote down verbatim the verses and passages she remembered as well as the gist of her studies and algebraic formulas. These would school her child.

On a blustery day in late March, Lael felt a pain that was nothing like the restless kicking of the baby during the past few months. She continued preparing the heart of a stillborn lamb to be cooked with rosemary and garlic but the cramping soon became so violent and regular that she had to sit down.

Engrâce looked at her sharply. "It is time?"

Lael nodded, damp with cold sweat. Beltrana rushed to her, clucking. The two older women helped her upstairs and to bed. Engrâce made her drink hot brews. Worn cloths were placed under her so that the good linen would not be stained. Between spasms Beltrana encouraged her to walk. The day wore on, passing into a blur of racking misery.

"Bear down." Engrâce's voice filtered into her separate

country, a world of agony. "Push! You must get the babe's head out!"

Panting, Lael tried to do her bidding but lost conscious control. When she slipped into awareness again, she heard Beltrana weeping, "She is too narrow! What can we do?"

"She should have purged herself of this," Engrâce said grimly. "But no, she must have her Moslem's get. She will be lucky not to die of it."

"I'll have my baby!" Lael choked. She remembered something that Abram had said about how Jewish women gave birth.

Dragging herself out of the bed in spite of the women's protests, she gripped the bedpost, squatting, forcing downward. A brutal, fiery hand seemed to wrench her vitals, twisting them, tearing. She screamed for the first time, screamed and hung on while she pressed.

The hand tore then, swirling her into flame-shot darkness. But as she slumped to the floor, she heard Beltrana cry, "It's coming! Hurry, andrea, the head is through!"

After all that, the child was not a boy. When they placed the silkily black-haired baby at her breast, Lael kept saying "he" and "him" even though they corrected her. The eyes were hazy like deep, misty water but the tiny fingers were perfect, with minute, pearly nails. The smooth brow wrinkled imperiously in Arslan's manner. Lael sighed, cradled her child and dropped into slumber.

Dreams. Phantasms. Snatches of talk, a baby's wailing. And through it all, burning that neither drink nor wet cloths could lessen. When Lael finally started to recover from the milk fever, Beltrana said that she had been sick for two weeks.

"But by the mercy of God and herbs your grandmother knows, you didn't lose your milk," the old woman said, her hooked chin wobbling. "You will not believe what a fancy the andrea has taken to the babe, maybe because she saved the little one."

"My Moslem brat?" thrust Lael, but in spite of jealous twinges when Engrâce crooned to the baby or, smiling, held out her finger for the tiny hand to clutch at, Lael was glad that her daughter would be loved by the redoubtable old woman.

Beltrana adored the baby, of course, boasting of her every natural accomplishment as though no other child had ever lifted its head so strongly, followed objects so quickly with its eyes or learned so soon to push up on firm, dimpled elbows.

Urta and Beltrana stood at the altar as the baby's godparents when she was baptized and solemnly named Kattalin Lucira after her grandmother and Engrâce's mother. Engrâce had wanted to ask rich friends of hers to be godparents but Lael had said, "I hardly know them. Urta and Beltrana love the baby. Please, grandmother, let them be her sponsors." And so they were, each so filled with joyful pride that their aged faces had seemed to light the church.

Kattalin's sweet flesh and dove's eyes had soon reconciled Lael to not having a son. Since her marriage contract had stipulated that sons were to be reared Moslem, she would have felt some guilt, a certain betrayal of Arslan, in doing otherwise.

As she took her newly blessed baby, she prayed that Arslan and Omar might know about Kattalin. She had already taken the baby to Abram's grave and had again felt her teacher's presence, as though he had smiled and lovingly admired the child.

Leaving the church, thanking the folk of the *parrokia* for their good wishes, she was happier than she had been since Arslan's father called him from the rose garden. But a vague uneasiness nagged and she glanced up.

Adam Otsoa stood in the men's loft. His eyes flickered as if they had captured the flame of the extinguished candles. He laughed down at her, teeth showing white.

She held her baby closer and went out quickly.

VI

KATTALIN GREW out of the cradle that Urta had carved for her and now had her own small bed in Lael's room. She talked in sentences before she was a year old, mixing Arabic with Bascoli, and toddled eagerly after first one, then another, of the household. The women dressed her in fine cotton and silk cut from Lael's garments, reserving only Lael's wedding clothes, though the child had wool, too, for winter. She had Arslan's gray eyes and Lael's auburn hair, with fair, translucent skin.

She was as much the life of the house as was the fire. Absorbed in her, busy with domestic chores, Lael was more content than she could have imagined possible without her men and all she had so loved in Cordova. She carried the child to pet Al Zirr, who now had a pretty blood-bay mare for company, and she looked forward to the time when Kattalin could start reading the "books" written down from memory on Abram's precious paper.

For some inexplicable reason, Adam Otsoa still came to church. Lael never looked up at the loft. Perhaps he just preferred this priest. Lael had almost forgotten her dread of him when, a few days after Kattalin's first birthday, she opened the door to a knock and found him standing there.

She stepped back involuntarily. He entered without invitation though he greeted her politely. "My grandmother is cleaning the church, if you have business with her," she stammered. Beltrana was upstairs napping with the baby and Urta was in the fields.

"My business is with you." The man spoke pleasantly enough but he closed and barred the door. "I have waited until you had your child and raised her through her first year. That is long enough to mourn the best of men. I've come for an answer."

"You had it long ago."

His eyes dilated. The curves of his nostrils showed white. "You still won't marry me? Be *etcheko andrea* of the best house and farm in ten valleys?"

"Of a thousand valleys."

She moved back, trying to put the hearth between them as she had before and seize some kind of weapon but he caught her arm and closed a broad palm over her mouth and nose. She fought till suffocation sent the room whirling into blackness. Reviving as he tossed her down on a rug of wolf skins, she started to scream. He brought his mouth down on hers in cruel stifling. She managed to move her jaws and bite his lip.

He cursed. A buffet seemed to jerk her head from her shoulders. Stunned, she felt only dimly the ruthless hilting of him, his lunging thrusts, but her senses returned as he lay drained on her, weighing her down with his spread-eagled body.

It could not be. Yet it was.

Her violated body shrieked its pain. Rage and humiliation surged redly through her mind, leaving cold, bright fury. Suddenly wresting herself from beneath him, she scrambled to the far side of the fire and grasped the iron poker.

"Get out," she said in a deadly voice.

He looked almost bewildered as he righted his clothes but by the time he was on his feet, he was able to set his head cockily at her and grin as he licked the blood trickling down his lip.

"If I've put a babe in you, you may pray to see me back."

"I'll have no babe of yours."

He shrugged, "Anyway, this may remind you that you need a man."

She could not believe his words. That brutal tumble on the floor was supposed to arouse in her an overpowering, primitive urge? His conceit was so ludicrous that she burst into astounded laughter. His eyes narrowed.

"You have a witch's mirth."

"Because I laugh at you?"

"You laugh when no decent woman would."

"Oh, should I cringe and kiss your feet now that you have

abused me? Be grateful that you want me in your house, where you could humiliate me all you please?''

"You may learn.''

He started toward her but she held the poker with the stance of a trained fencer and he halted. "Adam Otsoa,'' she said slowly, measuring each word, "I want no trouble for my daughter's sake, and what is done is done. But if you molest me again, I will surely kill you.''

"You are a witch!''

"No. I am a woman who will not be your toy.''

For a moment their eyes battled across the smoldering coals. He let out his breath gustily and wheeled toward the door. "You are crazed or the devil's!''

He flung himself out of the house. Trembling, Lael washed herself in water as hot as she could stand it before she hurried among her grandmother's herbs and made a purging draught. If a seed of his had lodged in her, she did not want to know.

Adam Otsoa came no more to their church. He danced the Horse before Lent, leaping high, high, higher into the air, and at other special occasions he was always invited to dance the principal part because of his grace and endurance. Apart from such times Lael did not see him but often as she washed clothing in the stream, sat by Abram's grave or rode Al Zirr with Katti before her in the saddle, she seemed to feel those yellow eyes following her.

Except for that and the fall dove-netting, which Lael detested, life moved tranquilly from one season to the next— enfolded within the rhythms of planting and harvest, the sheep going to the high pastures in spring with new lambs and returning in autumn, and the round of holy days celebrated in the little church, punctuated by christenings and buryings and marryings. On the Day of the Holy Cross in mid-September, people trudged up the mountain to the Basa Andrea's haunt and said their blessings to prevent storms; when it was droughty, they importuned Engrâce to ring the church bells and perform the rites for rain. And always, in sickness they came to the women of Etchahoun.

In the autumn of Katti's third year, Engrâce began to look

haggard and lose flesh. She dosed herself with many concoctions. "I am getting older," she said with asperity when Lael questioned her with concern. But though she ate heartily, she gained no weight and the skin pressed ever more tightly against the strong bones of her craggy face. She still did all of her work but she began to retire earlier.

Before she went to her chamber, though, she never failed to gather Katti into her arms and sing to her for a while or tell her a story. The precocious little girl especially enjoyed the times when Lael and Engrâce tossed couplets back and forth at each other, improvising till one or the other could no longer respond.

This was an esteemed talent among the Bascoli, one that Lael had cultivated by matching verses with her father. Now, though she was still quicker in Arabic, she won rhyming duels with her grandmother more often than she lost. And she, too, told her daughter stories, tales of the mighty Rustum or accounts of magical fishermen and genies, cave doors that opened to a word, wonderful lamps and flying carpets.

Others were Moslem legends such as the one told of Adam's first wife, Lilith, created out of flame. When he commanded her to prostrate herself before him, she cried angrily, "Shall a being of fire kneel to one made of clay?" For her pride she was banished, to become a spirit of the air and darkness. "But," concluded Lael, smiling into Kattalin's wide gray eyes, "she never knelt to a man."

Engrâce scowled as she opened a chestnut, peeled and offered it to the child, who ran and climbed into her lap. "Why do you fill her head with such dangerous nonsense? Adam's wife was Eve. Ezba. She and Adam were Bascoli and they spoke our tongue in their earthly Paradise."

Lael raised a shoulder good-humoredly. She and Engrâce would never love each other but respect and unwilling admiration had developed gradually between them and they were united in their love for Kattalin.

"I prefer Lilith to Eve."

"You would," said Engrâce dourly.

Several other men had by now offered for Lael, who rejected them with unflattering speed. Fortunately, since she feared to lose Katti, Engrâce no longer urged Lael to marry though on principle she considered continued celibacy unnatural for a healthy woman in her twentieth year.

Smiling as she stroked Kattalin's mass of burnished curly hair, Engrâce launched into a wonder-tale of El Cid. She spoke of how a coffer of sand that he had used as security for a loan was miraculously turned into treasure.

When the drowsy child took her turn in Urta's lap and fell asleep against his grizzled cheek, Lael looked up from her sewing. "Grandmother, you're the one who is telling noxious stories. Making a hero of Rodrigo Diaz!"

"Why, so he is! May God strengthen his sword to utterly vanquish the infidels."

"He promised grace to Valencia but what did he do? Bury the governor to the waist and burn him alive! He'd have done the same to the man's wife and children if his own commanders had not protested."

"They were faithless heathen. Promises to such are not binding."

Of course this was Moslem doctrine, too. It never ceased to amaze Lael that there was so much similarity, good and bad, between the warring faiths. She let the argument go, not adding that she saw some justification for El Cid's ferocity in that the governor had killed the former king, Moorish Alcadir, and stolen his treasure, including the fabled girdle of Zobeida, Harun al-Rashid's favorite wife.

Engrâce rose to her feet. "The child is asleep. Let me take her to my bed till you come up, Granddaughter."

Lael nodded. "I'll carry her. She's getting heavy as an acorn-fattened pig."

After she had tucked Katti in with the older woman, she made a strong brew of camomile and took it up to Engrâce, who sipped it and thanked her.

"Granddaughter," she said as she returned the wooden cup, "I was bitter at heaven when you came to my door looking like a Moorish lad, burdened with the body of a dead Jew. But you have blessed my life with this child. I am grateful."

They looked at one another in the dim light, worlds apart in their upbringing, each unable to understand the other however much she tried yet bound by common blood. Lael would have liked to kiss her grandmother but there had never been tender expressions between them. So all she did was brush her hand and say gently, "I'm glad you love Kattalin. Good-night, Grandmother."

Another year passed. Engrâce worked no longer in the fields. She still performed her rituals as the *serora* but Lael did the cleaning of the church. Though Engrâce did not say so, it was clear she was in pain that her remedies could not ease. Lael ached for her but her herbs, too, were useless. Engrâce seemed to live only that she might enjoy Kattalin.

On Saint John's Eve, Engrâce carried a bundle of burning laurel through the fields, chanting incantations against thieves, witches and vermin. At the end of the rite she collapsed and Lael and Urta had to carry her home.

Next day she did not come down for breakfast. Lael took her some barley mush and milk. It was the first time in her memory that Engrâce had not been up long before dawn.

Engrâce frowned in distaste at the food but forced herself to eat before she lay back on her pillows. "Lael, I have the wasting sickness."

"Oh, Grandmother, perhaps—"

Engrâce lifted a bony hand. "I saw my mother die of it, and my sister. I do not wish Kattalin to remember me as they were at the end." She smiled slightly. "I am not asking you for death. I have a medicine of my own. But first I must show you something." She sighed heavily. "It is a secret meant only for the women of our blood."

Lael's chin lifted. "Perhaps you would rather not. I am my father's daughter as well as my mother's."

"I must tell you." Engrâce's dark green eyes glowed as if they had drained all the color from her face. "You will pass the secret on to Kattalin."

Yes, there was that. Kattalin should have her heritage even though nothing of this cold north country could ever be Lael's. "We will do as you wish," she told her grandmother. "Shall I help you dress?"

It was toward the mountain of Basa Andrea's dwelling that

Engrâce directed Lael to lead her donkey. As Engrâce motioned for her to stop at the rocky gray cliffs, Lael asked, "Are we going to Basa Andrea's cave?"

"No." Engrâce's face was a mask of controlled pain as she dismounted, tried to walk without Lael's arm and then accepted it. "But we are going to a cave. Not the ones you already know of, where those of the Ancient Law painted beasts—but to a cave known only to one woman in each generation."

When they reached the small opening, Lael was surprised that anyone had ever gone inside. She slipped through the narrow aperture without much trouble but it was difficult for Engrâce and it was frightening to edge along between cold rocks on either side. Her torch protested at the thick, still air but in a few minutes they entered a vaulted chamber.

Lael caught in her breath. "Our Lady and her Son," she breathed. "The flying birds! And all the hands—"

Engrâce shook her head. "These were done even before the Ancient Law. We don't know who painted them, but she passed on these words: 'This is a place for the women of our blood and it will last long after the things that men hunt are gone. In our cave, it is always summer.' "

She took a packet from her clothes and unfolded a strip of hide smeared with reddened tallow. "There is your mother's hand," she said, pointing to a small one hovering above a shard with a small blue bird painted on it. "I brought her here after her first flow, as my mother brought me." Pressing her palm into the pigment, she selected a clear place on the wall. "Since your mother cannot pass on the secret, I will sign for her," she said, making her imprint and then offering Lael the paint. "You may make your mark anywhere you please."

Lael hesitated a moment. For the first time since leaving Cordova, she had a sense of belonging. Even more poignantly, she was aware of her mother and felt a wave of love and longing for the woman she had never known. Kneeling down by the blue bird, she placed her palm so that it touched her mother's.

"Well done." Engrâce looked weary to fainting. "One favor. When you bring Kattalin, show her my hand. Ask her to make her mark close to it."

"I will," Lael promised. She took one last sweeping look

around the chamber, locking its wonder in her mind before she led the way out, helping Engrâce as best she could.

That night Engrâce sat up later than usual, enjoying riddles and rhymes with Kattalin. At last she told Beltrana to bring wine and cups. "For fifty years I have been *etcheko andrea*," she said, pouring out the cups for Beltrana to pass around. "I am tired." She lifted her cup to Lael. "Granddaughter, you are now the mistress. Strive to direct this household wisely and well. Urta and Beltrana, faithful friends and helpers, salute the andrea."

They drank. With tear-stung eyes, Lael raised her cup to Engrâce. "You will always be lady of this house."

The two regarded each other across the hearth's glow. Then they rose and kissed solemnly before Engrâce took her lamp and started up to bed.

"Would you like Kattalin to sleep with you?" Lael asked.

The lamp wavered, betraying Engrâce's weakness. "No. We have had a happy time tonight." She went out the door to the stairway and the others finished their wine.

When Engrâce did not come downstairs next morning, Lael went alone to her chamber. The andrea lay as if asleep, face soft and smiling. A little wine remained in her cup. Whatever her remedy, it had been easy and kind.

As mistress of Etchahoun, Lael took the leading part in her grandmother's funeral rites and since there was no *serora*, the priest asked her to perform those offices too. When the *parrokia* chose its new *serora*, to Lael's great amazement, it chose her.

"The office has remained with your family for a long time," the priest explained. He was a middle-aged, rather unkempt man who always seemed nervous in the presence of Lael. "Also, people respect you as a healer."

And they probably think it is better to have a half-Moslem witch on their side than not, Lael thought with dour humor. But she accepted the duties, eager to do all she could to ensure Kattalin's place in the community.

She herself would always be a stranger—except in one place. She visited the cave often, marveling at the brightness of the colors as she tried to imagine the woman who had used them. She dreamed over the multitudes of hands, spinning fancies about their owners. Did any of them have stories as strange as Lucira's? Or her own, for that matter?

The birds fly free in our cave. They are not trapped in nets. The annual slaughter of doves weighed with increasing heaviness on Lael's heart. She was andrea now, and *serora,* in a way responsible for much that went on in the valley. The God of the church might not care about the netting of the birds but she was sure the mother in the cave did.

Lael racked her brain as snow appeared on the peaks and the time of migration neared. She decided that the flock must be frightened away from the great oak tree—but allowed near enough to it that the birds would not reunite and dive into it. Diverting them at the pass would be too soon. But if a block of wood could frighten them into the nets, it might also frighten them out.

She fashioned a piece of wood into a long heart shape and practiced throwing it until she could send it high and far. On the day that the flock came streaming darkly over the mountains, she climbed the outside stairway that was hidden from the *parrokia,* listening to the excited cries of the women and children as they formed into lines below.

The nets would be spread in the oak and the man with the hawk-wedge would crouch on his ledge. Lael took a deep breath. As the flocks darkened the sky above her, she lobbed up the piece of wood.

The birds flurried, calling their distress, scattered like a swirling of leaves in a whirlwind. Cries of disappointed anger from the netters frightened them even more. They flew high and dispersed over the valley. Only in the far distance, barely discernible, did they start merging into formation again.

There was much talk about the event on Sunday and several of the women asked Lael whether she was certain that she was correctly fulfilling her duties as *serora.* It was as though the devil had a hand in it, the way the flock had been coming in just right and then had suddenly flown off in all directions.

"My husband thinks a hawk flew up from somewhere near your house," an older woman said. "If there are hawks about, you had better get rid of them before the lambing season."

Loss of the doves would have been grumbled over and forgotten but then—even though the people had trudged up to say blessings at the Basa Andrea's cave—hail and winds devastated the crops just as they were ready to be harvested.

Lael sent Urta with gold pieces to the neighboring village and bought grain, which she shared with the people. Her neighbors accepted it but they cast dark looks at her. Several, in voices loud enough for her to hear, muttered that such things had never happened while Engrâce was *serora*.

Then plague broke out. Fever and retching led to death within a few days. None of Lael's medicines would check it. After her third patient died, no one sent for her and when she tried to visit a stricken household, the door was barred against her.

"You bring bad luck or worse," the mistress called from behind the door. "If my son dies, I will conduct his *yarleku* rites myself. Do not come."

Lael went home. She noticed Beltrana, Urta and Katti gathering chestnuts in the pasture as she washed in the icy stream before she went inside where she wearily stared at the fire. Could it be true? Had she somehow brought a curse on her mother's valley? One thing was clear. She could not continue as *serora*. The people had no trust in her.

Though she had never belonged among them, the responsibilities had given her a place. Now all was ruined. For herself she could bear it but what of Kattalin? Better no mother at all than one viewed with suspicion and hatred.

The door opened though there had been no knock. Adam Otsoa closed it and came to stand between her and the hearth. "Well, Basa Andrea, unless you can vanish in a golden whirlwind, you had better take a husband to protect you. A lad has just died and his mother cries that you came to the house minutes before he passed."

The boy had been a sturdy, handsome child, a few years older than Kattalin. "I wanted to help," Lael said. The words caught in her throat.

"They are saying now," the man went on as though he bore pleasant gossip, "that Engrâce's death was very sudden." He smiled winningly. "Suppose I tell how I saw you scatter the doves? And there's little doubt you brought the hailstorms."

"Why would I destroy my own fields?" she asked scornfully.

"Oh, you had to or everybody would have guessed at once." He took her hand and drew her toward him. "I can stop the whispers. No one would accuse my wife."

"Aren't you afraid to wed such a fearful person?"

He laughed huskily, framing her face with his hands. "Maybe you are a witch. I can't forget you. But you are the woman I must have—and I will have you."

Adam Otsoa—or a disgraceful death at the hands of desperate, sorrowing people. Lael sighed and made the only decision possible, the one she had seen as she stared into the flames.

"Go tell the priest we wish to marry. And give me until evening to make ready."

His eyes shone. He laughed with unbelieving joy as he caught her to him and kissed her numb lips. "When I come for you this evening, you will be dressed as a bride?"

She almost smiled at him. "Yes," she said.

Taking Kattalin away from her foraging, she promised Urta and Beltrana to return her shortly. Then she hurried the child, now in her fifth year, up to the forbidding gray cliffs.

Intrigued by the mystery, Kattalin cried out with delight as Lael blew the coal end of her torch into flame and led the way into the passage.

"Remember what I tell you, Katti," Lael urged. "This is a secret that you must keep until you give it to your own little girl or her daughter. Be sure to come here often enough that you will always remember the way."

When she had repeated the ancient words to the wide-eyed child, Lael opened the paint hide and showed the girl Engrâce's print. "Your great-grandmother made this. She wants you to make your hand close to hers."

Kattalin laughed mischievously. She smeared her palm and fingers well and placed them not by, but on, the larger hand. "We used to make hands together like that," she said.

"Good." Lael signed beside the double print and held Katti close for a moment as she felt the presence, comforting and invit-

ing, of all those who had gone before. Then she smiled gently at
the bright birds and led the way out.

Lael left Kattalin with the old servants, bidding them with
special emphasis to care for her daughter. Taking her bridal garments from a chest, she dressed carefully, thinking of Arslan
more deeply than she had in years. She mixed the Herb of Mary
with a little wine and poured it into a skin.

Had the old tutor brought along this cure in case his exile in
the valley became too harsh? She would have liked to visit his
grave but she would soon be with him anyway; the same heaven
took them all and she believed that if what she was about to do
was a sin, the Holy Mother would plead for her.

Whistling up Al Zirr, she climbed up on his back from a tree
stump, riding him with neither saddle nor bridle. That way,
there would be nothing to encumber him when he found his
way back home.

As she rode toward the mountains, she remembered the
day she had ridden outside Cordova and Arslan had pursued
her. She thought of playing chess with her father and of many
other happy, joyous times. The only thing that held her here was
Kattalin and now, as all had happened, the child would be better
off without her.

As she neared the pass, Lael tilted up the wineskin. The liquid tasted sweet and cool. She drank again, more deeply this
time. Her legs began to lose their feeling as she rode through the
pass. She stroked Al Zirr and signaled him into his smooth,
swinging canter.

The sun had never been so bright. There was a faint, distant
shock, a rushing in her ears.

Then she was among the roses and fountains with her own
dear love.

IV

Gran Chichimeca

I

MARYA KNELT at the *yarleku*, lit the candles and prayed for her father's soul. Cristóbal Urdin had been swept overboard in a storm as his ship was returning from a successful whaling season off Labrador after having been iced in for the winter. Though he could have lived luxuriously in Bruges where there was a stately Basque consulate and where Basque merchants enjoyed judicial immunity except for murder or maiming, Cristóbal preferred to leave the conduct of his various interests to his cousin, Perkain Artza, who, when he was not overseeing the iron smelter near Bilbao or the shipyard, or was not in Seville or Bruges or Cadiz on business, occupied the stone tower attached to the large stone house on the slope above the village.

Perkain had come and gone like a thin gray wraith for as long as Marya could remember, yet she never felt easy with him and was glad that he kept to the *dorrea*, cooked for and attended by his Moorish slave, a deaf-mute named Abu. Perkain was nothing like her adored, barrel-chested father, with his skin leathery from wind, sun and salt and his laughter that swept like a gale through the house when he was home.

Born to a Bilbao family that owned not only whalers but codding vessels, Cristóbal had loved the sea. When Marya's mother, Esteffania, had been alive, he had remained inland at her farm, Etchahoun, for as long as he could bear it between short voyages but after his wife's death ten years ago, when Marya was seven, he began to go with the whaling ships that left in summer and returned late in winter, unless ice bottled them up till spring, or he sailed with a cod vessel. Since it took quantities of salt to preserve the fish caught off Newfoundland, Basques from south of the Pyrenees often carried iron to a port such as

Lisbon or Seville and traded it for salt before sailing west. Such a voyage would keep Cristóbal at sea from January until autumn. Whether he went after whales or cod, he was gone the better part of the time.

Now he would return no more and Marya wept for him more than she had for her mother, who had been sickly and had not wanted a romping child in her room. The closest that she had ever felt to Esteffania was on the day that the ailing woman had rallied herself to take Marya to the cave and tell her what she knew of the ancestresses who had made the handprints surrounding the gently smiling mother and child among the flying birds.

These prints were Pita's, she who had danced before Queen Isabela at Gernika; this was the mark of Berengaria, a famed healer; here was the hand of Graciana, who had made the beautiful altar cloth in the church. And the small palm over the darker one? Oh, that was Kattalin's. She was the most famed *serora* ever known in the valley and her mark was over that belonging to her great-grandmother, Engrâce. The print just touching theirs was that of Lael, *La Morisca*, who was said to still ride the mountain passes on her great white stallion. For a time she had been buried next to the Jew's tomb but Kattalin, with great reverence and ceremony, had moved her into the churchyard, where now mother and daughter lay side by side.

Marya left the church presently, giving good-day to two boys who played at handball on the stone-paved *pelota* court, bouncing the stuffed leather ball off of the church's whitewashed wall. One was Martín Yriate's younger brother and the grace and speed with which he moved reminded her so wrenchingly of her betrothed that she fought back tears. She lingered beside the churchyard on the other side, where his family's plot was near that of hers. Ancient discoidal stones were sunken beside splendidly engraved markers bearing names and dates. Her father's stone, which David was carving, would be without a body. Would that also be true of Martín's stone?

Martín had sailed three years earlier to seek his fortune in Nueva Vizcaya, the province that its founder, himself a Vizcaíno from Durango, had hoped to govern under the *Fuero of Vizcaya*, the charter of rights solemnly affirmed by all Spanish rulers. The

Fuero had existed even before their Most Catholic Majesties, Ferdinand of Aragon and Isabela of Castile, also Lady of Vizcaya, had pledged to uphold the old privileges as they stood beneath the sacred tree of Gernika, where that region's *Juntas* had met from times unremembered to pass laws.

In 1526, Charles V, grandson of the famous sovereigns and father of the present king, Philip II, had reaffirmed the universal nobility of all long-time families of Vizcaya and Guipuzcoa because these provinces had never surrendered to the Moors.

Actually, the inhabitants of a number of valleys, cities and other regions had been collectively ennobled and granted charters, often in recognition of their service against the Moors. No one took this "nobility" seriously in a social sense but it was highly useful when it came to dealings with the rest of Spain, where only nobles were permitted to hold important religious and secular positions.

Among other things, the *Fuero* exempted Vizcaínos from taxes of maritime endeavors, granted every Vizcaíno the right to engage in commerce, guaranteed due process in legal cases and exempted men from obligatory military service outside of Basque territory.

Although Spain had refused to grant Nueva Vizcaínos these same liberties, the New World still lured men with gold and silver shipped back to Spain and persisting rumors of fabulous cities of gold. Martín would not even inherit his family's modest farmstead for it was being passed on to a daughter, already named *etcheko primu*. Cristóbal's wealth was such that he was more concerned with the character of his son-in-law than with his worldly goods but Martín had rejected Marya's pleas that he stay at home.

"I love you, Marya mine," he had said, pressing her hands to his face, "but I do not want to tend your farm or your father's smelter or sail in one of his ships. I have to bring something of my own to our marriage."

"You are all I want." She had put her arms around his neck. "Please, Martín! So many sail to the New World and never return."

"I will," he promised. "I'll come back with a fortune. No one shall snicker that I married you for your holdings." His blue eyes softened and he played with a strand of her curly chestnut hair. "Though they would be blind to say it, for you are the fairest maid in all Vizcaya. I love the way your eyebrows wing up over those green eyes. It's as if you are always asking a question. And your mouth—I can't see it without wanting to do this!"

He had kissed her then and their leavetaking had been both rapturous and sad. She had given him an amulet, a tiny blue bird that she had persuaded David to carve. It was modeled on the one in the cave, though neither man knew that. She had put it around Martín's neck and prayed to the spirits of the Mothers to bring him back safely. She did not think that God would concern himself with lovers but the women of the cave—they had all loved. They understood.

But perhaps their power does not reach across the ocean, Marya thought as she started home. Of course, though it didn't ease her troubled longing, she was not the only one of the women in her valley, Vizcaya and all of Spain whose man had taken eagerly to the seas.

In 1453 the Ottoman Turks had taken Constantinople and gained control of the land routes to the East, making it vital for Western Europeans to find a water route. A hundred years ago Vasco da Gama had followed Bartholomew Diaz' route around the Cape of Good Hope and sailed on to reach India. Soon Portugal was also trading along the Persian Gulf. Ships returned laden with spices, pearls and porcelain from China, rich Japanese brocades, precious stones and ivory from Siam. On the spiritual side, Jesuits had been welcomed in Japan in 1549 and they had also reached China.

Competing with these new routes to the luxuries of the East was the fabled New World. Columbus' flagship, the *Santa María*, had been Basque-owned and manned and the little cockleshell, *Niña*, had been crewed mostly by Basques. Their centuries of experience in building ships that could seek whales in northern waters after the great cetaceans became scarce in the Bay of Biscay had made the Basques the best shipbuilders and sailors of Spain, while their iron industry was crucial for the making of weapons of war and implements of peaceful colonization. But while commerce boomed and fortunes were made, probably most of the women of Vizcaya had lost men to the ocean or countries halfway around the world.

Martín had reached Nueva Vizcaya; that much Marya knew from a returned neighbor. Several leaders had been planning to explore the regions farther north in hope of discovering the golden cities that Coronado had failed to locate. Martín, Marya's neighbor said, had been excited at the prospect. It was likely that he had joined some such expedition. If he had, only God on High knew when he'd return.

He would surely come if he knew her father was dead. Though Cristóbal had not been home much of the time, she had felt protected by him. The loving old nurse who had raised her after her mother's death had died the year before and though Ana and Joseba, the middle-aged couple who attended to the daily running of house and farm, were kind and respectful, they were not really friends or people in whom she could confide. To them she was the young mistress and thereby a gulf was fixed. She was grateful for David, though, and smiled at the thought of him.

Saffron-skinned, with an absolutely bald head and eyes that matched the sapphire he wore in a slightly pointed ear, David reminded her of one of the genies in the book of stories, poems and lore that Lael had written down and which was Marya's greatest treasure. His real history was almost as incredible as those in the book.

Originally a member of a heretical Christian sect in India and a pilot on a trading ship, he had been enslaved and sold to a wealthy Moroccan Jew. Finding much to admire in his master's faith, he was converted to it, whereupon he could no longer be slave to a co-religionist. His master sold him to a Moslem. Once again David found beauties in the dominant religion, converted to Islam and was immediately sold, for Moslems, too, could not enslave another Moslem and thousands of their slaves had achieved freedom by simply espousing the Prophet and Allah.

Cristóbal bought David from the Moslem for a personal servant and because of the sea-lore that David had acquired while serving in ships plying the Mediterranean and the Indian Ocean. Cristóbal detested slavery. None of his vessels engaged in the West African slave trade that had started about thirty years ago, carrying unfortunate tribesmen to the New World to work on the plantations. He had given David his freedom and David had converted to Catholicism again, coming full circle, though he liked to say, "I've not been yet a Calvinist or a Lutheran or one of those English who thinks that his wife-murdering King Harry could make himself head of the church and forget the Pope of Rome."

It was David, two weeks ago, who had brought the news of Marya's father's death and he had remained at Etchahoun. "Your father counted on me to have a care for you if anything befell him," the lemon-skinned seaman had announced. "He was my friend and my good master. I'll just wait till you're more settled." He grinned. "Maybe that sweetheart of yours will come home and I can see you married before I go to sea."

So there was David. But she still felt lost. She helped with the work of the house, tended her herb garden and during the past few days had been helping the shepherd with the lambing for she was determined that no orphaned lamb should die. Because there were more stillborn lambs than dead ewes, usually it was possible for Juan, the shepherd, to skin a dead lamb and bind the pelt to an orphan, which would then smell to the deprived mother like her own. Marya was busy. But with her father dead and Martín still away, a great void seemed to open before her.

She stopped by Abram's grave and said a prayer for *La Morisca*'s old tutor, as had become a custom among the softer-hearted women of Etchahoun. A bit ashamed of her own faint-heartedness when she remembered Lael's tragic situation, Marya glanced up at the sound of a rasping voice. With no pleasure at all, she saw her second cousin approaching.

Perkain's skin looked almost as gray as his clothing and the hair that escaped his velvet cap was also gray. His eyes were colorless as ice water. A long nose bisected his narrow face and small, pointed, grayish teeth showed when his pallid lips parted, his closest approach to a smile. He had arrived from Bruges two days earlier. So far Marya had managed to evade him but now her luck had run out.

"My dear cousin," he said, his manner portentous. "My

very dear young cousin, I know that you are still grieving for your good father's death but it is time to consider the future."

Though she had just been doing that, his tone caused the back of her neck to prickle with hostility. "Thank you for your concern, Cousin Perkain," she said, "but I do very well here with Ana and Joseba. And David will be staying."

"That bald apostate to all religions!"

"He was father's trusted friend."

Perkain tried to draw himself up imposingly but the effect was spoiled by his thin shanks. He was dressed in city style, with tight hose, slashed, puffed, padded breeches and a stiff white ruff. "I am your father's business agent," he reminded her, "and kinsman to you both."

Again he gave that slight, unnerving smile while reaching for her hands. It was the first time that he had ever touched her and even though he was her cousin, she had to fight down repugnance. His touch was clammy and there was a faint odor to him that reminded her of rotting mushrooms.

"Sweet cousin, nothing could increase my interest in your welfare. I wish to formalize the guardianship that I am certain your dear father would have vested in me had he foreseen his unfortunate death." She stared at him uncomprehendingly. "I mean," he continued with a patronizing laugh, "that I am desirous of protecting you, shielding you from the harsh buffets of life. I want to be your husband, Marya, and under the circumstances no one will gossip should we marry soon."

Husband? She could not believe her ears.

Gasping, she jerked her hands from his as she would have eluded death. He was older than her father and if he'd ever had the slightest affection for her, he had concealed it admirably. But even if they had been friends, how could he possibly dream that she would consent to lie beside him, let those cold gray fingers trace their blind way over her?

He may have read some of her thoughts in her face for a sudden flush gave a tinge of color to his visage. Still, Marya didn't like to wound anyone unnecessarily. Mustering control, she spoke courteously.

"Thank you for your favor, Cousin Perkain. I appreciate your kindness but surely you will recall that I am betrothed?"

His brow wrinkled. "To that Yriate sprig? He's either been killed by Indians or has died somehow."

"No! Don't say that!"

Perkain shook his head. "Marya child, you have had no word at all of him in over a year. If by some freak he's alive, he must intend to remain in the New World."

"We are betrothed. I will wait for him."

The pale eyes blinked rapidly. "Cousin, it is dangerous and unseemly for a maiden of your years to remain unmarried. It provokes lascivious thoughts among men and makes you a target for smutty talk and perhaps worse. We must marry."

"I won't!" she hurled at him, goaded past restraint. "You—you loathsome old man! I'd rather be dead!"

"Would you?" Red spots blazed in his cheeks. "You hussy, to speak thus to a decent, godly man who offers you refuge!" He glared at her for a moment, then swallowed and said with a hollow effort at magnanimity, "I should have waited for a time. You are distraught by your father's death. We'll speak of the matter again when you're in better heart."

Already regretting the cruelty of her rejection, she said gently, "Cousin, I beseech you, let us be friends. I will be grateful for your advice and tutelage but speak no more of marriage."

He shot her a venomous look and turned on his heel. "You act as though you took your counsel from that dog of an infidel!" he spat.

His ankle turned on the foppish high heel of his shoe. He went down, sprawling headfirst. Marya rushed to his side. "Are you hurt, cousin?" she asked, trying to help him up. He glared at her.

"You—or that dead Jew—cursed me!"

"Cousin!"

He scrambled to his feet, his expression twisting between fury and alarm. "If you've witch powers, my girl, don't use them on me! I have friends in the Holy Office who are much concerned at the manner in which you valley people cling to heathenish ways. Your *serorak* do things proper to a male sacristan at best—and at worst, some have been proved witches."

"We had *serorak* before we had priests."

"Yes, worshipers of the Red Lord!"

"You are mistaken, cousin." If those ancient priestesses had worshiped any deity prior to God, it would have been the Mother Goddess, with her serpent consort. But there was no use in making Perkain angrier than he was. Marya could not resist saying though, "Vizcaínos don't like to have outside churchmen interfering. Don't you recall that when King Ferdinand himself came to meet with the *Señorío* of the province, the elected representatives, he brought with him the Bishop of Pamplona? The Vizcaínos refused to let the bishop enter the land and when he had retreated, they rubbed out the footprints he had left in the soil."

Perkain sneered. "That was over a hundred years ago. Ferdinand's grandson, Charles V, sent Dominicans and Franciscans into these mountains to teach the true faith and get rid of heathenish practices. Even before that there were thirty witches burned at Amboto. The inquisitors have often filled the jails of the Basque country. I well remember when I was a young boy that twenty-one members of a *serora's* family were imprisoned for witchcraft in Bilbao, all of them women but three."

"The inquisitors, I believe, are always men."

The pupils swelled over the pale irises of Perkain's eyes. "Do you mock the Holy Office?"

"Cousin, when I see the three *sanbenitos* that hang in our church, I do not feel like mocking."

Two of the sackcloth garments were black and painted with devils and flames, which meant that the impenitent wearers had been burned. It had happened before Marya's time but she knew a few people in the village who did not seem to believe that the two women had sucked children's blood or blighted crops, though they did not openly say so. That would have in itself been heretical and made them liable to punishment.

The yellow *sanbenito*, painted with red crosses, had been worn by a well-to-do farmer who had confessed under torture and so escaped the stake. His penance had been seven years at the oars of a galley and the loss of his farm and property. He died in the galleys but even had he returned, he could never have held an important post, worn silk, pearls, gold, silver or carried arms or ridden horseback.

Had he been burned, the penalties would have applied to

his children and grandchildren. In any case, the *sanbenitos* hung permanently in the church, marked with the names of the accused, the crimes and the dates of sentencing. They were potent warnings and indeed they did not leave one disposed to joke about the Holy Office.

"It is well that you do not mock," nodded Perkain, his thin lips puffed slightly with gratification. "But you had better reflect on how you may avoid the appearance of evil. It would be fitting to level the Jew's tombstone and let the infidel slip from memory."

"I cannot do that."

"Cannot? Why?"

Marya made a helpless gesture. "Abram was the teacher and friend of one of my ancestresses. According to the stories, he was a kind and good man. I will not dishonor his resting place, which he came so far to find."

"Was he a convert?"

"I don't know and I can't see that it matters."

Perkain's straggly gray brows lifted. "You know well that since 1492, only converted Jews have been allowed to live in Spain and they are watched closely in case of relapse."

"Abram died four hundred years before that." Angered to a degree of recklessness, Marya added, "In Abram's time the King of Castile permitted Moslems and Jews their faiths, just as the Moslems persecuted neither Christians nor Jews."

"Praise be to God that Their Most Catholic Majesties wrested all Granada from the Moors in the same blessed year that they expelled the Jews."

Marya said hotly, "Yes, and under the terms of surrender, Moslems were to be allowed their faith. But in 1499, the mosques were closed, Arabic books were burned and many Granadines were forcibly baptized. Then a few years later Isabela issued an edict that Moslems must convert or leave Spain but they could not take with them their sons under fourteen or their daughters under twelve. I wonder what happened to those children."

"They became Christians, of course, and were fortunate to be delivered from hell."

"There must have been many parents who couldn't bear to

leave their children and who converted in order not to be separated from them."

Harshly Perkain demanded, "You lament that the unbelievers were forced from the Christian lands they had overrun?"

"I am sorry that families were broken and people suffered."

"Have a care," he warned. "Pity for heretics is itself a crime. When the Edict is read, it is the duty of anyone who suspects another of heresy to so inform the inquisitors."

Marya detested the visitations of an inquisitor, during which time all adults were required to hear High Mass, take the oath of loyalty to the Holy Office and attend the half-hour reading of the list of heresies. Anyone who knew that someone else had said or done an offending thing was required—under threat of excommunication—to reveal it anonymously to the inquisitor.

Though the inquisitors were rumored to use fewer and milder tortures than secular authorities did, long imprisonment had broken many people. Further, the accused were not told of the nature of the charges or who had made them. It was up to the victim to prove innocence of an unnamed crime. Rarely indeed did an accused person appear at an *auto da fé* carrying a palm branch as a sign of acquittal.

"This is dismal talk for one already wearing black," she told Perkain.

"It is yet more dismal to lose one's soul. Marya—"

She drew her shawl more tightly around her shoulders. "I do not understand, cousin, how the matter of my marriage has become a question of my salvation. I pray you will excuse me. I have duties to attend to."

Making a wide swing around him, she hurried up the slope to the house.

II

DORREAK HAD been built throughout the Basque country as protection during the many clashes between warring powers. In 1456 a general order had caused many of them to be razed. Now it was forbidden to build them but a number, like the tower of Etchahoun, remained for use as storage, or the top story had been removed and replaced by a new roof. Etchahoun's broad, low "new" dwelling had a brown-tiled gabled roof and an arched *loriua*, or portico, where threshing and other chores could be done under shelter. Beyond this there was space for carts, wagons and implements.

The ox-byre, stables and *zelauria*, where fodder was stored, were still on the ground floor of the structure, which yet bore the house's name and motto, and its symbol of a sickle and a sheaf of wheat. On the lintel of the new house were incised the names of Marya's great-grandparents and words telling that the house had been built in 1499 with wealth made in trade with India and the East. Above the words were carved a sickle and a sheaf of wheat.

A delicious smell of baking bread came from the brick oven built into a corner of the portico. Marya went around to the kitchen on the other end of the ground floor and sniffed the mouth-watering odor drifting from the cauldron. The fireplace was built into the wall and its round chimney ran up through the next floor.

"It smells like we aren't having *talo* and *lapikoko* tonight, Ana." She smiled at the plump woman treadling the spinning wheel. Marya liked the bean soup and cornbread that had become staple dishes since beans and maize had been brought from the New World but sometimes she wished Ana relied less on them and dried cod.

"One of the old hens had stopped laying," Ana chuckled, "so now she's simmering with a ham shank, onions, garlic, carrots, chick peas and rice. It's time for the *chorizos*. Would you put them in?"

Marya put in four of the sausages she had helped Ana make last fall and gave the stew a careful stir, taking care not to knock off the legs or wings of the chicken. Ana shot her a sly glance from small dark eyes.

"Perhaps you would want to invite Master Perkain?"

"We never have except on feast days." Anger coursed through Marya again together with a cold shock of fear as she remembered how he had persisted in his obnoxious suit. "This is not a feast day."

She gave the fire a vicious poke and began setting the table with beechwood trenchers and pewter spoons from Nuremburg. Cristóbal had brought silver forks from Italy but Ana refused to use them and they remained in their velvet wrappings in one of the drawers of the great carved cupboard, the upper part of which displayed other trophies of its owner's journeys: fine Chinese porcelain and Japanese vases; gleaming brass and copper; blue, green and violet glassware; an astounding array of platters in silver and pewter and the lovely blue and white earthenware that Hermon Pietersz manufactured in Delft.

The table was made of heavy hand-hewn oak, polished by generations of use, as were the benches and chairs, but the massive candelabrum had been fashioned by Italian artisans. It held candles made from wax taken from Etchahoun hives, however, and the oaken floor was rubbed dark with the same wax.

Going upstairs, Marya passed the *sala*, where graceful Italianate chairs and tables were mixed with grim, solid, homemade furnishings. An El Greco painting of a saint hung on a wall there, and another done by Caravaggio. Persian carpets covered the seldom-trod floor. Across the narrow passage and on the other side of the *sala* were the bedrooms. Ana and Joseba occupied one. Cristóbal's lay between theirs and Marya's. The one opposite hers was empty. David preferred in warm weather to sleep on a pallet in the portico, where he could feel the breeze.

Marya's room was full of curious, often beautiful things Cristóbal had brought from a dozen countries: peacock feathers, fans, figurines of jade, rare woods and ivory, silk and brocade hangings and pillows, a rare Persian carpet, a Venetian glass mirror with a silver handle, golden scissors, a faience clock that had to be wound only once a week, and many, many dolls. Some were of leather, wood or cornhusks. Others had porcelain faces and were exquisitely dressed in satins and laces.

The lacquered jewel chests held everything from simple clay and seed and bone beads to precious stones set in gold and silver. But the best treasure was books. Cristóbal, who liked to read himself, had provided her with a number of *cancioneros,* books of ballads, the exciting tales of Don Juan Manuel—one of which the English dramatist Shakespeare had used in his *Taming of the Shrew;* the wonderful romance of Amadis da Gaula; Peter Martyr's history of the discovery of America, and the poems of Garcilaso de la Vega, who had died young while fighting Charles V's battles in Italy.

There were the lyrics of Gutiette de Cetina, who had been murdered in Mexico while serenading a fair lady, and the passionate works of San Juan de La Cruz, friend of the nun, Teresa of Avila, who had expressed the fervor of divine love in a way that made Marya tremble and think of her lover. But most of all she treasured the pages written down five centuries ago in archaic, vernacular Spanish by *La Morisca* on paper so excellent that it was still intact.

Of the many exotic robes and garments in the chests, Marya wore few. They would have been out of place here; she preferred her dresses of calico, the printed cotton that Vasco da Gama had brought from Calicut on his Indian voyage, to the city-style gowns of velvet and brocade which required a farthingale.

As she looked around at the presents Cristóbal had brought her—partly, she was sure, to make up for his long absences—she ached with grief and loss. She had clung to her father when she was small, begging him not to go away, asking him to take her with him, promising that she would learn to be a good sailor and even help to take the whales.

Growing older, she came to realize that girls did not go to

sea and she stopped her futile pleading but the loneliness had still been there each time he sailed, along with a bitter, if silent, rebelliousness. Had she been a son, Cristóbal would have taken her and for the sake of being with him, she would gladly have endured hardships and dangers.

And had she been a man, she would not have gone on wondering about Martín. She would have taken ship, made her way to Nueva Vizcaya and hunted for him. If only—

A thunderbolt drove through her lament, stunning her. She did not stop to reflect that had she been a man, she would not have had the same interest in Martín. Her hands trembled as she put down her comb and mirror.

A few women did go out to the New World with their husbands. She was heiress to her father's ships. If she could just escape without Perkain's knowledge—

Snatching up her skirts, she ran down the outside staircase and went in search of David.

She found him sitting on a sun-warmed gray rock, showing the shepherd's youngest child how to play the flute he had just made for her. At Marya's breathless arrival he glanced up keenly at her and sent the little girl off with the flute and a pat on the shoulder.

He started shaking his head, making the sapphire in his ear wink, even before Marya finished outlining her plan. "You could never make that voyage alone, lass. Men have mutinied for less than a pretty woman."

"But if you pretended to be my husband—"

His jaw dropped. He burst into astonished laughter before, noting that her mouth quivered, he sobered. "Before you can leave for the New World, you have to fill out papers. We'd never get through the masquerade." He scratched his bald head, troubled. "If you were a lad, it would be simple enough to smuggle you aboard one of the ships in Bilbao bound for Seville and then Mexico. Seville has a monopoly on New World trade but most of the vessels come from Basque ports, as do a big part of the trade-goods and sailors. Yes, that could be done. But you're no lad."

There it was again. Marya groaned with frustration. She

told David about Perkain's startling proposal. The furrowing of David's brow grew into a ferocious scowl.

"That old crow wants you to wed him?" he growled. "He fancies himself, to be sure. Thinking he should have you and your inheritance, the greedy spindleshanks!"

"I would rather die than marry him but I'm afraid he's going to keep after me. He *is* father's cousin and his business agent. I suppose that he'd inherit everything if I were to die." She grimaced at the prospect. "I—I'm afraid of him, David. He acts almost as though he thinks I'm a witch."

David said hopefully, "He never stays long. Maybe he'll shortly take himself off to Bruges and get drowned on the way." He gave her hand a heartening squeeze. "Hold a steady course, lass. Your father paid me well enough to put by some gold and now that he's gone, I would like to serve you if I can. I'll just slip down to Bilbao and see when a ship is bound for Mexico. Maybe I can find your Martín."

"Oh, David!" She flung her arms around him. "Will you, really? If you find him, I'll give you a ship of your own and—"

He placed his fingers on her lips. "If I bring your Martín home, what I would like best is a bench by your hearth, lass. I've enough of the sea and adventure, which, when you come down to it, usually means wondering if you'll make it alive through some accursed predicament."

"Bring Martín home and you can make flutes for our children and tell them great lies about mermaids and sea monsters, just as you did for me," Marya promised, laughing. "You don't know how happy you've made me! I guess I can put up with Cousin Perkain for a while longer." She gave David's arm a tug. "Come on, supper should be ready and it smells delicious."

David sighed. "I'd best enjoy it while I can. I expect I've eaten more worms than ship's biscuit and they probably tasted better at that!"

He left next morning after a breakfast of cheese, honey, half a loaf of bread and three cups of thick, rich chocolate, promising to return and let Marya know what ship he had found and when it would sail.

After he was gone, Marya slowly luxuriated over her second

cinnamon-spiced cup of chocolate, wondering how Spain had ever done without this drink that had become almost a national addiction. It was said that Montezuma, Cortez' unfortunate victim, had drunk fifty jars of it every day.

Much cheered by David's promise to look for Martín, she was able to dismiss Perkain's absurd suit with a certain amount of pity. Not that she thought he loved her. Her inheritance had to be the cause of his ardor. But he was so dour and dried up and joyless. It was a shame for anyone to be like that. She put him out of her mind and daydreamed about Martín as she churned the butter, chatting a bit with Ana and Elena, the shepherd's wife, who came over most days to help with the work.

Marya was too restless to spin or sew. She decided to go to the women's cave and dance off her nervous energy in the oak grove nearby, as she had often done since Martín went away. She liked to dance there for some of her ancestresses had been famed dancers. She believed that they might somehow join the measures with her.

Taking one apple for Blanca and bundling another and a piece of cheese in a cloth along with her tambourine, Marya told Ana that she would not be back for the noon meal. On the way she stopped by the field to caress her favorite mare, Blanca, and feed her the apple she had in her hand. Blanca, like the other three horses in the meadow, was descended from *La Morisca*'s famous stallion, Al Zirr. They kept an aristocratic distance from the cows, who wore bells that had been blessed by the priest.

"I won't ride you today," Marya told the mare, who nuzzled her arm and whickered softly. "But we will have a canter soon." She felt instinctively that it was more fitting to approach the cave on foot, as the early generations would have done.

Because it was close to the rocky cliffs, she stopped at the shepherd's hut to take a brand that had a smoldering end. It could be blown into fire when she entered the cavern.

Once there, standing in the flickering light of the torch, she smiled at the mother and child among the bright birds, lightly touched the blue-bird shard and slowly looked around at the countless handprints, large and small, that spoke from the walls. Her own childish print was between Lael's and her own mother's. Apparently even some of the women who shared this secret had feared close contact with *La Morisca*'s sign. Marya was glad that she had been able to fill that emptiness.

"Mother," she said to the woman whom she scarcely remembered, "Father must be with you now. Tell him that I love him."

Marya was silent for a long time, then, sinking into a wordless communion with these women of her family. A sense of their loves and griefs, vanquished terrors and endurance of hard times, strenghtened her. She had no living mother or kinswoman but she had the spirits and they were infinitely comforting. She did not aspire to prove herself stronger than any of them but she believed she could survive equally as well since they had proved it could be done.

After a time she murmured gratitude and farewell, and rubbed out the torch.

In the oak grove, she ate her cheese and apple with good appetite, threw off her black shawl and drank at a spring that wound past an exposed rift of gray rock. The top of the small cliff was flat, the stone overgrown with moss and flowers. It was her favorite place for dancing.

Taking off her sandals, she tossed back her head, breathed deeply of the sweet air while her naked feet enjoyed the texture of the weather-smoothed stone. Sun filtering through the boughs warmed her skin. She stood eyes closed, senses filled with the song of birds, the rich odor of old leaves mingling with new blossoms, the murmur of the stream, the touches of breeze and sunlight.

So good. It was all so good.

Barely sounding her tambourine, she moved into a graceful swaying that shaded gradually into advances and retreats, whirling steps, abandoned leaps that finished in dropping to one knee before, arms turning to the inner rhythm shaken out on the tambourine, she sprang upward and imagined that she was dancing with Martín, inviting him, tempting him, gliding forward before she spun away.

Oh, Martín! Oh, my love! Let David find you!

When she was exhausted, she sank down on the stone, arms flung wide. Dreamily thinking of Martín, she relived each time they had been together, the sweetness of his kisses, the hard young strength of his arms. She was almost in blissful sleep when a twig crunched.

Sitting upright, she saw Perkain. Snatching her shawl, she wrapped it around herself and rose to her feet, thrusting into her sandals.

"You can talk to me, when necessary, at the house," she said coldly. "You need not trouble to hunt for me."

His gray tongue flicked his lips. Her hope that he had just come upon her was shattered as he smiled and drew a step nearer. "Then I would have missed an interesting spectacle, wouldn't I? And I did not seek you, cousin. I followed."

A choking sensation knotted her throat. Followed? Then he must have seen her go into the cave! Reading her horrified thoughts, his smile broadened. "Yes. I saw you enter that crevice. And then I watched you dance. I could not see the Red Lord but no doubt you did, the way you strutted and wriggled."

"I—there wasn't anyone—anything! I was just dancing."

He shook his head reprovingly. "No need to act with me, cousin. You're young and were doubtless led into error by an older witch. I am still willing to marry you. A full confession, some lavish gifts to the right authorities—" He snapped his fingers. "As my wife, you will have nothing to dread of God or man."

Only you.

Fighting the nightmare, she insisted, "I am no witch! I have nothing to confess! Everyone dances, Cousin Perkain. There's no sin in it."

"Everyone doesn't dance in oak groves, flaunting themselves as you did. Especially not after spending an hour in a dark cavern." His nostrils swelled, revealing coarse black hairs that contrasted unpleasantly with the gray strands on his head. He caught her hands in a surprisingly steel-like grip. "Is that where the devil took you? Is it true that his member is like a great, swollen, blunt icicle that burns cold as he puts it in? Does he take you back or front?" Perkain's voice went husky. "From back is a sin, of course, but when you're with the devil, what does it matter?"

Marya shrank at his whispered perversions. He was dragging her to him, fumbling at her breasts. She could not wrench free. He laughed at her struggles. Marya brought up her knee as hard as she could, driving it into a stiffening that pressed at her through his padded short breeches.

He screamed, doubled and let her go, rolling on the ground. Marya fled. She didn't know what to do about him and his suspicions but for now she must get away from him.

For the rest of the day she half expected Perkain to come knocking at the door and try to resume his threats and bullying. Ana and Joseba were highly superstitious and she did not want to tell them about the encounter. She wished desperately that David was at Etchahoun but it would be at least several days before he returned.

Had Perkain really believed his accusations? She was tormented at the possibility that he might squeeze through the passage to the cave and discover the centuries' old secret. The fear that she might have betrayed the mystery, that the beauty and memories might be obliterated, worried her as much as fear over what Perkain might do about her. She had escaped him this afternoon but what if he threatened to desecrate the cave?

At that point she stopped thinking, gripped by a revulsion so overwhelming that it turned her physically sick. Marry Perkain? Submit to those claw-like hands, those thin gray lips? She would rather die, rather mate with the devil himself.

That desperate truth made her smother a hysterical laugh and turn her back to Ana as she hemmed a fine linen shirt she was making for David, who had, as always, come home ragged from the sea. Perhaps she really was wicked, liable to damnation. If being a witch would save her from Perkain or protect the cave, she would become one in an instant if she knew how.

She had no close relatives. One uncle was in Peru, another in Brazil. Three others had been lost in the defeat of the great Armada in 1588. One aunt had died in childbirth, another of fever. When people survived the ills of childhood, there were still many common ways for them to die.

Marya thought of taking gold from her father's chest and traveling to Bilbao in search of David but she had never been in the bustling port and was dismayed at the prospect of searching for him around the docks and shipping area.

He would be back in a few days. She could hold Perkain off until then, give him answers that were neither yes nor no. With that resolved, she tried to push her fears away but she did not enjoy supper that night even though it was one of her favorites, trout from the stream, thick vegetable soup and hot bread.

After she went up to her room, she lit a candle and read from Lael's book. At some time the old pages had been bound in leather but the book did not seem to have been often used. Until Cristóbal brought his books to Etchahoun and nurtured Marya's love of them, there had been few at the house.

"Oh, that I might die for you, my son, my son!"—Rustum's cry to Sohrab, yet surely the lament of many fathers, even as King David mourned his willful Absalom. And Sohrab's reply: "Father, don't mourn. I only meet today the death that at my birth was written down."

A prickling ran down Marya's spine. Was a person's fate decreed, inevitable? Because of the vigilant Inquisition, the Protestant fervor transforming Europe would never reach Spain but she knew of Martin Luther, who had died fifty years ago; of John Knox in Scotland, who had railed at Queen Mary for her "popery" and exulted when she was beheaded by Queen Elizabeth in the same year, 1587, that doughty Sir Francis Drake, son of a poor English hedge parson, had raided Cadiz and destroyed the Spanish fleet. Drake boasted rightly that he had "singed the King of Spain's beard" and it was a year before the Armada was ready to start for England and the shattering defeat in which many Basque ships and men were lost. Martyrs to both Catholicism and Protestant faiths had been burned in England, including saintly Thomas More, who had died "the King's good servant, but God's first" for refusing to sanction Henry's marriage to Anne Boleyn.

By an odd quirk, Henry VIII—after his secret, scandalous marriage to Anne Boleyn in 1533 following his divorce from Ferdinand's and Isabela's daughter, Katharine of Aragon—had declared himself head of the English Church in 1534, the same year that a Basque, Ignatius of Loyola, had founded the Jesuits, whose influence now reached around the world.

The religion that struck Marya as the most gloomy and fear-some, though, was that established by John Calvin. Not only did Calvinists burn heretics as enthusiastically as did Catholics and Anglicans but they believed only a small portion of mankind would be saved and these fortunate were already selected. Nothing that a person did could possibly merit salvation. It was hard for Marya to understand why people would accept such a dismal faith; even earthly princes were expected to deal more justly than that.

She turned with relief to Rabi'a, who, when asked if she hated the devil, had said, ''My love of God leaves no room for hating Satan.''

> *Oh, my Lord, stars glitter and the eyes of men*
>   *are closed,*
> *Kings shut their doors. . . .*
> *Here, I am alone with you.*

The words were addressed to God but their passion com-pelled Marya to think of Martín. She blew out the candle. Count-ing the hours she had spent with him as she would the beads on a rosary, she was drifting into sleep when a creaking brought her upright.

''What—?''

Hurried shuffling. Before she was sufficiently awake to scream or move, coarse hands closed over her mouth. Others held her roughly while still others twisted ropes around her hands and feet. A cloth was wadded into her mouth, stifling her outcries, and tied in place so cruelly that her jaws ached.

She writhed, flinging her body this way and that, trying to make enough noise to awaken Ana and Joseba, but then one of her attackers swung her over his shoulder. Blood rushed to her head. Panic blackened her mind, as if she were plunging into a bottomless pit. Hauled up before a horseman, she retched from terror and the acid stink of sweat and garlic.

And she heard Perkain's voice.

III

WHAT COULD he mean?

A stupor of dread paralyzed Marya. She had no sense of the direction in which they were riding, no idea of what Perkain intended. Simple abduction by him would be unutterable horror. Someone had wrapped one of her shawls around her. Swallowing the bile that welled up against the gag, she collected her strength.

Better, much better, to break her neck than suffer whatever Perkain had in mind. She waited until her captor's hold relaxed and then wrenched sideways with all her might, trying to hurl herself from the saddle.

"Whoring witch!" A brutal arm crushed her breasts as the man dragged her back in front of him.

Perkain rode alongside. "Throttle her if she causes trouble," he advised. "Just don't kill her." To Marya, he said, "You're going to need to talk a lot—unless you have the wisdom to say one short word to me." Cackling at his wit, he went ahead to lead the little procession.

Marya lost track of time, bruised by the pommel, cramped by the uncomfortable position that was changed only when the rider shifted her weight to ease himself. The wasted moon gave little light but enough for her to make out the shapes of buildings as they entered a paved road and the horses' shod hoofs sounded on the stones.

There were no lights in the town but a pack of dogs was fighting in an alley and there was a stench that almost blotted out the reek of the man who held her, a thick smell of human waste and rotting garbage. There was also the unmistakable tang of salt water. They had to be in Bilbao, which was built on the Nervion River and the estuary leading to the Bay of Biscay.

On the edge of town the horsemen stopped before a building at some distance from any others. One of the men came back to haul Marya down and carry her into the dark house. "Leave her trussed up," commanded Perkain.

The man snickered, his hands in the darkness mauling at her. "I would be glad to stay with her, sir."

"You will put her on the pallet in the corner and go your way," Perkain snapped.

There was a clink of coins as the others came to the door. One, whose voice Marya recognized as that of her captor's, said gloatingly, "I'd like to watch this one burn. It should be a rare sight to see the clothes scorched off her. I'd like to see her devil's mark."

A companion chortled. "You may wager that the devil marked her where you'd like to!"

"Be on your way!" snapped Perkain. There was another clinking of money. "Don't talk about this, mind you. It is my hope that my kinswoman will renounce evil and be restored to her own place."

Huddled on the odorous straw pallet, dressed only in her thin nightgown and shame, Marya shrank against the wall as the horses moved away and Perkain was briefly outlined against the door before he stood above her, speaking from the darkness.

"Sleep well, cousin. You will need your strength in the morning."

The gag had become sheer torment. Her wrists and ankles throbbed. He did not loosen her bonds, though, but locked the door behind him as he went out.

The night wore on, hell-like eternity. A rat ran over her feet, scurried off as she flinched. She managed to climb up on her knees and crawl painfully about the cubicle, hoping to find a sharp surface or object she could work against her ropes, but there was nothing except the rancid mattress. In the farthest corner, she struggled to drag her skirts aside enough to relieve her aching bladder. It smelled as if others had done the same and though the pallet was an abomination, she dragged herself back to it and sat leaning against the corner.

From what the men had said, there was little doubt that Perkain meant to threaten her with the Inquisition. He may have deliberately pounced while David was away. David, who must be here in Bilbao. The thought drove her frantic. He might never know what had happened to her until the public *auto da fé*, and that might not take place for several years. The Inquisition was careful and deliberate in its examinations. Since the accused, while trying to prove innocence, had to pay the cost of imprisonment, the Holy Office was under no pressure to hurry. Ana and Joseba had apparently slept through the abduction.

No one who cared would know where she was. Marya tried to pray but her way to God was blocked by the Holy Office. She thought of Martín despairingly. He was far away, might well be dead.

Only in remembering the Cave of Always Summer did she find any comfort, a sense of support. She summoned up all the stories she knew and tried to envision Lael and Kattalin, Engrâce and the others.

Help me, she implored silently. *Help me*. Jaws aching from the gag, wrists and ankles numbed by the ropes, she lapsed into fitful, exhausted sleep.

She roused to the sound of a groaning door and a flood of light that blinded her. The cell had no window. Blinking, she recognized Perkain beside a tall, skeletal priest who lit a candle as Perkain closed the door.

"I have brought you food and cider, cousin," said Perkain, bending to remove the gag and work at the knots.

They were so tight that he quickly gave up and severed them with his knife. Her nerves tingled excruciatingly as blood began to flow into her feet and hands but it was such a relief to have the ball of cloth out of her mouth that Marya scarcely felt the pain. In the dim yellow light her cousin smiled at her benevolently.

"Father Rojas wants to help you, child. Listen to him and nothing further will befall you."

Marya was hungry and parched. She drank the cider thirstily and slowly ate the bread and cheese, face aching from the exercise. She would do all that she might to keep up her strength.

A servant brought in three chairs, a small table, a quill, ink and paper. "Be seated," the priest said. His black eyes were set so deep in his skull that the sockets looked like empty hollows. His face and fingers showed bones barely covered by skin, the pallid white of fungus growing without sun.

He sat down behind the table. Perkain started to draw Marya to her feet. She avoided him and lurched to the side, tried to rise and fell back for a moment, restraining a cry of agony.

"Bring her," said the priest to the servant, who was waiting in the corner. The man hauled Marya up, half-carried her to the chair opposite the priest and tossed her shawl over her nightgown. Perkain sat to one side, crossing his arms.

"My child," Father Rojas said in a surprisingly deep, mellifluous voice, "you are accused of heresy and witchcraft but your orphaned state, your youth and the intercession of your cousin give me hope that your follies are not so deep-seated and pernicious as to require the Holy Office's most rigorous attention."

Leaving her to wonder what that meant, he asked her name, age and other mundane questions, noting the answers on the paper. Then, staring at her, he asked suddenly, "Do you wish to make a confession, my daughter?"

"I—I have nothing to confess, Father."

He clicked his tongue. "That you say so shows woeful ignorance and prideful delusion, which are in themselves sins." His skeletal finger jabbed at her. "Surely you do not claim to be without fault?"

"Father, I am neither that proud nor ignorant. I only meant that I am not a heretic or a witch."

The click of the tongue again. "You have been seen in acts improper to a Christian damsel."

Pausing by Abram's grave? Entering a cave, dancing in the ancient grove? "I have done nothing that my conscience counts an offense to the faith."

"Have you not?"

She stared at him mutely. More kindly, he said, "My child, the Holy Office does not wish you to suffer or die. You have lacked firm guidance. I am ready to believe that you have erred out of folly rather than wickedness. If you will promise to be governed by him and accept his instructions as your lord and husband, I will commend you to the care of your good cousin."

"He is not my good cousin!" Marya burst out. "He's a disgusting old man who wants my inheritance."

"You reject his protection?"

"Protection? He—he said things so foul and terrible that to repeat them would be a worse sin than any I have committed. I would rather die than marry him."

Perkain rose, quivering. "That you will do if you don't repent!" He said to the inquisitor in a voice half-strangled with rage, "If your mercy allows, Father, give her three days in which to consider. If she is humble by then, I will strive to lesson her in womanly subjection. If she remains defiant"—he shrugged his narrow shoulders—"then the Holy Office must have its way with her. I will reimburse you for her food and lodging."

"Out of my money?" Marya cried derisively.

He showed his small gray teeth. "Reflect, cousin. Have you ever heard of anyone leaving the Holy Office's hostelry with more than the rags on his back?" He went out abruptly.

The inquisitor's hollow eyes bored into her. "You have exactly three days in which to ponder your cousin's magnanimous offer. After that I will have no choice but to begin your interrogation. You would do well to admit your heresies at once even should you refuse to wed your cousin. Otherwise you will be persuaded."

He motioned to the servant, a burly man with powerful arms and thighs and an out-thrust jaw, his small black eyes glinting from beneath a shock of greasy black hair. "Jaime, tell this woman of some of the methods used to help accused witches purge their souls."

As though not fully comprehending what was meant, the man scratched his armpit for a moment before he brightened and turned to Marya. "Well, there be the cords. Fasten 'em on arms and legs, we do. I've seen them cut through the meat to the bone. Then there's hanging from your hands. Doesn't sound much but a few hours of it loosens many a tongue." He scratched again, like a dull student trying to satisfy his teacher. "Sometimes we pour water down a throat till the accused nigh chokes to death. One old gaffer did." He added benignly, "Mostly a year or two in a cell does the trick."

"The Holy Office does not like to use torture except when it may save the accused's soul by obtaining a confession." The priest's pale lips stretched in a wan smile. "It is never administered except in the presence of a notary, a recording secretary, a representative of the bishop and the Inquisitor. I thank God that only five of the people I have examined went to the stake recalcitrant and suffered the flames. The others all confessed and were either let off with punishment or strangled mercifully before the burning."

"But none ever carried a palm branch, Father?" asked Jaime eagerly. "None ever got off innocent?"

The inquisitor rose. "None."

At the door he faced around, a towering, dense shadow outlined by a wavering aureole of dim light. "Chain the prisoner, Jaime, and remove the candle, table and chairs." He solemnly crossed himself. His beautiful voice seemed to burrow through her ears and chase through the echoing labyrinths of her skull. "Believe me, child, I have no wish to see you suffer. I will return in three days. Should you find grace before that, tell Jaime when he brings your food and he will summon me. May God soften your rebellious heart before it's past my power to release you quietly."

Marya dragged herself to her feet. "How much has my cousin paid you?"

Sorrowfully the inquisitor shook his head. "You fall ever deeper into blasphemy," he rebuked. He waited till Jaime and another man returned with chains, an evil-smelling wooden bucket, water and bread.

"Repent, my daughter, while that will bring you life," he intoned and then was gone with a swirl of dark robes.

The blackness of the cell was all the worse because Marya knew it must be light outside. Utter silence intensified the darkness. Jaime and his helper had not tried to hurt her when they put on the manacles and leg-irons; in fact, they had been roughly kind, adding cider and fish to her breakfast, bringing water and a towel for washing. Still, the irons chafed at her swollen, bruised flesh.

She had eaten for she was young, she loved Martín and she wanted to live. She walked to the limits of the leg-chains, flexed her arms and moved in a weak pseudo-dance, trying to exercise. It was important to keep up her strength in case an opportunity came. When Jaime next brought food, she would see if he'd try to deliver a message to David.

Jaime seemed her only hope. She was resolved not to make a false confession and not to reveal the secret of the cave. Marrying Perkain was so far out of the question that she did not spare it a thought. Equally remote was any chance of appealing to higher authorities and being justified. Should she somehow manage to escape, she had to disappear. It galled her to leave Perkain in possession of her inheritance but she would gladly have given it all to be free again under the blue heavens, breathing the sweet air.

Why, when she had been able to enjoy those things and more, had she ever bewailed her lot or dared to be unhappy?

She was resolved. Yet when she fell into a stuporous sleep, she dreamed that she was being tortured or delivered to the stake. Would she be brave enough to endure? Could she bear the agony?

She thought she could if the final torment came now, while she was strong and in her proper mind. But what would happen after months or years of this dark, stinking cell with the only people she ever saw firmly convinced of her guilt and determined to make her confess?

Surely in such straits God would forgive her if she found a way to cheat the stake. But she would wait as long as she could before seeking that remedy.

Trying to steady herself, she again summoned her memories of the women of the cave, calling on them for courage. She recited aloud the poems of Rabi'a and the cadences of Sohrab and Rustum, the passages that she remembered of the epic of El Cid, even falteringly sang sailors' work songs that David and her father had taught her. She paced the length of her chains again and danced as best she could, trying to imagine with all of her senses that she was in the oak grove, able to feel the sun and wind and smell the fragrant air.

After that she lay down, invoked the Mothers and slept.

Light seeped in, watery thin and hazy, casting Jaime into silhouette as he set a candle on the floor and shut the door before putting a basket of bread and cheese on the floor beside Marya.

"My woman baked today so the bread's fresh," he said.

"And here are some dates!" exclaimed Marya as she picked up the half-loaf. "Thank you, Jaime. You are kind."

"I'm not," he said, hanging his shaggy head. "But I do hate to see a pretty young lady in this hole." Lowering his voice, he dropped to one knee. His clever, small eyes softened with pity. "Give them what they want, little one. Make up something, even. But get yourself out of here."

"Has my cousin paid you to speak so?"

The jailer spat. "He's an ugly, frayed piece to be sure, but he's the quick way out of here. Let me tell Father Rojas that you're ready to confess and you'll sleep this night in a fine bed, not on this filthy straw pad."

She shuddered, thinking of who might share that fine bed with her. Jaime said brusquely, "Many a young wife with an old husband has found a young gallant to ease her woes. You might manage to run off when he was away on business. At any rate, you'd be alive outside and able to take a chance if it came." He sighed. "You can do naught here, lady, but wait for the Inquisitor."

Whether he was in her cousin's pay or not, she had no choice but to trust him. "Jaime, my father's servant, a sailor named David, is in the town seeking passage to the New World. If you could get a message to him—"

"What could a sailor do against your cousin?" asked the jailer. A grin split his features for a moment before he shook his head. "He could put a dirk in him but that would worsen your case since it could be claimed that you witched it to happen." He turned to the door. "I'll leave the candle. Maybe you can go to sleep before it burns out. I had a daughter who would be your age if she had lived. Scared of the dark, she was. My woman said it was nonsense but I always saw that she had a rush lamp."

He closed the heavy door. The key grated in the lock. Marya, her one faint hope dashed, at first had no appetite but the crusty bread was good, the dates were sweet and the goat-cheese tasty. Most of all, the candle's glow kept her deepest terrors at bay, just as Jaime's sympathy saved her from feeling that she was lost in a terrible separate world, totally cruel and inhuman.

A mouse emerged from a cranny and watched her with bright eyes, its nose twitching. "If I feed you, small sister, will you not run over me in the night?" Marya asked.

She tossed it crumbs of bread and a few nibbles of cheese, glad of its company. Her hair was matted in knots. She loosened them as best she could with her fingers, drank deeply, availed herself of the bucket and arranged an edge of the shawl beneath her face so that her cheek did not rest directly on the malodorous pallet.

Her plight was just as deadly as before but the candle and good, if simple, food had heartened her, along with the knowledge that at least her jailer would not mock or brutalize her. She closed her eyes and conjured up Martín but his face kept fading away, though the recesses of her mind reproduced without effort the cave, with its myriad handprints and summer birds.

Willing herself there within its safety, she could almost believe that she heard the ancestresses' murmuring voices and comforted by the sheen of the candle against her closed eyelids, she drifted into sleep.

"Well," Jaime said as he opened the door the next morning, "are you ready for me to call Father Rojas?"

Sitting up, befuddled by sleep, it took Marya a moment to realize where she was but the inquisitor's name brought everything back to her in a rush. "No," she said. "I will not marry my cousin, Jaime. I would rather burn."

The jailer crossed himself. "God help you, girl." He ducked outside and reappeared at once with a new candle, bread, cheese and milk. He put a comb and a faded but clean dress in Marya's lap.

"The comb was my daughter's," he said gruffly. "The dress—well, it came from someone who won't need it anymore.

I thought that another night on that foul mattress might make you see sense but since it hasn't—"

He went out again and returned with a clean pallet that smelled of fresh new straw, filling Marya with a wave of longing for the fields at haying time. She moved to it gladly while Jaime took the other one out. Then he squatted on his heels as she ate, talking about his daughter.

"She seemed too fair and elegant to be got by me and my woman," he said. "Danced around the house like a sunbeam. Maybe she wouldn't have grown to be beautiful like you but she was the prettiest child I ever saw. She died of that fever. Wilted like a flower."

Marya listened, asking a question now and then since her interest seemed to help him to recall his Flora. As well as being grateful to him and touched by his loss, Marya was sufficiently self-protective to want to be on as good terms as possible with the jailer. He sighed and rubbed his bulbous nose.

"If Flora had lived, I'd have looked for different work before she was—well, you understand, lady—old enough to properly know what I do. She wouldn't even let us kill spiders in the house, she hated so to see anything hurt."

Marya could not think of anything to say to that and Jaime stared sadly at his stubby fingers. "They say it's godly work, looking after the Holy Office's prisoners. The priest tells me not to worry, that the sin would be to pity heretics. But there was a pregnant woman died under the cords. The way she screamed—" He shook his head unhappily. "She was accused of killing her own sister's babies, sucking their blood. Neighbors said she had caused blight on the maize and blasted the apples and chestnuts. She claimed she didn't though, right till her heart stopped. I drink heavy before I go to bed of nights but sometimes I can still hear her."

Rising abruptly, he unlocked the manacles on Marya's wrists. "I'll wait outside while you change into the dress," he said. "Then I'll have to put you back in the chains."

When he returned in a few minutes, Marya handed him her soft cotton nightgown. "Your wife may have it," she said. "I can't use it here."

He chuckled, twiddling the flimsy garment on one thick finger. "Bless you, she couldn't get it over her head. But I can sell it and buy you some candles. Your cousin is paying handsome for your lodging but I don't see much of the coin."

It took Marya an hour or more to remove the tangles from her hair. She spent the day in alternately exercising, reciting poetry and using her senses to transport her to the places she loved best. She even tried to imagine that she was in the New World with Martín but she knew so little of the region that she soon shifted back to the village and remembered how swift and strong he had been in hitting the ball in *pelota* and how well he had performed in the Sword Dance.

While all Basques danced, only a few of the most talented boys were trained from childhood in the difficult feats demanded of *ezpatadantzariak,* crouching with a sword, pirouetting, poising on one foot while twisting the other in the air. There was no one in the village now to equal him; in fact, the older people lamented that the Sword Dance was no longer the fine spectacle that it had been before most of the vigorous young men had gone out to the New World.

It was such a vast place, stretching from Peru and Brazil to the northern frontiers explored by Coronado. Could David find Martín there? If he did and if Martín were to return, would she still be alive, even as a captive in a cell? The Inquisition was slow but not that laggard.

For some reason the probability that none of those who cared about her would ever know her fate made that doom seem all the worse. It already seemed that she had been imprisoned for years, though there remained one full day and two nights before the inquisitor would begin his examination.

She prayed she could be brave.

When Jaime brought her food on the night before she would see Father Rojas, he again begged her to send for the priest and bend to Perkain's will.

Mumbling so that she could scarcely hear him, the hulking jailer said, "You could find an apothecary to give you something for a spicy dish, girl. It is no more than he deserves."

Marya knew that she might well take a knife to her cousin were she ever subjected to his perverted lusts, but then she would die for murder. She could not, despite his malevolent betrayal, bring herself to marry and then poison him.

"I can't," she told Jaime. "I wish I could but I can't."

He drew a long breath. "Well then, girl, God save you in the morning." He peered at her. "Whatever happens, you will know that I did my best for you?"

She nodded. Why reproach him for not seeking David? Without his kindness and—most of all—the candles, she might have been crazed by now.

"Thank you, Jaime."

He touched her hair, hesitating as if about to plead with her again. Then he sighed and went out. The momentary draft from the door made the candle waver. Cold terror paralyzed her.

When that door swung open again, the inquisitor would stand there.

IV

MERCIFULLY Jaime had brought her wine instead of cider. She drank all of it and was able to sleep. The candle had burned out before she awoke and the darkness gave no clue to the time, though she thought it must be morning.

Groping for comb and basin, she washed her face and did what she could with her hair. Her nerves began to tighten as if wound on a reel. Waiting alone in the silent blackness was so terrifying that she almost wished the inquisitor would come.

No wonder that prison, even without the infliction of torture, usually broke the strongest spirit. She could not endure weeks, months, years of this! If there was no way out of the cell, she must find a way out of life—before her mind frayed and she told about the cave or tainted her family with admitted witchcraft.

Suddenly she realized that the secret of the cave, so long cherished and handed down, would die with her. No more hands would press against the wall, no torches light the faces of mother and child and the flight of the summer birds.

This realization was as difficult to face as was the thought of her own end. It seemed wrong, wicked, that the shrine that had comforted and strengthened her succession of women throughout countless ages should be forever lost. The threat made her resolve to hold out as long as she could, for with her would vanish the birthright bequeathed by that ancient, nameless woman who so long ago had painted her dreams on walls of rock. Marya herself had no mother, and no daughter, but she was kin to all the mothers and daughters in the cave. That their secret depended on her called up a steadfastness that she hadn't known she possessed.

As the door opened, she rose to her feet. The light blinded her even though the figure of the tall, gaunt priest loomed in the doorway. As he stepped inside, followed by Jaime and another man, there was a sudden onslaught which Marya, dazed, could not fully comprehend.

Hooded men fell upon the inquisitor and grappled with the jailers. Taken by surprise, the attacked were quickly gagged, tied and dumped unceremoniously on the floor. One of the assailants yanked the keys from Jaime's belt and came over to test the lock of Marya's chains. The hood slipped enough that she could see his face and she started to cry out with joy but he touched a finger to her lips.

The third key that he tried undid the locks. As Marya stepped away from the chains, David grabbed her arm, wrapped a mantle around her and hustled her outside. His companions followed. David locked the door, then tossed the keys into a ditch of stagnant water.

They hurried along the street to the wharfs, where they ducked into an empty warehouse. "Thanks, lads," David said, counting silver into the hands of four of the men. They thanked him and made off. The fifth refused payment.

"The Inquisition sent my mother to the stake," he said. "I was glad to cheat them. Good luck to you, young lady." He nodded and was gone.

"David!" Marya cried at last, throwing herself into his arms. "How did you know?"

He disengaged her. "We're not shut of trouble till we sail," he said tersely. He reached into a crate and brought out clothes and shears. "Dress in these. The shirt's baggy but if you . . . show, here's a strip of cloth you can bind around you."

Holding up coarse pantaloons, Marya gasped. "These are men's things!"

"To be sure," David said impatiently. "There aren't many women going out to the New World and there will be a watch for you. Hurry! I have to cut your hair."

Within minutes she had donned the strange-feeling garments. Head atilt, David frowningly decided that she would have to bind her breasts. "Can't have the sailors finding out you're a woman."

"David! Tell me right now what we're going to do."

He grinned and started awkwardly clipping off her ringlets. "I had already signed aboard a ship bound for Vera Cruz when your friend Jaime found me—"

"He *did?*"

"How else would I know?" David chewed his lip in concentration as he clipped around an ear. "He didn't let you guess, of course, because had there been a slip-up and you were put to the torture, you might have given him away. He wanted to save you but he's also fond of his own neck."

"So that's why you tied him up!"

"Sure. He has to be just as mad and disappointed as anyone else that such a dangerous wench escaped." David shook his head. "That gray louse, Perkain! If I didn't have you to look after, I'd cut his throat."

Gathering up her shorn hair, he stuffed it behind a pile of bales. "If anyone ever finds that, it'll be too late to connect it with you." He swore as he noticed her raw wrists and ankles. "If your poor father knew . . . never mind, lass! We'll find your Martín. Then you can start a new life in a new land, or he may think of some way to settle with Perkain. The thing now is to get you snugged away on the caravel. I've paid for your passage, claiming you as a nephew with a weak back so that you won't have to work. But only the captain and pilot have cabins so don't expect comfort."

"After that cell, anything will seem wonderful."

David grunted. "I told the captain your name is Nico. Since we're not filling out papers for you, officially he doesn't know that you're aboard. I've rolled our pallets in a corner beneath the forecastle deck, where you'll at least be out of the worst weather."

Marya hugged him. "Don't worry. I'll make you such a good, obedient nephew that you'll wonder how you ever got along without one!"

Eyeing her with a twinkle that belied the severity of his tone, David said, "Obedient? You didn't stop till you got your way about going to the New World, did you?"

They dropped her dress on a garbage heap and made their way along the crowded wharfs.

* * *

The *Trinidad* was a three-masted ship riding low in the waters with her burden of two hundred tons of iron goods. Brawny men, naked to their waists, were scurrying about. To Marya's confused eyes, ropes and sails seemed to be everywhere. Though much of her family's wealth had come from ships, she had never seen one before.

"Hurry, Nico!" David urged, running along the plank that stretched from wharf to deck. Marya followed, hoping that she wouldn't slip.

"Looks like the tide's right," he observed, hustling her along the main deck and past two iron guns to the towering forecastle. The deck on which the forecastle was built sheltered the forward section of the main deck and David was not the only one to stow pallets in this comparatively protected place.

"Keep out of the way," he told her and hurried to help raise the great triangular sails, joining in a singing chant that set a rhythm for the task.

Shouted commands, the creaking of the ship and the singing of the men made Marya's blood tingle. She found a niche where she wouldn't be in the way and watched the sails fill as the vessel moved down the estuary, passing incoming and outward-bound ships as it steered for the famed Bay of Biscay.

How many times her father had sailed out of this port! She could almost hear his laughter mix with the other sounds and she laughed aloud herself, exulting in her escape—even more, in being on her way to find Martín!

She blessed Jaime and the nameless sailors who had dared the wrath of the Inquisition to free her, vowing to reward David should she ever find a way. To the spirits of the cave she whispered, "I'll come back if I can. I will try to bring you my daughter."

Then she turned to face the open sea.

The *Trinidad* and her cargo were contracted by a Cadiz firm but did not have to call in at the port. She sailed in sight of the coast until after midday, when she turned westerly, following the sun.

A yellow-haired sailor, his blue eyes startling in his sun-baked face, set down a pan holding several cleaned fish. He built a small fire in a box of stones that sat just under the edge of the forecastle. A wide strip of zinc stood upright at one side of the box, serving as a windbreak.

"If you'll cook these up for me, laddie, we'll share them," he said in strongly accented Spanish. "I'm Dirk Harris. Reckon you'd be Davie's nephew."

Marya tried to pitch her voice low. "Is this the kitchen?"

"Bless you," Dirk chuckled, "it's all we've got! That bolted-down chest beside you has cook pans and some victuals. No use going to salt cod and salt beef until we have to!"

Marya opened the chest, located garlic and a jug of oil and carefully tended the fish as they cooked golden. Her stomach had already felt a bit queasy from the motion and the smell of fish made her nauseated. She politely refused the share Dirk offered.

"Like that, is it?" he said, his tone between sympathy and amusement. "Here, chew on this bread. It will settle you if it doesn't break your jaws. *Calliorne*, they call it, same as the wooden pulley-block."

He was right. Chewing the tough bread and putting something into her empty stomach did make her feel better. As Dirk washed down the fish and bread with cider, he told her he was English. "Son of a son of a sailor," he grinned. "Went around the world with Sir Francis Drake in '79 when I was just a lad. But—well, there was a spot of trouble. Maybe I'll never see Devon again." He rose to his feet and gave her a wink. "Just chomp on the *calliorne* when your belly starts tossing," he advised.

She had recourse to the remedy several times that day. Though she didn't get retching sick, she was highly uncomfortable, an unease deepened by the knowledge that there would be no surcease from the rolling swells until the *Trinidad* had crossed the Atlantic.

"Will I get used to this?" she asked David when he came to eat his bread and cheese.

"Some do, some don't. If you're standing by the side, don't watch the waves close by but look a long way out." He dropped his voice. "I don't know exactly how to say this but don't let any of the men be hugging you or, well . . . sort of acting as if you were a woman.''

She frowned. ''But I'm a boy.''

''Right enough. But you're smooth-skinned and delicate. When men can't get a woman, sometimes even when they can—'' He broke off, a blush of red reaching to even his shining bald skull. ''Just shout for me if anyone gets too friendly.''

Nothing like that happened. As the days passed and the men came to the forecastle to cook, eat or rest, Marya gradually came to know them all by name. Most of the fifty mariners were Basque, with a number of Spaniards and Portuguese mixed in, and there were two Genoans, a Frenchman, a German, a Greek and a Fleming. About the only qualification demanded of a sailor leaving Spanish ports was that he be a practicing Catholic. Recent converts from Judaism or Islam were not allowed to leave Spain.

After Marya's nightmarish confinement, she was of no mind to complain. She was free, she could move about, breathe clean air and see the sun high in the blue skies. She was on her way to Martín. So it was with thankfulness that she prayed before the small image of the Virgin on the sterncastle, where the captain and pilot had their cabins.

At night Marya slept against the hull with David, who lay stretched out between her and the several dozen men who were lucky enough to spread their straw pallets in the sheltered area.

The rest of the crew slept on deck or in the unventilated space between decks where the cargo and supplies were stored. The diet was salt cod, salt beef, cheese that went hard and moldy, *calliorne*, biscuit that was soon crawling with weevils, and beans.

To help this monotonous fare there was oil, vinegar, garlic and onions—until the supplies ran out. Since the water in the casks went brackish, the men drank a lot of cider, a good thing in David's opinion and he admonished Marya to do likewise.

''Must be something in it from the apples that keeps folks' teeth from loosening and their joints getting all sore and swollen,'' he said. ''Sailors who get beer instead of cider can be a sight when they've been at sea for a couple of months.''

Dirk Harris put his faith in fresh fish and shared them with Marya. He often regaled her with tales of his father's and grandfather's voyages as he whittled surprisingly artistic little figures out of the gristle that comprised a good part of the "beef."

In spite of the necessity to stay clear of his homeland, he was proud of England and though he was not foolhardy enough to flaunt the defeat of the great Armada ten years ago, Marya wondered, from a few remarks that he dropped when they were alone, if he hadn't been with Drake when that bold commander devastated the Spanish fleet when it lay in port at Cadiz in 1587.

"Drake was a grand captain," Dirk boasted, hollowing out the sails of a miniature galleon. "Learned to command under his kinsman, old Sir John Hawkins, who made the queen's navy what it is. Lots of captains didn't like it when Hawkins lowered the 'castles' at bow and stern so he could mount big guns." Dirk shook his yellow head. "High sterncastles and forecastles give ships a proud look but cause a lot more rolling."

Marya was more interested in Drake, hated in Spain as a heretic devil. He had died just last year in the Indies' waters. "What was Drake like?" she asked.

"A great one to speak cheeringly and joke even though he had misery from two old Spanish hurts, a ball in his leg and an arrow wound in his thigh. He could be hard, though, when his undertakings were threatened. His friend, Doughty, talked mutiny, and after the other captains found him guilty, Drake took Holy Communion with him and had his head off on the old block where Magellan executed a mutineer fifty years earlier."

Marya shuddered at that, but she loved the mariners' tales of hardships survived, strange lands and stranger beasts and men. Most of the men were so clumsy with needles that she took over their mending. In return she was gifted with trinkets carved of bone and gristle and many a fascinating story.

When René Dubois, the wiry dark Frenchman, slashed his arm on a hook, she sewed it up neatly, although she winced each time the needle pierced his skin and after that the men came to her with their hurts even though she had little with which to treat them. David explained her deftness by saying that she had been apprenticed to a tailor.

Whether it was the shelter of the forecastle or something

about Marya that drew them, most of the men spent their spare time resting in the circle that formed around her. Hans Eber, a flaxen-haired German youth of angelic face and savage oaths, had a flute that he played beautifully and Pietro Savan, who had been captured by Barbary pirates and plied a galley's oar till he escaped, had a Jew's-harp from which he could coax amazing varieties of sound. The men sang in half a dozen languages and Marya never tired of listening to their rich voices.

She explored the ship, of course, and became familiar with the duties. In addition to tending the wheel, keeping watch and handling the sails and cordage, the pumps had to be worked so as to expel water from the bilge. No matter how well-caulked the seams were, they leaked and constant tossing by troublous seas had split the seams of many a ship, sending it to the bottom.

"It wasn't the English fleet that destroyed us as much as the mighty storm," Juan Mendez said. He had been with the Armada. "After we rounded Scotland on the way back to Spain, it was terrible to hear ships groaning as they struggled with the storm, had their seams twist open and went down in that black water or splintered into the rocks on Ireland's coasts." He nodded solemnly. "A ship has a soul, young Nico. When she dies, she cries out just as a mortal would."

"That's true," Dirk said. "And I pray for all men who are lost in that manner. But, Juan, have you forgotten that the Armada was defeated before it ran into those storms?"

"Defeated," agreed Juan, shrugging. "But, Englisher, the winds of God sank twenty times the ships that your queen's fleet did."

So there were seams to be caulked, repairs to be made high in the rigging, brasswork polished and decks scoured. Life was governed by the ship's bell, which rang according to time marked by the sandglass, dividing duty into "watches" of about four hours apiece.

The mate, a green-eyed, sandy-haired, bowlegged native of Bilbao, Carlos Echalar, felled any man who dallied or hesitated for a second at following orders but he seldom had anyone flogged. Sancho Diaz, the boatswain, signaled the crew with his whistle. Captain Vargas rarely came among the men and was usually to be found in his cabin. A large, dark man with a pointed beard and piercing black eyes, he had a few times stared so sharply at Marya that she tried to keep out of his sight as much as possible. No one seemed to know much about him and all agreed that they had no wish to test the mettle that lay beneath his grim demeanor.

"It's this way, lad," said Dirk, grinning. "A captain can birth you, baptize you, marry you, try you, hang you and even swive you. The only thing he can't do is get you in the family way. Captains are like God, Nico. Except for a few like Drake, God rest him. Tend to your work and hope they won't notice you." He sighed nostalgically. "My granddad went down with a fine captain though. Chancellor of Bristol, who tried to find a northeast passage to China."

"Did he?"

"No but he got to Russia." Dirk grinned. "Dined with Ivan the Terrible, who wore his robe of beaten gold and opened up the trade that has been a lot more valuable than the China route could ever have been. But on Chancellor's second voyage home to England, the ship smashed on the Scottish coast and my granddad drowned."

"That's how it is with sailormen," said David, who had come off his watch in time to hear the last words. "What is it they say? 'Man born of woman has but a short time to live. He goes up like a topsail and comes down like a rotted mast.' Was it Friday the thirteenth when your granddad went to sea?"

That day was accounted unlucky in memory of Good Friday and the thirteen diners at the Last Supper. Dirk shook his head. Pietro Savan glanced up from his Jew's-harp. "I don't believe that Friday bilge myself. Didn't Columbus sail on Friday, reach America on a Friday and sail into home port on a third Friday?"

"It's still bad luck," David said. "And sailors need all the good luck they can find."

No one argued with that.

Martinmas, when the White Mare visited the fields, was past. The *Trinidad* sailed now in waters infested by French buccaneers and corsairs of many nationalities.

Lookouts were doubled. Tension sparked quarrels among the crew, wearied of being shut up together for almost three months and even more tired of the biscuits that they pounded up with belaying pins and mixed with slushy boiled beef or cod. Mold flowed out with the cider; the drinking water was stinking and foul. Still, Dirk and David assured Marya that the voyage had been fortunate so far.

Often half of the crew would be dead or disabled by now but the *Trinidad* had lost only five men: two blown out of the rigging in high winds to crash into the deck, one swept overboard and two dead of pains in the belly. Everyone yearned for land. Men long-deprived of women began to tell bawdy stories and at night Marya often heard her companions thrash in their sleep and groan as their dreams relieved them.

Frightened and awed by the strength of an urge so elemental that it persisted even without women and thrived in a life as brutal as this, Marya was more careful than ever to pitch her voice low and be wary when she attended to her natural functions.

The men simply relieved themselves over the side of the vessel. Modesty apart, there was no way that Marya could do that without risking notice of her sex. David had brought a pail for her, which she used as stealthily as possible down in the hold and then dumped its contents overboard.

Having first looked all around the dimly lit space, Marya stepped behind a pile of plows and implements and was taking down her pantaloons when a rough chuckle behind her made her jump and quickly pull at the breeches.

"Easy, boy!" A calloused hand gripped her elbow. "I never saw a prettier bum even on a maid. Round and smooth as a peach! Let's have another look."

It was Lope Nerva, a hulking Castilian whom she knew by his especially depraved sexual bragging. She struggled, fearing exposure almost as much as she did his lust. She tried to bring up her knee as she had with Perkain but Lope was too close. Laughing huskily, he was stripping down her pantaloons, groping at her, when his eyes widened.

"A woman, by all saints!" His breath stank and his lips peeled back over rotting stumps of yellow teeth. "Well, now, let old Lope have a little of what you've been giving Davie and the Englisher!"

She started to scream. Horny fingers closed over her mouth and stifled her breath. He shoved her down. Engulfed by red-streaked panic, she regained her senses when his clutch loosened suddenly. With a gurgling shriek, he fell to one side. David dragged her from beneath him, hauling up her breeches and tying them hastily.

"The mate is just above with the captain," he hissed at her. "Don't say a word when they come down."

Lope thrashed in a last convulsion, clawing at the knife in the side of his throat. A gush of blood poured from his nose and mouth. He was dead when the mate's bowlegs skimmed down the ladder.

"What's going on?" he demanded. His green eyes widened as they fixed on Lope but he gave place to the captain, who had descended, bent over to avoid hitting his head on the top of the hold.

Vargas' black eyes moved from David to Lope to Marya. His brow wrinkled faintly before he turned to David. "You've murdered. Would you rather hang or be tied and cast off in a boat?"

"No, please—" Marya cried.

David's golden complexion had turned waxy but he motioned her to silence and spoke up stoutly. "Sir, Lope was about to bugger my nephew. You remember that I paid the lad's passage. Lope wouldn't stop. I had to do something before he wrecked the boy."

Something glinted for a second in the captain's eyes. "Ah, so that was the way of it?"

He glanced at Marya for confirmation. His expression sent a prickling along her spine. She nodded mutely, unable to check the hot blush that rose to her forehead.

Encouraged, David said, "I swear it on my hope of salvation, sir."

"Buggery is a mortal sin and merits death," mused Vargas, stroking his perfectly trimmed beard. "I suppose that you've saved me from hanging him. Get one of your mates to help heave the carcass overboard."

David gulped. "Thank you, Captain," he muttered, choked with relief. Vargas shrugged his thick shoulders.

"Your nephew is a fair lad and has paid passage. I'll protect

155

him from future trouble by letting him share my cabin." Vargas smiled at Marya but there was no kindliness in his look. "Come, boy, I'll show you where to toss your pallet."

Marya was horrified but David beamed. "May the Virgin bless you, sir, for your protection of a poor orphan. I've done my best but—"

"But men at sea too long cannot be trusted," Vargas finished. He turned on his heel, snapping his fingers at Marya as if she'd been a dog. She tried to hang back but the mate shoved her toward the ladder.

Resistance or protest would get David in trouble. She was being foolish. With his apparent horror of sodomy, the captain could mean her no harm. But her feet dragged as she followed him past the culverins and the lashed-down small boats to the cabin on the sterncastle.

V

THE CABIN had a single window, through which the captain could observe his crew. A chart covered one wall; a sword hung beside it and several seafaring instruments were tied to shelves. A small table was fastened to the floor and held the remains of the captain's lunch and a half-finished bottle of wine. One chair and a chest made up the rest of the furnishings except for the bed built along one wall with storage underneath. The only hints of luxury were a beautiful Persian rug and a mattress that seemed to be made of feathers rather than straw.

"I—I fear I will crowd you, sir," Marya stammered, fighting to keep her voice low and deep. "There's no need. Thank you for your kindness but I'll just go back to the forecastle—"

She was pushing at the door when he reached past her and pulled the bolt. He picked up the wine and filled a cup, passing it to her while he himself drank.

"Now, lad," he said pleasantly, "let me tell you how it is. You can amuse me and get back your passage money when we dock. Or you can be obstinate. I shall have my way with you anyhow and it will hurt a good deal worse should you refuse. And your uncle will hang for murder." He smiled silkily. "Which will you have?"

She shrank against the wall. "Sir, it is mortal sin—"

"I'll worry for my soul later, boy. Make up your mind. Does your uncle hang?"

There was nothing for it. Unable to speak, Marya unfastened her shirt, loosed the cloth that bound her breasts. Vargas' eyes dilated.

"A woman!" His face crimsoned. "Did your 'uncle' smuggle you aboard to tumble with the men and enrich him on the voyage?''

''No one knew,'' she whispered. Desperate, she pleaded, ''Sir, I am a virgin and betrothed. I beg you—''

He laughed unbelievingly. ''If you're a virgin, I'm a bishop! But you are very fair. I noticed you before and thought you the prettiest lad ever born.''

Suddenly a shout of alarm could be heard faintly, coming from outside. Marya cried urgently, ''Captain, there's something amiss! Listen!''

''Think you can fob me off like that because you've heard I'm deaf from cannon?'' he snorted.

More voices could be heard now, rising to a shouting clamor. ''Captain!'' she pleaded. ''Look outside!''

''Stop your tricks!'' he muttered thickly.

The cabin was so small that he reached her in one stride, stripped off her shirt and sucked in his breath as he feasted on the sight of firmly rounded breasts with rose-brown nipples. He touched them wonderingly, then cupped them so roughly that his nails bit into the flesh and she gave a startled cry of pain.

Catching her up, he tossed her on the bed and yanked off her pantaloons. Veins stood out in his forehead. He was breathing heavily as he took down his breeches.

The commotion outside swelled into louder shouts, the boatswain's whistle shrilled and the ship's bell clanged. Vargas checked himself as he was almost astride her, and listened for a second, the hard thing he had rubbed against her seeming to melt. Springing down, he pulled on his breeches and caught up his sword.

''Stay here!'' he ordered as he went out the door. ''Pirates are upon us!''

Pirates! Marya scrambled to her feet as an object thudded heavily against the door. She dressed quickly and tried to leave. The door would not open. Vargas had barricaded it.

The window was too small to climb through but by standing on tiptoe, she could see what was happening. A fleet, graceful ship bristling with gleaming brass guns had come alongside. Grappling hooks had clamped it to the *Trinidad* even before the gunners could fire the culverins.

The big guns did finally belch smoke and iron balls as pirates swarmed over the decks but the gunners were quickly cut down and Marya groaned in horror as she saw that one of them was flaxen-haired Hans Eber who had played his flute so sweetly.

Whatever else Vargas was, he was brave. Shouting to his men, he cut his way across the main deck, where he was confronted by a tall, broad-shouldered corsair in black. Each man drew a dagger, feinting and parrying, neither able to find an advantage. The corsair slipped in a pool of blood. Vargas slashed in a way that would have lopped the pirate's head from his shoulders had he not rolled to one side.

On his feet in an instant, he lunged up beneath Vargas' guard, carving into the belly. Staggering backward, trying to catch his spilling guts, Vargas crumpled. The victor cupped his hands to his mouth.

"Men of the *Trinidad!*" he shouted in Spanish. "Why lose your lives for some fat merchant? If you sail this ship to harbor for me, I'll pay you double wages and give you a small boat to take you to Vera Cruz or whatever port you wish."

"How do we know you won't murder us when we reach harbor?" demanded Dirk Harris, wiping blood from a cut on his forehead.

The corsair laughed. He had black wavy hair and even from the cabin Marya could see that his eyes were gray. "I want cargo, not men's lives," he said. "Well, what say you? Where's the mate?"

Carlos Echalar came forward, holding a slashed arm. "If you were English, we would fight," he said boldly. "But since you're not, lead us and we'll follow." He glanced around at the crew. "Be that your will, lads?"

Even in the brevity of the encounter, many had wounds and a dozen were dead. Marya breathed deeply in relief when she saw David limp down from the forecastle, supported by René, who propped him against the side of the deck. When none of the sailors wanted to continue the battle, the pirate commander started to give brisk orders.

The wounded were tended and the dead of both parties were tossed overboard, though the corsair did say a prayer for them. Marya could not be sorry to see Vargas go. David had been carried beneath the forecastle. How bad was he hurt?

Setting her shoulders against the door, she tried with all of her strength to dislodge the barrier. It would not move. She retreated and tried launching herself against the door but she only bruised her shoulder and jarred her teeth.

She must help David and the other wounded. She also thought it best to be out of the cabin before any pirates came to see if Vargas had anything of value in his quarters. Because she could think of no other course of action she again shoved hard against the door.

It gave way suddenly as there was a grating sound outside. The door was flung open, spilling her forward. Strong arms caught her, hauling her up. Deep gray eyes laughed down at her.

"So *you're* what the captain barricaded in his cabin! Was he afraid that you might fight and scar that pretty face?"

Marya said chokingly, "Please, my uncle has been hurt! Let me go to him."

The corsair's head lifted. He eyed her with an incredulous look that turned to grim humor. Stepping inside and closing the door behind him, he opened her shirt with deliberation, stared at the wrapping and undid it. For the second time within an hour Marya tried to cover her breasts but the black-haired man wrested down her hands with a scornful chuckle.

"So the captain had a cabin wench."

"I was not—"

"What? Maidenly airs? Spare me, pretty one. I don't like them." He drew her against him and raised her chin. "Come, you'll find me a pleasing lover."

He stopped her protests with his mouth, as hard and ruthless as the hands that stripped away her clothes. He held her naked body against him, stroking her back. She shoved and kicked at him until he swore and swept her up in his arms.

Lying down with her on the bed, he clamped her firmly with one long leg and thigh slung across her, held her wrists with one hand and explored her body with the other, caressing her flanks and breasts until a strange new feeling began to mingle with her fear and she trembled uncontrollably.

"Eager now?" he whispered in amusement.

"Please—"

But he kissed her mouth and stroked her till she felt dazed and drunken. His weight shifted. She opened her eyes to find him looming above her. Something warm and hard searched between her thighs, questing as if it had a life of its own. Marya tried to roll away, to free herself, but the corsair pinioned her wrists with one hand and lifted her beneath the hips, fitting her to himself as he thrust.

Marya screamed with pain though she stifled the sound as it broke through her lips. David was already hurt; were he to brave the captain, his life would certainly be finished. The man above her lay motionless now, though he still filled the secret place within her that he had penetrated.

Astonished eyes gazed into hers. He groaned. "I'm sorry, girl. There's no way I can put back your maidenhead but I'll be as easy as I can."

It still pained. Marya bit her lip as he moved slowly, gently, until at last he gasped and shuddered, plunging deep and gathering her close with a choking cry. She felt pulsing within her, the sensation of a warm fountain pumping out a golden spray that almost soothed the hurt.

Then he pulled her into the curve of his shoulder and rested. So this was what the mystery was about. Somehow she had always thought that losing her virginity would change her but now the ache between her legs and the sticky mixture of blood and fluid were not as shocking as her first flow had been four years ago, when she had thought that she was bleeding to death.

But would Martín still want her? Tears welled from beneath her eyelids. The man turned to her and kissed them away. "How could I have known, girl—you here in the captain's cabin like this?"

"He had just brought me up from below. He—he hadn't known till just before—"

"Out of luck, wasn't he, poor devil?" Sliding off the bed, the pirate poured some water into a basin and brought it to her with a towel. "Here, wash yourself and dress. You will stay in my cabin on the *Enara*." That was the Basque word for swallow—a strange name, she thought, for a pirate craft. When she made no move to obey him, he said roughly, "It's for your safety. I won't take you again unless you wish it." He smiled, touching her cheek. "I hope you will wish it, of course. Now dress and tell me why the disguise."

Somehow she trusted him. As she cleaned herself and dressed, she briefly explained her circumstances to his back. "So you have come to find your betrothed?" he asked when she finished. "Have you any idea of the size of Mexico and the unknown regions north of it?"

"I'll go to Durango in Nueva Vizcaya. If he's no longer there, maybe someone will know where he has gone."

The corsair swung around. "What if I don't let you go?" He captured her hands. His eyes were a deep gray, black-lashed, and they watched her in a way that made her body soften. She flushed as she remembered how he had held her, how he had. . . .

"You—you said that you would not force me."

"Nor will I. But I could keep you on my island or my ship until you changed your mind." His voice thickened.

He set one hand at the back of her head and turned up her face. His cool mouth warmed on hers, coaxing, demanding. When he let her go, she would have fallen had he not caught her. "You see?" His black eyebrows rose. "This is not love between us. I am not sure what love is. But this we have is strong, however much you try to deny it."

"We—we only met!"

He laughed. "Is that what you'd call it? Well, lightning need strike only once to scar a tree forever."

"I must find Martín!"

"Must you?" He eyed her somberly. "Even if you survive the journey, chances are good that your Martín is dead. What will you do then?"

She had never thought beyond reunion with Martín and she could not do so now. It would be cruel, too cruel to even contemplate, were he dead or vanished. The corsair's face took on a softer expression at her stricken look.

"Let your servant go to Durango. If he returns with your be-

162

trothed, I swear that I will give you a dowry, my blessing and let you go."

She could not imagine being near this man for months and not yielding to him. Shattering as it was to admit it, his strong arms, strangely gentle hands and ardent kisses had already dimmed the image of Martín in her mind. She tried to remember his blue eyes but they faded oddly into the gray ones searching hers.

She shook her head. "I must go."

His lean jaw tightened. Then he swallowed whatever he had started to say and turned toward the door. "Come. Let's find your David. I'm moving both of you to the *Enara*."

"But—"

"You've been lucky with your masquerade so far," he growled impatiently, "but I'm not going to risk you." When she hung back, he swore in exasperation. "Would I take your servant along if I meant you ill? Though what you find ill about life with me as compared to what you're facing is for one wiser than I to say!"

David had lost blood from a cut in the thigh and a slash across the shoulder but Dirk and Pietro had bandaged him and were having a hard time keeping him from going in search of Marya. The corsair, who had told Marya that his name was Ruy Narvarte, stopped to inspect the guns while Marya ran to drop on her knees and she and the golden-skinned little man assured one another that they were all right.

Ruy came over and glanced from David to Pietro and Dirk. "You two," he nodded at the blond Englishman and the dark Genoan, "help your mate aboard my ship. Toss his pallet and gear in the cabin." To Marya he added curtly, "Get your things. No, not that pallet."

All she owned was the comb Jaime had given her, an extra shirt David had taken from one of the dead seamen and an array of bone ships, birds, fish and animals that the men had carved. As he helped her scramble down into the smaller, lighter ship, Ruy said in her ear, "You need a bath. And clean clothes!"

In the cabin he ordered Pietro and Dirk to change ships and then went to supervise the disposal of the prize ship, explaining that he was putting his mate on board as captain, along with enough armed pirates to make sure the *Trinidad*'s crew did not repent its surrender. Once the ship was anchored at Ruy's island, a small one between Florida and Cuba, the crew could rest before taking a small boat to Mexico or any destination it chose in the Caribbean.

While the captain was attending to these matters, Marya poured wine for David, replaced the blood-soaked bandages with material torn from her extra shirt and told him everything that had happened except that Narvarte had ravished her.

David squinted his smoky eyes. "You blush when you speak of the corsair," he said. "Maybe you should bide with him while I hunt for Martín."

"I can't stay."

The bald, muscular little man shifted to a more comfortable position and swigged his wine. "You're afraid you'd never wait till I returned with Martín. *If* he's to be found."

That was most of it, but there was more. "I'm tired of waiting!" Marya blazed. "I know that you would search, David, and I'm grateful. I already owe you my life. But if you came back without him, I would always wonder. If I go myself and am satisfied that he can't be found, then I can finally put the hope out of my mind."

David sighed. "To be unlucky, you've had luck! Let's hope it holds out."

From the cabin window Marya watched the *Trinidad*'s sails dwindle as she sailed off at an angle from the *Enara*. Strange to watch the vessel that had been her world for three months recede into the sparkling horizon. She was glad that at least Dirk and Pietro were aboard the pirate ship. When Ruy Narvarte entered, ducking to avoid the lintel, she frowned at him.

"Won't it be dangerous for you to sail into Vera Cruz?"

"Not if big war galleons and slow merchant carracks were the only craft that might get after me," he shrugged. "But there might be other *gallizabras* like mine."

"*Gallizabras?*"

"They're small, strongly armed galleons designed to carry valuable, concentrated cargo such as silver, gold and jewels.

They can outrun English galleons but they carry enough guns to fight off most raiding craft that are able to catch up with them." He smiled. "Not all. But then I knew what a *gallizabra* could do and wouldn't rest till I had one. To answer your question, I won't take you all the way into port. We'll send you on the last stretch in a small boat—if you haven't changed your mind by then."

"I won't."

He only laughed. "At least change your clothes." Rifling about in a chest, he came up with a gown of blue cotton and a white petticoat. "You'll look better in these. There are women enough on the island that my men aren't so randy they'd mutiny for you." He added significantly, "There's French soap in that jar by the basin—and lots of water. You can use what's in the ewer."

The prospect of a dress and cleanliness was so overwhelming that Marya did not even try to think of a retort as he chuckled and went out.

Hair springy and soft from its washing, nails scrubbed, smelling faintly of the perfumed soap, Marya was clean for the first time since she had been thrown into prison. The simple dress was a little too big but it was a vast relief not to have to bind her breasts anymore, not to have to guard against discovery.

At a tap on the door she opened to find Dirk holding a wooden tray, which he almost dropped as he gaped at her. "Holy Saint Swithin! Nico, lad, you're a—a lass!"

She motioned him in, laughing, as David roused from sleep brought on by loss of blood and plenty of wine. He raised up on his elbow and stared, too, then leaned back with a nod.

"That's better, andrea. I've been sore worried all these months over what your father would say about you shipping as a boy but I couldn't think of any other way."

Marya quickly explained her role as a lad to Dirk, who whistled softly and grinned at her in wholehearted admiration. "I wondered why I enjoyed your company so much, Nico—I mean Mistress Marya. When Captain Narvarte sends us ashore, I'd like to go with you to hunt for your betrothed."

"It would indeed be good to have a stout man along," said

David, "but I've only a few pieces of gold left. We couldn't pay you."

"Narvarte has promised us double pay and his men speak as though his word's honest if his ways aren't."

"Then we would love to have you," Marya said, feeling much cheered.

Dirk went his way. She put the tray beside David and they shared the rich fish stew, crusty bread and delicious fresh fruits that David said were mangos and pineapple. When Dirk returned for the tray, Marya looked around for the captain. He stood silhouetted against the crimson sunset, talking with a man who was polishing the bright brass guns. Though she could not see Narvarte's face, his careless grace would, she thought, have made him stand out in any company.

A bit piqued that he hadn't joined her for the evening meal, she was surprised, disappointed and slightly annoyed when he didn't come to the cabin. Apparently he intended to keep his word. She was grateful for his scrupulousness and yet—he could have visited just to talk, couldn't he?

Narvarte seldom entered the cabin in the next few days as they sailed for the Mexican coast but he did show Marya their location on the wall map and pointed out to her the area northwest of the settled Valley of Mexico that he called Gran Chichimeca. The Chichimecas, unconquered Indian tribes that raided and harassed the silver trains, had given their name to all the vast frontier.

Her heart sank at the immensity. Where in all of that unexplored country would she find Martín? Of course he might still be in Durango or another frontier town. Ruy seemed to sense her consternation.

"You could always wait in Vera Cruz and send the men," he suggested.

Mute, she shook her head. Her heart leaped when Ruy approached. Sweet fire ran from his fingers when his hand brushed against her. She appreciated his forebearance while finding it a perverse challenge. But she still loved Martín. She was promised to him and she would honor that vow until she heard from his own mouth that he didn't want her or until she knew he was dead.

Ruy shrugged and took down one of his treasures for her. It was a beautiful book of maps, translated from the work of a Dutch pilot, Lucas Wagenaer. "Here's the Bay of Biscay," Ruy said. "See the spouting whales and the sea monster?"

Up along the Norwegian coast there were pictures of reindeer and wolves and the seas were enlivened by drawings of handsome ships, some engaged in firing broadsides at each other. "My father would have loved this," said Marya.

"So would mine," nodded Ruy. "He was captain of a whaling vessel."

"Father often sailed with one of his ships," Marya said. "I wonder if they knew each other."

"My father certainly knew of yours but I don't know that they ever met. Cristóbal Urdin was famed not only for his wealth but for his seamanship. He seemed to know where the stars are, even on a black night."

Marya felt a wave of longing for her father, for one of his boisterous hugs and a gust of the laughter that roared like the sea. Perkain might seize control of Cristóbal's fortune but he could not touch his good name and the way it would be remembered by sailing men.

"Is your father alive?" she asked.

"No. He fell sick on our last voyage. Died on the way back to San Sebastian."

"I'm sorry."

"Don't be." Ruy's voice grated and his hands clenched. "At least he never knew that while we were away, his wife and daughter were denounced to the Inquisition and died under torture."

Chilled at the horror of his words, Marya could not speak for a few minutes. "Your mother and sister?"

"Yes. My sister was thirteen."

"Merciful God!"

"There is none. I strangled the inquisitors, burned the house about them, but I couldn't bring myself to kill the eight-year-old boys who were the accusers. They had been tormenting a cat. My sister loved animals and she made the children stop.

She took the starving creature home and cared for it. So the urchins vowed that the cat was her familiar and that they had seen her and my mother blighting the crops. I couldn't stay among people who had done nothing to help—though what *could* they do? It's a sin to even say those accused by the Inquisition are innocent.''

Trembling with pity, Marya could only murmur, "I know."

"Five years ago." He swung away violently. "I still cannot think of it. I would go mad. There was no place for me on land or under law."

Marya shrank from asking, yet she felt she must. "Would it please your mother and sister to know you prey on ships?"

He seized her arm in a grip that bruised. "Don't mention my mother and my sister to me," he gritted. "I take ships, true, and I am glad to seize the king's treasure for it's the Crown that has made the Inquisition what it is." His gray eyes lit with a wildness that frightened her. "I have killed men who opposed me but the only prisoners I ever condemned were three inquisitors bound for Mexico. Yes, it has spread its tentacles even there! I didn't torture or burn them, though I wish I'd had the stomach for it. They were only flung overboard with dead men weighted to their feet."

Ruy did not speak again of his family, though he bitterly denounced Isabela and Ferdinand for reviving the Inquisition in Spain and making it a weapon of the Crown since it answered to the king and not the pope.

"The queen was no doubt sincere in thinking she did well in burning bodies to save souls," he said, "but Ferdinand used it as a tool to control his enemies and enrich himself. His own Jewish physician was burned for a heretic, yet Ferdinand himself had Jewish blood. So did Torquemada, his Inquisitor-General."

Marya thought of Abram, safe now in his grave, and tried to imagine a time when Moslems and Jews had been allowed to worship freely.

Ruy showed her how to read a compass and explained that the magnetic needle on its pivot would always point north. The instrument was from Augsburg, as was his astrolabe, which gave the position of celestial bodies. He had a Portuguese meteorscope, which he said was all but useless unless one was in a dead calm with nothing to do. The sundial was used with a table that gave the declinations of the sun. Instruments like this, faulty as they were, had led to an opening up of the world during the past hundred years. In 1494, Spain and Portugal had signed a treaty sharing the globe but King Philip had taken over Portugal in 1580 and bold explorers and captains of France, England and the Netherlands were making their nations' bids for new dominions.

"Though," said Ruy, laughing, "Magellan's men were upset when they sailed south of the equator and couldn't see the same stars. And the North Star isn't visible from the southern waters."

Marya shook her head. "I don't know how men ever dared sail out of sight of land."

Ruy threw back his head and roared with astonished laughter. "Yet you're going thousands of miles into a wilderness!"

"That's different. I have to."

He looked at her thoughtfully and touched her cheek. "Different people have to do different things. I could say I have to keep you with me."

Her flesh beneath his hand felt warmly sweet. Melting weakness seemed to dissolve her bones. She could offer no resistance when he took her in his arms. Though her will cried, *Martín! Martín!*, it was Ruy's hard mouth she answered, his heart that beat against her own.

"Stay with me," he whispered.

It was what she wanted to do. But she had made a promise, one that would haunt her unless she did her best to keep it. Putting her hands against Ruy's chest, she said desperately, "Ruy, you swore to put me ashore."

He tilted up her face. "Can you say you don't want me?"

Miserably, she said, "I am betrothed."

"You were only a child." His hands gripped her shoulders. "It is as a woman that you've given back my kisses. Marya, love is a thing that grows but it is also a fire. We have the fire."

When she only looked at him stubbornly, he demanded, "How do you know your Martín hasn't married? Or found a new love?"

"I don't know," she said wearily. "Oh, Ruy, please—"

He swept her roughly, tenderly close, taking her lips till longing and desire seemed to melt them into one. "Well, then, my relentless love," he said, "make me a promise."

"What?"

"If your betrothed is dead or vanished or bound to another, will you come to me?"

"How could I ever find you on the seas?"

"I am tiring of the life. With you I would even go back to our country. Somewhere deep in the mountains we could find a place of our own where greedy cousins and grim inquisitors could not reach us."

"I wish you would change your life in any case," she said. "If the dead know what we do, it cannot cheer your family to know you have innocent blood on your hands."

He colored to the roots of his dark hair. "Shall I become an honest merchant, trading in slaves? Or discover a mine and work Indians to death in it?"

"You know I didn't mean that kind of change."

He laughed at her severity. "You'd better hurry back and save my soul, little Marya! I have a friend who runs an inn in Vera Cruz. Should you want me, send a message through him." He scowled at her. "I've half a mind to go on this mad excursion myself. I don't like to let you out of my sight."

Her heart leaped at the prospect of not having to be separated from him but she quelled the temptation. "No, Ruy. This is my search. But—" she smiled tremulously, "if I do not find him, be sure that I will send for you."

"Highly flattering," he grumbled.

He took her in his arms and held her sweetly, not trying to kiss her until she was out of her senses but simply holding her close. That—more than anything he could have done—made her wonder how she could leave him.

VI

THERE HAD been nothing Marya could do to hasten the voyage and during the bittersweet days with Ruy, she had not even wished to but once on land, she was feverishly impatient to start out on what she knew would be a long and difficult search. Ruy had given her gold with which to buy horses and supplies. Pietro, with his double pay, had decided to strike out for the rich mines of Peru but Dirk still wanted to accompany David and Marya.

Though it was early November, this tropical seacoast was hot and sticky, with mosquitoes to add to the discomfort. Still, Marya enjoyed the bliss of a small room of her own in the inn run by Ruy's friend, Simon Altuna. Simon, a dark, rotund man with a peg leg, confided to Marya that he had been one of Ruy's men till a sea battle had cost him his leg.

"Then the captain set me up here," Simon grinned, "so that I, who had thought to end my life in either a wreck or a fight, should die decently abed."

He had married a pretty *mestiza*, granddaughter of an Indian woman and one of Cortéz' soldiers. Their four children were lively, handsome youngsters, showing their Indian blood in varying degrees, ranging from one who was quite dark to a little girl who was as fair as Marya.

In spite of her eagerness to press northward, Marya enjoyed the feeling of being in a home and finding the company of another woman after so many months at sea. Simon's wife knew little Spanish but they conversed with those few words, gestures and smiles. Her concoctions of fresh fish were delicious but even more, Marya reveled in the pineapples, mangos, bananas and other tropical fruits. Cortéz had left a garrison at Vera Cruz, thus founding the town; he then scuttled his ships to discourage grumblers who wished to return to Cuba and set out for Montezuma's city.

Departing and arriving ships kept the docks in a bustle for this was where supplies, settlers and missionaries entered and where Mexico's riches were shipped to Spain. The plaza was only a few blocks from the docks and dominated by the Municipal Palace and the cathedral. Out on an island towered the great mass of a prison-fortress, San Juan de Uloa. It was almost eighty years since the coming of the Spaniards and though Marya noticed many distinctively Spanish faces, most people appeared to be of mixed blood.

It took Dirk and David several days to find three reasonably good horses, while Simon helped Marya buy provisions and items that would be useful in trade with the Indians—bright cloth, small bells, mirrors and beads.

"You would be safer traveling with a supply train or people bound for the mines around Durango," Simon warned. "Why don't you wait for a party?"

"I've waited too long now," Marya told him firmly.

Part of her haste was to get far away where perhaps she wouldn't be haunted by memories of Ruy, or at least would be unable to weaken and send him a message. When she tried to remember Martín, she thought of Ruy. No matter how much she scolded herself, she longed for Ruy, burned with sweet fire when she remembered his kisses and worried about what might be happening to him. The life he led would destroy his soul if it did not kill him first and she prayed fervently that he would abandon it.

On the fourth morning after having left the *Enara*, Marya and her companions bade Simon and his family good-bye and set their faces to the west.

It was a relief to pass from the lowlands into higher country and beautiful to see Orizaba's snowy grandeur glistening in the sun. As they climbed higher, they were glad of the blankets that Simon had insisted they buy, especially those with neckholes that could be worn on chill mornings and evenings and then added to the night coverings.

172

Puebla, halfway between Vera Cruz and Mexico City, dazzled Marya with its handsome tiles that ornamented many of the buildings, especially the domed cathedral, magnificent though only partially completed. Colonists from Toledo had been offered lands if they would settle the city and they had brought with them their skill at producing glazed Talavera tile, graceful blue or yellow designs on a background of lustrous white, often embellished with added browns, greens or reds.

The travelers bought fresh provisions in Puebla and developed a taste for *mole*, a sauce invented by the nuns of the Santa Rosa convent. The innkeeper vowed that it contained chocolate, avocados, chile, tomatoes, spices, almonds and butter. Dirk made what Marya called his "English face" when he learned of the ingredients but he was not deterred from asking for another helping on his turkey.

At Puebla they left the road to Mexico City and took a route northwest toward Zacatecas, winding through wide green valleys and narrow passes between snow-clad mountains and entering high plains studded with dull green tooth-leafed agaves. Marya had ridden sideways at first but it was difficult for her to keep her balance and while they rested in Puebla, she slit a skirt and sewed it up the center. It still looked like a skirt when she walked but made it possible for her to journey astride.

They didn't push their horses. Since they had to be sparing with the grain they had brought, they let the animals graze for several hours each noon as well as during the night camps.

Accustomed to a spirited descendant of Lael's Al Zirr, Marya found her hard-mouthed little chestnut mare something of a trial; she was skittish from ill-treatment. After a few days of firm but gentle handling, Txori—or Bird, as Marya hopefully named her—stopped flinching at Marya's approach and moved along with considerable verve. David and Dirk had geldings, one dapple gray, the other a faded sorrel.

Neither of the men was used to horses and Marya had to show them how to rub down the animals at night and watch for any places where the saddles might have rubbed and made sores. She also insisted that they water and care for the horses before they themselves rested. In order not to attract possibly hostile Indians, they cooked their evening meal before dark and went to bed early, rising with the first gray light.

"Never thought I'd miss the deck of a ship," grunted Dirk, rising in his stirrups, "but I guess I'd rather ride the waves than this old nag! He has a gait that fair jolts the backbone, not to mention the backside."

"The food's better," reminded David.

"It doesn't take much to beat wormy biscuit," Dirk snorted.

Marya laughed at their bantering but her heart was in torment. What if she found Martín and discovered that he'd changed into a stranger? Sometimes she caught herself almost hoping that he would have found another woman, that at the end of this arduous journey there would be nothing more she could do but turn around and go back to Ruy. If he still wanted her.

Zacatecas, built along the steep slopes of a mountain named *La Bufa* because it looked like a wineskin, glowed pink from the sandstone used to make most of the buildings. It was the heart of a fantastic silver ore region that had been discovered over fifty years earlier and the first of a series of mines that reached to Durango and northward. Pack trains bringing in supplies and carrying out silver bullion made progress difficult through the cobblestoned streets. Marya's party bought supplies as quickly as possible and spent the night beside the Durango road.

Mines were tunneled back into the mountains and laborers could be seen bringing out leather buckets of ore, which were dumped into waiting carts. Several times groups of unhappy-looking Indians passed the travelers, and others, apparently coming from the mines, trotted by, some with lash marks on their coppery skin.

Marya didn't know much about Mexico but she recalled that Isabela had been outraged at the enslaving of natives and had forbidden it. That night a miner bound for the mines north of Durango asked to share their fire. Diego Perez, the squat, pock-marked son of a Castilian soldier and an Indian woman, scathingly explained the breakdown between humane laws passed in Spain and their application in the New World.

"I can work with my hands," he growled, holding out

scarred, horny palms. "And I'm going north to where I can make good wages because the big owners can't find enough *Indios* to work the mines for nothing like they do here."

"Don't they pay the Indians?" Marya asked.

"Pay?" Diego hooted. "*Indios* are paid with the lash if they don't move fast enough. Some of those holes go down fifteen hundred feet. Torches suck up the little air there is and the ore has to be hacked out before it's lugged up, two hundred pounds at a time, on rickety ladders and through tunnels a body has to crawl along."

Chilled, Marya faltered, "You mean the Indians are slaves?"

Diego shrugged. "Close to it. There's a law of *repartimiento* that lets conquered infidels be forced into labor. My father told me the Moors in Spain were made to build bridges and roads and plow many fields under that rule. Then there's *encomienda*." He spat sullenly. "Spaniards didn't come over to work but to become lords. An *encomendero* is given a grant of land and a certain amount of Indian labor. He's supposed to civilize his workers and make good Christians of them but you can imagine how that has worked out."

Isabela had abolished serfdom in Castile though the practice had continued in Aragon and of course there was still some slavery. David, after all, had been the slave of Cristóbal Urdin. But somehow Marya had dreamed of the New World as a place untainted by the savageries and hatreds of Europe.

"That's not all," Diego went on sourly. "Indians die fast of smallpox and measles and they're not used to working twelve hours a day. Often they just give up and die. I've heard there used to be five thousand *Indios* to each Spaniard. When that many could spread the work and tribute around, it wasn't a lot on any one person. Even in my lifetime I've seen the numbers drop until now I'd guess there are only about twenty *Indios* for each Spaniard. And the harder they're worked, the fewer there'll be."

Is that how Martín hoped to make his fortune? By forcing Indians to work under the whip? She pushed the horrid thought away but long after they had wished Diego Godspeed, she felt a pang of guilt each time they passed an Indian.

What have we done to you? she cried in her heart. *What have we done to ourselves?*

Durango was located on a river flowing through a plain that was surrounded on all sides by rugged mountains. It had been founded in 1563 by Francisco Ibarra, who had named it for his birthplace in Vizcaya. There was no cathedral as yet but the town had a plaza and wide streets. Drovers urged their burdened animals along and horsemen disdainfully crowded foot-travelers aside.

As in Zacatecas, grim excitement charged the air, a lust for silver and all it could mean to those who had been seamen, muleteers, swineherds or ruined *hidalgos* in Spain. There were a few tilled fields and herds of cattle spread along the river but it seemed that most Spaniards and Basques were more interested in rifling the mountains for riches than in growing food.

Marya gazed about, feeling great inner desolation. Ridiculous as it was, Durango had been a goal, a place where she must have unconsciously expected to suddenly find Martín. If he had ever been here, there was no telling where he was now.

"Let's find an inn," David said as if sensing her despondence. "Then we can start asking around."

They did not have to ask far. The innkeeper remembered Martín. "Stayed with me three months and worked in the mines. He wanted to go as a colonist with Juan de Oñate but when it was plain that Oñate couldn't start for months, if not years, Martín went off with some soldiers who had been up the Rio Grande in 1581 with three priests. The priests stayed to Christianize the Indians and sent the soldiers back to Nueva Vizcaya." The burly innkeeper shook his head. "Those heathens killed the priests the minute the soldiers were safely gone. In the next year Antonio Espejo organized a small expedition to look for the priests. When he learned that they were dead, he kept going north and west, now with only four men, up through the Moqui country and over great mountains and through deep canyons until he found the gold and silver ore Indians had told him about. That made a lot of people eager to explore the country west of the regions Coronado had traveled, where he found only hovels of mud and straw instead of the golden cities."

Dirk raised startled eyebrows. "Do men just plunge off into the wilds by themselves?"

"They're not supposed to," grinned the innkeeper. "But you can guess what it is when they sniff gold. After Espejo came back, he and several other men applied to the Viceroy for the contract to explore and settle those northern regions. It's no small undertaking. Oñate, Espejo and the other contenders each had to say how many colonists he could furnish, the sort of military force he would have and how he proposed to govern the colony and help the priests convert Indians. In his spare time he's supposed to map the shoreline—because the region must surely lie near the Pacific—and he's to hunt for the Strait of Anian that should lead into the ocean, that northwest passage that the French and English are also looking for."

Whistling, David tugged at his sapphire earring. "Why would anyone want headaches like that?"

"Oh," shrugged the innkeeper, spreading his hands, "if Oñate finds gold and silver, he can keep all but the Crown's fifth. He'll have rights of *repartimiento* and *encomienda*, which means that the Indians will have to give him some provisions and do a certain amount of work—at wages that have a strange way of never getting paid. He can give *encomienda* rights to his followers and create his own kingdom, not a small one either! He will be governor of Nueva México, captain-general of the troops and *Adelantado*, he who goes first."

"It all sounds very fine," said Dirk with a quizzical smile, "but if he doesn't find mines, it seems to me that all he has is hot-air glory and real trouble."

"Don Juan made a good bargain," insisted the innkeeper. "He'll be paid six thousand ducats a year and allowed to pick his land grant, over two hundred square miles. He can also open harbors and bring in ships to fetch supplies and carry ore." His plump face sagged dolefully. "I tried to get Martín to wait and go with him."

"When did Martín leave?" Marya asked faintly.

The innkeeper frowned. After a moment's thought, he snapped his fingers. "It is almost exactly three years. For my wife begged him to stay with us through Christmas, but nothing would do for him and his companions except to set out."

Three years? Marya's heart sank. "There—there's been no word?"

"None. But how could there be? Since Espejo's return in 1583, no one has gone north of the Rio Grande except Castaño de Sosa, who went illegally in 1590 and was chased up the river by the Viceroy's troops. He was chained, tried and exiled to the Philippines. After that no one was eager to brave the Viceroy's anger."

Except Martín?

The man answered Marya's unspoken question with rough sympathy. "Oh, a few men can go off, of course, if they're foolhardy enough." He sighed. "It's easy to see why, with someone like you waiting for him, poor Martín was in a hurry."

Marya shivered at the way he said "poor Martín" as if it were certain that he was dead. "Do you know the route he was taking?"

"The way that's easiest. Follow our river to the Conchos and then up that river to the Rio Grande, or Rio Bravo, whichever you choose to call it. As one goes north to the river's source, the Indian pueblos are found, where they can grow crops along the fertile bottom lands."

It sounded so far, so dangerous, so totally alien. After months of sea travel and weeks of the grueling overland journey, Marya was almost overwhelmed by temptation and the memory of Ruy. Martín would never have expected her to come searching this far. And now that he had gone off on an unauthorized, desperate quest among Indians who had every reason to kill trespassing Spaniards—

David said with quiet urgency, "It's enough, lady. Hunt for a man who vanished three years ago into those northern deserts? I am sorry but you must see that he's probably dead."

"*Probably*," Marya echoed, "but not certainly." She straightened her drooping body and managed the strength to smile at her companions. "Thank you for coming so far, good friends. I cannot ask you to go north. Yet I must."

Blue eyes widening, David said, "But Captain Narvarte's waiting! Who knows if he will be this time next year?"

"Only God." Marya repressed a wry smile. Apparently few secrets could be kept on a small ship. Turning to the innkeeper, she said, "This Juan de Oñate, do you think it would be possible for us to travel with him?"

Dirk and David refused to let her proceed alone. They rested for a few days, buying supplies at exorbitant mining town prices, and then set off for Santa Barbara, another mining town on the Conchos. The innkeeper had heard that Oñate was camped there, undergoing the final rigorous inspection by the Viceroy's representative. If the expedition had already departed, it would be easy enough for unencumbered riders to catch up, for the colonists were hampered by ox-carts.

Not only by oxen, Marya and her friends discovered as two days later they came in sight of an immense encampment spread out along the river above the mining settlement.

Thousands of sheep, goats, cattle, pigs, mules, donkeys and horses found what graze or browse they could, ranging up and down the valley. Dozens of wagons and two-wheeled carts were being used as the walls of makeshift shelters. Some of the women had recently laundered for clothing was spread on bushes near the river. Children wrestled and played and a pungency of wood smoke and cooking food floated across the water.

"Why, they're spread out for a league!" Marya gasped, wrinkling her nose at the dust.

"Or almost three good English miles," Dirk estimated.

Now that they were in sight of the expedition, Marya hesitated. She was nervous of approaching the leaders, especially since she had no intention of becoming a colonist. Although there was no resemblance between them, she was identifying herself as David's niece but since he and Dirk were obviously neither Spanish nor Basque, their little group might not be welcome.

"Maybe we should just follow the expedition but not try to join it," she suggested.

David tugged at his pointed ear. "There's no hurry," he said after a moment's reflection. "They can't run away from us, that's certain. I'll scout about in the camp a bit tonight and see what kind of people they are. There are hundreds of them, women and children, too. If they seem friendly, maybe we could just blend in."

It seemed a reasonable plan. Santa Barbara appeared so raw, crowded and uninviting that the travelers decided to camp in the shelter of some big trees along the river. David started for Oñate's camp while Marya and Dirk cared for the horses and began cooking parched corn and chilis. It was good to walk and stretch after a tedious day in the saddle and Marya wandered down along the river in search of more firewood.

She was passing a welter of debris left from a flood when she heard muted whimpering. Stopping, she moved back to a fallen tree and peered around its snaggled roots.

A small gray-yellow dog was making the pleading sounds. It kept trying to creep under a brown arm that lay outstretched, as lifeless-looking as the broken, decaying branches around it. Marya stifled a scream.

In the dimming light she saw that the man's back was caked with dark blood, dried-up rivulets that followed down the grooves of slashes that crossed and recrossed the prone body.

Was he dead? She could not detect any rise and fall of breathing but when she knelt and fearfully touched the Indian, he groaned and stirred. The little dog went into a frenzy, licking the young man's face.

A runaway or a worker beaten and left to die, who had crawled into this sheltered place? Fighting a surge of outrage and nausea, Marya tried to lift the man, realized that she could not and started off at a run to find Dirk. As she emerged from the trees, she almost collided with a horse and rider. Controlling his frightened mount, the stranger, whose face was a blur in the twilight, called in a rich, deep voice.

"Is something wrong, *señorita?*"

What if he were a persecutor, one who would take the Indian back if he were an escapee? Gulping for breath, Marya said, "I—who are you, sir?"

"Luis Sandoval de Torres, at your orders," he bowed, sweeping off a plumed hat. His tone hardened. "You are breathless, *señorita.* Has someone molested you?"

Something in his voice and manner made her trust him. "Are you from the town, sir, or with Juan de Oñate?"

"I am a colonist. If you have an uncle named David, I know

enough about you to assure you that you have nothing to fear from me.''

She hesitated for a second and then decided to follow her instincts. ''Don Luis, there's a badly hurt man back there in the trees. Will you help move him to our camp?''

Dismounting at once, he motioned for her to follow. When he bent over the crumpled body behind the uprooted tree, he choked back a strangled cry. ''I'll put him across the saddle. Merciful God, is this how we bring religion to the heathen?''

Marya helped him, speaking softly to the dog, who yipped and seemed frantic at not being able to reach the Indian. ''Come along,'' she told the starved creature.

The Indian, his face down so as to spare his wounded back, seemed insensible but when they reached the camp and Dirk helped lift him down, he opened his eyes. A look of terror transfixed his face.

''We're friends,'' Marya said gently.

If he knew any Spanish, it would not be those words but as he looked at her, he slowly relaxed. The men placed him on blankets and the dog curled up beside him. In the light of the fire, though he had a man's growth, the Indian looked very young. He had shoulder-length black hair and in spite of the season, he wore only a coarse breechcloth.

Don Luis said, ''I have a good ointment. Let me bring that and some clothing and blankets.'' Mounting, he vanished into the darkness and in a few minutes the sound of his horse splashing across the river came wafting back.

''Let's get some wine into him,'' David said, carefully lifting and supporting the youth.

Dirk held the skin while the Indian swallowed. Marya mashed up some corn so that it made a gruel and slowly spooned the thick liquid between the grayish lips.

''Not too much at once,'' cautioned Dirk. ''He looks as hungry as his dog but a quick bellyful will make him sick.''

They fed the dog, too, who seemed unable to believe that he wouldn't be kicked or cuffed away from the ham bone that David gave him. Marya decided to do nothing about the savaged back until Don Luis brought the salve.

''Who is he?'' she asked David.

"A good man who will welcome us into his household for the journey," David assured her. "I walked up to his people and he was with them, not with the other *hidalgos*. I didn't have to ask if we could join his group. He asked me. And when I told him just a little about you, nothing would do but for him to ride over to extend his personal invitation."

"He seems kind," said Marya thoughtfully. "But—"

Before she could express misgivings over such unusual concern and helpfulness, Don Luis returned. She studied him closely for the first time as he took clean cotton and carefully washed the lash cuts with wine.

The Indian set his thin jaw but did not make a sound. After Don Luis had deftly applied a sweet-smelling salve to the wounds, he helped the younger man into a fine white shirt that flowed loose but would protect the raw cuts.

Don Luis tried speaking to him in several dialects. The Indian only stared but when Marya offered him cheese and bread, his face widened into a smile. "Good," he said in Spanish.

As he ate and drank more wine, using gestures and his meager Spanish, he told them that he was Ruri, of a people the Spaniards called Tarahumar. The men of his valley had been forced to take turns working in the mines and were never paid. Yesterday an elderly Tarahumar had collapsed down in the nearly airless mine. Ruri had dragged and carried him out and tried to revive him. The overseer started to lash the old one. Ruri tried to catch the lash. He had been tied and whipped unconscious, then cut down and left to live or die.

He woke in the night to find his little dog pressed against him. Groping about, he had found the lifeless body of the old Indian. Running away before his allotted time of servitude was out would mean another beating, perhaps a killing one, but Ruri thought that he would rather die than slave longer for the Spaniards. He crawled away from the mine, racked with pain at every movement, and at last huddled in the shelter of the fallen tree. Early this morning he had crept to the river and drank deeply, then laboriously returned to his refuge and lapsed into a stupor.

"Dead if you no help," he finished, watching them with bitter pride in which there was no trace of pleading. "You feed dog. Maybe no give me back to mine?"

"We'll help you," Marya said before she even thought to glance at Don Luis.

He was nodding. "The Captain-General has sent his nephew, Vicente Zaldívar, ahead to find a route to the north shorter than the one that follows the Conchos. By the time the caravan's ready to move out, Ruri should be able to travel."

"How will we take him back to his people?"

Don Luis smiled faintly. "I'm sure he can manage that himself once we're a safe distance from Durango." Their speech had been too rapid for the young Tarahumar to follow. Slowly, with motions, Don Luis explained enough for Ruri to understand that they would take care of him.

Since the meal was ready, Don Luis joined them and then helped them load the disgruntled horses, who had thought their day's journey finished. "It's just over the river," Marya whispered in Txori's pricked-back ear. "Don Luis says that we should join his group tonight lest we attract attention in the daylight."

Dirk had volunteered to lead his horse across the river so that Ruri might ride. Although it must have been agony to be hoisted into the saddle, the young man tried to sit erect and made no sound. David extinguished the campfire.

Then, in what seemed almost total blackness, they followed Don Luis across the river and into his camp.

VII

ALL COLONISTS were under the command of the Captain-General. Some of them were members of large family groups and others were of the households of the *hidalgos*. The latter tended to stay together and since Don Luis' people were fiercely loyal to him, there was no gossip about the strangely assorted people whom he had added to his entourage. Marya was clearly of good birth and breeding, though her "uncle" had a foreign look. It was assumed that Ruri and Dirk were servants.

By the time Don Juan gave the order to start four days later, Ruri was able to keep pace with the wagons, his dog, Lofa, staying close as a shadow. Timidly, at night, Ruri sat at the edge of the campfire like a wild creature who might vanish at any moment into the darkness.

Both Marya and Don Luis had told him that he could go back to his people when he felt strong enough but as the column tediously progressed, the Tarahumar remained with it. Sometimes he ranged off to return with a rabbit for the cooking pot, brought down with a sling he had fashioned. Although Marya kept expecting that he would disappear some night, the mornings found him still with them.

She learned that there were four hundred men, one hundred and thirty women and a number of children as well as a few Tlascala Indians in the camp. Of the farmers, craftsmen and ordinary soldiers, most were *mestizos* but many soldiers were Spanish, especially the *caballeros*, who loaded their armor on extra horses and mules when the sun beat down in hot dazzlement. Although these haughty adventurers had equal swagger, Don Luis explained that there was a sharp distinction between *criollos*, those born in Mexico, and *gachupines*, or *peninsulares*, natives of Spain. *Gachupines* held the most powerful offices and seemed to think that all Mexican Spaniards had some Indian blood in their veins. The *criollos* marveled sardonically at upstarts who put "Don" in front of their names and acquired a coat of arms immediately after setting foot in Mexico.

"It was different during the conquest," Don Luis said. "Cortéz' officers married into the Indian nobility and their children were *grandees*. Juan de Oñate was proud to marry a granddaughter of Cortéz and great-granddaughter of Montezuma. She is dead now but he has his twelve-year-old son along. No doubt he hopes to make him heir to the kingdom he plans to establish. On the frontier, *criollos* and *mestizos* have a better chance of gaining honor and wealth."

"Are you *criollo?*"

"No. I am from Madrid." He stared toward the mountains. "I came over when I learned that the Inquisition had arrested my cousins and aunt. But by the time I reached Mexico City, Don Luis Rodriguez de Carvajal, with his mother and beautiful sisters, had been burned at the stake in the plaza of San Ipolito with all the great ones of Mexico City looking on."

Marya cried out. Don Luis added softly, "They were strangled first. They had been horribly tortured and recanted their Judaism at the last. So a good Catholic would think their souls saved."

Shuddering, Marya told him about her own escape from the Holy Office and asked if the Inquisition in Mexico persecuted the Indians.

"Usually not, though an Indian can be executed for returning to his old faith after baptism. It's about the only legal ground for a death sentence on a native." Don Luis' lip curled. "The laws are meant to protect Indians from corruption. They must live separated from the Spanish and are forbidden to wear European attire, own horses or weapons or run up a debt of more than five pesos. But they can be whipped for countless reasons and many are beaten to death. It could all have been so different."

"What do you mean?"

"When Cortéz came, the peoples who had been forced to send sacrificial victims to the Aztec altars were glad to turn and fight against Montezuma's warriors and be rid of their old vassalage. A happier, freer world could have been nurtured here.''

Marya looked at the almost haggard young man with sudden understanding. "Is that what you hope will happen in Nueva México?''

He nodded. "I had felt for a long time that I could not breathe in Spain. After what happened to my cousins and aunt, I detested Mexico City and I lived for a while in Nuevo León, where I have other relatives. I could not breathe there either for the misery of the Indians, so when I heard of this expedition, I viewed it as a chance to begin a new life in a new place with new ways.''

Glancing through the dust toward the front of the line where burnished armor flashed, Marya asked doubtfully, "Won't the leaders seize Indians to work for them? Won't it be as it has been in the mines?''

"Not in my lands," vowed Don Luis. "Ten *mestizo* men came with me, three with wives. They should prosper and have children. If any Indians want to work for me, I will pay them and treat them well but I won't depend on them for labor or take land they are using. I think that I can show other settlers that they will fare better by living in peace.''

"I hope you will," said Marya. But watching Ruri as he walked beside David, she wondered.

She wondered, too, about Martín. Had the New World changed him into a harsh, ruthless man, eager to gain riches by any means? She thought of Ruy also, especially at night. Though she tried to summon Martín's smile, it was Ruy's she saw against the darkness of her eyelids before she drifted into sleep.

Don Luis took his meals with her small party and nearly always rode beside her. He seemed like someone she had known forever, yet he was always startling her by voicing thoughts she had never heard before. Although in repose his face was somber, he had a warmly delightful smile, like sun emerging from behind a cloud. He would go out of his way to avoid stepping on an ant and once he stopped one of his men from killing a rattlesnake.

"God has given him life, let him live it," he said.

When the wife of one of his retainers gave birth, he had a litter rigged for her and took his turn at helping carry it until she was strong enough to hold her baby and ride a donkey. He stood godfather when one of the Franciscan priests accompanying the settlers christened the child and feasted the household as best he could from the monotonous staples.

He was a kind, wise, gentle man. Marya grew fonder of him daily. She liked to imagine that Lael's teacher, Abram, had been like Don Luis, that perhaps they were even distantly related so that in this generation the essences of people who had previously known and loved one another might again meet and kindle the same love.

Of the three thousand sheep with the colonists, a thousand were his, *churros*, the common, bare-bellied, thin-fleeced, long-legged sheep of Spain.

"Why didn't you bring some merinos?" Marya asked. "Their fleece is much finer and thicker."

"*Churros* are tougher," shrugged Don Luis. "It takes hardy animals to survive this journey. Do you know what happened to Coronado's sheep?"

"I didn't know he had any."

Don Luis laughed disdainfully. "He had five thousand and a lot of cattle, intended for provisions. He lost most of both herds before he reached Culiacán. He claimed to the Viceroy that the sheep lost their hoofs in the mountains. Out of five thousand, only about twenty-eight sheep and lambs reached Nueva México. Coronado left them with a few priests, who were later killed by the Indians. No one knows what happened to the sheep."

"Did your family have sheep in Spain?"

He shook his head in amusement. "No. We were councillors, physicians and investors. But if King David was a shepherd, why shouldn't I be one?"

"I used to help with our sheep," Marya said, a lump in her throat as she remembered her home.

Those happy, protected days at Etchahoun seemed like a dream. Was Perkain enjoying her inheritance? When the bitterness of his treachery sometimes threatened to overwhelm her, she turned her thoughts to the women's cave and communed with the memory of the possessors of those handprints, each of whom must have known that loving was more important than having.

Don Luis' dark eyes watched her with something deeper than concern, a look that made her suddenly uncomfortable. Bit by bit she had told him most of her story, except that the corsair who had rescued her from the villainous captain had ravished her himself and then wooed her in a way she had scarcely been able to withstand.

"Marya," said Don Luis softly, "if you do not find your Martín, you will always have an honored place in any home that I may have."

"Thank you," she said in confusion. "But I—"

"It's nothing to say yes or no to right now," he cut in swiftly. "Only for you to know."

Should she tell him that she had promised to return to another were she unable to find Martín? She could think of no simple way of explaining the matter and decided not to try. Don Luis was only being kind, as he was to everyone in distress.

To turn the subject, she said, "Do you think Ruri believes he should go with us out of gratitude? We must long ago have passed the way to his home."

"He knows he's free," Don Luis assured her. "When I asked if he wanted to live in my colony, he said no. All I could get him to say was that he must stay with us till it was time for him to go to his own people and that he would know the time."

"Maybe he wants to travel so far from the mines that no Spaniards can ever find him," Marya speculated.

Don Luis grimaced. "Who could blame him?"

The journey seemed interminable. Ox-carts, groaning along on wooden axles, forced a slower rate of travel than even the vast herd of animals. The direct route to the Rio Grande that Zaldívar had scouted would cut off many weary miles and lessen the journey by weeks but along the way water was scarce and the grazing sparse.

Marya could not believe any country to be so vast. Wheels and axles splintered and had to be replaced. Horseshoes wore out, keeping the blacksmiths busy. Sheep and cattle whose hoofs split or cracked were butchered and eaten. The priests held Mass and ministered to the souls of the colonists but there was nothing to ease their bodies except hope—hope that this exhausting journey would bring them at last into a fertile land where they could make homes and prosper.

The *caballeros* no doubt had dreams of gold and silver, rich estates and power, but the humble men and women, mostly of mixed blood, simply hoped for a place where the caste system would not press down on them so rigorously, where hard work would bring rewards. Marya sympathized with them but at the same time, looking at Ruri whose back would forever carry scars, she prayed that the Indians of the Rio Grande would be more fortunate than those of Mexico.

As it was Eastertime now, every stopping place or landmark was given a name to commemorate the season. The colonists encountered a small miracle on the first of April when, after having marched all day without water, a heavy rain left so many pools that the thousands of thirsty animals were able to drink all they wanted. Eight days later sand dunes seemed to stretch endlessly in all directions.

In order to water their animals at the Rio Grande and avoid the sand dunes, they broke up into detachments. It was a weary group that finally reunited at a sluggish stretch of the river and followed it upstream to a pass the waters had worn between the great masses of mountains. Here they rested. On April 30, 1598, before the assembled throng, Juan de Oñate, Captain-General and *Adelantado*, scooped up a handful of earth and scattered it to the four directions, claiming the land for God, King Philip—and himself.

Marya glanced at Ruri. Did he understand? If he did, what was he thinking? His thin brown face was expressionless but later she saw that he laughed when the play written by Captain Farfán, one of the leaders, was enacted. It was a great fiesta, with a sermon and religious ceremonies as well as the fun-filled comedy. The actors were awkward and had to be prompted on their lines but the people had reached the border of their new country. They were ready to rest and rejoice.

Oñate's patience must have been worn thin by the tedious slowness of the herds and ox-carts. He also feared that such a mass of foreigners would frighten the Indians away. Therefore he went ahead with sixty *caballeros* to announce to the pueblo dwellers that they were now subjects of the King of Spain.

The main expedition followed along the east side of the Rio Grande, cheered by having reached the great river along which they would settle. However, after about a week's journey above what they called the Pass of the North, the mountains cut them off from the river and forced them into an arid valley bleached with alkali.

The vast expanse of grayish-green wasteland had its thorny, surprising beauties—yellow blooms on prickly-pear cactus; long, spiny ocotillo tipped with flame-colored flowers; incredible snowy white blossoms crowning spiky yuccas. But there were parched white flats where nothing grew and the mountain ranges to the east and west loomed starkly barren and merciless.

They pushed on, hoping to find water for the animals but failed and had to make a waterless camp that night. Drinking water for the humans was carefully doled out. Marya and Ruri gave little Lofa some of theirs. There was no way to water the horses and herds. The animals could go without water for another day but after that their plight would grow desperate. There was not even any dew-laden graze to relieve them.

Surely, surely, their way would curve back to the river tomorrow or they would find a stream that flowed into it.

They did not. The mournful blatting of the sheep and lowing of the cattle increased. Lambs sank down, could not be coaxed up and had to be slaughtered. Some of the soldiers drank their blood. Don Luis' group led their horses, though two children were lifted into the saddles. Marya carried Don Luis' godchild for the mother was staggering. The Don and Ruri went ahead to look for water.

Water that day was given to soldiers and children. The wine was finished. Marya's tongue was thick like a wad of cotton in her mouth. Her throat felt cracked and hollow. No one spoke or made an unnecessary motion.

Somewhere ahead there was water. Somewhere. They had to keep moving until they found it. At the noon halt it was almost impossible to force down dry food. The baby wailed as he sucked at his mother's drying breasts. As the colonists began to move on, there was a commotion up ahead—and despair as the word filtered back.

One of Oñate's captains had returned to warn the main group of this terrible parched desert. He had hoped to catch them before they left the river and tell them to fill every container for it would be days before their course returned to the river.

Days! People looked at one another with dread.

"We'll have to open veins in the animals' throats and drink blood," said one soldier, a survivor of other desert journeys. "But we had best wait as long as we can for that will weaken them."

Holding the dying baby, Marya trudged through the afternoon with her eyes half-closed against the blazing sun. She tried to imagine herself and the child in the cool, restful cave and she called up a vision of the flying birds and comforting hands.

Would they all die here, from the most hardened soldier to this poor infant, who seemed to be withering by the moment in her tired arms?

The priests moved among the people, encouraging them, urging them to pray and press onward. The cooling night brought some surcease but there was no water left. Ruri and Don Luis had not returned and though Marya was worried about them, she fell into heavy sleep almost as soon as she sank down between Dirk and David.

By morning the animals were thirst-crazed but with persistence the herders prodded them on the way. The long caravan straggled on through sand where the wheels stuck and exhausted people had to dig out in front or push from behind in order to get the ponderous carts and wagons moving again.

The baby was quiet against Marya's breast, its skin beginning to shrink against the small, delicate bones. Could he drink blood? Much as Marya shrank from the thought, if the humans were to survive, they would soon have no choice but to tap the veins of the horses and cattle.

God, if only there were water! How could she ever have taken it for granted, spilled it on the ground or wasted it? She was beginning to hallucinate, envisioning people who could not possibly be here. Her father, laughing, faded into Perkain, whom she hastily dismissed. He was followed by Ruy, who held out a goblet of sparkling, crystal water that dimmed as she tried to grasp it. Martín would not come, though she labored to see him.

At first she thought Don Luis another phantasm but suddenly he was holding a waterskin to her lips. It hurt, the trickle of liquid down her throat. She swallowed, choked, laughed weakly and then wept as she brought the skin to the baby's mouth while Don Luis and Ruri handed around other bags.

There wasn't enough for everyone to get even the taste of water that Marya had taken but a great echoing murmur of relief and thanksgiving swept through the colonists as the news spread.

Ahead—just a few hours' march—was a side canyon with a clear, cold spring. Lofa had found it, sniffing and whining when Ruri and Don Luis would have ridden by. They had dug out a natural trough where the animals could water. On, then! Just a little farther!

There was no way, of course, that the suffering beasts could understand why they were now urged on remorselessly. People who were strong enough and were not herding animals went ahead as fast as they could, led by Ruri. Lofa, instead of being scorned and kicked aside as a half-coyote mongrel, was now praised and petted and promised more bones than she could have eaten in the course of several lifetimes.

Don Luis made Marya mount his horse and walked beside her, carrying the child, whose mother had been given enough water to start the restoration of her milk.

Marya's eyes stung though she had no tears. "It is a miracle," she whispered.

Don Luis pressed her hand. "No. It's only the result of your having saved a beaten runaway."

"Do you think he knew this would happen?"

"No or he'd have warned us when we left the river. But Ruri is used to these deserts. He probably figured we would run into trouble sometime. That's why he wouldn't leave us."

Marya did not speak further. It hurt her throat. She was in a kind of stupor when there was an uproar of squealing, bleating, braying, lowing and neighing.

The animals had scented water. Fortunately the men who had gone on ahead had scraped out holes along the sandy track where the stream only trickled after gushing down from the rocks. Even so, the herders were hard put to prevent trampling.

People were frantic. Dropping to their knees, they scooped up water in their cupped hands or lowered their faces to drink. Some were so faint that water had to be carried back to them. It took a long time but at last every living creature had its fill. Camp was set up. For a few days they would rest beside the water before they filled every possible container, drank deep themselves, thoroughly watered every animal and started on. With such preparations, Oñate's messenger assured them, they could safely reach the river.

Lofa was feasted that night, many people bringing her special tidbits and lingering to stroke her coarse hair. Ruri thriftily tucked the excess offerings into pouches, pleased, too, to accept a rosary from one woman, several shirts, a wool shawl and a good knife.

Marya tried to give him a gold coin but he recoiled. "That why my people die!"

Flushing in shame as she understood, Marya handed the gold back to David. Sweeping her arm to include the vast camp, she said in a breaking voice, "You saved us, Ruri."

A smile flitted across his face. "Lofa save. But Lofa need water too." He did accept some of the bells, beads and mirrors that Marya had purchased in Vera Cruz.

Next morning he was gone.

It took three days to reach the river. There was no way to carry enough water for the thousands of animals but the toiling oxen were watered from leather buckets. No one had died during the frightful ordeal except one of Oñate's advance party, whose raw grave they paused beside while the priests held Mass.

"I wish that Ruri had said good-bye," Marya told Don Luis as they journeyed on.

He shrugged. "He had paid his debt. Maybe he thought nothing needed to be said."

"Do you think he can find his way home?"

Don Luis snorted. "Even I could follow the track these carts and herds have made. He took a blanket, a waterskin and food. When he gets back to his own people, he will have plenty to tell them."

"I hope he tells them to move deeper into the canyons where Spaniards cannot find them," Marya said. But even as she spoke, she wondered if there was any refuge where, sooner or later, the Spaniards would not penetrate.

It was the end of summer when the main body of colonists caught up with their Captain-General near a scattering of pueblos, baked-earth cities where the Indians dwelt, irrigating their crops with the river's waters. The Tewas had welcomed Oñate. He had held a great meeting, telling them about the King of Spain, who would now protect them from their enemies, and about baptism and the salvation it offered.

It was difficult to guess at how much of this the Tewas understood but the chiefs had kissed Oñate's hand and made what he thought was an oath of allegiance to Spain. They had paid homage to the church, too, by kissing the hand of Father Juan de Escalona.

"The Tewas were probably just being polite," muttered Don Luis.

Marya agreed with him. Why should the Indians want to be subjects of a faraway king, one who would authorize these strangers to force them into labor and change the easy-going rhythms of a way of life long adapted to the country and its seasons? She also suspected that they had a perfectly good religion of their own for some of Oñate's advance party had talked of circular underground *kivas*, where the men communed with the spirits and deities who made corn and squash grow and brought the proper rains.

As Oñate proceeded up the river, stopping at each group of pueblos to explain his presence and receive the homage and submission of the natives, Marya, aided by Dirk, Don Luis and David, inquired among the Indians for Martín. They had acquired a few words of Tewa and with these, combined with signs, believed their questions were understood but the Tewas,

194

clad in their brief garments of wild cotton which they spun and wove, could not help them.

Long, long ago, a few old people remembered, soldiers in armor had passed through and killed many Indians farther south. They must have been Coronado's men. There were garbled memories of murdered priests and Espejo's astounding excursion with only five men. But when fingers were counted as years, heads were shaken and everyone consulted, there was no memory of any white man within the last few years.

At the place where the Rio Grande joined the Chama River, the expedition rested briefly in a pueblo which the natives hospitably yielded. Then it moved to the west bank of the Rio Grande and began a settlement, calling it San Gabriel de los Españoles.

The church was finished on September eighth and consecrated with a great fiesta attended by delegates from the Indian villages that had accepted the Spaniards. The chieftains were given batons as a sign of their rank. After the solemnities Indians and colonists alike gathered in the plaza to applaud a presentation of an old play dramatizing the struggle between Moslems and Christians, *Los Moros y los Cristianos.*

All Nueva México was divided into seven missionary districts, with a Spanish *alcalde* appointed for each. Oñate organized a central government to rule the immense, mostly unexplored region that stretched from the Pass of the North to the furthermost northern pueblos and from Pecos on the east to the high Moqui villages on the west.

Smiths, wheelwrights and carpenters went to work. Farmers selected land. Herdsmen moved the sheep and cattle from place to place as the animals devoured the grass. Don Luis' people, with the help of hired Indians, were building their homes in a fertile valley. Don Luis had given sheep to the Indians, who were delighted for though they wove rabbit fur into garments, wool would be warmer and easier to get.

Marya had been glad enough to rest for a time but as the leaves of the trees bordering the river began to change color, she realized with a shock that she had been a whole year in the New World, traveling from Vera Cruz into this wild new land, and still knew no more of Martín than she had when she left Bilbao.

That evening as she filled dishes for the men, she took a deep breath and looked into Don Luis' face, which by now had become familiar and dear.

"I must go," she said. "I must go and search for Martín."

VIII

DON LUIS would not hear of Marya traveling with only Dirk and David. After some dispute as to whether or not to join one of the several exploring groups Oñate was sending out, they decided to go alone. Marya thought that if the Indians did know anything about Martín, they would be more likely to disclose it to a small, peaceful group than to one of soldiers armed with swords, lances, crossbows and alarming harquebuses that belched smoke and flame.

The great pueblo of Zuñi lay to the southwest. It was probably the one that Fray Marcos de Niza had declared larger than the City of Mexico. Ácoma, another big pueblo of the Keres people, lay between the Rio Grande and Zuñi. Farther north were the high plateaus of the Moquis.

"If we find no trace of Martín in those places," Marya said, "then I must believe he has died in the wilderness or wandered so far away that he will never return."

Don Luis looked at her. "I hope you will come back then and become mistress of my home." His voice dropped. "Even, Marya, if you cannot marry me."

Marry? Shock went through her, followed by a physically painful regret. This good man had been her companion, protector and friend. She loved him, but not as he would wish. Out of concern for what he might think of her, she had blundered tragically in not telling him about Ruy.

Swallowing hard, she put her hand on his—and told him. Expecting scorn or derision to flare in his eyes, she watched him steadily, ready to accept any rebuke as earned. But he gently covered her hand with his other one and lowered his head for a

197

moment. Then he looked up and smiled, sadly, wistfully, but without bitterness.

"It was only a dream, Marya. But I will have my dream of you after you are gone."

"You must think ill of me—to love one man when I am promised to another."

He shook his head. "I honor you rather that you searched for your Martín when it would have been simple and pleasant to stay with your new love." He raised her hand to his lips and kissed it.

He still insisted on going with her. Leaving his most trust-worthy man, the father of his godchild, in charge, Don Luis rode out with the others one crisp November day.

The Captain-General himself had traveled this way a few weeks earlier, searching for treasure and an outlet to the Pacific. They journeyed down the Rio Grande, got directions at Santo Domingo, now the center of religious administration, and struck west. Should they have to travel as far as the Moqui towns, winter would be upon them and so in addition to the gear that the horses could carry, they took along a pack mule laden with extra blankets, provisions and the trinkets that Marya had not yet given away.

From a far distance they could see the red sandstone butte that must be Ácoma rearing into the deep blue sky above the valley below. There were still signs of Oñate's passing. Marya wondered whether the Indians were as friendly as those encountered along the Rio Grande. Unless the dwellers of the sky village *were* friendly, she did not see how anyone could ever reach it for the few accessible routes up could be defended by rolling down boulders or shooting arrows.

As they neared the butte, Dirk whistled. "Must go over three hundred feet straight up! Can't take the horses. Are we going to shinny up that crack they seem to use for a trail?"

"Maybe we ought to shout," Marya said doubtfully, almost wishing they had an escort of soldiers. If the Indians were upset at the coming of the Spaniards, this would be an excellent chance for them to do away with a small party which could be thought to have just disappeared in the wild, measureless country.

As the travelers hesitated, several men appeared high above. They called to each other, pointing. Gleeful laughter floated down. One man hurled a rock. Then a hail of stones followed. The nearest shelter was against the cliff itself. As the little party huddled against the wall, Marya heard a scream and saw an object hurtling downward that was not a boulder.

It was a body, a small golden body. The hail of rocks from above halted as a groan went up. Marya braced in the saddle and held out her arms. They jerked with the impact but the child was safe.

Chubby, dark-haired, the little girl appeared to be less than two years old. She was naked except for a little blue bird amulet she wore around her neck. For a moment, before she burst into a howl of fright, she gazed up at Marya with blue, blue eyes.

Swarming down the cliff, the villagers brought a boy to care for the travelers' horses and welcomed the group to the town. The little girl who had toddled off the cliff was the niece of one of the leading men. Her rescue was a sign from the gods that these strangers were holy.

Siki, the child's mother, knelt to Marya and tearfully kissed her hands before she could prevent it. To her further astonishment, Siki spoke in halting Basque.

"My husband—his spirit send people like him, save baby."

The eyes. The blue bird. There could be only one answer to the child's parentage—and it left many questions.

"Your husband's spirit?" Marya asked slowly, involuntarily glancing around to see if among the coppery faces there was a paler one.

Pausing often to search for words, Siki explained. Two springs ago she and a few other women had been gathering cattail shoots in a small marsh near the river below when a band of raiding Apaches, comparative newcomers to the region, had tried to carry them off for slaves or wives.

Martín, with a single companion, had ridden up. Swords and horses put the Apaches to flight but not before Martín's thigh had been pierced with an arrow and his friend had been mortally wounded. Someone from the high village had seen the fray. Warriors had hurried off after the Apaches. Others had buried the dead Spaniard and carried his companion to Ácoma, where Siki had nursed him.

She smiled. A beautiful young woman with a short nose, a shapely mouth and silky hair, she must have seemed like a vision to Martín after his grueling journey. Along with her grief, Marya felt a pang of jealousy.

Siki said softly, ''Mar-teen, his wound heal. My brother give me to him. We happy but . . . sometimes his heart sad. I learn his tongue.'' Her head drooped. ''He still—need something more.''

He had remained long enough to see his baby and leave the little blue bird for her to wear. Then he had departed with two young Keres to hunt for the precious ores that Espejo had discovered. Three days later a hunting party had found their stripped bodies. One broken arrow was Apache. The horses, weapons and equipment had been plundered.

So that was the end of Martín's dreams, of his young life. Marya could not help it. She turned her head and sobbed. Whether she loved him still, she could not have answered but she had loved him long.

A strong yet soft arm went around her. ''You know Mar-teen?'' Siki asked wonderingly.

Unable to speak, Marya nodded. Siki made a soft sound of shock but her comforting embrace grew firmer. ''You hunt Mar-teen,'' she said positively. ''You wife?''

''No, but—'' Marya broke off. Why say anything to alter Siki's memory of her husband?

Siki said quite matter of factly, ''Mar-teen tell me he love woman across big water. Say some day he go back to her. You that woman?''

Again Marya could only nod.

Siki sighed but she was still smiling. ''It good you come far, look for Mar-teen. Show strong spirit. And you save his child.''

Yes, there was that. Marya looked down at the little girl, at her beloved's clear eyes in the eager, questioning face, and although her throat ached, she did not feel like crying anymore.

* * *

The travelers were feasted and given rooms in one of the terraced houses where they could rest. Martín's daughter, Xia, often cuddled in Marya's arms but she was especially charmed by Dirk's yellow hair and David's bald head and gleaming earring.

After taking counsel together, the travelers had decided to rest for a few days, as Siki urged them to do, and then return to Mexico. Don Luis insisted that he would go with them as far as Durango, where he would recruit a few more colonists.

Ácoma was a secure and prosperous stronghold with great cisterns carved out of rock to catch rainwater, communal buildings two and three storys high and ceremonial *kivas*, looking like big, roofed-over wells, which were entered by descending a ladder. Zutucapan, Siki's tall, haughty brother and one of the headmen, was grudgingly courteous to the strangers but Marya felt certain that he had been one of those hurling rocks and that he would be glad when they were gone.

She wanted to leave but delayed because of the daunting prospect of the journey back and the feeling that the animals and her companions deserved a good rest before they started. And she loved Xia. Although the venturesome, sunny child was doted upon, Marya still felt a strange guilt at leaving Martín's child here.

A week passed. The packs had been brought up from below and Marya and the men gave away extra blankets and the remaining mirrors, bells and beads.

"We will leave tomorrow," she told Siki, who looked stricken but then gave her a hug.

"You sister. Not forget you."

Next morning Siki was packing food for them—ground corn, dried squash and meat—when there were excited shouts from the edge of the cliff. Hurrying to look, Marya saw perhaps thirty mounted Spaniards below, sun glinting off their helmets, mail and swords.

Warriors clustered about Zutucapan, who lifted his fist and made fierce exhortations that were greeted with laughter and shouts of approval. Then his gaze fell on Marya's small group. He gave a brief, harsh order.

Siki, eyes flashing, defied him. There was a murmur of support. The headman shrugged, gestured and tossed a few contemptuous words over his shoulder as he strode toward the path leading up to the stronghold.

Siki took Marya's arm. "Come," she said. "Tell friends come. You stay in room. I stay with you."

Several of the warriors followed them closely, not touching them but leaving no doubt that they were guarded. Siki led them to the most remote building of all and escorted them into one of the higher rooms, where they couldn't see what was going on. The warriors remained just outside the door.

Xia climbed into Marya's lap. Marya held her absently and asked in a whisper, "What—what will happen?"

Siki glanced away. "My brother say Spaniards make slaves. Say kill them."

Marya's heart dropped. After all she had seen, she knew Zutucapan was right. But to sit here helplessly while her countrymen died?

"What does Siki say?" asked Don Luis, who had no knowledge of Basque.

When Marya explained, he leaped up as did the other two men. A warrior signaled. Within seconds Marya's companions were overpowered and bound with braided leather thongs.

"You be safe," Siki promised. "When my brother say you die, too, so no tell, people say no."

Far away, there was a sound of confused shouting. Then there were screams, oaths, the clash of steel. One of the guards who could see the melee described the scene, his voice hoarse with excitement. In answer to Marya's imploring gaze, Siki dropped her eyes and translated haltingly.

"Fifteen came up. Others stay with horses. Zutucapan welcome them. They start to walk around. Warriors attack. All dead but five. They at edge of cliff. Fight."

At a cry of wonder from the guard, Siki sprang up and ran to look. In a moment she returned. "They jump!" she gasped. "They jump from cliff!" And in another moment: "Two— three—all but one get up! Fall in sand."

The exultant jubilation mounted. The guards ran down the path to join the fray. Marya closed her eyes.

She did not want to think of what was happening as the Keres mocked the dead bodies, assuring each other that the Spaniards, after all, were mortal and could die like other men. Siki's urgent hand startled her.

"Mar-ya! There more soldiers?"

"Many more."

"The soldier chief, he be angry?"

"Very angry," Marya said and trembled as she thought of the vengeance that would be exacted for this affair.

If the Spaniards were to remain in the land, they could not allow such a massacre to go unpunished but they would not kill a mere eleven men, or even fifteen. The warriors of Ácoma far outnumbered Oñate's force but they lacked swords, armor and firearms.

"More soldiers will come?" pressed Siki.

"Yes. They will come."

Siki was silent for a long moment. Then, with a flint knife, she began to cut the thongs tying the men. "People smell blood, maybe kill you. Come. I show other way down."

It would be death to go without provisions. They slipped back to their rooms and caught up the packs and weapons. They did not glance down to the center of the village, where wails for the Keres' dead mingled with cries of triumph.

Siki led them to the side of the terraced houses and pointed out a narrow way between the rocky crags. "Boy watching horses moved them out of sight when soldiers come," she said. Holding Xia close to her, she looked Marya in the eyes. "You take Xia."

Marya stared at her in amazement. "But—you love her! She belongs to you!"

"She Mar-teen's, too. You save her once. Maybe gods send you to save Xia again from when soldiers come."

"Do you want to come, too?"

Though she held herself proudly, there was something forlorn about Siki as she stood outlined against the bright sky and the high pueblo. "No. This my place."

She hugged Xia to her fiercely and tears flooded her eyes as she handed her to Marya. Just then, Zutucapan came around the buildings. With a shout, he ran toward them, brandishing a sword he must have taken from a dead soldier.

"Go on!" Don Luis told the others. "Go!"

He unsheathed his sword and advanced. There was a clash of blades. Don Luis' weapon was knocked from his hand. In a twinkling, he seized the headman around the waist. They wrestled for a moment, teetering on the edge of the cliff, then hurtled over the precipice.

Everything swirled before Marya. Xia cried out in fright. Dirk took the child and David gripped Marya's arm.

"Siki!" Marya called desperately. "Will you be all right?"

"Until soldiers come." Siki motioned her to go on down. "When Xia old enough to understand, tell her I love her."

The young woman knelt then and began to lament her dead brother. Marya, between the men, started down the cliff.

They left Zutucapan's body for his people to bury but dug a grave for Don Luis where the morning sun would bless it. The Spanish horse-guard and cliff-jumping survivors were already gone. Marya wept for the Don but she thought that now at least he would not have to endure the pain of watching his dreams for a land of refuge and hope disintegrate as the Indians were cast into a hell of servitude and worse.

They placed his sword beside him and Marya found one little late desert flower and placed it in his hands.

There was no pursuit as they started for the Rio Grande. Except for Zutucapan, no one had wished them dead, though some might have followed his lead in the flush of triumphing over the Spaniards. To reward the boy who had guarded the horses and mule, Marya gave him Don Luis' horse and riding gear. He was overwhelmed for he had come to love the animals and was especially fond of Don Luis' splendid black Arabian.

From the start, Xia was enchanted with the horses. The riders took turns holding her. She played with the horses' manes, stroked their shoulders and even the glum-natured mule lowered his head for caresses and crooning.

She cried for her mother, especially at night, but both men were good at diverting her, riding her on their shoulders or playing counting games in which they seized one of her little toes or turned their fingers into steeples. At night, though, she slept cuddled close to Marya. To the child's shift of woven rabbit's fur Marya added a cloak made from a brightly embroidered shawl. Xia was proud of it and patted the flowers as she rode along nestled in Marya's arms.

Santo Domingo was ablaze with news of the slaughter of Juan de Zaldívar, nephew of Oñate and brother of his second-in-command. For the eleven dead soldiers there would be bloody retribution when the Captain-General returned from his westerly exploring.

Marya, still mourning Don Luis, could see both sides. The pueblos already had a way of life that suited them, orderly and civilized. Why should they want to be ruled by a distant king and abused by Spaniards, who were all too near? On the other hand, the colonists could not allow such atrocious murders to go unavenged or they would all be butchered. Fear and awe were the only tools that a comparatively small force could use to control many times their number of Indians. It was rumored that Ácoma was sending now for Navajo allies to help resist the Spanish assault they expected.

"Let them!" cried a one-eyed soldier who had lost a brother on the cliff. "We'll haul up the mortar and blast in their walls! Kill them as long as the devils fight. Make slaves of the rest. Lop a foot off each of those warriors and they won't be so ready to lure good men to death!"

Sickened by the cruel fate that might befall Siki and her people but knowing of no way to prevent it, Marya held tightly to Xia as, reprovisioned, the party rode out of the pueblo and followed the Rio Grande.

South this time.

Free of herds and ox-carts, the return was much faster. Before the mountains would shunt them east of the river and into the region that was becoming known as the *Jornada del Muerto,* Journey of the Dead, they rested their animals for several days, watered them deeply and filled every waterskin before riding into the treacherous wasteland.

With gratitude to Lofa and Ruri, they halted for three days

at the canyon spring, peeling bark from the white-trunked trees to feed the horses and mules. Xia thought this great sport and squealed with glee as the animals ate from her hand.

As they resumed their journey, snow fell, melting during the day but collecting at night. They huddled together for warmth, Marya and Xia between the men, but the snow provided the animals with moisture and Marya was able to refill the waterskins.

It was easier wayfaring than on the journey inland, mostly because they were unencumbered, but partly because they knew where they were going. Where the river cut through the mountains at the Pass of the North they decided to take the longer but easier and unmistakable route down the Rio Grande to the Conchos. A severe snowstorm could utterly blot out the tracks of Oñate's *entrada* and along the river there would be water.

Dirk kept track of the days, marking them on a stick and crossing the marks for a week. Days into weeks and weeks into months. Xia did not cry anymore for Siki, although Marya often wondered what had happened to the lovely and compassionate woman who had given Martín a way to live on.

Xia had been just learning to talk when they left Ácoma. Now she seemed to have forgotten the Keres tongue and prattled in Basque, Spanish and a little English. On even their weariest days, it made the travelers smile to hear her launch shrilly into one of Dirk's sailor ditties or whirl and stamp a hornpipe.

When they came to good grassland, they stopped for a few days to let the gaunt animals rest and graze. It seemed to Marya that she had never known a life other than this endless journeying. She thought of Ruy often but without daring to hope that she would ever see him again.

By Dirk's reckoning it was early March as they rode southwestward down the Conchos. Trees along the river were greening and a few bold wildflowers sparkled on the banks and in the rock crevices. Marya felt the stir of winter breaking, of what Basques called *llurun*, earth's living breath. She began to amuse Xia with little stories and in them the hero was always tall and dark, with gray eyes. Later, when Xia could understand, there would be time enough to tell her of Martín and gentle Siki, the mother who had loved her enough to send her away.

Early one morning they were approaching a narrow defile when they heard shouts and a commotion. Quickly taking cover behind some rocks, they saw a dozen Indians spill out of the pass, scattering as a horse and rider burst through their midst.

Several more Indians followed, winging arrows and lances at their formidable prey, who wore chain mail but no helmet. He kept them at bay with his sword but his horse was flagging, thrust through with two lances and wounded by arrows.

"Ruy!" Marya shouted in astonishment.

Heedless of all but his danger, she thrust Xia into David's arms and heeled her mare around the rocks, startling the Indians away from their intended victim, who now stood behind his fallen horse, using its body as a barrier.

An arrow pinned her mantle to her dress but she scarcely felt the sting. Dirk and David had come, too, leaving Xia behind the rocks. They grouped around Ruy, still outnumbered but armed with Toledo steel.

In the end, by using arrows, the Indians could have taken them but one young man had run forward, lifting his arms as a sign to the warriors to stop. A little coyote-like dog ran at his heels.

"Ruri!" Marya cried.

He gave a brief smile while shouting to his comrades. A low murmur of disappointment was swallowed by a lifting of bows and lances as though in salute and then all of the Indians except Ruri vanished.

"You back," he said to Marya. He nodded to Ruy, squinting curiously. "He your man?"

"Yes," she cried joyfully, thankfully. "Yes, Ruri. He is my man!"

Ruri nodded gravely. "My people live far back in canyons now. Spaniards no find." To his astounded recent enemy, he said politely, "Horse dead. Tarahumar eat?"

"No need to waste meat," Ruy said, slowly recovering. As

Ruri signaled his companions to a feast, Ruy came over and lifted Marya down, taking her into his arms.

"I can't believe that you are really here," he whispered, "but even if you are a dream, I'll never let you go."

Ruy's few wounds were little more than deep scratches. The pack mule's load had lightened so much that they apportioned the supplies to their saddlepacks. David insisted on yielding his dapple-gray to Ruy, saying he was sure the mule would be a lot more comfortable.

As they rode along, Marya explained the presence of Xia, who was entranced with the handsome new man in her party. After that Marya asked, struggling to frown through her bliss, "What are you doing here?"

He grimaced and chuckled. "Looking for you, what else?"

"But your ship?"

"It's waiting at the island, all properly refitted, to take us home."

"Home?"

He nodded. "I couldn't get you off my mind, little witch. I bought false papers and thought to wait for you in Vera Cruz— not revealing myself, of course, should you return with your Martín. But the wait became tedious. Besides, news came from Vizcaya that I thought you should have."

"What?"

His gray eyes chilled. "Your Cousin Perkain got his due. There was blight and pestilence in the fields of people with whom he had quarreled and then some children died after he'd had words with their parents. The people were so sure that he was a witch that they didn't wait for the Inquisition. They hanged him, but not till he had prayed for it."

Marya closed her eyes. She had seen too much suffering and death to wish ill for anyone. Ruy touched her hand. "So his charges against you were declared false, sweeting. Etchahoun is yours again. Is it your wish to return?"

She nodded, unable to speak but smiling through her tears. Surely the Mothers would understand if she took Xia to the cave, where their presence might help make up for the mother the little girl had lost. And someday—someday she and Ruy would have a child, too.

There was no shadow between them as he reined nearer to draw her into his arms for a long, sweet kiss.

V

The Scattered Fire

I

DOMINIKA KNELT in the dark by her mother's grave, glad to at last be alone with her grief. Maria of Etchahoun had died suddenly on Monday. Since then the public rituals had given Dominika a pattern to cling to when loss threatened to overwhelm her but there had been no time for private weeping. At night physical exhaustion sent her quickly into dream-ridden slumber which failed to refresh.

Even as she bathed her mother in holy water, dressed her in her best black dress, sealed the gentle, dark eyes with drops of wax from a blessed candle and fastened her hands on a crucifix, the nearest neighbor, Elena Bigatzi, was bustling about the room, draping mirrors and furniture with special funerary cloths made from Etchahoun flax and embroidered through generations by women of that house.

"Just to go like that!" Elena sighed as she poured hot water into a dish on the bedstand and set a laurel leaf to float in it. "But she had many sorrows in this life. Now she is in glory." The raw-boned, red-cheeked woman stared at Dominika with narrowly set black eyes above a beak-like nose. "It will not be decent for you to remain alone in the house with such a young stepfather. We will arrange a quiet wedding for you and Nicolas."

Big, clumsy, well-meaning Nicolas was the Bigatzi heir. It had been assumed by both families that he and Dominika would marry. She was fond of him in a rather pitying way but thus far she had not met the man to make her ready to leave Etchahoun.

Her mother not yet cold and she was already being pressed to wed! Shocked past making a soft answer, Dominika said, "I will not marry Nicolas."

The older woman took the words like a slap in the face, then blinked rapidly and pursed her lips. "You're too upset to think properly, my girl," she said with forced patience. "We'll speak of it later."

Dominika scarcely heard. She gazed down at Maria's face, which looked almost young again in its relaxation, and her heart cried, *Mother! Mother!*

All that night masters and mistresses of the neighborhood came to watch with the body, as well as relatives from the next valley and the village. Dominika's stepfather, Esteban Lexa, sat with his golden head bowed in a corner of the *sala*. Several women murmured approvingly that he was grief-stricken but Dominika had suspected that he was drunk.

As he probably was now, over at the tavern where the banquet was being served. Dominika curled her lip though a wave of desolation swept over her. A handsome young husband with a taste for drink and women was one sorrow Maria would bear no longer. Did she have any knowledge of the dozens of candles lit for her this morning at the service held on the first Sunday after her funeral or of the loaves of bread placed by brass candlesticks on the *sepulturie* or *yarleku* belonging to the House of Etchahoun? Or of the Low and High Mass, held just before the last and biggest of the funerary banquets?

Maria had been devout, so much so that several women had remarked that the many Mass donations were wasted since she would not be long in purgatory. Still, the making of *artu-emon* donations, "to give and to take," was the accepted way to show respect for the dead and their house. Such donations were given by the mistress of each household to the sacristan, who recorded them in a small book which he then gave to the bereaved family. When someone from a family that had given a donation died, the mistress of the previously mourning household looked up the amount of the donation and gave the same or a larger one.

The ritual of death and mourning was marked deep by centuries, there to be followed when needed, like the coffin road linking each neighborhood with the village church. But even after the night watch, funeral, *novena*, later services and banquets, the dead were not forgotten. For a year, on Sundays and holidays, the mistress of the house would light candles on the *sepulturie* and bring a bread offering. At the end of the year there would be a service with High Mass and many candles to mark the completion of prescribed mourning but anniversary Masses were often held for many years after the death of a husband or wife.

And there was All Saints' Day, the first of November, when the mistress of each household lit candles on its *sepulturie*. There was Mass, a procession to the cemetery and prayers. The next day, All Souls', saw the ritual repeated except that women put candles on the *sepulturie* of the household into which they had been born.

Christmas dinner was begun with a prayer by the master for all those who had ever lived in the house, worked its fields and been remembered at its *sepulturie*. Farms were rarely sold but when they were, the *sepulturie* remained with them. The entrance to the house of this life was inextricably joined to the entrance of the next. To Dominika, though, the Blessing of the Fields was the most practical and beautiful way of remembering the dead.

After Easter, when the new crop was sprouting, each neighborhood chapel was visited by the priest, accompanied by the sacristan and altar boys, especially pious folk and someone from each household which had that year carried a member down the coffin road. After Mass the priest blessed a large bowl of salt that was placed on the altar. The master or mistress of each neighborhood household came forward with pieces of paper to be folded around handfuls of salt dispensed by the altar boy. Crude wooden crosses were also blessed and these, thrust into the edge of each field, ensured a rich harvest.

Someone from each bereaved house attended all the neighborhood services and brought back salt from each. This communal salt was then mixed with holy water and sprinkled over the family's fields. That rite would mark the time when Maria's spirit would hover close to earth if it could. She had not only tended the garden but had said when it was time to plant corn, wheat, barley, flax and root crops, sow clover and when it was time to harvest. The family coat of arms, a sheaf of grain enfolded by a sickle, truly suited her.

It was hard to believe that dark-haired, bright-spirited Maria lay under the earth in spite of all the rites and services that said it was so. A blooming peach tree cast its petals on the raw earth beside the grave of Dominika's father, killed ten years earlier by a falling tree, and her spritely grandmother, who had told her stories of Mari, Queen of Witches and her father, the Basa Jaun, and taught her to dance.

There was no stone for Dominika's only brother, Blas, who had been the best dancer and *pelota*-player of the village. His chestnut hair, ruddier than Dominika's, had pillowed itself in Australian soil five years ago when he was shot during an argument. He had gone to earn the money to buy back some of the fields sold by Etchahoun after the Second Carlist War ended in 1876. Don Carlos had sworn by the Tree of Gernika to uphold the Basque privileges granted in the ancient *Fuero*, or charter, and the Basques, unwilling to be absorbed into a liberal, anticlerical Spanish Federal Republic, had supported his claim to the throne just as in the Carlist War, beginning in 1833 and lasting seven bitter years, they had supported the claim of dead King Fernando's brother, the first Don Carlos, against that of Ferdinand's three-year-old daughter, Isabela. The Bourbon dynasty's rule in Spain had brought with it the Salic law, which stated that women could not inherit, but Fernando had returned to the earlier Spanish law of succession, giving the throne to the eldest child.

In both disastrous wars the Basques had fought on the losing Carlist side, not so much to uphold the monarchy as to protect their way of life. Much fighting had taken place in the Pyrenees and after each war the Basque villages had been heavily fined. Many had to sell off their commons to raise the money. But the master of Etchahoun, Dominika's grandfather, who had led a guerrilla band from 1872 until the end, had insisted that the village keep its commons. Etchahoun, he said, had much more land than any other house. His neighbors had already lost enough by following him. Etchahoun would pay the retribution.

He had died before Dominika was born, died heartbroken at having sold off ancestral lands. True, Etchahoun still possessed its timberland, meadows for pasturing five cows and growing hay, an orchard of cherry, plum, pear and apple trees, and fields where wheat and corn alternated with a winter crop and clover, which put richness back into the soil. But Dominika's grandfather had died believing that he had been an unworthy keeper of Etchahoun.

His son-in-law had worked hard to save purchase money but although the house was almost self-sufficient, the only cash came from cheese, butter, eggs, an occasional calf and the aged cider for which Etchahoun was famous. Farm products could be bartered in the village shops and used to pay church tithes and the doctor. Even so, the slowly accumulated money went for taxes and to provide dowries for Maria's brother, who had gone to America and never been heard of again, and for her sister, who had married into a household in the next valley.

As heiress to Etchahoun, Maria had inherited the farm since it was the custom to prevent the land from being divided into tiny lots that would support no one. It was also custom for the heir to provide brothers and sisters with money to make their start in life, though as long as an unmarried member of the family wished to stay at home, he or she could, giving labor or wages earned outside to the household and remaining under the authority of the master or mistress. Elena Bigatzi's husband's aging uncle had returned after thirty years of sheepherding in Wyoming, bringing with him his saved wages, thousands of dollars, and he had been content to hand it to his nephew, who then allotted him spending money. He was only one of many whose wages from the American West had helped to keep a family farm going in the hard times after the Carlist Wars.

Since only one child could inherit the farm, Basques had been emigrating for centuries—many to remain—to South America and Mexico and more recently to Australia and America. Some stayed in America only long enough to save enough money to buy a business or a farm or pay off debts on the old one. Others remained for the span of their adult lives and returned just in time to die in their childhood homes.

Blas had not returned. So Etchahoun had continued, diminished but comfortable, almost self-sufficient from spinning, weaving and sewing home-grown flax and wool into clothing and house linens, fattening a pig each year and butchering it in the fall, collecting honey from its beehives and chestnuts, walnuts and firewood from the commons as well as bracken for animal bedding, which would later be excellent fertilizer. Since the land was cropped frequently and much fertilizer was used, the neighborhood had built a big lime oven. After rock was hacked out of the mountain and brought to the oven, a fire had to be kept going for many days. Then neighborhood men took turns at the chore and divided the lime when it was ready.

The last descendant of Al Zirr had been sold to help pay the village's fines to Madrid but fawn-colored cattle pulled the cart used for hauling wood, stone or crops or for the rare occasions when it was necessary to go to the nearest market town, Gernika. Also, protected by blankets and red-fringed sheepskin headdresses to keep away flies, the cows drew the plow through the fields. The funny little donkey, Birri, was used for lighter loads.

Dominika could scarcely miss what she had never known. Her grandmother's stories of proud Arabian horses and fields stretching to the mountain pass had been part of the lore of Abram, whose grave was still maintained under the huge old oak, sprung from earlier trees that had shaded it for almost eight hundred years; of Lael, whose book had crumbled but whose stories were still told; of Marya, who had sought her lover overseas and returned with her handsome corsair and a blue-eyed Indian child.

That little girl's palm-print was in the cave close to that of Marya's and her blood daughter's. She had been given the secret in partial recompense for the land and the mother she had lost. No one had ever learned whether Siki was one of the hundreds of Ácoma folk killed when Oñate's men avenged the killing of Zaldívar and his men but it was known that seventy-five warriors had been enslaved and lamed by having one foot chopped off and that many young women had been sent to a Mexican convent, never to return. Siki's daughter had married a young man who was going to Santa Fe as a colonist, so she had returned to those bright blue skies, broad plains and jagged mountains.

Strangely enough, thirty years after the devastation of Ácoma by Oñate's men, a priest who hoped to build a church on the mesa caught a child who fell off the cliff above. The Indians welcomed him after that and helped him build his church.

Brave, fabulous stories to hear in a snug kitchen in the old house nestled in the Pyrenees. Dominika had thrilled to them while quite content to live at Etchahoun and, when the time came, to become its mistress. But she had expected that to be many years away, long after she had married a man whom she could love and who would make up for Esteban's lack of industry.

After Blas went to Australia, Etchahoun had no man for the heavy work and although Maria was comely, there were few eligible. Four years ago she had married Esteban Lexa, from a valley on the other side of Gernika. He was the eldest son of an old farm household, passed over as heir in favor of a younger son. He claimed that was because he had not married a girl whom they considered suitable; in fact, hadn't married at all, though the younger son had. That may have been part of it for the master and mistress rarely relinquished control of the farm until the heir had married, but though Maria had seemed to love her roistering husband to the last, she could scarcely have failed to notice that without her quiet but firm persistence, little would have been done.

He was not exactly lazy. It was just that he always intended to do something next day or when the weather was a little warmer or a little cooler. His plowshare was never sharpened, or his scythe, so that he always had small, readying tasks to do before he could begin the actual work. He was much in the tavern, drinking, playing cards and exchanging couplets in verse duels with anyone rash enough to challenge him, for he was ready of tongue and wit.

Esteban could have been better, but might have been worse. He was good-natured and affectionate to Maria, though it was whispered that he sought out old sweethearts on market days. Further, he did not attempt to assert a father's control over Dominika but behaved toward her more like an older brother or an uncle.

But now, with Maria dead, what would happen? Dominika touched the moist earth of her mother's grave and got stiffly to her feet.

She was heiress of Etchahoun. Had she married, there would be no problem. Esteban could have stayed on until he died and was buried out of Etchahoun. But for them to be alone together in the house was as unthinkable as it was for her to marry nice, dull Nicolas Bigatzi.

Desperate thoughts rushed through her head as she trudged homeward. The household's carefully hoarded cash was in a little wooden chest in the bottom drawer of Maria's bedroom dresser. After the funeral banquet was paid for, would there be enough to persuade Esteban to go away? Probably not. But if in addition the thirty sheep were sold and all but two of the cows?

Overwhelmed by grief, confused by plans and fears, she bit her lip to keep from sobbing. It was too cruel, too terrible, to have to worry about Esteban. Yet very quickly they must reach some kind of understanding.

Tonight, she was too exhausted to think of it. Tonight, she would sleep. But there was one last thing she must do.

Entering the kitchen, she took the ash bucket and scooped the smoldering coals from the hearth into it. In the light of the sickle moon, she walked to the junction where the house road crossed the coffin road.

There she spilled out the coals of the fire that had been Maria's to the four directions, commending Maria not only to God but to the ancient spirits of the Summer Cave.

May you be with Father and Blas. May you pass quickly into heaven, where it is always summer and where bright birds fly. Dominika huddled there in her shawl, saying her private goodbye to her mother long after the last coal had winked out.

Back in the house she lit a lamp and folded the funeral cloths. Removing the embroidered shrouding from Maria's large mirror, she beheld her own face with sudden shock.

Hair that looked black in the dim light, though it showed reddish glints in the sun, framed an angular face softened by a widow's peak. The strong chin was saved from severity by a dimpled cleft. Her eyes were swollen from weeping but small golden flecks lightened the deep jade green. Dark eyebrows feathered to questioning tips at the edges. Not a beautiful face but even with the softness of youth, an unforgettable one.

The new mistress of Etchahoun?

The face stared back with neither pride nor affirmation. *I am Dominika. What else, I cannot tell.*

Putting the funerary linens into the great carved chest in the parlor, Dominika left the lamp on the kitchen table and went upstairs to bed.

She slept heavily but woke still exhausted. Putting on the black she was already beginning to detest, garments that Maria had worn for her husband and then for her son, Dominika stopped halfway down the narrow stairs.

Esteban sprawled snoring on the goatskin-covered bench by the hearth, a wineskin in his hand. He had not stoppered it and a dark red seepage stained the floor around him. A golden stubble showed on his slack jaw.

Disgusted but somewhat pitying, Dominika mopped up the wine, milked the cows, fed the pig and chickens and kindled a new fire on the hearth. This was not the manner in which she had meant to light her first fire, with a drunken stepfather spraddled five feet away, but she struck a spark on the tinder with steel and flint and fed it to a blaze.

Pouring milk into a kettle, she broke old cornbread into it, set the kettle on the hook above the fire and stirred the mixture to a mush. Part of a smoked ham hung from the rafters beside red peppers, pearly strings of garlic, yellow onions and a basket of round yellow cheeses but Dominika was not disposed to fry up any of it for Esteban, along with the several eggs he usually had. She did brew coffee though, strong and black, and heated milk to be mixed with it, half and half.

She ate her breakfast while sitting on the stone step, feeling empty and lost now that the funeral observances were over and it was necessary to pick up life and go on without Maria.

Maria's things needed to be washed. Rather than put them away, Dominika decided to give them to old Violeta, the widow who took care of the *sepulturie* and helped the sacristan's wife clean the church. For this Violeta received a portion of the bread offerings and a little money but she was very poor and would welcome the gift of serviceable clothes.

The garden had been neglected during the past week. It

needed weeding. Peas and tomatoes had to be picked. The cream must be churned and there was bread to bake. Oh, yes, the days would fill as they always had and as she worked hard and days slipped into weeks, the ache for Maria would begin to lose its jagged edge. Through the open door, she heard Esteban groan. Rising, she went back in.

She brought him a mug of coffee, which he took with a shaky hand. "I thought that banquet would never end," he grimaced. His pale blue eyes were bloodshot. He fumbled in a pocket and brought out a piece of paper. "Here's the bill. I couldn't make it out last night but now I want to see what that thief at the tavern charged."

Shaking out the paper, he gaped at it. "It's not possible! Forty-two pounds of stew meat, fourteen pounds of veal, twenty pounds of tripe, three pounds of bacon—"

Wadding up the bill, he tossed it away but Dominika picked it up and smoothed it out. "There were eighty people," she reminded him and finished reading the account. "Five pounds of garbanzos, seven of navy beans, fourteen sausages, eighteen loaves of bread, twenty peppers, fifty liters of wine, coffee, liqueurs, spices, wood, coal, four broken glasses, one smashed platter, salary for the cook and four helpers—"

Her head spun at the total. Two hundred and seventy pesetas! More cash than Etchahoun spent in an entire year.

Dread gripped her. She had been dreaming that there would be money to give Esteban. Etchahoun had always paid its debts and would now, but there'd be little left with which to bribe her stepfather into leaving.

"Fine neighbors we've got," he growled, burying his bright head in his hands. "Buy a few Masses and gorge themselves! Why, most of them only bought the cheap prayed Mass instead of the sung one."

It was true that the *onrak* banquet was becoming something of a scandal, although givers of the minimum *artu-emon* were provided with plain food, no cigar or cognac, and had to share a bottle of wine with eight people. Some families had been forced to sell livestock and skimp for years in order to pay the cost but a household that refused the Mass donations was considered shameless or close to poverty.

Dominika strangled the urge to tell the bleary-eyed, still-handsome man that had he himself not gotten drunk, encouraging others to do likewise, much less wine would have been consumed. Pouring him more coffee and dishing up his mush, she took the bill and went into Maria's bedroom.

To her relief, the money box was heavy and clinked as she placed it on the dresser. She tried not to look at the bed where her mother had died. It had not been slept in last night. Dominika had a fleeting twinge of pity for Esteban, who would have to find his rest there. How many times would he reach out, half-waking, to find that his wife was gone? Perhaps the dread of that loneliness would make him glad to leave. If there were enough money—if enough could be raised.

Dominika had seldom handled money and now she found an awed fascination in counting out the coins. At first she feared that there might not be enough to cover Esteban's debt, but when the whole amount was put aside, there was still a respectable store of pesetas and small coins.

She was sweeping the tavern's money into a pouch when she heard the stairs creak. She hurried to put the box back in the lower drawer when Esteban appeared and stood leaning against the door.

"What are you doing with the money?"

"I am going to pay the tavern."

He looked amazed. "What's the hurry? Let the robbers wait a while."

"Etchahoun has never let its debts grow whiskers."

"God on High!" he said with a surly laugh. "So young and you already sound like your mother."

"If that is so, I'm proud of it." Dominika took the pouch and waited for him to step aside.

Why was he looking at her like that? Something hot and greedy flared in his light blue eyes.

"Dominika," he said in a husky voice. His breath, sour with wine, made her stomach twist. "We should be friends, comfort each other, you and I." He took an uncertain step forward, leaving room for her to dart past him.

223

"We have to talk," she called over her shoulder, "but I hope that you will have a clear head!"

She hurried down the precipitous stairs and could not tell whether the sound following her was a sob or a curse.

The tavern paid, she took the laundry to the stone trough hollowed by the spring, let it soak with homemade soap and then with a wooden beater thumped it clean against the smooth wooden washboard, aged by years of use. It was noon before she had rinsed and wrung out the last sheets and garments, spreading Maria's over the bushes with special care. There was something sad about a dead person's undergarments and personal things such as comb and brush. They seemed too private to use or give away.

Esteban was nowhere to be seen. Dominika had a hasty lunch and spent the afternoon working in the garden, which had been Maria's pride and pleasure. She was not looking forward to the talk that she and Esteban must have but the rich smells of earth and growing plants lifted her spirits and began to ease her back into the rhythms that she had known all her eighteen years.

She was washing tomatoes, carrots, peppers and lettuce at the spring when she heard footsteps and looked up to see Nicolas Bigatzi. Though he was under thirty, his hair had already receded beneath the edge of his beret. He had dark eyes, a long, rather lugubrious face and big hands and feet.

A good man. Kind. Hard-working. But dull. With Nicolas there would never be delighted surprise, a thrill of wonder, a leap of the heart. Drying her hands on her apron, she greeted him with a sigh. He blushed and shifted his weight from one leg to the other.

"Dominika," he began. "Dominika—"

"My stepfather is not here," she told him. "Shall I send him to see you?"

"Yes—no—I mean, it's not necessary." His Adam's apple worked convulsively. "It's you I came to see, Dominika."

He was nice, she had known him all her life and she hated to wound him. But there was nothing for it. She was searching for a way to refuse him clearly but indirectly, sparing each of them embarrassment, when he wrung his beret between his large, chapped hands, squeezed his eyes shut and blurted, "Our parents always hoped that we would marry, Dominika."

"Yes, Nicolas. But we are not our parents."

He opened his eyes and stared at her. Apparently it had not occurred to him that he might be refused. "But—but—it's not seemly for you to stay at Etchahoun alone with your stepfather."

"I know. I don't intend to."

"Then what will you do?"

"I'm not sure yet."

He gave the crushed beret another twist. "Grief has befuddled you." His tone gained confidence. "Of course, that's the trouble. Trust me, Dominika, and all will be easy."

Even while she knew that she could never marry him, her brain ticked off the advantages. He could help her deal with Esteban and he would work hard for Etchahoun as well as for his own farm. He was sober, industrious and thrifty. He would never give her a moment's worry.

Or a moment's joy.

"I'm sorry, Nicolas. Some woman will be lucky to wed you. But I cannot."

"Cannot? Why?"

Since he had not spoken of love, it would sound ridiculous for her to mention it and so she only shook her head.

He sputtered, then jammed on his beret and wheeled about. "I won't ask you again," he flung over his shoulder as he strode away. "If you come to your senses, you can ask *me!*"

Though she was sorry for the injury to his pride, Dominika had to smother wild laughter at the thought of contritely beseeching him to be her husband.

"*Give me a dancing young man!*" her grandmother had sung. "*A player of castanets! A player of cards, no!*"

It was not Nicolas' fault that he wasn't a dancing young man, one with dash and gaiety. Dominika had not met hers yet but she was certain that he existed somewhere.

Esteban did not come home for supper or while Dominika ironed Maria's clothes, folded them neatly and put them aside to take to old Violeta. The Nuremberg clock struck nine as Dominika allowed herself the luxury of a cup of spiced hot chocolate, curling her feet up beneath her as she sat on the hearth bench and let her gaze rove from the acorn loaves drying on a fishing cord to the cupboard boasting glass, porcelain, pewter and copperware that had been in the family for hundreds of years.

Her grandfather's *makhila,* or shepherd's crook, was above the mantel, where several guns were racked. A wineskin hung from a stout peg close to a pigskin bag holding cider that was ten years old. At last, though she didn't want to, she had to look at the empty chair by the hearth.

Her throat ached. Tears blinded her. Finishing the chocolate quickly, she rinsed out the cup and went upstairs. *Eltzekarea,* "everything in the pot," was staying warm at the back of the hearth. Esteban could eat that when he came in—if he did.

Soon they must have their talk.

II

SHE WOKE thinking that she was still gripped by a nightmare, one that weighted her down while a hot, wet mouth clamped over hers, while rough hands fumbled beneath the neck of her nightgown for her breasts.

It was no dream. Somehow she knew that it was Esteban even before he moaned against her throat. "Be good to me, Dominika. Be nice. You'll like it—"

Revolted, outraged, she doubled her knees, toppled him away and sprang up while he groped after her. "You drunken fool! Get out of here!"

"No way to talk to a sad man." His speech was slurred. "I'm not much drunk, girl, just a bit. 'Nough to tell you plain what I know sober. No way can we live together in this house and me not come to your bed." His tone took on a wheedling note. "Your mother wouldn't mind. She would want you to be nice to me."

"I don't see how you can mention her name!" Dominika moved around to her dresser and picked up a heavy candlestick. It was too dark to see Esteban's face but the pallid near-dawn let her discern his shape. "You're right about one thing. We can't stay in the same house. How much would you take to leave?"

"Leave?" He chuckled thickly. "I'm not leaving."

A cold weight seemed to press on her heart. "You know that I'm heiress of Etchahoun, the *etcheko primu.*"

"True. But I am the master."

"You don't like to farm. There is some money left. You can have it and we can sell the sheep. I will even send you half the cash from the apple crop and if you will let me keep the cows, you can have half the money from the cheese and butter."

227

His voice came hard, no drunkenness blurring it now. "I'm not going anywhere."

"But—but you were not born to Etchahoun. You can't care about it as I do!"

"I'll tell you how I care about it," he said sharply. "As long as I didn't marry, I could live at home, even if I had been cheated out of the heirship by my goody-goody brother. Now the only roof I have is this one."

"You're young yet. You could go to America, save your wages and come back with enough to buy a farm or town house."

He laughed unpleasantly. "Now why should I do that? This house suits me very well. Of course, if you're going to be like ice, I'll have to marry again or get a pretty hired girl."

"It isn't fair," she said desperately. "This is my house."

"Am I turning you out? Marry that young bull Nicolas if you want or some other man who will help with the work. That's the way a household is supposed to be, isn't it? The older couple, the younger couple and any brothers, sisters or children. I don't begrudge selling sheep for your wedding banquet, Dominika, but nothing can be sold that's enough to send me to the streets."

Rising, he straightened his clothes and contrived to swagger as he moved toward the door. "Think it over, little one. You could do much worse than make yourself agreeable and remain the young mistress of Etchahoun."

Dominika barred the door behind him and thought she heard him laugh.

She did not go downstairs till long after the door down the hall closed and she thought he must be asleep. As she prepared coffee and toast, she wrestled again with her choices, all of which seemed unthinkable. Becoming Esteban's mistress was not even a choice. His very presence now would make her feel defiled. And to stay here while he brought in another woman who would think herself the andrea? It wasn't to be borne.

Marry, protect her body and position by bringing a husband to Etchahoun? She would if she knew of a man whose touch she could welcome, but Nicolas? Forcing herself to explore beyond her immediate rejection of him, she tried to imagine him in her bed, tried to imagine having his children.

Huddling into her shawl, she knew that she could not take him. In shamed truth she had to admit that physically even Esteban was more appealing.

"Give me a dancing young man—"

There were none here. She would have died to protect Etchahoun but wrong-headed and disloyal as it might be, she could not now stay under the same roof with Esteban nor could she marry a man for whom she had no love.

She must leave Etchahoun. Grief curved through her like a slow, thick blade. This, in its way, was as shattering as her mother's death. In leaving the house she had expected to preserve, she left also the patterns, the old, sure ways. There had been rituals, the support of the neighborhood, to guide her through the shock of Maria's death. There was no support or help for what she must do now.

Her aunt living in the next valley might take her in and let her work for her keep but there was no fondness between them. There were distant cousins in Bilbao and Gernika but none to whom Dominika felt that she could appeal. They would all agree that she should marry Nicolas or some other suitable man, the quicker the better.

Some of the young women went to large cities, or even to France, and took work as maids or cooks or children's nurses. This idea seemed almost as distasteful as drudging for her board in some neighboring farm household.

A nagging little thought in the back of her mind burst into clarity. She straightened and took a deep breath, laughing in the mingled and somewhat frightened surprise of having reached a decision.

She would go to America.

If men could save their wages and return to salvage a family farm, perhaps she could. At any rate, if she had to leave her home, she preferred a sharp and utter break, a fresh start in a place that would not constantly remind her that her destiny had been scattered with the fire from her mother's hearth.

That week she cleaned the house from top to bottom, blinking back tears as she rubbed beeswax into the ancient, polished floors, cleaned the brass and copper, burnished old chests, chairs, cupboards and dressers, laundered the curtains and coverlets and even washed the cows' blankets and sheepskin headdresses.

She baked and churned and tended the garden, all the while her heart throbbing as though a small, secret wound were leaching away her blood.

Painfully she decided what to put in the heavy sack and small, battered satchel that a man of the house had once brought back from his journeys. She would not take mourning clothes. Maria would understand. It was not good to enter a new life in black.

Dominika packed her holiday red skirt and green vest, her everyday skirts, blouses and aprons, undergarments, kerchiefs for her hair, extra white wool stockings and her best shoes with laces that criss-crossed around the ankle and halfway up the leg. There was her grandmother's prayerbook and acorn rosary, her mother's wedding ring, a small, faded picture of her parents at their wedding.

And there must be something from the Cave of Always Summer.

When the small blue-bird shard was securely wrapped in a shawl, Dominika felt a sense of finality. She had not told Esteban or anyone of her intentions but she had taken all but a few coins from the money box. It was her rightful dowry.

Esteban said nothing further. They did not speak on the rare occasions when they were both in the kitchen at the same time. He worked a little in the fields but went to the village in the afternoons. She was always asleep, her door barred, before he returned and was busy at milking and other chores before he came downstairs in the mornings. She feared to leave the animals in his careless charge but she anticipated that he would soon sell them to the Bigatzis, who were looking for more cows and chickens.

On Sunday morning she was up before dawn. After milking the cows, she caressed their soft brown shoulders and told them good-bye as she turned them out of the byre. She stood in the garden, where for so many years she had helped to plant and gather the food, gazing with tear-blinded eyes at the blossoming trees.

She, too, was rooted in this earth, this place. How could she tear herself away from it without leaving behind the very center that gave her balance and nourished her spirit? But there was no help for it. She must leave. She armed herself with the thought of Marya, who had endured her perilous journey to return with her love.

Might not something similar happen for her? She leaned her cheek against a branch of the oldest apple tree before she went inside and began to dress for church.

During Mass she lit the candles on the *sepulturie*. They shed soft light on the loaves she and Elena had brought. Beneath the formal words of the service Dominika's urgent prayer was sent to Maria, to the other women of the family who had knelt there and to those who had tended the family shrines long before there was a church.

Please forgive me. Understand. I will never forget you. Be with me in the new country and help me to return.

She sat in Maria's wicker chair among the *etcheko andreak*. On the mourners' bench near the altar, Esteban sat in his black mourning cape, and she prayed to be forgiven a surge of sheer hatred. Once, glancing over his shoulder, Nicolas gave her a hurt, puzzled look. If people weren't already lifting eyebrows over her living alone with her young stepfather, it wouldn't be long till they did.

Dominika kept her spine stiff although she knelt at the proper times and kept her head bowed. When the service was over, she waited to speak with hunched, frail old Violeta, to whom she had already given her mother's clothes.

"Violeta," she said, counting coins from the pouch, "this will buy candles and bread for the year. I am going to America."

"America?" Watery old eyes widened in their wrinkled seams. "But, child—"

"I have to go," Dominika said roughly.

She hurried out into the sunlight. In the graveyard she knelt for the last time where blossoms still drifted softly to Maria's grave. *Good-bye. Good-bye.* She was raw with leave-takings, yet how could it be otherwise when all she loved was here, in this ancient land?

Passing the tavern, she heard Esteban inside and she hurried up the road to Etchahoun.

The master and mistress of a household in a neighboring valley, people whom Dominika knew only by sight, were going visiting in Bilbao and gave her a ride in their wagon. When she told them that she was going to America, they kindly offered her work in their house but did not insist that she accept. The master, Sebastian Aguirre, had for a time worked as a herder in Idaho and explained that she would need documents, both to leave Spain and to enter America.

"Do you have friends or relatives there?" he asked.

"My uncle went over years ago but we have never heard from him," Dominika replied.

Sebastian puffed out his ruddy cheeks and shot her a searching glance. "You're bound to go?"

"Yes."

"Then the best and easiest thing for you to do is to get a job at a Basque hotel. The proprietors won't take advantage of you and you can learn English and American ways a little at a time." He winked. "You'll meet lots of young, lonely Basques, and some not so young, who've started their own ranches. Yes, that's the best plan."

He and his wife would not hear of letting her out on a Bilbao street. They took her to their cousin's and on the next morning Sebastian went with her to help fill out the required forms and find passage to New York. When the Aguirres departed for their farm, they left their cousin, also a returned *Amerikanuak*, in charge of seeing that she had her papers and was safely aboard. She paid for her food and lodging, but it was not nearly as much as a hotel would have cost.

The ten days that it took to process her papers seemed an eternity but at last she was on the ship with what Sebastian had assured her was enough money to take her to Idaho and convince the American authorities that she was not an undesirable immigrant. None of it seemed real and she did not even cry as she stood at the rail when the ship moved away from the dock.

At Etchahoun and in the cave she had already said good-bye.

Dominika could remember only a blur of people and strange, bewildering places from the time she sailed until she reached Idaho. Two men on the ship were Basques, now prosperous California ranchers, who had returned to their home valleys for a visit. They helped the non-English-speaking Basques through immigration formalities and got them aboard the proper trains. One sketched a sign for Dominika which read "Boise, Idaho," and she tied it to her satchel. She looked at the coins and green folding money for which her pesetas had been exchanged and hoped that they would last till she could find work.

Strange money, a strange language, strange people. Dominika remained in her corner seat except when the conductor made her understand that she must change trains. She was afraid to get off at the short stops and buy food for fear that the train would leave without her; she slept only in exhausted snatches.

Once when she changed trains, she bought three apples and a sandwich from a vendor and on the last day an ample, friendly woman, who had heaved herself into the seat beside Dominika, dug into a hamper and insisted that she share roast chicken, pickles, boiled eggs and a huge chunk of chocolate cake. They could not converse but the woman's smiling kindliness comforted Dominika's spirit as much as the good food did her body.

Still, she was full of misgivings. Had she been mad to come to this country, so vast, so different, where she could not even speak the language?

In Boise the conductor hailed a loitering urchin and gave him some instructions, motioning for Dominika to go with the lad, who took her sack and started off. As the boy led the way out of the central district of the city, Dominika noticed that the dwellings sat apart from each other and that the streets were wide. The sun was dazzling and she was grateful for the shade of the big trees.

The boy stopped at a two-story, frame building on a side street, pushed inside and plunked down her sack next to a high counter. He said something with a wave of his hand, grinned at her and bobbed his red head as she gave him a coin. The small, dark-haired, mustachioed man at the counter said, "You are Basque."

He spoke the dialect of Guipuzcoa but it was so wonderful to hear her own language again that Dominika could have embraced him.

"I am Basque," she told him. "I need a place to stay. And I must find work."

He frowned at her in surprise. "You have no family here? You are not meeting a man who wishes to marry you?"

She shook her head. He banged on a door behind the counter and a large woman appeared. As the man described Dominika's situation, shrewd brown eyes scanned her. Only when Dominika apparently passed inspection did the big woman smile.

"You look ready to drop, child. I well remember how I felt after that trip. Come have some dinner while we think about what to do."

Dominika felt better after two cups of sweetened strong coffee mixed with hot milk, a big bowl of mutton stew and a beautiful omelette with tomatoes and peppers. Marta Irigay refused payment.

"The food goes with your room," she said. "And you can settle that after we've found you a place to work. I am sorry that we can't use you here but our daughters and daughter-in-law can handle things." She studied Dominika closely. "I know some good Basque ranchers who need wives. Would you want to meet a few of them?"

Dominika flushed and refused. She had not denied Nicolas and traveled all this way only to marry without love.

"I would rather work on a farm or at one of the ranches," she said. "I will keep house, cook, wash and iron, tend children—anything."

"Except marry?" There was a twinkle in Marta's eyes.

"Oh, I want to marry some day," Dominika said earnestly. "But I want to—to know the man first."

Marta chuckled. "You mean you want to love him. You needn't be ashamed of that, my dear. Now let me take you to your room. The girls will bring hot water and a tub. You can have a nice bath and sleep as long as you want. Meanwhile I'll ask around and try to find you a good place."

The tiny upstairs room was crowded with a narrow bed, chest of drawers and washstand but it was luxurious to have a place where she could take off her travel-grimed clothes and marvelous to take a bath. After she had helped one of Marta's buxom, cheerful daughters carry the tub downstairs and dump it, Dominika went back to her room, undressed and slipped naked between the clean white sheets.

It was daylight when she closed her eyes and daylight when she opened them again. Someone was knocking on the door. "Dominika!" came Marta's hearty voice. "Dominika! We may have just the place for you!"

Calling that she would be down in a moment, Dominika sprang out of bed, washed her face in cold water, dressed hastily and struggled with the knots in her hair, securing the dark, auburn-tinted mass into braids that she fastened primly at the back of her head, although wayward ringlets escaped to soften the excited young face that watched her from the small mirror.

Work already? What would it be? Marta had sounded pleased so it must be a good opportunity. Dominika ran downstairs. Marta, beaming, beckoned her into the dining room. A man rose from a table by the door and came forward, smiling.

He had thick, tawny hair, and the bluest eyes she had ever seen laughed down at her from a sun-browned face. The hand that gripped hers was warm and strong. Something wildly sweet flowed between them at the touch. Almost trembling, Dominika drew back but she could not take her eyes from his.

"Give me a dancing young man—"

She didn't know if he could dance but his eyes did. He was tall and there was a fluid grace about him. It was like being drenched with ice water when she heard Marta say, "Mr. Rawlins needs someone to manage his house. His wife is an invalid.

When their last housekeeper left, Mrs. Rawlins asked him to look for someone young who would be pleasant to have around."

He was married. Dominika almost refused the job. "The foreman's wife cooks dinner and helps with the housework," Marta went on, aglow at her protégée's prospects. "The wife of another cowboy does the laundry. So you see, you'll have an easy time. And the pay is good. Fifty dollars a month with room and board."

It seemed a fortune, especially since most of it could be saved. "But I speak only Basque and some Spanish," worried Dominika. "The wife of Mr. Rawlins must want someone with whom she can talk."

Rawlins shrugged as this was translated. "She'll enjoy teaching you English. A Scotswoman didn't work out and neither did the last companion brought over from England." Marta squeezed Dominika's hand bracingly as she translated. "You'll be all right. One of the cowboys is Basque. In a pinch he can interpret."

Dominika still hesitated. If this man belonged to someone else, she did not want to be around him. But that was ridiculous! How could she stay here and run up a hotel bill when she was being offered a much better place than she could have hoped for?

"I'll get my things," she said.

Marta patted her shoulder. "That's right, dear. You'll do very well. But sit down and have something to eat with Mr. Rawlins. It's noon and his ranch is a four-hour drive away."

Her new employer held a chair for her at the red-and-white-checkered table. He filled her glass with deep red wine and raised his, inclining his head. Then he drank, slowly, savoring the taste. His eyes never left her face.

When she tried to pay her hotel bill, Marta said that Brant Rawlins had already taken care of it. "It's all right," she assured Dominika. "He's very glad to find you and he can afford it."

Brant carried her sack and satchel downstairs and out to a wagon that was loaded with supplies. He helped her onto the seat, climbed up beside her and started the gleaming bay horses with a word and a lifting of the reins. Marta waved from the door of the hotel. Dominika waved back until they passed out of sight.

Brant Rawlins glanced sideways at her and said a few words in his deep voice before he shrugged and laughed, amused in his realization that she could not understand him. Then he gave his leg a slap and pointed to a building.

"House," he said and looked expectantly at her.

"Ho-use?" she repeated.

"House," he encouraged firmly.

She echoed him till he was satisfied. Pointing to the peaks that towered above the valley in a way that made her long for her home mountains, he taught her *mountain* and then *river* and *tree*, *horse*, *wagon*. She learned *thirsty* when they stopped to drink at a sparkling stream, *water* and *good*, *grass*, *flower*, *bird* and *sky*. He pointed to the sky and then to his eyes, which were still dancing.

"Blue," he said. "Blue eyes." He waved at the sky. "Blue." She thought that she would never see a bright, bold sky without remembering his eyes, which sobered as he watched her.

"Man." He touched himself. His long, brown fingers lightly brushed her shoulder. "You. Girl."

"Girl?"

He gazed at her. Sweet wildfire flamed through her veins. The golden air between them seemed to vibrate. "Woman," he said. "Not girl. Woman." His hand moved toward her as if irresistibly drawn before he jerked it down and spun away.

III

THE RANCH lay in a long, wide valley watered by a creek and little streams that zig-zagged through grassy meadows and across gentle slopes where red cattle with white faces grazed. High, jagged mountains reared at a distance in all directions.

Much of the western country Dominika had passed through had been monotonous, drab plains or forbidding, barren mountains. She was relieved to see the fertile green expanse and the trees that forested the hills and grew along the creek.

A white, two-story house rose among stately trees. A pillared veranda ran the length of it, softened with ivy and flowering vines. Brant drove around the house to a stable next to a barn, other outbuildings and large enclosures he told her were corrals. Between the barn complex and the big house there were four small, neat cottages and two big buildings, all of white-painted frame. Flowers and shrubs grew around the smaller houses and a large, fenced garden lay between them and the barn.

As Brant stopped the horses, a man quit chopping wood from a huge pile ricked behind the long buildings and strode forward, taking the reins. "Hi, boss," he called.

Sweeping off a battered, wide-brimmed gray hat, he grinned shyly at Dominika and asked something in a bantering tone. Brant answered before he jumped down and came around to help Dominika out of the wagon. He nodded in the direction of the skinny, freckled redhead.

"Harry."

Dominika repeated the name and smiled.

Harry blushed and mumbled something that sounded like, "Pleasedchameetcha, ma'am."

It was fun to know she could affect an American man in that way even though he was a very young one. Repressing a chuckle, Dominika started to get her satchel but Brant took it along with a parcel, indicating that Harry would bring her sack and the other things.

She was a strong walker and Brant wore high-heeled boots but she had to lengthen her pace to keep up with him. They went in the back door of the house, through a large pantry and a kitchen dominated by a big, black iron stove, and passed into a hall that led past a room with dishes and crystal sparkling in glass-windowed cabinets and a long, polished table of dark wood surrounded by matching chairs upholstered with rose brocade.

An arched door opened into a thickly carpeted, velvet-draped room where she caught a glimpse of an organ. Spiraling stairs led upward past walls hung with family portraits.

Brant motioned her to precede him. Upstairs a hall divided the rooms to each side until it ended at another archway. Putting Dominika's satchel down by one of the brass-knobbed doors, Brant escorted her through the arch.

The woman framed by windows that filled the whole side of the wall was the most exquisite being that Dominika had ever seen. Long hair the color of moonlight waved around her shoulders. She had clear, flawless skin and wide-spaced violet eyes fringed with ash-colored lashes. She half-reclined on a brocade couch that had a high, curved arm at one end against which silken pillows were heaped. A spy glass, books, periodicals and a clutter of other things Dominika could not identify ranged along the window seat behind her. A wicker chair set on a platform with high wheels was shoved against a wall as if pushed there in a fit of temper.

The young woman straightened with a cry of joy as Brant entered, held up her arms to him so that a light blue robe, frothily trimmed with ivory lace, fell back from her slender wrists. He bent to kiss her, smoothed her hair and put the parcel in her lap.

Stepping back, he smiled encouragingly at Dominika, who came forward slowly, aghast at the fierce spasm of pain their embrace had caused her. She was neither awkward nor coarse but she felt both as she stood before the woman, surely not much older than she, who was to be her mistress.

Yes. The *etcheko andrea* of Brant's fine house. And however beautiful and pampered, this woman was an invalid. Shamed at her jealousy, Dominika looked with respectful steadiness into the other's eyes.

A flash of something sparkled in the violet depths and was gone. "Dominika?" The soft, almost childish voice repeated Brant's introduction. She smiled, banishing the downward droop of her prettily bowed lips. "Nika?"

Playmates had called her that sometimes. Dominika nodded, daring to smile back. Brant's wife caught her hand and squeezed it.

"Lucie," she said, touching herself.

"Lu-cie?"

The other laughed and spoke delightedly to Brant. Tearing open the parcel, she squealed at sight of the gold-paper box, opened it and held it out, motioning for Dominika to take one of the chocolate candies, insisting until she did.

"Thank you," Brant supplied the words. Dominika repeated them to Lucie Rawlins, who laughed and sampled one of the sweets herself, made a face and tried another.

Then Brant gestured, nodding toward the arch. Dominika understood and went out, scarcely tasting the delicious chocolate. Lucie, she thought, was a fairy princess who seemed to be kind as well as pathetically hungry for diversions. This was a beautiful house in a lovely valley. Her new position was incomparably better than any for which she could have hoped. Still, she felt like grasping her satchel and running outside, taking the long road back to town.

How could she see Brant every day, hear the caress of his voice, thrill at each inadvertent touch, and not fall ever deeper in love with him? If she left now, she would get over it, she would recover.

"Dominika." He had opened the door at the end of the hall. His eyes held hers, drawing her as though she were magnetized. A trembling started within her. She moved swiftly past him.

It was too late to leave. It had been too late since the moment she saw him.

* * *

After Harry brought up her sack, bashfully muttering words that she could not understand except that he seemed to be calling her "ma'am," Dominika looked out the window to the green slopes stretching into the high, distance-purpled range beyond. She was blessed to have mountains.

And the room! It had a postered bed with a rose-printed coverlet and big ruffled pillows, matching curtains and an easy chair cushioned in the same fabric. A deep rose rug lay on the burnished oak floor. A gilt-framed mirror hung above a dresser. Beside the window there was a graceful little writing desk and chair. As she shook out her few garments and hung them in an armoire with mirrored doors, she wondered where the washstand was.

It was strange that such a thoughtfully furnished room would lack that essential. She peered through an open door at the end of the room and gasped in amazement.

What were all these gleaming white articles with odd-looking metal and crystal fittings? The long, white trough with thick towels hanging above it could be nothing but a tub. Then she realized that the rectangular porcelain box fastened to the wall high above a sort of oval, closed-in stool was a more elegant version of the facilities that she had used in public buildings and trains during her journey, as was the small marble basin set in a corner.

As she frowned in wonderment, there was a rap on the door. Dominika answered and a tall, ruddy-faced, brown-haired woman breezed in. She set a tray holding a steaming pot and plate of small cakes on the bedside table and then she gave Dominika's hand a hearty shake.

Her warm brown eyes appraised Dominika, who was somehow sure that this woman's judgments, while uncompromising, would always be leavened with kindness. "I'm Sarah." At Dominika's questioning look, she tapped herself. "Sarah."

Dominika smiled and groped for the phrase that Brant had taught her. "Thank you, Sarah."

Sarah whooped with delighted surprise and said a spate of words so rapidly that Dominika could only shake her head, crestfallen after her brief triumph. Sarah, realizing the problem, stopped in mid-flow and gave Dominika a hug and pat on the shoulder.

Dominika assumed that she should go to work at once but Sarah made her understand that she could begin the next day. Now she should have a bath and rest till dinner time, when a bell would ring.

With a reassuring smile, Sarah departed, leaving Dominika to gratefully sip the strong, hot fluid which she recognized as tea. She had tasted it only a few times before in her life but if it was what people drank here, she would get used to it.

Succumbing to temptation, she ate all of the delicious little cakes and then, with some trepidation, approached the bathroom. Everything worked. Experimenting with the crystal knobs, she found that hot water flowed from one and cold from the other.

Could there be an unlimited supply of water? She did not believe it possible and so she was sparing in her use, although she did wash her hair with the fragrant, rose-scented soap. After she had rubbed herself briskly with one towel, she wrapped herself in another and sat by the window, fluffing her hair so that it would dry faster.

She was tired from her long journey, feeling yet as if her real self were at Etchahoun while an empty body moved about this strange, new country. But she had found a place to stay, a place where her shadowy self could acquire substance. She must not ruin it by desire for a married man.

Rising, she opened the satchel and carefully unwrapped the blue-bird shard. She placed it on the dresser along with her grandmother's prayerbook and rosary. Though Violeta would be faithful in offering bread and candles, Dominika wanted a candle of her own that she could light each Sunday and pray for her mother and the dead of Etchahoun.

The acorn beads polished by her grandmother's fingers, the sheepskin-bound parchment pages used by generations, the blue bird as miraculously bright as if painted yesterday—these time-hallowed relics strengthened Dominika. Life had not been easy for her mother or grandmother or for any other ancestress she knew anything about. Why should she expect it to run smooth for her?

But she was so far from home!

She fought an overwhelming surge of homesickness, savagely combing tangles out of her hair. No whimpering! She could have married Nicolas or put up with some woman of Esteban's. Instead she had chosen to make a fresh start.

So she must make it. And no nonsense about another woman's husband even if he did have the bluest eyes she had ever seen and a smile that made her feel like a tight-curled leaf tempted to unfold and bask in the sun.

At the distant sounding of a bell, Dominika hurried downstairs. Lucie was already seated at one end of the table enthroned in a high-backed, padded chair, her feet resting on a cushioned stool. She had changed into a violet robe that matched her eyes. Her silvery hair was caught back with velvet bows of the same color. Diamonds and amethysts sparkled on her fingers as she smiled and indicated the place set between herself and Brant.

"Nika," Lucie said as though she liked the name, giving it a lilt. She spoke further, at which Dominika could only look at her blankly. Then Lucie remembered and shrugged prettily, saying something which Brant answered as he came to hold Dominika's chair for her.

"Chair," he said as he pushed it in.

Lucie's small pout faded. She touched the polished wood. "Table," she said.

Dominika didn't feel like having a lesson that night but she repeated the word. Lucie laughed with delight. After that it was plate, fork, knife, spoon, napkin and as Sarah brought the food, Lucie enjoyed teaching Dominika to say soup, roast beef, tomatoes, green beans, potatoes, bread and butter.

The food was good but to Dominika's taste it lacked flavor. She thought longingly of how peppers, onions, rosemary and garlic would have enhanced it. As she helped Sarah clear away the dishes, the older woman gave her an encouraging little hug and said something with a sympathetic smile.

Still, Dominika had to learn. She told herself that she was lucky to have a mistress who was interested in teaching her rather than one who would be angrily impatient because she had not miraculously absorbed English along with the fresh American air.

There was apple pie for dessert and dishes of a soft, cold delicacy, ice cream, that melted in the mouth. To finish, there was coffee. The cups were almost filled and in spite of the rich cream that was added, Dominika preferred the half-milk Basque coffee. She wanted to help Sarah with the dishes but was shooed away briskly. Lucie called to her and Brant signaled for her to follow as he picked up his wife and carried her into the spacious adjoining room.

Settling her into a big easy chair, he tucked a footstool beneath her feet. She motioned for Dominika to sit nearby on a fan-backed sofa. Then Lucie clapped her hands and suggested something to Brant that he answered with a smiling nod.

He pulled a drapery at one end of the room, exposing a large, white square of heavy cloth. From a closet he took out a case and set up the contents on a table. There was a box-like platform fitted with a strange apparatus resembling a footed telescope embedded in a fluted case connecting to a rear box and something that looked like a small, round metal chimney. He lit this, did some adjusting and slipped a small card into the machine.

Dominika gasped. The image of an elephant covered the far wall, darkened as Brant pulled the window draperies closed. A lion climbed onto a platform at the command of a man with a whip. Plumed horses seemed to be in the act of prancing about a ring. A man and woman in spangled, tight-fitting costumes hung by their knees on high rope swings. Monkeys. Tigers. Animals that Dominika had never seen even in books.

Next came pictures of gigantic idols, beautiful castles and magnificent buildings, people of different races dancing, working in their fields or posed beside thatched huts, mud abodes or other dwellings. Dominika was dazed by the exhibition but when it was finished, Lucie made another request.

Lighting a triple-globed lamp, Brant put away the magical pictures and turned a crank on an instrument that was dominated by a big horn attached to a metal bracket. A platform holding a disc revolved beneath a needle set on the small end of the horn.

Dominika had never heard such music. Flutes, violins, piano, instruments that she could not name, all playing at once like a grand orchestra. Lucie squeezed her hand and said, "Graphophone."

The next disc was that of a woman singing, the third of a mixed chorus. Brant wound up the machine again and they heard some marches. By this time Dominika could scarcely hold her eyes open. The pictures and the talking machine were amazing but she wondered if Brant and Lucie spent all their evenings watching and listening to them. They sat in silence now.

Feeling like an intruder, Dominika rose. "Thank you," she said and pointed toward the stairs.

Lucie's slim white fingers, soft yet surprisingly strong, closed on hers. "Good-night," she smiled. Brant stood up, somber in a dark suit, although the lamplight cast a rich, golden sheen on his thick, slightly wavy hair.

"Good-night, Nika."

"Good-night."

She would learn. A few more words each day, a little more awareness of how things were done. What would be much harder was to school her heart not to leap when Brant's eyes touched her, to quell the trembling that started within her when he spoke her name.

Holding her grandmother's rosary that night, she prayed for him and Lucie and then for Etchahoun and her mother's soul. Last of all she asked to be spared temptation—but it was a hollow prayer. Already, she could not imagine a world without Brant. Temptation would be the price of seeing him but she must resist it.

As she stretched out on the softly firm mattress and snuggled into the fluffy pillows, she had an unwelcome flash of wondering what was going on in the big room at the end of the hall.

Was Brant helping his wife prepare for sleep? Did they share the big brass bed at one end of the chamber? And Lucie's infirmity, did it mean there could be no lovemaking? Dominika had seen animals couple but she did not know how to precisely translate the act into human terms. Blushing at forbidden and disturbing thoughts, she closed her mind to further speculation and reviewed the words she had learned during the day.

But that was dangerous for Brant smiled at her again as his glance changed and he said, "Woman." She forced herself to recall the dinner foods. Somewhere between green beans and apple pie, she fell asleep.

During the next days a pattern evolved. Dominika at first helped Sarah make Lucie's breakfast and then completely took over that light duty. Brant ate much earlier, breakfasting with the men down in the dining hall connected to the bunkhouse, where an old peg-legged cowboy, aptly called Pegleg, cooked the hearty fare. In order not to disturb his wife, Brant slept in a room across the hall from Dominika.

While Lucie had her breakfast on a small teak table, Dominika had hers from a tray. Afterward she helped Lucie out of one of her lacy silk gowns and into a pretty wrapper. Lucie had dozens of wrappers in various fabrics and trims, and slippers of velvet, brocade and glove-soft leather. She had an invalid chair upstairs and another below but she detested them and used them only to move from one place to the next. Her bathroom was specially fitted so that she could manage alone except for baths. After a few weeks she let Dominika help her slide from her chair to the stool in the tub, soap her back and rinse her.

Lucie had many diversions: books; magazines; a stereoscope with hundreds of views; needlework; a mandolin that she played charmingly; an easel for sketching or painting; another Graphophone, this one with cylinder records; and a magic lantern that enlarged slides to a size of almost three feet. Besides a spy glass, she had binoculars that let her see clear to the ends of the valley. She had everything money could buy—except the use of her long, beautiful legs.

It might not have been so bad for her had she been born crippled but according to Marco—the swarthy, lean Basque cowboy who was sometimes borrowed from his duties to translate and teach Dominika words that could not be acted out—Lucie's greatest pleasure had been riding. Three summers ago, only a year after her marriage, her horse had bolted. Knocked to the ground by a low-lying tree limb, she had been dragged by an ankle caught in the stirrup. Her spine was severely injured and she had lost the baby she had been carrying at the time.

Lucie had wanted more of Dominika's story than Brant had learned from Marta Irigay and so Marco had transmitted the simple facts. Lucie reached out to clasp her hand and spoke with a catch in her voice.

"Mrs. Rawlins sorry you had to leave home," Marco explained. "But she hope you find a man, stay here."

If she only knew.

Still, in spite of her feelings for Brant, Dominika grew increasingly fond of Lucie and felt much the older of the two. Lucie was the indulged youngest daughter of a prominent widowed Denver lawyer. For one brought up to find a wish fulfilled almost before she could express it, she had accepted her crippling with surprising fortitude, though at times she could be childishly demanding. It never seemed to occur to her to use her invalid chair downstairs rather than expect Brant to carry her. There must have been evenings, too, when he would have liked to read or rest but Lucie demanded entertainment. If not the Graphophone or stereopticon, there must be cards or dominos or Brant must play the organ or guitar and sing in his resonant baritone.

He never showed resentment at Lucie's control of his leisure. Probably, like Dominika, when he tired of catering to Lucie's unquenchable thirst for diversion, he had only to remember that he could walk and she could not.

If he was working near the house, he came home for the noon meal but more often he was gone all day and Dominika prepared a light, tempting meal to carry upstairs. Apart from being almost constantly at Lucie's call, her duties were few. She preferred to take care of her own room and kept Lucie's straight since she could do that without leaving her. Sarah cooked the main meals and made sure that Mollie Slade, the full-breasted, yellow-haired wife of a lanky cowboy named Tex, properly dusted and polished, ran the carpet sweeper, cleaned the baths and mopped the oilcloth rug in the kitchen and on the back porch.

The kitchen fascinated Dominika although she thought wistfully of the one at Etchahoun, which had been the heart of the house. Here, in addition to the great cast-iron range, with its warming oven and porcelain-lined water reservoir, there was a kerosene range for use in summer. The white-enameled kitchen sink with its drainboard stood next to a big ice chest that held a hundred pounds of the ice that was cut from a nearby lake in the winter and stored through hot weather in a shed insulated with sawdust.

Half of the porch was fitted with granatine laundry tubs, a small coal stove to hold the copper-bottomed boiler in which the white laundry was stirred in hot, soapy water, and a washer with two cylinders that rotated in opposite directions as the crankshaft was turned. There was a wringer equipped with benches to hold the tubs, and a mangle. The ironing board and sadirons were kept here, too. Beneath a window in the pantry there was a sewing machine with which Sarah or Mollie could quickly mend torn sheets and clothing.

"Brant knows we have a lot to do," Sarah told Dominika. "He's always looking for ways to make things easier; most men never give it a thought." She laughed. "My Mac's a good man but he thinks a house takes care of itself and doesn't want to know any different."

Dominika did not understand every word but she could now follow the drift of most that was said to her. Lucie had begun to teach her to read. As her English improved, Brant explained the stereopticon scenes, though he stammered in embarrassment when he remembered that the slides showing the United States' new possessions, Cuba and the Philippines, must remind Dominika that Spain had lost these vestiges of her empire in the brief Spanish-American War in 1898.

Dominika, with some hauteur, informed him that Basques were not Spaniards but had undertaken much of the early exploration of America's Southwest. Haltingly, she told the story of Marya and her journey.

"And she married her handsome pirate and lived happily ever after," Lucie applauded, violet eyes shining. She cast Brant a teasingly amused glance. "Dear, let's hear no more of your ancestor who helped make John sign the Magna Carta and I won't boast about my kin who helped colonize Maryland. I think

Dominika can trace her family back a lot further than either of us."

Back to the caves, thought Dominika and felt a sudden rush of longing for a certain secret, dream-like chamber.

She enjoyed seeing the pictures of strange cities and countries, the Paris Exposition, the Pan American Exposition and the life of Christ. She did not at all like scenes from the Boer War or Queen Victoria's funeral cortege and was amazed that Lucie viewed with zest even a ghastly survey of the Chicago stockyards.

Dominika had grown up knowing that living animals could be turned into meat but one pig or calf killed yearly could not be compared with the nightmarish scene of countless cows hoisted by the leg to be clubbed and slaughtered. She did not like to watch the assassination of President McKinley, either.

"You like president?" she inquired on perhaps the fourth time that Lucie asked Brant to show the sequence.

"Of course!" Lucie's eyes widened. "He led us through the war with Spain. When he was killed last year, everyone mourned him."

Brant's puzzled look changed to one of comprehension as he seemed to read Dominika's face. The awareness, tormenting but sweet, that was always between them tautened.

He said quickly, dropping his hand over Lucie's filmily clad shoulder and smiling down at her, "I think, dear, that Nika can't understand why we like to watch the president getting shot if we liked him so much."

"I don't *like* to see him shot!" Lucie cried indignantly. "It's a way of—" She floundered. "It's a way of showing respect."

"Respect?" Dominika did not know the word.

"You can't understand," Lucie charged pettishly, smoothing her skirts. "You're a foreigner."

It was the first harsh thing that had been said to Dominika in this house, the first to make her feel like a blundering, stupid outsider. Blinking back tears, she stood up. "You show respect. I go to my room."

"Nika!" protested Brant.

Lucie caught her hand. "Don't be a big silly! Brant will show us the views of Paris and the Exposition."

He did and the rest of the evening passed companionably. But when Dominika was holding her grandmother's rosary and saying her prayers, she wondered if she would ever understand these people or feel at home in their country.

IV

AT FIRST Dominika had felt herself to be little more than a shadow, as though her substance and spirit had remained at Etchahoun. As days grew into weeks and weeks into months, the balance slowly shifted. She was in Idaho now, under Brant Rawlins' roof. Only a wraith lingered now to wander between Etchahoun and the women's cave.

She had asked for some candles to be charged against her wages, which Brant, at her request, was holding for her. On Sundays she lit the tall white taper that flickered above the blue bird and prayed as if she had been kneeling on the household's *sepulturie*.

Brant and Lucie were Episcopalians but the long, jolting drive to the church in town was impossible for Lucie. Sunday was a day of rest at the ranch, except for necessary chores. The cowboys sometimes threw horseshoes or lounged around outside, although their principal recreation was playing cards.

Autumn crisped the air and chilled the nights. Snow geese winged south. Aspens and maples on the mountainsides made patches of brilliant yellow and red against evergreens. Along the creek, cottonwoods, ashes and alders blazed with golden glory before they began to fade.

It was time for what Brant called "beef work." The chuck wagon, complete with Pegleg, and the bed wagon, hauling bedrolls and tents in case of bad weather, would move around the huge ranch gathering the cattle that would be trailed to the railroad and shipped to those same stockyards that Dominika had viewed with the stereopticon. Calves missed at the spring roundup or born since then would be branded now and marked. Sarah explained that marking meant cutting the ears so that it would be easy to identify the calves and castrating all but the few that would be kept for breeding.

Brant stayed out with the men during the beef gather. He was gone for two weeks. Lucie fretted and Dominika was hard-pressed to keep her in reasonable spirits. Once Dominika and Sarah carried her downstairs for dinner but Lucie decided that without Brant it was not worth the trouble. After that Dominika carried trays up to her.

"At least Brant won't go to Chicago," Lucie sighed one golden afternoon as she scanned the valley with her field glasses. "He lets Mac take care of the selling. I suppose I should be glad for that. Men can get into a lot of trouble in town." Her tone took on an edge of bitterness. "I couldn't blame Brant if he did want to go to Chicago. It can't be much fun for him, having a crippled wife."

"But he loves you!" Dominika protested quickly.

It was the first time that Lucie had mentioned to Dominika the effect that her disability might be having on Brant. Now she sent books and magazines flying off the table beside her with an impatient sweep of her arm.

"How can he?" she demanded, beautiful face contorting. "I'm no good to him! We'll never have children—" She burst into sobs.

Dominika put her arms around her and murmured soothingly, aching for both the handsome young people who had been so kind to her, vowing to try even harder not to dream of Brant's laughing eyes, to discipline that rush of warm joy she felt when she saw him at the end of the day.

Lucie clung to her. "I don't know what I'd do without you, Nika. The last woman was dull and pious and the one before that was always sneaking off to meet some cowboy." She straightened, wiping her eyes as Dominika picked up the scattered books and magazines. "This must be tedious for you though, being always in the house. I've been selfish. When Brant comes home, he must choose you a horse so you can go riding."

"I have only ride donkey," Dominika said. Horses were beautiful but she was rather afraid of them. "At home I always walk."

"Well, you're in America now, out West, and you'll have to ride," Lucie said gaily. "You can have my riding habit and divided skirts. In fact, dear, you might as well have lots of clothes I'll never wear again. I like your skirts and blouses but when they wear out, you'll have to change to American clothes. You might as well make a start."

Enthusiastically, Lucie wheeled herself to the big double armoire. For the next few hours she was happy, only now and then regretful as she remembered wearing a gown at an elegant function in Denver, or Chicago, or Boise. As though she were dressing a doll, she insisted that Dominika try on a few of the dresses.

"That green challis never did much for me," she said, "but it's beautiful on you. It brings out the color of your eyes and hair. Of course, you really need a corset. There are several in that box."

When Dominika saw one of the boned, laced garments, she shook her head. "That squeezes—hurts. I want to breathe."

Lucie frowned before she dissolved into laughter. "You're right about that. The only good thing about my trouble is that I don't have to wear corsets anymore, or bustles."

Most of the stunning array of clothes were unsuited to Dominika's daily life but she was glad of warm underwear, several light wool dresses and some sateen waists and skirts, serviceable shoes and a dark-green wool cape lined with taffeta. She declined the elegant chocolate brown velvet riding habit, saying that should she ever ride, she would like to try the comfortable-looking divided skirts.

"Take them," Lucie said, wheeling back to the window. "And will you please make us some of that wonderful chocolate with cinnamon and tell me more about your family?"

Always attracted to things new and different, Lucie particularly liked to hear about Etchahoun and the people who had lived there, especially Lael and Marya. She asked many questions about the Inquisition and seemed a bit disappointed to learn that it had been abolished in 1820. When Dominika mentioned the splendid sword-dancing, Lucie listened with bright eyes.

"Do you dance, too?"

Dominika stared. "Every Basque dances unless—"

Flushing, she caught herself but Lucie finished. "Unless he's lame? Please show me, Nika."

Dominika said helplessly, "I need music."

"Surely there's some tune the Graphophone could play?"

A few of the cylinders did have music that had set Dominika's feet tingling and her main task was to keep Lucie entertained. So, even though it felt strange to be dancing here in this room, so far from Etchahoun, Dominika found a suitable record, wound up the Graphophone and moved into the dance that showed a woman beating out laundry, wringing it and spreading it about on the bushes.

Lucie clapped her hands with delight. "Why, Dominika, you're wonderful! You could dance on the stage if it weren't indecent. Do some more."

At first, Dominika was oddly uncomfortable and self-conscious but these sensations eased into the pleasure of matching herself to the music. Since many dances required a partner, she improvised, doing the *jota* brought from Aragon within the last century, snapping her fingers to keep time as she held her body proudly erect and whirled and turned.

She was laughing and breathless when the music began to slow.

She froze as she saw Brant standing in the archway. How long had he been watching? There was something in his gaze that she had not seen before, a look that pierced to her depths, arousing a slow, insistent, inner quivering. To hide her feelings and the blood suffusing her face, she turned abruptly, went to the Graphophone and removed the cylinder.

"Darling!" Lucie held out her arms to her husband.

He went to her, gathering her close with a murmured endearment. Dominika left them but the feverish longing within her burned.

She danced often for Lucie after that for it seemed to give the invalid a vicarious pleasure but once when Brant suggested that he accompany her on his guitar, she had said that she was too tired.

She felt it unsettling, and even dangerous, that she saw him every evening. But to display herself, to move so that her blouse molded her breasts, to make an offering, no matter how formalized, of her body? The most bitter part of all was that had things been otherwise, she would have gloried in dancing for Brant, sounding her tambourine or castanets to match the beating of his heart. For she knew that he wanted her. He might not love her as she loved him but there could be no mistaking the naked hunger she caught sometimes in his eyes before they both looked quickly away.

Should she leave? She wrestled with the question. It was torment to see him, yet it was joy.

Never to hear his voice again, never to see him smile, would be like banishment to a world without music or sunlight. Besides, she had become genuinely fond of Lucie and there was no doubt but that the lonely young woman found her an interesting companion. On the purely practical side, though Dominika was much too troubled to pay attention to practical matters, it would have been impossible to find another place where she would be so appreciated, live so comfortably and be able to save all of her wages.

But now that she was able to be out of the house for a few hours on most days, she felt a sense of relief. Brant had selected a gentle buckskin mare for her, with dainty hoofs and an inquisitive velvet muzzle. Each day when the weather was good she went down to the corrals and one or another of the cowboys roped Honey and saddled her. While Dominika didn't think that she could have stayed on the sidesaddle hanging in the shed, in a divided skirt she soon decided that there was no way in which she could fall out of the saddle, with its big horn, high cantle and stirrups that Brant himself painstakingly adjusted so that her knees were slightly bent.

"You make a mighty pretty cowgirl," he said. "Just don't you go hiring on with any other outfit!"

She was both relieved and disappointed that he did not escort her on her first ride but instead detailed skinny, red-haired, freckled Harry with friendly brown eyes that worshiped her like a puppy's as he taught her how to hold the reins and get Honey to turn or stop.

Except for Mac, who was the foreman and Sarah's husband, a graying, stocky man with charcoal-colored eyes, Tex, Mollie's husband, and Marco—who seemed to have taken a brooding dislike to her, perhaps because he was from Navarre and thought that Vizcaínos were arrogant, clannish people—all of the cowboys vied to catch Honey and go riding with Dominika. They were exceedingly gallant and touching in their eagerness to please her. Usually, though, Harry went with her, or Ollie, a round-faced, rosy-cheeked boy with golden hair.

Without having to hunt for passes through the mountains, it was possible to take many varied rides up and down the valleys and into side canyons. At the far upper end of the valley, nestled in a small box canyon, there was a line shack. When winter closed in, Ollie explained, a couple of men would stay there to make sure that the cattle did not drift off their range during storms. The men would feed any cows that looked weak and cut the ice on the watering holes.

After the fall beef gather, the bulls had been collected on the southern range, where they could be fed during the cold, and the calves were weaned from their mothers so as to give the cows a better chance of surviving till spring grass.

When these chores were done, Brant had laid off the half-dozen extra hands he had hired in the spring but there was plenty of work to keep the regular outfit busy until spring roundup, when new calves would be branded and marked.

"Do you ever take time off?" Dominika asked Ollie. He grinned and let one eyelid droop in a slow wink.

"In between spring roundup—that's usually early June—and fall beef work, there are two or three weeks of haying and riding fence. That's when I go down to Boise and turn my wolf loose."

"Your wolf?"

"Never mind, Miss Nika," he laughed. "Let's just say my hand don't fit a pitchfork or wire-pliers."

It fitted a rope, though. Brought up on a New Mexico ranch where he had been trained by *vaqueros* whose skill with the *reata* was legendary, Ollie could work magic with his cherished eight-strand rawhide rope, though he admitted to Dominika that for roping heavy steers he used a hard-twist Manila rope that he could dally around the saddle horn.

"That means you give the rope a turn so there's some give with a thousand-pound steer at the other end, or so you can just let the critter go if you have to," Ollie explained. "Out in California, hands use a long rope and dally. Texans use maybe a thirty-three-foot rope and tie fast like they do in New Mexico and Arizona Territory. Up north and into Canada we dally more than we tie fast and like you might expect, in Colorado, Utah and Indian Territory, they do it both ways."

It took only a simple loop to catch the docile Honey but when an obstreperous pony had cast a shoe and needed another, Dominika would see Ollie forefoot him by tossing the loop to just the spot where the pony was running and bring him down neatly. This looked brutal but Brant said that it was a lot easier on the horse than catching him by the neck and choking him into submission.

Ollie could throw overhand or under, toss a *peal* on an animal's hind legs, catching each in half of a figure eight, or go slowly up to a horse and then frighten it into the loop by stepping suddenly to the right so that the horse roped itself when it jumped. Dominika discouraged him, though, from showing off his prowess when they were out riding together.

He also taught her many interesting things about cattle, including how to tell their age. "You've got to look at the teeth to be sure," he said, "but most range cattle have horns and starting with the third year, there's a ring for each year. There are rings the first two years, too, but they fade away as the critter gets older."

The white-faced, red cattle on the ranch were nothing like the tawny, cream-colored cows that Dominika had milked and protected with blankets and fringed sheepskin bonnets. Would they ever stop, these painful flashes that made her long for Etchahoun, nestled among its orchards and stone-walled fields?

Ollie tried to kiss Dominika one day when they had dismounted to sit on a rock and admire the towering mountains, now crowned with snow. When she pushed him away and sprang up in amazement, he apologized abjectly.

"It's just that I'm crazy over you, Miss Nika," he blurted. "I know I'm young but—oh, if you'd marry me, I'd work real hard—even in haying—and we could get a little ranch of our own."

She put her fingers gently on his lips. "Ollie, you're like my brother."

His boyish face was tragic. "You—you don't care about me at all?"

"Of course I do! I care much. But not that way."

He spun away from her. She was afraid that he was going to cry but when he turned back to her, his tone was matter of fact. "Let's get moving. The boss promised to skin anyone who didn't get you home well before sundown."

That night she told Brant that she could ride well enough now and knew her way around the ranch sufficiently so that she did not need an escort.

"Why, you'll break Harry's and Ollie's hearts," he teased, though there was a quick leap of question in his eyes.

"No, I won't," she said grimly and after that she rode alone.

She was rounding the canyon by the line shack one afternoon when she saw a woman run out and mount a tethered horse. Yellow-haired Mollie. She rode off toward the ranch while Dominika frowned in puzzlement.

What was she doing here? Perhaps her husband had moved up here for the winter—

But it was not lanky Tex Slade who stepped out of the line shack. Brant stretched broadly before he buttoned up his jacket, set his hat lower and strolled toward his horse.

Although Dominika smothered a cry, a small sound escaped her—or Honey moved or Brant somehow sensed her presence. He turned. The smile of gratified satiation was stricken from his face.

"Nika!" He glanced after Mollie, who had by now vanished behind the slope. Swallowing, he managed a sickly grin. "Just checking on the shack."

She stared at him, clinging desperately to the saddle horn. Swearing, he came forward. "You saw, didn't you?"

"I saw." The words were coals on her tongue.

"Don't look like that! What can you know about what a man feels when—well, you can't understand."

I know only that I love you. And I have yielded to your wife but how can I bear this? You with that yellow-haired slut, kissing her loose, wide mouth, touching those swelling breasts!

"Nika," he said in a pleading tone. He reached for Honey's bridle.

"Don't worry!" Dominika cried, veering away. "I will not tell."

She sent Honey into a lope and cried heartbrokenly as she rode, fiercely uttering every bad word she had ever heard, even the cowboy curses that she did not understand.

How could he? How *could* he?

If she had been tortured by his marriage, it was nothing to the furious hurt and jealousy that seethed in her now. She almost hated him that evening as he spoke tenderly to Lucie, carried her from room to room, and at her request, strummed his guitar and sang old English songs:

> "Oh, I have dreamed a deadly dream,
> It fills my heart with sorrow.
> I dreamed I pulled the rowan green
> With my true love, on Yarrow. . . ."

Dominika listened and her heart ached even as it burned. It could not be easy for him. She knew that. But—Mollie! Was the way he had looked at her a lie, then? Or was it just the way in which he gazed at any attractive woman?

She could have schooled herself to accept Lucie's claim on him, but this? She scarcely slept that night.

Next morning, after she had brought Lucie her breakfast, she took a deep breath and nerved herself. "Lucie, you very kind, very good, but I—I want to get work in town."

Lucie's violet eyes widened incredulously. "You what?"

Flinching inwardly, Dominika found that she could not

meet the other woman's startled gaze. "I—I better work in town."

"Why?"

Dominika's English deserted her but even had she known the words, what could she say? As she stood with her head bowed unhappily, Lucie caught her hand. "I thought you liked me, Nika."

"Oh, I do! You very good. Very sweet."

"Is it wages? With board and room you're making more than you could anywhere else but we've planned to give you a raise at Christmas anyway."

Miserably shaking her head, Dominika said, "Not wages. You pay much." It had not occurred to her that she might have to invent reasons. She wasn't used to dissimulation but after a moment's floundering, she decided upon an excuse that was valid enough, although it would not have driven her from the ranch. "I miss Basque talking, Basque people."

"Yes, I suppose you do." Lucie's grasp softened and her tone was so insistent that Dominika could no longer avoid looking at her, nor could she avoid thinking of the invalidism that the other woman could not escape, the perpetual confinement which Dominika knew her presence had eased. Brant would find another companion eventually but Dominika felt much the guilt she would have in abandoning a child.

There were tears in Lucie's eyes. "Please stay, Nika. I don't know what I'd do without you."

Whatever Brant did, he was Lucie's husband. That put him beyond Dominika's reach. She was a fool to torment herself over him and because of that to desert Lucie, who had befriended her. Everyone had a burden. Loving Brant must be hers. Beneath her conflicting feelings, she was glad that she would still be seeing him.

She must discipline herself to be grateful for that and never ever think of him with Mollie, holding her close, venting in her all his hunger and splendid strength. *Stop it!*

With the gesture of one taking a vow, she pressed Lucie's hand to her cheek. "I will stay." And with a touch of irony she remembered an old proverb: "The Basque is faithful."

* * *

One thing to make resolves. Another to keep them.

Dominika slept poorly. She could not banish images of Mollie taking those kisses, those caresses she herself so longed for. When Lucie prattled trustfully to Brant, Dominika had to fight an urge to scream, "You think your husband's faithful. And all the time he's sneaking off to tumble that yellow-haired whore!"

Only riding brought her any relief. For a few days a fall of snow kept her inside but the white covering soon melted off in the valley and she could ride again. She never went near the line shack, though Tex and Ollie were staying up there now. Even with her husband gone, it would seem foolhardy to use Mollie's house for adulteries.

On All Saints' and All Souls' days, Dominika lit extra candles during her prayers and thought of how, in her village, black mourning cloths would cover each *sepulturie* while the *etcheko andrea* lit candles and the priest moved from one household's place to another, offering prayers before leading the black-clad procession to the cemetery.

At home people were strongly and constantly connected with the past and with family, which in a way were the same. It was on holy days and Sundays that Dominika felt the greatest loneliness, the deepest separation from Etchahoun and the village and all that she had ever known.

V

MARTINMAS PASSED, when men costumed like a white mare had visited the corn fields, and a few weeks later it was time for the American Thanksgiving, with a big, wild turkey that Brant had shot, cranberry sauce and pumpkin pie. All of the hands were invited to dinner in the big house that day. Ollie and Harry compromised by saving the seat between them for Dominika, who perched there when she was not helping Sarah serve. To her delight and homesickness, there was apple cider to drink but it tasted nothing like the aged cider in the pigskin bag at Etchahoun.

The northern skies were piled with heavy gray one afternoon when Dominika went down to the corral. Harry cocked a red eyebrow at the lowering clouds. "Sure looks like a storm, Miss Nika. Maybe you'd ought to stay in today and keep your feet warm."

Honey neighed, trotting up in anticipation of the apple that Dominika always brought her. Dominika stroked the mare's creamy neck and laughed at the young cowboy.

"Honey wants to go, too, Harry. We watch sky. Come home fast if it snows."

He scratched his head. "I don't think the boss would like it, ma'am."

And just where, Dominika wondered darkly, *is the boss?* Hardening her jaw, she said, "All right, Harry. I saddle Honey."

He cast her a glum look and went into the tack shed. As he cinched the saddle and tied a slicker behind, he asked hopefully, "Maybe I could go with you, Miss Nika?"

262

"Thank you, Harry, but I—" She searched for words. "I need loneness."

He did not argue further but he was scowling as she rode away.

It was one of the days when Honey wanted to run. Dominika let her, finding surcease in the sting of the wind on her face, its wild tugging at her hair. Even when Honey's first exuberance was spent, she moved at a brisk trot and before Dominika realized it, she was farther from the house than she had ever gone, following one of the jagged little streams so thickly tufted with grass that it was not visible until she was almost upon it.

Clouds nearly covered the sky now. Lightning flashed toward the mountain above and there was a rumbling growl of thunder.

Dominika reined in to marvel at the expanse of broad valley and the embracing ranges. In Vizcaya every valley hosted a village and a hundred or more farms clustered in small neighborhoods. This country was so vast, so empty, that it was easy to imagine it was still uninhabited. Scanning the mountains, Dominika tried to picture Mari living among the crags and could not.

As for Basa Jaun, what would he say to cowboys? She laughed at the thought of such a confrontation. Ollie would forefoot Basa Jaun and tie him hoof to tail. No, there might be spirits here but they would be Indian ones.

She was jarred from her reverie by a clap of thunder that sent Honey skittering. Heavy drops splattered slowly at first but by the time Dominika pulled on the poncho, rain was slashing down in driving, sluicing sheets. There were no nearby trees large enough for shelter. Besides, she had been warned several times not to seek such refuge. Tall trees drew lightning.

At least if she and Honey were to start home, the slant of the rain would be at their backs and less blinding. Dominika patted the mare's neck and turned her.

"Let's go, pretty one. I'm sorry I got you into this."

There was a dazzling brilliance, a reverberating crash. Dominika, half stunned, marveled at the way the rumble echoed and resounded in the earth, actually making it shake. Then she saw it was not thunder she heard but the stampede of cattle panicked by the sound. They streamed past, bellowing, their eyes wild, and one, swept far to the side, stabbed a horn into Honey's neck before it disengaged and fled onward.

Honey gave a scream and leaped forward convulsively. "Honey, Honey! Steady, girl!" Swinging down from the saddle and pulling the mare a distance from the streaming cattle, Dominika blanched at sight of the deep red pouring from the wound.

She did not know what to do. In a blind effort to check the gushing flow, she put her hand over the hole but blood immediately seeped through her fingers. Sickened, she pressed her other palm a little above the gash. It took her a moment to realize that the trickle between her fingers had almost stopped. Blinking rain out of her eyes, Dominika saw that she was pressing against a vein.

Prayerfully she increased the pressure and removed her other hand from the wound. Only a little blood oozed out, quickly washed away by the rain.

Almost at once Dominika's relief was overwhelmed with dread. Apparently for as long as she could apply pressure to the vein, the bleeding would be checked but how long could she continue to do that? Her arm and hand were already feeling the strain.

If only someone could sew up the injury . . . But they were miles from the ranch. She was afraid if she tried to walk the mare, the motion and slipping of her hand would let the blood flow again. Fighting down her panic, she forced herself to search her memory for any hint of what might be best to do.

She had cut herself often enough to know that such hurts eventually stopped bleeding, although a person could bleed to death rather quickly from a serious wound. Was Honey's injury such that were the blood stanched long enough, it would clot? Or would that gush of deep red start again the instant that Dominika's hand could no longer press strongly against the pierced vein?

If only she had let Harry come with her—or had stayed in to start with! She was sure there would be a search if she wasn't home by dark but by then it might be too late for Honey.

The way that she was pressing on Honey's neck reminded her of how five years ago she had set her paint-dipped hand against the wall of the Summer Cave, her print joining the hundreds already there. Now she called on those women, all of them a part of her, especially Lael, who had loved her milk-white Al Zirr.

She had to shift to using her other hand, moving swiftly. Only a little blood escaped. Softly, to comfort Honey and herself, she spoke of the cave and its women, and of Mari, who sometimes took the form of a mare and who was known to pity animals, especially her favorite lambs.

The fury of the storm had thinned into a drizzle. The cattle had run themselves out near the distant narrowing of the canyon and were spread out now, seeking any refuge they could find. The air seemed colder but perhaps it was only that Dominika's feet and lower skirts were soaked and rain had found a way down her neck and into the poncho.

When one arm and hand grew nerveless, she changed to the other. There was no other reality. Keep the pressure on. Hold back the blood. Dominika was shivering now and it seemed to be getting darker. She did not know how long she could last.

Her hand was numb again. In the second that passed between the time she moved it and put the other in its place, she saw no seepage of blood from the wound.

Had a clot formed?

Cautiously, scarcely breathing, Dominika eased the pressure. The flow did not resume. But would it when Honey moved? Dominika was afraid to test it yet. She stretched her cramped shoulders and arms, rubbed warmth into her face and hands and was just wondering if she dared to lead Honey slowly homeward when she heard a shout.

Turning, her heart swelled with joyous relief. A rider was coming, mounted on a big iron gray. Brant! Calling his name, she ran forward. He swung from the saddle.

Without a moment's strangeness or hesitation, they were in each other's arms.

For just such accidents or barbed-wire cuts, Brant carried

needles and waxed thread. "That horn may have nicked the jug-
ular vein," he said as he sewed up the wound. "Whatever, the
blood has clotted and made kind of a patch. You ride Shadow
and I'll lead Honey."

He fired his revolver twice to let the searchers know that
Dominika was found. When he had come in from feeding poor
stock when the storm began, Harry had told him that she had
left early in the afternoon, riding off in the direction of where the
storm had subsequently raged.

"I was afraid something had happened to you," he said
huskily. "We all turned out to look." He gave her a shake.
"God, Nika, you could have been gored instead of Honey!
Knocked off and trampled—"

He found her mouth again. They clung to each other there
in the rain. His lips warmed her, sent her chilled blood coursing
through her.

"I love you," he said, cheek wet and cold against hers before the touch warmed both of them. "I love you, Nika."

He helped her into his saddle. A little farther down the valley they met Marco and Harry. Brant sent them to check on the
cattle and tend to any injured in the stampede.

"You ride on," he told Dominika. "Get out of those wet
things and have a hot tub. Sarah will bring you something hot."

Dominika shook her head. "I will stay with you."

Their eyes met. Physical shock went through her at the blue
fire of his gaze. She looked away as he said her name and she did
not answer. But deep in the tumult within her there lay a rock-
hard core of fatalism, of exhausted surrender.

When he had kissed her, she became his. It *was*. Whatever
she might do.

It was after dark when they reached the corrals. Mac, with a
lantern, came to put Honey in a stall, rub her down and give her
oats. He whistled at Brant's brief explanation and his charcoal
eyes slanted an admiring if puzzled glance at Dominika before
Brant hustled her off.

Neither of them spoke. Without his arm beneath hers,
Dominika would have fallen. In fact, she would have liked to
fall, have him catch her up and carry her in his arms. In the

kitchen Sarah took her in charge, having her sit by the big range and sip steaming, sugared coffee while she, Sarah, hurried upstairs to light the kerosene heater in the bathroom and run a hot bath.

Brant's face was grim as he stared at Dominika. There was no tenderness in his eyes now but something close to anger. "Lucie will be worried about you, and me, too. I have to tell her that you're all right." He stopped in the doorway. "After you're cleaned up, come and see her for a minute if you're able. Then have something to eat and go to bed."

"But—"

"Do as you're told!"

He swung his back to her. In a moment she heard his boots on the stairs. She took a scalding swallow of coffee and smudged away her tears. Why had he turned so cold and harsh?

Was he sorry he had kissed her? Sorry for what he had said? Dominika finished the coffee, rose and wearily started upstairs. Sarah, clucking, forbore to ask many questions but helped her out of the sodden divided skirt and took it, her wet boots and stockings away with her.

"Lucie already had a tray," she said, pausing in the door. "Would you like one or will you feel like coming down for a bite?"

"I'll come down," Dominika said, dismayed at all the trouble she had caused.

She finished undressing and lowered herself by inches into the hot water. In spite of her distress over Honey and Brant's suddenly hostile manner, the scented water relaxed her and dissolved much of her soreness and fatigue. She soaked until the bath began to cool and then stood on the thick mat to towel her hair and body. After she was dressed, she brushed her hair and tied it back with a ribbon before she hurried down the hall.

Lucie gave her a tempestuous hug, scolded her for staying out when it looked like a storm brewing and asked a dozen questions.

"Easy, love." Sitting by his wife's couch as he carved a steak and helped it down with potatoes, gravy and biscuits, Brant gave an indulgent chuckle. "Nika can tell you all about it tomorrow. Let her have a bit to eat and tuck in early."

Lucie patted Dominika's hand. "You heard the boss, dear. Run along and get rested. I'll hear the whole thing at breakfast."

Dominika said good-night and went down to the kitchen, where Sarah again gave her the rocker by the stove and ladled up a portion of the creamy soup that she had made for Lucie, buttered biscuits and poured a little whisky into hot milk.

"This should chase off any coughs and sneezes," the motherly, brown-eyed woman said. She wouldn't let Dominika help with the dishes but sent her upstairs as soon as she had savored the last of the toddy.

Drowsily climbing between the sheets, Dominika shivered at their chill but relaxed as they gradually took on the heat of her body. She imagined herself in Brant's arms again and felt his lips warming her cold ones.

He had said he loved her.

If that was all she would have of joy to last through a lifetime, it would be enough.

He was kissing her, his hands gently running through her hair. But they were not in the rain. Long fingers stroked her tenderly, curved around her breasts, stroked her sides and back. Dominika roused slowly from dream to awareness.

He was here! He was in her bed!

She should have pushed him away. She should have shamed them both with the thought of his wife only a few doors down the hall. She could have done those things for she knew that she could do whatever she must. But with heart, soul and body, she loved this man.

Shunting away the image of Lucie, she gave back Brant's kisses and offered herself to him wildly, recklessly. He did what he could to ease his entry. She bit back a gasp of pain and then moaned softly at the hurt and wonder and marvel of feeling a part of him within her, sheathing deeper and deeper, throbbing and pulsing like the vein in Honey's throat.

He filled her utterly. She arched her body against him, smothering a cry. Then he was the storm, surging, primeval, sweeping her away with him, cresting, gasping aloud as the force pumped from him and he fell to one side, cradling her in his arms.

"I tried not to come," he whispered. "I have no right. But, God, I love you!"

She felt a great wave of tenderness, equaling the awe that his passion had evoked in her only a moment before. "And I love you," she murmured, smoothing his thick hair, pressing his head against her.

When she woke in the morning, he was gone. Had it been a dream? She both hoped and feared that it had. Then she moved, wincing at the ache that assured her he had been very real.

Overpowered by the memory and a rush of trepidation, she closed her eyes. Surprisingly she felt no guilt, no sense of sin, though the thought of Lucie filled her with discomfort. It never occurred to her to blame the unaccustomed whisky, her half-waking state or Brant. The power drawing them together was too great. This would have happened sooner or later unless she had left the ranch and put a great distance between them.

Now she could not even think of that. Only of the next time he would take her in his arms.

Within three weeks Mac pronounced Honey sound again. Dominika rode when the weather permitted but as winter settled in, the days were trance-like. She and Brant did not always make love. Sometimes they simply held each other and talked softly. Though he did not say so, she gathered that Lucie, even before her crippling, had enjoyed courtship but not its consummation.

When conscience pricked her, Dominika told herself that a man must have release and it was better for Brant to be with her, who would cause no trouble, than frequent prostitutes or Mollie. Spiteful over having lost him, Mollie had extracted not-very-subtle blackmail.

"I hope Tex never wonders where she gets so much extra money," Brant said ruefully, "but I expect she hides it away."

Mollie's smolderingly suspicious eyes rested sometimes on Dominika but at a direct glance from her, they dropped sullenly. After Thanksgiving Mollie drove to Boise with Mac, who was buying provisions, and when he was ready to return, she was nowhere to be found.

"I finally checked at the railroad station," he reported to

Brant that night, embarrassedly twisting the rim of his soiled Stetson in his rough hands as he avoided looking at Lucie and Dominika. "Sure enough, a pretty, yellow-haired woman had bought a ticket and caught the train to San Francisco."

"Have you told Tex?" Brant asked.

Mac nodded his grizzled head unhappily. "Yeah. He just cussed and said—well, never mind what he said. And he got out his whisky."

Rumors that eventually reached Dominika through Brant claimed that Mollie had once been a small panhandle rancher's wife and that she had talked Tex into running off with her. She had never been content with his position as a hired hand so it was no great surprise that she had apparently saved her wages and left to hunt better pickings while she still had her looks.

"Did you pay her to go?" Dominika asked Brant.

He stroked her cheek and then let his fingers trail lightly to her breast. "You bet I did. Cheaper to pay her once and for all and get her out of the way. There was no telling when she might shoot off her mouth. Anyway, she had begun to wonder about you."

Mollie may have been mercenary but it jarred Dominika to hear Brant speak with such brutal indifference. She turned from him. He caught her shoulder.

"What's wrong, sweetheart?"

"I would die—" The words broke in her throat. "I would die if you talked that way about me."

"Nika!" He gave her a shake and laughed in amazed exasperation. "Hell, darling, I never gave a hoot about that woman. She kept putting herself in front of me at a time when I sure needed something."

"I—I hate it when you talk so!"

He laughed in masculine amusement. "I guess good women can't get it through their heads that a man doesn't 'love' or even like most of the women he beds."

"I'm not a good woman," she said stiffly. "If I were in confession, the priest would tell me that this is great sin."

Brant was silent for a long moment. "Does it bother you? A lot?"

"Not as much as it should," she answered truthfully. But

she did not pray for herself anymore. On Sundays she lit the candle for her mother and hoped that the prayers for her soul would be heeded, even from a sinner.

Sighing, he gathered her close, nestling her head on his shoulder. "Nika, if I could, I would marry you. You must believe that. But there's no way I could divorce Lucie."

"No. That would be wicked." Dominika could not imagine her child-like, fragile mistress existing without Brant's attentive care and devotion.

Now he kissed Dominika's lips and then her hands, slowly, gratefully, as if in homage. "I can promise you this, though. In my heart you are my wife. I feel as responsible for you as if you really were. I will always take care of you."

They made love solemnly then, though at the last their restraints were stripped away and they swept each other through a wild crescendo into that vast, calm ocean, where they lost their names and were blissfully part of all that was eternal peace.

Later, though, Dominika wondered what could be the end of it. Would she ever return to Etchahoun? And if she did not, how, unmarried, would she bear the children to send back in her place, especially a daughter who would visit the cave? Most of the time, however, she did not allow herself to think of the future. Except for short rides when the weather was fine, she spent the unreal days with Lucie and lived for the nights, when she would be Brant's love.

There was no *sepulturie* to hold the bread and so on Christmas Eve she took a big loaf and crumbled it for the birds before she went down to the gala dinner that Sarah had prepared, assisted by Mac's widowed sister who had been glad to assume Mollie's duties and get back to a ranch after several years in Boise as a doctor's housekeeper. Lorene wore her graying hair in a tight knot but her rare smile was warming and she kept the house in better order than Mollie ever had. She had lost a daughter of Lucie's age and treated her mistress with a quiet solicitude that quickly drew Lucie to her.

After the festive meal, Brant carried his wife to the parlor and lit the softly glowing candles on the Christmas tree. The tree continued a custom that his father, the younger son of an earl, had brought from England to this home that he had established in the wilderness.

"But the tree's not an old English tradition," Brant smiled, pouring eggnog for the women. "Prince Albert brought the custom from Germany and of course Queen Victoria thought anything he did was perfect." He surveyed the tree with admiration. "This was one of his better notions."

Dominika had knitted shawls for Lucie and Sarah and several pairs of warm wool socks for Brant. As Brant handed out the presents, she quelled a rush of longing for Etchahoun, where this night would have been set aside for a family dinner and gifts would be given on January sixth, Three Kings' Day. With some bitterness she wondered if Esteban would hypocritically open the Christmas feast with the ritual prayers for all who had lived in the house he had wrongfully claimed. He probably had another woman there by now and—

"Come back to us, Nika," Brant teased, passing a hand before her face as he handed her another parcel. She had never had such gifts—a hooded velvet cape, furred house slippers and warm flannel nightgowns. From Brant there was a music box and perfume.

Although he made much of the socks and modeled the brocade smoking jacket that was Lucie's principal gift to him, it was really Lucie's celebration and she reveled in it, eyes sparkling as she opened each present.

Luxurious wrappers, slippers, perfume, bonbons, books, records, ivory dominos, a silver brush and mirror set. She exclaimed her way through the trove but still she seemed not quite satisfied.

"Well," said Brant, laughing down at her, "there *is* one more thing."

He whisked the covering from a machine sitting on a table at the back of the room and pulled down the big screen.

"Are you ready?" he asked with a flourish, turning the lamp down and putting it in the hall.

There was a metal tank beside the machine. He worked with it for a moment, made adjustments to the flickering images wavering on the screen and when he had a clear picture, he cried triumphantly, "The one, the only Edison Kinetoscope! Real moving pictures!"

Lucie gave a cry of delight and squeezed Dominika's hand. They watched enthralled as the horses on the screen really galloped in a thrilling race and as yachts vied to pass each other. Indians danced and Niagara Falls sparkled in its downward plunge.

"Isn't there more?" Lucie asked when after more than an hour Brant shut off the illumination.

"Yes, my love." He bent to kiss her and a flash of pain shot through Dominika even though she sincerely wanted Brant to show Lucie affection. "You'll be able to see the Oberammergau Passion Play, trains, fire-fighting, funerals, wars, expositions and comedies. But not tonight!"

He wanted to explain that the strong light needed to project the film was generated by burning hydrogen and oxygen gases on a lime pencil, thus producing "lime light." In order to always have plenty of fuel, Brant had bought a gas-making outfit which produced hydrogen by evaporating eighty-eight-test gasoline.

"It supplies about seven hundred candle power," he gloated like a boy with a fascinating new toy. "An electric arc lamp would be better, of course, but I don't suppose we'll ever have electricity out here."

"That's interesting, dear," Lucie said, patting back a yawn.

He grinned at her obvious boredom. "Well, my love, since I've put you in a sleepy mood, let me take you up."

"It's a lovely surprise," she murmured drowsily, folding her arms around his neck. "You're so good to me, darling, and I'm such a—"

"You're such a beautiful lady that I never quite believe you," he said firmly. But as he turned at the doorway, his eyes met Dominika's.

VI

CANDLEMAS CAME, February Second, when the *etcheko andrea* of each household had candles blessed for use in ritual occasions throughout the coming year. The money that Dominika had left old Violeta would keep candles and bread on the *sepulturie* until the anniversary of Maria's death. In the spring Dominika must send money so that candles would be lit on the special holy days.

She did not trust Esteban to do it. Of all the grievous thoughts about losing her inheritance, the one that plagued her to ferocity was the fear that he might marry again and a usurping woman would fill her place, actually supply the candles and bread and kneel on the *sepulturie* of Etchahoun.

It would not be long, either, until the blessing of the fields. Dominika yearned for spring. Snow stayed on the ground for weeks at a time and even when the trails were comparatively clear, the cold was so biting that she seldom rode.

Ironically, the short winter days seemed endless and the long nights brief. There were never enough hours when she and Brant were together. At night, to please him, she wore the diamond ring that he had given her for Christmas, though there was never a time that she could wear the matching earrings. The lavish gift had made her feel strange, as if he were buying her, and she took the glittering pieces only when she saw that he would be genuinely hurt if she did not.

She no longer agonized about their loving but did all she could to keep Lucie amused. How could anything so natural and powerful be wrong? Rather than abating, their passion swept them into ever-mounting discoveries and delights. Dominika did not think ahead or plan or worry but gave herself entirely to her lover.

The first soft greening was showing along the valley when Dominika realized that her monthly flow was late. Early in their affair Brant had assured her that he was taking care that she would not get a baby and although she had wondered how that could be, she had believed him. Almost from the beginning, her periods had been as regular as the moon's phases.

She went riding but nothing happened. She took long walks but the familiar cramping, always before detested but now desperately wished for, did not come.

Sometimes she had let herself dream of the child, a boy with eyes and hair and a smile like his or a girl who would look like Maria, but she knew that a child was one of the many things denied by their position. Had they been married, or even had Brant been unmarried, her feelings would have been very different from the dread that seized her.

When, falteringly, she told him, the arm on which she was lying stiffened. "Are you sure?"

She said miserably, feeling at fault even though he had assumed responsibility, "It is ten days now. I am never late."

"Good Lord!"

The silence between them grew thickly suffocating. She wished that she could see his face. She felt as though a weight crushed in on her, limiting her breath.

"Perhaps the Irigays can give me work at the hotel," she said. "Or know of a place."

Turning roughly, he gripped her shoulders. "What are you talking about? You're not leaving!"

Relief that he did not want to be rid of her mingled with anxiety. "But I can't stay, Brant. In three or four months I'll grow big."

"No. You're going to develop some kind of problem that will require a Denver doctor to cure and Lucie will agree that I should take you there. When we come back—well, it will be just as it has been except that I'll be damned careful every time."

"What do you mean?"

He sighed and patted her shoulder. "I mean, my sweet-

275

heart, that you're going to a doctor who'll be well paid to take care of things. You won't have the baby. Though God knows I'd give anything if you could!"

She thought about his plan. Even though she had hoped that the long rides and walks would bring about the very thing that he was suggesting, she shrank from the thought of a deliberate operation. To have a surgeon intrude into her body and take away the small life she longed to cherish—that was wrong.

"I cannot."

"Nika, you have to!" He drew her against him, stroking her hair. "I hate it, too, darling, but there's no other way out."

"Yes, there is. I can have the baby."

"But you can't and stay here. Unless—"

"Unless?"

His unwilling tone held a note of grudging hope. "I don't like this notion one bit but it would be a way to keep the child. Ollie's wild for you. So is Harry. You could marry one of them."

Dizzied, her brain whirled in disbelief. She pulled away from him. "It would be like Tex and Mollie? Very easy for you!"

He shook her hard. "It would be hell! But we could have the baby, he could grow up here!" He had a sudden thought and added eagerly, "I could even leave him the ranch since I won't be having children by Lucie."

"I won't do that. Ollie and Harry are too nice."

"Well, how about Marco? I bet if I paid him enough, he would consent to marry you and then disappear. That's the best idea."

As he talked, the confusion in Dominika's mind had narrowed to unshakable conviction. She would be glad if the baby left her body naturally but if it did not, she would have it. That decided, she knew deep in the core of herself that she could not, married or single, stay at the ranch and continue to be Brant's mistress as her child grew up and inevitably came to know that Brant visited his mother's bed under cover of night.

What was possible to her as a woman was not possible to her as a mother. "I cannot stay at the ranch," she said.

"Sure you will. You'd be crazy to go anywhere else." He gathered her possessively into his arms. "You're upset now, sweetheart, but you don't have to worry. It'll work out."

She did not argue further but when he kissed her, her lips were unresponsive. In her heart, she had already left him.

It wasn't that simple, carrying out her resolve. She still loved him. She was a stranger in a strange land. She had no family, and away from the ranch, no friends except perhaps for Marta Irigay. Dominika's courage often ebbed but there was no time to lose if she were to find work before her figure began to show that she carried a baby. At least she now spoke fairly good English, thanks to Lucie's perpetual teaching and correcting, and she had her saved wages and Brant's diamonds to help her through the time that she would give birth.

Maybe by then she could find work in a home where she could take care of her child and still earn their living. She could not worry about that yet. It would take all of her strength just to leave the ranch. The hardest part of all was telling Lucie. Dominika waited for a day when Brant had ridden up to the line camp and would be gone overnight.

After she had helped Lucie dress and they had breakfasted, she took a deep breath, steeled herself for what would follow and looked into the beautiful, child-like face.

In spite of the secret barrier between them, Dominika had come to love the other woman and she dreaded to hurt and leave her. For a moment she wished that they were Mormons, who had once allowed a man more than one wife. Then they could all have lived together without shame or subterfuge. She would never aspire to Lucie's position but she would have given anything for a decent, open place of her own.

The hardest thing that she had ever done, harder even than sealing her mother's eyes or leaving Etchahoun, was to meet that violet gaze and say, "Lucie, I must go to town, find a different work."

Lucie's eyes dilated in shock before her slim brows drew into a frown. "Again? Don't be silly, Nika. Just tell me what you want. And in the future please do that rather than threaten to leave."

"I do not threaten." The sting in Lucie's words braced Dominika. "I have nothing to ask, you are too good to me. But I am lonesome so far from town."

"Then I must be very poor company," Lucie said with a brittle little laugh.

Dominika flushed hotly. "That is not how I mean."

Lucie's brows shot up in sudden contemptuous understanding. "You're lonesome for men? You want a husband?"

It was probably the best thing for her to think. Dominika nodded mutely although her whole being stormed: *It's your husband I want—and he wants me! You should be grateful that I'm going away.*

Lucie stared at her for a moment in scornful affront that could not entirely hide the stricken pain in her eyes, the pain that stabbed Dominika deeper than the scorn. "Very well," Lucie shrugged. Her tone was icy. "You've been here long enough to know what you want, evidently. Tell Mac to drive you to town as soon as you can pack. Lorene can move into your room. She's a quiet, restful person, thank goodness, who's too old for ridiculous romantic notions."

Dominika would have given much not to have to ask for her money but she would need it. "If—if you could please pay me? I owe for sixteen candles."

With a disagreeable laugh, Lucie reached into the drawer of a stand beside her and took out the checkbook she kept handy for ordering things that caught her fancy in the catalogues. "Candles? I should have known that a superstitious little Roman Catholic foreigner couldn't have much on her mind but getting married and having some man father her litters!"

Swiftly she wrote out a check. As Dominika reached for it, Lucie let it slip through her fingers so that Dominika had to stoop to pick it up. Cheeks burning, sorrowful over the unhappy leave-taking, Dominika said hesitantly, "Lucie, please—"

"Get out!" Lucie shouted, her face suddenly contorting. "Get out of my house and if you don't like what happens to you in town, don't crawl back here!"

Tears sparkled in her eyes but Dominika dared not touch her. "Good-bye," she said through numb lips and stumbled blindly through the arch.

In anticipation of Brant's absence, she had packed the day before and then taken a farewell apple to Honey. After some debate she took most of the things that the Rawlinses had given her. They would be of no use to anyone else and the gesture of pridefully leaving all but what she had come with was one that she could not afford.

Lacerated by Lucie's attack, she sobbed as she finished putting her last belongings in the sack and small case, carefully tucking in the blue bird. *Oh, Mothers! I know that I have done wrong but you who were mortal once, help me now! Help me and my child.*

Rinsing her face in cold water, she waited until the red blotches around her eyes faded before she put on her cape and went down to the foreman's house.

Sarah, although her brown eyes were puzzled and concerned, gave Dominika a warm embrace of farewell. "We'll miss you, dear. But it's dull for a young thing away out here, especially in the winter. Good luck to you—and if you need friends, you know where we are."

"Thank you," Dominika said. Mac helped her into the wagon in which Brant had brought her to the valley in last summer's brightness, when all the leaves were green. He spoke to the horses and they were on their way.

"Weren't the Rawlinses good to you?" demanded Marta Irigay, dark eyes peering closely at Dominika.

"Very good."

"Then why are you back here asking for work? I can't pay what a rich rancher does."

"You don't have to. I—I was just lonesome."

Marta clicked her tongue. "Ah! You missed the language and Basque people." She nodded at the solved mystery. "Good, I can use some help right now. My daughter married and moved to California and the place is full of sheepherders who won't have work until the spring lambing. You can have your old room and start right away."

So for board, room and half the wages she had earned at the Rawlins', Dominika had shelter and work. She put her money in a savings bank and when she learned that it could earn interest, she sold her diamonds to a jeweler, who exclaimed at their value, and put what seemed like a small fortune in the bank with the wages.

With mournful pride she considered the money from the sale of the diamonds as Brant's gift to his child. Before her condition was visible, she needed to find a cooking or housekeeping job but for the moment she welcomed the busyness and clamor of the hotel, the heartening sound of her own language and the twenty or so wintering herders whose foibles and personalities gave her something to think about besides her troubles and the dull, constant ache of longing for Brant.

At least she was too tired at night to lie awake missing him. She sometimes wept into her pillow but not for long. The day started before dawn and she had to brew the strong coffee, heat milk to go with it and slice the loaves of fresh bread.

As the men came downstairs, they poured their own coffee, adding milk and taking small glasses of whisky. These they carried with slabs of bread into the dining room. Thus sustained, they would not hunger before Marta cooked the big breakfast of eggs with bacon or ham or *chorizos*. Marta's young sister-in-law, Mariana, a slight, dark, pretty girl who had just come over that fall from a valley south of Bilbao, helped Dominika serve and clear tables.

There was an occasional rancher or traveler passing through but the twenty winter boarders were all herders, ranging from seventeen-year-old Sabino Goiro, who blushed when one of the girls came near him, to Domingo Artza, whose age no one would guess. His mahogany skin was weathered as tree bark. He had a silver mane and beard of waving hair, stood six feet tall and was bull-chested. In spite of his intimidating appearance, he had a gentle voice and a quick smile. He liked to joke with Dominika and Mariana; most of the men were tongue-tied except when asking for more food or coffee.

While Marta did the mounds of dishes, the young women went upstairs to make the beds and empty the chamber pots. Once a week they cleaned the rooms and changed each bed.

The laundry was done in the hotel bathtub on washboards in water heated in tubs on the wood and coal kitchen stoves. A neighbor boy filled the woodboxes and coalbins from the shed next to the two outdoor privies. Dominika and Mariana rinsed and wrung the sheets by hand before hanging them outside on clotheslines, where they often froze before they dried.

It was hard, almost continuous work even though Marta and her Joanes were kindly. The boarders might play handball on the court a few blocks away but they spent most of their time in the hotel, playing cards or dominoes in the bar, reading American or Basque newspapers and books, some of them studying English or the requirements for becoming a citizen.

After supper someone always started singing. Paunchy, middle-aged Luis Escudi fetched his accordion and Domingo took out his *alboka,* a curious instrument made of two cow horns linked with a pearwood yoke. Often the men would move the tables and dance but though Marta urged both her helpers to join in, and sometimes did herself, Dominika had no heart for it. She stayed downstairs after her work was done only if Domingo entered into a singing duel of verses with anyone rash enough to challenge him.

"A real *bertsulari,* that one," Marta laughed as Domingo ended his defense of sheep as opposed to cattle with a nimbly versifying cattle-rancher who had told how he had got rid of his dumb sheep and their dumber herders. Grinning at his opponent, Domingo set his big hands on his hips and lilted:

> "When the shepherd lies down at night,
> He knows where his sheep are;
> The cattleman doesn't want to know
> Where range his cattle. In his heart
> He's hoping they're eating
> The grass of his neighbors."

There was a roar of applause and the clatter of stamping feet. "What can you expect of sheepherders?" grumbled the bested rancher.

He went upstairs. Dominika was starting to follow, intending to retire, when a gust of cold outside air made her glance through the lobby to the door. Strange for a traveler to come so late.

It was no traveler.

Brant strode to the dining room and looked at her. Her heart stopped, then throbbed painfully like a numbed leg or arm whose circulation has been suddenly restored. The men had started to sing again, boisterous at their triumph over the cattle-man.

Feeling weak, as if her legs were heavily weighted, Dominika stepped into the lobby. "Where can we talk?" Brant demanded.

He was leaner. His eyes were darkly ringed. He looked as though he had been sick. In spite of herself, Dominika felt a wave of pity for him. Women were not allowed in the bar and she would not have dared to take him to her room even had it been permitted.

Although the lobby was drafty and unheated, she crossed her arms and said, "We can talk here. How—how is Lucie?"

"She's made a mother out of Lorene, who's moved her cot in so she can be there if Lucie wants something at night." He grimaced slightly. "Lucie may be having a little too much sherry in the evenings but she says she needs it to help her sleep."

"And Sarah?"

"Sarah's fine," he said curtly. "So are Mac and Ollie and Harry and Marco. Everyone's fine, including Honey." He took a gusty breath and made a gesture at the crowded dining room. "Nika, this is crazy! It's been hard but I've waited till you had time to get tired of hustling tables and dumping thunder mugs. I guess you can't come back to the ranch but we have to agree on something sensible."

"We don't need to agree on anything." Fortunately her voice sounded stronger than she felt. "The Irigays are very good to me."

His blue eyes widened. White showed at the rims of his nostrils. "You'd really rather wait on these damned sheepherders than live in a nice house?" He glanced with contempt at the men in the other room, suspicion sharpening his scrutiny. "I suppose they've all asked you to marry them. Or warm their beds for an extra dollar."

In spite of refusing to dance, Dominika had already refused four offers of marriage. Shrugging, she said, "Herders are like cowboys. They will propose to anyone in skirts. As for anything indecent, not a one of those men would say a bad word to me. If he did, Marta would throw him out."

Brant stared at her in helpless anger. "You can't run up and down stairs and carry heavy trays when you get closer to your time." His voice dropped. The pleading hunger in his eyes tore at her. "Nika, it's been hell without you. Can you look me in the face and say you don't love me?"

Sorrowfully, she shook her head. In that moment, she was unable to speak. Seizing her hands, he urged imperiously, "Stop being a fool. I'll buy you a house tomorrow, put it in your name. You can pretend to the neighbors that you're a widow. I'll come in from the ranch as often as I can. We'll have to be careful but—"

It was barely possible that other people might not find out but sooner or later the child would learn.

He stared at her. It was hard to do but she met his pleading look. The muscles above his jaws stood out. "What will you do?" he asked wearily.

"There is money in the savings bank, enough so I won't have to work until the baby doesn't need me all the time." He scanned her waist significantly. Flushing, she said, "In six weeks or two months the boarders will be hiring out. Marta won't need me. Then I'll look for a housekeeping job where they will let me have the baby."

"Sweet Jesus! You hard-headed little Basco—"

She turned her back on him and went up the stairs.

Next morning Marta, with a keen glance, handed her a letter. Thanks to Lucie's teaching, Dominika could read most of Brant's message: *"At least let me give you a house and money till the child is school age. I will not visit you unless you ask me. You can reach me through my lawyer."*

The lawyer's name and address followed. That was all. Dominika did not even consider the offer. Should she accept anything from Brant, a foundation for future claims and entanglements would be laid. In spite of disillusionment at his suggestions for disposing of the baby or pushing it off on one of his cowboys, she still loved him too much to trust herself to leave any ties between them.

She put the letter in the stove. Her heart felt as if it curled and withered with the paper.

Physically she had been fortunate in her pregnancy. The queasiness that she had felt for a few weeks passed and although she was entering her third month, the slight rounding of her belly was imperceptible when she was clothed.

In the room she shared with Mariana she lit the Sunday candle for her mother beside the blue bird, prayerbook and acorn rosary. She went to Mass but neither confessed nor took communion, though to do so would have been a comfort. She did not intend to continue in her sin with Brant but neither could she honestly repent. She was sorry for the outcome but not for the love she had known.

At the end of March she took sufficient money from her wages to buy candles for Maria on holy days and the postmaster helped her send it to Violeta. Every cent of the rest of her earnings had gone into savings. It seemed a fortune, more than enough to see her through her confinement, but as time approached for her to begin hunting other work, she began to worry.

Marta knew that she wasn't married. If Marta were to help her find a position, Dominika could not pretend to be a widow. Marta would have to know about the baby and it was likely that she would guess the truth. As kind as the older woman had been, Dominika was certain that the fewer people who knew about the child, the safer the secret would be. Later, when the baby was old enough for no one to be counting months, she could visit the Irigays and let them assume that she had lost the baby's father—which was true enough.

The work was never really finished, but Marta gave Mariana and Dominika an afternoon off each week. On one of these days Dominika took an address and advertisement that she had copied from the paper and by asking directions, she finally located an imposing, two-story house on the edge of town, on spacious grounds among splendid tall trees.

It took courage to approach such an impressive edifice but the occupants *had* run an advertisement and she certainly was capable of doing housework. Even so, she walked by twice before she braced her shoulders and went up the long, paved walk. She knocked shyly. When no one answered, she knocked harder.

The door swung open. A grim-faced woman in a maroon dress and starched white apron looked down a long, thin nose and asked, "What do you want?"

Dominika produced the advertisement. "You need someone to help with housework?"

"You should have gone to the rear door," said the woman. "Go around and I'll talk to you there."

Since they were already talking, the order made no sense to Dominika. This prospective employer filled her with dismay but she could not expect everyone to be like Marta or as kind as Lucie had been until that last terrible day. Following a narrow walk to the back of the house, Dominika waited till the starched woman appeared and somewhat dubiously invited her into the big kitchen.

"You have a nice house," Dominika said politely.

The woman's nail-thin lip curled. "This is the residence of Mr. and Mrs. Bridwell. I am their housekeeper. My name is Mrs. Thaxton. What is yours?"

Except for that final, desperate deceit that she had imposed on Lucie, Dominika had never lied and now she felt her face reddening as she said faintly, "I am Mrs. Urdin. Dominika Urdin."

"You are Mexican? Spanish?"

"I am Basque."

The woman shrugged. "That's Spanish. Anyway, it scarcely matters. At least you have rather good English. How long have you been in this country?"

"I came last summer." *And my love drove me through the mountains to his valley and taught me my first words.* It seemed a lifetime ago. Yet at this time last year Maria had been in good health and Dominika had never dreamed of leaving Etchahoun.

With her first hint of approval, Mrs. Thaxton said, "Well, I must say you've learned quickly. I've no use for foreigners who want to live here but won't learn the language. Where have you been employed? Will your husband need work, too?"

"He—he was killed in an accident," Dominika invented. "I am working at a hotel."

"One of those Basque places? They have the reputation of being decent." Her eyes narrowed. "Why don't you stay there, among your own kind?"

Dominika felt sicker than she had through all of her pregnancy. Her palms were clammy and her tongue was thick and clumsy as she forced herself to meet her interrogator's probing stare. "I will have a baby next October. It would not be proper to work in the hotel during the last few months, though I could still do ordinary housework. And in a house it would be easier to take care of the baby in between my duties."

"A baby!" The housekeeper bristled with outrage. "Of all the nerve! What you're looking for is easy work and free lodging for you and your brat! It's out of the question."

She marched to the door and held it open. Unutterably humiliated, Dominika fled. Tears welled to her eyes as she hurried down the street. Was that the way she would be received wherever she turned in this strange land?

VII

THE CRUSHING experience haunted Dominika for days afterward. Perhaps she should leave the town. She knew that there were Basque hotels in many western cities: Elko, Nevada; Reno; Buffalo, Wyoming; San Francisco; Los Angeles; Salt Lake City; and a number of other places.

The Basques were a practical people, and hotel-owners liked to employ Basque help. In a different city she could work hard till the baby came, forego wages during the few weeks she would not be able to do chores and take less money in return for being allowed to keep the child in her room.

That seemed the best plan. She hadn't seen any other advertisements and even if she had, the encounter with Mrs. Thaxton would have made her apprehensive of applying. Still, she was reluctant to leave this region with which she had a familiarity. It would be difficult to summon the strength to begin all over just at a time when her natural bent would be toward an inward turning to the life growing within her. How wonderful it all might have been had she been sheltered by Brant as her time approached! For the first time since childhood she wanted to be taken care of and she longed for her mother.

Meanwhile, her tasks kept her busy. In addition to taking care of the rooms and waiting on the tables, the bar from which Joanes served the herders' favorites—Picon punch; Amer Picon mixed with soda water and brandy, sometimes sweetened with grenadine or lemon syrup; or Izarra, a green or yellow liqueur of aged Armagnac flavored with herbs and flowers from the distant Pyrenees—had to be constantly stocked with appetizers.

Easiest of all her chores was setting out bowls of plump green olives, fat Spanish peanuts, almonds and pine nuts or walnuts, sometimes blanched, fried and salted. Neither did it take long to slice cheese, salami or ham or to open cans of sardines and anchovies. Canned tuna, sprinkled with vinegar, oil, salt and pepper, was often served on Fridays and hard-boiled eggs were popular.

On Sundays there would be delicious little meat balls, *albondigas,* simmered in wine and tomato sauce.

The men consumed so much food in the bar that Dominika never understood how they could still tuck away three large daily meals. For dinner there was always soup, rice, beans or garbanzos, and then a stewed mixture of vegetables and plenty of mutton, beef, ham or chicken, or steaks or mutton chops. Bread and butter, of course, and hot chocolate or coffee.

Bar bills were separate but for the bounteous food and lodging a herder paid a dollar a day. Some of the men had run out of money months ago for after the fall gathering and shipping of sheep, comparatively few herders were needed to tend the reduced flocks through the winter till lambing time. Joanes and Marta always gave credit, however, and never had they been cheated. Year after year herders returned to the same hotel, often relying on the hotel-keeper to take care of mail and money, advise him on financial matters and help find work. Since the Irigays were Vizcaínos, so also were most of their boarders. The herders liked to stay at hotels that were run by people from their own provinces and often they would travel to a more distant city in order to do that. Or they would patronize year after year the same hotel to which they had gone when they first arrived in the States.

Domingo seldom missed a chance to pass a few words with Dominika. Because their names were similar, he called her *Tocaya,* namesake, and told her that she reminded him of his younger sister, although by now that sister had become a grandmother.

"Won't you ever go back?" Dominika asked.

He shook his magnificent silver head. "No. In my mind it is beautiful and just the way it was."

"It's still beautiful, *Tocayo.*" Dominika's voice was tinged with yearning. How she would have loved to have her baby born at Etchahoun!

"Yes," Domingo nodded, "but those who have visited and returned say that everything seems so small there, so crowded. They're glad to see their families and valleys but they don't belong there anymore. They're happy to get back to America." There was a twinkle mixed with the sadness in his eyes as he added yet another carving to his *makhila*, or staff. "I would rather dream here of my valley than go back and think it was little."

He was an excellent *muz* player, much sought as a partner because of his skill at bluffing and rattling opponents with a boisterous flow of nerve-rattling challenges and warnings. Partners signaled each other with twitches of the eyebrow, hand gestures and quirkings of the mouth.

Eights, nines and tens were tossed from the deck and twos played wild with aces, threes with kings, so that there were eight of each, kings being high. Domingo was the acknowledged champion of the hotel but he said that the best player he had ever known was Joe Uhalde, a sheepman for whom he had worked on several occasions.

"Joe, he's quiet but he's got four kings when you think he has nothing. He knows sheep and his herders always get the best food. I'd hire on with him year-round if one of his herders quit or went back to the old country."

Luis bumped his accordion against his paunch. "You, Domingo? Work all year except for a few weeks or a month? I thought you always said that a man who stays with sheep through the year forgets how to talk to people."

Stubbornly Domingo shrugged. "I would still work for Joe Uhalde. I hope he hires me this spring."

Luis nodded. "In the fall I never want to see another sheep but after a winter's loafing, it will be good to trail a band up to the high country."

"After lambing," Domingo grinned. Luis groaned. "After lambing."

Hiring time would put an end to Marta's real need for Dominika. As April began, Dominika was increasingly worried, slept poorly and was always tired. "You don't look well, *Tocaya*," Domingo told her kindly. He went to the bar and brought her back a glass of *panash,* half beer, half soda. "Drink this. It will calm your nerves."

His thoughtfulness was more cheering than the drink but Dominika felt more desperate each day at the prospect of going friendless to a strange place and starting over as the days of her heavy-bodiedness approached. She felt the instinctive, primeval need of women to hide away during their period of greatest vulnerability.

One noontime as she was hurriedly serving tables, she noticed a large, broad-faced, middle-aged woman in an enormous plumed hat and braid-trimmed traveling suit. With her was a pleasant-looking man upon whom she beamed fondly. Dominika paused to see what they might want.

"We've heard that you have good food here and it certainly smells like it," the woman boomed. "Bring us big plates of whatever you're giving the others." Her eyes held Dominika's for a moment. "No rush, my dear. Take care of your steady boarders first."

"Thank you," said Dominika.

As she turned, a tray of empty soup bowls in her hands, Sabino, late for his meal, ran into her. The tray went flying and the bowls crashed to the floor. In her overwrought state, it was too much. Dominika burst into tears as she knelt and hastily began picking up broken stoneware.

"I'm sorry," Sabino said but he didn't offer to help, hurrying on to his table.

Domingo, who was close by, patted her shoulder and bent to pick up some of the shattered bits. To Dominika's astonishment, though, the elegantly dressed woman was already kneeling down beside her, helping her.

"Men can sure be hogs," she said comfortingly, handing Dominika a lace-edged handkerchief. "And that boy's not old enough to know that a man's more of a man when he can clean up the messes he makes."

It took only a few minutes to pile all the broken crockery pieces on the tray. Heaving herself to her feet, the amazing woman gave a rumbling chuckle that made several of her chins vibrate.

"Take three deep breaths and laugh," she advised. "That's

what I did when I was running my boardinghouse and some clown dropped a snake in the soup or tracked up the floor.''

Was the woman mad? Her gaze was clear and steady. To humor her, Dominika took the three deep breaths, laughed shakily and did indeed feel better. She took the tray to the kitchen, mopped up the traces of soup and finished serving the boarders. When she brought the strangers their meal, the woman looked at her intently although she smiled.

''I'm May Arkwright Hutton,'' she announced in her carrying voice. ''This is my husband, Al. We own most of the Hercules mine up in the Coeur d'Alenes. It has the richest silver ore ever taken out of those mountains, although now we're having to fight the Guggenheims and the Lead Trust, who're trying to squeeze us out. You must be from across the water.''

''From Vizcaya. I am Dominika Urdin. Would you like more coffee?''

''Sure, when you can sit down and have a cup with us.''

It was to be Dominika's afternoon off and though she was puzzled by the woman, she was also drawn to her. After the other diners had departed and the Huttons' table was clean except for the cups, Dominika poured coffee for them and a cup for herself.

''Sure beats our log shack at the opening of the Hercules' tunnel,'' May Hutton said, stretching expansively. ''We'll be millionaires out of that mine but we worked for it. While the men used drills and picks, we womenfolk took in washing, hired out to do housework and I picked those hills clear of huckleberries so I could make pies. Sold dozens of 'em.''

Her husband, an unusually nice-looking man of average size, regarded his wife fondly. ''You pulled on overalls, too, May, and mucked out right along with the men.''

She put her fingers on her lips. ''Shh!'' she laughed with elephantine coquettishness. ''I'm a lady now and don't you forget it. Al, dear, don't you want to go along to the bar and have a drink?''

After a mystified stare, he sighed, grinned and said, ''Nice to meet you, Miss Dominika. I can promise that my wife's not crazy even though she sometimes acts that way.''

May hooted after him but her laughter faded as she turned

to Dominika, reached across the table and took her hand. "Honey, you're in some kind of mess. No one cries that hard over a few broken dishes. Want to tell me about it?"

Dominika froze, involuntarily glanced at her waist and flushed as May gave a brisk nod. "You're going to have a baby. And you aren't married."

There was no condemnation in the words, yet the revelation of her secret snapped something in Dominika. Although she was horrified at herself, she couldn't help it. She buried her face in her arms and wept. When the storm subsided, she felt that she had acted the fool but she also felt better. May handed her another handkerchief, this one embroidered, and said matter of factly, "Now that's over, let's decide what we're going to do. Your baby needs a daddy, you need a husband and I know a mighty fine man who needs a wife."

"But—I cannot lie! Or marry just anyone."

"Joe Uhalde's not just anyone. He's a sheepman now but he got his start working in the mines. Lived in my boarding-house." The folds around May's eyes crinkled. "Had a letter from him a few months ago saying he was sure tired of his own cooking and if I ran into any nice girl who would live on a sheep ranch, he'd sure like to meet her even if she wasn't Basque. Joe is," she added unnecessarily, for Dominika had already connected the name with Domingo's favorite employer, the laconic *muz* champion.

A spark of hope ignited within Dominika. "I can't marry a man I do not know. I don't want to marry anyone. But I would cook for him and keep his house if he would let me keep my baby."

May looked ready to argue but something in Dominika's face changed her mind. "All right, honey. That'll do for a start." She got to her feet with amazing lightness for a woman who must weigh over two hundred pounds. "Maybe, like Al says, I butt in where I oughtn't but my gracious, what are we if we can't help each other a little? I've known lonesome miners and ranchers who sure wanted wives and the ones I've matched up with girls who needed daddies for their babies have raised the children same as if they'd been their own. I'd never send some girl off with a mean man. She'd be better off alone."

Ending this homily with a puffing out of her round cheeks, she paid the bill, called loudly for Al and told Dominika that they intended to stop off to see Joe while they were down this way. Dominika was to be prepared for him to turn up at the hotel shortly.

It was a week. Sheepmen had been coming in, drinking at the bar and sizing up prospective herders, who in turn sidled over to learn from Joanes or Marta what kind of boss the man was and how well he fed. Most of the men signed with one rancher or another and bade the Irigays good-bye until the fall. Domingo had numerous offers but he turned them down, saying to Dominika, "I wait for Joe Uhalde."

"You must like him, *Tocayo!*" Dominika had not told Domingo that she hoped to be offered a job at the Uhalde ranch. If Uhalde wanted a wife, he might look further rather than hire a woman who said at the start that she was not interested in marrying.

Domingo blew his *alboka*, fingering out an old dance tune. "It's more than 'like,' *Tocaya*. I can work for a man I don't like if I respect him. Joe Uhalde, I respect." Domingo's solid belly rumbled with laughter. "I *like* him too, even though he always beats me at *muz*."

So nervously Dominika waited. Maybe he had already hired in another town. Now that most of the rooms were empty, she and Mariana gave them a thorough cleaning, washed and ironed the curtains and polished the windows. When these chores were finished, Marta would not need her anymore. She couldn't wait for Uhalde much longer. He might not even hire her. And she was almost four months pregnant.

Then one day there was a dark-haired, broad-shouldered man sitting at a table with Domingo. He rose as Dominika stopped to serve them, took the tray from her and shook her hand. His big, work-hardened fingers swallowed hers, warm, not crushing. His hazel-colored eyes were bright in a weather-burned face that had high cheekbones and a strong jaw.

"You are Dominika Urdin," he said, still holding her hand. He had good white teeth and she could see now that his thick black hair was streaked with a beginning gray.

His gaze seemed to gather in all that there was to know about her. Suddenly, he drew her away. Baffled, Dominika stared questioningly at him as they stopped out of earshot of anyone.

He said softly, "My good friends, the Huttons, say that you will cook and keep my house. That's good. You have the job if you want it." He hesitated and then said in a rush, "I would rather marry you, though."

"You don't even know me!"

His eyes smiled but there was a steadiness in them that told Dominika that this man was not to be trifled with. "I know enough."

"Please! You—you're very kind but—" A terrible thought rocked her. "Did Mrs. Hutton tell you—"

He finished the sentence for her. "That you will have a child? Yes. And it will be a beautiful one." It was the first happy and hopeful thing that anyone had said to her about the baby. In her own mind she had been able to think of it only as a burden, a punishment she must bear.

She could have kissed his scarred hands in gratitude. Fighting back tears, she gave him a joyous smile.

"Thank you, Mr. Uhalde. I will be very glad to work for you."

Two hours later they were on their way, Dominika tucked in between Uhalde and Domingo on the seat of the wagon, which was loaded with supplies. The rancher had talked with the Irigays, old friends of his. To oblige him, they had agreed that Dominika could leave that very day.

"But if you get tired of being stuck out there on a ranch, you can come back next fall," Marta assured her as she paid her and added a little extra. She gave Dominika an affectionate hug and twinkled at Uhalde. "I bet you figure to get this poor girl so far from other people that after a while you'll start looking handsome to her and she'll marry you!"

Joe just laughed. "How did you know?"

As they jolted along, the men talked about the sheep, the weather and the shearing crew that Joe was hoping to hire following the lambing.

"Better shear before," Domingo urged. "That way you don't have to fool with all the lambs."

"I've tried it both ways," Joe said. "The handling the ewes get from the shearers makes it a little more likely that they'll have trouble lambing and it seems to me the lambs don't thrive quite so well."

Domingo shrugged. "You're the boss."

"I'm not," Joe grinned. "What decides is the weather. And the shearers." He explained to Dominika, "If it rains, the sheep can't be sheared until they dry out but they can die if it rains or snows after shearing."

If bad weather struck after Etchahoun's sheep had been clipped, they could all be sheltered in the byre and storerooms of the old *dorrea*. "How many sheep do you have?" Dominika asked.

"Right now pretty close to eight thousand. They're split into four bands and after lambing they'll be split up again so that dry ewes and yearlings won't be in with the mothers and new lambs. They'll trail into the high country for summer and come back next fall. Then we ship the two-year-olds that aren't kept for breeding along with any old ewes whose teeth are so worn down they can't feed very well. After that—" He opened a palm toward heaven and laughed. "After that," he resumed, "Domingo spends the winter playing *muz* and feasting while I hope it doesn't snow too hard and that the sheep are finding enough to eat."

Domingo said, "I'll stay through the winter and worry with you if one of your regular herders quits."

"Old Paco may. His nephew, an *etcheko jaun*, has been trying to get him to come back to the farm, although Paco talks about opening a tavern."

"How would he stand the company after thirty years with the sheep?" Domingo asked skeptically.

Joe chuckled. "Old friend, you know men are always wanting what they haven't had."

Did his side-glance touch her for just a second? Dominika wondered. What a relief it was to have someone share her secret! After the long, anxious weeks, it was unspeakably blissful to have found a place where she could have her baby.

Joe's obvious steadfastness would have earned her trust even had May Hutton and Domingo not praised him. As for his immediate proposal, she did not take it too seriously. Since he had been wanting a wife for some time, he probably would have proposed to anyone who was young and reasonably pretty. One of Marta's continual laments was about the difficulty of keeping Basque maids. Herders or ranchers were always taking them away as wives.

It would be nice to be living on the same place as Domingo, too, though apparently he would soon be taking a band of sheep to high country for the summer. By the time he came down in the autumn, she might have had the baby. Somehow she did not worry over what he would think. He seemed past the sort of pettiness that called a child "bastard."

Feeling herself safe and protected as she rode along between the two men, Dominika was happy for the first time since she had suspected her condition. Breathing in the sparkling air, reveling in the caress of the sun, she watched the countryside eagerly as the wagon bumped along ruts that seemed to twine endlessly through sandy, flat, sagebrush land, broken only by rocks, always surrounded by snow-tipped mountains in the distance. Junipers studded the hills but it was mostly a dun and dull green landscape, the dazzling sky holding the only color.

Her first elation quieted as the hours wore on and her spine began to ache from the jolting and sitting upright with nothing to lean against. When they stopped to water the horses at a stream and let them rest briefly, Joe offered her the wineskin.

"I make my own wine," he said proudly. "Almost have to in order to keep the herders supplied."

"It's good wine," Domingo grinned, "but I hope you don't flavor it like one boss I had who tramped the grapes out barefoot instead of wearing his gum boots."

They passed a number of corrals which Joe said were the shearing pens, and the small log cabin used for cooking for the men during the three or four weeks of lambing, when they would be too busy to cook for themselves. There were also a few crude sheds for the ewes who were having a hard time birthing and had to be helped.

"One of the camp-tenders does the cooking, though," Joe

said hastily. "You won't have to come down here, M'nika." He had shortened her name and the new term was sufficiently different from Brant's "Nika" that she was not hurt by it.

"I know you have to hire extra men for the lambing," she said, positive that had she not been pregnant, he would have expected her to at least help cook for the crew. "There's no use in tying up one of your hands with work that I can do."

He raised a heavy eyebrow at her and said to Domingo, or God, "Already she's telling me how to run my ranch. Thank you many times, M'nika, but this season you will stay at the house. If you want to, you can bake the bread. That will keep you busy." She suspected what she was later to know, that when he used that gently firm tone, it was useless to argue.

Joe's ranch was spread out in the head of a canyon, protected on three sides by towering rock palisades that were softened at ground-level by a mixture of freshly leafing trees interspersed with darker evergreens. Wherever there was a little soil, trees and bushes creased the stone and cottonwoods grew thick along a stream that meandered down from the rocks.

There was a big barn and several buildings that Joe pointed out as the blacksmith shop, ice house and granary, a chicken house and fenced yard, scattered sheds, corrals, a garden and two log cabins. "One cabin's the bunkhouse," Joe said, halting the team in front of the other. "I live here."

Two dogs came running out to bark a joyous welcome, one white and black, the other gray and yellow. They had tulip ears, intelligent dark eyes and plumy tails. "Kato, Xagu, how are you?" Joe spoke to them as he would to people before he said to Dominka, "They were my dogs when I was a herder. They've worked hard and have earned their rest."

He carried her sack and small satchel through a big kitchen-dining room to the far end, where there were two doors. Opening the right-hand one, he entered and put her things down on a blanket-covered bed. There were pegs for clothes, a small chest of drawers and nothing else except for a sheepskin rug on the floor beside the bed.

Joe seemed to be somewhat embarrassed. "This isn't nice enough for you," he blurted.

"It's fine," Dominika said. The luxury of her quarters at the Rawlinses' certainly had not eased her misery.

"I'll fix it up after lambing," Joe insisted. "You be thinking of what you'd like." He went out to help Domingo unload the wagon. Through the one small window Dominika saw the small building she badly needed. There was another outside door in a hallway close to the bedrooms. She hurried out and realized that at last she was really in the Wild West.

There was one major labor-saving aid in the kitchen, though, a pump anchored by the sink, with a washbasin and bucket beside it and towels on a rack above. The woodbox, at one side of the big range, was stacked with cookwood and there were plentiful cupboards and shelves, though skillets and a few enameled pans hung on the wall by the stove. A long, heavy table was protected by the same oilcloth covering the floor, of yellow and blue with serpentine leaves and tendrils meandering across.

Instead of a fireplace, a cast-iron stove with mica panels occupied a brick dais at the side of the room nearest to the door of Dominika's room. Close to the stove was a big chair and a table holding a lamp, newspapers and magazines. The dining-room table was flanked by a dozen chairs and covered by red and white checkered oilcloth that had been scoured patternless on top.

The porch just outside the kitchen held a big ice chest, wash tubs, a copper-bottomed boiler, an assortment of muddy boots, both leather and rubber, rain gear, sheepskin vests and coats and a pile of neatly stacked wood.

It was a man's house, furnished for function. The ornamentation consisted of antler gun racks and a calendar depicting two stags with their horns locked.

Still, the windows looked out to the magnificent walls of the canyon, the house would certainly be easy to manage—and there was that wonderful pump!

It was twilight now as Joe entered the house after Domingo had taken the team down to the barn. He gave Dominika a reassuring smile as she moved around the kitchen, trying to locate things and decide what to cook.

"We'll just open cans tonight and have the beans from yesterday and the pies I bought in town," Joe said, tossing small pieces of wood into the stove in order to start the coals. "You'll have plenty of time later to make lots of good Basque food."

Joe had been in Nampa the week before, where he had hired the hands who would help with the rush of lambing and shearing. Some would herd until fall. "Then you didn't have to come to Boise at all!" Dominika exclaimed.

"Sure I did," Joe grinned, unabashed. "You were there."

VIII

IN ADDITION to Domingo and Joe, ten men sat down at the table that night. Joe introduced Dominika, saying that she would be keeping house for him, and named the herders. For last names a few used those of their home villages. They nodded shyly and quickly turned to the food. During the meal Dominika felt short, curious glances directed at her and she indulged in some of her own, trying to remember which name went with each man.

It would take time to identify them but the oldest man, with a tonsure of white hair and melancholy black eyes, was Beltran Zabala. The slender, green-eyed boy with smooth, olive skin was Kepa Artzaina, just arrived from his valley and probably homesick. He was the nephew of old Paco, one of the herders who would soon arrive with his band.

Andres Recalde, hunched and gnome-like, with wide, child-like eyes, she had met while preparing supper. He brought in jugs of milk from the goats and stacked the woodboxes even higher. Joe explained to her that Andres did such chores and helped out wherever he was needed. He had once been a very good herder but had begun to hallucinate a few years ago and could no longer be left alone with his band. He had no close family left in his homeland and so Joe had given him tasks at the ranch, which Andres accomplished with faithfulness and great satisfaction, especially the planting and caring for a big garden.

Dominika had heard of the hallucinating illness when she was at the hotel but it seemed eerie to be with someone who smiled and spoke while his mind was elsewhere. At least, he seemed to be perfectly content.

After supper Joe and Domingo, with their partners, had a spirited session of *muz*. A stocky man with straight black hair and bushy eyebrows, Vicente Isasti, played Basque tunes on his guitar. Beltran moved his lips as he read one of the papers that Joe had brought back from town. Young Kepa pulled out a harmonica and settled down close to Vicente.

The music cheered Dominika as she washed the dishes and got things ready to cook next morning. This house in an Idaho canyon was six thousand miles from Etchahoun, yet she felt more at home than she had since coming to America.

She did not mind the work. It was good to be needed. And most wonderful of all, she had at last found a refuge where she could have her child.

By the end of the week there was no one left at the house with Dominika except for Andres. The sheep had started lambing. Five thousand pregnant ewes would be having their lambs, twenty-four hours around the clock, for the next three weeks or so and Dominika had only to multiply her experience with Etchahoun's small flock to understand something of what would be going on. If there was time before the shearing, the lambs would have their tails docked for sanitary reasons and the males would be castrated.

Seventeen hard-working men consume a lot of bread. Dominika baked twelve loaves a day, making it in two batches, and sent it by Andres, who seemed to enjoy his glimpse of the hustling activity for he always returned wearing a wide smile.

In the time between kneading the dough and letting it rise or bake, Dominika reorganized the kitchen and the pantry that adjoined it and held bins of potatoes and onions, now depleted, barrels of flour, sugar, corn meal, lard, beans, lentils, garbanzos and rice, strings of garlic and red peppers, and shelves stacked full of canned fruit and vegetables, bags of nuts and a supply of delicacies like sardines and tuna. Part of a ham hung here and there was more smoked meat in the smokehouse, as well as fresh meat in the ice house.

Andres brought twenty or more eggs to the house each day, taking delight in counting them out before Dominika. He also promised that it would not be long before there would be succulent little new potatoes, onions and radishes. He often brought

Dominika wildflowers, which she placed in a glass on the dining table.

Once she was prepared to handle the cooking, she thoroughly cleaned the house and bunkhouse and washed the windows, thinking that it might be a long time before she had another opportunity. She caught up on the laundry, grateful that except for Andres and Joe the men used bedrolls instead of sheets, and she went over Joe's and Andres' garments, mending, patching and sewing on buttons as she sat by the stove at night until she grew sleepy.

After being constantly with people at the hotel, even sleeping in the same room with Mariana, Dominika welcomed this solitude. Throughout the strain of the last months and during that now dream-like period spent with Brant, she had not felt really herself but like a stranger caught in a snarl that Dominika Urdin of Etchahoun could scarcely believe possible.

Now as she worked in her new home and sometimes took an hour or so to walk up the canyon and enjoy the bright weather, the primroses and columbines along the creek, the flash of white on the black wings of magpies or the high soaring of a redtail hawk, she began to once more belong inside her body and her feelings. When she lit the candle by the blue bird on her dresser, she felt as if someone again heard her prayers.

The dogs usually accompanied her. Occasionally Kato would chase a rabbit, something he had not been allowed to do in his working days. When he returned, panting, Xagu cast him a scornful glance as though to say that male dogs never did grow up. Between them they had produced a fine line of dogs for Joe's herders and other fortunate sheepmen.

Easter came while the men were still hard at work. It was the holy day when Dominika would most of all have wished to kneel at the *sepulturie* and light the candles. It would soon be time for the Blessing of the Fields. Who had gone in her place? Esteban? Some woman whom he had married?

Overwhelmed by memories, Dominika tried to combat her loneliness by thinking of something that would give the men a special holiday treat. She would have liked to make crisp, golden Easter doughnuts, flavored with cloves and orange peel, but those had to be eaten as soon as they were fried. Instead she made sweet quince loaves and almond cookies and rode over to deliver them herself, riding the gentle mare that Andres saddled for her. Her divided skirt was snug through the waist but she could still wear it.

As she approached, the whole plain seemed to be filled with ewes who had had their lambs, ewes who were having them and ewes who did not want them. The pens were filled with mothers who wished to evade the knobby-legged little creatures who were trying to suckle. A few of them, Dominika noted, wore jackets cut from dead lambs in order to persuade a bereft ewe that an orphan was indeed her own. The men were scattered about, helping with difficult births, trying to get ewes to mother their newborn, who sometimes had to be shown how to suckle, and trying to find mothers for lambs whose mothers had died.

Joe had one hand and forearm thrust inside a ewe. This was no time to bother him or anyone. Dominika hastily put the cookies and quince loaves in the cookhouse, where several herders were gulping coffee and wolfing meat and bread, wished them a blessed Easter and was turning to go when Domingo hailed her.

"Could you take these little fellows home and feed them?" he asked, a lamb in his arms and another tagging behind. "Their mothers died and all the ewes with stillborns have other lambs now. These will die unless you want to coddle them."

"Of course I'll take them," Dominika said.

Domingo put the lambs in bags, which he hung pannier-fashion on each side of the saddle horn. Dominika led the horse home.

Andres helped her feed the hungry, gangling little animals by squirting goat's milk into their mouths with a syringe. They huddled together for warmth in a bed of old tarps behind the kitchen range. Dominika left her bedroom door open so she could hear if they bleated in the night.

They did of course, several times. After feeding them all they would take, Dominika built up the fire to keep the chill off the air and smiled sleepily as she thought this was a foretaste of motherhood.

In a few days the lambs were frolicking outdoors in the daytime, leaping and kicking with glee, running up a slope and trying to butt the other down it, rollicking up to Kato and Xagu, who growled at them in annoyance as if saying they had long ago served their time with stupid *ardiak*. Because they reminded her of dancers, Dominika called them Jautzi and Arin-arin, "Jump" and "Quick-quick."

They came to the porch and bleated pathetically when they were hungry and at night they were brought in to cuddle behind the stove but during the day they played with such abandon that it was hard to believe they would ever become placid and mournful-looking like their elders.

"Ones raised like this have more sense than most sheep," Andres said as they fed the lambs one day after the little animals had graduated to rubber-nippled bottles. "They usually become leaders." Though part of his mind was clouded, he hadn't forgotten anything the long, lonely years had taught him about sheep.

"I hope Joe will keep them for breeding," Dominika said, rubbing Jautzi between the ears. "I don't like to think of their being shipped off to make mutton."

Andres looked at her incredulously. "But, M'nika, that's why sheep are raised. For meat and their wool."

Dominika knew that and had certainly eaten her share of lamb and mutton. All the same, she hoped the carefree foundlings would die of old age up in the mountains.

It was the middle of May when Joe sent word by Andres that Dominika might enjoy riding over that evening. Shearing would be finished today. Tomorrow the herders would trail their bands to summer range. Tonight there would be a dance. Maybe she would like to join the celebration. It would be attended by wool-buyers and other people from Boise as well as neighboring ranches.

"Neighbors?" asked Dominika, frowning. She had not seen any signs of habitation except off in the distance as they had traveled up from Boise.

Andres laughed. "Pete Falxa has a place ten miles south of here. Then Gabe Esponda—he's a French Basque—he just bought part of an old cattle ranch on the other side of the canyon. Maybe fifteen miles as you go by road."

Shaking her head in bewilderment at the vastness of the

country, Dominika started to say that any ten miles of the Basque region would contain several villages, each acting as a hub for thirty or forty households.

But she didn't voice her thoughts because they might make Andres sad. He never talked about his home valley but sometimes she thought that he had, by some merciful trick of the mind, made this canyon into his old home.

"You're going to the dance, aren't you?" she asked.

He beamed. "Of course! The boss said for me to drive you over in the wagon. And to bring plenty of wine."

Andres did the chores early and Dominika fed Jautzi and Arin-arin. It seemed a time for Basque clothes so she put on her full red skirt, green bodice and white blouse and laced the ties of her rope-soled sandals around her ankles.

"Give me a dancing young man. . . ."

Unbidden, Brant's face rose before her, laughing as it had been until—until— She must not think about him. This was the last time in her life that she would go to a dance as a maiden. No one else would know it but the lacings of her bodice were at least two inches wider than the last time she had worn the garment. There was something implacably final about the slow march of days that was leading to the time when another life would emerge from hers, one for which she would be responsible for many, many years.

She had forfeited her right to wish for a dancing young man, but for this night she wanted to forget. She wanted to feel young again, and dance and laugh and sing.

Andres had wrapped a red sash around his waist and he wore his beret. As Dominika climbed into the wagon, Xagu and Kato watched her longingly, wagging their tails slowly.

"Can't we take them?" she asked Andres.

He looked surprised, then chuckled. "They deserve a party, too, and to see their children and grandchildren. Kato! Xagu!"

At his gesture the dogs jumped into the wagon. Both seemed to be grinning. When the wagon reached the lambing camp, it took only a word of permission from Andres to send them bounding off to reassert their dominance over the younger dogs, all of whom they had trained.

Since the Mexican shearing crew had many other ranches to work on their journey north, they had left in mid-afternoon, just as soon as they had clipped the last fleece from the last ewe. There must have been thirty or more people in the camp, though. Besides the men whom Dominika already knew, Andres pointed out the five regular herders. The heavy, sandy-haired man was Paolo Esponda and the thin, wedge-visaged, nervous-footed man with curly black hair was Pete Falxa. Both were bachelors and were accompanied by several of their hands. It was pathetic and yet amusing to see the eager way in which they glanced toward a buggy that was approaching.

Mariana and several other Basque girls employed at the hotels jumped down, giggling and pretending not to notice the stir their arrival had created. Joanes Irigay had brought them out. He had been a herder himself and still enjoyed a taste of his former life.

He greeted Dominika warmly and gave her Marta's good wishes before he went off to visit old acquaintances. Mariana and Dominika embraced and Mariana introduced her to the other young women before she squeezed her hands.

"Have you decided to marry Joe yet? Marta was sure you would wed him."

With some dismay, for seeing Mariana and Joanes had made her realize that she would not be able to keep her baby's birth a secret even on this isolated ranch, Dominika shook her head and turned the subject. "Aren't you marrying soon?"

The pretty, dark-haired girl shrugged. "Tony wants to get another band first. Always more sheep! He thinks I'll wait on him forever." Her rebellious gaze drifted to the men, many with red sashes about their waists and all with clean shirts. "If he puts me off again he may be in for a surprise!"

There was stew in a big kettle for anyone who was hungry, the bread that Dominika had sent over earlier in the day and skins of wine. Reunited, lambs and shorn ewes were tucked into their bands spread around the pens, guardianed by watchful dogs. As twilight thickened, lamps were lit in the cook house and kerosene lanterns were set in safe places outside.

Contests in wood-chopping and weight-lifting gave way to competition in the high kick and the high leap. Kepa Artzaina, slim and green-eyed, won both of the latter. He had been trained as an *ezpatadantzari* in his village, he said shyly, and Dominika felt a wave of sympathy for this boy who would soon be going alone into the mountains of this strange country.

Pete Falxa took a long, expert squirt from a wineskin and began to sing verses about his ranch and how nice it was—except that it lacked a mistress. Gabe Esponda puffed out his red cheeks and let everyone know that his ranch was much finer. It only lacked a woman. This year he had sent for his sweetheart, but God on High!—she had married and was a grandmother.

"An old man needs a nurse, not a wife," Pete Falxa sang and went to rhyme, declaring with a sweep of his hat to the women that if any of them cared to inspect his dwelling, they were welcome.

One of Falxa's men had an accordion. Vicente Isasti took out his guitar, Kepa produced his harmonica and Domingo experimented with his *alboka*.

"*Zazpi Jautziak!*" shouted Beltran, looking much younger than previously with a beret covering his bald skull.

The men formed a circle for the Seven Jumps, performed to affirm the common heritage of the seven provinces, three in France, four in Spain. The dancers began with two walking steps, a turning step toward the center and a shift of weight to the forward foot and back to the inside, followed by a sequence of turns and steps until the dancers shouted "Bat!" or "One" and leaped. The sequence was repeated to clapping from the onlookers until seven jumps had been made and called. Dominika was surprised to see that although Joe had a solid body, he was as agile and graceful as slender young Kepa.

Next the men formed a line. Joe was pushed into leading it. At the end of the line was Pete Falxa. Joe burst into an amazing display of leaps, turns and side kicks. Pete responded in challenge. Joe doubled and whirled and sprang, spinning to the shouts and wild clapping. Having outdone his challenger, he made an arch with Kepa and the other men passed under it. One man had already drunk so deeply that he was staggering. The bridge-makers made a shearing motion as though to cut off his head and he retired from the dance.

After a few more steps Joe whispered to four men who then

came to Dominika, sweeping off their berets, and escorted her to stand in front of Joe. She did not have to feign the timidity that she was supposed to show while Joe danced before her.

It was a bold, ardent dance of courting, the male showing his strength, speed, endurance and artistry to win his partner. Joe's face was set as though he were listening to music far away from that which the players were making. He was so assured, relentless and primitively dominant that Dominika suddenly felt that she did not know him at all.

A thrill of danger shot through her as he took her hand and led her into the dance. Kepa, Pete Falxa and Beltran claimed the other women by dancing before them and then the whole group burst into a spirited fandango, forming a circle, taking quick, intricate steps and making half turns and full turns to the sharp snapping of fingers.

Dominika loved to dance and this would be her last opportunity for a long time. She threw herself into the kicks and turns, knowing that she had never danced better. Joe smiled at her from across the circle, his earlier impassiveness lost in admiration. She knew that the rhythm he kept with his fingers was especially for her. From across the space between them, as they exactly mirrored each other's steps, she felt a sudden unwelcome but undeniable awareness of him as a man.

She could have laughed in self-mockery. He was one of her people. He could have been her dancing man though he was no longer young. But she had loved a stranger, a man whose wife was her friend. Or had been.

Her memory flinching from Lucie's last bitter words, Dominika danced on mechanically for a while. Then the music, clapping and shouting swept her into the spirit again. Head high, torso erect in the ancient stylized figure, she made a rapid turn and as she did, something moved within her. It took her a moment to recognize the first perceptible movement of her baby.

Afterward, she would always remember that it had quickened while she danced.

She didn't want to dance too long lest she harm the child who had just announced its presence. Joe must have had the same thought. After the fandango he made her sit down on one of the benches from the cook house and brought her a cup of wine before he accepted a challenge to see who could toss a heavy weight the farthest from between the legs.

Flushed and breathless, Dominika wrapped her shawl about her and sipped the wine. A hard voice behind her said, "So that's Joe Uhalde. He's certainly strutting his stuff for you!"

The cup almost dropped from her fingers. Her heart constricted and then raced as she slowly turned. Hands jammed into his sheepskin jacket, Brant stared down at her. In spite of, or perhaps because of, the angry hurt in his voice, a fiery current pulsed between them. He looked thinner and creases that she did not remember had formed around his mouth.

I still love him, Dominika thought despairingly. *I have come this far, lived all these days and still I love him.* The knowledge gave her an odd, fated sense of imprisonment but she managed to keep her tone steady.

"You don't like sheep." After weeks of speaking only Basque, the English words felt stiff and awkward on her tongue. "Why did you come?"

"You know why I came."

She could find nothing to say. Silence drew taut between them as a tortured vein. When he spoke, a note of desperate pleading sounded through his assumed reasonableness. "Nika, this is crazy. Slaving for a bunch of Basco herders, living in God knows what kind of a shack—"

"I'm Basco myself," she broke in fiercely. "Joe has a good house! And I can live in it without deceiving anyone."

Even in the flickering yellow lantern light, he showed pale around the lips. "God damn it, you can have your own house! Nika—"

"Why did you come?" she asked miserably. "Why, *why* did you?"

"When I asked for you at the hotel, Marta said that you'd gone to work for Uhalde." His blue eyes drilled into her. "Say, you aren't planning to marry him, are you?"

"Why shouldn't I?" she demanded wrathfully. "You were ready to see me married to one of your cowboys."

He colored and she saw his hands clench inside his jacket. "I don't want my kid calling some Basco 'Daddy.' "

"You should have thought of that before you put your baby in me."

His hands came out of his pockets curved as if he would strangle or shake her. "I should never have let you go," he said thickly. "I should have hog-tied you and hidden you out somewhere till you woke up to what was good for you."

She laughed in scorn. "It is good for me to have your bastard?"

He flinched. "Are you going to try to foist it off on Uhalde?"

She sprang up and would have slapped him except for the attention it would attract. "Go away!" she hissed under her breath. "Haven't you done enough? Go back to your wife and your whores and leave me alone!"

With their eyes locked, their wills battled. They each jumped as Joe Uhalde spoke from the side in groping English. "Mister, you welcome dance or drink or eat. But no talk this lady. She no like."

Brant, taller than Joe though not so broad in the shoulders, threw him a glance of contempt. "I talk this lady," he mimicked. "She used to work for me, Uhalde. We have unfinished business."

"She owe you money?" Joe persisted. "She do, I pay."

"It's none of your business," Brant grated. "Get that through your thick Basco head. I came out to see this woman and by God—"

Neatly, almost without a betraying preliminary motion, Joe felled him.

Brant lay stunned for a moment. Shaking his head woozily, he pulled himself to his knees, then to his feet and charged Joe in a vicious rush.

Joe side-stepped, put out his foot as Brant surged by and as he tripped, Joe clubbed the side of his palm down across the back of the cattleman's neck.

Only a few men had noticed the fight, so abrupt and short at the fringe of the gathering. To one of his herders Joe said, "When this one comes around, help him on his horse. And make sure he heads for town."

Taking Dominika by the arm, he marched her to the wagon at the far end of the camp and quickly hitched up the horses. As they started off, she saw Brant shake loose from several men who were trying to help him. Reaching his horse, he yanked his rifle out of the scabbard, readied it and aimed.

Dominika gasped as the weapon pointed at her and Joe. Then before the men surrounding Brant could knock the rifle askew, he shoved it back into the sheath. As he rode away, Dominika felt as if her bones had turned to water. It was an awful thing for a man like Brant to be humbled in that way but the pity that tainted her outrage changed to fear as she caught Joe's arm.

"Joe, you shouldn't have hit him! He may—"

"He'll stay away," Joe said grimly. "He's a fair man. I know from herders who've worked for him when there were no sheep jobs. He knows he shouldn't have come here tonight."

"I couldn't bear to make you trouble!"

He laughed but there was a husky sound to his voice. "M'nika, seeing you causes me more trouble than a dozen men like that." In a deliberately expressionless voice, he asked, "Rawlins, he's your baby's father?"

"Yes," whispered Dominika, feeling that she would die of shame.

Joe knew, for she had told him, how kind Lucie had been to her. What could he think of a woman who had betrayed her crippled mistress?

Silence stretched between them but when he spoke, there was no condemnation in his tone. "You still love him, M'nika?"

"I—don't know. I hated him tonight but—"

Joe sighed. "Beneath hate there can be love. He loves you."

It was like a sentencing. She trembled. Just when the memory of him was no longer an aching throb, just when she was beginning to feel that she had left the past behind and could make a good life for her baby! She fought against the sobs that racked her but a muffled sound escaped.

Joe stopped the horses and took her in his arms. Smoothing her hair, he let her cry till some of the unbearable weight lifted from her. Then, drying her face with a big handkerchief, he said as though advising her to come in out of a storm, "You had better marry me. That man, he won't give you up as long as you're single. And your baby needs a father, M'nika. You and I get married, no one's going to say much. Otherwise—'' He let her mind finish the ugly thought. ''You don't want that.''

No. She didn't want that. And she lacked the strength to go elsewhere and start over with a pretense of widowhood. She did not want to leave Joe. She didn't see how she could love him when she felt as she did about Brant but she trusted him, liked him and craved the strong, sure protection with which he enfolded her.

''Joe, it wouldn't be fair.''

''You let me worry about that.''

''But—''

Reading her thoughts, he said, ''You don't have to sleep with me until you want to. Someday you will.'' He stated this, not boastfully, but as a matter of fact. Then he kissed her lightly. ''The thing we have to do now is give your baby a name. What's wrong with Uhalde?''

Everything he had said was true. He was old enough to know what he was doing. She let herself relax and gave in to the comforting clasp of his arms as she laughed shakily and raised her hand to touch his face.

''Uhalde is a beautiful name.''

He kissed her, carefully, gently at first and then with controlled passion that sent wakening flame through her. She might not love him in the wild, tormenting way she had loved Brant but there could be an ardor between them, a deepening bond that would ensure that Joe was not cheated in his marriage.

''As soon as the bands are off, so will we be,'' he said. He started up the horses but kept her hand nestled in his and though the night wind had risen, she wasn't cold at all.

IX

IT HAD been a good lambing. Of five thousand ewes, only a small number had died. Stillborn lambs had been replaced with one of a set of twins or an orphan. Close to ten thousand ewes and lambs were now split into five bands trailing toward summer range. Domingo and Kepa had charge of a band of three thousand yearlings and dry ewes. Dominika was glad they would be together and that Kepa would not spend his first herding summer alone.

Rams were let in with ewes only at breeding time. The rest of the year they were herded in a separate band made up of the rams of all the sheepmen in the area. This year one of Pete Falxa's herders had them.

The extra hands departed to look for other work as soon as they had helped drive the wagons loaded high with three-hundred-pound wool sacks into town and back. Joe had sold his clip to a Boise buyer on the night of the dance. He and Dominika took the last of the wool into town, along with the paid-off herders.

Joe treated the men to a big meal and Picon punch at the Irigays' hotel, telling the delighted Marta that he and Dominika would be married that day and spend the night at the hotel. Mariana squealed and gave Dominika a hug.

"Why didn't you tell me at the dance?"

"That's when we decided," Dominika explained.

Joe knew the priest. Dominika went to confession that afternoon and as the priest absolved her, she vowed to be a good wife and to never let Joe be sorry that he had married her. Marta and Joanes attended the wedding and afterward hosted a celebration attended by the many people who knew Joe and wanted to wish him and his bride joy. Dominika wished that May Hutton could have been there. It was late before the dancing was over.

Drowsy with wine, it seemed only natural to rest in Joe's arms when he climbed into bed beside her. He did not kiss her mouth but his lips gently touched her eyelids. Soon the tension in his body roused her to consciousness that this was his wedding night. No matter what he had promised, he deserved more than this.

"Joe—" she whispered and caressed the corded back of his neck, heavier and wider than Brant's.

No! She must not think such things. She pressed closer to her husband, wishing that she had not put on a nightgown.

His warm lips brushed hers swiftly and his fingers lightly touched her breasts before he made a muffled sound and got out of bed.

"I'll wait, M'nika. Until I can have all of you." He lay down on the other bed.

In spite of the wine, it was a long time before she slept.

She wanted to use her own money next day to buy things she needed for the baby but Joe handed her a roll of bills and said in a tone that allowed no argument, "You're my wife. I can pay for anything you want for our baby."

While he bought supplies and attended to his business, Dominika bought flannel, cambric and nainsook with which to make the infant's clothes, diapers and sheets. The clerk tried to sell her some rubber diapers but she shuddered at the thought of these cold, stiff wrappings holding a wet or soiled cloth against a baby's delicate skin. She did buy rubber sheeting, though, to protect the pad she would use for a mattress in one of the willow laundry baskets.

Putting away the memory of the Etchahoun cradle, in whose downy softness generations of babies had been rocked, she selected knitting wool dyed pretty shades of pink, blue and yellow. Then she chose some gray wool that she would use in making Joe's socks. She would knit most of the baby's things but she did succumb to buying a flower-embroidered, eiderdown sacque with booties and bonnet to match.

Joe had told her to buy whatever she would like to have for

the house, too. She bought the heaviest linen she could find and many skeins of blue embroidery floss with which to make a bedspread like the ones at home, turkey-red damask to dress the table for special occasions and an oak-leaf-patterned oilcloth for everyday use.

Both frightened and intoxicated by spending more money within a few hours than she ever had in all her life, Dominika resisted a beautiful double-globed lamp, rugs and pretty dishes. When she knew Joe better, perhaps she could persuade him to let her use some of her savings on luxuries. Every towel at the ranch was full of holes, though, and so she bought a good supply of Turkish toweling to cut and hem.

After one of Marta's substantial meals, Dominika and Joe told the Irigays good-bye, collected their purchases and started home. *My husband*, Dominika thought, stealing a glance at Joe as the wagon rumbled along. *My husband*.

She closed her mind to a stabbing image of Brant's furious, anguished eyes. He had to make his own life now, as she must make hers. The past was finished.

The evening sun flamed against the eastern wall of the canyon as they rolled toward the house. Jautzi and Arin-arin frisked out to meet them, getting in the way of Kato and Xagu. Andres hurried to help unload.

"I've got good sourdough bread baked in the Dutch oven," he boasted. "Garbanzos with *chorizos*, stewed hen and new potatoes with little peas. Welcome home, boss and andrea!"

Dominika gasped. Joe helped her down and grinned. "That's right," he said softly. "Welcome to your house, *etcheko andrea*."

Jautzi and Arin-arin butted softly against her legs. The dogs thrust their heads up to be petted. Dominika caressed them all and did not stop the flow of her tears.

This was her house now. She would make it a home.

Joe helped Vicente Isasti with the camp-tending. Each of six bands had to be visited every week and as they ranged into the foothills and on to higher ground as the summer progressed, Joe and Vicente were often gone overnight with their pack mules. Since the camp-tender baked the herders' bread now, that chore was ended but Dominika tried to make something special, cookies or nut cakes or pies, to be sent each week to the men.

Andres' garden yielded abundantly. She blanched and dried green beans, peas and carrots and preserved tomatoes and sliced cabbage in brine. She gathered enough huckleberries to make several dozen jars of jellies and preserves and by fall there should be enough potatoes, onions and turnips to fill the pantry bins and garlic and peppers to hang in the kitchen.

She had a lot of time in which to sew and that was fortunate for she had to add panels to her skirts and increase the waistbands as well as salvage the ranch's worn sheets by cutting out the frayed parts and reseaming the strongest portions to form a new sheet. This task, and hemming the towels, was made immeasurably lighter by the sewing machine that Joe had bought for her without her knowledge.

At first she had been afraid of getting her fingers caught under the rapidly stitching needle but after a little experience she thought it a wonderful invention and blessed it as she quickly hemmed three dozen flannel diapers. She also used it for seaming the small gowns and wrappers, though she did the finishing by hand as she sat in the comfortable rocker, another gift from Joe, while Andres played wistful tunes on his harmonica or told her stories about his years with the sheep.

When Joe was there, Andres would sit with them for a while after supper, often whittling, the shavings going into the woodbox, but he went off to the bunkhouse as soon as Joe had given them all his news about the herders and the sheep.

Next day Dominika would help Vicente and Joe fill the herders' lists as faithfully as possible and then wave them off before resuming her own work. Since Vicente and Joe were often home at unexpected times, she always had a heartier meal prepared at night than she and Andres needed. If Joe was home, Vicente would have a glass of brandy before retiring. Otherwise he went straight from the table.

Dominika did not know if her condition embarrassed him or whether he was only shy of women. Her belly seemed enormous to her at the start of her seventh month. She felt heavy and lumbering, found it difficult to bend over and wondered how Joe could still gaze at her admiringly and want to hold her at night.

He had never made love to her beyond kissing and caresses and now she was certain that he would not till after the baby came. On a few occasions, waking in the night to feel him close to her, she had been tempted to arouse him so that he might take her before he knew what was happening but something had deterred her. Perhaps, though he had never said so, he did not want to enter her while she carried another man's child.

On the anniversary of her mother's death she lit four candles, prayed with the acorn rosary and read from the aged prayerbook's parchment pages before she took a new loaf of bread and crumbled it for the birds. She had sent money for a proper ceremony to mark the year of mourning but she felt it keenly not to be there herself to kneel at the *sepulturie*.

She kept the blue-bird fragment on the dresser by the candle that she would continue to light on Sundays, not only for Maria now but for the memory of Etchahoun.

Joe had never questioned her about the shard but she felt that it should not be lying about where anyone else could see it. She had searched along the canyon for a cave where she might put it but found only a few shallow grottoes or hollows too small to enter and was about to conclude that there was no suitable place for it.

She had gathered all the ripe berries along the canyon. One afternoon she wandered into the adjoining valley and followed a sheep trail as it wound around the mountain. Verdure sprang up in places where there must be a seep or a spring. Continuing on the trail, she found serviceberries and followed them where they grew along the rugged rock cliff.

Reaching for some especially choice fruit, she tugged at the bush within her reach, revealing a cavern. Putting down her pail, she went back a few steps and found that it was possible to enter the hollow by parting the shrubs and slipping between them and the rock.

She had to stoop a little but the mouth led into a cavity perhaps ten feet wide that narrowed as it led farther back into the cliff.

It was not like the Summer Cave. There was no mother and child, no red-brown handprints speaking from beyond the grave. But it held between its walls the primeval spell of all hidden places deep within the earth, its shadows whispering of the ancient womb which had nourished so many living creatures and, as their brief shapes crumbled, received them again.

It was for Dominika both more and less, providing her with a shrine in this strange country. Although the long walk had tired her, she went straight home and returned that very day with the shard, fitting it into a small niche just inside the entrance. In the unlikely case that anyone duplicated her discovery, the bird would still escape notice.

The little cave was too far away to visit daily and her increasing heaviness made the ascent taxing, even somewhat hazardous as at one side of the bushes there was a steep drop of fifty feet to the jagged rocks below.

Still, the bird once more rested in the earth. She carried the refuge in her consciousness as leaves began to turn and patches of yellow aspen began to show amid the firs and pines of the higher mountains. Joe began to worry.

"Maybe we'd better get you into town," he suggested. "There would be a doctor close and you could stay at the hotel."

Dominika wavered for a moment. She, too, had been wondering if there would be time to get the doctor out from town or send for Marta, who often acted as a midwife. Thinking aloud, she said, "I don't want to be away from the ranch for two months. Jouncing over that road if we wait till next month would probably send me into labor. They say that first babies usually take a long time coming." She laughed, trying to ease his concern. "We can send for Marta the first time I have a pain."

"But that should be about when we're taking sheep to market," Joe fretted. "We ought to hire a girl or woman to come out and stay with you. She could help with the work till you get your strength back."

It was hard to find good female help for remote ranches. Dominika did not want the other kind. "Andres can help me," she said. "And he'll be here while you're sorting sheep. I can send him for Marta when it's time."

"I want you to have the doctor. Just in case something goes a little different."

"I would rather have Marta." In truth, she wanted her mother now.

"We'll get both," Joe said firmly. "What are we going to call him?"

"Him?" Dominika bridled.

He laughed disarmingly. "Well, if we have a girl, you probably want to name her for your mother. But a boy—"

For as long as she lived, would she feel that heartbeat of raw, aching pain whenever she thought of Brant? Meeting Joe's warm, hazel eyes, she said, "I would like to call him after you."

Joe blushed with pleasure. "I'd like that. But if you don't mind, maybe we could call his first name after my father and use Joe for the second?"

Dominika lifted a questioning eyebrow. "What was your father's name? Eulalie? Something awful?"

"It was Faustino," Joe said with dignity.

"We'll wind up by calling him Foss."

Joe shrugged. "That's no worse than most nicknames."

"All right," Dominika nodded. "But if we have a girl, she will be Maria May."

"For Mrs. Hutton?" Joe asked in pleased surprise.

"Who else?" smiled Dominika.

Early in October the bands trailed down from the high country. The ewes had to be "mouthed." Those with severely worn-down teeth would go to market along with two-year-olds that were not being saved for breeding. All animals not being sold had to be dipped to prevent scabies, just as they had been dipped at lambing time.

In November old ewes would be put with coarse-wooled Shropshires to produce lambs for mutton. Young ewes would receive the attentions of fine-wooled merinos or Rambouillets.

"Do they fight much?" Dominika asked.

"Not as much as you might think, although once in a while there'll be one who'd rather fight than—well, anything. They wind up real fast as mutton."

"How can you tell if a ewe—" Flustered, Dominika broke off. Farm-reared, she had grown up with a knowledge of breeding but had never discussed it with a man.

"Some owners use a 'bucking' harness that holds chalk and rubs off on a ewe. I don't bother with it. The ram knows." Joe's eyes crinkled with laughter. "And the ewes either all look beautiful to him or he doesn't give a snort."

Five months later, after being kept on the lower winter range, ewes would drop their lambs and the whole cycle would begin again. *By then,* thought Dominika as the baby stirred insistently, *there will be a new little person with us, Faustino Joseba or Marie May.* The infant who grew now within her darkness would laugh with joy and reach for the rays of the sun.

Joe came home at nighttime now but was gone from before daylight until after dark. He would not let her bake for the herders, saying that Vicente could do that while he was cooking. He took Jautzi and Arin-arin down to their kindred, whom they examined with disdainful wonder before they made a dash for the house. It took several trips before they finally began to lord it over their ewe-raised contemporaries. They had no fear of dogs and had to be nipped a few times before they concluded that these bossy, relentless beasts were very different from Kato and Xagu, who had only wanted to be let alone.

A week passed, ten days, and Dominika began to hope that the baby wouldn't come till Joe had finished marketing. Andres stayed so close by that she was sure Joe had instructed him to. She was big and unwieldy now and she deplored the slowness of her steps. She felt as if she always needed to urinate and the child seemed to have even compressed her lungs so that her breathing was labored. It was difficult to get out of bed, rise from a chair or go down the steps. Her temper frayed easily and she sometimes cried from sheer vexation at her bulk and nervousness.

Somewhere she had heard that women had easier birthing if they kept active and walked. She did, walking each day though she no longer trusted herself to go up the canyon. One afternoon she put on an old jacket of Joe's and was going down the steps when her ankle turned.

She called out as she fell, instinctively twisting sideways and throwing out her hands to protect her belly. Waves of shock vibrated through her body. Her palms were numb and as she slowly raised herself up, she saw that they were bleeding from tiny grains of rock that had ground into them.

"Are you all right, andrea?" The old herder's face was pale as he helped her to her feet. "Oh, your hands!"

"Only skinned." Dominika tried not to wince at the bright, shallow sting. "I'll wash the dirt out and—"

Suddenly a cruel hand gripped her entrails, squeezing and wrenching. She could not check a cry. Andres gaped at her, terrified.

The twisting came again. Dominika bent double with it. Panting, she gasped, "Go for Joe! There's not time for Marta."

"But—but I better help you to bed, andrea."

"I'll get there," she said grimly. Sweat broke out on her as those brutal fingers clutched again. "You just hurry for Joe!"

She needed him *now*. She was afraid, afraid that something had gone wrong. Andres ran for the corral. She set her teeth and crawled up the steps as the malevolent grip tore at her.

Somehow she managed to wash her hands, put water to boil and spread a rubber sheet on the bed. She washed her sewing scissors in soapy water. By then the spasms shook her as a storm shakes a young tree.

Was she going to die? She gripped the rail of the bed. Fiery raw pain engulfed her. At the back of her mind she saw the women's cave. The hands seemed to move toward her. Then everything was blackness, vaguely pierced by the sound of a woman's screams.

"Push!" Joe ordered. He was somewhere off in a swirling mist but she could grasp his hands. "Push!"

She tried to obey. She had a hideous sense of being split in two, of being broken. Then there was a burning hollow within her, as if that hand had ripped out her entrails. Gasping, she braced for the next assault.

Instead, there was a wavering cry. She opened astounded eyes to see Joe holding a small creature which he swaddled in a soft blanket and placed in her arms.

"Here's Faustino."

In spite of the fall that had brought on her labor, Dominika quickly regained her strength. It had been time for the baby and he seemed bright and perfect in every way. He had fine soft black hair and creamy skin from the start, never being red like most babies. The first unnameable, vague color of his eyes changed to blue but if this gave Joe a pang, he did not show it. He was enthralled with the infant from the first, marveling at the tiny fingernails and the grip of the little hands.

Foss didn't sleep for long at a time and by evening he was often crying with what seemed to be colic. Nursing only seemed to make him worse until Joe found a way to soothe him into a nap before his feeding. Leaning back in a chair, Joe would croon lullabies or old songs as Foss lay on his chest.

Apparently the warmth of the man's body and the rhythm of his breathing combined with the sounds coming from his chest and throat to lull the excitable baby into slumber. He looked comical, his little rear hoisted slightly aloft, as he perched there on Joe's massive chest. It was a good place to be, next to that heart. After such a nap Foss would nurse with appetite but without the frantic gluttony that could send him into screaming cramps.

Joe had insisted on sending for the doctor, who had only confirmed that Dominika was fine. She had torn with the exit of the baby's head and would have to heal, but that often happened. Joe would not leave her for the first few days after the baby's arrival and then went only for a few hours at a time to supervise the division of the bands and the breeding.

"We have to take the baby down and get him baptized," he said, looking past Foss's elevated rump to Dominika.

Dominika laughed. "Are you afraid that a witch will steal him?" Witches seemed very far away from this country, along with Mari and Basa Jaun, though she sometimes wondered whether Mari's sheep hadn't led her to the cavern where the blue bird waited.

Joe grinned. "I notice that you keep garlic and salt tied to his basket. And I don't think you burn candles at night just to find your way to him when a lamp would do as well."

He had her there. Even though the old customs did not seem fitting in Idaho, she would have been nervous had she not followed them as best she could. And there was so much she missed!

322

Poignantly, keenly, she longed for her mother. Often she could not keep from weeping when she realized afresh that Maria would never hold this child, never love and praise him. And there was the infant's meal that Elena Bigatzi and the other neighborhood women would have hostessed, the time when the mistress of each household centering around the village would come to see the baby, admire him and bring gifts. Dominika despised tears but though she was enraptured with the baby and delighted at Joe's love for him, she seemed to cry a lot.

Tears brimmed in her eyes now. "What's the matter?" Joe asked anxiously.

She blew her nose and tried to smile. "I—I was just thinking of the *aur bazkaria.*"

"Yes, that's a nice thing," Joe agreed. "And when I was a boy, we all hurried down to the church when there was a baptism and pounced on the treats the godparents tossed among us. If they were stingy, we used to yell, 'May a rat eat the baby!' or 'It's a bastard!' "

Dominika shrank against the pillows. Joe muttered exasperated words of self-chastisement and jumped up quickly, although he took care not to startle Foss. Folding Dominika in his arms beside the child, he growled softly, "There's no bastard in this house, my sweetheart. Only our son, Faustino Joseba Uhalde."

In all the world, there could not be another man like this one.

"I love you, Joe."

He stroked her hair and said, "I know you do." He did not add what they both knew, that she could never feel for another man the reckless passion she'd had for Brant, whose blue eyes would always look out at her from Foss's small face.

Had they been in Vizcaya, one of Joe's parents would probably have been a godparent and one of Dominika's the other. Since Joe's parents, too, were dead, it was simple to ask Domingo and Marta to act as godparents. In her heart, though, Dominika always considered May Arkwright Hutton the godmother.

323

Marta and Domingo must have known that Joe could not possibly have sired little Foss but they asked no questions. They hosted a festive meal at the hotel and the next morning Joe and Dominika drove home with their son.

X

THE SHEEP were divided into five bands for the winter. Paco, the oldest herder, had drawn seven years of accumulated wages and gone back to his valley to buy a tavern. He might even find a wife, for the streaming out of Basque men to America and other countries left many women without hope of marriage unless they were willing to follow the men. Domingo took Paco's band and now young Kepa was alone except for his dogs.

"I found him dancing the other day," Joe said, returning from one of his camp-tending visits. Through the winter he could have left this chore wholly to Vicente except when weather made traveling difficult but he believed the herders needed to know that he wanted to see for himself how the sheep were pasturing and make sure that all was well with the men. "He said he wanted to stay in practice so he wouldn't make a fool of himself when he goes home. I reminded him that there's good dancing wherever there are Basques." He paused for a moment, frowning. "I think I'll give Kepa's band to Vicente for a few weeks at Christmas while I camp-tend."

"Were you lonesome when you first herded?"

"I thought I'd die," Joe said honestly. "I was up in the California sierra within a week after reaching New York. I used to build a big fire every night to fight the darkness and scare off bears and all the other wild things I was sure were just waiting to gobble me or the sheep. The camp-tender came once a week but he didn't speak Basque and he just brought my things and left except for when he moved camp." Joe sighed, looking back twenty years. "A friend who had come over from my village cut his throat in a Basque hotel that year and I think I might have, too, if it hadn't been for my dog. She was Xagu's grandmother. I bought her when I left that boss and moved into Nevada.''

''Vicente seems like a good camp-tender.''

Joe nodded. ''He knows what it's like. He kids with the men, catches them up on any news he's heard, maybe tells some jokes about women. When he thinks a herder's getting 'sheeped,' I try to get that man into town for a few weeks.''

Foss yawned and stretched. Joe supported his reared-back head and before he could yell his hunger, nestled him beside Dominika.

By Christmas Foss was sleeping through the night and Dominika was doing all the housework again. She was also baking for the herders now that Vicente had taken Kepa's band while the boy spent two weeks at the Irigays'. During his stretch as sole camp-tender, Joe usually came home at night but was gone nearly every day. Dominika missed him but she was glad that Kepa was having his holidays in town, where there would be dancing and fun and plenty of Basques, even some pretty girls.

Foss was too young to understand, of course, but she often talked to him and to lift her spirits during the lonely days, she even told him stories that her grandmother and mother had told her, rocking him gently while Andres whittled.

''This was in the time when all animals and all things spoke,'' she began and told the story of the princess who was dying because she could not smile. Her father was desperate and offered half his kingdom to anyone who could save her but nothing helped until a band of gypsies appeared and danced beneath the princess' window. Her lips curved in a faint smile.

'' 'Dance on!' the king begged.

''And the gypsies danced. Three days, three nights. Their shoes fell off and their feet bled. One by one they had to stop, and the princess was dying.

'' 'Dance!' begged the king to the one remaining dancer, a handsome young man who was faint with hunger and weariness. 'You shall have half my kingdom!'

''The dancer's eyes flashed. 'I dance for your daughter's hand,' he cried and the king dared not say no.

"And then the princess smiled. She ran down to bring the gypsy a glass of her father's wine. They were married. And since they lived well, they died well."

"A pretty story," complimented Andres but when she told Foss about the first Christmas and how to this day, all sheep face to the east on Christmas Eve, the old herder snorted.

"Andrea, don't spin the babe such cobwebs! Sheep face east just about every evening."

He stumped out to do the chores. Foss was sleeping, dark lashes fringing his flawless cheeks. Dominika, amused rather than rebuked by Andres' realism, put the baby in his basket, which she kept near the stove in the daytime. She stirred the thick, good-smelling stew that simmered at the back of the range and was working out the bread for its last raising when there was an abrupt knock on the door.

Puzzled, for they never had callers, she washed her hands and had started for the door when it opened. Brant stood there.

Dominika froze. Blood and breath seemed to drain from her. "You—you shouldn't be here!"

Blue eyes, hauntingly like Foss's, searched hers. He looked gaunt and deep lines seamed his face. "I had to see you. I heard in town that your Basco was camp-tending so I figured this might be a good time."

She shook her head. The sight of him caused such pain that she could scarely speak, though mixed with it was a bittersweet rush of longing. "There's no good time. You're married. And now so am I."

He did not answer but strode past her to stare down at Foss.

In spite of herself she wanted to hear him say that the baby was beautiful, a child to be proud of. "I guess all babies look alike for a while." Turning, he caught her hands. "This is all wrong, Nika. We belong together."

She laughed in speechless bitterness. He reddened to the edges of his tawny hair but doggedly went on, "I know you can't stay around Boise. Not now. But look, we can go to Denver, buy a house, be Mr. and Mrs. Somebody-or-other. I won't be there often but it will be perfectly respectable for you and the boy—"

"And a lie."

327

He looked at her with such suffering that she pitied him beneath her anger. "Nika, I've offered to do everything I can."

"I know. I don't blame you for what has happened." She swallowed and moved toward the door, feeling as if her bones had turned dangerously brittle. "But I will blame you if you don't leave me alone now."

He approached almost as if he were stalking her. As she reached for the doorknob, he caught her against him, forced back her head and found her mouth. For a moment she fought, struggling and arching back. He crushed her arms to her sides and kissed her until she moaned. Her knees could barely support her when he stepped away.

Opening the door, he said, "You still love me." A chill wind blew past him, piercing her. His eyes were as wintry as the sky. "I'll stay away if that's what you want. But if you ever change your mind, get in touch with my lawyer."

The door slammed with the extra force of wind behind it. The baby cried in alarm and Dominika went to him as if in a dream.

On the Day of the Three Kings, Dominika put warm wool socks by Andres' plate, socks and a red muffler beside Joe's. Joe had fleece-lined boots for her, a beautiful red challis dress and emerald earrings.

"Gold and green like your eyes," he laughed, smiling with pride as she put them on.

Andres had carved a wooden rattle for Foss and Joe had bought him an ingenious swing and jumper which straightened into a bed should the baby go to sleep. Foss was too young to sit in it without pillows but he laughed gleefully at the gentle swinging and the fuzzy twin lambs that Dominika had knit for him, one black, the other white.

They sat snugly around the stove that night, sipping spiced chocolate and munching roasted chestnuts, enjoying the marzipan and special holiday nut cups like those Joe had already taken to each herder. Dominika rocked the baby. As they sang the songs of their home country, she realized with a pang that home, to Foss, would never be Etchahoun.

Would she herself ever go back, ever redeem the farm?

Etchahoun was where she dreamed but she had married in this country and her son was of it. If men reared in Basque valleys found it difficult to return, how could a boy born in this vast wilderness possibly live enclosed by neighbors and small, stone-walled fields?

On that Epiphany she accepted in quiet sorrow the certainty that her American sons would never be heirs of Etchahoun. But a daughter—a daughter might be different. For a daughter could be given the secret of the cave, the mystery handed down from before there was a house. A daughter could take the blue bird back. She must have a daughter.

Kepa did not return when his holiday was up. Joe shrugged and said, "Sometimes it happens. I've had a couple of men go to town to get a tooth pulled or see the doctor and never stop until they were back in the old country. But perhaps he just got drunk and will be along when he sobers up."

"He didn't seem much of a tippler," Dominika said.

"They're the ones whisky hits the hardest," Joe sighed. "If he's not back in a couple of days, I'll have to leave Andres with a band while I go in and find Kepa or hire someone else."

He did not have to do that. Next day one of the temporary herders he had hired for lambing turned up to bring the news and to see if Joe would like him to take over a band.

Kepa, olive-skinned, green-eyed Kepa, had cut his throat from one side to the other. He had danced brilliantly that last evening, balanced on a wineglass and leaped higher than any-one had ever seen the Horse spring in his final triumph over death and gelding. He had left a note, asking that his wages be sent to his mother. Beside the note Marta had found a letter from a girl back in his village. She was not waiting. She was marrying the heir of a wealthy farm.

Dominika had cried out at the horror of it. For weeks the im-age of such a sorrowful death haunted her and as she prayed for Kepa's soul, she prayed for the men with the sheep and for all people who were alone. She did not really believe that it was the letter from the far Pyrenees that had made Kepa despair. No. She thought it was facing the endless stretching of lonely days into lonely weeks beneath the boundless sky.

So gripped by the sadness of it one night that she could not sleep, she huddled close to Joe, slipping an arm over his steadily rising and falling chest. Sleepily he turned, drawing her close. He kissed her. She let it last. He caressed her shoulder. She stroked the back of his neck. His warm, strong fingers brushed her breasts, traveled along her flanks.

She had turned to him for comfort. It was that and more that grew between them. Her senses, long dulled by thwarted love for Brant, pregnancy and its aftermath, aroused now and responded eagerly to Joe's ardor.

He was tender—but he was a man. When at last he took her, she did not fly apart in the raptures that she had known with Brant but she felt good, happy that the barrier was down. She was really Joe's wife now. And they might have a daughter.

When Joe went to town to hire extra herders, he brought back six young apple trees that he planted where Dominika could see them from the main room. They were her birthday present and nothing could have pleased her more.

She had planned to cook at the lambing camp this spring but Joe sternly said, "With Foss starting to crawl? Listen, dear, you'll do very well to get the bread baked!"

And he was right. Foss never napped for more than an hour and would not stay long in his jumper-swing. His diapers and sheets had doubled the laundry. She did manage the baking but at the end of lambing and shearing, she was as exhausted as Joe. Even so, she went to the dance held on the last night and Domingo held Foss and entertained his godson while Dominika danced.

At about the time the sheep came down from summer pasture, Dominika knew she was with child again. She was glad. In spite of her closeness and contentment with Joe, Foss's eyes could still send a twinge of longing regret through her before she forced away the memory of his father. She hoped for a daughter but in any case, a child of their own would make her marriage to Joe completely binding and final.

Foss was old enough to enjoy his toys from Three Kings' Day—the rocker with a seat between two rocking-horse panels, a gingham dog sewed by Dominika, beautifully carved blocks that

Domingo had made for his godson while up on the summer range and a pair of belligerent rams shaped by Andres' deft knife.

"Ardi!" Foss crowed, banging them together. Joe laughed but sobered as he glanced at Dominika.

"M'nika, you'd better start speaking English with the boy. Better he learn young. Me, I'll never speak well. The first time I tried to buy a rooster, I couldn't think of the word and finally I had to say I wanted a 'bull-hen.' " They all laughed but Joe said earnestly. "Foss will go to school with Americans. English will help him."

There was no arguing that and so during the day Dominika made it a point to speak often in English and teach Foss the English names of everything. In a way it seemed to be returning a part of him to his natural father and she did not like that but it was the only sensible thing to do. Foss, after all, *was* an American.

That winter she and Joe studied the questions for citizenship and in the spring they took the tests and became citizens. Dominika had a sense of unreality as she swore allegiance to the United States. She had never felt herself a citizen of Spain but always, even if she never saw them again, she would belong to the Summer Cave and Etchahoun. Such things had nothing to do with governments. The deepest allegiances streamed in the blood.

It began to seem that she was destined never to cook for the men during lambing and shearing. She had grown big much faster this time and was by April already heavy on her feet. In June, a month before the baby was due, the head seemed to drop, pressing against her pelvic bones so that she was in great discomfort.

Joe had been arguing that she needed help for the next few months. When he saw how painfully she moved, he went to town and "borrowed" the young woman who had replaced Mariana, now married to Pete Falxa after having grown tired of the procrastinating Tony.

"Marta said it was fine as long as Panchika is back in time to get ready for the wintering herders," Joe assured Dominika when she remonstrated with him. "After all, she wants to be sure you have time to take care of her godson."

Panchika was such a shy, doe-eyed girl that it was hard to imagine how she had ever summoned up the courage to leave her village until one day she confided in Dominika that the man she loved and expected to marry had instead wed the heiress of a substantial farm.

"I wanted to forget him," Panchika said, tears in her eyes, "but being so far from home only makes it worse."

"It will get better," Dominika promised. "Stay busy, laugh all you can and keep your eyes open for the man who's bound to come along. If your sweetheart behaved like that, he wasn't worth having."

"Yes, but—andrea, you don't understand! You have your good husband and baby and—"

"I didn't always have them," Dominika said. Although she was only three years older than Panchika, she felt as if she belonged to another generation. She concealed a smile. "Isn't it strange that Gabe Esponda's brother, Paolo, finds so many errands to bring him here?"

Panchika blushed. "He is from my village. I think he's homesick."

Dominika laughed and gave the younger woman a hug. "I think that he wants a home. With you in it."

From the way that Panchika's blushes deepened, Dominika thought it would be wise to warn Marta that she had better start looking for another maid.

At this birthing, in late July of 1905, there was time to send for both Marta and the doctor. The pains began one evening and it was noon of the next day before Marta put a squalling, red, boy-child into Dominika's arms. Hazy with her ordeal, she kept calling the baby "her" and "she." It was several days before she acknowledged fully that the child was a boy, not the longed-for daughter who would carry on the magic of the cave.

She adored small Vachel, plumply dimpled, soft brown of eyes and hair. Her delight poured out in a wholehearted fashion, untainted by the guilt and memories of Brant she often felt when she encountered Foss's clear blue eyes. Mariana Falxa was godmother and Andres was exalted into unspeakable pride and joy when he was asked to stand godfather.

Panchika stayed for a month after the christening and returned to the hotel to celebrate her wedding to Paolo Esponda. Dominika and Joe attended the service and dance. With a new baby in her arms and Foss on Joe's knee, neither joined in the dancing but clapped from the side lines. Dominika felt very married and almost middle-aged.

She said something of this to Joe on the way home next day. He chuckled incredulously. "Why, M'nika! You were the prettiest woman there!"

"Joe, I wasn't! My waist—"

"Your waist is just fine." He leaned over to kiss her. "Maybe I shouldn't tell you this and make you so proud you'll think yourself too beautiful for an old man but the children have made you—" He groped for words, found none and made an eloquent curving gesture with his hand.

When they got home, he gave the children over to Andres and before they even had dinner, he swept Dominika into their bedroom and proved past doubt that to him, at least, she was as exciting and desirable as ever.

It buoyed her spirits. By the time the sheep came down to winter pasture, her waist was as small as it had been. She had a devoted husband and two sound, handsome children. If only she had a daughter, there would be nothing more to ask.

Almost nothing.

Why did her heart still contract in an agony of longing when a sudden turn of Foss's head or a fleeting expression in his sunny eyes made her remember Brant?

During the lambing of 1906 she brought Andres to look after the children while she cooked for the lambing crew. For almost a month she kept coffee and stew on the stove all around the clock for, contrarily, more lambs were born at night than in the day. She was still nursing Vachel and it seemed that whenever she managed to slip into her tent for a few hours of sleep, the baby would find her and whimper for cuddling and milk. She began to feel a considerable sympathy for ewes that tried to discourage their importunate offspring.

Jautzi was with the rams but Arin-arin was the mother of twins that year, both of them black. She had tried to sneak away from them at first but Domingo had caught her back leg with his sheephook and tethered her to a bush. Surrounded by two little voracious black lambs, Arin-arin had sniffed them suspiciously and apparently decided that they were hers and she would have to put up with them. By the time Domingo turned her loose, she was ridiculously proud of her twins and hung around the cook house as though to show them off to everyone who passed.

There were three orphans that year. Joe thought it best to kill them since Dominika was so busy but she took on their feeding with help from Andres, though the lambs still went "bumming" among the ewes, approaching from behind and trying to steal a few swigs of milk before they were kicked away. As a result of nuzzling beneath the ewes' tails, their heads were stained dark. When Dominika took them home after the lambing slackened sufficiently so that Vicente could do the cooking, she energetically scrubbed the evil-looking fleece but it took several sudsings and long bleaching by the sun to efface the telltale color.

Foss, wiry and quick at two and a half, loved to play with the lambs. He ran along the road with them, laughing with glee, although he did learn from repeated tumbles not to challenge their control of the hillocks.

He seemed indifferent to Vachel now, though at first he had been wildly jealous. Joe had spanked him hard when he had been caught trying to dump Vachel out of his basket and after that Foss had kept his distance, announcing that he was a "big, big boy, not a *baby*."

Now and then Dominika found him watching her with an expression of having been betrayed, but she told herself that she was imagining it. Still, she redoubled her efforts to pay him more attention and was a little hurt and bewildered when he would wriggle down from her lap.

"It's as if he thinks I don't love him and so he's showing me he doesn't need me," she told Joe.

He laughed and tweaked a strand of her hair. "He's just a boy, M'nika. You ought to be glad he keeps out from underfoot."

It did make her busy life less hectic than if he had been constantly tugging at her apron but it also left her with a small, nagging worry.

Running the household and caring for two small children, she had little time to wander alone up the canyon, though with the children and Andres she did pick berries to justify her occasional escape from the house. She was seldom able to visit the blue-bird cave but it strengthened her to know that it was there, that the talisman from before there were nations or races—even before time—waited for her within the mountain.

Life at the ranch moved with the cycles of the sheep but some of the events of that year of 1906 were so notable that they reached even the herders' lonely camps. Vicente Isasti's brother had been killed in the collapse of a Basque hotel in the earthquakes that shook San Francisco that April, starting terrible fires. The toll of seven hundred would have been even worse had not automobiles been requisitioned by the military to move people out of danger and rush the injured to hospitals.

Meanwhile, the activities of the woman whom Dominika regarded as her own godmother as well as Foss's were reported in the papers that were brought home and read along with the Basque-language periodicals. May Arkwright Hutton had entertained Theodore Roosevelt when he was stumping for his successful election in 1904; she had joined the National American Woman Suffrage Association and given a banquet for Susan B. Anthony in Portland, Oregon; she was the first woman to run for the Idaho legislature and came within eighty votes of beating her Republican opponent.

Wealthy now, she was still sympathetic to working men and unions. Bitter strife between owners and miners was raging. Out of the Western Federation of Miners, there emerged the more radical and socialistic Industrial Workers of the World, or IWW.

Early in 1906, Big Bill Haywood, the leading spirit of the IWW, and two other union leaders were arrested for complicity in the assassination of the ex-governor of Idaho, Frank Steunenberg. May thought that the labor leaders were being railroaded and when a shaggy-haired young lawyer named Clarence Darrow came out to defend them, she gave Darrow and his family a place in her home during the long and impassioned trial.

Dominika marveled at the wide-ranging involvements of her benefactress, the more because she was sure that big, plain, childless May was still helping desperate young women to find homes for themselves and their babies.

Dominika and Joe talked with wonderment and some fear about the problems that always seemed to be erupting within this unimaginably vast and bewildering country.

"There is so much here for everyone," Joe said in puzzled sadness. "Why is there all this trouble?"

"Maybe it's because there is so much," Dominika suggested. "In other countries everyone has a place and usually stays in it. Here a person can become anything. Everyone expects a lot."

Still, these events seemed worlds away from the seasons of the sheep. That October, Dominika cooked again while the herders sorted out the sheep that would go to market but she did not go to Boise with Joe when he went to sell the animals and buy supplies. It would be no vacation for her, having to manage a bouncy, inquisitive three-year-old Foss while carrying around Vachel, now a sturdy, placid fifteen-month-old toddler.

"But you need a change," Joe argued. "We can stay at Marta's for a couple of days and you can shop and go to Mass and—"

"And wrestle with the boys," she concluded, laughing, giving him a quick hug and kiss. "You're the best husband in the world but there are some things even you don't understand! Next year we'll all go."

"If you'd let me hire a woman to help you—"

She silenced his growl with a light touch of her fingers to his mouth. "When the ranch is paid off. When you can hire another camp-tender so that you don't have to work all the time!"

Although wool and sheep had brought good prices over these past few years, expenses were high, too, and Joe was barely paying the interest on the mortgage. Still, he hadn't had to mortgage his sheep as many owners had been forced into doing and so he was satisfied with his progress. Considering that he had arrived penniless in the States, even owing for his passage, Joe Uhalde had done very well.

Dominika waved him off to town and returned to the house. She would never let Joe suspect it but to her his occasional absences were a blessing, allowing her a break from the cooking of the three big daily meals that he needed, a chance to sew or clean house without interruption except from the boys and even a little time to leave them in Andres' charge and take a delightful, leisurely walk.

XI

ON THE first day she sewed a shirt for Joe and made Foss two pairs of denim overalls. The next morning she baked and scrubbed. When Vachel was tucked in for his afternoon nap, she asked Andres to keep an eye on Foss and started for the cave.

It was a beautiful afternoon, sunny, with a fall crispness in the air. Snow whitened the purple mountain crests but aspen cut broad swaths of yellow through the evergreens and here and there she could see a blaze of scarlet maple. An eagle climbed toward the sun and then seemed to float in a lazy circle.

Dominika breathed deep and laughed in the sheer joy of being alive on such a glorious day, basking in the slightly wicked luxury of taking a few precious hours for herself. Joe would return by evening and if he reached home before she did, he would simply be glad that she was taking his advice to take life easier. How lucky she was to have a husband who never complained or found fault.

Lucky—

Yes, she was. And she was going to enjoy this afternoon without tormenting herself with thoughts of Brant. She had not seen him since the day he had stopped to see Foss almost three years ago but Marta, with a strange look, had told her that he stopped to eat at the hotel occasionally and always asked about Dominika. He was drinking quite a lot but perhaps he was worried about his wife. A discharged cook had grumbled around town that Mrs. Rawlins drank so much that she couldn't appreciate good cooking.

Dominika had ached for the young woman who had once been her friend. It was sad. Sad, too, for Brant—

Don't think of him.

Striking the sheep trail that led along the ridge toward the bushes that covered the cave, she sent her thoughts back to that other cavern so far away; called it vividly to mind and all that she could remember about the women she knew by name. Stories she would tell her daughter. She would tell the boys about their ancestresses, too, of course, but she suspected that they would be more interested in the Saracen nobles who died defending Cordova, in the whalers who reached Newfoundland or Marya's dashing corsair. She herself never saw sheep without a consciousness that Marya, over three hundred years before, had marched with the first sheep to produce descendants in what was now the United States, the sturdy *churros* tended by women of her family before there was history.

But Marya had gone back to Etchahoun. Dominika wondered if she herself ever would, or if the closest she would ever again be to the Summer Cave was this small cavern, where she had enshrined the blue bird.

Entering, it took her eyes a few minutes to adjust to the dimness. Standing there in the hushed cool, she studied the heaven-bright bird and hoped that it wasn't lonely here. She did not think it was for almost magically she could conjure around it the shimmering images of other birds and the tree, the mother and child, the dozens of blessing hands.

Rapt, she scarely noticed the first crunch of footsteps but then they were so close that she realized they could not belong to a bighorn sheep or any other four-footed animal. Andres?

If something had happened that sent him in search of her, surely he would have called out now and then. A hunter or a trapper?

The bushes stirred, limbs were pushed aside. A man stooped to enter. She knew that curly, dun-gold hair before she saw his face.

"Brant!"

He did not speak, only moved toward her. She felt turned to stone; yet paradoxically a sweet wildfire stirred within her, long-buried coals fanned from ashes to burst into flame.

Even as her knees trembled, she dodged to one side and tried to slip past him. He caught her against him. His mouth claimed hers as his lean, hard body imprinted itself on her. A raging torrent of desire swept her along. Her cry was strangled by his lips. And then they lay together in the soft dust. There was no world but this one, no man but this one.

Avid and longing, a severed half seeking to be whole, she met him in utter abandon, hurtled into exploding, cresting wonder that she had never known before, swept into a timeless ocean, flowing, disembodied, moving with the eternal pulsing rhythm of all that had ever lived.

"You have to come with me," he said at last. "I'll rig it so Lucie will think I've been killed and we'll take your boys and go away. Start over and—"

Dominika roused from beatitude. She could feel no shame, she could not be sorry, but she knew that this must never happen again. Sitting up, she began to straighten her clothes.

"Brant, we must each go home. And stay there."

He seized her wrist and gave a harsh, cutting laugh. "Don't go prim and pious, Nika! You wanted me just as much as I wanted you. When I saw Uhalde in town and figured that he'd be gone for a day or two, I couldn't come out here fast enough. But I don't like this. We belong together."

"Lucie—"

"Lucie needs a nurse, not a husband. And her whisky. It does more for her than I can."

"I'm sorry. But however that is, I am not leaving Joe."

"That damn Basco?" Brant's eyes narrowed, glittering like ice in the shadows.

Dominika rose to her feet. She had taken two steps when he brought her down. She heard her own cry, echoing as though it came from someone else.

Then there was another cry, one of such pain and shock that it would forever resound through her being. Brant sprang up, dragging at his clothes and looping his belt as Joe leaped on him. They grappled on the earth, Joe reaching for Brant's throat.

Brant wrenched away and tried to roll free but Joe was on him again. Wildly Dominika shouted their names, with no effect. They were locked in elemental battle, where words and reason had no part.

They crashed through the bushes at the entrance, still embraced in fury. Dominika looked about frantically for a rock, a branch, something with which to stun one of them. There was nothing. They struggled on the ledge.

"Stop!" She tried to drag them apart. "Stop! You'll fall—"

Brant heaved backward. Joe fell over him and momentum carried him past those few spare inches. The sound as he fell was more of thwarted rage than fear.

His neck was broken. He was dead before they reached him. Lifting him in her arms, Dominika whispered, "We—we killed him!"

"Did you want me to let him choke me?" Brant growled. "Hell, I tried to get away."

Numbly Dominika shook her head. After the scene that Joe had witnessed, there could be only death for one of the men. She could not have blamed Joe had he killed her, too, though she felt terrible regret that he had not known how it had been, that it was the first time—that it would never have happened again—

Was she herself so sure of that, even as she held Joe's broken body in her arms?

"He fell." Brant's voice pierced her through swirling black mists. "It will be better for everyone to stick to that."

There was nothing to be served by telling a sheriff *why* he fell. Even were the facts known, Brant had fought in self-defense. Joe's death had been an accident.

It had also been murder.

"I'll take him home," she said. "You had better ride to town and send out the coroner." She knew that was necessary because a coroner had been called when Kepa cut his throat.

"Dominika—"

"Help me get him to his horse."

"Listen! This doesn't change—"

"It changes Joe to a corpse. Leave me alone. I never want to see you again."

There were marks on his face and throat. She supposed that he could turn up his collar and pull down his hat. "You don't know what you're saying. I'll come by later when you're not so upset."

Joe's bloody head rested against her breast. Cradling him, she said in strange, calm voice that she did not recognize as her own. "We have killed Joe. Shall we do the same to Lucie?" He shrank, his eyes stricken. She went on pitilessly. "If you come to Joe's house, I will kill you."

"You're crazy."

"You'll be dead."

Wordlessly he managed to position the dead man over his shoulder. Dominika followed him up to the waiting horses.

Joe, returning early, must have come looking for her and noticed Brant's tethered horse. He had probably died thinking that he had discovered only one of many trystings. Brant fastened the body across the saddle, casting her a haggard glance.

"Can you get him home, Nika? You won't—do anything?"

"I will bury him. And raise his sons."

Brant flinched at her use of the plural. He started to speak but stopped at what he saw in her face. He climbed into his saddle and let the horse pick its cautious way along the narrow trail. Once he was on level ground, he nudged the big gray into a trot.

Till he was out of sight, Dominika soothed Joe's horse, nervous from the smell of blood, and then she led him homeward.

Candles for Joe, and prayers.

He had died in the throes of killing anger and despair but God, who knew all, surely could not charge that against him after a good, kind and honest life. Nor did God need to add the sin to Dominika's guilt. Her conscience had already done that.

She had loved Joe. Not with the mindless, all-consuming passion she'd had for Brant but with the deep sharing of every day's living, working and quiet pleasures. She found it impossible to remain at the ranch even had she felt herself capable of carrying on the sheep business. With the help and advice of the Irigays, she sold the sheep and other animals to Pete Falxa and Gabe Esponda, except for a band of two thousand which she gave to Domingo.

She cleared the mortgage on the ranch and sold the property to the neighboring sheepmen, who split it between themselves. Panchiko and Paolo Esponda would take over the ranch house.

Joe was buried on a ridge above the canyon, where wild roses grew. Kato lay across the grave. He would not eat or drink although Dominika took his favorite foods to him. Each day he grew gaunter and weaker but he would still give his frondy tail a thump when she approached. He was an old dog and the nights were freezing. Andres rigged a shelter for him but on the fifth morning he was dead.

Xagu had stayed with him through most of the days but she had come down at night. The boys wept for Kato, who was buried next to Joe. For their sakes, to hold on to something of their familiar life, Dominika decided to take Xagu with them. She had to go far away, to a life as different as possible from that of the ranch, one where she would be with many people and stay so busy that she would have little time or strength to think about the past.

She could not take her own life and except for her sons, she might have taken an uglier way to self-destruction, become the harlot that she felt herself to be, humiliating and punishing the flesh that had betrayed Joe. Because of the children, that penance was unthinkable as was her first confused impulse to give away the money she received from Joe's estate. It would have served her right to have to slave for a bare living, but Foss and Vachel deserved better.

Since Joe had no close family, she sent a lavish sum to the priest of his home village, asking that High Mass be said on each anniversary of Joe's death for the next ten years and that the rest be distributed among the needy. She left money with the priest in Boise for the same purpose and more with Marta and Joanes to use in succoring herders like Andres or to send home those like Kepa, who could not endure a return to the loneliness.

Loneliness. It was a bleak, terrible wasteland within her, one nothing could reach. She felt like a hull as she packed clothing, the children's favorite toys, her rosary and prayerbook. Also the blue bird.

She had dreaded going back for it. The cave of refuge had become a place of horror. But she needed the talisman. When self-loathing and despair overwhelmed her, when she woke sweating in the nightmare of that deadly struggle and Joe's fall, the memory of the women's cave or touching the sweet, sleeping bodies of her sons were her only defenses against madness.

At last everything was done. She took the boys to pray for a last time beside their father's grave. Vachel, in her arms, was too young to understand but Foss sobbed. He left a bone on Kato's mound and thrust his greatest treasure, a beautifully carved small staff, into the rocks covering Joe's body. "Maybe Daddy walk with it in heaven?" he asked hopefully.

Dominika hugged him and finally managed to speak through the aching tightness in her throat. "Yes, Foss. Your daddy will like it."

Andres was going with them. Domingo drove them into town, saw Xagu safely placed in a spacious box in a freight car and hugged the children. Tears glistened in his black eyes as he handed Vachel to Dominika.

"I would come with you, andrea, but all I know is sheep." He hesitated. "Now, if you were opening a Basque hotel—"

She had thought of it but almost immediately rejected the idea of being in a place where she would always see herders and be constantly reminded of Joe. Running a boardinghouse would suit her need for people and hard work. She was going to Goldfield, Nevada, the fabulous, high-grade gold strike that was drawing people from all parts of the country.

Pressing Domingo's rough hand to her cheek, she smiled through her tears. "I would rather think of you here, Domingo, trying to keep Arin-arin from stealing all the black lambs. But when you take a holiday, come stay with us. Maybe, when the boys are older, they can help summers with the sheep."

"Ah! That would be good." Hope shone through Domingo's mournfulness. "Good fortune, andrea. If you ever need an old man's help, send for me."

He kissed the boys again, squeezed Dominika's hand and rushed away. Bells clanged. The engine started up. Foss and Vachel squealed as the train lurched forward. Dominika took one last look at the town where she had begun her life in America.

A little over four years ago? In that time she had been Lucie's friend, Brant's mistress, the Irigays' hired girl, Joe's wife, the boys' mother. Each identity took her further from *etcheko primu* of Etchahoun.

From it all she remained only the boys' mother. And Dominika, heiress of the cave. Yes, there was still that. That, beneath all. She closed her eyes and conjured up that ageless refuge while the train bore her and these innocent, vulnerable young lives to a new and different world.

At Las Vegas, Nevada, the track gave out. Tent saloons and restaurants clustered around the depot and the Goldfield passengers had a greasy, high-priced meal of tough steak and half-done beans before crowding into a Rockaway stagecoach that was to bounce and jostle them across a hundred and ninety miles to the boom town.

Xagu, although she whined plaintively as her box was placed beneath the feet of the passenger riding beside the driver, had by far the best of the journey. Crushed in a corner, grateful that Andres, holding Foss, was sitting between her and a drunken blacksmith, Dominika tried to cushion the tired, fretful Vachel against the worst jounces and avoid the knees of the cadaverous man seated across from her who cheerfully announced that he was an undertaker.

From bits of conversation she gathered that of the six other passengers jammed into the coach, one was a lawyer and another a doctor. The painted face and fancy garb of the only other woman left small doubt as to what profession she followed and the handsome, pale man with beautiful, well-kept hands was almost certainly a gambler. Dominika entertained herself with wondering how he would fare in a game of *muz* but then Vachel began to howl.

Abjectly embarrassed, Dominika tried desperately to quiet him. The lawyer glared, the undertaker tutted and the blacksmith soddenly tried to interest the baby in a gold watch.

Vachel thrashed and screamed on. Dominika was nearly ready to scream, too, when the woman leaned across and said in a surprisingly gentle voice, "Let me take him, ma'am. I—I had a bunch of brothers and sisters. I can usually make the little ones happy."

At her wits' end, not knowing how to decline without seeming to consider herself above the other, who beneath the rouge and eye shadow had a young, rather sad face, Dominika reluctantly handed Vachel over.

He blinked at the transfer, gulped in amazement, then cast Dominika a reproachfully furious glance and sucked in his breath, preparatory to a shriek. Dominika cringed. Foss's tempers came swiftly, vented themselves and passed. Vachel, rarely perturbed, boiled over only on occasion and when he did, he was a devil.

Before his wrath could burst eardrums, the languid, black-clad man scooped him away from the woman, swung him as high in the air as possible, settled him on his knee and began to rock him even more violently than the stage itself rocked.

"Tired, little guy?" asked the gambler. "It's a tough world for us boyos, isn't it?" He had a lilting, deep voice that checked Vachel in mid-shriek. "Let's see if you like the cards."

Shifting Vachel so the child leaned back against him, the man produced a deck from inside his coat and riffled it. He fanned the cards, making them seem to flow from one to another. Then he made one disappear and plucked it out of Vachel's collar.

"Pretty!" Vachel said, patting a queen.

"Clever lad!" applauded the pale, handsome stranger. "You may have her. And here are her husband and son so she won't be lonesome." Including Foss in the game, the gambler said, "Can you count?"

Foss proudly stuck up three fingers. "I'm this many!" He gave his brother a derogatory look. "Vach's a baby. This many." He held out one finger and crooked down another to make a half.

The man gave him a trey. "Here's what you are. The four's what you'll be next year. The five has as many hearts as you have fingers on one hand." Turning up one of Vachel's chubby fingers for each count, he put down seven, eight, nine and ten. "There you are. Ten spades, ten fingers."

He handed the counting cards to Foss along with a set of face cards. A joker showed in his hand. "Who's that?" asked Foss.

"He's the wild one." The stranger's tone roughened. "Better not play with him. He'll make you think you've got winning cards when you don't." For the first time he looked directly at Dominika. "Take a good, solid jack any time."

346

"Madam," interposed the balding lawyer, "are you going to sit idly by while your children are perverted and trained in card-sharping?"

Slim, black eyebrows raised. "Perhaps, sir, I did not hear you correctly." The gambler's words purred silkily. "If I did, I would remind you that there's a question as to which of our professions boasts the greater number of thieves. I will be happy to make my argument more convincing when we reach Goldfield."

"I'm not a gunman," spluttered the lawyer.

"Neither am I," shrugged the gambler. His sunny smile showed his white teeth and stopped short of smoky, fathomless eyes. "That's one reason I don't say more with my tongue than my fists can back up."

"Gamblers don't fight with their fists," sneered the lawyer. "It ruins their hands."

The pale man made a fist and studied it reflectively. "Doesn't seem to have hurt mine."

The lawyer hesitated. "Oh, very well!" he said with ill grace. "I withdraw my remark. If people don't care enough about their children to—"

"Stop while you're ahead," advised the gambler.

"Thank you very much," Dominika said. "I can take Vachel now."

Smiling at her above Vachel's dark hair, the stranger said, "I assure you, ma'am, I'm enjoying the novelty. Let me hold him." He chuckled. "Of course if the lad starts squalling again, I'll promptly return him."

Dominika had to laugh. When they stopped at a way station to change teams and eat, the gambler introduced himself as Shelby Truro. "My parents came over from Ireland," he said, "but I'm thinking that you aren't all that long from . . . is it Spain?"

"No. I am Basque, of Vizcaya. Dominika Uhalde."

"Basque, it it? Well, then, we're both Celts. Cousins, you might say."

Dominika knew that her blood ran back beyond the Celtiberians who had fought the Romans but saw no need to argue with this helpful man, who fed Xagu and with Foss took her for a walk. When the stage rolled onward, Shelby saw that the other young woman was seated opposite Dominika. The undertaker had to splay his legs around the lawyer's tight-pressed knees. Then the gambler took the sleeping Vachel on his lap.

"Please," said the painted young woman, leaning forward, "could I hold the little boy for a while?"

Beneath the rouge and lip salve her face was vulnerable and young. She had curiously misty gray-blue eyes. "Why," said Dominika, "that would be kind of you. Mr. Truro, wouldn't you like a change?"

"I'll share the pleasure," the Irishman said and added gallantly, "Were the boyo a tad older, there's no doubt whose lap he'd prefer!"

The girl blushed. Taking the child, she gazed down at his smooth olive cheek with such yearning that Dominika sensed unhealed grief and to divert the young woman, she introduced herself.

"I'm Sherlottie Winston," the girl responded. "From—St. Louis."

"Not always, I'll bet," said Truro. "You came from some little town where people called you Taffy because of your hair."

She stared at him with fear that turned to wonder. "How did you know? I mean—"

"Well, now, what else could one think of when your hair's thick and rich and shines like taffy when it's just been pulled to silver-gold?"

Dominika drifted into an exhausted doze as the two talked softly but she awoke at a convulsive movement of Sherlottie's knee against hers.

"I can't!" the girl was saying. "It's too late!"

Truro said quietly, "It's never too late till you think it is."

"I can't go back."

"Maybe not. But you can go forward. Take that paint off your face when we get to town, buy some simple clothes and look for an honest job."

"I've tried working as a clerk. You can't live on the pay unless you have a home." Dominika had kept her eyes closed during this exchange but now she thought of offering to employ the girl. She would need help with a boardinghouse and if Sherlottie really wanted to make a fresh start— "I need money," Sherlottie was saying in a suddenly hard voice, "and there's only one way I can get enough, Mr. Truro."

Dominika straightened. "I'm going to buy a boarding-house. If you would work for me, I'd pay better than most jobs do."

Hope seemed to flicker for a moment in the other woman's eyes before she shook her head. "Thank you, ma'am. But I'm afraid I have to earn lots more than that."

Somewhat affronted, Dominika shrugged. "It's up to you, of course."

They lapsed into silence.

XII

GOLDFIELD STRADDLED a wind-scoured saddle between barren brown peaks. At one end was the railway station, a business house or two and several freight yards crowded with wagons, horses and mules. On four corners in the heart of the bustling town four large gambling-hall saloons vied for the miners' wages. There was a bank and a stock market in addition to stores, restaurants, rooming houses and livery stables. Farther along was a section of saloons, dance halls, sleazy restaurants and establishments that Dominika could not identify.

The driver let the passengers out in front of several boardinghouses. Undertaker, banker and lawyer gripped their baggage and went into the most respectable looking of the buildings. The blacksmith lurched into a saloon. Sherlottie took a small valise and, head defiantly high, started for the seedier end of town.

Dominika stifled an impulse to call after her but Sherlottie seemed to know what she wanted. If she preferred life in the tenderloin to the brutally hard work of a boardinghouse, Dominika was not the one to blame her. Xago, pathetically glad to be out of the crate, licked Dominika's hand and Foss tugged at her skirts, telling her in Basque that he needed the toilet. Andres, in these surroundings almost as dependent on her as were the boys, held Vachel and gaped at the stream of people, wagons, buggies and even a few automobiles.

Dominika felt dazed herself. With a trunk and valise, her family made a small, lost island about which the human flood eddied and ebbed.

"Do you want to stay in a boardinghouse?" Shelby Truro asked her.

She nodded as Foss whispered urgently, in English this time, "Mama! Wee-wee!"

"If that means what I think it does, you better come with me, young fellow." Truro hustled Foss into one of the buildings. They had scarcely disappeared when a blond youngster of perhaps twelve or thirteen came out and looked sullenly at the trunk.

"Can't heft that by myself," he grumbled. He squinted a sharp glance at Andres. "Can you take one side, mister?"

Translating the request, Dominika took Vachel and was staggering under his weight combined with that of the valise when Truro returned and took the bag from her. In the hall, where the landlady, gray of face and hair and frostily gray of eye, looked her over with a doubtful expression, Truro murmured, "Do you have enough money?"

"Yes," Dominika answered. "Thank you."

"I don't take dogs," the landlady said, eyeing Xagu with disfavor. "And children—well, the poor things have to stay somewhere, I suppose, but they make a lot of extra washing. Really, missus, you better go someplace else."

Dominika was tired. Parting with Xago was out of the question, nor did she feel like going to some other place and finding herself refused on one count or another. Giving Vachel to Andres, she said, "How much will you take for this house?"

The woman's pasty jaw dropped. "What? I got no time for jokes, missus!"

"I do not joke." Swaying with weariness, Dominika leaned for a moment against the wall. "I want to buy a boardinghouse, run it for a living."

"Now I know you're daft! Anyone who wants to cook and clean and slave—" Bitterly the woman hunched her shoulders. "My husband thought it was a great way to earn enough for our old age but what does he do?" Snorting, she answered her own question. "Has heart failure and now I have to wait on him and do everything else, too."

"Sell it to me," said Dominika firmly. "You won't have to work so hard and I'll have a place for my children and my dog."

The woman squinted at her suspiciously. "Let's see your money."

Dominika started to oblige but Truro stepped forward. ''If you're serious about this, let me handle it,'' he advised Dominika. To the older woman he gave a cool smile. ''With these changed circumstances, ma'am, I assume you don't object to giving Mrs. Uhalde a couple of rooms while we work out the sale. Maybe you could give the boys some bread and milk? And fetch some water for the dog? After they're settled, we can have a discussion.''

By the time she went to bed that night, Dominika was the owner of a boardinghouse.

Mrs. Harlidge had agreed to stay on for a week while Dominika settled in and learned the management of the house. Thanks to Shelby Truro's knowledge and shrewd bargaining, Dominika had a little money left over to put in the bank, and the boardinghouse would bring in a steady flow of cash. The twelve rooms upstairs were shared by twenty-two men, two of whom preferred solitude and paid an extra dollar a day for it. Board, with a shared room, was three dollars a day and about ten other miners took their meals in the dining room for a dollar a day.

Shelby Truro had a room to himself and was the only boarder who did not work in the mines. He dealt cards for Tex Rickard's Northern, named for the gambling hall that the entrepreneur had operated in Nome. Shelby left the house after supper and did not return until breakfast. Then he retired till late afternoon, when he usually stopped by the kitchen to play with the boys and have a cup of coffee while he chatted with Dominika.

''He ought to be down in the tenderloin with his own kind,'' Mrs. Harlidge sniffed. ''He won't do your reputation any good, missus. If you ask me—''

''Thank you, Mrs. Harlidge, but I didn't ask you.''

The gray woman's sharp nose twitched. ''Well, if it's that way—''

''The only way it is, is that Mr. Truro is my friend.''

Dominika did not know why that should be so, but it was. She could not discuss her worries and problems with Andres any more than she could with the boys but Shelby was always ready to listen and offer sound, humor-laced advice. When she worried that she was charging the miners more than half of their five-dollar-a-day wage, he choked with laughter.

"Bless your heart, there may be a few honest miners in town, but most of them are taking out a hundred dollars or more a day in high grade. They say God didn't put gold in the mines just for the owners."

Multiplying that sum by the thousands of miners in town, Dominika gasped. "Why don't the owners stop it?"

"They'd dearly love to. Been trying to make the men use changing rooms when they come off work but the union has been able to block that so far." Shelby raised a lazy shoulder. "Someone has to get the ore out. The owners can fire one bunch and hire another just as bad. When there's jewelry-grade ore handy, a lot of it's going to walk off. So don't you worry about overcharging your boarders, my dear."

Certainly none of them ever complained. Dominika encouraged Ah Sung, the Chinese cook she had inherited from Mrs. Harlidge, to put better and more plentiful food on the tables and she often made a thick stew herself, or bean or dried-codfish soup in the Basque fashion. The foul air of the mines caused numerous stomach complaints among the miners and left them with poor appetites. They craved sharp, salty flavors. She did not think that an excess of these was good for them and tried to entice them with tasty, healthier dishes.

She didn't have much time for cooking, though. Maids were so quickly snatched up by the wife-hungry men. Katie, the pretty Irish girl who had been there when Dominika arrived, married a miner from her home county the following week. Dominika had hoped to keep Eliza, a shy Mormon girl who demurely served tables without ever seeming to look at the men. But she must have looked at some time or another for during the second week of Dominika's taking charge, Eliza wed a man with his own claim and left for Tonopah.

There were no other single women wanting work but by appealing to her boarders, she acquired the part-time services of Brigid O'Malley, a middle-aged, red-faced woman who joked with the men as she waited on tables, urged them to save some of their high grade for the church and clouted them if their humor exceeded the bounds she considered seemly for a well-married woman to hear. Brigid's Michael earned good money and doubtless high-graded more but he was fond of drink and cards. For this reason she was glad to be sure of enough cash to pay the exorbitant rent on their little shack that was still better than the tents, framed-up tents or tin-over-frame shacks in which many of the miners lived. There were also adobes, a few neat brick or frame houses and even some made of bottles mortared together with adobe.

Ah Sung's cousin ran a laundry and Dominika was glad to let him pick up the sheets and other laundry each week. Andres emptied chamber pots and washbasins, refilled the pitchers in each room and brought in wood for the kitchen range and the pot-bellied heater in the dining room. Dominika changed sheets and towels, kept accounts and, with Brigid's help, cleaned, waited on the tables and bought groceries and supplies.

Meals were served to overlap shifts at the mines. Breakfast, from six to eight, caught those going to work at seven as well as the men who were coming off shift then. The meal served between two and four took care of the three-o'clock shift change and men coming to or going off the eleven-o'clock shift helped themselves to the stew and coffee that were left on the big range along with the crusty bread that Dominika baked.

Up before five, she went steadily all day except for time taken to eat with the boys or have coffee with Shelby. When the rush of her work ended sometime after eight, when all was in readiness for the graveyard shift and the next morning, Dominika relaxed with her small family in their quarters behind the kitchen. Xagu lay by the little stove in the tiny parlor, tired from shepherding the boys for she had appointed herself their guardian now that both Andres and Dominika were so busily occupied. Andres held one of the boys and Dominika took the other. Then the old herder would play his harmonica or sing, or Dominika would tell stories, those she had heard from her grandmother.

"As happens to all who were, are or shall be in this world," she would begin. Or: "This was in the time when all animals and all things spoke."

Before she tucked the boys into bed, she made cups of rich, spiced chocolate for all of them. Foss shared one of the bedrooms with Andres and Vachel had a crib in Dominika's room. Although the bedrooms were frigid, Xagu slept near Foss—in his bed, Dominika suspected, though the wise old dog never let herself be caught there.

There was no time to grieve or brood even though Dominika still had nightmares of Joe's falling and was often reminded of him with a cruel stab of pain or surge of aching loss. If she had let herself mourn in the way she wanted to, she would not have been able to keep going and so she welcomed the hurried routine. At night she fell at once into exhausted sleep.

Some day she would think about it. Some day she would cry. But for now she had to manage for the children's sakes and raise Joe's sons to be happy and strong.

The miners came from other camps: sourdoughs from Nome and Fairbanks in Alaska; copper-miners from Utah, Arizona and Montana; from the Coeur d'Alene; from California's Mother Lode and from the restless Colorado camps of Telluride, Cripple Creek, Leadville and Ouray. They also poured in from Australia, Canada, Mexico, South Africa, Peru and England.

Since the slump in Cornish mining began in 1840, followed by the copper crash of 1866, skilled "Cousin Jacks" had left Cornwall by the thousands, flocking to the mines of the western United States. They had been joined by desperate Irishmen during the potato famine in 1846 and the brutal years afterward. The Welsh, miners from antiquity, also came in multitudes. By the turn of the century western bonanzas drew Scandinavians, Italians, Serbians and men from Austro-Hungary so that it was a mix of many nations that thronged Goldfield.

The Chinese had been bloodily excluded from mining except in places where they independently worked low-yield or abandoned placer areas but they dug ditches, laid track and became cooks, laundrymen and house-help. Thrifty and hardworking, they endured much to save enough from their comparatively low wages to return to their homeland or remain to rear their children in this country, which though alien and often cruel, provided undreamed-of opportunities to anyone who would work and save.

Of the twenty-nine miners who ate at Dominika's boarding-house, ten were Cornish, six were Irish and the others were a conglomeration. There was even one Basque from Chile. When the men sought her out every two weeks at payday in order to settle their accounts, they tried laughably hard to find her alone.

Many were too shy to do more than pay and mumble something about the good food and clean rooms but others engaged in clumsy flatteries, boyish worship or fairly blunt speculation as to why such a pretty "widder-woman" had not chosen some lucky man to protect her.

"That Shelby Truro," grumbled a husky Australian who had thrice invited her for a Sunday drive and been thrice declined, "maybe he's as lucky with ladies as he is with cards."

"I'm mighty lucky," Shelby drawled, lounging into the small lobby which served as Dominika's office. "Lucky to room in the best boardinghouse in town. And so are you, Derry."

The Australian glared at the Irishman for a moment but, although he was much bigger, he decided not to quarrel. As he sauntered off, Dominika suddenly felt uneasy at something in the smoky, dark eyes that watched her gravely, belying Truro's careless grin.

"Shelby," she demanded, "do you lurk around the corner on paydays?"

She hadn't thought about it before but this wasn't the first time that he had happened in when the situation was becoming a trifle embarrassing. He shrugged, not at all disconcerted.

"Never know when a lad may stop by a saloon and be plastered when he comes to settle up."

"You don't have to feel responsible for me."

"I don't but I do."

The sense of comfort and support that his presence always brought her was now obscured by a flash of awareness. For the first time the female in her responded to his masculinity.

Disturbed, she bent over her record book. When she looked up, he was gone.

Christmas was nearing. Dominika had little heart for it but

one morning she entered the dining room and blinked. A small but perfectly formed spruce tree occupied a barrel in the middle of the room. It was decorated with strings of popcorn and tinsel, and a gilt star sparkled at the top.

Ah Sung, behind her, smiled broadly. "Mr. Truro, he fetch tree and bought star. I make popcorn. Little Foss, he like?"

"He will like it very much. Thank you, Ah Sung."

Foss did enjoy it, especially as presents began to appear beneath the boughs. The miners were delighted with the tree and added their own ornaments—arrowheads, bits of shiny fool's gold or quartz. As the stack of presents grew, Dominika saw that they were all meant for the boys.

"Don't spoil the men's fun," Shelby advised her when she worried about it.

Dominika waved a hand at the heaped-up gifts, some wrapped in newspaper or paper bags, some in expensive gilt tissue. "But the boys don't need all this. There must be children in town who won't have much. Weren't three men killed in a cave-in last Thursday, two of them married?"

"Yes and they had tykes," Brigid said, taking off her shawl. "There be a lot of miners' widows, mum. The union pays for the funeral and usually gives the family a hundred dollars but then the woman be on her own, with little mouths to feed. They most take in a few boarders and scratch a living that way."

Dominika thought for a minute and then she smiled. "Every child in this camp is going to get a toy and any clothes he needs! We'll have a party—two of them, really, one for each shift except graveyard, with different children at each one. Brigid, Shelby, will you help find out who ought to be invited? Brigid, will you help me talk to the men? We have to ask if they mind letting most of the presents go to other children."

They not only didn't mind, they raided the shops. Piles of nuts, candies, oranges and apples accumulated in a corner of the big kitchen. Toys were stacked along the dining-room wall. Some of the men ventured to buy clothing but most of them gave money to Dominika or Brigid.

"Get what the kids need," was a typical remark. "If you run out of cash, let me know."

Word of the celebration spread. Strangers came in to leave

money for the "kids' Christmas," some shyly asking if it would be all right for them to happen by and watch the festivities. Dominika assured them that they would be welcome, though they might have to stand up. She had planned to buy and pay for the clothes herself but since the contributions made that unnecessary, she added a sum to the accumulating cash that she planned to divide and give to the mother of each family. The fund was trebled when square-jawed, golden-haired Patrick O'Brien, an ardent IWW man from Cripple Creek, brought her a purse collected from local members, almost bumping into Cornish Davey Trefax carrying donations from the WFM, the Western Federation of Miners.

The two, each a boarder, had apparently once been close friends but now Davey resented the IWW's take-over of the WFM local. His green eyes flared beneath unruly black hair tangling low on his forehead as he gave Dominika a pouch of money and turned to look Patrick up and down.

"Well, old son, don't be spoutin' Wobblie guff at they young'uns or buy' un toy sticks of dynamite to blow up they mines!"

Patrick's blue gaze darkened. "And don't you be teachin' them it's fine for the bosses to make a man strip and parade mother-naked past company men who poke around where even a doctor's got no business! Maybe you like that but—"

Going scarlet, Davey growled, "Come outside and I'll try to pound some sense into 'ee hard Irisher skull! Damme, 'ee never learned to stand upright till 'ee got behind they wheelbarrow!"

Patrick let out a roar and would have grabbed the Cornishman by the collar had Dominika not stepped between them. "It's wonderful that your members want to help," she said, laying a persuasive hand on each forearm. "One of the stores sent over these garlands that would look pretty hung above the windows and doors. I can't reach that high—"

"We'll do she," said Davey grandly, although he was scarcely taller.

By the time they had finished festooning the room, they were caught up enough in the holiday spirit to offer to stand each other to drinks. Dominika heaved a sigh of relief as they strolled off arm in arm.

She was buying warm clothes for twin babies whose father had died in a blasting accident a few days before they were born when a hand touched her apologetically. It took her a moment to recognize the thin, nervously attractive young woman but the misty blue eyes were the same without their mascara and shadow and the taffy-colored hair caught such light as there was on that dull winter day.

"Mrs. Uhalde, I—I heard about the orphans' party." Sherlottie Winston pressed an envelope into Dominika's hand. "Please use this to buy a little boy something."

Dominika had a flash of the sort of memories that Christmas must bring to a woman like Sherlottie, something of the terrible loneliness.

"Thank you," she said, smiling as she took the envelope. "Why don't you come for one of the parties on Christmas Day? There will be one early in the morning and another in the afternoon."

"Oh, I couldn't do that!" But longing filled the sad, deepset eyes.

"Of course you can," Dominika countered briskly. "We have to feed the boarders and see to the parties besides so I could certainly use some help. The children will be served cake and cocoa and the presents have to be handed out and some will need help in getting them open. Please come."

A smile lit the heart-shaped, almost translucent face. "Are you really sure?"

"I need you," Dominika said.

Sherlottie glowed with eagerness. "I can come both times. I'll help clean up afterward and it will be a pleasure. We—we don't work on Christmas Eve or Christmas."

Impulsively Dominika took the younger woman's hand. "If you'd like to come to work for me—"

For a moment hope turned Sherlottie's face pathetically young. Then it hardened and she drew her hand away. "Thanks, Mrs. Uhalde, but you can't pay as much as I have to earn."

Repelled at what seemed a thirst for luxuries at whatever cost in degradation, Dominika cooled her voice. "You must be the judge of that." She had turned back to the baby clothes when Sherlottie caught her wrist.

"It's not what you think, Mrs. Uhalde! I—I have a little crippled boy back with an aunt in Missouri. He has to have doctors, special food, special things. His daddy—well, he's married, a respectable businessman. I never even let him know about Tommy."

Dominika could think of nothing to say. Before she could recover, Sherlottie was gone.

She came to the Christmas-morning party though, wearing a holly-green dress, her face scrubbed as clean as the children's to whom she passed out plates stacked with fruit, candy and cake. If any miners recognized her, they never said so, although the women probably wondered how Dominika had held on to such a pretty maid.

Patrick O'Brien squeezed his accordion and they all sang carols. Sherlottie had a true, lovely voice and knew the songs so well that Dominika was certain that she had belonged to a choir at some time in the past. Dominika had made nut cups, almond cookies and marzipan molded into stars and colored fruits. With chocolate, coffee and Ah Sung's cakes, everyone feasted, though the children couldn't take their eyes off the graceful little tree and the mountains of packages.

Sherlottie, Davey and several of the other miners handed out the gifts and clothing. Each child received two toys and whatever clothing he or she most needed. While they fell upon their parcels with cries of delight, Shelby presented the mothers with envelopes that he and Dominika had assembled. Depending on the number of children and the financial need, the envelopes held from a hundred to five hundred dollars, in some cases enough to enable a widow to return home to her relatives.

"I know that some of your men lost more than you liked at cards," the gambler said quietly. "So you should know that my—colleagues contributed handsomely to this effort to brighten your holiday."

"It's glad I am to know that," snapped a bird-like little Irish-woman. "For I'd never want charity. But my poor Michael, God rest him, lined every pocket in the tenderloin so it's glad I am to be getting some back!"

Shelby joined in the laugh. "That's the way, ma'am!"

Sherlottie, as good as her word, picked up plates and cups, swept the floor and straightened the chairs. "You have a beautiful voice," Dominika said. "Would you sing a few songs alone this evening?"

She flinched at the sudden anguish in Sherlottie's eyes but the pain was quickly hidden and the girl's voice was steady. "I'd love to. Would it be all right if I sang some of the old songs my grandmother taught me?"

"That would be especially nice," Dominika said.

It had been a great success but there was still the second party to attend to and she was tired. As soon as Sherlottie was gone, Dominika went back to her little parlor.

Foss was playing with a wind-up automobile while Andres and Vachel were enthralled with a frog that jumped and squeaked when Andres pressed a rubber air-ball. Xagu had retired behind the stove to be out of the way of such noisy creations. As Dominika sat down, the boys swarmed over her with their treasures—tops, a bird-shaped whistle, balls, a model of the *Maine*, a red wagon, a balky wind-up mule.

When all had been demonstrated to Dominika's admiring ohs and ahs, the boys settled on the rug with Andres. Putting her feet before her on a footstool, Dominika leaned back, happily weary. Joe would have loved the celebration.

It was the first time that she had been able to think of him naturally—as the good, loving husband and friend he had always been until those last awful moments—the first time that she had been able to remember him without overwhelming despair and guilt.

Going into her bedroom, she wept in a cleansing, freeing way, grieving without self-hatred, affirming her love for him, and her gratitude. When she went back to the children, she half-expected to glimpse Joe playing with them.

His body was not there, of course, but she felt that his spirit was. Peace filled her with the certainty that he knew she had not seen Brant behind his back and that there had been only that one, fatal meeting.

She had continued to light a candle for her mother on Sundays beside the rosary, prayerbook and blue bird. Today she lit a candle for Joe, too, and at last she was able to pray.

XIII

THE FORGIVENESS she had never dared hope for was not Dominika's only special Christmas gift. Domingo arrived in the middle of the afternoon with his white beard and long hair giving him the appearance of the Santa Claus that American children expected.

"But of course I had to see my godson," he laughed, hoisting a rapturous Foss above his head before he more gently did the same to Vachel. "One of the wintering herders at the hotel was glad to keep the band for a few weeks and earn a little more money for *muz*. You own this place, andrea? Then you must keep busier than even Marta!"

For the boys he had carved wooden sheep, imitating fleece with great skill and carving two "black" ones out of dark wood. There was a dog for each child, painted to resemble Xagu and Kato.

"I want them to remember the *ardiak*," Domingo said, smiling as the boys abandoned their store toys to group their new animals with those Andres had made for them.

"No danger of that as long as you come to see us," Dominika laughed, going to the kitchen to bring him a plate of food.

He had his *alboka* and played at the afternoon party, adapting to Patrick's accordion. When Sherlottie sang, though, both men stilled their music. Her pure, silvery voice quieted even restless babies as it soared in "Oh, Come All Ye Faithful." Those who knew the words joined in on "The Twelve Days of Christmas" and other songs but Dominika thought the loveliest of all was one that Sherlottie sang alone.

Joseph and Mary walked in an orchard good
Where were cherries and berries as red as any
    blood. . . .

Mary's request for fruit and Joseph's harsh response to her pregnancy were poignant:

Go tell you that man and tell him straightaway
That cherries and berries mean nothing to me!

The stigma that Christians placed on children born out of wedlock made Dominika wonder afresh whether they realized that Jesus had been considered a bastard until God had proclaimed Himself the father. Might not God then be called the very special father of all those who had no earthly one?

Then there was another feast, another joyous opening of presents, shared by miners going to their shifts and returning. When the widows and children left in the early twilight, it had been a long day but Dominika urged Sherlottie to sit in the parlor for a while with the family.

The young woman hesitated. "Stay a bit," Shelby urged for he was invited, too, along with Ah Sung. "I'll see you home."

So Sherlottie stayed and had crunchy almond cookies with chocolate while Andres and Domingo played their instruments and sang old Basque carols. Vachel's curly dark head was nodding. Sherlottie glanced at Dominika for permission. When it was given, she gathered up the child and cradled him, humming softly to the music. When Vachel was sound asleep, she handed him to Dominika and spoke softly.

"Thank you for a beautiful day." Shelby helped her into her coat and they went out together.

Sometime later in the night Dominika roused from heavy sleep to the sound of Shelby's voice at her window. "Nika! Sherlottie's—sick. Can you come?

"Just a minute!"

Pulling on her coat, she let him in. He explained quickly that the girl had taken poison but the doctor was with her now. She had been made to vomit until her stomach seemed empty. The doctor thought that she might live. "But she won't want to if she has to stay in that place," Shelby finished. "It's a lot to ask but could you bring her here?"

"Of course. Do you know why she has to earn such high wages?"

He shook his head. Leaving the bedroom door open as she stood in a corner and dressed, Dominika told him. "I wish I'd known that," he muttered as she joined him. "I thought she was just a little gold digger for all those big spiritual eyes."

He berated himself as they hurried through the bitter cold toward the lights still blazing in some of the saloons and dance halls. Sherlottie had been so quiet when they left the boarding-house that he had suggested they stop in one of the saloons for a final drink.

"It had a piece of sagebrush set up for a tree," he said, his face twisting. "And the prostitutes were ganged around the piano, trying to remember carols. They'd given each other presents and decked out their pimps but it was— Compared to your place, it was hell! So we had one drink, I took Sherlottie home and—well, she sort of hung on to me and I made another damn-fool mistake."

"She said they don't work on Christmas."

"It wasn't work," he said with bitter self-mockery. "She made it clear that it was on the house. But there was something about the way she said good-night that worried me. Couldn't get her off my mind. After I had another drink—two or three of them—I went back."

Sherlottie would not wake up. He had called the madam, who had seen this kind of thing before. She had started the girl vomiting while he rounded up the doctor, who had just finished giving morphine to ease the death of a prostitute who had drunk carbolic acid.

The outside of the frame house was simple, although it was one of the few buildings that were painted. Shelby steered Dominika through a foyer hung with gilt mirrors and into a thickly carpeted parlor that was furnished with velvet sofas and brocaded chairs. At the far end there was a bar and a grand piano, dimly lit by a single lamp.

Upstairs, in a room at the end of the hall, they found the

doctor taking his leave. "Feed her lightly for a few days," he was saying. "Better not let her work until she's strong." Giving Dominika a puzzled glance, he tipped his hat slightly as he brushed past her.

A woman with a heavy but still voluptuous figure was bathing Sherlottie's colorless face. She gave Shelby an unfriendly stare from shrewd hazel eyes. Her hair was an unnatural auburn but she was still a handsome woman.

"What'd you do to upset her, Truro? One of my best girls! Never drunk or rolling clients or making a fuss. Just right for the quality. What did you say to her?"

"That's none of your business, Helen. Pack her things. Mrs. Uhalde is going to take care of her."

The madam's gaze swung to Dominika. Her scowl slowly faded. "Oh. You're the one runs the Basco boardinghouse. Gave the kids a party." Her tone softened although it held an edge of perplexity. "Sherlottie was tickled pink that you asked her to come." The keen hazel eyes narrowed. "You reckon one of the widows or some big-mouth miner said something mean to her?"

Sherlottie's eyes opened. She gave a weak shake of her head. "Everybody was nice. Real nice." Tears brimmed through the thick, dark-golden lashes and spilled down her face.

Easy enough to understand, Dominika thought. The children had made her think of the boy back in Missouri. After the warm, happy sharing, after she had sung like an angel to the hushed miners and families, she had gone with Shelby to a grim foreshadowing of the future holidays stretching before her. Then even the needs of little crippled Tommy had not been enough to keep her from trying to escape.

Kneeling beside her, Dominika took her hand. "I want you to come home with me. We'll manage to take care of your Tommy. Maybe he could even come out and live with us."

Sherlottie gave a half-glance to Shelby and flushed deeply. "Mrs. Uhalde, I'm no good. Not fit to be around you."

"My luck has been better," Dominika said.

Helen cleared her throat. "Sherlottie, you better go with the lady. I don't want girls who're apt to take poison, stir up a mess." She gave her dyed hair a toss. "I'll get your things together.'' The harshness in her tone was not echoed by the look in her eyes, though, as she bent over and for just a second hugged the girl to her heavy bosom.

Shelby hired a livery carriage to transport Sherlottie and her small trunk. When they reached the boardinghouse, he carried her to the parlor, where Dominika hastily made up the couch. Sherlottie would convalesce better in this warm place than in the icy bedroom. Dominika made coffee for Shelby and warmed milk for Sherlottie, which she gave her along with a sleeping powder the doctor had left.

When Sherlottie seemed to be asleep, Shelby, who had been staring at the pot-bellied stove, put down his cup. Rising, he took Dominika by the wrist and drew her into the kitchen, closing the door. ''Nika, I know your husband hasn't been dead long. I meant to wait another six months, maybe a year, before I said anything. But you must know that I love you.''

''Shelby, I—''

He searched her face. ''You know it, all right. I hope you won't be angry if I say that sometimes you seem to have felt a little of the shock I get deep in my guts when our hands brush or you smile.'' He took a long breath. It was strange to see this brash, assured man nerving himself. ''Maybe you don't know yet, Nika, but you ought to have some notion. Will you ever love me?''

Distressed, she faltered, ''Why, Shelby, I do love you as friend but—'' How could she explain that she thought she would always mourn Joe, be too full of guilt to love another man?

He covered his ears in mock horror. ''That's enough! Next you'll say I'm dear as a brother. It's what I was afraid of but I had to be sure.''

''Shelby—''

He laughed at her bewilderment. ''Don't look stricken, my dear. I'm not one to hang around and eat my heart out. Pretty tired of this life anyway. If Sherlottie will have me, I'm going to marry her. We'll send for her Tommy and maybe have a few kids of our own.''

''But—what will you do?''

''Think all I can do is fan the pasteboards?'' His dark eyebrows arched up and he chuckled. ''This may surprise you but

I've always wanted a farm. I have enough saved to buy a good one. If Sherlottie likes the notion, that's what we'll do.''

Dominika had relied on him more than she had realized until that moment and though she had not been ready for courtship and doubted that she ever would be, Shelby's admiration had reaffirmed her as a desirable woman. A wave of desolation went over her but she swiftly controlled it.

"You, a farmer?" she laughed. "Why, that's wonderful, Shelby! I think Sherlottie's very lucky—and you are too."

He fumbled in his pocket. "I haven't given you your Christmas gift." The ring that he put on her finger was of intricately worked gold set with a big ruby surrounded by smaller ones.

"You should give it to Sherlottie," she protested.

"I bought it for you. Just something to remember me by." The smile left his face as he gathered her close. "I want something to remember, too."

He kissed her tenderly, long and deeply. The awareness that had smoldered between them broke into flame. Dominika's blood was racing when Shelby let her go. He smiled crookedly.

"You'll remember," he said. "Not enough to make you sad. But you'll remember." He dropped a kiss on her forehead and was gone before she could move.

The wedding was held in Dominika's parlor a week later, and following a festive meal served with champagne, Mr. and Mrs. Shelby Truro took the Rockaway stage for Las Vegas and the train to Missouri.

Happy for them but feeling lonely, Dominika waved them off and turned her collar high against the piercing wind. Domingo had left the day before, the holidays were over, Shelby was gone—

But she was at peace with Joe. She had two dear children, faithful Andres, Ah Sung and Brigid. And a boardinghouse to run! There were sheets to change today and it was time to add *garbanzos* to the thick stew. She hurried home, drew off her gloves, gazed at Shelby's ring for a moment and then smiled as she threw back her shoulders and went into the kitchen.

1907 saw almost open warfare between members of the IWW and the WFM. In Idaho, Clarence Darrow had won acquittal for Big Bill Haywood and other union officers in the dynamite murder of former Governer Steunenberg but the WFM was trying to distance itself from the IWW and its reputation for radical lawlessness. Some miners who belonged to both unions switched to one or the other.

"Damn Wobblies want to give dishwashers same as miners!" growled Davey Trefax one day as he came in from work and Patrick O'Brien was just leaving. "Damme, they be even letting in the bunch of pimpin' musicians!"

Patrick slammed down his lunch pail. "Hadn't been for the IWW, there'd aye be changin'-rooms by now. Ye'd have to shove that high grade up your arse or leave it for the company, ye bandy-legged, monkey-armed, shoutin' Methody Cornishman!"

Davey tossed down his lunch pail and peeled off his jacket. "Why, 'ee igerant, Papish, pot-muchin' Irisher, 'ee don't know as much as 'un pig about politics. All 'ee I Won't Workers! Ee can't run 'un mine! But 'ee can get 'un closed down and throw us all out of work!"

"Patrick! Davey!" Dominika hurried out of the kitchen and stood between them. She picked up their lunch pails and handed each to its owner. "I would hate to lose either of you but you know the rules about fighting."

"I couldn't fight such a little banty rooster as that anyway," Patrick said scornfully. He swung out the door.

"Come get your breakfast while it's hot," Dominika urged the spluttering Davey.

She had managed to keep fights from breaking out in the boardinghouse but there was many a melee in the tenderloin. WFM miners boycotted the dance hall where IWW musicians played and IWW men stopped patronizing places employing non-union musicians. The conflict spread to the cribs and parlor houses so that, as Davey taunted Patrick when he did not know that Dominika was in earshot, "Un good man's not gonna catch they Wobblie clap from some IWW whore!"

"Didn't know ye had anything to catch it with," blasted Patrick but when Dominika walked in, they fell silent, contenting themselves with glowers.

As winter passed Dominika was appalled at the ways in

which a miner might die and the numbers of them that did. Use of dynamite, electricity and machine drills had sent the men ever deeper into the earth and killed an increasing number of them.

Cave-ins had become more common because proper timbering was often neglected when the shaft was a long way from the outside. Dangers of fire, poison gases, water and heat increased. It was more difficult to dispose of the men's wastes, and many caught pneumonia from working in wet areas and walking home while soaked garments froze to their bodies. Foul air was the worst problem, though. Miners often grew dizzy or lost consciousness from lack of oxygen and in hard-rock mining that could mean tragedy.

Dynamite, kept at forty-two degrees for safety, had to be warmed before use and though larger mines employed specialists to unpack, thaw and deliver the explosive to blasting sites, in smaller operations the ordinary miners might thaw it before a fire, place it in the hot ashes of a blacksmith's forge, put it on the back of a boiler or even heat it by a candle flame. Few people, including engineers and superintendents, understood much about electricity, and faulty wiring in a wet shaft often led to an electrocution.

Slower but perhaps the worst killer of all was phthisis, or "miner's consumption." Dominika grew to hate the sound of the hacking cough and shortness of breath that gripped some of her boarders. The machine drills made a fine, razor-edged dust that cut into lung tissue and made the men easy prey to tuberculosis or pneumonia.

Companies were often sued, of course, by men, or the families of men, who were maimed or killed but as she gathered from a heated argument between Patrick and Davey, there were several widely accepted doctrines that often excused a company.

"I had a mate got both eyes blown out, lost his hands and was burned terrible," snarled Patrick. "What'd the company do? Lawyer argued it was me mate's place to refuse to go lookin' for that missed charge—and they'd have fired him if he hadn't!"

Davey shrugged. "Everybody knows mining's they devil. That's why pay's good, ole son."

" 'Assumed risk,' " mimicked Patrick. " 'Contributory negligence!' Holy Mither, that be a lot to feed kids on! Use a man up, blow off his legs and arms and throw him out. And it'll be that way, ye blockhead, till workers own the companies!"

"Butte local owns shares in Amalgamated," growled Davey in disgust. "Ever since Comstock began, miners bought shares. Right up they road at Tonopah, WFM and they operators get along fine. Plenty of bosses were miners once. I do hear that John MacKay over on Comstock wouldn't cut wages to three and a half dollars like they other owners wanted. Said he got four dollars a day when he was working and when he couldn't pay 'un, he'd quit."

"Faith and ye sound like a boss yourself!" scorned Patrick. Suddenly he laughed. "If my poor ould dad could have made even three dollars a day, he'd have thought he'd gone to heaven!"

"My da came over to keep from going on they parish," Davey remembered.

"Mine came to keep from starving," Patrick said. Their eyes met and for a moment they were friends again.

Bickering continued between the WFM and the IWW but as summer deepened, all thoughts turned to the gala Fourth-of-July celebration that was the high festival of every mining camp. Drill and hammer were the main tools of the hard-rock miner and experts came from all around to compete for the prizes in drilling.

Patrick and Davey, it turned out, had been unbeatable in double-hand drilling, "double-jacking," but when one of the boarders asked Patrick if they were competing as a team that year, he shook his wild golden head after a questioning glance at the silent Davey.

"Machine drills make a mock of what men can do," Patrick said.

"But without you and Davey, the Mohawk may lose!" objected the other miner.

Patrick shrugged. "Oh, there be other good double-jackers, Willy." He sounded wistful, though. A sparkle came to his eyes as he flexed his long, battered fingers. "I may single-jack."

" 'Ee would," grunted Davey. "Seeing as 'ee left hand is

same as 'un right to 'ee, 'ee hast advantage over they right-handed.''

''Man does the best he can,'' Patrick retorted jauntily.

The morning of the Fourth began with a parade led by the union band and hose-cart races between the volunteer fire departments. Foss and Vachel enjoyed these but grew restless at the ball game played between married men and bachelors. When compared to the speed of *pilota*, Dominika found it a dull and confusing contest. She took the boys home and assumed the cooking so that Ah Sung might watch the foot-races and tugs-of-war that he enjoyed.

That afternoon they all went to watch the drilling. They were yielded places near the heavy platform to which a one-ton ore car had been lifted. On the ground below, perhaps eight feet beneath the end of the car, a plank bin held a ton of rock debris. When the starting pistol fired, a miner started heaving the rocks into the car, using his hands for the big chunks, a scoop for the smaller. He was panting and sweating when he pitched the last bit of waste into the car along with the scoop. His friends shouted and the scorekeeper chalked up his time while the car was upended in order to dump the rock back into the bin for the next contender.

This ''mucking'' was a warm-up for the events of skill in which winners might become legendary. The ore car was trundled away and attention turned to the great block of granite, six feet high and flat on top, that was placed flush with the height of the platform.

''That be Vermont granite,'' Patrick explained. He had come through the crowds to Dominika and now he lifted Foss in his arms so the boy could see better. ''Costs a mint to ship it in but it's the thing for drilling. Basalt's too tough, soft rock's no good, quartzite chews up a drill. And ye can just bet they've looked that rock over to be sure it's not got cracks.''

''Are you going to single-jack?''

Patrick grinned. ''Depends. I'll see how the others do. Not going to work up a sweat if there's no one worth beating.''

The first contestant knelt on the block. At the signal he planted the drill steel and swung down the four-pound hammer which was attached to a wrist-thong. On the backstroke the driller loosened his fingers, relaxing them for the instant before they gripped the steel for the next blow. As one drilling steel dulled, he tossed it aside and without missing rhythm put in a new, longer one. An official hosed water at the crevice to wash away the filings.

The driller hammered with expert concentration for fifteen minutes, stopped at the signal and rose to thunderous applause. Grinning, he wiped his face and jumped off the rock as the depth he had reached was chalked on the scoreboard.

"Fair," Patrick shrugged. "But if no one's deeper, I'll just stay nice and clean."

The fourth man's motions flowed with a precision and grace that was wonderful to see. A great cheer greeted his score. "Twenty-five inches?" frowned Patrick. With a sigh he handed Foss to Davey, who had shouldered his way over to them. "Begorrah, I'll have to see if I can beat that!"

" 'Ee should," groused Davey. " 'Ee swings as mean left hand as 'ee do right. That be they tramp miner up from Bisbee, Pat. Show 'un how we drill at Goldfield!"

Goldfield partisans were shouting Patrick's name. With a lordly smile he fished a pouch of drilling steels and his hammer from beneath the platform and went to kneel on the great block of granite. His hammer echoed the start-off pistol crack. With his fair hair blazing in the sun, he looked like an ancient hero-god as he sledged the hammer blow after blow, discarded steel and shifted hands all as smoothly as if it were play.

Goldfielders yelled themselves hoarse. The Cornishman using the hose was supposed to be neutral but he was a shift-boss at the Mohawk and as he rinsed away the filings, he shouted, "Come on, old son! Hit she just 'un fast and just 'un hard as 'ee can."

When the pistol sounded, the scorekeeper called out the time before he chalked it up. "Patrick O'Brien of the Mohawk— twenty-six and three-quarter inches!"

No one tried to better the record. Patrick, flushed and gulping for breath, was given a box on which to sit and plied with cold beer. When one of the officials, a mine superintendent, brought him the two-hundred-and-fifty-dollar purse, Patrick accepted it negligently and said in a voice loud enough for all to hear, ''Thank ye kindly, sir. I'll be givin' this to the local to help widows and orphans.''

The superintendent gave him a hard look but it was time for the double-jacking to begin and attention turned to the shirt-sleeved pair that strode across the platform with their bundle of steel. One carried a double-jack, a hammer that could not weigh more than nine pounds.

XIV

THE PAIR were liquid force and power. At the end of a few minutes it was clear that this team was hitting the steel oftener and harder than anyone before them. Sounds of dismay rose from the crowd, mingled with unwilling cries of admiration. A champion driller, Dominika thought, was to miners what a great *pelotari* or *ezpatadantzari* was to Basques.

"Look at 'un!" groaned Davey as they changed places without missing a stroke. "Damme, she drill bits be each just a hair smaller, slide in nice and easy after they one before. These be no tramps," he finished gloomily. "These be canny lads as go around she camps bragging big and silly till 'ee bets agin 'un. Then 'un clean up."

At fifteen minutes the pair had put down forty inches. Heaving, soaked with sweat, they collapsed beyond the platform, grinning at the applause that echoed from the mountain. They had been magnificent and even those who had lost heavy wagers gave them their due. Patrick was one who took them beer and a wet towel. While he was congratulating them, the hose-operator from the Mohawk hurried over to Davey, his plump face red and looking as if oiled.

"Davey, old son, 'ee and they Wobblie Irisher have to make 'un team!"

Davey shook his head. "We've not drilled together in 'un long time. Don't have they steel."

The Mohawk man looked around desperately. "We can get 'ee steel."

"Patrick's wore from she single-jack."

" 'Ee going to let they tramps get 'un horselaugh on Goldfield?"

375

"We're out of practice," Davey growled. "Don't think we could beat 'un."

Still, he glowered through the next performance and swore savagely when the steel broke off. The next team put down only thirty-five inches.

There was one team left now, older men. "They know how to dress they steel," Davey said, watching closely as they apparently debated whether to even try to go against the daunting record. "Sometimes that, with skill, makes up for speed. But not today 'un won't."

Abruptly the driller with the hammer went over to Patrick and the other came to Davey, proffering the cherished, finely honed steel. "Come on, Davey. You and Pat show those guys!"

The Cornishman hesitated. He looked across the granite to where Patrick was facing the man with the double-jack. Davey raised a black eyebrow.

"Old son?" he called and though the question was not loud, Patrick's square-boned face broke into a grin.

"Let's do it!" he whooped and grasped the hammer.

Davey held the "starter" while Patrick swung and from that first second no one would have guessed that they had not been practicing together for months. Patrick was younger and bigger but Davey had formidable power in his brawny shoulders.

Someone beside Dominika whispered, "That hose-squirter, be sure he's put some beer in the water so's the foam'll bring the cuttings up faster!"

Dominika had winced before at the force of the hammer blows, fearing what would happen should the hammer slip even a fraction and strike the holder's hand. Now, with men whom she knew and liked facing that danger, she could scarcely breathe.

"Seventy-five, seventy-six, seventy-seven!" the official counted at the end of one minute.

The crowd roared wildly.

The pile of discarded drills grew bigger every time the men changed place. Eight minutes were gone. By Dominika's calculation they were tied, or even a few strokes ahead. If their blows were driving the steel as deep, they had a good chance to win.

Their motions were so splendidly gauged, so flowingly perfect, that she began to relax, even starting to enjoy the spectacle without that anxious fear.

Patrick brought the hammer down. It glanced. Davey flinched. There was a moan from the crowd. The hammer stopped. Blood dripped from Davey's hand. But he glared up at Patrick.

"Lay it on, 'ee!"

Patrick brought down the sledge. They had barely missed a stroke. Men shouted. A woman screamed as each blow of the hammer seemed to shock more blood from the injured hand. When it was time to change, Davey somehow took the hammer. There was no wavering as he swung, though blood coursed down his arm and dripped into the hole so that the hose washed away red water with the filings.

The camp doctor ran up. Davey cursed him back. He changed with Patrick once more, holding the last, long five-foot steel. Blood poured from him and his head drooped but he gave Patrick a savage look. The double-jack descended. Again and again.

The crowd was hushed. Apart from the ring of the hammer, the only sound was the tortured breathing of the men at the rock.

"Seventy-eight, seventy-nine, eighty—eighty-one! Time!"

Patrick dropped the hammer. He gathered Davey into his arms, cradling him and weeping while the throng went mad.

They had won with a fraction under forty-two inches. Championship drilling, the official announced, close to the forty-two and a half put down in fourteen minutes at the 1903 Mining Congress in El Paso.

The doctor cleansed and bound up the crushed hand. He thought no bones were broken. The main danger would be from infection. Patrick carried Davey home, put a basin under the bandaged hand and doused it with whisky.

Davey howled. " 'Ee blockhead Irisher, wastin' they good whisky!"

"There's plenty more for ye," Patrick said. "Ye take the purse."

"Half belongs to 'ee," Davey said faintly. He was drained of color and Dominika hurried to bring him some wine and a bowl of soup.

"Ye won't work for a while," Patrick said. "Money's yours. We wouldn't have it if ye hadn't held on."

He was determined as were the miners who came in all the rest of the evening to praise Davey and give him a share of their winnings. He was the camp's hero. Dominika babied him for a week with special foods, until his strength returned. The hand healed gradually, the splayed, oozing wound closing itself a little more each day. When Patrick was off work, the two men sought the gambling halls and saloons together, comrades again. There was even affection in the way they argued over the IWW.

Vachel had turned two that July, still chubby and dimpled, his rosy cheeks giving a tender flush to his warm skin. Foss was thin with straight black hair and those disconcerting blue eyes that reminded her of Brant. Bitterness and shame still welled up within her when he entered her mind. She quickly forced his memory away.

Foss considered Vachel a baby and he usually played with the slightly older children of the livery-owner down the street. Vachel did not lack for attention, though. Ah Sung spoiled him scandalously with tidbits and Andres was content to sit on the floor with him and play by the hour with blocks or the toy sheep and dogs.

The relentless round of work, welcomed at first, was beginning to wear on Dominika. Goldfield was all right as long as the boys were small enough to keep track of but she did not want them growing up in the feverish hustle of a boom town. With longing she remembered the quiet of Joe's ranch. Sometimes it had been oppressive when Joe was gone most of the time but if only she had the chance to wait for him again! If only—

In a year or two, she decided, certainly by the time that Foss was ready for school, she would sell the boardinghouse, buy a home in a small, settled town and perhaps start a restaurant. Maybe at Reno, Carson City or Elko, where she had heard that there were many Basques. It would not torment her to serve Basques the good food of their homeland now and while her sons were American and spoke English more fluently than they did Basque, she did not want them to lose all touch with her people.

She was lonely, too, in a way strange for one who was constantly among people. She missed her talks with Shelby, the knowledge that he cared about her and could be depended on. She was fond of Brigid, Ah Sung and most of her boarders, especially Davey and Pat, but there was no one in whom she could confide, no one to ask for advice or share her private thoughts with. She did go to Mass but no Basque was used in the service, of course; there were no *sepulturie* and she felt almost as if she were attending alien rites. Where at home centuries and tradition linked Etchahoun with the church, here there was no connection and for Dominika the loss was grievous.

Richard Andrews, the young, blond mining engineer who had rented Shelby's old room, invited her to ride in his automobile and made it clear that he wanted to be more than friendly but although he was nice-looking in a freckled, snub-nosed way, she felt twice his age and refused his invitations and overtures.

"You don't seem to think I'm dry behind the ears!" he burst out one day when she had laughingly evaded his attempt to take her hand. "I'm twenty-seven. How old are you, Mrs. Uhalde?"

She actually had to stop and think. "Twenty-three," she said in surprise.

He looked startled, too, but recovered quickly. "Well, then, you've no reason at all to pat me on the head. I thought you were at least twenty-six. Not that you look old," he added hastily. "But to have the boys and run this business and all—"

Something about the situation struck her as hilarious. She leaned against the bannister and laughed until, bright crimson, he turned on his heel and marched away. He moved when that week's rent was up and although she tried to apologize, his youthful male outrage and wounded pride again caused her to laugh irrepressibly. He gave her a last furious glance and stalked out, his large ears red above his stiff collar.

Dominika sobered after he had gone. It was not really funny. Would there never be another man for her? She was young and healthy and occasionally she dreamed that a man held her and loved her, although she could never see who he was. Since the time that she had felt attracted to Shelby, no man had seemed even faintly possible. With other men, she felt as old as Mari, as secret and inaccessible as the spirits of the cave. Perhaps she measured them against Joe. Compared to him, most men would fall short.

October came. Foss was four years old and Dominika felt as if she had already lived her life.

Not long after Foss's birthday Dominika's growing dissatisfactions were blotted out by a business panic that began in the East with the collapse of the Knickerbocker Trust Company and Westinghouse Electric, causing banks to close throughout the country.

The run on the Goldfield bank was stopped only when Tex Rickard of the Northern sent wheelbarrows of silver dollars for display in the bank's front window. Since he trusted the bank, people decided that they could, too.

In the East, J. P. Morgan and other financiers combined to import a hundred million dollars in gold from Europe. This action checked the worst of the crash but in many mining towns, including Goldfield, the operators paid in scrip that was good only in places where it was accepted.

The use of scrip added insult to temptation when men worked with ore worth ten to forty dollars a pound. "Owners been't takin' she profits in scrip," Davey said as he apologetically paid his board in the detested paper. "I never high-graded before but damme if I'm not about to start."

Even after the railroad had reached town two years earlier, the prices of groceries and other necessities had remained at the high rates charged when all supplies had to be freighted in by wagon. With high-grading at its peak, the operators decided to force the use of changing-rooms. They claimed to have lost at least a million dollars to high-graders in 1906 and were determined to stop what they considered thievery but the miners considered almost a right in such rich ore, especially when they were being paid in scrip. Only three of the fifty-four assayers handled ore that had not come to them through "lunch-pail shipments."

"Company don't want us catching cold," Patrick chuckled wickedly when he settled his bill. He paid in money. "We'll be aye healthier to take off our wet 'diggers' and change to dry things—only they want us to strip and walk a couple hundred feet in front of a bunch of gawkin' watchmen."

He did not tell her, but Brigid did, that some of the watchmen checked under the men's armpits, high between their legs and even in their mouths and rectums. The three hundred men at the Mohawk, including Patrick and Davey, rebelled. They agreed to change to underwear before walking to their street clothes but they refused to walk naked past company men who felt empowered to handle them as if they were so many mules.

The men went on strike in some of the mines. In others they were locked out from fear of sabotage. The simmering struggle between the operators and the IWW-dominated local exploded into threats. The owners persuaded Governor Sparks to ask for Federal troops. By December sixth President Theodore Roosevelt's orders to General Funston had brought in soldiers from California and had them camped at a vantage point from which the mines could be watched.

There were no riots and the Federal investigators who arrived on December fifteenth notified the President that the camp was peaceful and agreed with General Funston that his men should be withdrawn. "Owners put up such a howl that the President left two companies," Patrick said in disgust. "They'll sit on us till a State police can be got together and sent over to enforce they bloody change-rooms!"

"Camp be full of scabs," Davey added, scratching his ear. Between sorrow and anger, he said to Patrick, "This be what 'ee IWW did to the union."

"Local passed a resolution in October for WFM to keep hooked up with they IWW," reminded Patrick. "Change-house is what's wrong here—strip searches and scrip pay."

Davey sighed. " 'Ee be right there, old son. How's Tonopah sound to 'ee?"

"Operators up there wouldn't mix into this row," Patrick

pondered. "They get along with the union. Any camp's better'n this now we got army or police on us." His blue eyes were bright with regret, though, as he looked at Dominika. "It's sorry I be to leave the best place I ever stayed, Mrs. Uhalde."

"You have to go where you can find work," Dominika said. "I'll miss you both but I wish you all the luck in the world."

They gave her the rest of their scrip, saying it would be worth nothing outside of Goldfield, and left that day for Tonopah. Dominika had been paid in paper ever since the strike began and now she was not being paid at all. At least grocery prices had come down twenty per cent, for the mine owners had threatened to set up commissaries unless the independent stores reduced prices to a reasonable level.

Because of the panic there were many unemployed workers who were glad to break the strike at three and a half dollars for unskilled and up to five dollars for skilled. Applicants had to sign a "rustling card," stating that they would not join a union. The hated changing-houses were used.

Most of Dominika's boarders were union members but many stayed on, hoping that when the troops left, hiring would ease and they could return to their old jobs. Dominika wished that it would happen soon. Her sympathies were with the men although she did not approve of high-grading. She was resolved not to put them out but she was beginning to draw on her savings in order to put food on the table. That could not go on much longer.

Even so, she organized another Christmas party that year, although most of the money for gifts came from the madams and the saloon and gambling-hall operators. Her boarders had no money but they had gone around to all of the widows' homes and made any necessary repairs. They also brought down a tree from the hills and trimmed it.

On Christmas morning the dining room was crowded with mothers and children and many unemployed miners. There was spiced chocolate or coffee for everyone, with fruit, *almendrados* and nut cakes. Patrick's accordion was missed but another man played almost as spiritedly and the carols at least briefly swept away the troubles brooding over the camp.

Dominika was having coffee in her parlor, smiling at her

sons' delighted rapture with their new toys, when a knock came at her private entrance. That was unusual. Callers ordinarily came through the kitchen and she suspected that Ah Sung discouraged unsavory visitors.

Rising, she opened the door to a stranger, smartly dressed in a dark, pin-striped suit and derby hat. He had a ruddy, moon-shaped face, a fat neck and black eyes set so deeply in surrounding flesh that they seemed pushed in like raisins.

"May I step in, Mrs. Uhalde?" he asked politely. "I'm Lyman Falks from the Businessmen's and Mine Operators' Association."

That was the group that had called in the troops and instituted the "rustling cards." Dominika stepped back to let him enter but she did not ask him to sit down. "What can I do for you, Mr. Falks?"

He beamed. "Madam, the question is, what can I do for you?" He paused, seeming disappointed when she did not respond. "I assume that you're running this boardinghouse as a business, not a charity," he continued briskly. "Perhaps you hope to receive your due when these strikers are rehired but I can assure you that will never be. They're finished in Goldfield."

Dominika shrugged. "I should think this is a thing to tell the men."

"They've been told. They just won't believe it." Falk's heartiness congealed. "If you weren't harboring these malcontents, madam, they'd have to move on."

Dominika looked at him steadily. He reddened but went on. "My Association is prepared to indemnify you for the arrears owed by these malingerers."

"That's kind. But why?"

He made a sound of exasperation. "Madam, from all I hear of you, you're not simple-minded. Of course you'll send these Wobblies packing. As long as they're here, they can stir up trouble. We want them gone before the troops leave."

"Mr. Falks, the Association doesn't own my boardinghouse. My arrangements with my boarders are none of your concern."

"You're crazy!" His eyes sank even deeper into the pale fat. "Or maybe you're paid by the Wobblies! Is that it?"

She opened the door. He caught her wrist. "Well, my girl, if you're a Wobblie whore, you might think of switching to the Association. We pay better—"

Dominika slapped him so hard that he stumbled down the steps, losing his derby. As he stooped to dust it off, a seam in his pants ripped.

Holding the hat behind him, he said thickly, "You're as stupid as these damn miners and you're going to be just as broke!" Dominika shut the door. She was trembling with outrage though a chill of fear quickly followed.

If the Association was determined to see the union men gone, there was no telling what it might do. "Who was that man, Mama?" Foss demanded, tugging at her skirt.

She ruffled his dark hair. "He came to the wrong place, dear." But for all her brave words, she did not know how much longer she could pay Ah Sung's and Brigid's wages and feed twenty-eight men.

She awoke coughing. For a moment she drowsily thought Ah Sung was having trouble with the stove but the acridity was too great for that. Wide awake in an instant, she caught up Vachel and opened the door. Fire and smoke leaped at her, sucked by the fresh oxygen. Shutting the door, she banged her fists on the wall that separated her from Andres and Foss.

"Andres! Fire! Get Foss and Xagu! Go out the window!"

His distant voice reached her. "Yes, andrea!"

She opened the window, snatched up the rosary, the prayerbook and the blue bird, wrapped Vachel and herself in a blanket and climbed out. She and Andres shouted the alarm. A roused neighbor ran for the nearest fire department. Boarders were piling out of the house, bringing whatever they'd had time to catch up. Dominika left the boys with Andres and ran back inside to look for Ah Sung, who slept in a little room off the kitchen.

She found him pumping water at the sink and tossing it onto the flames that were licking at the kitchen wall, having eaten through from the parlor. Smoke was rolling through the house, pushed along by darting billows of fire. Dominika dragged at the cook's sleeve.

"Ah Sung, we can't save it! Come on! Now!"

For a terrible moment she thought he would refuse but then he seemed to wake out of a daze of compulsion. They ran through the front door as the stairs crashed behind the last miner out and the fire wagons rolled around the building, hosing water on it from both sides.

It was hopeless but at least no one had perished and the volunteers had prevented the fire from spreading to the surrounding flimsy buildings. Dominika stood there in the night, barefoot and shivering in the blanket she had again wrapped around herself and Vachel.

The fire had not started in the kitchen. Nor upstairs. Nor from a careless smoker. It had started in her parlor despite the fact that the fire in the stove had been down to ash-covered embers when she had gone to bed.

She could not prove it and there was nothing she could do, but she would always believe that the fire had been set at the behest of the Association.

One of the miners' widows who had attended the party that day came over and put an arm around Dominika. "Come along with 'ee, Mrs. Uhalde. 'Ee'll catch thy death like that."

"The men," Dominika faltered.

One of them standing near her gave her a lusty hug. "Don't worry about us, bless you, ma'am! We can stay with mates for a day or two or at the union hospital. It's time we left for other diggings anyway. But how will you make out? We owe you money and you've lost all this—"

"I have a little in the bank," Dominika reassured him.

He still looked worried, as did the other men who had gathered around. "Tell us where to send our back board and when we're working again, we'll pay you," said one of the miners whom she had nursed through pneumonia.

There was a chorus of assent.

Dominika looked at the rough, whiskery faces. She had not been as close to any of them as she had been to Patrick and Davey but each was a friend. Their concern took away some of the devastating sense of loss. Her work had not been wasted. She had lost almost everything material but a score of fatherless families had been given hope and a new start because of her parties, and her boarders, she thought, would always be a little kinder in the future and readier to share.

She had felt for months that she should leave Goldfield but she realized that her resources would not be enough to buy a home or a business. That would have to wait till she earned a new stake and the place to do that was in a mining camp.

"I'm going to Tonopah," she told the men.

Ah Sung remained in Goldfield with his laundry-owning cousin. When Dominika went to see if he had enough money, a smile broke over his broad, tea-colored face. "Ah Sung going to ask missy same question. Missy pay good, Ah Sung have room and meals, save allee else. Many dollars in bank."

"Why, that's wonderful!" Dominika said with heartfelt relief. She had been afraid that Ah Sung might have lost his hoard in the fire. "Are you going to start your own restaurant?"

Ah Sung shook his head. "Want to return to Flowery Kingdom. Marry, have family. But, missy, Ah Sung want to leave you money."

"Thank you." Tears stung her eyes as she pressed his hand. "That's very good of you, Ah Sung, but I'll get along all right. Good luck to you, and a good life."

He had been in America for twenty-five years but he had not the slightest doubt of where home was. Dominika envied him. Etchahoun was the home of her heart, the cave was the home of her soul, but day by day her life was further bound to this new world.

Should she break the ties, work and save enough to take her sons back to the Basque country? If she ever meant to go, it must be soon, while they were young enough to adapt.

But the truth was that she could not imagine either of them, especially Foss, growing up in that small, green country and accepting the traditions that she had absorbed with her mother's milk. If she could have taken them to Etchahoun, if one of them could have become the heir, she might have tried to make the journey but Esteban would keep the farm for many, many years and should he have children, she might face a terrible battle to regain the holding after his death.

No. Her sons were both American. She would raise them in America. At least, to strengthen her, she had the blue bird.

XV

THE TONOPAH ORES, mostly silver, had been discovered in 1900 by Lazy Jim Butler, a former Comstock miner who with thousands of others had drifted away when the original Comstock lode was exhausted at the end of the century. The use of cyanide to extract gold from tailings or low-grade ore kept the Virginia City-Gold Hill region in operation but the bonanza was over. Butler had turned to ranching and prospecting and one day while he was hunting for his burros, his wife noticed a yellow glitter in a rock among those where she sat waiting.

Founded and run by experienced prospectors, Tonopah had been an orderly town even in its great boom period and was in this year of 1908 a steady and substantial city, with many permanent homes and businesses. It had its saloons and tenderloin but it also had an opera house, a movie theater, schools, churches and a fine hospital that had been built by the union. Most of the mine-owners had been miners at one time and had maintained good relationships with their union workers.

It was only a brief train ride from Goldfield to Tonopah. When Dominika arrived with her sons and Andres and Xagu, she found it difficult to believe that such a short trip had entirely changed the nature of her world. The town spread out along the street toward the mines lying ahead on the sides of two steep mountains. To the west gleamed the snowy Sierra Nevada, seeming closer than it had in Goldfield.

Bewildered, she stood there on the platform unmoving, surrounded by her little group and its single valise. She had not seen fit to buy things only to carry them, although she would have to outfit all of them quickly. Fortunately, while most of her money had been invested in the boardinghouse, a neighbor had paid her a fair price for the lot and she'd had some savings in the bank. She would be able to rent a comfortable place and take care of the boys and Andres but she must find work as soon as possible.

So there was no time to stand here woolgathering! She took Foss by one hand, Vachel by the other, and was turning to ask Andres to bring the valise when Foss gave a shout of pleasure.

"Davey!"

"Right on 'ee, son!" The stocky Cornishman swung Vachel to a shoulder and gravely shook Foss's hand before he gripped Dominika's. "Patrick or me's been meeting every train from Goldfield, ma'am, since we heard 'ee was coming. Couple of our old mates came up to work day after they fire. We'd have come down but they said 'ee was bound 'ere."

"It's good to see you!" Dominika cried, much cheered by being so remembered. "Do you know of a good place for us to stay till I can rent a house?"

"If two rooms'll do 'ee, 'ee can stay at our house," Davey said. He grinned at Dominika's startled glance. "Oh, it be proper and all. I married 'un nice widder lady last week. We board Patrick but Annie's got no mind to have the extra rooms full of miners."

"Well, if I can pay rent—"

"We can settle that later," Davey said. "Maybe you'd like to help run our restaurant."

"Restaurant? You're not in the mines?"

"They bloody hand, she never got quite right. Hurt bad after I'd worked a few hours. So Annie, she figgered that was no good and I could help her with they restaurant." He added with quick pride, "I paid off her house with they double-jacking prize and still have 'un bit in mine stocks. We're doing right well with they restaurant, too."

Annie was a tiny, bird-like woman of middle years who doted on her husband and warmly welcomed the strangers. "You stay as long as you like," she told Dominika. "It'll be rare fine to have tykes about. But if you feel crowded or find something you like better, you don't need to be embarrassed to say so."

Dominika was more than pleased with the two rooms at the

back of the solid brick house that Annie had operated as a rooming house before she bought the restaurant. They were freshly papered and the larger one contained a heating stove and several comfortable chairs. When Patrick came in after work, the boys ran to meet him and everyone went to the restaurant for supper. Dominika could not believe her luck in having so quickly found nice quarters and the support of good friends.

Next day she took Andres and the boys shopping. She outfitted them, bought what she needed for herself and purchased a few things to make the rooms more homey. The day after that she started work at the restaurant.

She had refused to accept a normal salary since the Trefaxes were charging her a ridiculously low rent of only two dollars a week. She soon discovered that she could have worked for no wages, for the miners were generous with tips, especially those who had known her in Goldfield.

At first she waited on the tables and helped Davey with the dishes but then a few of her former boarders started pestering Annie to have Dominika make a boiled dinner or codfish soup and so she was soon helping Annie cook. There was no room in the kitchen for the boys but Andres and Xagu looked after them and Patrick played with them when he had time.

Since the house was only a block from the restaurant, Dominika was able to go home several times a day and though the restaurant served till the graveyard shift, Annie insisted that Dominika spend the evenings with her sons. Andres brought them in to eat, too, and they quickly became favorites of the regular patrons.

Dominika began to think that were she able to buy a home, Tonopah might be a good place in which to settle. While it was true that more people probably went to the Big Casino, a brothel and dance hall that took up a square block of the tenderloin, than attended all the city's churches, Tonopah was not merely a free-spending mining town. It was the county seat, had five newspapers, five banks, served as headquarters and outfitting center for hundreds of prospectors and flourished as the trading hub for the region. Some of Nevada's most lavish homes graced the residential section.

Dominika did not think of marriage although she'd had three proposals during her first week at the restaurant. Shelby Truro was the single man since Joe's death to have awakened a response in her. Only in her dreams did she know passion, and now she could envision the man.

It was Brant. She locked him out of her thoughts by day but she saw him in her dreams. Not often but often enough to make her wonder despairingly if she would ever be free of that consuming, forbidden but ecstatic love which must be forever tainted by guilt.

She had wondered why Domingo had not come to visit at Christmas. One busy noontime she glanced toward the white-bearded, dark-skinned man just coming in the door and gave a cry of delight. Running to embrace him, she introduced him to Annie. Davey shook his hand and took him off to see the boys. They all returned after the rush of diners thinned and Annie made Dominika sit down to eat with them.

Severe weather had delayed Domingo's Christmas journey by several weeks. When he had at least reached Goldfield and was shocked at the sight of the burned building, a neighbor had told him where the little family had gone. Arriving in Tonopah, he had planned to go through all the stores, restaurants and hotels until he found her.

"I was going to write to Marta and Joanes so they could tell you where we were," Dominika said contritely.

"Never mind, I'm here." Domingo took a boy on each knee as he finished his meal. "My godson's almost old enough to start learning sheep. When are you going to send him to me for a summer?"

"Oh, he's not five yet," Dominika protested but for the first time she realized that her sons would soon grow up. Foss would start to school in a year and a half.

They would both be gone in fifteen years. What would she do with the rest of her life? If her sons were in America, she could not happily return to her valley but what kind of life could she have here alone?

Domingo stayed for a week, sharing Andres' and Foss's room. He had brought them carved animals and puzzles and small red berets. "You don't want them to forget that they are

Basque, andrea," he said with a hint of rebuke, though he added with a smile, "I'm glad they know the old songs and stories."

"Those are the only ones I can tell them," Dominika said. And it was true.

Her sons would hear other stories, go to school with Irish, Cornish, Scots, Welsh, Swedes, Mexicans, Austrians, Chinese and Italians as well as Americans. So many nationalities, each with its own legends and history. They would study not their own countries but the American Revolution, the Civil War and the spread westward.

She would make certain that the boys were aware of her homeland's proud past but would their children care? A daughter would be different. She could be shown the blue bird and be sent on pilgrimage to become part of the mystery that would forever link ageless past with unknown future. At a distance from both, Dominika knew that Etchahoun, though beloved and very old, could be coveted by men and taken over by them. The cave, no matter what happened in the outside world, would always be a sanctuary of peace and comfort for its women, a place of always summer.

Before Domingo left, he took Dominika's hands. "Andrea, if you want to come back, I can add onto the cabin."

Although his presence had made her homesick not only for her life with Joe but for her own people, she did not trust herself to be that close to Brant nor did she want her American sons to grow up in the isolation of a small Basque sheep camp.

So she only thanked Domingo and sent him away with a kiss.

She was twenty-four that April of 1908. Peering into the mirror, she could not see that her face had changed much since she first came to America. It was thinner perhaps, the cheekbones more pronounced beneath dark-lashed, green-gold eyes. Her thighs bore the faint pale stretchmarks of pregnancies, her waist was slimmer, her breasts fuller, but otherwise there was little to show for the years of tumult, love and sorrow that she had lived through.

Several young engineers, wearing riding breeches, welltailored flannel shirts and high-laced boots, had recently taken to eating regularly at the restaurant, loitering over many cups of coffee until a chance came to invite Dominika to the opera, a movie theater or one of the dances or parties that were given almost nightly among the town's society.

"Why don't you go?" Annie fussed, head atilt. "Do you good to have some fun, dearie."

Dominika knew that it wouldn't be long until any young man would want to do more than hold her hand, especially since she was known to be a widow. She did not want proposals, honorable or otherwise, and when she was forced to ponder the matter, she concluded with surprise that she did not *feel* single.

Nor was she bound to the memory of Joe. The blessed sense of reconciliation she had felt right before the first Christmas in Goldfield had allowed her to remember him fondly but without the anguish of guilt. No. Impossible as it was, Brant still dominated the secret, dreaming core of her inner self.

The absurd hopelessness of the feeling made her angry. Damn him, was she to wither into an old woman, never to know love again, because of him?

John Parrish was a tall, sandy-haired engineer with frank hazel eyes and an infectious grin. The next time he invited her to the theater, she went with him to a Florence Lawrence film.

It was a mistake. Instead of losing herself in the romance of "the Biograph girl," as this first star was called, Dominika found herself remembering the times when Brant had shown films for Lucie. It was a miserable evening. She declined Parrish's invitation to ice cream or coffee with the excuse of a headache.

With a puzzled sigh, he helped her into his Packard and drove her home. Standing awkwardly on the porch, he blurted, "Have I done something wrong, Mrs. Uhalde?"

"No, certainly not." She held out her hand in contrition. "You've been very kind. It was my fault. I'm afraid that I haven't yet recovered from my husband's death."

A lie of sorts but one that spared his pride—and would also, she hoped, prevent his further pursuit. But he was not that easily discouraged.

Grasping her hand, he said earnestly, "I honor your devotion, ma'am, but you're young and beautiful! It's not right to hide away." He coaxed boyishly, "If you'll go out with me, I promise to be a gentleman."

"You're very kind, Mr. Parrish but—"

A darker shadow detached itself from those beside the porch swing. "Young man, the fact is that this lady's going to marry me."

Dominika gasped. In the dim lamplight coming from the window she saw Brant's face. She also saw Parrish's face turn crimson as he dropped her hand.

"Do you know this man, Mrs. Uhalde?"

"I—I—" The words would not pass her throat.

Why was he here? What could he mean?

With perplexed bitterness John Parrish said, "I don't understand what's going on but it's pretty clear that I'm unnecessary. Good-night, ma'am."

He took himself off. Dominika whirled on Brant. Wasn't it enough that he tormented her dreams?

"I don't know why you're here," she said, trembling with fury and desire. Even in the near dark she could see the flickering light deep in his eyes. "Why don't you leave me alone? Why—"

She pushed vainly at him as he brought her into his arms, forced back her head and found her lips. She moaned, dizzied, trying to deny him, but her body softened, swept with engulfing, wild sweet flame. When he let her go, they were both gasping.

"You lied to that youngster," Brant said roughly. "Don't lie to me. It's not Joe Uhalde you can't get over, Nika. You still love me."

"Yes," she blazed, throwing back her head. "I love you. But it doesn't change things."

He spoke quietly, taking her clenched hands. "Things *have* changed, Nika. Lucie is dead."

She stared at him in shock. "Oh, my God, you didn't—"

His grip tightened savagely, "Of course I didn't! In spite of—everything, I always loved her."

"Then how—"

"She had been drinking a lot. Taking morphine for the pain that started a few years ago because of some degeneration of the spine. I guess she forgot how many pills she'd had. She died two weeks ago."

Aghast at the news, feeling a surge of grief and pity for the beautiful young woman who had been her friend, Dominika said cruelly, "I suppose it's something that you do not come straight from the funeral."

He slapped her across the face.

She staggered and hit him back with all her strength. His teeth cut into her palm. His mouth began to bleed. Then they were in each other's arms once again, tasting blood and tears, weeping for all that they had lost but aching still, longing and cleaving one to the other.

She felt as if she tore apart her own flesh when she pushed away from him. "Go away, Brant. Leave me alone."

He caught her arm, gripping it so savagely that she winced, at the same time welcoming the hurt since it combatted the deeper, hidden pain. "You love me, Nika. You still do." Desperate triumph rang in his voice. "You always have."

"Yes. Even when it was wrong." The words were like ashes in her mouth. "We can never marry, Brant. Not over two graves."

"That's crazy!"

"It's true."

As though forcing himself to be calm, he took a deep breath. "Nika, sweetheart. I've wished a thousand times that I'd died instead of Joe. He was a lot better man than I am. He was good to my son, a real father. Do you think I don't know that? But do we have to punish ourselves for the rest of our lives?"

When Dominika was silent, he stroked her hand. "Let me pay Joe back by raising his son. Don't wreck the good that we can all still have, darling."

She was tempted by his plea but something deeper than reason cried that she must not surrender to her long, agonized passion for this man who had killed her husband, her good, faithful Joe.

Stepping back sharply from Brant's persuading touch, she said brokenly, "I hope that you can have a good life, Brant, but it cannot be with me. We—we would always remind each other. Go away."

Blindly she hurried inside but as she shut the door and locked it, he was still standing there.

When Dominika came home from work the next day, Brant was playing ball with the boys. Foss proudly flourished a shiny, small bat. "Look at what Brant gave me, Mama!"

Vachel ran forward with the ball. "Look at what he gave *me*, Mama!"

Brant knelt beside him. "Yes, son, but you have to learn how to throw it." His long fingers fitted gently but firmly around the small, chubby ones. "Like this, see? Now bring back your arm and let 'er go!"

"Let me try!" cried Foss, jumping up and down with eagerness.

Furious at Brant for flouting her decision, Dominika felt a stab of regret as he stood there with the boys, watching her with the blue gaze of their son.

Their son.

Guilt-laden as that bond was, it was real, one of blood and flesh. Was she wrong to deny it? Patrick and Davey loved the boys but neither could take the place of a father.

Torn and bewildered, Dominika said coldly to the boys, "Come inside. It's time for supper."

"Oh, Mama!" Vachel wailed. "Do we have to?" Foss groaned.

Brant gave them each an admonishing pat on the shoulder. "Go in with your mother, boys. I'll come back tomorrow if you want me to."

"Will you?" shouted Foss happily.

Brant chuckled. "Wild horses couldn't keep me away." He looked deliberately at Dominika before he strode up the street.

For three weeks Dominika contested with him and her own desires. For herself she could have and would have refused him. But since there was no bringing Joe back, did she have the right to forbid Foss his real father and Vachel one who owed the child's father a very special debt?

Annie had already guessed the relationship between Foss

and Brant. "Why don't you have him, dear? It's plain that he's daft about you and the wee laddies."

"Oh, Annie, some of the things that have happened—"

Annie shook her head. "What's happened is over. You and the boys have to live now."

That was true.

So one evening when Dominika called the boys in to supper, she invited Brant. When Foss and Vachel did not want to go to bed because of him, Brant hoisted them on his shoulders and bundled them off, promising them a buggy ride next day if their mama agreed.

When he and Dominika returned to the parlor, Annie and Davey had discreetly retired. Dominika looked at Brant; he was so much the image of her eldest son that it seemed wicked to persist in holding them apart. And he was haggard still, as if he were not sleeping.

"Well?" he asked softly. "Well, my love?"

Dominika no longer knew the best course. She knew only that this man had inextricably worked himself into her sons' lives and that she loved him.

With a fated sense that he was her destiny, she went into his arms.

Brant refused to be married in the Catholic Church. Dominika did not insist upon it for although the union now seemed inevitable, she still felt that it was something forbidden, so unthinkable and beyond the rules that marriage rites scarcely mattered. Joe and Lucie were dead but memories of them were not. These, unlike physical bodies, could appear at any moment, slip unexorcised between enraptured, naked flesh.

And in spite of the haunting past, they were enraptured in each other's arms. They took a short honeymoon in San Francisco. Brant delighted in buying clothes that set off her slender, womanly figure, her gold-green eyes and dark auburn hair. Elegant shops, restaurants, the theater, their luxurious suite—ten days passed like a dream but by the end of it Dominika was anxious to see the boys and eager to reach their new home and start their real life.

To her vast relief, Brant never suggested they live in the

house that he had shared with Lucie. He had, a few years before, acquired a ranch in northeastern Nevada, south of Elko in the Ruby Valley. It was close enough to the home ranch that he could still travel up there quickly when necessary, though careful, experienced Mac could manage it alone.

Brant had ordered modernization and additions to the existing ranch house and by the time the family arrived from Tonopah, two bathrooms were completed, the kitchen was equipped with sinks and a new wing was being added. They bought all the furnishings and equipment they could in Elko and ordered the rest from San Francisco.

From its start as a construction camp for the Central Pacific Railroad in 1868, Elko had become a thriving cattle capital, with schools, churches and an opera house as well as saloons and gambling halls. The state university opened there in 1874, although it was moved fifteen years later. Vicious blizzards in 1888 and 1890 starved and froze thousands of cattle. The animals had gone through Elko streets, lowing for food until it was only merciful to kill them.

The great Spanish Ranch, started by the California Basque Altubes, claimed a loss of ninety per cent. Many cattlemen were forced out of business. Sheep losses had been closer to twenty-five per cent and so when the ranges were restocked, it was often with sheep instead of cattle.

Sheep had been passing through that part of Nevada since 1852, when Kit Carson drove a herd of merinos from New Mexico to California. Other herds followed but by the seventies, sheep from California were being driven back to Nevada to feed miners and railroad-builders and to stock the first Nevada sheep ranches.

Though some cattlemen detested sheep, many now raised them as well as cattle. Prosperity had gradually returned to Elko, especially when the Western Pacific came through in 1907 and when the mining activity revived.

There were several Basque hotels in Elko, one opened just that year by a young couple from Vizcaya, Domingo and Gregoria Sabala. To please Dominika, Brant agreed that they stay there and enjoy the good Basque food. The Overland was a social center, catering special occasions from weddings to wakes, and darkly pretty Gregoria told Dominika that the family must be sure to come in for the big Feast of the Three Kings that would be held in January.

"I don't know," Brant said when Dominika enthusiastically mentioned it to him. "The boys are American, darling. Why confuse them with all this Basque stuff?"

She stared at him with such hurt that he quickly hugged her and said of course they would come if she wanted to. But they were having trouble over the boys. Brant, unused to children and obsessed with Dominika, was almost childishly jealous of her time and love. The boys, accustomed to her complete attention when she wasn't working, and bewildered when Brant changed from indulgent friend to disciplinarian, declared war on this man who had appropriated their mother.

Vachel, just turned three, started wetting his bed. Almost every night he would come pounding on the bedroom door, which Brant had taken to locking, sometimes while they were making love. After the first few times, Brant, tight-lipped and furious, caught Dominika's wrist as she started to get out of bed.

"I'll take care of him, Nika."

"You—won't hurt him!"

"No." Brant pulled on his trousers. "I just bet that when the little bastard finds out that he can't get your attention this way, he'll dry up mighty fast."

He unlocked the door, took Vachel firmly by the hand and led him off. Dominika listened for sounds of trouble carrying from across the hall but although Brant's voice was firm, it was controlled and if Vachel said anything, it was quietly indeed.

She was furious, though, at the name that Brant had called her little son. When he returned to bed and reached for her, she slid away from his arms.

"Vachel's not the bastard," she said coldly. "But *your* son would have been had Joe not given him a name."

Brant groaned. "My God! I didn't mean it like that."

"You'd better learn to say what you mean then! If you call either of the boys a name like that again, I'll take them and leave."

"Nika! That's crazy! Getting all upset about one little word."

"It's not the word, it's my sons! If you don't want them, I'll take them away and raise them myself."

"By God, you would, wouldn't you?" he said with a wondering, half-grudging, half-admiring laugh.

He gathered her against him and drowned her protests with hungry, melting kisses. Her anger peaked into an urgency as great as his. They took each other with avid ruthlessness, demanding, challenging, only in that last surging release merging into oneness.

Afterward, his head on her breast, he said wearily, "I try, Nika. They're smart, handsome kids. I really do care about them. But damn it, I want you to myself sometimes. The way it was in San Francisco." He laughed suddenly. "That's the answer! We'll hire a housekeeper. She and Andres can take care of the kids now and then while we have ourselves a trip."

"Another part of the answer is for you to spend more time with the boys as if you really enjoyed them—the way," she said bitterly, "that you played with them while you were trying to convince me that you would be such a good father."

He sighed. After a moment he nodded. "You're right. I'll make a point of doing something with them every day. That's only fair."

"Fair! If you're going to begrudge it—"

"Sweetheart, be reasonable," he pleaded. "I try but I can't be the kind of father Joe was because I'm *not* Joe. My own dad, hell, I can't remember his paying any attention to me until I was big enough to start helping with the cattle."

She supposed that it was true. From what she had seen of Americans, there was often more rivalry than affection between fathers and sons. But she could not help contrasting Brant's manner with the way in which Joe would have fathered the boys.

She held her husband against her breast, loving him though troubled at his self-centeredness, and said gently, "If you love me, Brant, love my sons."

"Foss is mine, too," he reminded her. "Of course I love them. I just don't show it like a woman, that's all, but I'll do better."

* * *

He honored his word and set aside time each day for the boys, who responded to the attention by gradually accepting him as a part of their lives although without any of the first worship they had had for him when he was their playfellow in Tonopah.

Brant followed up on the other part of his plan too, hiring Moira Flaherty, plump, motherly and carrot-haired, the widow of a railroad man, away from her job as cook in an Elko restaurant. Childless, she spoiled the boys so thoroughly that they seldom came now to their mother. When Dominika heard one of them come running inside with some triumph or discovery, shouting, "Look, Mo'a!" or "Mo'a! See what I found!" she felt a pang and a sense of loss. At the same time she was grateful that the children seemed happy and secure again. When Brant took her to Denver for a week, she worried about them till it tainted her response to him.

"You love those kids more than you love me," he accused when she received him absently, preoccupied with the fear that the children might feel deserted.

"It's not that at all," she retorted, stiffening. "But they're little, Brant. Vachel is almost still a baby. They need me."

"They need good care," he growled. "They have that. Damn it, Nika, I need you, too. I've waited for so long—"

In that moment he seemed as vulnerable as either of her sons. She held him tenderly, smoothing his hair, cradling his head on her breast. Smiling up at her, he began to trace the contours of her breast with the tip of his tongue. Quivering, languorous flames spread into her loins. He nibbled gently, excruciatingly, somehow reminding her of a deer feeding on ripening buds. He caressed her until she opened to him, pulled him on top of her and met his thrusts with equal insatiability.

The rest of the time they spent in Denver was like their honeymoon. They feasted on each other, sometimes with butterfly lightness, sometimes with the savagery of battle. But when they were home again, Dominika's feelings were bruised to discover that the boys now wanted Moira to put them to bed.

As time went by, Dominika felt increasingly like a stranger standing at the edge of her sons' lives, yet she felt it would be wrong to try to make herself so important to them that they would suffer from Brant's possessiveness or fret when she was away. She wanted another baby, a daughter for the Cave of Always Summer, but Brant took precautions.

"We have plenty of time, sweetheart. I want you to myself for a while."

Strangely, Brant got along better with Vachel than with his own son. Easy-going, quick to forget a rebuff or harsh word, Vachel lived in the moment and took Brant as he found him, staying out of his way when he was tired or irritable, joining in when Brant spread out an inviting leg or offered to play ball.

Foss eyed his father warily, sulked for days at a reprimand, and those two pairs of blue eyes, so piercingly alike, often clashed. Foss was afraid of horses. Brant took this as a personal affront and insisted that the boy learn to ride. While Vachel tumbled happily off and on a gentle old burro, Foss had to sit on a gelding that looked formidably tall and dangerous to Dominika, though Russ Evers, the grizzled, rangy foreman, assured her that Domino was patient and well-trained.

"Why, the kid could fall between his legs and Domino wouldn't step on him," Russ promised. The image gave Dominika a cold sensation in the pit of her stomach, especially when she saw that Foss's lips were white with fear, although he would not beg to be let down.

"Brant, if you would just give him a little time—"

Brant took her arm and led her toward the house. "Nika, please leave this to me. You're scared and the boy knows it. He has to learn and the sooner, the better."

Halting, Dominika demanded, "Why does he have to learn?"

Brant's jaw dropped. "Why, damn it, he'll have the ranch one day. How's he going to run it if he can't ride?"

She said grimly, "Maybe he won't want to run the ranch. Or maybe he'll have sheep instead of cows."

"Sheep!"

"Lots of ranches stock them," she said defiantly. "Foss played with lambs when he was little. I think he likes them a lot better than he does cattle."

Brant was speechless for a moment. "If being raised by a

Basco sheepman has turned that kid funny, I'll work it out of him if it kills us both!''

''Joe was a better father to Foss than you are,'' she blazed. ''I don't think you care about the boy at all. You just need a son who will be everything you want without your spending any time with him or taking any trouble.''

Angry as she was, she shrank from the look he gave her. ''I'll spend time with him,'' he said tightly. ''And I'll take trouble. My son's not going to be a damn sheepman.''

''Brant—''

''He's my son, too, Nika.'' Brant shook off her hand. ''I won't hurt him. But there are things he has to learn.''

He swung away from her and strode back to the small boy sitting high on the big black gelding. ''Arms looser, son. Now then, move your rein hand this way. Easy, but like you mean it. That's good. Now let's see you ride.''

XVI

BRANT ATTACKED the boys' range education, especially Foss's, in the way that a general might conduct a campaign. Nearly every day he took Foss riding, teaching him not only horsemanship but how to tell the age and condition of cattle, how to spot loco-weed and how to judge when it was time to move a herd to better graze.

Instead of almost ignoring the boys at meals, Brant now often quizzed Foss. "How did you think the hay looked in the near meadow?" "How old, about, do you reckon that cow was that I pulled out of the bog?" "Why do you reckon Domino tilts an ear back toward you?"

Dominika could not venture a guess as to how Foss felt about this sudden shift from neglect to vigilant tutoring. At least he seemed to have conquered his fear of horses and he never forgot the answer to a question. She tried to tell herself that it was proper for Brant to take an active part in raising the boys, yet she could not escape a troubled intuition that Foss still resented Brant but, young as he was, had the judgment not to engage in a battle that he could not win.

The ranch lay between the Ruby and Goshute Mountains, watered by the Franklin River and several creeks. Its broad meadows grew wild hay that would be cut to feed through the winter, for the 1890 disasters had convinced cattlemen that it was dangerous to leave their stock scattered far out on the range to fend for themselves. Including the Idaho holdings, Brant owned a hundred and fifty thousand acres as well as having access to countless thousands of acres of public lands. He owned thirty thousand Hereford cattle, upgraded by the use of purebred bulls imported from Herefordshire, and four hundred blooded horses wore the Lazy R brand.

As heir apparent, Foss rode the Nevada domain with his father, a small figure beside the man but just as proudly erect. That fall Brant took him on the roundup of the cattle that would be driven to market in Elko. When Brant returned from selling the herd, he brought a tutor with him. Pink, blond Eldridge Sommers from Boston stammered when he spoke to Dominika but she liked the steady, honest blue eyes that peered at her through thick, steel-rimmed spectacles.

"All right, love!" Brant said to her that night, undressing her with the long, brown fingers that could always send her blood racing and cause her chest to tighten with the acuteness of her desire. "Russ Evans will keep up Foss's riding, Eldridge will start teaching him his books. There's Andres and Moira to look after him and Vachel. The check for the fall beef is in the bank. And now, my beautiful green-eyed wife, we're going to San Francisco!"

That became the rhythm of the years, dictated by the cattle. During the first part of April, steers, yearlings and dry cows were turned out of the fenced pastures to forage. Only cows with calves were kept in. In early June calves were gathered and branded. Then there was haying. It took nearly a ton of hay to feed a cow through the winter and an acre of meadow was required to produce that ton.

The beef roundup began by September. All late-born calves were branded with the Lazy R on their left hip. After the cattle were shipped off to be fattened for the slaughterhouse, the early spring calves, now seven to ten months old, were weaned and put in a feed lot. The stronger cattle that could survive on winter range without feeding unless there was extremely severe and prolonged snow and cold were turned out. The main bunch—cows, calves, yearlings and weaker steers—were kept close enough that they could be fed hay, although they grazed, too. The poorest cattle and those near calving were held in closest to feed and care.

Besides all this there were other chores. Fences had to be ridden and repaired, stock fed and kept from drifting in the winter and when weak ones bogged down in the spring mud, they had to be pulled out.

Brant supervised branding and the fall gather. The routine work bored him. He left it to Russ Evans to oversee while he took Dominika to Denver or San Francisco for a month of shopping and high life.

The Feast of the Three Kings, though, was always celebrated at the Overland Hotel in Elko, where Domingo never failed to meet them. He had visited the ranch on that first Christmas but though Brant had been courteous, there had been unease. Domingo had not directly refused to come to the ranch. He simply met them in Elko instead, and rather than bringing the boys whittled toys, he took them on a spree through the shops, enjoying the expedition even more than they did.

"No sheepherder has to buy my kids presents," Brant grumbled to Dominika. "And I wish to hell he wouldn't call Foss his godson."

"He says it in Basque," Dominika pointed out. "Besides, he has been a very good godfather."

Brant looked at her sharply but did not follow the argument. For a few years she had hoped that at least friendship would develop between Brant and Foss but grievous as the truth was, she had been forced to admit that the boy did not like his father. He respected him, grudgingly admired him, perhaps even feared him.

There was never any warmth in Foss's deep blue eyes when his father complimented him on a riding feat or a Latin essay. Vachel, on the rare occasions when he had earned such favor, wriggled with pleasure and glowed but Foss only said, "Thank you, sir."

Helplessly, loving them both, Dominika watched the distance deepen as Foss grew older. She did not know if Brant loved Foss but he often looked at him with pride and a sort of baffled affection.

"Dad and I never got along until I grew up," he told Dominika one day when Foss had made some politely curt answer and escaped as quickly as possible. "I guess I can't expect it to be different with Foss and me."

Brant did not make demands on Vachel but whatever Foss

did, Vachel copied. He was a natural rider and liked nothing better than helping to handle and break the young horses. Foss would not play *muz* anymore, not even with Domingo, but Vachel loved cards and spent most of his spare time in the bunkhouse, playing with the cowboys.

Foss was agreeable with the men but he never seemed to belong with them. Even in his early teens he had preferred long discussions with Eldridge Sommers about politics, philosophy and history. Dominika did not understand much of their argumentation but she slowly realized that Foss was absorbed in the uses of power, where it came from and how it was wielded. He was also fascinated with automobiles and learned to keep the machines, which Brant could only curse, in good repair.

As one year slipped into the next, Dominika wondered where time went. She made few requests of Brant, although after the fall gather of 1914 she did ask him to take her to Spokane to see May Arkwright Hutton, who was said to be in failing health.

"Why do you want to visit that loud, vulgar, socialistic suffragist?" he scowled.

"I want to thank her," Dominika said. "It would become you to thank her, too. She helped me find a home for our son when I was desperate."

He bit his lip. They left the next day, driving in their Coey Flyer touring car to Spokane and the white-frame, pillared mansion with a view of Mt. Baldy.

May, in an invalid chair, had lost so much flesh that only her broad smile and indomitable blue eyes remained the same but she recognized Dominika at once, greeted her warmly, gave Brant an appraisingly frank stare and rang for refreshments.

After a quick catching-up on personal matters, May chuckled and raised her tea cup in a salute. "I see that Nevada women won the vote this fall." She slanted a challenging glance at Brant. "May I ask your sentiments on that, sir?"

Dominika knew that he had voted for the measure but he gave May a teasing smile. "I think there's much to be said for the view of the Ely paper whose publisher wrote that suffrage is the descent of a goddess from Olympus to mingle with mortals and become contaminated. It is the abdication of her throne."

"Bull feathers!" returned May. "For every woman that's protected and treated 'like a goddess,' there are a thousand ground down, overworked, beaten or deserted by their husbands. Give us a fair shake and we won't need your protection."

Giving her a glance of surprised respect, Brant inclined his head. "Well, madam, if ever you run for president, you have my vote."

She beamed and patted his hand forgivingly before she made a face. "Some of the presidents we've had! When I think that I once feted Teddy Roosevelt, that hot-air hero of the African jungle with his army of press agents. He had the nerve to say that a decent woman's name should be in the paper only when she marries and when she dies. Served him right to get trounced by Woodrow Wilson in 1912."

May passed to the happier subject of the plan she and her husband had to establish a settlement for orphans on a site up the Spokane River. Children would live in real homes, with a motherly woman in charge of each cottage.

"There will be a big barn with cows for the boys and girls to feed and milk." May's face brightened at the thought. "They'll grow lots of their own food and learn to cook and take care of themselves. Those who want to will go to college. Al and me never had kids but this way we can have lots of them."

She was tiring. Although she urged them to stay to lunch and see her Al, Dominika and Brant took their leave.

Almost a year later they read in the papers of her death. Brant did one of the things that could still surprise Dominika and thrill her with love for him. In her name he sent the check for that fall's beef gather, the whole year's income, to the orphans' settlement that Al Hutton was going to build as an ongoing memorial to the homely, bastard orphan-girl from Ohio who had given so much to others while having a grand time herself.

1917 was the year that Pershing was recalled from Mexico after almost a year's futile chasing of Pancho Villa through the northern mountains. It was the year that war was declared on Germany, the July Fourth of "Lafayette, we are here," the November of the Rainbow Division's arrival in France with men from every state in the Union.

It was also the autumn when Eldridge Sommers was released with a generous bonus and Foss, nearly fourteen, and twelve-year-old Vachel were sent to attend high school in Elko, staying with a family that boarded several boys from ranches during the school terms.

Dominika missed their handsome young faces, Vachel's merry brown eyes and Foss's startlingly blue ones, their half-embarrassed good-night hugs and kisses, but it seemed to her, really, that she had lost them long ago—when she had married Brant.

Brant subscribed heavily to the Liberty Loan, helping Nevada to become the first state to raise its quota, and even exceed it by over ninety per cent. In 1918, November brought Armistice Day and joyous celebrations across the entire nation, with the blowing of sirens and whistles, the marching in parades and the lighting of bonfires. Never again a war! But a hundred and twenty-six thousand young American men were dead, almost double the number that were wounded.

What if Foss had been only two years older? Dominika shuddered, grateful that her sons had been spared, yet feeling guilty because they were.

Nevada passed Prohibition laws that year and in January of 1919 the United States Congress ratified the Eighteenth Amendment. Annoyed at such meddling, Domingo Sabala kept a bar with an entrance through the back alley at his hotel. The Sabalas were public-spirited. When Elko had been ravaged by the World War I flu epidemic, the Overland had overflowed with dozens of sick people, all nursed back to health by a squad of volunteers headed by Gregoria. But when it came to saying that Basques could not have their Picon punch or Izarri, the Sabalas put tradition above new law.

In 1920, when May Hutton's ghost must have stood up and cheered when the United States Government gave women the vote, Foss outraged Brant by announcing that he wanted to study law at Harvard. He got his way by calmly insisting that he would work his way through college if Brant refused to help him. Dominika was then thirty-six, ripe-breasted but slimmer of waist and thigh than she had been as a girl.

"White hairs," she muttered, noting a few among the rich

cascade of dark auburn hair. Her skin was as creamy and soft as ever.

Brant came up behind her to cup her breasts in his strong, tanned fingers and kiss the nape of her neck before he laughed at her in the mirror. "You were a beautiful girl but now you're a magnificent woman. The woman's more than a girl could ever be."

Catching her up, he swept her onto the bed. She gasped, briefly tried to escape and then surrendered to his loving. It was always wonderful. In some ways she felt herself to be older than Brant, almost regarding him as one of her sons, but in bed he was her man. She regretted the rivalry he still showed now and then with the boys but she could not be sorry that she had married him—not even when he drank too much, which he did rather frequently in the winter when he was often confined to the house. He would go to his office, drink himself into a stupor and spend the night on the leather couch.

One of the first times that it happened, Dominika, at bedtime, had gone in to see if he was all right. As she draped blankets over him and pulled off his boots, he roused and stared at her glassily.

"Lucie? Darling—"

He collapsed, mumbling incoherently. Stricken motionless, Dominika had felt an eerie creeping of her flesh along with guilty shock. She glanced behind her. Only shadows moved in the dimly lit room. Shivering, she had finished covering her husband and retreated to bed.

She did not speak to him about it nor had they ever talked about Joe's fall. These were the secret, buried chambers of their marriage which they dared not open. Dominika sometimes felt they had been almost too lucky in finding so much joy together when Lucie and Joe were dead. Half-consciously she kept waiting for retribution.

True, Joe's fall had been an accident. True, she and Brant had desperately battled their passion before betraying Lucie, who had almost certainly never guessed at the truth. But beneath logic and reason, Dominika felt that both of the deaths were on her head and Brant's. She hoped they might be forgiven but should fate exact punishment, she was prepared not to whimper.

In the autumn that the boys went off to high school, Andres and Xagu died within a few days of each other. Vachel shed tears over the grave of his godfather but both boys wept for the old dog who had guarded them from infancy.

Saddened at the double loss and missing her sons, Dominika began to take frequent rides by herself when Brant was busy. Her favorite way followed a creek into a mountain canyon that was studded with wildflowers—shooting star, larkspur, violets and brilliant red paintbrush. Stunted willow and pine gave way, as the trail climbed, to mountain mahogany and the graceful white-trunked, trembling aspen that turned the slopes to a glory of yellow in the fall.

Riding through eroded cliffs into higher reaches splashed in summer with thick beds of lupine, blue elephant's head and other flowers, she passed yellow pine, manzanita, columbine and snowbush until she came to a sub-alpine terrace of rock that seemed to her like a great natural temple, its knotted, twisted trees sculptured by time and weather into fantastic shapes.

The buttresses of a huge trunk often appeared smooth and polished and most of the tree seemed dead but here and there live bark and green branches jutted out of the dead-looking wood, proclaiming to sun and sky the tree's survival.

"Bristlecone pine," Brant told her when he accompanied her one day. "Really tough wood. Lasts forever. The power poles on the Goldfield road are made of it."

"That's awful!" Dominika cried. "These trees—why, they look like they've been here since the world began. They ought to be left alone."

Brant laughed and tweaked her hair. "You mean that I can't start a fire for our coffee with limbs taken from one of these?"

"No," she replied, not even smiling.

She could not have said why but these ancients reminded her of the Summer Cave, a persistence of life that echoed down through centuries. Since it was a long day's ride, she did not come often but when she did, she knelt at the base of one of the gnarled old trees and embraced it, closing her eyes to remember that distant sanctuary. She would ride home feeling renewed, mystically attuned with an indefinable power that had no boundaries.

She was sad, though, that it seemed there would never be a daughter to whom the secret could be entrusted. Although Brant had stopped taking precautions several years ago, she had not conceived.

Well, there should be a granddaughter. And she herself still had time. Each Sunday she lit a candle for her mother and Etchahoun, prayed with her grandmother's acorn rosary and then she held the blue bird and promised the spirits of the cave that, somehow, their magic would not die with her.

A decline in livestock prices started in the twenties and continued, even though Brant kept predicting an upswing. "Anyway," he would reassure himself and Dominika, "I have enough in stocks and bonds to tide us through."

When she suggested that they economize, forego the expensive trips to San Francisco or get along without a cook-housekeeper, he hooted derisively. "Honey, it's a mistake to *think* poor. That makes it come true." He kissed her and chuckled. "Don't you worry. Prices are bound to go up. Americans like their beef."

But prices stayed low. And in 1925, when Foss finished law school and went to work down in Reno for George Wingfield, Brant drank heavily for a week.

"Who's going to take over?" he demanded when Dominika ventured into his office with coffee and food. He stared at her as though it were her fault. "If I could have had the boy from the start, he'd know today where he belonged."

"And if he'd been born heir of Etchahoun, he would be caring for its fields and apple trees," Dominika shrugged. "Brant, what is, is."

"If we'd had another son—"

"It seems unlikely now," Dominika said, thinking with pain of the daughter for whom she longed. "Drink your coffee, Brant, and eat. Come back and live with me or I'm going into town."

"Why?"

"Because I can't stand it when you shut yourself away."

"I love you."

"Then live with me."

He recovered from the spell of deep depression but when Foss came home to visit, Brant made such disparaging remarks about Wingfield that Foss said angrily, "I didn't drive twelve hours over that lousy road to hear you blast the man who really runs Nevada, Dad."

Wingfield, enormously rich through his Goldfield mining stock, owned a chain of banks and other interests. He was the Republican National Committeeman and since one of his lawyers was the Democratic National Committeeman, Wingfield had power in both parties that extended beyond Nevada.

"And what's he running?" Brant demanded. "Baby Face Nelson and Scarface Sullivan hanging around Reno, crooks from Chicago and New York coming there to hide out or launder hot money in the gambling halls!"

Foss turned red. "Reno's the hottest town between Chicago and San Francisco," he said. "Plenty of society folks from the East come out and Hollywood people—"

"Sure," Brant derided, laughing unpleasantly. "Ever since Mary Pickford got her divorce there, it's been the stylish place to end a marriage. It's a cesspit, Foss. You may be wading now but someday you'll slip—go in up to your nose."

Foss was ambitious. If he served Wingfield well, he could advance swiftly in politics. His lips tight, Foss stared with eyes as furious and blue as those looking back at him. "If I'm not mighty wrong, Dad, I saw your name on some mortgages Mr. Wingfield holds. Seems you think his money's clean enough to keep buying purebred bulls when beef prices are ridiculous."

"Hey, cut it out!" pleaded Vachel before Brant could explode. "I came to see Mama, not to listen to you two fight. Dad, why don't you bring Mama over for a week?"

"Why?" growled Brant. "So she can watch you deal illegal games?"

Vachel loved to gamble. He had spent several lackadaisical years at the university in Reno and then dropped his studies to deal cards in The Willows, one of Reno's fancier bar-restaurant-gambling houses. Now he shrugged cheerfully. "Well, Dad, we could have been sheepmen."

413

"Over my dead body!"

The men laughed. Dominika was angry at what she considered a slur on Basques but she did not touch off another argument. Her sons seldom came home and it was not just because the Reno-to-Elko road became impassable every fall.

She loved her sons but she could not understand them. And the more she understood her husband, the more her once-passionate love shifted to pity. He was no longer young and his son and foster-son had rejected the cattle kingdom he had built. She saw him age greatly in the drought year of 1929; he was hollow-eyed and haggard when he decided to sell off cattle no longer able to survive on the remaining grass and water.

When the stock market crashed that October, not even J. P. Morgan could check the panic-selling as he had back in 1907. Brant never told Dominika exactly how much he had lost but she knew it was a staggering amount. This time he did not resort to the bottle.

"I'm going to sell the Idaho ranch," he said just before Christmas.

"But it was your family's!" Dominika protested.

"I don't have anyone to carry it on," he said soberly. He managed a smile and she felt a rush of admiration, a feeling that she rarely had for her husband anymore. "I'd rather sell it than our place here, Nika. Wouldn't you?"

She shivered involuntarily at the very thought of going back to live in that Lucie-haunted house. Putting her arms around him, she rested against his heart. She would always feel that she had lost her sons for him and that he had given up his home for her. She could not have measured all the bonds, some dark, some happy, that ran between them and she did not know if she loved him now. But they were bound as surely as though their bodies had grown together.

"We could let the cook go—" she began.

"You funny little Basco! Two thousand a year won't sink or save us, either." He laughed and the tension eased. But Dominika worried, the more because he had never explained his finances and there was no way that she could really help him.

Their fate depended on weather, range and the price of cattle, each beyond their control. 1930 was a drought year. So was 1931.

"I have to borrow and ship the cattle to Colorado for grazing," Brant said desperately. Dominika knew the depths of his trouble when he asked Foss to help him obtain a loan from Wingfield, who had for the last few years been almost single-handedly financing the states' stockgrowers through his banks.

Most of the cattle were trailed to Elko and shipped to fatten on Colorado's public lands. The whole nation was gripped by the Great Depression. The erosion of plowed lands in Kansas and Oklahoma broke thousands of farmers and put more out of work. Grasping at any hope, they streamed west in old flivvers and trucks, hoping to pick fruit or crops or, lacking that, do anything in order to live. Tramps rode the boxcars, scavenging however they could. It was a nightmarish time, seeming to Dominika like a rising tide that lapped slowly but inexorably at the ranch.

When she visited the ancient bristlecones and leaned against their twisted, weathered roots, she gained courage but now Brant was drinking again. This time nothing she could say would stop him but she could not leave him, go in to Elko and take a job at the Overland. He had sold his home for her. She must stay by him.

1932 came. Midwestern farmers who managed to grow wheat on their ravaged lands saw it drop to thirty-two cents a bushel—two dollars below the 1920 price. President Hoover tried to break the grip of the nation-wide curse by cutting government spending and granting credit to industry. He cut his own salary by twenty per cent and persuaded his cabinet to take a similar reduction.

That terrible year found the Nevada range still locked in drought, barren where once there had been high meadows. George Wingfield's empire collapsed. In order to continue lending to the stockmen, he had illegally siphoned off funds from his savings banks and slipped them into his commercial banks. He had advanced over four million dollars to Nevada's ranchers. Only a fraction of it could be repaid.

When they heard the news over the radio, Brant turned white. Then he went to shave and dress in his well-tailored suit and hand-stitched boots.

"I've got to go into Elko," he said in a colorless voice. "Have to see if there's any way—"

"I'll go with you," Dominika said, catching his arm.

He shook his head. "No, honey. I can manage whatever comes up better if I'm alone."

He kissed her and went out to the Pierce Arrow he had bought the year they sold the Idaho ranch. She stood on the porch and waved as he drove away.

XII

THE NEXT time she saw him, he lay in the mortuary. His face was covered. He had put the barrel of the gun inside his mouth before he fired.

Gregoria and Domingo Sabala had driven out to tell Dominika and bring her to town. They had also notified Foss and Vachel, both of whom arrived that night. The bank-closing was going to wipe out all that the Sabalas had built up over thirty years but they showed none of their strain as they made Dominika at home in the Overland and gave her Brant's letter.

"The ranch will be foreclosed on," he wrote. *"Everything's gone. You will be better off without me, Nika. You're strong. The boys will help you. I love you, believe me, but I just can't face it."*

That was all. All, after twenty-four years of marriage. Dominika was numb and she willed herself to stay that way, for the anger within her, the sense of betrayal, was so great she feared she would explode if it surfaced. All through these years he had refused to tell her anything about his business affairs, never asked her advice, and when his empire crumbled, he left her alone, abandoned.

The same misfortune had befallen countless people all over the United States. Brant was not the only wealthy man to kill himself when faced with financial ruin. But most men went on as Domingo Sabala did. In a few weeks his hotel, theater, cattle, sheep, mining interests and other properties were lost but he had taken a job as janitor at the county courthouse.

I would have helped, Dominika thought as the days began to penetrate the frozen casing around her heart. *We both could have worked. We would have gotten by.* But she knew that Brant could never have tolerated the situation. He had never been poor, never done other people's bidding. If such a large part of his character had depended on his position, what kind of man had she loved? It was like reaching to touch a face one had taken for real and watching it disintegrate like charred curls of a paper mask.

Foss and Vachel each wanted to take her back to Reno. Foss was doing what he could to salvage some of Wingfield's holdings. The fall of his patron was a setback but he could keep afloat. He intended to run for a Senate seat. Vachel had lost his investments but shrugged and laughed, appearing younger than his twenty-seven years.

"Come along and keep house for me, Mama. Gambling has been legal in Nevada since last year and those California folk sure come flocking over! As long as I can deal cards, we'll have enough to eat."

She thanked them both but she had no wish to squeeze into some corner of their lives. She would not be a sad little foreign widow dependent on her sons. She let them take her to the ranch to collect her personal things and tell Russ Evans and the hands that they could remain there until the mortgage-holders decided on the disposition of the ranch and its stock.

The boys were chagrined that they did not have the money with which to buy her a small town house but Dominika assured them it was just as well since she wasn't sure that she would stay in Elko. The furnishings of the ranch house were mortgaged, too. She packed quickly, taking in addition to her clothes only her jewelry, her grandmother's rosary and prayerbook, and the blue bird.

At her insistence her sons went back to Reno to cope with their own devastated affairs. The Overland was in its last days of operation. It was heartbreaking for Dominika to watch Gregoria try to be cheerful as she cooked and set out food in the hotel that had been like home to so many.

Dominika looked for work as a cook but none of the restaurants or hotels were hiring. Neither was there an opening for a maid or housekeeper. She was about to buy a ticket to Boise and see if perhaps the Irigays had survived the crash and could hire her when Domingo knocked on her door.

He must have been close to eighty but he was unstooped.

His beard and hair were still thick and of a silver that made his brown, lined face seem as lasting as the roots of a bristlecone. His dark eyes embraced Dominika as he took her hands.

"Andrea, I came as soon as I heard."

At last she could weep. This old countryman who had known her for so many years held her as he would a child, clumsily patting her hair but not trying to stop the cleansing tempest.

When she was calm, he said briskly, "Wash your face. We'll have a good dinner and talk about what's to be done."

Dominika was forty-eight, the mother of two grown sons. She could not have guessed how comforting it would be to place matters in the hands of someone who had been mature when she was young. She managed a shaky laugh, washed her face, combed her hair and they went down to dinner.

Prolonged drought and a particularly cruel winter had hurt Domingo, too. He had lost half his sheep but had managed to save all of his ewe lambs and would build up the bands again. He wanted to borrow on his sheep to stake Dominika to a fresh beginning in a restaurant or boardinghouse but she shook her head.

"Let me help with the sheep, Domingo. I would like to do something completely different, away from here."

He looked shocked. "But, andrea, my house, it's not much. And the work—God on High!"

"I lived on a sheep ranch," she reminded him, smiling. Heart lighter than it had been since Brant's death, she got to her feet. "It's close to lambing time! We'd better be getting back."

Domingo's range was considerably south of the house where Dominika had lived with Joe. From the band that she had given the old herder, he had developed four bands totaling ten thousand sheep and acquired additional deeded land. The drought years and the killing cold of the past winter had used up Domingo's savings and reduced his sheep to five thousand.

"My sheep are in pretty good shape, and I expect the clip to pay off most of the loan. I had corn trucked in to feed them. There are about three thousand ewes going to lamb so in two years we'll have quite a few young ewes ready to breed."

She marveled at his resiliency and it strengthened her. He insisted upon giving her the bedroom of his two-room cabin but they left in a few days for the lambing pens, several miles down the valley. Dominika was in charge of the cook wagon, which had a cot for her at the rear behind a curtain.

Since fewer ewes were lambing, Domingo hoped to handle them with his three herders and the camp-tender while the fourth herder held the other band and moved it around to graze until shearing. "Columbias make the best mothers," he said, "and that's mostly what I have. They mother up faster so it saves trouble."

A few lambs had already dropped by the time Domingo and Dominika arrived. Dominika put on coffee and water, started a pot of rich stew, set bread to raise and insisted that Domingo show her how to help the ewes before the rush started.

He looked at her doubtfully. "It is not pretty, andrea."

"It's the starting of life."

"Some lambs, some ewes, die."

"I might be able to save a few." She smiled at him. "Anyway, *Tocayo*, there's more life than death."

After a final measuring glance, he nodded his head. "Come with me."

They quickly found a ewe bleating in pain, sounding shockingly like a woman in labor. "Roll up your sleeves and scrub with soap and hot water," Domingo said, taking out the olive oil. "Then coat your hands and arms with this."

Dominika almost lost her nerve as she knelt by the suffering animal. "You have small hands," Domingo assured her. "You can slip in much easier than any of us."

So, biting her lip, Dominika gently slipped her hands and arms up the slippery canal, murmuring quieting Basque words. She was awed as her fingers touched a small head and tiny legs.

"The head?" asked Domingo. "The front feet?"

Dominika moved her fingers searchingly. "Here's one. I don't feel the other."

Domingo sighed. "There's the problem. Bring the one foot forward." He did not have to caution her to use care. "Locate the other foot," Domingo prompted. "Now bring both feet as far as you can. The head needs to rest between the hoofs."

Dominika concentrated on timing her motions with the ewe's increasingly strong contractions, which now gripped her arm. "Harder," Domingo called. "Pull a little harder. She needs more help."

With the next muscular clamping the ewe's passage seemed to expand to accommodate the feet and head. The lamb slipped into Dominika's arms, the little baby covered with a golden membrane. Dominika's proud awe changed to dread as the little creature lay still and unbreathing. "Is it stillborn?" she cried.

Domingo was already peeling membrane from the tiny nose, breathing into the mouth and trying to start the breath. Nothing happened. Then he thumped its body across his knee.

The lamb jerked, breathed and gave a wavery "Maaa!" almost all at once. Domingo settled it down by the ewe, who sniffed and began to lick it. The lamb could not seem to find a teat, and so after a few minutes Domingo opened the lamb's mouth and squirted into it a rich, golden fluid. "This is 'first milk,' " he explained. "It gets the lamb off to a good start and prevents sickness. The regular milk will start tomorrow."

Leaving the ewe with her now eagerly nursing baby, they moved on. The next stop was not so happy. A fine ewe lay racked with the agony of a breech birth. The lamb could not be shifted. Sweating, his dark eyes miserable, Domingo said, "Maybe you better go away, andrea. I have to kill her and take the lamb or they'll both die."

"I must know how to do that, too."

He clipped the ewe's heaving side, lifted her head and drew his keen knife across her throat. Even as blood gushed, he opened the belly and took the lamb. Chico Loyola, a thin, hatchet-faced young herder, called out that he had a stillborn. Within minutes a skillfully cut jacket of the dead lamb's hide clothed Domingo's waif and it was presented to the bereaved mother. She sniffed. The scent was right and she licked the baby who settled hungrily to nursing. Domingo moved on and Dominika followed.

When lambing ended three weeks later, she was the best midwife in the camp because of her small hands and empathy with any creature in labor. She was also feeding a little black "bummer" which she liked to think was descended from Arin-

arin. She called him Jautzi after one of her first orphans and also because he was from the start a fearless, joyous leaper.

The shearing crew had finished at Pete Falxa's place as Domingo's lambing tapered off and the men moved over one night with their trucks and tents in order to start early the next morning.

Since the grass was used up around the lambing area, the shearing camp was set up in fresh graze down the valley. It was bedlam, dogs barking to send sheep down the chutes, herders and shearers swearing in Spanish, Basque and English, and above it all, the frantic blatting of separated ewes and lambs. Even with hand clippers, these expert shearers could average a hundred thick fleeces a day, yellow beneath as egg yolks.

On the ninth day, the crew moved on to the Espondas, leaving Domingo's men to dock the lambs and castrate all the males except those saved for breeding. Herders held the lambs, while the tips of their scrotums were cut and the testicles pushed forward to be sucked out by Domingo or Chico. These lamb fries were a delicacy but it made Dominika sick at her stomach to prepare them. And now there could be no doubt that there was another reason for that.

She was going to have a baby. This was the second flow that she had missed. The first had been due a few days after Brant's suicide, but she'd scarcely thought about it then, and when she had, she had attributed its lateness to shock. During the lambing and shearing she'd been too busy to think much about anything but the meals and work. But now she could no longer ignore the tenderness of her nipples, the queasiness that assailed her at the smell of hot grease.

Would this be the son Brant had wanted for the ranch? Or the daughter for whom she had longed, a girl child to make that pilgrimage to the cave? It was strange. When Dominika thought of Brant now, he seemed to be someone whom she had known and lost long ago. She had experienced the weeks in Domingo's camps like years. It seemed impossible to be with child by someone from whom she felt so distanced.

Her remoteness had to be a defense against the angry, desolate sense of abandonment that had agonized her right after his death. He had left her; this would not be his baby, but hers.

Oddly, she found herself remembering Joe and the concern he had shown when she was pregnant. In her heart he seemed more the father than Brant.

A buyer with wagons bought the clip for enough money to pay off most of Domingo's loan on his bands. The ewes and lambs were split into three bands and trailed off to higher range. Dry ewes and yearlings made the fourth bunch.

Domingo had hired an extra herder, freeing himself to act as camp-tender. Upon returning to the cabin, Dominika quickly fell back into the pattern she had followed when Joe was alive, baking the bread and gathering the food and supplies that Domingo must take weekly to each of the scattered bands. She had young black Jautzi for company, a spotted goat called Nani and several old dogs, retired after years of faithful herding, though they still kept coyotes out of the chicken pen.

Mariana and Pete Falxa had come to see her but after reminiscing over old times, they had little to say to one another after the passage of so many years. Marta and Joanes Irigay had sold their hotel before the crash and returned to their valley to buy a farm. Dominika was glad to learn that they had not lost everything.

By August, Dominika was heavy on her feet although the baby wouldn't come until December. Her feet and legs had swollen and she felt puffy and gross. She wanted the baby but not the distortion and cumbersomeness. Her state seemed grotesque—she could have been a grandmother several times over by now had either of the boys shown an inclination to marry.

They came to see her late that summer, handsome young men, Foss tall, Vachel stocky, who hugged her and looked both embarrassed and horrified at her condition.

"Mama, you can't stay up here at a sheep camp when you're going to have a baby," Vachel blurted.

"Both of you were born on a ranch without a doctor," she said tartly.

Foss scowled. "But, Mama, you're older now. Hell, you shouldn't be having a kid at all. Did Dad know?"

Dominika shook her head. Blue and brown eyes exchanged

worried glances. "You have to come to town with us," Foss said in the tone that he probably used to stupid clients. "If you don't want to live with either of us, we can rent you a little house."

"I don't want to live in town again," she said, trying to be patient because of their concern. "I like this better. Mariana Falxa can be sent for when I'm near my time."

"Don't women's bones harden?" Vachel asked, reddening. "Won't this be worse than having us?"

"How do I know?" she snapped. Controlling her temper, she took their hands. "You're good boys to care but please believe that I'm old enough to judge what I want to do. Aren't you hungry? I baked just this morning and there's bean soup and rice. Come sit down and tell me your news."

When the sheep trailed down in September, Domingo did not want Dominika to cook any longer for the crew.

"I promised to take care of you," he argued. "Do you want to make my godson angry at me?"

"He won't be able to drive out here again till next summer," Dominika shrugged. "*Tocayo*, I cannot sit with my feet up from now until December! I feel better when I'm doing something."

He sent two thousand wethers and old ewes to market, buying hay, corn and cottonseed cake with the proceeds left after paying interest on his loan. The remaining sheep were split into two bands for winter range, saving the wages of a herder.

In November the baby's head dropped within Dominika. She continued to bake for the two herders and did the housework and cooking but her pelvic bones ached and she was now quite content to sit for long spells in the one comfortable chair, her feet on the stool that Domingo had made for her. She was making baby clothes from the soft flannel that he had bought for her in Boise and in the little bedroom there stood a cradle he had carried.

In the evenings he often played the *alboka* or sang the old songs. It was good, almost like being at home again, though this little cabin was so different from Etchahoun. Was Esteban still alive? Had he sired children? Would they inherit the property that he had usurped?

Now that Brant was dead, Dominika realized with a stir of wonder that she could save enough for the passage fare and return to Vizcaya. Even if Etchahoun was occupied, she could find work at somebody's farm. But when she searched herself, she knew that she did not want to go. Her sons were here. She had become accustomed to these wide spaces, these mountains and valleys. She had lived longer in America than she had in her home province, thirty years to eighteen.

She would not return to live in Vizcaya. But if she had a daughter, when the child was old enough, they would go back together. Enter the Cave of Always Summer, pay homage to mother and child and touch the handprints. The secret would not die.

XVIII

SNOW WAS falling as she waked that late November morning. Strange, she could not hear Domingo in the kitchen. He always had the fire going and coffee on the stove before she managed to stir. Rising, she dressed as quickly as her bulk allowed, teeth chattering in the frigid room.

At eighty-three Domingo was entitled to his sleep, she thought affectionately. She would make breakfast before she called him. He was due at Chico's camp today, fourteen miles up the valley. The bread she had baked yesterday was already packed with the other things in leather panniers—two dozen wrapped eggs in tin buckets, canned meat and fish, peaches, preserves, red peppers, beans and soups, a bar of soap, a gallon of wine, coffee, potatoes, a clean towel, matches, Basque papers, tobacco and another blanket. Each week the herders told Domingo what they wanted and he filled their orders as faithfully as possible from the storehouse-pantry built on to the kitchen.

A few coals smoldered under the ashes in the cookstove. She stirred them and added kindling, put coffee on and fed the fire before she covered it, being as quiet as possible. Preserves went on the table along with slices of bread. She poured some of Nani's milk into a pan to heat for the coffee. No matter how long he had lived in America, she had never met a Basque who did not insist on blending very strong coffee with hot milk in just about equal parts. Brant had preferred his coffee black. She had always shuddered at it.

She sauteed onions, red peppers and tomatoes, whipped up five eggs and cooked them, now making enough noise to rouse the old shepherd. She did not hear a sound from him.

426

"Domingo!" she called. "*Tocayo*, your eggs are ready."

Still no response. A coldness crept over her. Automatically switching the eggs to the side of the stove where they would not scorch, she hurried to the bunk at the far end of the main room.

Domingo's jaw gaped. He gave no sound or sign of breathing. Unbelieving, she touched his face. It was cold. When she caught his shoulder and shook him, his head fell back. One eye was slightly open.

He was dead. His heart? A stroke? Mind whirling, unable to accept this, Dominika stripped back the blankets and pressed her ear against the brown chest matted with silvery hair.

No breath. No heartbeat.

"But he was fine last night!" she wailed aloud. "He played the *alboka* and said that he must practice up on lullabies."

Her voice echoed in the room that seemed suddenly even more chill. She covered Domingo's face and murmured a hasty prayer. From the bedroom she took the candle that she still lit for her mother and Etchahoun, placed it beside him and lighted it.

She had no holy water with which to sprinkle him, no funerary cloths in which to drape his house. But she would wash and dress him and send for the priest.

There was no one to send. And there were the herders to be supplied.

Shuddering violently, she fought down her panic-stricken grief, went to the stove and poured a bracing mug of coffee and milk. She would need strength for whatever she did next and so she took a plate of eggs and bread and sat close to the stove to eat and try to decide what to do.

Domingo was past help. At this time of the year, when a storm might blow in and make travel to their camps difficult, it was vital not to let the herders fall short of supplies. Chico's band was closer than Pete Falxa's house. Since she had to go somewhere for help, she might as well deliver supplies while she was about it.

And then?

She could not plan right now except to know that the sheep must be cared for and that a camp-tender must be found. Chico could ride to town and hire a man, stop at Falxas' on the way back and ask them to come help with the funeral and the settling of Domingo's affairs. Dominika would have to stay with the sheep for the day or two that Chico would be gone but it seemed the best solution.

Domingo had been her friend since those days so long ago at the Irigays' hotel. She was still too stunned to feel that he was dead. Mechanically she milked Nani, fed the chickens and dogs and rubbed Jautzi's head, giving him a handful of grain. She also grained Domingo's bay horse and the pack mule, glad that they were in the corral.

The snow had stopped and the wind had already blown it off higher ground to lie in hollows and sheltered spots. The skies were gray and heavy, though, as if bloated with storm. Dominika's belly bulged under the sheepskin coat and her pelvis ached with the pressure of the baby's head. Riding was not something she would ordinarily do this late in pregnancy but she had no choice.

Inside, she blew out the candle and folded Domingo's gnarled brown hands over the crucifix he had kept on the wall. Kissing his forehead, her numbness threatened to give way to a surge of loss but she braved herself against it, trying to concentrate on the duties that he had left in her hands.

Kissing his closed eyes, she prayed for him again and then prepared to ride.

It was almost noon when she rode up to Chico's tent, pitched where a rock ledge broke the wind. Most of the night's snow had been scoured away and the band was spread out along the slope, grazing contentedly.

Rising from his cookfire, Chico stared when he recognized her. His pitted, narrow face full of concern, he hurried to help her dismount. "The boss? Is he sick?"

She shook her head, unable to speak. Chico led her to the fire and poured her a mug of coffee drenched with hot milk and sugar. The brew steadied her, warmed her.

"Domingo died in his sleep." She said it fast, before her voice could break. "It must have been quick—easy."

"But he was fine last week!" Chico cried.

"He was fine last night."

The dark young herder stood for a few seconds as if frozen. Then he took a blanket, spread it and made Dominika sit down by the fire. "You shouldn't be riding," he blurted.

"You needed supplies. You can ride into town, hire a camp-tender and then send the Falxas over."

"The sheep—"

"I will stay with them." At his horrified stare, she gave a weak smile. "The dogs do all the work anyway, don't they? They know me. If you tell them to watch the sheep, they will."

Chico watered the bay and the mule, gave them some corn and unpacked the mule, hobbling him so that he could not disappear. Finishing his meal of corned beef and potatoes, Chico glanced at Dominika in an agony of indecision.

"The boss—"

"The boss would say get a new camp-tender. Don't try to come back at night. Stay over and rest the bay." Rummaging in her pocket, she found a pencil stub and pad and wrote down Foss's phone number. "Call my son in Reno. Domingo was his godfather."

Resignedly Chico took the paper. He stroked the flop-eared black and white dogs, who had frisked out to meet Dominika but then lain down unobtrusively as though they sensed something wrong.

"Take care of the lady," he told them softly. "Watch after the sheep. Txiki, don't let some silly ewe start them moving in the night. Arri, look out for coyotes."

Straightening, he turned to Dominika. "I'll bring the wagon for you when I get back," he said. "Or send Pete Falxa with his truck. Yes, that would be better! Just stay at the tent, andrea. Let the dogs look after the sheep."

"We'll all still be here when you get back," she assured him briskly.

She waved him on his way but when he had vanished behind a slope, she felt utterly exposed and alone. Calling the dogs, she petted them, drawing comfort from their intelligent, sympathetic eyes as she promised them—and herself—that their master would not be gone for long.

* * *

The sheep had salt and they were close to a little creek. Chico would need to move them to fresh graze in a week or so—but there was really nothing for her to do but be alert for any disturbance. This band had three hundred "markers," black sheep or the biggest belled wethers. She counted them before dusk settled in, relieved that they were all there, though it would have been hard for any to sneak off as closely as she had been watching.

She blessed the good supply of firewood as she added a small log and several small branches. The ride had made her back ache and she had felt an occasional twinge that afternoon but the baby had been moving a lot during the last few weeks and she had learned to ignore most of the uncomfortable thrashing about in her abdomen. She warmed stew and had a bowl of it along with a soothing cup of hot chocolate before she fed the dogs.

It was dark by the time she had washed the dishes. She sat huddled near the fire, grateful for its light, remembering how Joe had told her that he had been so afraid during his first year as a herder that he had kept a roaring fire going all night long. She wondered if Domingo had also been frightened long ago when he was new to America and the care of the sheep.

She prayed for him, hoping he knew that she had not wanted to leave him unattended. His death still seemed a bad dream from which she would awaken to find him smiling at her. It was early but she was exhausted. She banked the fire, wedging in a log to hold coals until morning, washed her face and gave the dogs a good-night caress.

The whiff of unwashed male that exuded from the bedroll as she opened it made her realize that she should have brought her own bedding. At least there was the clean new blanket. She took off her coat and boots but left on the rest of her clothes, folded the fresh blanket around herself and climbed into the bedroll.

Someone was thrusting a red-hot docking iron into her belly, snipping at veins and arteries, tearing out bits of flesh. The baby—her baby! Her own stifled cry woke her. Quick, anxious dog tongues licked at her face.

"It's all right," she told them, weakly pushing them away. But it wasn't. As pain wrenched her, she gritted her teeth.

The baby was coming. Almost a month early. Chico could not return earlier than tomorrow noon. There was no one to help her but herself. When the spasm eased, she worked on her boots and coat and crawled to the tent flap. Snow had fallen and was drifting down in soft fleece, burying the fire.

She scraped away the white fluff and sighed with relief as the underside of the log glowed brightly. From under the tarp protecting the wood she brought out kindling and got the flames going, put in bigger limbs and set a kettle of water on to boil.

In the tent she located and lit a kerosene lantern. Chico's clothing sack yielded one clean undershirt. There was a sharp knife among the cooking utensils.

She sweated in fiery torment as she made her few preparations. Had she ever hurt this much before? It was the first time that she had been alone in labor and she was old for birthing. What if she died, or the baby did?

Don't be silly, she scolded. *You're not so different from a ewe. Most of them have their babies without help.*

But some did not. Some strained and battled and . . . . *Don't think of such things.*

She twisted as a pitchfork seemed to fasten within her, rotating cruelly. The dogs whined uneasily. Panting, she fell into the bedroll. These pains were not coming with a purposive, increasing rhythm that she could try to follow, could work with to deliver the child. They gripped her in breathless agony that made her writhe, clutch at her stomach and try to tear it open to be rid of the gigantic, rending claws.

She had become the pain. It was all she was, crowding out every other thought and memory. She was in a deep black cavern that endlessly echoed with her pain. But then the sides of the cavern bore the prints of hands, hundreds of them, blessing, encouraging, the hands of women who had suffered as she suffered, speaking to her now from the other side of the agony.

We are with you. It was not a voice but a whispering impression planted in her mind, calming her dread. The tent was full of comforting presences. She felt as if her mother were close, lending her own will to endure, helping her to bear down against the hurting.

Then real hands gripped hers. Strong, live fingers. "A little more," came a deep, pleasant voice. "Come on now! Get those pains working for you."

She bore down with all her might. Useless. Gasping, she looked up into a tanned face with a stubble of light brown beard, a long mouth and gray eyes. A stranger! But there was such kindness in his voice and hands that she felt no shame at his presence, only great relief, a certainty that he would help her.

He offered encouragement, holding her hands tightly until she lay exhausted. He swore softly. Then he said, "Ma'am, I have to see whether the baby's turned wrong. I'll be easy as I can."

She could not repress a moan as his hand probed and searched. He sucked in his breath. Then there was a lurching sensation. "Shoulder in the way," he said. "All right, ma'am. I know you're wore out but can you try again? Yell if it helps. Cuss me out. But hang on and give it all you've got!"

Again, he braced her with his hands. Again, she summoned the remnants of will and strength. Something was changing. The contractions seemed to come of themselves.

Rending, crimson-streaked pain, animal scream, searing, ripping passage—then a lapsing into feathery warm darkness in which she was buoyed up by an ancient, mystical pulse.

Floating. Drifting. Empty of blood and pain.

Those strong hands raised her. She rested against a shoulder. "Drink this, ma'am."

Coffee, with the sting of brandy in it. She swallowed and coughed, swallowed again. Her eyelids fluttered up.

"My baby—"

The arm that was cradling her tightened. The man turned his face away. "I'm sorry, ma'am," he said in a husky tone.

She struggled to sit up. "Where is she? Where's my baby?"

"Now how did you know it was a little girl?" he asked under his breath before he eased her back against him. "The baby was born dead."

Dead? Her daughter? After years of waiting and all that pain?

"I don't believe it!" she cried against his breast. "Where is she? Let me see her!"

Sighing, he reached for a small bundle at the foot of the bed-roll. Unwrapping Chico's clean shirt, the stranger showed Dominika the body, still bearing traces of blood and mucous. Lots of fine black hair, curved dark eyebrows, little flattened nose, minute fingers closed in fists.

Her daughter had never breathed earth's air. The only life this small, perfect creature had known had been within the warm cradle of Dominika's womb.

Dominika took the tiny blood-moist hand, opened it to press against her own. *Go to the cave,* she told her daughter's spirit. And of the presences that had sustained her, she implored silently, *Take her with you. Keep her always.*

Julian Matthews was the camp-tender whom Chico had hired. A Kansas wheat-farmer who had watched his soil blow away in clouds that had darkened the sun, he had taken his tubercular wife to Colorado, doing any kind of work he could to keep them alive. She had died that fall and he decided to move farther west. He had herded sheep last summer, and so he knew something about it.

"When Chico said that you were with the sheep and pretty near your time, I didn't like the sound of it," Julian said in his warm, soothing drawl. "Got directions from him and came on out. But it's a good thing you had that fire built up or I couldn't have found you until morning."

She might have been dead by that time. Dominika shivered as he fed her some more soup. Devastated as she was by the loss of her daughter, she was glad to be alive, glad to be succored by this man who was like no one she had known. He had washed her and cleaned her up as much as possible. Now he spread his bedroll beside her, covered her snugly and took her in his arms.

"Go to sleep," he said.

Drained, she lay against the calming, even beat of his heart. It lulled her, lengthened her breaths, steadied the erratic pulse of her blood. She felt safe and protected as she had not since Joe's death—and this time there was no pent-up desire for Brant to blight her peace.

Her body and spirit still ached but she knew, as she drifted into heavy slumber, that this man cared for her and, already, that she cared for him.

XIX

THE BABY was buried beside Domingo on a little slope above the house, first to get the sun in the morning, last to have it at night.

Vachel and Foss had taken the train to Boise and driven out with the priest. They had been a bit suspicious of Julian at first, especially when the banker who handled Domingo's affairs produced the old sheepman's will, which left everything to Dominika.

"Pete Falxa has offered to buy the land and sheep if you'll give him credit, Mama," Foss urged. "Losing the baby should have shown you that a sheep camp's no place for a woman. Come back to Reno with us."

"No."

Foss scowled past Dominika to Julian. Vachel took her hand. "Mama, you won't have to be beholden to us if that's what you're afraid of. Falxa can pay enough down to buy you a nice little house."

"And then?"

He looked puzzled. In Vachel she could always see and love the child he had been. Foss was different. She loved him but he had grown away from her early. Marrying his father had completed the estrangement. He smiled somewhat contemptuously now as Vachel floundered.

"Well, Falxa's payments will give you enough to live on, Mama. Foss and I can stop by every day, nearly. You won't have to worry about a thing—"

Dominika burst out laughing. When he looked at her as though he thought she had lost her mind, she could only laugh the more. Recovering, she was suddenly not as amused. Addressing them in Basque, she said slowly, "My sons, I am forty-

435

eight, not ninety-eight. Shall I live for your visits, the scraps of your busy lives? I'm far from ready to sit by the fire and knit.''

''But, Mama—''

''I thank you for coming,'' she said courteously. ''It will always pleasure me to see you. But Domingo has left me the way to start again. I'm going to.''

Her sons must have recognized that tone. They did not argue further. They stayed for another day while Julian supplied both of the herders. By the time the men would need food next week, Dominika planned to be back on her feet but for now she was resting and regaining her strength. Let the boys hustle for her for a while! She was not as decrepit as they seemed to think but it took her longer to recover.

She smiled against her pillows as she heard Foss say grudgingly to his brother, ''I've had some pretty long talks with Matthews. Turns red as a kid when I mention Mama. He's daffy about her and,'' he concluded glumly, ''he may not be smart but he's honest.''

Vachel snorted. ''Didn't think you knew any honest guys!''

''Believe me, I can spot a con man.''

''I'd hope.'' Vachel pondered for a minute. ''Isn't Matthews younger than Mama?''

''Eight years. But he's grayer than she is and, hell, Mama looks better than some of the women I court!''

''I wish 'em joy,'' Vachel said after a little thought.

Dominika straightened. ''Thank you,'' she said demurely.

Her sons stared at her, blue and brown eyes startled, a little guilty. When they saw that she was smiling, unwillingly they began to laugh. She joined in, holding out her arms to them. As they embraced, she felt closer to them than she had since their childhood, yet she felt an irrevocable separation.

They were grown now. And she was a woman who had found a new man.

Two months later she and Julian were married. It had been the natural, inevitable outcome ever since he had come to her on that night of her agony and loss, but though he had kissed her and held her, trembling with desire, he had not tried to know all of her until their wedding night.

He was a tender, eager lover, worshipfully delighting in her, humbly proud that he could lift her into unfolding joys, ever brighter and more intense, like the sun-wooed blossoming of a rose. Her flesh glowed, her hair and eyes took on a sheen and she had never been more conscious of herself as a woman, more confident and proud. Their loving was as rapturous as any she had ever known with Brant but with it came also the warm cherishing that Joe had lavished on her. In spite of the little grave beside Domingo's, she had never been so happy.

Franklin Delano Roosevelt was sworn in as President that March of 1933, while the panic accelerated and still more banks closed. Yet the sheep had wintered fairly well and the spring clip, even with low prices, brought sufficient to pay off the last of Domingo's loan and leave enough to buy winter feed. Julian was new to sheep but not to livestock and he listened to Chico's and Dominika's advice. That fall they saved all of the young ewes again and had to hire another herder for now they were running close to nine thousand sheep.

Julian and Dominika listened to Roosevelt's "fireside chats" on the radio and hoped that better times were coming.

"With Prohibition getting the ax, things are bound to pick up," Julian chuckled. He helped both of them to hot, spiced cider, toasting Dominika gaily.

The radio in the isolated cabin brought in other news, much of it disturbing. A man named Hitler had been appointed Chancellor of Germany; Communists were accused of firing the Reichstag in Berlin and Dominika heard the phrase "concentration camps" for the first time. After the Spanish Revolution of 1931 had seen the departure of Alfonso XIII, the brief Republic succumbed in 1933 to the conservative right wing and a sinister fascist group, the Falange, was taking shape.

"If they would only give the Basques independence!" Dominika cried. "We don't want their fascists or communists or monarchies—just the rights we've had even before there was a Spain!"

Julian had the sense not to remind her that she was now an American citizen. She appreciated that, as she did so many things about this tall, deliberately moving yet decisive man.

He had never had a child. His wife's frail health had led to several miscarriages; after that he had taken precautions. At first Dominika hoped she might conceive again but as the months passed, she reluctantly decided that the dead baby's conception had been the last fruitfulness of an aging body and seldom thought of it. Foss and Vachel would marry sometime. Surely one of them would have a daughter fit to know the secret.

There was good spring grass in March of 1934 but by the April lambing the weather was cold and windy. Drought wiped out what little grass the sheep missed and Julian had to find a place to trail two of the bands. After some searching, he leased meadowland south of Elko. Dominika's questions convinced her it was part of the ranch that she and Brant had owned.

"Does that bother you?" Julian asked quickly.

She shook her head. "No. If the sheep can eat, that's fine." Brant would have detested the sight of "woolies" on his land but she felt no loyalty to his prejudices.

The Taylor Grazing Act, passed that year, put an end to the grazing of sheep on public lands by nomadic herders unless they owned enough land and water to carry their winter herd. Many Basques and other sheepmen had made their start that way, saving their money to buy a band which could then be pastured on free graze. Like Joe, most of them bought land when they could and now they were members of the local livestock grazing boards set up in each district to apportion leases of Federal lands.

Stock raisers who had freely run their animals on National Forest graze grumbled at being told when they could bring their sheep or cattle and how many were allowed, but the surliest of them knew that something must be done to halt the race for the best Federal grass. As long as this range was open to anyone, the first user tended to let his herds tear up even the roots because the next comer certainly would. Further, there was no incentive to let worn-out graze renew itself because some herder would soon move in on it and ruin it anyway.

"We haven't had any idea of what we've been doing to the soil," Julian mused. "My daddy homesteaded in Kansas. I've turned many an acre of virgin sod over, fighting those tough

hunks of roots that locked the long prairie grass to the earth."
He shook his head. "Now when it gets dry and the wind blows,
the soil just goes along with it."

"Domingo always moved the sheep when the grass got
short."

"Yes, he did a pretty good job, lots better than most, but
this fall we need to either sell off quite a few sheep or get some
more land."

It was a good thing two of the bands had been moved to the
Ruby Valley because that summer saw the worst drought in per-
haps a hundred years, searing Midwestern crops, shriveling up
Western grass, drying the streams.

Sheep on the Idaho range got so scrawny that Pete Falxa
and Julian shipped three thousand ewes and lambs to Colorado,
where there was good graze on abandoned homesteads in Park
County. This almost turned into disaster. Several dozen sheep
died before a farmer told them that the animals must be pulling
up the roots of a variety of wild onion. The tops of the plants
were safe but eating too many of the bulbs would kill animals. By
moving the sheep away from the onions and feeding them on al-
falfa, the men managed to save the rest but since the drought
continued, they both sold their sheep in Denver rather than ship
them back to the withered Idaho range.

Roosevelt's New Deal program had set up all kinds of
boards and bureaus in order to try to defeat the Depression. The
year 1934 brought thirty-three new government agencies and
twenty-four thousand new Federal employees along with a
twenty per cent increase in the national debt. At the same time
only fifty-eight banks failed—a striking contrast to the years
since 1921 when it was common for nine hundred to fail annu-
ally. One small part of the vast Federal spending that year was
for the purpose of buying sheep at two dollars per head.

"Even for a sixty-pound wether, that's a terrible price," Julian said disconsolately. "But we can't carry the sheep through
the winter, not all of them. Even if we could afford to buy corn
and cottonseed cake, there's not much for sale because of the
drought."

So that fall, black Jautzi, now the bellwether, marched all
but the best ewes and strongest yearlings down to Boise.

One shepherd with one band stayed down in Ruby Valley. "The bank has had to foreclose on the last owner," Julian told Dominika that fall. "That's better range than we have here. I'd hoped we'd make enough money this year to talk about paying down on some of your old ranch but all we've managed to do is keep from running into debt."

"That's something," Dominika stated. "Gabe Esponda went broke and had to go back to herding. So have lots of stockmen."

She looked out to the graves on the slope. Domingo belonged here where he had lived; it comforted Dominika to know that the little daughter rested beside him, ewe lamb with a good shepherd.

The ranch in Ruby Valley had been Dominika's home longer than any other place in America. It was where her sons had grown up and she had found the bristlecone pines. She willed herself to remember Brant and found that she could do so now without anger or grief, though she would always feel regret.

Crossing the room, she rested her hands on Julian's shoulders, feeling fresh and happy as she saw the way his gray eyes softened for her. Her times of wishing for a dancing young man were long over. She wanted one now who would walk with her, not showing off for anyone who would watch but matching his stride to hers.

"Why don't we see if Pete Falxa still wants this place? Try to make a deal with the Elko bank?"

"You want to move down there?" He studied her closely.

"Yes. It's beautiful country. We'll be careful and bring back the grass." She gave him a hug and sighed with anticipation. "After lambing next spring, we'll ride up into the high mountains. I'll show you the bristlecones."

"Now what are they?" puzzled Julian, laughing at her enthusiasm.

"You'll see!"

The drought broke in the spring of 1935 as though to welcome Dominika back to the valley between the mountains. It was a beautiful sight to see lambs frisking pell-mell on the green slopes while their mothers fed nearby. When the bands moved to summer range, Dominika picked a day when Julian did not have to supply the herders, packed a sumptuous picnic and brought him along the flower-spangled canyon and up the rocky way to the ancient trees.

She knelt by her favorite tree and pressed her face to its polished roots. Surviving drought, storm, wind, the weather of century after century, these trees awed her with the same sense of persistent, enduring life that she had felt in the women's cave.

"Better than a church," Julian said. Reverently he touched the dead trunk from which the green half sprang. "It's a place for thinking. I'd reckon a man could live his whole life while this tree adds on a couple of inches of rings."

The high place and the aged trees appealed to something locked deep within the prairie-bred man. Without being told he knew that it was a place Dominika liked to visit alone. After the first time he did not return with her but he sometimes made his way there on his way back from camp-tending.

Prices rose a bit that fall. They saved all the ewes and were still able to pay on the ranch. Dominika went to Reno for Foss's wedding to a niece of one of the out-of-state millionaires whom Norman Biltz, a Lake Tahoe subdivider, had lured to the region during the Depression by showing them how they could pay substantially lower taxes by changing their residency. Since Nevada had never provided the public with many of the services that other states did, taxes were comparatively low. Foss guessed that Biltz had enticed at least fifty extremely wealthy people to settle in Nevada.

With the six-week divorce law, legal gambling and good roads to California and the East, Reno was booming again. Vachel had acquired a third interest in a casino and was engaged to a partner's daughter, a willowy, green-eyed redhead named Sarah who treated Dominika sweetly.

Foss's tall, blonde bride, Madelaine, fussed over Dominika, demanded of everybody to know if her accent wasn't "completely darling," and made her so uncomfortable that, the wedding over, it was a relief to escape back to Julian, who had been invited but had felt that his presence would be an intrusion.

"So how do you like your daughter-in-law?" he asked her when he met her train in Elko.

It felt wonderful to be back in his arms. She laughed a little to cover her reservations about Madelaine. "She's very beautiful. She says she thinks that sheep are—are romantic!"

Julian hooted and seemed to know that Dominika did not want to voice her misgivings. If Foss were suited, that was what counted. But Dominika could not imagine a daughter of the chic, brittle Madelaine as one who would be able to appreciate the cave and its secret.

She sighed and pinned her hopes on Sarah.

Although things were going better with the sheep, and the country on the whole seemed to be coming out of the worst of the Depression, Dominika was chilled at the news coming over the radio.

Germany had broken the Treaty of Versailles and was conscripting men. Jews were being deprived of their rights as citizens by the Nuremburg laws. Stalin's purges continued in Russia. Fascist parties seemed to be springing up in many countries. The whole world boiled with unrest.

Julian and the Sabalas had liked each other immediately and usually the two couples had a meal or drink together when Julian and Dominika were in Elko. Domingo kept up with the explosive developments in Spain and gloomily peered at his braced fingertips as he spoke of the elections set for February of 1936.

"The Popular Front will set up a leftist, anti-Catholic government but it does support Basque autonomy. The right is Catholic but won't give the Basques much freedom." Domingo shrugged unhappily. "However it goes, the Basques will catch the devil. If Spain would just leave us alone—"

"Not likely when so much of the heavy industry is in your region," Julian pointed out.

"For Christian civilization! For Basque liberty! For social justice!" Ironically, Domingo quoted the Basque nationalists' official slogans. "The first words show that they're not Marxist. The next insists on autonomy and the last separates them from the rightists."

When Dominika and Julian next saw him, it was after the election and he was downing straight brandy instead of Picon punch. "The Popular Front won in Spain but in the Basque country it's a mess! Nine nationalists, eight rightists and seven Popular Front!" He spread his hands despairingly. "If we can't unite, how can we win independence?"

He would never go back; he had been in Nevada since 1898; his seven children were American. Yet in his heart he was forever Basque. Dominika understood. It was so with her.

That spring Julian leased enough forest land to carry the increased bands and hired two new herders, young men from Vizcaya who brought grim accounts of strikes, riots and increasing hatred between left and right. In July the Fascist right, led by General Franco, revolted. The seething country exploded. Revolutionary worker groups swarmed into city streets and armed themselves. In parts of Spain still dominated by the Republican government, there were slaughters of non-leftists, including many priests. The Basque country was more fiercely conservative and Catholic than any other part of Spain but this struggle saw Catholic pitted against Catholic over the question of autonomy.

It was in that troubled month of July that Dominika incredulously realized that she might be pregnant. It was possible of course. Though she was fifty-two, her flows were still regular; but it had been so long—

By the next month she was sufficiently certain to whisper the news to Julian. He laughed and swept her close. "That's wonderful, honey! I hope we have a little girl just as pretty as you!" The delight in his eyes changed to sudden concern. "But should you?"

She lifted her chin determinedly. "Of course I should! I want this baby more than anything—that is, anything I don't already have."

"Then so do I. But we're going to take mighty good care of you." He chuckled, caressing her cheek and throat. "Babies must be catching. Foss ought to call us most any day now."

He did, on the fifteenth of August. "Hello, *amona*," he greeted, using the Basque word for grandmother. "Faustin Robert Uhalde was born about dawn this morning. Will you come and stand godmother?''

That October the embattled Republican parliament voted to grant Basque autonomy and sent most of its fleet to Bilbao, along with badly needed supplies. Only Vizcaya and the western part of Guipuzcoa were still holding out against Franco's forces when President Aguirre took his oath under the Tree of Gernika.

Freedom at last, but at what a time!

And the whirlwind was rising everywhere. China declared war on Japan. The Rome-Berlin Axis was formed and German troops marched into the Rhineland.

All this made Dominika's head whirl. And it saddened her. But it was the plight of her homeland that oppressed her the most during that winter and the spring of 1937. The United States had remained neutral but hundreds of American men had paid their own way to Spain and taken up arms against Franco. Both Foss and Vachel were more concerned about Hitler than they were about the Civil War, though they were outraged that Germany and Italy were supporting Franco and that German bombers were being used against the Republicans. That spring Julian hired a new herder for the lambing, a blond, hazel-eyed youngster of about sixteen.

The image of Esteban! Dominika's breath tightened in her chest. When Julian said, ''This is Koni Lexa,'' the boy smiled shyly.

''Are you kin to Esteban Lexa?'' she asked.

''He's my grandfather.'' The lad flushed with eagerness, obviously pleased to find someone in this new country who knew his family's name. ''You knew him, andrea?''

The past was not the boy's fault but Dominika had to swallow before she could say casually, ''Long ago I knew him. Is he well?''

Tears showed in Koni's eyes. Averting his smooth young face, he muttered, ''*Aitona* was killed when the bomb fell.''

Late in March Franco had advanced on the Basque country, now called Euzkadi. What had made the struggle devastatingly unequal were the hundred and forty planes, nearly half of them from the German Condor Legion. Euzkadi had no more than thirty-five planes and almost no antiaircraft guns.

"Bomb?" Dominika echoed, flinching. The baby lurched within her. Blindly she put out a hand and would have fallen had Julian not supported her.

"I was in the village," Koni said, his face twisting. He clenched his hands. "It was a gray plane—one of the Condors. Maybe it meant to hit the village. The planes have been strafing and bombing, trying to make us surrender. However it was, a bomb blew up the house." The young voice cracked. "*Aitona* and father were dead when I got there. Mother lived for a little while. She—she made me promise to leave." His voice broke. "My uncle smuggled me up through France and put me on a boat for America. It—it all happened before I knew it." He began to sob. "I should have stayed. I should have stayed to fight!"

Dominika put her arms around him and soothed him. "No. Your mother was right, Koni. Euzkadi will have to live in our hearts until a better time." When he was quieter, she said, "The house is gone then? Etchahoun?"

Koni frowned, "You knew the farm?"

Dominika nodded.

"All that's left is a little of the north wall of the old stone tower."

All that is left of Etchahoun after a thousand years?

"Honey," ordered Julian, "you lie down and rest. I'll take Koni down to the lambing camp."

She managed somehow to smile at the boy and tell him to let her know if he needed anything but as soon as Julian had driven off with him, she walked as if in her sleep to the bedroom, lit the candle by her grandmother's rosary and prayerbook and took the blue bird in her hands as she sank to the floor in an abandonment of weeping.

The shock was worse in some ways than if a loved one had died. She marveled now that she could have contested Esteban for the house; at least he had not wanted to wreck it. Waking and sleeping, she recalled it in vivid detail: the hearth, the old clock, the beeswax-polished floors and furniture, the embroidered linens of Etchahoun's flax, the cider skins from its orchard.

No, even though she could never live there again, the knowledge that Etchahoun was there had been a foundation to her life. For once it did not help to think of the Summer Cave. The home of her childhood, the home of generations, was shattered, and with it, part of herself.

Julian had hired a cook for the lambing and shearing, insisting that Dominika stay at the house. She had not argued. The baby should come late that month. She moved heavily, was short of breath and was forced to realize that she was old for childbearing.

The destruction of Etchahoun blighted her happiness. In a world where such things happened, where there was war and strife everywhere, what use was it to have children?

Julian had to be at the lambing during the day but he came home each night and tried to cajole, startle or anger her into rousing from her grieving melancholy.

"If you don't snap out of this," he growled, "I'm going to get the doctor out."

"I don't need him."

"You need something!" He gripped her shoulders, hurting her in his frustration. "That house is gone, damn it! Think about our baby."

She did but somehow it meant nothing. She went numbly about her daily chores. The baby, as if absorbing her hopelessness, almost stopped moving. Was it dead? In her desolation it would have been fitting that she carry a dead child in her womb. She was heavy, heavy, longing to be free of the weight, although now she felt no joy at the thought.

She kept the radio turned on, listening for the sparse news from Spain. Blockaded, shelled by artillery and strafed by planes, Euzkadi, scarcely born, writhed in its death throes, the bitterness increased by internal struggles and the assault of Narvarrese fellow-Basques. Durango was bombed and many killed.

On April 26 wave after wave of Condors flew over Gernika, dropping their loads of death. It was market day. There were few air-raid shelters and those were flimsy. The planes swooped low to machine-gun people as they ran for safety.

The town began to burn, the wooden rafters catching fire. After loosing high explosives, the planes dropped incendiary bombs. Shocked from her apathy, Dominika knelt and prayed, the blue bird in her hands, as the radio droned on.

For three hours the bombing lasted. Three hours to raze a little town of six thousand people, the heart of Euzkadi, site of the ancient oak where the Lords of Vizcaya had always sworn to uphold the freedoms, where Isabela had sworn, and Ferdinand, the luckless Don Carlos, and only months before, President Aguirre.

Gernikako Arbola. . . .

The song of Basque freedom sounded in her ears as the pains she had scarcely noticed insisted and grew strong. Her water broke as she was climbing painfully to her feet.

The baby was coming. As Gernika smoldered, her baby would be born. Julian came in at that moment, took one swift look, and lifted her to the bed.

Two hours later, before the doctor could arrive, Kattalin was born. During the labor Dominika's primeval struggle to bring forth a child cleared her mind. Etchahoun was gone but somehow, miraculously, in the little town of Gernika with twenty-five hundred people dead and wounded, the Tree still stood.

She cradled her daughter to her breast and looked up thankfully at Julian, her man who had brought her through death and through despair.

Her life lay with him now. But Kattalin—oh, Kattalin would journey to the Cave.

VI

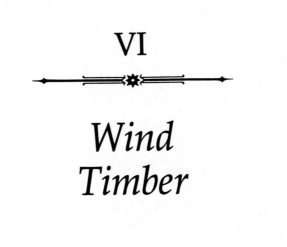

Wind
Timber

I

THE FEARSOMELY beautiful angel with a flaming sword was shoving Eden off the crumbling hillside and into a dark abyss. Catching at his feet, she pleaded. God sat on a throne beyond them, gray-green, horned like Moses in her father's books. He reached for one of the thunderbolts stored under his throne and she screamed, clinging to the angel's legs.

Hands gripped her shoulders. She opened her eyes, a cry breaking on her lips, expecting to see the angel. Instead, her father's blue eyes stared into hers.

"What's the matter, Eden?"

His tone was harsh. He did not like for her to cry or make noise or come into the big, sunny room where he had all those wonderful paints and brushes. She tried to gulp back her sobs but the terror of the nightmare was still upon her. She began shivering uncontrollably.

He almost never touched her but now he gathered her into his arms and held her against him in his wheelchair. His legs would not support him but his shoulders and arms were strong.

"Bad dreams, little one?" His voice had softened.

She took a gasping breath that hurt and yet seemed to unfreeze her lungs. "God was sending me to hell."

His fingers bit into her till she winced. "What?"

Frightened, she could not speak and buried her face against his unfamiliar shoulder. Stroking her hair, Magnus Lowrie spoke in a way that permitted no evasions. "Has Mrs. Parrish been telling you a lot of rubbish?"

"She—she told me I would go to hell if I didn't get saved. She said if I prayed, God would save me—and I did pray but nothing happened."

Mrs. Parrish had said there was something wicked in her heart. During the day Eden could forget but she'd had the dreams every night for so long that she couldn't remember how nice it had been when she used to snuggle up in the pillows with Lambie and Tigger and just go to sleep. At the moment, so unexpectedly cuddled in her father's arms, Eden almost felt that the luxury was worth the price of nightmare.

"God doesn't send people to hell," Magnus said slowly. "People do that. What else did you dream, Eden?"

When she finished, he shook his fair head decisively. "Mrs. Parrish is dead wrong, child. Hell isn't a hot, dark place down below us. It's here, when people do awful things to each other or to animals or the earth. Hell is in people's hearts. It's nothing for you to worry about for a long, long time.

"But Mrs. Parrish—"

"Mrs. Parrish is leaving. Her hell and her god are going with her." Settling Eden back in bed, his stern mouth curved into a smile. "I'll paint you a picture, though. One that will keep away bad dreams. Would you like to come in my studio tomorrow and watch me start?"

What joy! For him to want her, to let her see him work! Unable to speak, Eden bobbed her head. "Go to sleep," Magnus said, covering her up. "I'll leave your door open and the hall light on."

He turned off the lamp but she caught the glint of his wheelchair as he maneuvered it through the door. Sighing, she hugged Lambie and Tigger. When the scary images tried to form, she told them: *Daddy says you're not true.* She filled her mind with glorious thoughts of watching him work the next day, making a picture just for her. She would take her crayons and draw something for him. It was going to be wonderful!

You're not real, she scolded the angry, gray-green god. Remembering the warmth and strength of her father's arms, in that haven she drifted into sleep.

Twenty years later Eden straightened the painting that Magnus had made for his frightened child and stepped back to enjoy it. Except during her three-year marriage to Fowler Drake, Ygdrasil had always hung on the wall above her bed. It seemed immediately at home in this rough Forest Service cabin that she had permission to use while she assessed the lower, privately owned lands for Earth Heritage.

Magnus had died two years ago but when she studied the painting, she always felt close to the complex, embittered yet visionary man who had been her adoptive father. It spoke of his surviving faith, an unquenchable trust that life and beauty would always arise out of destruction.

The deep-rooted Tree of Life stood in the storm of Ragnarok, the end of the old world, while in back of it bright Asgard of the gods crashed behind the wavering Rainbow Bridge. Amid the blaze and swirling muck, the Tree endured while within its translucently glowing trunk and limbs there were men and women, animals and birds, that would replenish the better world to come.

Eden still remembered with what rapture she had watched her father create the painting and how at her request he had painted the suggestion of Lambie and Tigger into the branches. He had bought her a little easel and for an hour or so each day had taught her how to mix colors and how to use a brush. He had also delighted her with quick sketches of the Gambel's quail that paraded through the yard, topknots bobbing; the stalking road runner as he lowered his crested head and streaked after a lizard; rabbits, big and little; chipmunks and squirrels and javelinas with dainty hoofs, slim flanks and heavy shoulders topped with hairs that bristled at alarm, sometimes followed by their young, looking exactly like dark, tiny piglets.

One morning a doe came to the stone water trough. As she drank, lifting her graceful head and listening between swallows, her fawn came up and lifted his nose to hers.

"They love each other," Eden whispered, her throat aching at their loveliness.

"Of course they do." Magnus sounded angry.

She gazed at him, uncomprehending. He said with a certain weariness, "There are many excuses for killing and hurting animals. I'm ready to allow honest hunger or self-defense. But don't ever let anyone tell you that animals don't feel love and fear and pain." Savagely he added: "It was once the fashion to say that it was all right to kill and torment animals because they had no souls. Then when there began to be doubt that people had any either, the argument was that animals couldn't reason. Both alibis are stupid. Animals hurt with their bodies when they're shot or trapped or vivisected, not with their intellects or souls.''

It was not until she started to the ranch school ten miles away that she realized that people ate animals. Most of the eleven other children attending the one-room school were vaqueros' children and brought tortillas wrapped around beans but the ranchers' children usually had meat sandwiches and occasionally fried chicken and venison. Eden could never taste flesh. It always made her see the animal from which it had come.

Her real education was in Magnus' studio, his library, and the hours she spent wandering through the desert and mountains, although she rode a bus thirty miles to high school. Through Magnus' contacts, by the time she finished school, she was selling her wildlife pictures and rock etchings, some of them reminiscent of the ancient cave paintings of the Pyrenees that she dreamed of someday visiting.

At some point she learned that she had been adopted when Magnus and his wife despaired of having children. On the way home from the Tucson hospital where Eden had been born, a truck had hit their car, killing Magnus' wife instantly and leaving his legs paralyzed. It was easy then to understand why, until her nightmare had reached him, he had preferred to leave her to housekeepers and see as little as possible of a child who had cost him so much. Eden, named by her adoptive mother at the hospital, did not unduly puzzle over her real parentage. Magnus was her father and her teacher and she loved him.

He died in the year that she finished high school. She rented the house to another artist and with her small cash inheritance, she bought a camper-van in which she traveled around the West, often leaving the vehicle while she walked back into a rugged canyon or followed an animal trail up a mountainside.

Vistas of purple ranges fading one into another until they merged with sky; streams trickling through rocky passes, creating stands of white-trunked sycamores, gnarled oaks and walnut trees; myriad tracks in sandy washes or along dunes, fragile hieroglyphics of lizards, quail, snakes, rabbits, coyotes and deer;

the crunch of pungent pine needles underfoot—all of these she loved. But there were things that outraged and haunted her.

In her own Arizona smelter smoke belched in dark plumes that spread out and hazed the valleys fifty miles away. Automobile exhaust fumes covered cities with a thick yellow pall. Phoenix, where people often moved for their health, issued pollution alerts advising those with respiratory ailments to stay indoors. Rivers, drained for agri-business, were dry, while irrigation practices mindlessly squandered fossil water sucked from water tables that could never recharge. Cattle and sheep had devastated hundreds of thousands of acres of Western public lands.

In Monument Valley on the Navajo Reservation she sat under a ramada, watching Jess Windsinger's wife sprinkle the earth with water for cooling and listening as the wasted man spoke weakly of his years as a uranium miner. "No one told us it was dangerous. We worked seven hundred feet underground in bad air. Sometimes the company sent in air for a couple of hours to settle the dust in the main tunnel."

"Where did you get your water?"

"From pools where water seeped out of the rock." Windsinger's skeletal face twisted. He was middle-aged but he looked ninety. "We didn't know to change clothes or wash when we came home. Lots of my friends have died of lung cancer. Lots more will die."

"Our healers can't cure it," said his wife bitterly. "But neither can the white doctors."

"I'm scared for the children," Windsinger said. "They play around the old tailings. They swim in the pools in the old pit mines."

"Cattle and sheep drink there, too," said his wife. "There are some warning signs posted but animals and children can't read."

At the other end of the state, north of the Grand Canyon, Eden talked with people downwind from the nuclear testing site in Nevada. "The testing moved underground in 1963," said one graying woman, "but they still had all kinds of seeps and leaks. Why, fallout was even tracked to as far away as Texas and

Minnesota! We have twenty times the average leukemia rate here. And they're still setting off bombs every couple of weeks."

Eden had supposed, somehow, that testing had ended long ago. "Why?" she asked, aghast.

"They have to set off the old warheads. Guess they're like canned food—go bad after a while. And of course they're trying out new weapons." The faded woman glanced westward. "I just wish that everybody who likes nuclear weapons would live here where they could get good and acquainted with them."

In less than a hundred years man had so polluted and poisoned the earth that it seemed to Eden that Ragnarok *had* come and that if the land she loved was to survive, she must do all that she could. For this reason she had become a volunteer field-worker for Earth Heritage, a powerful and dedicated group formed to study threatened wilderness areas and buy them as preserves in order to protect the threatened plants, trees and wildlife.

During her marriage to Fowler she had taken a staff-artist's job with a magazine to help put him through medical school. Fowler was annoyed when she spent her weekends in working for Earth Heritage and tried to keep up her art at the same time. A few weeks before he finished his internship, Eden's darkly handsome young husband told her that he had found a woman who liked to spend her spare time in doing "fun things" rather than "mucking around" with turps and paints or roaming in inaccessible places. Further, the woman was a physician whose father conveniently had an opening in his group practice for Fowler.

That was two months ago.

Eden took a deep breath and wondered when she would stop feeling completely rejected and humiliated. Maybe, she reflected dourly, it was what she deserved for mistaking a powerful sexual attraction for love, worth giving up almost everything for—even parts of her work.

She would never do that again. Not for any man. Right now she was too raw and hurt to even be tempted. The rent from her father's house supplied her basic needs. The publishing division of Earth Heritage had commissioned her to do the paintings for a book on bristlecone pines. The tree was the organization's symbol.

Already she had sketched the enduring, wind-tortured shapes of the bristlecones in Arizona's San Francisco Peaks and the doughty individuals in California's White Mountains facing west to the Sierra Nevada. She believed that she had found Melah there, the world's oldest living thing, some forty-hundred years old. From her present base in the Ruby Mountains, she could do the Wheeler Peak bristlecones, only half a day's drive south, and develop her sketches into paintings by studying the bristlecones only a short walk from the cabin.

Hanging the Tree of Life above the blanketed cot had been her first touch of settling in. She had swept out the debris, lined the shelves and filled them with food and a few dishes and cooking utensils. Her clothes went in the old dresser with the veined mirror, except for a couple of skirts and blouses that she hung on pegs. The wood stove had taken the chill from the air and the teakettle was simmering.

Home. Sweet home?

You bet it's going to be! she thought, giving Fowler a mental kick. She was lucky to have a project as exciting and beautiful to work on as the book and when she needed a change from painting, she would negotiate her way down that gullied service road and look over the region that Earth Heritage wanted to acquire before its aged owner died.

Right now, though, she was going to find the trees.

The bristlecones were not tall. The burnished yellow, dead branches and the living stubby ones tufted with short needles seldom thrust more than twenty-five feet into the brilliant sky. But they were awesome, magnificent in the shapes that had been sculptured by centuries of lightning fire, fierce winds and rain, scoured by storm-driven sand and ice.

A tree no taller than she might be a thousand years old. Scraggly crowns, blasted branches protruding, often topped massive trunks with buttressed sides and roots that dug like talons into the stony earth.

Wind timber. That was what they called such trees in Colorado. They were buffeted by storms, crushed by snow and ice, survived on tiny amounts of moisture and had a growing period of perhaps only three months a year. A bristlecone's rings did not necessarily tell its age. Some years, when the snow never melted, were so cruel that the tree could not grow at all.

It had been a hundred and ten degrees at Las Vegas this morning, ninety in Ruby Valley, but here it was forty and snow lay in sheltered places. Thrusting her hands deeper into her warm jacket and turning up her collar, Eden wandered through the stand of pines, content for now to reverence them and experience the wonder of their existence.

"You like the trees?"

She whirled at the deep, soft voice. The man reminded her at once of the bristlecones. His face was as weathered as the wood. He was tall in spite of the slight, dogged hunch to his shoulders that made him look as if he were used to walking in high, cold winds. Pure white eyebrows bristled above keen gray eyes. He was clean-shaven but thick white hair grew shaggily beneath his ears.

Eden had learned to be wary of strangers in solitary places but this one belonged here. He was no stranger. Smiling, she said, "It would be presumptuous to like such trees."

He nodded. She noticed that his big, ungloved hands were as gnarled as the roots of the pines. They stood in companionable silence for a few minutes. Eden felt immediately comfortable with him, as though he were somebody whom she had known for a long time. Squinting at the westering sun, he turned back to her.

"Sun's about to slide behind the cliffs. Going to cool off in a hurry. Are you staying in the old forest cabin?"

"Yes."

"Then why don't you come along to my place and have some beans and cornbread?" When she hesitated, he chuckled reassuringly. "I'm two miles from you by road but there's a trail cuts off more than half of that. Of course I won't let you wander home in the dark by yourself."

She cast him a quick glance, remembering several aged lechers whom she had been amazed to find that she had to ward off, but though he was as strongly masculine as any man she had ever met, she would have sworn that not only now but never had he embarrassed a reluctant woman.

"Sounds great!" she said.

He adjusted his long stride to her shorter one and they started down the slope to the saddle and the road.

Julian Matthews had not prepared Eden for Trace Steele. Except for his height and gray eyes beneath straight eyebrows, it was hard to believe that he was Julian's grandson. He had jumped up when they entered the cabin, plainly startled, and acknowledged the introduction curtly.

When, obviously trying to ease the awkward tension, Julian explained Eden's picture-drawing undertaking to Trace, the young man looked arrogantly down his straight, rather long nose.

"That's all we need—a big, splashy inducement for everyone with a four-wheel drive to come tearing up to see the bristlecones." He reached for his Stetson and jacket. "Guess I'll get on down the hill, *aitona. Amona* will be expecting me."

"No one, least of all your grandmother, is foolish enough to do that," Julian said firmly. "And she knows that I haven't seen you since before lambing. You'll stay for supper."

Trace shrugged and pulled on his jacket. "Okay. I'll split some wood before the light goes."

"I can do that myself," Julian growled, deftly concocting the batter. "If you're so blamed energetic, stay over tonight and chop up a supply for Miss Eden."

"Oh," she protested, "that's not necessary."

"I'd hope not." Trace yanked his hat on over his tousled black hair. "Woman's got no business up here unless she can take care of herself."

"I certainly can do that, Mr. Steele. And even if I couldn't, I wouldn't ask you for help."

"That's a relief," he said nastily and strode out the door.

Eden almost choked with anger. She whirled to Julian, who was pouring the yellow mixture into a pan. "I really think I'd better not stay. Your grandson—"

Slanting her a quizzical glance, the old man grinned provokingly. "You going to let that rascal do you out of a dandy meal? Make you run for home? I sure had you figgered for more spunk than that."

Maybe they were related after all. Eden tossed her head. "I don't care what your grandson thinks, Julian, and I can't see why I should be glowered at through a meal."

"He's scared of you," Julian said with a smile, putting the bread in the oven. "And he wouldn't be scared if he didn't think you were dangerous."

Eden snorted as Julian placidly stirred the beans. "Trace doesn't know much about women. His mother died when he was a baby and his *amona*, my Dominika—she's almost ninety-seven—raised him. Trace had the bad luck to marry a floozie who caused him a lot of grief before she finally took off with some hotshot entertainer she met in Reno. But hell, that's two years ago. He needs to meet a nice girl before he gets mean and tempery as an old he-badger."

"He already is," Eden muttered. Julian's last name had registered with her when he mentioned his aged wife. Cocking her head at him in surprise, she asked, "Do you own the land below in the Ruby Valley?"

"Dominika does. Trace runs the ranch."

Eden scowled. "Then I'll have to talk to him sometime. I might as well stay to supper if you'll give me leave to kick him under the table."

"Kick him anywhere you want," Julian invited. Then he grinned wickedly. "Just don't damage any vital parts you may—well, be interested in later!"

Fat chance, Eden thought. But she did run her fingers through her hair. Julian raised an eyebrow. "Why do you need to talk to my grandson?" By the time she had finished explaining the preservation goals of Earth Heritage, he was frowning slightly.

"I wouldn't mention it to Trace right away. His two cousins have big plans for the ranch and he's pretty tired of fighting them off." Julian pondered. "Best thing would be to get Dominika interested, though I doubt that she'll sell. I'll take you down to meet her one of these days. Till then, as far as Trace's concerned, maybe you'd better just be an artist.''

''Whatever you think,'' Eden chuckled ruefully. ''Somehow I don't believe we'll have any trouble in finding plenty of other things to quarrel about.''

''Pour it on,'' said Julian.

II

IT WAS the best cornbread that Eden had ever tasted. Crispy, slathered with butter, the whole panful melted away along with helpings of the spicy beans. Mugs of mulled cider were delicious and Trace had brought a tin of crunchy almond cakes sent by his grandmother.

Julian had led the conversation, asking Trace about the lambing. Talking past Eden, Trace ignored her as much as possible. He sat between her and Julian and so it was difficult not to notice him, although she would have let her tongue wither before she would have asked him a question.

By the time Julian filled their cups with steaming coffee, she knew that Trace had a lean jaw accentuated by the shadowed clefts below his cheekbones. There was a white rim around his forehead where his hat shut out the sun, and his ears, though well-formed, were rather large. His thick hair was not curly but neither was it straight. Once when Julian spoke directly to her, Trace glanced at her sideways.

His gaze seemed to pierce her and Eden's pulse leaped. Something electric flared between them. His long mouth tightened before the gray eyes turned hostile and he turned back to face Julian.

Damn him, she thought, angered and confused by the sudden flash between them. *He's in for a shock if he thinks that I'm out to trap him—and what's the matter with him anyway? I have just as much reason as he does to play "burned child."*

She insisted on washing the dishes. To her surprise, he dried and put them away, all the while keeping up a flow of talk with his grandfather, who nursed a fragrantly odorous pipe and eyed them quizzically.

"Thank you for the dinner," Eden said, drying her hands and taking her jacket from a hook. "I have all the fixings for a great mushroom quiche. Will you come over tomorrow evening?"

"That's the best offer of the decade," Julian laughed, helping her into her jacket. "Trace will drop you off."

"That's not necessary."

"It's sensible," Trace said coldly. "No use stumbling around in the dark when I'm going right by."

She stared at Julian, who said blandly, "I'd walk you, Miss Eden, but the old arthritis sort of gets me after dark."

Argument made the small favor more important than it was. "If it's no trouble—" she began ungraciously.

"If it were, I wouldn't do it." His lips tight, he yanked on his coat and waved her out the door.

As if I were one of his sheep! she fumed inwardly. Hurrying to avoid his opening the door for her, she was climbing into the nearest pickup when he called infuriatingly, "Mine's over here."

He held the door, insisted that she buckle her seatbelt and slammed the door. No wonder his wife had left him! Not a word passed between them till he pulled up in front of the cabin. To her surprise, he stopped the engine and climbed out.

Scrambling to reach the ground before he could reach the door, she said a little breathlessly, "Thanks for the ride."

"It's nothing." Turning on a flashlight, he motioned toward the cabin door. "I'll wait until you light a lamp."

Feeling foolish, perhaps even a trifle disappointed that his delay had a practical reason, she hastily led the way inside, silently admitting that it was a good thing he had waited. Expecting to be back before dark, she had not taken her flashlight out of her pile of duffle or filled the kerosene lamp on the table.

Aided by the beam of light, she started to do so now. The screw-on wick section was stuck. After she had twisted it vainly for a few minutes, Trace made an impatient sound, handed her the flashlight and took the lamp. She was glad that it wouldn't turn until his second effort. He poured in the fuel and screwed on the wick-holder.

Lighting the lamp with a match of his own, he put on the

chimney and regulated the wick so that it gave the best light without sooting up the glass.

"If you'd wash the chimney, you'd get more light," he rebuked.

Eden's cheeks burned. "I got here just today," she reminded him.

His gaze traveled slowly about the single room—looking for more evidence of slovenliness or incompetence, she thought angrily. She was glad that the bed was made and her clothes were neatly hung up.

He stared at the painting of Ygdrasil. "It's funny to see something like that up here."

"I've always kept it over my bed," she said defensively.

"No matter what was in it?"

For a moment she could not believe her ears. Then she thrust the flashlight into his hand and flung open the door. "Get out!"

He laughed, took the lid off the stove and tossed in some wood. "I'll build up your fire first."

Trembling with anger and something else, a taut excitement that built until she felt that she must either scream at him or attack him, she stood by the door. Finished with the stove, he was beside her in a stride, catching her as she gasped and spun to race through the door.

He shut out the cold and the night and swung her up in his arms.

He didn't ravish her. Swept past normal restraints, she was as eager as he was. The smoldering, unwelcome attraction that had coursed between them all evening broke into flame. Fowler had been her only other lover. For the first year they had been passionately enraptured with each other but after that the barriers growing between them had distorted their lovemaking. He'd had to look at pornographic magazines in order to work up an interest in her and she had felt dirty and used, a receiver of lust forged by obscene or pathetic fantasies. For the last few months before their break-up, he had lost even that prurient desire.

Trace made love to her, fondling and delighting her, his ardor searing away her fears until she could touch him, too, taking pleasure in the hardness of his thighs, the broad shoulders and chest above the slim, tight belly. A rider's body, strength in the torso and flanks and legs. When he finally took her, he climaxed quickly but she was so feverishly ready, so eager for that wonderful, deliberate filling, that she cried out as he drove deep and rocketed into that expanding, swirling loss of self even before he did.

As they lay together peacefully, she reached to touch his face, filled with tenderness and gratitude. What a marvel that people could give such joy to each other! She felt cleansed, too, blessedly rid of Fowler's occupation of her secret parts.

Trace's eyes opened. In the dim light she could not see his expression. Rolling away from her and off the bed in one motion, he dressed quickly.

Not a word? Not a touch?

In disbelief she sat up, tugging a blanket around herself. "Good-night," he said, picking up his jacket.

While she shrank from the cold words, her knee still felt the warmth of where he had lain. That had not been trivial—or, if it had, if she could have been so mistaken, she had to know.

Springing up, willing her nakedness to compel the truth from him, she demanded fiercely, "Is that all you have to say?"

The tanned mask of his face crooked in a faint smile. "You want me to thank you? All right. Thanks. You're the best lay I've had in a long time."

She took one step and slapped him.

His eyes blazed but he closed his fingers into fists, and put them behind him. Her fingerprints showed white against his dark cheek. "You bed down with a man a couple of hours after you meet him and you want a big fuss?"

Flayed by the scorn in his voice, she cried out, "If it doesn't mean anything, why did you do it?"

He said brutally, "I needed a good tumble and so did you. We had it. Even Steven, lady." He reached for the door. In spite of his words, she still believed the consuming awareness that had flamed between them was more than simple sex hunger. She was not going to let him leave with slurring remarks that he could comfortably believe.

Barring his way, her hand on the doorknob, she refused to

flinch or retreat as his gaze raked her body. When at last, with a shrug, he looked straight into her eyes, she asked, "Why?"

The words seemed dragged from deep within him. "I didn't want to think about you—to wonder—after I went down the mountain."

That was the truth and it moved her away from the door.

"But you would mark my bed on my first night here. How can I not remember you when I lie here?"

He made a fending gesture. "Isn't it a little late—both tonight and in this century—to fake outraged virtue?"

"Virtue has nothing to do with it. It's being fair with another human being." Her eyes stung. She had compelled him with her exposed body but she would not show him tears. Turning her back to him, she managed to hold her tone steady. "You clearly don't think women *are* human. Go on down your mountain!"

She could sense his hesitation.

"If you expected more than you got, I'm sorry," he said stiffly, "but I didn't make promises. And if you let a man first try—"

She whirled on him. "Isn't it late—tonight and in this century—to think like that?" she mimicked savagely. "Get out! Get the hell out!"

His harsh, handsome mask slipping, he took a step forward before he pivoted and wrenched open the door. It slammed behind him. She threw herself on the bed and wept with such bitter fury that she scarcely heard the truck start and grind its way down the road.

She woke next morning thinking that he was beside her. When her searching hand found emptiness, her eyes flew open. Damn him! she thought wryly. It hadn't helped much to strip off the sheets that remembered him if she couldn't forget!

But she would. He was not going to ruin this beautiful place for her.

Thrusting her feet into quilted houseboots, she belted her heavy robe and coaxed a few ruddy coals into a fire before she looked out the window. Sun had not yet reached the cabin but there were only a few vague clouds nesting in the hollows of the mountain. It was a good day to go to work—and that was what she was here for.

She would not attempt to deny that she was powerfully drawn to Trace Steele. She even could have loved him. But she would not waste time and herself in yearning for a man who, because he'd had a dismal marriage, chose to see women as throwaway disposables. Hurt, as she knew from her own experience, certainly led to caution, but to wholesale condemnation and suspicion?

No. For all his strong, rugged stance, Trace was a coward. She did not need a man like that.

As soon as she had breakfasted, she arranged a few books on a shelf, finished putting away her possessions and shoved the duffles under the bed. She pumped a bucket of water from the creaky pump outside the door and set it on the stand, where she had decided to keep the flashlight. Brushing her long hair, such a light brown that it just missed being yellow, she fastened it back with a beaded ribbon and regarded herself in the mirror.

What had Trace seen last night? Inquiring eyebrows that feathered at the edges, eyes that changed from russet to tawny, a high, broad forehead softened by a widow's peak, a full mouth beneath an adequate, freckled nose.

"You have great bones," Magnus had told her once when she had lamented that she was not pretty like some of the girls in her class. "You'll be beautiful long after the glow has left your friends."

His words hadn't consoled her then but she had rather come to like her looks. They were exertion-saving at least, for she looked as attractive with a touch of lip gloss as on those rare occasions when she invested half a painstaking hour in trying to be glamorous.

Frowning at herself now, she scolded aloud, "You're not to wonder what that obnoxious man thought of you. He had an urge and you just happened to be handy."

But she had forced him to admit there had been something more than that. *Stop it!* she commanded herself. *He's scuttled down the mountain and back to business. Maybe you'll be lucky and never see him again.*

She put on her jacket, took her sketching things and started for the sloping, rock-strewn crest.

It was late May, early for flowers, but she shared her trail mix with several inquisitive golden-mantled ground squirrels, doughty-crested Steller's jays and gray-headed and Oregon juncos. In spite of the brilliant sun, the air was so cold that she frequently thrust her hands inside her parka to warm them and walked briskly to keep her toes from numbing.

She saw a few deer trailing along a lower ridge but she was grateful for the squirrels and birds for there was little to feed most of the creatures up here. Magnificent as the ancient trees were, their immense age and endurance made her acutely conscious of her own brevity and glad to be among other creatures who moved and felt and lived in measurable time. The ground squirrels were especially companionable. Usually at least one would be around, sunning lazily on a rocky ledge if it was not hunting food.

A harlequin-faced, red-capped acorn woodpecker labored at a blasted limber pine and she heard the shy twitter of pygmy nuthatches. Catching a glimpse of one hanging upside down by a pine cone, she sketched a fast impression of him and then scattered the last of her trail mix widely so that all the birds and squirrels could have a chance at it.

She would work in the warmth of the cabin for a while and then return to work on blending the colors by sight. The leached gold of the dead trunks, the dark green of the tufted needles, the purple in the cones, and the red-brown of the living bark—all of these hues would require careful experimentation if she was to even approximate them.

In butter she cooked onions to yellow translucence and sliced several scrubbed potatoes that she put in with them, letting them steam. Then she added milk, cheese and dill. This was her favorite winter soup. She enjoyed a bowlful of it, standing by the window and pondering where to hang her bird feeders. After that she took out her sketches and paints, arranged the easel to catch the best light and settled to work.

The trouble with her first position was that she was facing the bed. That would never do. She moved five times before she finally arrived at reasonable illumination without at least a partial view of that offending piece of furniture. By that time she was so angrily resentful of the way Trace had made her uncomfortable in her own dwelling that she decided not to go back to the bristlecones that day but to spend the afternoon in reclaiming her territory.

She worked doggedly till failing light warned that she had better start preparations for the company that was coming. By the time Julian arrived, whistling melodiously, she had not only tidied away her work and hung the bird feeders but she had set the table with woven-grass placemats, unglazed stoneware and silver goblets and silverware she carried in the van. It was durable luxury that lifted her spirits.

"Smells gustable, as my Scots granny used to say." Julian wrinkled his nose at the fragrant odor of the quiche and produced a bottle of wine. "Did you get lots done today? I saw you up on the crest but you looked busy so I didn't pester you."

"Stop by anytime," she invited, tossing a salad. "It's not as if there's a parade marching past."

"That's the truth," he chuckled. He did not seem to appraise the room but she was certain that he could have described it in detail. "You've made the old shack real cozy. That's quite a painting."

"My father did it for me when I was about five," she explained. Julian smiled as he turned from studying the picture.

"Not many people would find it comforting to sleep with the end of the world over their beds."

"But the tree lasts. And the creatures in it will start a new world. A better one."

"Ah," said Julian, "I suppose that's what we have to hope for."

During the next days Julian came often to watch her work. After she had made a few sketches of him, she said reflectively, "You're a sort of human bristlecone, Julian."

"Lord, I'm not that old!"

"No, but—you look *carved*, as though everything that isn't essential has been honed away."

He chuckled, throwing back his head so that his white-silver hair shone in the sunlight. "It's time for that, I reckon. I'm eighty-nine. But when you meet my Dominika—well, then you'll really think of bristlecones. She has lived many lives but at the core she's stayed the same."

Rising from a log, he went over to touch the tree that Eden had sketched that morning. "This tree might have been a young thing when the Roman Empire ruled the world. Some bristlecones go back to when the pyramids were being built. Most of this one is dead, but it takes only a tiny vein of living matter to keep part of it alive, a part that can survive storms and drought in places where few other things can even grow. The cones of trees four thousand years old can still produce fertile seeds. I like being with them."

"Do you stay up here all the time?"

"I have for the last five years, ever since Trace took over the ranch. Of course I go down every few weeks to see Dominika and during the warmest season I bring her up here for a while. She has always loved these pines."

"I'm looking forward to meeting her. It's beginning to sound like an event."

"It will be," Julian said quietly.

Eden was grateful that Julian never asked her what she had thought of Trace. With stern self-discipline she continued to banish him from her conscious thoughts but sometimes when she was drifting in and out of sleep, she felt the touch of his hands and his hard, sweet mouth and woke herself by moaning in desire.

It was a good thing, she thought, that she had an absorbing task. Each bristlecone was so different from any other that she was actually painting portraits, working to capture an essence of character.

Apart from the familiar birds and squirrels, she once glimpsed Rocky Mountain goats on another peak. Julian said that the Fish and Game people had planted them in the Rubies. He also showed her a memento of a Basque shepherd, carved on a gray-white aspen.

Back in 1898, Luis Gamboa of Durango, Vizcaya, had engraved his name on the tree and beneath it some Basque words.

"He says that eternity is no lonelier than this," Julian translated. "But he's one who had his own bands and his great-grandson runs sheep north of Elko."

"I've heard of the shepherd carvings," Eden said, touched by the old words even though she regretted the gouging of the wood. "There's a photo exhibit of them called 'Mountain Picassos.' "

Julian laughed. "Some of them look like those cave pictures—hefty women, with not much attention given to their faces. Come on, I have something else to show you."

He paused behind a thick cover of snowberry bushes, motioned for quiet and pointed toward a rugged outcropping of rock that overlooked a rubbled gully washed by wind and water. In front of a grotto, warmed by the sun, a mountain lion drowsily watched three kittens at play. She must have been seven feet long, frosted with white on her belly, chest, ears and muzzle, tawnily magnificent. The kittens, the size of domestic house cats, had dark spots and ringed tails.

The faint breeze was blowing toward the humans and could not betray their presence. They watched for a long time until the small ones tired of their game and trotted over to nurse at their mother's side.

"That was marvelous," Eden whispered when she and Julian were some distance away. "I saw a lion once in Arizona but I have never been able to see the babies. The father doesn't help raise them, does he?"

"No. He shows up to mate and then departs, the way some men would like to. But Mama manages pretty well. She teaches the kittens to hunt and they stay with her till they're about two years old."

"I'll get some photos and sketches."

"Sure. But take your binoculars and telephoto lens. You don't want to upset Mama."

"Do you have any more surprises?"

"Not like that. But I've got macaroni and cheese in the oven."

"Wonderful," Eden said. "Let's pick up my lemon sesame loaf for dessert." They walked along companionably, sharing the crimson glory of the sunset. Mixed with the pleasure she found in his company there was always regret that his grandson apparently had inherited none of the old man's kindness and little of his wisdom.

Nearly every afternoon after that she went to see the lions, careful to take advantage of the prevailing wind, sitting on a distant ledge and watching through her binoculars. She took several rolls of pictures and slides and made a whole pad of quick impressions. The lioness was probably taking a deer a week in order to feed herself and her family but apart from a few bones, Eden never saw evidence of any killings around the den.

"Didn't you poison lions when you were ranching?" she asked Julian.

He shook his head. "No, and I didn't put out 1080 for coyotes either. Coyotes and lions keep down the number of deer and rabbits that eat sheep and cattle forage. I figured that losing some sheep to them was just like paying a range-control specialist, only a lot more efficient."

"Does your grandson think that way?"

"Trace wants to get out of the sheep business. It's a sore point between him and Dominika."

Julian did not volunteer further comment on the matter and Eden did not press him but her curiosity was aroused. Was it possible that Trace might become an ally should Earth Heritage try to buy the ranch?

She had been on the mountain for three weeks. Encouraged by the longer, warmer days, purple fringe and butterweed grew along the ridges and scarlet paintbrush began to flower. Snapdragon-like rose and yellow figwort grew in damper places while fuschia shooting stars studded the meadow below the cabin. Eden still needed three blankets at night but after the sun banished early morning chill, the days were beautiful. Sometimes, wearing only shorts and a halter, she sunned as indolently as the mother lioness or the golden-mantled squirrels, although she knew that soon now she should go down and start looking over the land for which Earth Heritage might make an offer. She wanted very much to meet Dominika but when she thought of encountering Trace, her hard-won peace frayed.

She had hoped that he might return but he hadn't. When she, of necessity, visited his grandmother, she must make sure that he couldn't believe she was pursuing him.

One morning Julian stopped by to say that he was going to town for supplies. Would she like to go or did she need anything? She commissioned him to buy fruit, cheese and salad greens and although she had chosen to remain and work, she felt surprisingly lonely when he had rattled off in his old blue pickup.

She was sharing her lunch with the squirrels and birds when a flashy black RV painted with gold arrows churned past the cabin and butted part way up the bristlecone ridge.

Eden ran down quickly and held up her arms in warning. "Hey, take it easy! These trees are valuable."

A stubble-faced, sandy-haired man surveyed her and the bristlecones with equal scorn while his dark companion swept the neighboring ridge with binoculars. They neither looked nor acted like bird watchers. Uneasily conscious that Julian was gone, she answered their questions briefly.

No, she was not some kind of ranger and no, she hadn't seen any mountain goats but she was sure they were not supposed to be hunted.

The men laughed unpleasantly, backed into a bristlecone, scarring it, and shot off down the road. Eden was glad to see them gone but the invasion disturbed her. About mid-afternoon she heard a shot, then two almost at the same time and then a final one.

The likely thing was that the men had poached a deer but the firing came from the direction of the mountain lions' den. Hastily collecting her materials, she put them in the van and then struck out on foot. She hurried but it was an hour's hike to the den and shortly after she veered off the road to cut across the field, she heard the distant roar of an engine.

The men could have been shooting just for the fun of it. People often did. Look at all those saguaros in Arizona, riddled with bullets for no reason at all except sheer destructiveness. But the shots had not sounded like spontaneous vandalism. They had been purposively spaced.

Maybe they had missed their target. Anyway, there were

other things to shoot at besides the lions. Still, the dread that filled her heart intensified and she began to run wherever the footing permitted.

She smelled smoke before she saw it.

III

STOPPING, Eden looked around fearfully and gasped as she saw smoke sifting through the trees above her and coming from the ridge where the lions' den was. At almost the same moment she saw a bloody body hanging from a limb and screamed in revulsion and horror.

They had taken that proud head with those jewel-like eyes which had so tenderly watched the kittens. The paws were hacked off, and the long, sinuous tail. But they had not wanted the meat, only the hide to tan and peg to a wall or spread on a floor.

Eden retched, sobbing. She would gladly have killed those men had she been able. But the smoke was rolling in thicker now. While the poachers were scouting around, they might have built a cookfire or dropped a smoldering cigarette butt. She had seen hundreds of square miles of timberland burn from just such criminal heedlessness. No one could ever guess the numbers of animals and birds caught in the infernos, nestlings too young to fly and helpless, trapped young animals.

Like the lioness' kittens.

Jays were shrieking. Birds winged out of the smoke. Two deer ran past. The orphaned kittens had no one to rescue them. They had been trained by their mother to stay hidden in the den while she was out hunting. Had the grotto been deep, they might have wriggled back far enough to escape the strangling fumes and heat. As it was, they would burn.

Eden turned from the flayed carcass and ran toward the gully.

Instinctively fearing the smoke, the kittens crouched in the rock depression, laying back their ears and spitting as Eden approached. They were little, but their claws could shred her arms.

"Hey, fellas," she pleaded, "you have to help me or we won't get out of here!"

They snarled at her. Eden remembered then that falcons were hooded so they could be controlled and panicked horses could be led to safety if they were blindfolded.

It was worth a try.

Stripping off her jacket and sweater, she dropped the sweater over the small heads and followed it with the jacket, which she lapped around those vicious claws. To her vast relief, the strategy worked. Neither kitten struggled as she picked them up.

Which way to go?

Fire, not just smoke, was traveling down the ridge, cutting off the way to the cabin and her van. Ygdrasil! Her sketches and all her work on the bristlecones!

Unencumbered, she might have tried to save them but she could not move quickly with the little lions. Flames seemed to erupt in the crown of a pine and leap to the branches of the surrounding trees. A sudden crackling roar chilled Eden but sent her into motion.

She had never followed the gully but she thought that it came out on the road half a mile below. Once on that, she could go faster, though whether she could outrun the fire—

Holding the kittens tight against her to keep their coverings in place, she scrambled along the gully. If flames overtook them, she would shelter in the deepest ledge she could find and pray to stay alive until the blaze swept over the eroded watercourse.

The bristlecones? The wind was not blowing in their direction and the denser trees left off at the cabin slope. The crest where most of the bristlecones grew was almost barren. Chances were that flames could eat part way up the summit but would falter and die in the rocks. Besides, many of the trees had already survived fires. It took only that small skein of persistent tissue.

Smoke stung her eyes and nose and throat. She stumbled but managed not to fall. There was nothing to check the fire in this direction. Vegetation was thicker from the yellow pine belt to the scrub juniper and sage expanses at the bottom. Of course the Forest Service would spot the fire and come to contain it sooner or later. The trouble was that for her and the lion kits it might be later.

She could see the road ahead. It was not wide enough to act as a firebreak. She glanced behind her. Smoke and fire.

Along the gully she had glimpsed no cavern that promised safety. Rather than huddle under a ledge and pray to escape, she decided to risk the road.

Would the baby lions move on their own? She could certainly double her speed without them. But she was afraid that they would wait for their mother and become too confused to run from the threat. She jogged wherever the road permitted and went as quickly as she could where it was rough or more sharply downhill.

A stitch in her side cramped agonizingly. Breathing hurt. Her nose began to bleed. The road leveled out for a stretch and she started to run. Her foot came down on a rock that she hadn't noticed, her ankle turned and she went down. Even as pain sickened her, she managed to twist sideways so that she did not fall on the kittens or let go of them. Exhausted, she felt acutely, desperately sick.

Gritting her teeth, she crawled part way up and tested the ankle. It would not hold her. For a moment terror blacked out everything else. Then she looked around, suddenly feeling that she was not here at all but must give advice from a distance to a frightened, lamed woman who sat in the path of a fire and clutched two lion kittens.

That gully down the road only a hundred yards away. It was broad, with high sides. There might even be an overhang or ledge that she could not see from here. It was a chance. The only chance. Cradling the lions with one arm, she set her other palm on the ground and began to crawl.

''What the hell?''

Eden had not really believed the sound was that of a vehicle until a pickup spun around a curve and stopped. Trace sprang out.

''Where's Julian?'' He reached down to lift her up.

She fended him off with her free hand. "Be careful! I have some lion kittens here. Julian went to town."

"No one's up there?"

"Some hunters were but I think they've gone down. They got their trophy."

He took the bundled kittens, helped her to her feet and supported her to the pickup, thrust her inside and put the lions in her lap. "Are you hurt?" he asked roughly, sliding under the wheel.

"Just my ankle."

"There's blood all over you."

"I had a nosebleed. Have the rangers seen the fire?"

"Yes. We'll meet fire-fighters on their way up and they've phoned for a plane to drop slurry. I'll go back and help as soon as I get you out of the way." His gray eyes swept sideways. "What the devil are you doing with lions?"

She explained. He gave her a surprised look but said nothing. Reaching behind him, he took out a canteen and handed it to her.

The water tasted wonderful. She drank thirstily, hoping that it wouldn't be too long till she could get some milk for the kittens and let them out of their blindfold. She pulled a handkerchief from her jacket, wet it and scrubbed the crusted blood off her face.

"There's a candy bar in the glove compartment," Trace said. Reading her intention to refuse the offer, he snapped, "Eat it, damn you! I don't want you passing out on me. Can you describe the poachers' vehicle?"

"Black two-door with golden arrows." She added as much as she remembered about the men.

"You can tell the rangers that. Lions are a game animal here, with no set season, but I doubt that those guys had a permit. Maybe Fish and Game can catch them, hide and all."

"I bet they started the fire, too."

"That will be tough to prove unless there's evidence around an obvious campfire."

"Do—do you think the bristlecones will burn?"

Again he stared at her before turning his attention to the

road. "It's pretty hard for flames to reach them. But the cabin will go, and your van most likely."

If she had not come so close to death, the loss of her father's painting and her own work would have been crushing. As it was, she gently hugged the kittens. "The important thing is to be alive. Thanks for driving up."

"I was worried about Julian."

That hurt.

"Thanks all the same," she said.

They met three Forest trucks that were just starting up the canyon. Trace stopped to tell the men that they need not worry about Julian or Eden, what he had observed of the fire's course and dimensions and to advise them to watch for signs of poachers. The rangers used their radio to relay an alert for the black vehicle and then sped on up to their battle.

By the time Trace reached the mouth of the canyon, he and Eden had passed half a dozen volunteers and more Forest people. A battered old blue pickup came in sight. Trace honked repeatedly. Julian pulled off on a shoulder of the road and Trace swung over beside him.

"You've got Eden!" Julian's voice was husky with relief.

"You can have her now." Trace leaped out and opened her door. He lifted her together with the lions and carried her to the other pickup, depositing her on the vacant seat with a finality that all but shouted, Good riddance! "She hurt her ankle. May need a doctor. I'll go help the rangers."

"But—"

"Take care of your neighbor and her pets," Trace said. He banged the door closed and was headed up the mountain before Julian and Eden could do more than look at each other. Her ordeal must have been obvious. Julian took her in his arms.

"The mother lion—" she sobbed.

When she could stop trembling and crying, he wiped her tears, made her blow her nose, produced a thermos of coffee and turned the truck around.

"I'm taking you to Dominika. Now tell me what you have in your jacket. Tell me all about it."

* * *

They stopped at a campground where he got some ice from a well-equipped group of campers and packed it around her ankle, propping her foot on an old sleeping bag that he took from the rear of the cab. He also cadged half a carton of milk. Down the road a way he pulled off to the side, poured some of the milk into the thermos lid and, one at a time, keeping their paws muffled, he inveigled the kittens into testing the fluid. They were thirsty and quickly lapped it up.

"Dominika's going to fuss when she sees them," Julian predicted, "but when she knows what you did to rescue them, they'll be safe."

Their bellies soothed, the little creatures seemed to relax and went to sleep shortly after the pickup was on the road again. Eden kept their bodies well-wrapped, however. For miles around she could see smoke rimming part of the mountain.

"It's too bad that the men who started the fire don't have to put it out," she said. "I hope they get caught with that lion pelt."

"Even if they do, not many judges in ranching country are going to fine 'em for killing a lion."

"Then I hope there's some way to prove they started the fire."

Julian shrugged wearily. "I don't remember how many forest fires I've helped fight in my life but I do know that no one was ever brought to account for one." He squinted into the rearview mirror. "There's the slurry plane. That ought to help."

It was sunset when he turned off the main road, taking one that wound up a gentle slope to a sprawling house that had a broad veranda on the front. Corrals, a big barn, outbuildings and a windmill lay below the house and huge cottonwoods made a haven of shade in the broad, green expanse of meadow. It was the best grass that Eden had seen in Nevada, almost unbelievable to find on a long-established ranch.

"There's not much sagebrush and cheat grass here," she remarked.

"Shouldn't be, the way Trace went after it when he took over. It took a while but he cleaned the other stuff out of the meadows and brought back the Great Basin wild rye that used to grow here. Add blue-bunch wheat grass and Idaho fescue and you have mighty good range." He gestured toward the valley, where a collection of pens and sheds were clustered. "You'd never know that eight thousand sheep were here during lambing and shearing. Enough grass that they didn't have to eat it right down to the roots and they left lots of good fertilizer as a thank-you."

When he parked by the house, Eden started to get out of the pickup but he said, "Keep off that ankle!" and carried her and the kittens up the stairs and inside as a dark, pleasant-faced, middle-aged woman opened the door for them.

"Thanks, Estevannia," Julian said, perching Eden on a kitchen stool. "We've got a pair of orphans. Reckon I can fix them a box in the pantry while you rustle them some bones and milk?"

An old rug in a cardboard box made a comfortable den. "What are they?" Estevannia demanded suspiciously and muttered prayerfully in a strange language when he replied, "Mountain lions." All the same, she left considerable meat on the bones that she put down for them.

"You won't have to worry with them long," he assured her. "I'll take them back up the mountain with me when I go." He told her about the fire, introduced Eden and glanced toward the door that connected the large kitchen with the rest of the long, rectangular house. "Is Dominika in the front room?"

"They're all front rooms," Estevannia said pertly, "but yes, she is in the *sala*. And we will eat in thirty minutes."

"*Bai*, Estevannia," he grinned, adding to Eden, "that's 'yes' in Basque—a useful word when dealing with the women in this house. How's your ankle? If it's more than a sprain, we'd better get you to a doctor."

Testing it, Eden winced but found that the joint worked. "I don't think anything is broken."

"Good. I'll just fix you a proper ice pack and we'll keep your leg elevated as much as possible for the next few days. That will keep the swelling down." He gave her his arm. "Come meet Dominika."

Was this the woman about whom she had heard so much

that she had pictured a sort of ageless goddess? The small woman in the big carved chair looked fragile and withered as a winter-blighted leaf but when her green-gold eyes weighed Eden, the younger woman glimpsed a flash of the beauty that Julian's beloved had once possessed. There was warmth and vitality in the low-pitched, faintly accented voice.

"You are welcome." Small, veined hands closed over Eden's fingers in a curious, almost blessing gesture. "But you must sit down and let Julian tend to your ankle. The fire, it is a bad one?"

"If it's spread into side canyons, they'll have to go after it with shovels and light equipment," Julian replied. "I wouldn't expect Trace for a day or two. Tomorrow I'll go see if I can help."

"You have fought enough fires."

He shrugged. "What can I do when it picks my mountain? Are there any clothes that Eden could wear? Her things are all up in the Forest cabin."

"A shame."

"I can get more clothes." Eden ached at the thought of Ygdrasil curling in flames along with the sketches and paintings that had taken her so many hours. Resolutely she said, "If you get out of a fire with your life, you have to feel lucky."

Dominika nodded. "That is true. If there is life, one starts again. Julian, give her the back bedroom. I have given away most of the things I used to wear but there's a garment bag full of special things in the closet. In the chest of drawers are some jeans and shirts that one or another of Foss's and Joe's lady friends have left behind." She gave an earthy chuckle. "Between them there has been such a variety that you should find something to fit. My Reno grandsons like so many women that neither can settle on one."

Not like your other grandson, Eden thought but she only smiled and thanked her hostess as Julian helped her down the hall to the last door on the right.

"Estevannia is right across the hall. Dominika is between her and the front room and when I'm here, I have the room adjoining this one. Trace uses the foreman's house, though he comes to the big house for supper." He opened a door. "Yep. Plenty of clean towels and a bar of that stinky soap. Dominika broke her hip a few years ago and had to use crutches for a while. Let me see if I can't find one of them for you.''

Eden managed to take a badly needed shower and when she hobbled out of the bathroom a neat pile of white underwear and a hairbrush, toothbrush and comb lay on the bed. A crutch leaned against the footboard and when she opened the closet, she saw that her jacket had been hung up. The sweater would need washing. She brushed her hair, donned hand-embroidered cotton lingerie and peeked into the garment bag.

What lovely things! But they looked like attire for a folk festival: full skirts of red and green, exquisitely worked white blouses, a laced vest to match each skirt and, resting on the bottom, several pairs of black espadrilles stored beside white woolen socks.

They were obviously heirlooms. Strange that Dominika had even mentioned them. Rezipping the bag, Eden found in the handsome walnut chest of drawers a plaid shirt and jeans she could wear. She was grateful for the stretchable house slippers since her hiking boots were clumsy and she could not have forced one on anyway.

Taking the crutch, she found it helped immensely. She hopped through the now-empty living room, with its enormous fireplace, and into the adjacent dining room, where Julian was preparing to seat Dominika.

The old woman smiled and took Eden's hand, holding it as she blessed the food. Eden wondered why she should feel, deeply and immediately, that she had forever been searching for this woman, why it should seem that—for the first time in her life—she had come home.

Eden was up early the next morning but Julian had already left for the mountain. ''He promises to take those lions back as soon as he can,'' Dominika said, regarding Eden with some severity. ''Let us hope they don't remember the way back and visit us at lambing time.''

The kittens seemed to be thriving. While Dominika napped after breakfast, Eden begged clean shelving paper and a pencil from Estevannia, sat on a rug with her ankle pillowed and did a dozen quick sketches of them as they tumbled the length and breadth of the pantry, penned off by a board that Julian had rigged.

After dinner the night before, Julian had bluntly told Dominika about Earth Heritage's possible interest in acquiring the ranch. Dominika had said nothing at the time but as she and Eden, after lunch, sat in front of the huge window that faced the towering mountains, she looked up from sipping her coffee-milk and said with simple directness, "None of my grandsons is married but it has been my hope to leave this place to someone of my blood."

"I can see why you would want to."

"Ah, but Foss and Joe won't live here. They have other ideas of what should happen to the land." Wearily she pushed back silvery hair that was coiled at the back of her head. "This weekend they will be down to argue further about it."

"Trace seems to have done a lot to bring back the grass."

Dominika frowned. "Once I thought he was crazy—selling off sheep and keeping them out of the meadows. But things are better now than when I first came here over seventy years ago." Her gaze probed Eden. "Sometimes I think that Trace will never marry again or have children. I will not leave this ranch to anyone who won't be able to pass it on within the family. So I will listen to you talk about your Earth Heritage, although I tell you frankly that I will sell to strangers only if I despair of my own blood."

Eden was in the midst of detailing some of Heritage's achievements in preserving the nation's key lands when Julian's pickup came into view, followed by Trace's.

"Thank heaven!" Dominika's relieved smile showed that she had been anxious. She thumped hard on the window.

Trace looked up at her and grinned, waving. He was charcoal-smudged and dirty, with a black shadow of beard. Julian, behind him, did not look much better. "The fire's out, *amona!*" Trace called. "We'll be in as soon as we clean up."

"You come in right now and kiss me!" Dominika ordered through the open window.

He made a rueful face but obediently came in after stamping his boots on the outside mat. He slowed at the sight of Eden,

484

gave her a cool nod and bent to kiss his grandmother. She hugged him, embraced Julian and then rubbed her cheek.

"You feel like porcupines!"

"You asked for it!" they chorused, laughing.

"Yes, well, now I'm asking you to shave and shower and then have a nice drink while you tell us about it."

"There's not much to tell," Julian shrugged. "It didn't get up to the bristlecones and we stopped it before it spread to the other canyons. Seemed to have started at a campfire." He touched Eden's shoulder. "Both our cabins burned. Your silverware and a few such things will clean up but that wonderful painting is gone."

Eden had expected it but she felt a twisting sense of loss and had to look away as she fought tears. "Your van, though, was just far enough away to escape," he went on. "I brought your sketches and paints and locked the van until we can bring it down. How's the ankle?"

"Lots better," she said through the tightness in her throat.

"Good. Come on, boy." Julian grabbed his grandson's arm and they went out through the kitchen.

Dominika leaned over and took Eden's hand. "This painting—it was treasured?"

"My father made it for me." Eden told her about her nightmares and how Ygdrasil had banished them. Then she managed a shaky laugh. "I suppose it's fitting that the painting perished in flames—like those it showed licking about the tree."

"You're a painter, too," Dominika said gently. "Could you do it over?"

Eden considered for a moment. The thing that had made the picture so special had been her father's caring. She drew a long breath and looked toward the mountains.

"No," she said slowly. "I'll paint a bristlecone."

IV

TRACE HAD only snatched a few hours of sleep the night before. Shortly after dinner he kissed his grandmother good-night and went off to his own house.

"I'm tired, too," Julian said, smothering a yawn. "Eden, a game-warden picked up those men. They had the lion skin all right, but the judge let them off with a twenty-five-dollar fine. Seems that since he lost twenty lambs to lions this spring, he was more of a mind to give the poachers a reward."

"And they burn down a mountain and get away with it!"

Julian sighed. "There wasn't enough proof."

Eden seethed helplessly as he moved stiffly down the hall. He was old for fighting fires.

"Will you show me your bristlecones?" Dominika asked. "Sometimes I have thought about trying to grow one down here but it wouldn't seem right. They belong to the mountain."

Glad to get her mind off the poachers, Eden took the sketches from the table where Julian had placed them. Dominika went through them slowly, smiling at the acrobatic pygmy nuthatch and the lazing ground squirrels, narrowing her eyes at the mother lion with her kittens and studying with care the dozens of bristlecone portraits.

"Like people. Each one is different."

Eden nodded. "That's how they are."

One of the last drawings was of Julian. "Why, you've made him look like a bristlecone!" Dominika cried in delight. "Oh, will you let me buy it?"

"Please have it," Eden urged, detaching the page. "I can make it into a real portrait if you would like that."

"I would rather have it just as it is." Dominika admired the small canvases on which Eden had used color. A strange look passed over her face as she gazed at the younger woman. "Far, far back in my family there was a woman artist. I have seen a tree that she painted. And she painted birds."

"Really? I haven't been to Europe but if you'll tell me where her work is, I'll try to see it when I do go."

"It's in a . . . a very private place." Dominika again studied the drawing of Julian and smiled. "Trace will look like him someday. Do you know, I have seen bristlecones brought down to softer country. With more rain and less wind, one makes a handsome tree, neat and civil and with a proper spire shape." She laughed, gesturing. "Sooner or later, though, its wild spirit takes over. Branches jag outward and up, twist and curve, and it loses all claim to being a tame, pretty tree."

"I'm glad."

"So am I." Dominika took her hand. "My Eden, you're something of a bristlecone yourself."

"I'm not that strong."

"You're not that old." When Eden smiled skeptically, Dominika said, "I wasn't strong, either. I just lived through whatever happened."

Her gaze turned inward. Eden knew that she was remembering the past, loved ones who were dead and, perhaps, her distant homeland. Feeling herself an intruder, she quietly said good-night and limped down the hall.

Trace was gone before breakfast the next morning. Estevannia said that he'd had two cups of coffee, asked her to tell his grandparents he'd be back in a day or two and had driven off.

"Drat him!" Julian growled. "He knew I wanted him to help bring Eden's van down."

"That would be a good thing to do this weekend when his cousins are here," Dominika soothed.

"You just bet it would!" He bolted down a cup of coffee and frowned. "Are Foss's bigwig Washington buddies coming to the ranch?"

"No. He has suites for them in Joe's Elko hotel. They're coming for the Basque festival."

"Sometimes I wish that whingding wasn't getting so popular," Julian grumbled.

"I'm glad for it," Dominika defended. "It's good for young Basques to remember the old ways."

Julian rose. "Well, I'm going to drive into town today before the crowds start coming and see if I can buy one of those cabin kits. Can't go felling trees for building anymore and I'd like to get a new place up before winter."

Within the hour he was gone, too. But in spite of Eden's disabled ankle, time did not lag. She visited the baby lions, sat on a stool while she did the morning dishes and then asked Dominika if she might do some drawings of her.

"Shouldn't you work on your trees?" the old woman asked.

"I gave Julian a list of canvases, paints and other materials," Eden said. "I can't do much more till I have them."

So she sketched Dominika from several angles and did a number of studies of the aged hands, finding them exceptionally interesting. They looked as though they had done so many things. In their conversations some of Dominika's life had been mentioned, though as yet she had not dwelled on the past. Even so, Eden gathered that she had lived on cattle as well as sheep ranches, worked in a hotel and run a boom-town boarding-house.

"I like hands," Eden remarked as she worked. "I guess there was never a child who didn't like to make palm-prints. You find them in old caves—almost everywhere that people have been, I suppose. And when an Indian woman was bound for suttee, she would stop on her way out of the city and press her paint-dipped hand against the gate. Just imagine, all those hands across so many years."

Dominika opened her palms and regarded them broodingly. "Kattalin, my daughter, had lovely hands. She married very young and died when Trace was born."

"You brought him up?"

"We let him grow. I was seventy then, too old to be very firm with him, especially since I lost my two sons within a few years of each other." She added so wistfully that Eden suspected she had voiced the same plaint to Julian, "Grandparents should be able to spoil their grandchildren in peace and not have to worry about their character.''

''Your grandson has plenty of that,'' Eden said dryly.

She and Dominika were sitting by the window next day, enjoying a mid-afternoon cup of frothy spiced chocolate, when a black Mercedez-Benz pulled up in front.

''God on High!'' said Dominika as two men got out, one with vibrant silver hair, the other black-headed and swarthy. ''Joe and Foss! I didn't expect them until tomorrow.''

The older grandson waved as they came up the steps and the other blew his grandmother a kiss, glimpsed Eden and blew her another, his dark eyes sparkling. After Dominika had embraced them, she held each by the hand.

''Eden, my grandsons, Faustin and Joseph Uhalde. Boys, this is my guest, Eden Lowrie.''

''Call me Foss,'' said the silver-haired one, smiling and showing perfect teeth. His tanned skin was smooth except for a few etchings about his eyes and mouth. Eden was not so sure now that he was older than the shorter, heavy-shouldered man who shook her hand and held it for a caressing moment.

''I'm Joe,'' he told her. ''It looks like you've had a mishap.''

Dominika explained Eden's fall. ''It's a shame to have this happen to you in Nevada,'' Foss regretted. ''Let us make amends. Be our guest at the Basque festival this weekend.''

''I'm sure you have other guests,'' Eden protested.

''None that won't be delighted to meet you,'' Foss assured her. His green eyes lingered on her mouth so that in spite of his courteous, polished charm, he made it clear that he found her desirable.

''I'll phone right now and arrange a suite for you,'' Joe said. ''Don't worry about Foss. I won't let him get you in a corner.''

''Go,'' urged Dominika, patting her hand. ''The dancing is beautiful.''

''Could you go, too?''

The old woman shook her head. ''I must save my strength and there is another journey that is more important. A shame that you cannot dance but you must wear one of my outfits or Kattalin's and look like a real *Vizcaína!*''

"It's decided then," Foss said. The smoothness of his voice was belied by the way his lazy eyes enjoyed her as though in anticipation.

Disturbed at the raw awareness that he caused in her, Eden resolved not to be alone with him. His and Joe's attentions were flattering balm after Trace's boorishness but each, in different ways, radiated power and ruthlessness. They were not the kind of men whom she could trust or really like but, frustrated by Trace, she could imagine falling prey to either one in an unguarded moment.

And no matter what Trace thought, she was worth more than that.

The men were good company though, regaling Dominika with the latest Nevada gossip, ranging from Las Vegas and Elko to Reno and points in between. Estevannia made them a special Basque meal with three kinds of meat, which they devoured while pitying Eden for her omelette.

"At least your weird ideas haven't affected your health," Joe allowed good-naturedly. "It seems to be a kick that lots of folks go on these days."

"A lifelong kick for me," Eden told him. "And you couldn't exactly call it a passing fad with the Hindus."

"Oh, Hindus," Joe shrugged.

Dominika tilted her head. "Is it your religion?"

"In a way." Because she saw that the older woman was genuinely interested, Eden tried to explain. "If I were starving, I would kill something just as I'd not blame it for killing me out of the same necessity. But to end a life when there's another choice—no, I can't do it."

Foss groaned. "I come home on vacation and have to listen to more Right-to-Life talk!"

"Not exactly. I think it's disastrous for someone who doesn't want a baby to have one. But once life is here, I do respect it. Except," she admitted hastily, "that I swat flies and mosquitoes. I'll defend myself."

"Is that why you carried the spider outside the other day?" Dominika asked. She pursed her lips, frowning meditatively.

"Well then, when our herders kill coyotes or bobcats, it is also self-defense."

Eden smiled wryly. "I see what you mean but from the sheeps' standpoint, I expect they would as soon be killed on the range by coyotes as shipped off to slaughter."

"Abel raised sheep," persisted Dominika, still puzzling.

"After his parents were driven from the Garden," Eden pointed out.

Slanting an amused glance at her, Foss raised his glass to his lips and watched her as he savored his wine. "So you dream of an earthly Paradise?"

Daring his cynicism, she met his cool green eyes. "I want to see the Kingdom of God on earth. This world is so beautiful in the places we haven't ruined that I don't need another heaven."

"I sort of lean to the Moslem Paradise myself." Joe rolled his eyes blissfully and tossed down his wine. "Countless gorgeous women, flowers and shade and plenty to eat and drink—hey, that's just what I've got in my Reno club! Grandmother, shall we teach Eden how to play *muz* after dinner?"

They played until midnight. Deuces wild with aces, threes wild with kings, with aces low, kings high. Joe and Foss kept up a running war of boisterous bluffing, chortling or groaning over their cards.

Time after time, though, Dominika quietly met the early bets, then raised on the last and collected with high, low, a pair or thirty-one points totaled from the four cards counted as in blackjack. Eights, nines and tens had been discarded from the deck. Distracted by the men's constant psychic warfare, Eden found it difficult to concentrate and did not bet on most hands but she won once with three kings and another time with low.

Joe grinned at her as he shoved her winnings across the table. "You won't get rich that way, Eden. We're finding out that if you bet, you've got the cards. Takes the suspense out of it."

"Yes," said Foss, "be like Grandmother. She usually has a good hand to stay in but she bluffs just often enough that we bet to keep her honest."

Eden saw the wisdom of the ploy but although she began to

bet on hands that were dubious, the others always seemed to know. "Bless you," said Foss, spreading kings and queens, "your face gives you away. I'll have to teach you inscrutability."

"A senator should be good at that."

"I am. When it serves."

Dominika took the last stakes and said that she was tired. Estevannia had long since retired but Joe volunteered to make hot chocolate which he served with a plate of almond cookies. When Dominika rose to go to her room, Eden also stood up, reaching for her crutch.

"My arm's better," Joe said, crooking his elbow.

Before she could guess what he intended, Foss swung her up in his arms and carried her down the hall. "Can't waste an opportunity like this," he laughed softly.

But Joe was in front of them, opening the door and leaning the crutch against the chair by the bed. "See how I protect you, Eden?"

Foss put her down reluctantly. "Now I know why I went to Washington. To get a good long way from my cousin!"

"Don't believe him," Joe said. "It was because he couldn't stand having everyone think he was my uncle, what with all that white hair. Come along, Foss. I'm not leaving till you do."

Foss brushed a light kiss across her cheek. "Good-night, Eden."

"Out!" Joe insisted.

Eden laughed her good-nights but her amusement faded along with their bickering. They were burlesquing tonight, reverting to boyishness in their grandmother's home, but Foss was an influential congressman with a lamentable record on public-lands use and Joe was a successful Reno club-operator. Neither occupation bespoke innocence and Julian had said that each had plans for the ranch. It behooved her to be wary.

All the same, after Trace's chill behavior, his cousins' warm if exaggerated admiration gave her a glow. Careful she would be, and alert to Earth Heritage's interests, but she would go to the festival and have fun. If she were lucky, for several hours she might not even think of Trace.

Foss moved the seat beside him far back and arranged cushions to support Eden's ankle during the drive. Dominika waved from the porch as they started out. That morning she had come to the back bedroom to help select Eden's attire. Kattalin's rose-scented costumes were a trifle large but Dominika's fit exactly.

"You look like a proper Basque," Dominika had said happily, lacing the snug green bodice. The white cotton blouse had full, long sleeves and a gathered, scooped-out neckline. Touching the crimson wool skirt that swirled over a flounced white petticoat, Dominika mused dreamily. "This is made from Etchahoun fleece, carded and spun by my mother and myself. Eighty years and it still looks new. That's more than one can say for me!"

Eden knew something of Dominika's feeling. It surprised her when she put on a garment that she had worn as Fowler's wife to think that clothes could outlast marriages. But there was a good side to the durability of things as compared to people.

"I like to think that some of my paintings will last long after me," she had said. "And the birds and animals that I paint will exist in my pictures even after they're gone."

"Ah, yes," Dominika agreed. "A painted bird may live for centuries. But clothes should be worn. I am glad that you're taking these to the festival."

In the car Joe sat in the back seat and grinned broadly at Eden. Because her seat was pushed back, she was almost facing him. "Nice arrangement, Foss!" he teased. "You just watch the road like a good chauffeur while I blandish Eden with my wit and charm."

Actually, since the two men had not seen each other for a time, they fell into talk about business and politics. They seemed to know nearly everyone of any importance in Nevada and California and it fascinated Eden to hear Foss speak with familiarity of people whom she knew of as cabinet members, bureau heads and chairmen of important congressional committees.

She listened carefully when Joe grumbled, "I'd just as soon you boys picked some other lucky state for storing radioactive waste. West Texas sounds like a good bet to me. Or Utah."

"A salt basin one place or the other will be tested with an exploratory shaft in mid-1983," Foss said. "They'll probably test the basalt at the Hanford Reservation up in Washington on the

Columbia River. That's Federal land with a reprocessing plant for the extraction of plutonium for nukes from spent fuel. There's already a lot of high-level radwaste in temporary storage tanks.''

"So let 'em have it all!"

"It's not that easy. After the trouble at Three-Mile Island, people are edgy. Basalt's fine but the Hanford site lies between two permeable, water-bearing layers. We need to find out whether there will be leakage and if so, where.''

"Of course," said Eden, "we might just stop manufacturing nukes.''

When both men looked at her as if she were crazy, she told them about the Navajo uranium miners who were slowly wasting from the poison and of the leukemia-ridden sections of Arizona and Utah.

Foss shrugged. "You have to think of those people as soldiers. If their deaths are caused by radioactivity—which I don't admit, mind you—they died in their country's defense.''

"Without volunteering? Without knowing what was going on?''

"We have to be ready to defend ourselves.''

"I agree. But we can have deterrent force without lacing babies' milk with Strontium ninety and poisoning our water and soil. If war comes, neither side is going to need a lot of warheads. If we would seek peace as zealously as we arm for war, we'd come closer to having it.''

"Artists are a visionary lot," Foss said indulgently.

"Like hell we are! Is it visionary not to want the nightmares you call reality?''

Foss gave her a searching look. "What's the name of that organization Grandmother said you work with?''

"Earth Heritage.''

His eyebrows lifted in surprise and his mouth quirked down. "Noisy bunch.''

"We have to be.''

"I could ask what's a nice girl like you doing with a crowd like that.''

"I care about what happens to the land—and the people and wild things that depend on it.''

"Bless you, so do I. We just have different routes to the same goal." He blandly ignored her glance of disbelieving wonder and spoke over his shoulder to Joe. "Studies of the Nevada Test Site have been speeded up to meet the Department of Energy schedules. A waste repository in welded tuff surrounded by non-welded tuff might work well. But the region is geologically complex and needs a lot more research."

"But," interjected Eden, "since we have radwaste coming out of our ears, or at least stored around in tanks and resting in the bottoms of pools of water near nuclear reactors, the researching of sites may not be as thorough as one would wish." She counted on her fingers. "The timetable that I've seen calls for tests to begin at depth in 1985, the selection of the repository in 1988 and waste to be emplanted in 1989. If nothing catastrophic happens, it will be in full operation in 1998."

"It seems to me," Foss said stiffly, "that the government is taking extreme care. Testing three types of rock—"

"For ten years? When the life of that stuff, or rather its kill capacity, is thousands of years?" Eden laughed sharply. "What if an earth tremor splits the insulating layer? What if the waste eventually leaches even basalt? Remember, those miners are dying twenty years later. It's insanity to go on creating poisons when we don't know how to get rid of them."

Joe said peaceably, "Don't get too torn up about it. Some whiz-kid scientist will figure out a way to orbit the junk or sink it in the ocean or something."

"That's good?"

Joe patted her hand. "What you need is to come to Reno and let me show you a good time. You shouldn't be hanging around old uranium dumps on Indian reservations and listening to horror stories from those Arizona-Strip Mormons. No wonder you've picked up some weird ideas."

Eden was angry. Before she could reply, Foss smoothly ended the futile argument. "A friend of mine from the Department of Energy will be in Elko," he said. "I'm sure he'd be interested in your views. Who knows? You might convert him or he might reassure you."

He shifted the talk back to some tax legislation about which Joe was concerned and they finished the drive without further contention, though Eden was sorry that she had so thoroughly revealed her thinking. She might have learned many useful things had she kept quiet. Still, it went against the grain to use Dominika's sponsorship as a means to deceive anyone. And for all of Foss's rational-sounding eloquence, she knew him for the enemy, as he now knew her.

They arrived at the park in time for the outdoor Mass celebrated in Basque. A bandstand displayed Basque and American flags. Many of those attending were in Basque dress, the women in attire similar to Eden's, some with red or green silk kerchiefs around their hair, the men in white shirts, bright sashes and berets. Some had on jeans or dark slacks but others wore close-fitting pants that ended just below the knee.

After Mass the band began to play. "I've got to pick up my friends at the landing strip," Foss said, glancing at his watch. "Do you want me to drop you at the hotel, Eden, or are you holding up all right?"

"Oh, I'm enjoying it," she assured him.

"Take care of her, Joe, or I'll sic the IRS on you," Foss warned as he turned away.

"Back at you!" Joe called.

Pulling a chair up beside Eden's, he shouted and clapped for the weight-lifters, wood-choppers and the men who swung a heavy weight between their legs before coming erect to hurl it. "That thing weighs a hundred and five pounds!" Joe said as a roar greeted the final contestant's winning throw.

Suddenly he jumped up and hugged an older man whose blue beret slanted rakishly across hair that still retained glints of yellow in its white. "Koni! Have you bet and lost all your wages yet?"

"Lost?" demanded the other indignantly. "I bet half a year's wages on Ramon and he just won, as you saw! It's much better to wager on a man you know than on cards you don't."

"Koni is Grandmother's boss herder," Joe explained after introducing him to Eden. "If Cousin Trace does you out of your job, Koni, you come deal *muz* for me."

The weathered old herder chuckled. "I don't think many Basque herders show up in your fancy casino," he said and

496

drifted off to watch a game played with a hard ball and a long, curved wicker scoop that Joe said was *pelota*. "Our *muz* goes back before written history and *pelota* is just as old. Almost every American Basque community used to have a court but the game lost out to American sports in Idaho and Nevada during the years when the immigration of Spanish Basques was pretty much stopped. Since French Basques weren't hit as hard by restrictions, they kept coming to California and *pelota* remained popular there. Boise has restored its court now and this one in Elko was built in 1975 with the help of the Spanish government."

"Do you play?"

Joe patted a waist that was starting to thicken. "I do well to play nine holes of golf. In high school I played football and Foss was Reno's top basketball-player." He grinned. "We were also pretty fair brawlers. Those were the days when we were still called 'black Bascos' and got kidded about having ewes instead of girlfriends."

The spicy smell of barbecue filled the air; food was being served from the long tables beneath the shade trees. Foss wove his way through the crowd, stopping to shake hands frequently and visit with old acquaintances and possible new constituents. Four well-dressed, assured men were with him and when he reached Eden, he introduced them: an official from the Department of Energy; a senator from California, Donald Selwyn; a ranking official in the Department of Defense, gray-haired and with a tight, nervous smile; and red-faced General Bixby Scott from the Pentagon.

"Eden is with Earth Heritage," Foss told his guests. "She's also an artist."

Donald Selwyn winced perceptibly before his narrow teeth showed in a weak smile. "Well, Miss Lowrie, you're considerably prettier than your Washington lobbyist. I hope you're more reasonable."

She smiled back. "Compared to me, Toby's a moderate."

"Food before debate," Foss ruled.

Dancing clubs from towns across the state as well as from Idaho, California and Oregon put on performances throughout the afternoon while the spectators feasted on stewed or roast lamb, salad, beans, crusty bread, relishes, ice cream and almond cookies. Those who could squirt wine from a *chahakoa* did so. Both Foss and Joe were adept at this and gave their guests lessons while explaining the dances.

Zazpi Jautziak, the seven jumps proclaiming the unity of the three French and four Spanish Basque provinces; *Makil Dantza*, performed by eight men with sticks; *Txontxonquilo*, where a dancer seemed to die, be lifted by the others and in the end put down to dance again.

"Grandmother thinks that it's the remnant of a sacrificial rite performed when Basques used to offer a man to the sun," Foss said.

"Terribly phallic, all those sticks," tittered Selwyn, his dull pink tongue touching his lips.

The dancers moved into a spirited fandango. Joe clapped to the tempo, as most of the crowd were doing, and said to Eden, "Grandmother came to the first National Basque Festival at Sparks outside Reno back in 1959. She danced like a girl though she was seventy-five. She said she never danced again because she wanted to remember that day."

"A lot of Basque communities had big summer picnics before that," Foss added. "The Sparks' affair started a lot of Basque clubs. Most of them put on festivals that were more or less open to the public. Elko started billing its shindig as the National Basque Festival in 1964."

He feigned modest surprise as the announcer called him up to the grandstand to "say a few words" but he must have had them ready. Holding his arms over his head, he greeted the throng in Basque, bowed at the proud cheering and then held up a hand for silence.

"Thank you, my friends, fellow Nevadans, Americans and Basques! I appreciate your trust that places me in our government and I assure you that my first and unswerving commitment is to this wonderful state we call home."

There was wild clapping. He paused, laughed boyishly and continued. "I remember as a kid when we used to run races, even some black youngsters said—without thinking about it— 'Last one in is a black Basco!' Gatherings like this today remind us and show others that we have a proud and glorious heritage that enriches, not weakens, our American citizenship. One of the marvels of this free country is that the grandson of an immigrant sheepherder can become one of its lawmakers. I am deeply grateful for the confidence that has made me your voice in Washington but I will never forget that I am one of you. Don't you forget it, either! Write me, call me—come see me if you get to the capital. And remember me when you vote!''

The band burst into a triumphant march. It took Foss some time to work his way through the clusters of well-wishers and importuners, shaking hands and chatting as he went. Just as he reached his party, a commotion broke out at the edge of the crowd behind them. The smile congealed on Foss's mouth.

''Now what's he doing?'' he muttered.

Eden glanced around, startled as people scattered, revealing three men. The dark one, crawling to his knees and shaking his head in befuddlement, was one of the hunters whom she had seen on the mountain. As Trace drove a fist into the other man's midriff, she recognized him as the second poacher.

The man gasped and locked his arms around Trace, who tripped him and they rolled on the ground. Jackknifing to his feet, Trace met the flailing onrush of the black-bearded man, threw him hard. The sandy-haired man reached into his shirt. A revolver glinted. A woman screamed as Trace knocked the gun up and a shot resounded.

The two men wrestled for the gun. Trace wrested it away and clubbed it against the other's head. The man dropped. The dark-haired man still lay as though stunned.

Trace, shirt torn, face and hands bleeding, panted for breath as he leaned against a tree. Several policemen hurried up. He handed them the gun, wiped blood and sweat from his eyes and shook his head at a question.

''Son of a bitch!'' Foss growled. ''Joe, go over there and see what you can do. I'd just as soon not have my cousin jailed for assault on the day I give a speech.''

The announcer called for medical assistance but by the time a doctor reached the downed men, they were stirring. Joe was talking persuasively to the policemen, who questioned some of the witnesses. After a few minutes the officers collected the hunters, who had been quickly checked over by the doctor, and escorted them to a patrol car.

Trace straightened up. One eye was swelling and his lips bled. His gaze lit unbelievingly on Eden as she sat gripped by fierce, conflicting emotions. The savagery of his fighting had appalled her, yet she had thrilled to know that the wanton killers of the lioness had received some punishment. Most of all, she wanted to wash Trace's hurts and do what she could to heal them.

Reaching for her crutch, she started to rise to her feet. Foss took her arm in a cautioning, proprietary way. Trace's eyes chilled. His split lips twisted and he turned away. The crowd closed behind him.

Foss said softly, "Barbaric, but that's my cousin for you! You've had a long day, my dear. Let me take you to the hotel so you can rest before dinner."

Eden did not argue. But as she walked between Foss and Joe, followed by the distinguished visitors, she felt the stabbing impact of Trace's gray eyes and deep within her some untouched, primeval core melted in yearning for him.

There was a banquet that evening, followed by an open-air pageant that depicted Basques as shepherds, seafarers, merchants and explorers. It ended with the Flag Dance and the crowd joining the chorus in singing the national anthem, "Gernikako Arbola."

Entrancing as the vignettes and dancing were, Eden kept watching for Trace but she did not see him. After the pageant Foss had matters to discuss with his friends. Joe offered to stake her at roulette or whatever she pleased but she truthfully pleaded fatigue.

He insisted on seeing her to her suite. "Shall I have Room Service bring up wine or a nightcap?" he asked after he had opened the door and made a production of handing her the key.

The air was sweetly heavy with the scent of roses Foss had sent. "Thank you," Eden told Joe firmly, "but I really am going straight to bed."

He grimaced. "What a waste." He let his hand trail along

her cheek. "There'll be other times. Never let it be said that I took advantage of a lady on a crutch."

Chuckling, he retreated, closing the door behind him. Eden hooked the chain lock. As she showered, she wondered where Trace was and hoped that he was all right.

His pickup was parked beside the windmill when Foss stopped the Mercedes in front of the house the next afternoon but Eden did not see him till he came to the house for a drink before dinner. His lip was swollen and one eye was puffy and bruised but none of the cousins made any reference to the fight in Elko.

Dinner passed comfortably. Dominika was eager to know who had been at the festival and how old acquaintances of hers were looking. When she heard that Koni had won a big bet on the weight-lifting, she laughed in delight.

"Good! I only hope he didn't lose it on his next wager." She turned to Eden. "It's strange that he grew up at my family's home, Etchahoun. His grandfather was my stepfather. It all is so long ago."

After a full report had been given, she arched her eyebrows at Foss. "And your important guests?"

"They ate it up." Foss smiled reflectively. "I learned from Dad that the best way to accomplish things with busy Washington folks is to get them away from the rat-race, show them a good time and then talk things over in a relaxed way."

Trace said harshly, "I suppose one of the things you relaxed over was trashing Nevada with MX missiles."

"They have to be put someplace," Foss said benignly. "A thirty-billion-dollar project will bring a lot of money into the state."

"It'll tear up arid land that will have to be revegetated to keep airborne dust levels tolerable. That'll take water. So will construction and maintenance. Nevada doesn't have that water and you damn well know it."

"We'll get it from the Columbia River," Foss said airily. "It's the only river in the West that hasn't been piped to dry areas. Time it gave its share."

Slowly Trace said, "You're ready to destroy this state's best grazing land and drain its water?"

"The Great Basin—and some of it's in Utah, remember—has sparse population, little development and just makes good sense for such a system." Foss spread his well-manicured but blunt-nailed hands. "I truly believe that Nevada's overall prosperity will increase with the MX located here. And more, it's vital to our defense."

"I don't want missiles on the ranch," Dominika said positively, glancing from one grandson to another in a bewilderment both helpless and angry.

Joe patted her hand. "*Amona*, let me develop a small part of the land for a really gorgeous vacation-retirement complex and the place will be less desirable as a missile site. But you'd better make up your mind so I can get started before the Air Force does."

She looked at Trace. "Don't let him hustle you," he advised grimly.

The old woman lifted her head, regarding her grandsons. "I always thought that one of you, maybe all of you, would marry, have children and live here after I am gone. Now Foss talks of missiles, Joe of complexes and you, Trace, want to get rid of the sheep." A sheen of tears glistened in her eyes. "I don't understand any of you!"

Foss pressed her hand against his cheek. "Don't worry about it now, *amona*. I know that you love America and when I explain all about how we have to defend her, you'll understand, I promise." Changing the subject as Estevannia brought in coffee and custard, he smiled challengingly at Eden.

"Why don't you come to Washington and help Earth Heritage's lobbyist? We'd rather listen to you than to him."

Did she imagine it or had Trace's jaw hardened? "Maybe I will," she said.

After dinner they played *muz* again. "You learn fast," Joe approved as Eden won with kings over aces. "Why don't you go back to Reno with me for a few days, take in the shows and let me take you out to my place at Lake Tahoe?"

"Joe!" scolded Dominika.

He laughed heartily. "Don't look so scandalized. Friends

from Sacramento are staying at the lodge this month. Eden would be well-chaperoned."

"Don't believe him," Dominika warned.

After the second game Trace scraped back his chair and made his good-nights. When he kissed Dominika, Eden's breath constricted. Desire for him surged through her. But he did not even look at her before he turned away.

Foss escorted her to her room that night, stepped inside, put her crutch aside and took her in his arms so swiftly that she was utterly surprised. Holding her close, he kissed her lightly, testingly, and then with seeking urgency.

The tension that had smoldered between them, half playful, half earnest, flamed now, weakening her. His lips swept down her throat as his skilled fingers curved beneath her breast.

Her knees were trembling but she managed to set her hands against his chest and draw away. He tried to take her mouth again but when she averted her head, he shrugged and took her hands. "You're not a child, Eden, and you *have* been married. What's the harm?"

"I don't love you."

The words sounded naive even before he laughed. Her face burning, Eden wished that she had invented something more artful and then she realized that it didn't matter—she had spoken the truth.

" 'Love,' Eden?" Foss asked caressingly. He moved his hand through her hair, sensuously entwining it in his fingers. "I don't know about love but I do know that you're attracted to me."

"Do you go to bed with every woman who attracts you?"

He looked startled but recovered and smiled. "I do my best. There aren't that many. Not as I get older and wiser."

"Thank you for what I think is a compliment. But it infuriates me for a man to think that the only valid reason for a woman's not leaping into the sheets with him is that she's a virgin. There needn't be a reason. It's simply a choice."

He hung his head in mock contrition. "Consider me chastised. I would have been more gradual but I do have to get back to Washington tomorrow. I was hoping to ensure that you would come up for a while."

"If I come, it will be on Earth Heritage business."

"Fine. I'll help you with contacts." His eyes danced as he captured her hands. "But there will be the evenings, Eden. And eventually there will be a night."

He kissed her quickly, a light brush of cool lips on hers. "If you don't come soon, I'll be back. Waiting for what I want has the charm of novelty, my dear, but it's not my natural habit."

After he was gone she wished that she had thought quickly enough to convince him that there would be no affair. His experienced, elegant stalking was flattering after Fowler's rejection and Trace's scornful neglect but it was stalking all the same. There was something about Foss's manner that hinted at ruthlessness should he be thwarted. Right now he could afford to be indulgent about her views on land use and the MX, a sign that he did not consider her or those for whom she spoke as a threat.

If he ever did—then she could expect to see another face. For a purely recreational affair, Joe would be a better partner—but that was not what she wanted.

She wanted the man living in the foreman's house.

Tensing herself against a wave of longing, she limped to the rear window and pulled the curtains aside. A light still glowed from the dwelling near the windmill. She was too restless for sleep and she wanted to tell him that she was glad he had given the fire-starting poachers a little of what they deserved. Apparently that was to be a secret from Dominika.

Before she could waver, Eden took the crutch as she listened at the door. Everything was quiet. When she opened the door carefully, only a night light burned in the hall.

Setting the crutch down each time with caution, she quickly reached the back door and slipped outside.

V

THE BREEZE was cool. Eden shivered as she rapped softly. What if Trace were sarcastic? Or saw through the admissible reason for her presence to the need she had for him? She wouldn't mind that if he could care about her, too. But the way in which he had looked at her after the fight when he saw her with Foss and Joe; the way in which he had been only coolly civil that evening—

No, this wasn't right. She would find another time to tell him she had appreciated his "brawling." Pivoting on the crutch, she had taken only a few steps when the door opened. The light pinioned her, making her feel exposed and defenseless. She stepped into the shadows.

"I—I came to thank you for fighting those men."

"I didn't do it for you."

"You did it for the mountain. Maybe for the lions. That's why I wanted to thank you."

He stood quietly in the dark. She could not see his expression but he wasn't helping her a bit. Lifting her chin, she said "Good-night" and started away.

His voice traveled after her. "My cousins' bidding for you was more interesting than their bets on *muz*. Which won? Or are you waiting for the bids to go up?"

"It's none of your business."

He overtook her in a stride. "Foss would be a useful contact. From what I hear, he gifts his mistresses royally. If you want to be the Mata Hari of the environmentalists, you could do a lot worse. Or are you holding out for a trip to Washington with entree to key people?"

Bracing herself against her crutch, she slapped him as hard

as she could. Her fingers stung and she took savage pleasure in the sound.

He crushed her arms against her sides, swept her up in his arms. His mouth fixed cruelly on hers. Dimly she heard the crutch thud on the barren ground as he moved through the shadows, going around to a side door which he kicked ajar. He dropped her on a bed.

"Trace—"

She tried to scramble up but there was the sound of a buckle hitting the floor and the clump of discarded boots. His shirt was still on, it was open, for his naked chest was against her as he found her lips and moved his hands over her in a passionate claiming she could not deny. She moaned, put her arms around him and gave back his kisses.

He came into her as she was arching her body in unbearable need, answering her supplication with a slow, deep filling of her so that she cried out with engorged sweetness. When he moved within her, she felt her muscles embrace and hold him.

They communed wordlessly in this sharing as he moved gently, deliberately, as if to explore and savor her most secret depths. Then, when she was almost fainting with rapture, he withdrew. When she gasped, he thrust deep and began a rhythm that peaked to a crescendo with blinding, melting waves of delight that flowed into a deep sea, where they seemed to float, purged, almost bodiless.

He broke that peace by sitting up abruptly, swinging his legs off the bed. "I'd better take you back to the house."

While his tone was matter of fact and not hostile, she felt that she had been slapped. "I can manage if you'll bring my crutch."

"It's just as easy to carry you," he said, pulling on his pants and boots. "You're a light weight."

"Am I?"

"Why do you want to fight?"

"Why do you—" She broke off. *Why are you my lover one minute, a stranger the next?* "If you can't stand to talk to me or be my friend, how can you make love to me?"

He sighed wearily. "Look, you don't really need a short course in male anatomy, do you?"

She sat speechless, then located her clothes and quickly dressed. When he started to pick her up, she thrust him away angrily. "I can manage." She hobbled toward the door.

His arms clamped around her. Struggle would only add to her humiliation. She held herself stiffly though, not letting her head touch his shoulder as he carried her to the big house.

"You can make it from here," he said, putting her down. "Wait a minute and I'll bring your crutch so no one will wonder about it in the morning."

As he returned with it, he hesitated for a moment. "If you didn't come to me tonight simply for what you got, I'll beg your pardon. But get this straight, that's all I'll give you. I can't match Foss's bids, or even Joe's."

He swung away from her. His harshness pierced her as deeply as had his earlier loving, wounding her in the same vulnerability. The night wind rose, chilling her. Inside, she threw herself on the bed and gave way to bitter tears.

She would never go to him again. In a few more days her ankle should be well enough that she could drive. She would miss Dominika but she could no longer stay around Trace. She still had the van. With it she would complete her study of the ranch for Earth Heritage and find out whether Dominika was remotely disposed to sell. A few days more spent with the bristlecones would enable her to finish their portraits. Then she would leave immediately.

The decision and a long shower were comforting but when she started to drift into sleep, Trace's arms seemed to close around her. When she reached for him, she roused, again remembered his brutal words, writhed and despised herself for loving a man who felt toward her as he did.

She could not help loving him but she could certainly go where he couldn't use her. And she would, just as soon as her work was finished.

Joe and Foss left the next morning after a lavish breakfast, each seizing a private moment to renew his invitation to Eden. Although Trace, talking to his grandmother, could not possibly have heard them, she caught a savage look on his face when she gave Foss a noncommittal reply. Foss laughed and turned up her palm to give it a warm, lingering kiss before he said good-bye.

Dominika stood on the veranda to wave at her grandsons as they drove away. Trace had already gone outside when the old woman joined Eden by the window, sinking into her chair like a fragile brown leaf seeking shelter.

"I love my grandsons," she said bluntly, "but I do not want this land to be a rich people's resort or a site for missiles. That means I cannot leave a share in it to either of them." Her green-gold gaze held Eden's eyes. "I do not understand all that he does but Trace, he loves the land. Still, if he will not marry, if he has no children, who will care for it after he is gone?"

Her look demanded an answer. Reluctantly, for she felt that she was meddling in family matters, Eden said carefully, "If you sold or donated the land to Earth Heritage, there would be guarantees that it would not be resold or used in ways of which you disapprove. Your lawyer could advise you but I'm sure that you could also leave the place to Trace for his lifetime and then pass it on to Heritage or a similar organization."

Dominika pondered for a moment and then grimly shook her head. "Let me try to tell you. With Basques in the old country, the *basseria* or farmstead, which included the *sepulturie* in the church, almost owned the people rather than the other way around. The owner was only the steward, taking care of it until the trust was handed to the next generation. If there was no worthy natural-born heir, one might be adopted, for the important thing was for the *basseria* to continue, even if the family line had to change." She closed her eyes for a moment. "Your Earth Heritage sounds very fine but I do not want this place to go to a big organization. It is for a family, a place for children to grow up and beget children as it was at Etchahoun."

Eden was moved at the thought but honesty compelled her to shake her head. "Dominika, Americans are so restless—"

"Are you?"

Startled, Eden had to consider. "I love traveling the wild lands. I think I always will. But someday I do want a home, a place to belong, to raise children—" She broke off, realizing that she was almost echoing Dominika's words.

"But first you must find your man?"

"There may not be one for me." Eden meant the words as a joke but they sounded sad.

Dominika touched her hand. "There will be. I was so in love with a dancing young man that I didn't love my first good husband as I should have and when I finally got my love, it was—it was not what I had expected. Julian came to me when I no longer dreamed. He was the one I had needed all my life. If only Kattalin had lived. . . ." The worn, yet rich voice trailed off.

Not knowing how to respond, Eden waited while Dominika seemed to regather her strength. At last the wrinkled eyelids raised. "Until a few years ago I went every summer to all of the sheep camps. I saw the ewes and lambs and knew all the dogs. This summer I want to go again but I can no longer set up a camp as I used to. Sometimes my hair is so heavy that I can't brush it and I need help to dress. Will you go with me?"

The admission of weakness could not have been easy. Apart from being strongly drawn to the older woman, Eden felt that she owed her gratitude for having so warmly taken her in.

"It won't take me long to finish my work," she said after only a moment's thought. "I will be leaving after that but I can take the journey with you."

Dominika straightened and chuckled. "Will your ankle be strong enough in a week?"

Feeling a bit as if she had been maneuvered, Eden said, "It should be."

"Good. Trace and a couple of the men are going up to help Julian raise his cabin but he'll be back by the weekend and he says that we can start on Monday."

"What does Trace have to do with it?"

"He will drive, of course."

"But—"

"I'm sure that you're a good driver," Dominika interrupted, her eyes glinting with mirth, "but the camps are very hard to reach and I don't know the locations. Trace has to drive."

"Um."

"Trace can't brush my hair and he's a terrible cook."

Eden sighed, shaking her head reproachfully. "All right, I promised. Do you always get your own way?"

Dominika grinned. "At my age, who's to argue with me?"

"Not I," said Eden ruefully. "I see now why Joe's good at cards and Foss is such a skillful politician." Dominika leaned back contentedly and crossed her feet on the velvet stool.

"Now that we have the house to ourselves again, why don't you bring your easel here to the good light? I like to see you work."

She wore such a beatific expression that Eden could not resent her maneuvering; was, rather, forced to admire it. "I have to do another portrait of you," she grumbled. "Dominika as the Godmother, pulling all our strings."

"I am not Italian," Dominika said innocently and chuckled at Eden's snort.

Eden put in long sessions of work, showing a fascinated Dominika the results, and by Friday night when Trace returned she had done most of what she could until she returned to the real bristlecones.

"*Aitona* just about has the cabin up," Trace said as he wolfed a bowl of stew and a half-loaf of Estevannia's crusty bread. "The dealers had already run the concrete slab and the rest went pretty fast." In a neutral tone accompanied by an expressionless look, he said to Eden, "You're invited any time if you'll bring your own sleeping bag and help tack up insulation."

"Now that's off your mind," interposed Dominika, "perhaps you can do a favor for your other grandparent?"

"*Bai*, andrea," he teased. Eden would have given much were he to speak to her in that tone of tenderly affectionate joking. "At your orders."

"Good. Monday I wish to start a visit to the camps."

"All of them? *Amona*, it's a jouncy ride through those mountains."

"Fine. We'll save the camp-tender a trip."

"Do you really feel up to it? The herders can give you their wagons, of course, but—"

"The herders can keep their smell of dirty socks. We'll take a tent, just as I used to. Don't scowl so," she added demurely. "Eden's coming along to take care of me."

He all but recoiled physically. Staring at Eden, the planes of his face grew bleaker as his grandmother continued. "You must know that Eden's organization, Earth Heritage, is interested in the ranch. We will be on Forest land some of the time but this will give her a good opportunity to really see the property."

His face registered such shock that Eden hoped he did not notice her equal amazement. "*Amona!* You wouldn't sell the place!"

She lifted her thin shoulders in a disclaiming shrug. "Unless I am sure that it can stay in the family, I would rather know that it has a worthy guardian."

"You don't trust me?"

"Where are your children?"

His eyes narrowed. "You know what I think? You're trying to bluff me—or Foss or Joe—into getting married."

"Think what you like," she said sweetly. "We leave Monday?"

"If that's what you want." His voice was tinged with bitterness as he confronted Eden. "While we're at our southeast camp, there's an exhibit at Wheeler Peak I want you to see. It would make quite a picture for your book."

He sounded as though he wished to punish, not enlighten, her. There was not a trace of sexual provocation in his tone. Puzzled, yet uneasily intrigued, Eden said, "It's kind of you to think about improving my book. Of course I'll be interested to see anything that you think might be included."

"This should be."

Dismissing her, he turned to his grandmother. Annoyed as he must be with her, his voice still softened. "I'm bushed, *amona.* I'm going to tuck in but tomorrow I'll start getting things ready for your queenly progress around your fiefdom."

She embraced him, touching his cheek as he bent to kiss her. Then he was gone, without the flick of a glance toward Eden.

She saw him only at dinner the next two days and then not for long. If he had been suspicious of her before, now his resentment was like a withering blast.

"Why," she asked Dominika reproachfully, "did you hint to your grandson that you might let Heritage have the ranch?"

"To start him thinking. He has a thick head."

Eden groaned. "If he's thinking, it's how to murder me and ditch the body. If I had known that you were going to tell him such a fib, I would never have promised to go with you."

"But you did, dear, and I can't manage without you. Besides, I didn't lie. I said I *might* leave Heritage the land."

"And it might snow in hell!"

"That would be nice for the sinners," Dominika said with maddening tranquillity.

Provisions for two of the camps were stowed in the back of the pickup along with the camping gear. They stopped only for lunch at the first herder's wagon, nestled in the higher foothills. The dark young Peruvian, in his third year of herding, was both flustered and flattered by Dominika's visit.

Because she had attended school with the children of *vaqueros*, Eden could understand the conversation that centered around the band of ewes and lambs who placidly fed along the slopes.

"I'm glad there was a letter for him," Dominika said as they drove away.

"I brought him a copy of *Playboy*, too," Trace said. "He claims it helps him with his English."

"He doesn't get much chance to use it," Dominika sighed. "Not so many Basques come anymore. About half of the herders recruited by the Western Range Association are from Mexico or South America. The rest are mostly from Spain but perhaps only a quarter of them are Basques."

"Why are so many herders imported?" Eden asked.

"The wages aren't terrific," shrugged Trace, "but it's probably the loneliness. Before it can bring in a herder, the Association has to let the employment services of every Western state know that the position is open. Only a handful of United States citizens apply and darn few of them stick it out the first season."

Koni's camp was an hour's drive to the south. He was delighted to see them and he made Dominika sit in his director's chair while he poured cider for them and regaled them with his account of the Boise festival and news of herder friends whom he had encountered there. By the time he had reported on his band, the sheep were bedding down. He piled a stone on top of a pile of rocks that stood higher than he was.

"One for each day," he responded to Eden's questioning glance. "And these are for only those spent in this camp. But a lot of years, young lady. A lot of years and a lot of days."

Supper was a cooperative effort. Koni supplied bean soup, sourdough bread baked in a Dutch oven and spicy sausages. Eden made cheese omelettes with Spanish sauce and they finished with hot chocolate and nut cakes from the big container Estevannia had filled.

After Eden and Koni did the dishes, the sprite, aging man took out a curious two-horned instrument and drew sounds from it that resembled those of a bagpipe.

"You gave me this," he reminded Dominika. "A very good *alboka*."

She looked back through time. Her voice deepened with remembered love. "Yes. It was Domingo's. One of my first friends in this country," she explained to Eden. She stroked the dogs that had curled up near her feet. "These seem young. Are they the new Xagu and Kato?"

Koni nodded. "Old Xagu died not long after you were here last. Is it four summers? And Kato died that winter. These are their pups." He grinned. "And we've a new black Jautzi and a skipping Arin-arin."

Dominika smiled, absently caressing the dogs. "It was long ago when I raised the first Jautzi and Arin-arin. They played with the first Xagu and Kato, who were retired and hated to be bothered by silly lambs. Play some old tunes, Koni."

He did. Intermittently Dominika sang in a still sweet though cracked voice. "That one," she told Eden, "is about a young bride whose husband is poisoned by a jealous woman on their wedding day. The bride kept him in her chamber for seven years and washed him with lemon water every Friday morning."

"*Amona!*" chided Trace. "The song doesn't say how he must have smelled!"

"My mother used to sing me a lullaby," Koni said, humming a few bars. "Would you sing it, andrea?"

"With pleasure." She sang for him and then translated for Eden.

> *Bonbolontona*, my darling,
> Do not go to sleep in the wood,
> Or the wicked eagle will come and take you
> As if you were a little hare.

"You used to sing that for me, too," Trace remembered, his gray eyes darkened by the night outside the fire.

She seemed to scarcely hear him but said to the shepherd, "You must have been the last child to hear that song at Etchahoun."

"I was the youngest," he nodded. "Grandmother told me stories, too. I used to be afraid to be out after dark because of the witches."

Dominika laughed and then sighed wistfully. "I wonder if people still see Mari, the Basa Andrea, in the rainbow or in a cloud of fire. When they see a light at her cave, do they still say that she's baking her bread? I have missed her here, and the *Lamiñak*, and Basa Jaun."

"I would as soon not meet Basa Jaun," laughed Koni. "It is strange that no matter how crazy a herder might go in America, he never claims to see Basa Jaun."

"This country has no fairies or brownies," Dominika regretted. "We don't know the Indian spirits and so we don't meet them."

"From what the young herders say, no one believes in *Lamiñak* or Basa Jaun anymore," Koni said.

Dominika smiled. "Oh, but in countries where they lived for so long, such folk can linger on and on in their groves and grottoes." Painfully she rose to her feet. "The night air chills these old bones. Thank you for your music, Koni."

"Thank you for your song," he said formally, bowing like a courtier.

Eden retired into the tent with Dominika. The fire gave them light to make their bedtime preparations. By the time they were in their sleeping bags, padded by foam rubber for protection against the rocks, the voices outside had stopped. All the same, as Eden wearily snuggled into her small pillow, she was keenly aware that Trace, somewhere nearby, must by trying to sleep, too. She only hoped that the thought of her disturbed him as much as the thought of him disturbed her.

VI

BY THE TIME Eden and Dominika emerged next morning, the sheep were browsing and the rich smell of coffee filled the air. Eden went to the stream to wash and then made golden brown French toast in the cast-iron skillet. When the dishes were done, Trace looked down at her as if ordering her to a tribunal.

"Let's leave for Wheeler Peak so we can be back before dark."

"Go ahead," urged Dominika. "Koni and I have many things to talk about. You had better take a lunch."

The road was little more than ruts and demanded Trace's full attention as they drove through rusty-rose hills with green shadings of juniper and white-capped mountains towering above. Eden made one or two remarks but Trace's curt replies ended her attempts at conversation.

She fixed her attention on the terrain but it was impossible to suppress the taut electric aura between them. She tried to divert herself by counting birds, although she could only guess at the flocks of red-winged blackbirds and sparrows. There were handsome black and white magpies, shaggy crows, sage grouse and before they reached the highway, she saw a kestrel and several redtailed hawks.

They drove along on flat land until they turned right, taking the road to Wheeler Peak. Sagebrush, snakeweed and scrub willow stretched up the ascent till the pickup reached a level that was beautiful with wild roses, aspens white against evergreens, and gnarled mountain mahogany.

"How's about lunch before we get up to where it's cold?" Trace suggested.

"Why not?"

He pulled into a site on the little creek where grass was luxuriant. Primroses grew along the banks and phlox, dandelions and shooting stars peeked through the grass. Eden gazed down at the dull green expanse stretching to distant mountains and then took a long breath as she looked up at the snowy side of what must be Wheeler Peak.

"From the highway no one would ever guess that this was here."

One of the great delights of the forbidding desert country was that a stream or run-off from melting snow could create a lush, hidden wonderland far back in a canyon or along a higher elevation, a place of shade and flowers, water and food for animals and birds.

"It's special," Trace admitted grudgingly.

Sitting on big rocks, they disposed of sandwiches, apples and cookies. Trace had a bottle of beer and Eden sipped tomato juice. It could have been wonderfully companionable had he not been so stony-faced.

"How's your throat?" she asked solicitously.

He frowned. "My throat?"

"I suppose it must be sore. Otherwise even you should manage more than a few monosyllables."

He reached over and pulled her down into his arms, found her lips and possessed them. Fiery sweetness shot through her. Starved for him, scarcely knowing what she did, she slipped her arms up and caressed the hard, muscular back of his neck, the thick, dark hair. His hand reached inside her shirt, covered her breast, avidly exploring her. Then he stood up, holding her against him.

"The hell with talking," he said thickly. "This is what I want with you."

He thought it was that easy! Fury slashed through Eden's drugged yearning. Setting her hands against his chest, she plunged her body downward and twisted from his arms.

Gasping, she said, "Do you think you can freeze me out, refuse to say a decent, friendly word and then have me when you feel like it?"

His mouth quirked as his astonishment faded. "Don't pretend you haven't enjoyed it."

"I won't. But there has to be more than that."

"Do you want a lot of garbage about true love?" he taunted. "Sorry. I'll see that you have as good a time as I do. If that's not enough—"

"I don't need lies." Her throat ached. "But you could treat me like a human being."

For a moment something flared in his eyes before his features locked into a cold, handsome mask. "Let's get on up the mountain."

They parked at a picnic ground and took a trail that wound through firs and spruces and then passed along flower-spangled green meadows, some of which had deep, green lakes that reflected greener trees, clouds and the jagged white profile of the peak looming above.

They were climbing at over ten thousand feet. The thin air made Eden's head ache slightly and her heart labored. It hurt her pride to have to rest but she felt better when Trace, also breathing heavily, seemed glad enough to halt. Their way lay past a great glacial cirque, smiling drowsily in its brief summer, then along a tortured warp of glacier-scoured rock that splayed down from the gleaming peak.

"We'll take the easy route," Trace said, leading the way back into trees that were smaller now, spreading dense branches close to the rocky earth.

The snow was not more than five or six inches deep but it made the jumbled rocks over which they toiled treacherous and uncertain. It was a relief to find more solid footing beneath the snow as they began to encounter bristlecones.

In spite of her bewildered anger toward Trace, Eden yielded herself to experience the place with all of her senses. Coming upon the golden, sculptured wood, sometimes only a relic of what had been, more often buttressing a living tree still partly clothed with bark and needles, was like meeting beloved friends. There was no time to sketch now but after the camp circuit with Dominika, she would make this her next stop, camping while she did her impressions.

They took the trail to the ice field, where they were able to look far over the green sides of the mountains to the misty desert and other ranges near the Utah border. Then they were amid bristlecones again, each one a starkly eloquent creation of living tree struggling against centuries of weather that most organisms could not survive.

Trace stopped.

She looked past him and cried out.

The great chain-sawed stump of a bristlecone rose from the snow, other chunks scattered around it like the amputated pieces of a body.

"This is WPN-114," said Trace. "It was two hundred fifty-two inches around, had four thousand, eight hundred forty-four countable rings, a nineteen-inch strip of bark, a dead crown seventeen feet high with a living shoot of eleven feet." His voice grew savage. "It was also the oldest living thing on earth. Till 1964."

"Someone cut it?"

"You bet they did."

She moved her head in grieving wonderment. "But who? Why would anyone do such a thing?"

"To see how old it was."

"But you don't have to cut down a tree to date it. Dendro-chronologists take core samples about the size of a pencil."

"This geographer didn't. The Forest Service gave him permission to cut it down so he could date Ice-Age happenings and that's exactly what he did."

The desecration was so appalling that Eden felt as if her own body had been attacked. She faced toward the shining peak so that Trace could not see her tears.

"After the scientific gentleman had killed the tree and collected his data, the Forest Service organized a team of dendro-chronologists to search the Wheeler Peak region to see if they could find a tree as old or older than poor old WPN-114," Trace went on. "None came within twelve hundred years of matching it. Man is a weird creature. He can't make a tree or live much more than a hundred years himself but it doesn't bother him to take his little chain saw and kill the most ancient living thing on all this earth."

Eden knelt by the stump, tracing its patterns, its memories of drought, moisture, lightning, wind and ice. *I'll put you in the book,* she promised. *Maybe that will help keep other trees like you from dying. But I'll paint you, too, the way you must have looked while you were living. That's nothing like your being up here on the mountain but it will keep you for all the people who will never come here.*

"This is what happens when agencies take over," Trace said bitterly, "and it's why I don't want some big, impersonal organization like yours getting hold of the ranch. I damn well know that I'll take care of it. I can't be sure about anyone else."

"You have your cousins to contend with."

"So we'll contend. At least they're in the family." His eyes raked her. "You really have a nerve to try to sweet-talk an old woman into selling or giving away a place that has heirs. Are you forgetting about Julian?"

"And you?"

"I took a degree in plant biology and range management in order to bring this ranch back to something like the way it was before the white men came. Even you should be able to see the difference in our meadows and most range land."

The slurring "even you" made her furious but as she rose from touching the vandalized testament of nearly five thousand years, she kept her voice level. "When your cousin is trying to get the ranch included in the MX system, don't you think a national group with support from other conservationists would have a better chance of blocking that plan? You could only argue personal interest. Earth Heritage would be protecting it for the future."

His face seemed all graven angles. "However you wrap it up, I think it's sleazy."

"If you want to think that, go right ahead."

As they left the bristlecone sanctuary, again traversing the mirrored lake, the green forests and flowered meadows, she resolved that she would never tell him that his stewardship of the land had already decided her, should the rest of the tour confirm her judgment, to advise Heritage that the ranch was in the care of a man who loved it intelligently and was working for its regeneration. Heritage could best spend its money where this was not the case.

She would have bitten off her tongue, though, before telling him that.

* * *

She dreamed of the mutilated bristlecone that night. Even after she awoke, it haunted her. She exorcised the dream to a bearable degree by making a few sketches of the bristlecone but she would have to spend several days up in that secret place of eternal snow in order to capture the majesty of the once-living tree, along with the mute reproach of its devastation.

Now Dominika's little expedition came down from the foothills and cut through the basin, where a national wildlife refuge covered thousands of marshy acres and ponds. Innumerable canvasback and redhead ducks skimmed the water with their young. There were ruddy ducks with incredible china-blue bills; sooty black coots against thick, pink milfoil; grebes; a white-faced ibis with long cerise legs and green and rose iridescence in its wings; cinnamon teal, willets and phalaropes; yellow-headed blackbirds like bright leaves in high sedges; terns flying over; a great blue heron stalking in shallow water; elegant gray sandhill cranes with maroon skullcaps, and a breath-taking glimpse of two dazzling white trumpeter swans gliding like royalty among the lesser birds.

A muskrat swam along a dike, parting dense bulrushes. Among the tussocks a coyote made a shadow of darker ombre. Deer bounded away, merging quickly into high grasses.

Water, marsh, land and air teemed with varied creatures, imposing, comic, entrancingly graceful or beguiling with their young.

"In Pleistocene times all this was covered by a lake of four hundred seventy square miles, maybe two hundred feet deep," Trace said. "During the ages the lake dried up till it left only the Ruby and Franklin Lake marshes. All the early diarists who traveled through here mentioned the swarms of geese and ducks."

Eden nodded. "Yes, this is on both the Central and Pacific flyways. It must get birds from the Great Salt Lake, the Klamath Basin and the Colorado River as well as from the Humboldt. Establishing an MX system in the Great Basin and ferrying fake and real missiles around to confuse the Russians is bound to play havoc with a place like this, even if the demand for water doesn't finish draining the supply left us by the centuries."

They had their lunch at Cave Creek, where subterranean

waters flowed out of an unfathomed cavern. "This was the major route to the West," Trace said. "The Donner party camped here before they went on to face cannibalism and death. It's supposed to be haunted by the ghost of a soldier who was drowned while trying to find the water's source."

It was difficult to believe in ghosts or despairing starvation here on the grassy bank thick with heavy spires of violet beard-tongue, brilliant monkey flowers, showy lemon blazing stars and everywhere the sweet honeysuckle-like odor of elderberries in snowy blossom around the cavern. Butterflies drifted like rootless, languorous flowers and bees hummed in this rare plenitude. Even Trace seemed becalmed so that it was Dominika, rousing from the briefest of naps, who said that they had better move along or they wouldn't reach the next camp before dark.

Angling along the northeastern boundaries of the ranch, they left private land for National Forest and followed a creek up a canyon where paintbrush, sego lilies and sunflowers contrasted with purple tones of lupine and larkspur. Blue grouse whirred up out of shelter but Franklin grouse merely watched the vehicle. Deer faded into an alder thicket. High above, a golden eagle circled.

It was late afternoon when Eden saw the white, arched canvas top of a herder's wagon in a high meadow dotted with hundreds of sheep. The middle-aged, short, stocky herder was Jacopo Garay, a nephew of Koni's, putting in his tenth summer with the sheep.

"Andrea," he said dolefully to Dominika as they had their meal by the campfire, "this fall instead of paying me off, you keep most of my wages. Otherwise I'll spend it all this winter just as I've been doing and I will never save enough to go home and buy a little bar or inn."

"I'll remind you," she promised between a sigh and a twinkle. "But you say this every summer, Jacopo."

He nodded, groaning. "I can lose at *muz* in a few days what I work eight months to earn. The only way is for you to pay my board bill in Elko and send me a little cash each week."

"All right," his employer agreed. "I will try hard to convince you when you bring the band down this fall."

Her words seemed to cheer him. He brought out his accordion and treated the group to a concert that lasted until long after dark.

They spent several days at the next camp before moving out of Forest land to the northwestern high pastures of the ranch. There the herder was from Madrid and he had known nothing of sheep until he came to the ranch three years ago but Koni had trained him well.

That day some of the sheep had gotten into foxtail and the spikes had burrowed deep into their fleece. If around the eyes, the spikes could cause blindness and the intolerable itching of the barbs could, according to Trace, make the animals so miserable with scratching that they could lose several pounds of weight in only a day. The herder was busy cleaning out the animals' eyes and ears. Since there were many to tend, Trace and Eden helped him while Dominika squirted medication into eyes that needed it.

They finished by lantern-light, working late so that few of the sheep would have to endure the torment throughout the night, and went to bed as soon as they had scrubbed the dusty lanolin from their hands and enjoyed Eden's casserole of layered hominy, cheese, green chilis and corn.

Next morning they checked the band for scratching sheep and sore eyes, cleaned off a few that had been missed in the darkness and carefully examined the dogs again, for the arrowy points could cause terrible abscesses in their ears, noses and paws. Eden found one spire at the base of the ear of a spunky little tri-colored dog and the herder extracted one from between the paw pads of the Australian shepherd.

During lunch the young herder somewhat fearfully admitted that he had lost three ewes to bloat at his last pasturage but he had been using the meat from one and the camp-tender had taken the others to be divided among the herders.

"It happens," Dominika said. "Sometimes they can be saved by sticking in a knife to relieve the pressure but if the bloat is that serious, they never seem to be strong again."

She, Trace and the herder launched into a discussion of the ills that afflicted sheep: blue tongue, pinkeye, blue bag, foot rot, a wasting away called *errezelatu* and various sorts of abscesses. Some could be treated by the herders, others required a veterinarian and in many cases the sheep would die anyway.

"Domingo always said that by the time a sheep was *eria*, it was too late to help it and that if it did live, it would be sickly and have weak lambs," Dominika said. "You've had no trouble this year with coyotes or mountain lions?"

"No, thank the good God. There must be enough deer and rabbits."

After yesterday's exertions with the foxtail, everyone was ready to laze around camp that afternoon. Eden made a big bowl of *tabouley*, letting oil and lemon juice permeate the nutty bulgur, adding parsley and the last of the onions, tomatoes and cucumbers they had brought in the ice chest. She made cornbread in the big skillet, enhancing it with grated cheese, whole-kernel corn, pimientos and green peppers.

This herder did not know Dominika and seemed shy so after some desultory conversation around the fire, they went to bed. "Our last night in these bags!" Dominika muttered as Eden brushed out her long, silvery hair and braided it into a single plait to keep it from tangling. "I have loved seeing the bands again in the summer pastures but I will be glad to be back in a real bed." She cocked her head at Eden. "I hope you don't regret coming."

"It's been fascinating," Eden said truthfully.

Being near Trace had also been harrowing but their forced proximity would end on the next day. Very shortly she would leave the ranch for good. She would visit Wheeler Peak again to sketch the ruined tree and then go back up the mountain to complete her work there. And when the book was finished she would ask if Heritage would give her another assignment, one far, far away—where she could forget the clear gray eyes that pierced to her heart and lips that could woo so tenderly and then say cruel things.

VII

IT WAS NOT that easy for Eden to break away.

Dominika was tired when they returned to the ranch but there was a peace of accomplishment in her weariness—as if she had said farewell, graciously and in good time, to what had been a large part of her life.

"Thank you for going with me," she said to Eden on the day after their return, while Eden was trying to think of the best way to say that she was leaving. She rested her brown, fragile-boned hand on the younger woman's arm. "I am very old, Eden, and there is one more thing I wish to do."

"Why, you'll outlive most of us," Eden began but Dominika hushed her.

"My only daughter died. As you know, my grandsons have no children. I must trust that someday there will be a great-granddaughter. For her I have a secret and a story." Dominika rested for a moment before her gold-touched green eyes fixed again on Eden. "It is not likely that my great-granddaughter will read Basque and I have never learned to write English well. Will you take down what I want her to know?"

"Oh, Dominika!"

Eden stared helplessly at this woman whom she had come to admire and love, the woman who had in an amazing way become mother, grandmother and all the nurturing women whom Eden had never known. "Look, a secretary would be better, one who could take shorthand or even work from tapes—"

"Tapes? That's a good idea," Dominika smiled. "It is nice to think that a child of my blood—one whom I don't even know yet—may someday hear my voice. But I want this in written words, too." Her tone and gaze filled with a supplication that was also imperious. "I must put down things secret to my family's women long before there was history. You are the only one to whom I would tell them. If you will not help, the heritage will die with me."

A chill passed down Eden's spine. She laughed, trying to lighten the moment. "Dominika, you're a schemer! First you needed me on the sheep pilgrimage. Now it's this. What next?"

With a simplicity that totally disarmed the younger woman, the older said, "I would like to keep you with me until I die. You have become my heart's daughter. And yes, of course it is my hope that you will marry one of my grandsons."

To such honesty Eden could only say, "I love Trace, Dominika, but I must forget him. He doesn't want love." She bit her lip. "That's why it's hard for me to be here."

Dominika nodded. "Since his wife, he has visited only whores and it has come to my ears that he never uses the same one twice. Doesn't that show that he can still love but is afraid to?"

Startled at the revelation, Eden stiffened as contradictory feelings of outrage, amusement and hope battled within her. Did he consider her a whore? How could he? And what, then, was she to make of his readiness to take her to bed at every opportunity even though he had made it clear that it was without commitment? She quickly dismissed the question.

She had more important things to do with her life than wait for Trace to work through his woman-hating. She was still too emotionally raw from Fowler's rejection to court further hostility.

"I don't know what Trace is afraid of but it needn't be of me. If I stay, it's because of you and in spite of him." Taking Dominika's hands in hers, she leaned forward and demanded severely, "If I agree to take down your story, will you promise not to invent delays?"

"I won't invent," Dominika pouted, "but should I get sick or tired—"

"You're never sick and I'll get tired before you will."

Dominika breathed out a grudging sigh of surrender. "Very well. We will work for two hours in the morning, two in the afternoon. But," she concluded hopefully, "you may have time off whenever you want it."

"Thank you," Eden said gravely although her lips twitched.

"I will expect to pay you, of course."

"You're feeding me. That's enough if we finish within a reasonable time. I guess I'll need to go up the mountain for a few days and back to Wheeler Peak in order to finish my book. So you'll have a few breathers."

They began that afternoon, sitting by the window. Estevannia had a recorder on which she taped messages to her large and scattered family and she had been glad to loan it until another one could be bought in town. Equipped with a thick legal pad and several felt-tipped pens, Eden toasted Dominika with a glass of iced tea and said, "Any time you're ready."

Dominika folded her hands and leaned back in her throne-like chair. "I was *etcheko primu.* . . ."

What began to unfold was not only the story of a dispossessed young woman who had come to America, but a treasury of folkways and customs reaching back to unrecorded times. When she came to a song, Dominika would carefully write in Basque and then translate the lines so that Eden could transcribe them into English. Since Dominika also had to spell out most of the Basque words, the part of the tale set in the Basque country took a long time. Dominika told what she remembered of Lael and Lael's grim old grandmother, Engrâce, a line of *seroras*, healers, craftswomen, mistresses of Etchahoun; Marya, the first to come to the New World. Dominika could not name all of her ancestresses, of course, but it was remarkable that she could give brief stories of some who had died nine hundred years ago.

"How do you know all this?" Eden asked her after several days had passed.

"That's the secret. I will tell you before we begin the American part." The vigilant, strangely youthful eyes rested on her. "Eden, you may give this secret to one of two people if either comes into being: your daughter or my great-granddaughter."

"My daughter?"

"If my line does not continue and your daughter would honor the knowledge."

"You will have a great-granddaughter," Eden said briskly. "I'll type all of this and then we'll put it in a strongbox with the tapes so that it will be ready for her."

Dominika did not argue but the stubborn set of her head declared that she had not yet abandoned hope that her great-granddaughter and Eden's child might be the same.

Trace had been gone most of the week, appearing only twice for dinner and leaving immediately afterward. He did bring a recorder and dozens of tapes from Elko.

"With these," he said as he handed them to Eden, "I can't see why *amona* needs a secretary, too."

"I can promise you one thing," Eden told him hotly. "I'll be out of here just as soon as we finish. Whatever you think, I'm doing this only because your grandmother wants it very much."

Turning her back on him, she marched down the hall and all but slammed her door. The conceited churl! He seemed to think that she was in league with Dominika, hanging about in order to wear down his suspicions. She would fulfill her promise to Dominika but she certainly would not languish around him or give him another opportunity to treat her like the only kind of woman with whom he seemed to feel safe.

As engrossing as she found Dominika's memories, her consciousness of Trace kept her hurts raw and so it was a relief when Foss flew his private plane to Elko on the weekend and drove down to the ranch in a rental car.

"Good to see you without that crutch," he laughed, sweeping Eden close for an exuberant kiss that might look boyishly impetuous to Dominika but was in reality demandingly sensuous. He bent over to hug his grandmother and kiss her cheek. "I tried to phone last week and Estevannia said that you were gallivanting around the sheep camps. When are you going to start growing old gracefully?"

"Never," she replied. "Can you stay long?"

"I have to be back in Washington by Monday night." His eyes, Eden realized, were the sparkling green of those glacial lakes just below timberline, chill beneath the surface warmth.

"Sprained ankles don't last forever so I thought I'd better pay a visit before Eden jumps in her van and heads for parts unknown."

"She'll be a while," Dominika said smugly. "We're working on my life story."

"Now that I'd like to read!" Foss teased, greeting Estevannia and thanking her most charmingly for the iced Picon punch she brought him. "Telling all, are you?"

"Enough," Dominika answered.

Trace had gone up the mountain to help Julian with the finishing touches on the cabin. After dinner the three of them played *muz* until Dominika yawned ostentatiously and said that she was sleepy.

"So am I," Eden said. She made her good-nights and escaped before Dominika, laughably taken aback, could even rise from her chair.

Eden had showered, slipped into a nightgown and was brushing her hair when there was a soft but positive rap on the door. "Come talk for a while," Foss urged plaintively. "If you don't, I'm going to huff and I'll puff and I'll blow the door in."

"You know what happens to wolves."

"Have a heart, Eden. I had a hell of a time getting away but I wanted to see you before you vanished."

"That's very flattering but you're wasting your time."

"Come out here and tell me that." As if he could see her frown, he said coaxingly, "I'll sit on my hands if you say so and I won't keep you up for long. But I'm going to stay here till you come out and if you hear heavy breathing—"

"Oh, for heaven's sake! Now I see why people groan when you start a filibuster. Just a minute."

"Wear what you don't have on," he called hopefully.

She hastily dressed in old jeans and a sweater and padded out in her house slippers, scowling darkly. Foss grinned as he took her clenched hand and led her up to the kitchen, where they would disturb no one.

"Shall I make hot chocolate?" she asked, uneasy at his frankly desirous stare.

"I'm drinking whisky." He leaned against the cupboards as

she heated milk and melted chocolate into it. "When are you coming to Washington?"

"No sooner than I have to." She added stick cinnamon to her drink and sat down to enjoy it.

Foss prowled, one hand thrust into the pocket of his perfectly tailored trousers. The silver hair against his dark skin made him look supremely vital and magnetism radiated from his lithe body, his sexuality heightened by the aura of power.

"My grandmother says you're leaving as soon as you finish her memoirs. How are we going to get to know each other if you don't visit my town?"

She smiled. "I don't see why we need closer acquaintance."

"We don't as far as I'm concerned." He halted, set down his glass and took her hands. "I want to marry you, Eden."

"But—but we scarcely know each other!"

"See?" he triumphed. "How can you turn me down on that score and then refuse to give me a chance to convince you?"

"You can't be serious!"

His eyebrows lifted. "Say the word and we'll have the wedding just as soon as we can get a license."

She had to believe him in spite of her utter bewilderment. Why should he set his mind on her when certainly he had his choice of glamorous and exciting women who would be political assets where she would be purely a liability? More troubled than flattered, she decided that the only way to shake his apparent determination was to tell him the truth.

"Foss, we're worlds apart in politics. That alone would wreck us. But you're exceedingly attractive." She looked him in the eyes, controlling the urgent awareness that passed like an electrical jolt between them. "My pride still suffers from being rejected by my husband for another woman. An affair with you would certainly boost my ego, apart from what I'm sure would be a fantastic time in bed."

"My dear," he cut in, "if you prefer an affair, that's fine with me. I thought, simply, that you would prefer marriage."

She shook her head. "I wouldn't marry you in any case. But I would probably have an affair with you if I weren't in love with another man."

He dropped her hands as if they had burned him and moved back a few paces to scan her face. The pupils of his eyes dilated, almost blotting out the cool green rim of iris. Although he did not make a menacing gesture, she was suddenly afraid. She had spoken to a debonair, sophisticated man—and raised the most primitive of responses. She breathed more freely when he gave a thin smile and relaxed slightly.

"It's nice to know that I at least appeal to your baser instincts. Who's the lucky target of your true affection?"

"I don't think that concerns you."

He laughed harshly. "For starters, I'm vain enough to want to know whom you could prefer to me."

"He's not at all like you," she said and added dourly, "It's beyond me why I should care about him."

"Your husband?" Foss persisted.

"Foss, I don't want to talk about him. I'm just not up for either marriage or an affair, thank you very much."

She rinsed out the mug and was turning to the door when strong arms swung her around. Foss ground himself against her, trapping her against the wall as his mouth plundered hers.

"You promised!" she gasped, twisting away her face.

With one arm he pinned her hands above her head and with his other hand he fondled her breasts, keeping her thighs against the wall by the pressure of his own. "Sweetheart, I'm an old hand at making promises. That's the way to get the opposition into a vulnerable position."

He kissed her again. She stood frigidly immobile until he sighed in defeat. "I guess I can't believe that the way I want you, Eden, could be one-sided."

"You'd better believe this: If you did somehow get me into bed, I would hate you for ignoring what I've told you."

His lip curled. "For sullying your integrity?"

"Whatever you choose to call it."

Eyes locked, they confronted each other like wrestlers. Then his shoulders moved as if shedding a weight and he smiled, surprisingly put out his hand to touch her face. "All right. Don't look so beleaguered. It's corny to say I want to be your friend and it wouldn't be true. I want to be your lover. But at least let's

531

not be enemies." He seemed to mean what he said. After all, his years in the Senate had taught him how to lose gracefully.

"Fine. Let's not be enemies."

He kissed her lightly, not touching her body, but she would never be off guard with him again.

"Good-night," she said and left him quickly.

Though his trip was an erotic disappointment, Foss evidently decided to salvage some benefit by pleading the MX cause with Dominika. He was thus engaged when Eden joined them Sunday for a late breakfast.

"*Amona,*" he was saying persuasively, "do you really understand nuclear strategy?"

"No, and I don't think anyone else does."

"Well, at least let me show you why we need the MX."

"You can try."

Eden buttered a *churro*, a crunchily golden finger of deep fried batter that was tastier than a doughnut. "I'll keep you honest."

He cast her the flick of a smile. It was hard to believe that this assured, confident man had courted her passionately but futilely only ten hours ago. "Before the development of MIRVs— that stands for multiple independently targetable re-entry vehicles—we faced the Soviets in a sort of perpetual standoff. Nuclear war meant mutual destruction, making it unlikely that either side would touch things off. MIRVs changed the situation in much the way that a repeating rifle made the old single-shots obsolete. Instead of a single missile, with MIRV one missile can launch many. This development restored the chance that even in nuclear war, whoever struck first with the most would win. A whole new ballgame." He made a cathedral of his blunt fingers. "We deployed our Minuteman and Poseidon missiles in 1970. The Soviet Union was deploying its MIRVs by 1975."

"So what could we expect?" Dominika frowned.

"What we got. Russia now had ICBMs with MIRVs focused on our thousand Minutemen and fifty-two Titans."

"How will MXs help that?"

"They'll protect our missiles against surprise Soviet attack," Foss said eagerly. "*Amona,* I fought MIRVs but now that we have them, there's no turning back. The Department of Defense wants to hide two hundred MXs, each equipped with ten deadly accurate MIRVs in forty-six hundred protected shelters in the Great Basin—mostly in Nevada but also in part of Utah. The idea would be to shuttle the MXs around the countryside from shelter to shelter so that the Soviets won't know where they are.''

Eden had lost her appetite but she took a second cup of coffee. "And apart from the damage to the land, it will cost ten billion dollars and all because MIRVs weren't banned in the first SALT talks.''

"That's under the bridge,'' Foss shrugged.

"Why make it worse?'' Eden challenged.

"Worse?'' he mocked.

"The Soviets can build forty-six hundred warheads and hit all the shelters, fake and utilized, at one time,'' she said. "Why tighten the screws so that a crisis would force Russia into a first strike? The MXs' two thousand warheads would threaten their whole ICBM system, three-fourths of their striking force. ICBMs are a quarter of our strategic strength. It's stupid to escalate. If we don't learn how to take care of our radioactive waste, we'll finish ourselves without any help from the Russians.''

Dominika nodded. "That's what I think. We need weapons but not such powerful ones that our enemies will decide they have to take us by surprise.''

Foss recoiled. His eyes blazed and for the first time Eden understood that he really believed in the missiles and was dedicated to proving their necessity. "And just what would you suggest to the Secretary of Defense?'' he demanded sarcastically. "I'm seeing him tomorrow. I'm sure that he'd be delighted to hear your solutions.''

"Great. I'm against having the MX at all but if you're hellbent on it, some experts think that it would be better to base them on small submarines that can move around at sea. And don't make them so accurate that the Russians are scared into doing something drastic to protect their ICBMs.''

He bowed sardonically. "I'll tell the Secretary that. Also that you're appallingly unrealistic.'' Pushing away his unfinished plate, he glanced at his watch and rose to his feet. "I'd better be on my way."

Dominika looked at Eden with troubled eyes. He was back in a few minutes with his overnight case. He kissed his grandmother, gave Eden a probing stare and cold nod and left.

"I love him," Dominika said, eyes dark with pain, "but he makes me afraid. Do you know what he wants?"

Eden laughed, trying to drain some of the anxiety from the older woman. "To be President?"

That won a chuckle but Dominika sobered as she dropped her voice. "He wants to be Secretary of Defense."

"But his good friend is that!"

"Yes, but the man is sick and wants to resign. Foss is sure that if he 'sets an example' of his belief in the MX by turning the ranch over to the government it will ensure his appointment. The Secretary has promised to recommend him and the President is favorable." Stunned, Eden could say nothing. After a moment Dominika went on. "It . . . it is not just the power. Foss thinks that he can save the country by being in that position."

"Save it?" Eden laughed bitterly. "That sounds like the old Vietnam strategy of destroying in order to save."

"I don't know about that," Dominika muttered, "but there will be missiles on this land over my dead body."

Eden tried to cheer her. "Even if the MXs are housed in Nevada, there's so much Federal land available that annexing the ranch wouldn't be necessary. It might be good propaganda for Foss's position but he can't make you sell."

She hoped that was true.

VIII

THE DEATH of Maria of Etchahoun, the journey down the coffin road, the ritual public mourning and Dominika's private grief. When she reached the time to embark at Bilbao, she paused, regarding Eden as though weighing an all-important decision before she leaned forward to touch her hand.

"Come to my bedroom."

She led the way, moving a bit stiffly. She seemed sometimes short of breath and easily wearied but the marvel was the clear mind in a body that still functioned well in spite of its ninety-eight years. Eden had never been in her room before but from what Dominika had told her, it could have been a room at Etchahoun except that it had electricity.

A woven white coverlet embroidered in blue lay on the postered bed of dark, carved oak. There were rugs of goatskin on the polished floor, blue and white curtains at the windows that looked off to the mountains. A great chest was adorned with a coat of arms, a wheat sheaf with a sickle.

"I have told you of Mari," Dominika said, caressing the design. "The sickle is her emblem and these are the arms of Etchahoun, going back to the time of the building of the old stone tower. Julian carved the chest for me. He made this furniture from my descriptions so that I could feel at home." She smiled and added softly, "It was his love that did that, after so many years."

A big mirror framed with aged bronze embedded with azure enamel hung above a dresser; it reflected a bouquet of dried blue flowers, gold and rose-hued grasses and winter pods. A crucifix hung above the bed and one wall was filled with photographic portraits, snapshots and a few sketches.

"These are my sons, Foss and Vachel," Dominika said, pointing out the pictures of men who bore a resemblance to the grandsons whom Eden knew. Dominika touched several faded old photos. "This is May Arkwright Hutton, whom I'll soon tell you about. This is Joe, my first husband. This is Brant."

Her voice softened as she indicated a white-haired old man with a carved shepherd's *makhila* in his hand and several dogs at his feet. "That's Domingo, my *tocayo*. And here's Julian when we were married."

The ruggedly pleasant face was so much like Trace's that Eden caught her breath. Dominika nodded and smiled. "Yes. They are very alike."

In the center of the gallery there were a dozen pictures of a girl. They ranged all the way from childhood to the beauty of a young woman in a white wedding gown with roses in her arms. "This is Kattalin. She did the sketches of the rest of us."

The pen-and-ink drawings depicted Julian and Dominika with zest and insight. There were also horses, dogs, a wily goat, raptors with spread wings and a pair of coyote pups.

"She raised them when the mother was shot," Dominika said. "We thought they might turn into sheep-killers but they never did. They bred with our dogs and now our best animals have a streak of coyote in them."

"But she was an artist!"

"She might have been. I was glad when she took to it so early. It seemed a sign that she was the one to go back to the cave."

"The cave?"

Dominika moved past the pictures to a niche in the wall. A white taper in a brass holder presided over an ancient-looking, sheepskin-bound book, a necklace of acorns, polished by use, and a piece of rock on which there flew a bird painted a vibrant blue.

Putting the bird into Eden's hands, Dominika said in a trembling voice, "What I tell you now has come down from one woman of each generation in my family. *Time out of mind, when only men made pictures in the caves, a woman of ours made true this dream for us, a place, hidden and secret, where it is always summer. . . ."*

* * *

When Dominika had finished, Eden gazed at the bird, thought in awe of the women who had treasured its promise of spring within the depths of that distant sanctuary. Feeling herself unworthy to hold the beloved relic, she handed it back to Dominika.

"Why—how—could you share this with me?"

Replacing the shard in the little shrine, Dominika sank down on the edge of the bed. "I want you to take the blue bird back."

"But—"

"It has comforted me all these years but it belongs with the tree and the mother and the child. You are an artist, like that first one. I think that you were sent for this." She added slowly, "You might have been my granddaughter."

A tremor prickled at Eden's spine. "But if one of your grandsons has a daughter—"

Dominika gave a sad, small shake of her head. "Even if one is born, she may not care anything about this. The bird might be broken or thrown away. No, I took it. I will not rest easy until I know that it will be returned, and by one who reverences the secret." Her face lifted imploringly to Eden. "It is the last thing that I will ask of you."

How strange it was that Eden had wanted since childhood to see those caves, the hairy mammoths and aurochs and reindeer, the prints of those hands long gone to dust. "I will go," she said, straightening, "but let's finish our story first."

"Yes, we will do that."

Disclosing the secret had exhausted Dominika to the point that Eden decided that she would go up the mountain and work for a few days. Julian's cabin was complete now except for some finishing touches. She slept in the half-loft, helped with the cooking and painted steadily the rest of the time.

The lion kittens still drank milk and seemed to relish the dry dog food that Julian served them. They inherited soup and steak bones, which they tumbled and wrestled over.

"They need their mama to teach them how to hunt," regretted Julian. "But they catch a squirrel now and then and I expect that when they're ready to mate, they'll go wild all the way.''

He had rigged a mock cave for them outside, a wooden crate covered with dirt and rock, and they came and went at will, beautiful creatures, still spotted and retaining enough of their kitten appearance to tempt cuddling, though Eden did not attempt it. She thought, as Julian did, that the less they were tamed, the better it would be for them but she did make several studies of their antics.

Did they ever return to their den? The thought of the burned slope and the memory of the slaughtered mother still enraged Eden. The forgiveness of nature had already sent up new grass and flowers and although some trees had been killed, others had managed to survive in whole or in part, generating new limbs from charred trunks.

"How's Dominika?" Julian asked one night.

Eden pondered. "She tires more easily, I think. Sometimes she's short of breath. And she's worried about Foss's plans for the ranch. Julian, won't you take over when—" She faltered but he did not wince.

"When Dominika passes? No. I don't want to run the ranch or bother with those things. Dominika and I arranged it long ago. I have savings enough to keep me for the rest of my life. The land will go to whichever of the grandsons seems the best guardian or to whomever she picks. It's nothing to do with me." He frowned. "If you're going on to Wheeler Peak from here, I think I'll drive down and see her. I've been lax about it, knowing that you were there."

Eden spent two days in working on the ancient bristlecone and reconstructing what she thought it had looked like before the data-gathering chain saw had ended its millennia. Julian had come and gone when she returned to the ranch after six days. Dominika seemed refreshed and eager to return to her story. Trace was away on business.

Did that, Eden wondered harshly, include visits to his once-only whores? Someone should tell him that he would be less likely to pick up a venereal disease if he chose a selective, non-professional girlfriend and stayed with her. She told herself to be glad that he wasn't around to distract her, sending those stabbing throbs of hurt or hope through her whenever she caught even a glimpse of him.

In the meantime it steadied her to listen to Dominika's passionless remembrance of passion: her "dancing young man," the long-ago fears of a husbandless woman about to have a child in a foreign land, the kindness and protection of Joe Uhalde. Then flamboyant Goldfield, the destruction of all that she had worked for, Tonopah, and at last the marriage with her first love, which for all its periods of fulfillment, carried its dark taint of guilt and obsessiveness that ended in Brant's suicide. Another collapsing world and then a pregnant woman in the middle of her years starting again in a rough sheep camp.

When Dominika told how Julian had saved her and how she had commended her dead little girl to the spirits of the cave, she lay back, spent with reliving that cruel loss.

"Julian knows the rest," she said. "But this is what I want my great-granddaughter to read."

"Your grandsons and great-grandsons should know it, too," Eden said, venturing the conviction that had been mounting within her since she had realized the broad, epic grandeur of the narrative. "It's not just a women's history, or your family's, or even the Basques'. In a way, it's the story of humankind."

Dominika's weary eyes opened to glint with mischief. "Well, to properly relate the men's side, you would have to bring in Jaun Zuria, the White Lord, who fought off our enemies, and tell of how we routed Charlemagne and resisted the Moors. Then there would be my kinsman, El Cano, the first to circumnavigate the world, and those who sailed with Columbus and—"

"What we have here will do just fine," interjected Eden. "Is it all right with you if I type up one version suitable for everyone to read and then do a private section just for your great-granddaughter?"

"Yes. And if I never have one, tell the story to your daughter or granddaughter. It is too precious to be lost even should my line end." Her eyes danced. "But at the finish of both versions, you can put the same thing. I have been blessed all my life to usually be in a place where I could feel and hear and sense what

we call in Basque *llurun*, earth's living breath. I have loved it—
and my life. I wish that fortune to everyone.''

Her story told and secret shared, Dominika seemed to be
happy but drained. It was as if her energy had spilled out with
her words. She went to bed early now and took a long nap each
afternoon. Even so, she still dozed in her chair. Eden watched
her with love and a growing sense of inevitability.

One day soon Dominika's sleep would deepen into that
long one from which she would not wake. Although bright-
spirited, she seemed to be drifting across the border, speaking
much of her mother, Joe, Domingo, Andres, Kattalin, her dead
sons and old friends. She never spoke of Brant, the man who
had dominated such a large part of her life and then left her to
face alone what he could not.

Such rememberings humbled Eden. How dared she feel
that without Trace, life had no savor? Love of many, many kinds
was the energy of life, an integral part of Dominika's *llurun*.
Even if Trace could never love her, she could love *llurun*, paint it
and work ceaselessly for it.

She had applied for her passport and was typing Dominika's account and working on her bristlecone book while making arrangements to take the blue bird back to its cave. She hated
to leave Dominika but all of her resolutions and common sense
went out the window when she saw Trace. She ached for him,
desired him, but most of all she wanted to share his thoughts
and feelings, be his friend.

That, clearly, he would never allow. He was deliberately
staying away from the ranch. That hurt, though it eased the situation a little.

Two weeks after Foss's visit, Joe came for a day, giving
Dominika all the Reno news. He had brought Godiva chocolates
and bushels of long-stemmed red roses for both his grandmother and Eden but to Eden's relief, his gallantries were good-
naturedly careless. After Dominika had retired for her afternoon
nap, he came to watch Eden working on her picture of the ancient bristlecone.

''Eden, you have a lot of influence with *amona*. Can't you
make her understand that Foss is determined to use this land for

the MXs? There won't be a viable operation left anyway if the government takes over the leased public lands, as it surely will. It would be better to give in gracefully and sell for a nice price."

Eden pushed away from her easel and stared at him. "What happened to your resort development?"

He grinned, looking like a chubby, overgrown boy. "That was just to make *amona* see the kind of thing that could happen—that it's stupid to hope this place can continue as a ranch. Its location is too valuable."

"I hear that every time farm land is given over to housing. But where will our food come from when all of the land is covered with people?"

He chuckled. "You'll convert us to eating seaweed and soybeans, I guess. Anyway, Foss tells me that he's being pressured to assure the Department of Defense that it can use this land. He hates to push *amona* but he can't wait much longer. You'd do everyone a favor to make her see reason."

"She's very old and seems to be a little weaker every day. Certainly Foss can't intend to bully her."

"He doesn't have much choice."

"I thought he loved her."

"He does. And he's taken quite a fall for you—which is one reason I'm not pouring blandishments in your ear. Foss and I often compete for women, but when one of us is really serious, the other backs off." Joe frowned. "Don't think anything comes before power with my cousin, though. On top of that, he believes in the MX."

"Do you?"

Joe shrugged. "I take Foss's word."

"Besides, MX site construction would bring in thousands of well-paid people, most of whom would find their way to your casino."

"Why not?" Joe's face lost its soft contours and his dark eyes turned cold. "Foss has a big yen for you, honey, but don't push your luck. I know what happened to a few people who tried to block him."

Trembling with anger and alarm, Eden put down her brush and rose to her feet. "If you're speaking for Foss, and I assume you are, tell him I hope with all my heart that your grandmother never gives in to him on the land.''

She started to add that wrangling with a frail, ninety-eight-year-old woman could kill her but she checked the words, suddenly convinced that, in extremity, Foss might hope for just that.

Presumably, as things now stood, the three grandsons would inherit equally. With Joe under his sway, Foss could force a sale of the ranch over Trace's objections. It was such depraved strategy that Eden did not want to believe Foss capable of it. Yet, chillingly, she did.

"Eden," Joe pleaded, "Foss and I love our grandmother too.''

"But you would poison her last days for the sake of power and money. God damn you both.''

She turned away and went to her room. When she joined Dominika a few hours later, he had already started back to Reno.

In a quandary, for she was sure that Foss would not wait long to force the issue, Eden debated how best to protect Dominika. Julian should be called down in any case. Dominika was always animated during his visits and he didn't realize how, since she had completed her revelations, she drifted more and more toward her final sleep.

His presence would support Dominika, and perhaps deter Foss to an extent, but Julian, too, was old. Reluctantly Eden was driven to seek out Trace, though it was three days after Joe's visit before he turned up at the ranch.

Desperate to catch him before he could vanish again, Eden went out to the cabin and knocked at the door. Her heart seemed to be wedged in her throat and she had an all-gone feeling in her stomach.

His eyes widened in surprise. "*Amona's* all right?''

"She's fine.''

Eden's tongue stuck clumsily to the roof of her mouth and she felt a hot rush of blood to her face as she saw the leap of cynical amusement in his gaze. She was humiliated as thoroughly as if she had sought him out for any crumb of attention that he might deign to give her.

"Come in," he said, stepping aside.

She entered, passing him quickly to stand by the far door that opened out of sight of the house. "I think you should know this," she said and told him what Joe had said.

"Hell," Trace growled. "I knew that was coming." He stayed where he was but his eyes fixed on the pulse of her throat.

The force between them dizzied her, tautened her body to demand the sweet surcease that she found only in his arms. She put a hand against the door to steady herself. "Well, can't you do something?"

"Short of killing Foss, what would you advise?"

"For one thing, you could stay closer to home so you'll be here when he comes."

"I was trying to do you a favor," he mocked. "Things must be really tough if you're asking me to stick around."

"You won't have to put up with me much longer. I got my passport a few days ago. My book should be ready to mail next week and as soon as it is, I'm leaving."

A muscle went rigid in his jaw but his tone was flippant. "Never to return?"

She wanted him so desperately that she almost went to him. The hint of a smile on his lips told her that was what he expected. He would take her to his bed and she could caress him, hold him, meet his passion, hurtle with him into that rapture that expanded into peace—and then he would close her out, treat her like a whore because that's what it suited him to pretend all women were.

"Why should I come back?" she cried savagely and burst out the door before he could move—even had he intended to.

Over her shoulder she hurled at him, "Julian should be asked to come."

"I'll go after him in the morning."

His words should have relieved her but the exchange left her so shaken and tortured that she scarcely slept that night, wrenching her thoughts from Trace only to worry about Foss.

IX

TRACE HAD left before Eden joined Dominika for breakfast. "I hope that he won't be away for long," Dominika fretted in a way so unlike her that Eden glanced up sharply.

"He just went to see if Julian is finished with the cabin and to persuade him to come down and rest for a while."

Dominika brightened. "Ah, good! I know Julian needs the mountain but I miss him more now that I don't seem to have much energy. If Julian's coming, it would be nice to have Joe over, too. Would you call him?"

"Of course."

Eden did not remind her that he had just been there. She hesitated, fearing that Dominika would also want her to phone Foss, but the old woman straightforwardly disposed of that problem.

"We won't invite Foss. He's busy. Besides, I don't feel like arguing with him over what he sees as my patriotic duty."

Rising, Dominika swayed and then steadied herself by gripping the chair. She smiled dismissingly as Eden sprang up to support her. "I think that my old brain doesn't get enough oxygen. Maybe long ago I should have learned to stand on my head. I would break my neck were I to try it now." She took Eden's arm, something she had never done before. "Help me to my chair, dear."

"Maybe you should lie down."

"When I just got up?" Dominika scoffed. But her weight rested on Eden as they moved into the living room toward the big window and Dominika was breathing in short, starved gasps when they reached the chair.

Alarmed, Eden said, "I should call your doctor."

Dominika's hand lifted in a detaining motion. After a few minutes she was breathing more easily and gave Eden an amusedly affectionate smile. "My illness is mortality, child. No doctor can cure that. It's nothing to fear or lament." Her eyelids dropped. "The dreams I have now of Etchahoun, the cave and my loved ones are as real to me as you are. I am journeying into light and love. You must not be sad."

Eden turned her face away to hide sudden hot tears. "Call Joe," said Dominika. "Then sit near me and work. I like to watch you."

"Is *amona* sick?" Joe asked worriedly.

"No." Eden swallowed hard. "But she's weak and short of breath. You had better come. She might just slip away at any time."

"Have you called the doctor?"

"She doesn't want him. Joe, she *is* ninety-eight."

He sighed gustily. "True. All right. I can fly to Elko and be down in time for dinner. Are you calling Foss?"

"She doesn't want him."

"But—hell, he's her grandson!"

"And she loves him. She just doesn't want to wrangle anymore." When Joe was silent, Eden went on persuasively, "This isn't an official family gathering, Joe. There's no reason to call a busy senator away from Washington. A big row could push her over the edge. None of us wants that."

She could almost see Joe chew his fleshy underlip. "I guess you're right. Okay. See you tonight."

Eden had worked often while Dominika looked on, sometimes drowsing, but today she felt tension and found it hard to concentrate on her painting. Dominika's breath came so lightly that several times, glancing up, Eden's heart froze. Once the old woman was so still, her mouth slightly open, that Eden went over to watch for a pulse. When Dominika looked up at her, Eden flushed.

"Would you like some tea or chocolate?"

The excuse didn't fool Dominika. She smiled. "Chocolate would be nice. And maybe you would help me to the bathroom?"

Eden did so and they talked for a while before Estevannia brought the chocolate. Because moving about seemed to exhaust Dominika, Eden coaxed her to have a tray by the window but she refused.

"I have a long time to rest." Her eyes twinkled. "While you were off painting bristlecones, I saw my lawyer and the priest. I have no chores left to save myself for."

She ate sparingly but with appetite. "You make good bread, Estevannia," she told the housekeeper. "I hope you know that I enjoy and appreciate it every day even though I do not tell you so."

Estevannia stared at her mistress in surprise and with a certain fear. "But, andrea, one always has bread. It is nothing to thank for."

"But I do thank you." Dominika added some teasing words in Basque at which Estevannia laughed and shot back a retort, chuckling as she cleared the table.

"Do you want to rest now?" Eden asked, giving her arm to her hostess as they rose from the table.

"All I do is rest," grumbled Dominika. "I'll sit in my chair."

Her lips were pallid by the time Eden had her settled where she could look out across the green meadows to the mountains. "Trace says that this is how the grass used to look," she said when her breathing came more steadily. "Maybe he's right. Maybe we had too many cattle and then too many sheep. I never meant to harm the land." Her fingers gripped Eden's suddenly with surprising strength. "You will take back the blue bird?"

"Yes."

"Bring me the acorn beads and the old prayerbook. They were my grandmother's. I would like to hold them."

Eden brought the use-polished rosary and the sheepskin-covered little book. Dominika took them and caressed the beads. "Are you tired, Eden, or will you paint some more?" Eden was tired but since she did not want to leave Dominika alone, she slipped on her paint-smeared smock and went back to the easel.

She was painting a bristlecone, yet as she worked, the tree and Dominika seemed to merge until the tree was the woman and the woman the tree, stretching wounded yet enduring arms to sun and sky.

This was the tree that would hang from now on at the head of Eden's bed, a Tree of Life, the eternal loving and living spirit of Dominika worked into its weathered grandeur. Never had Eden worked with such sureness and absorption, the vision a rapt communion between her and the weary, magnificent woman in the chair.

When Trace and Julian came in, both women roused. Eden hastily put away her supplies and changed her clothes for dinner. She was numb with weariness and yet unspeakably grateful for the afternoon. Glories had fused. She had been privileged to catch some of that. Now Dominika would be with her always.

Joe arrived as they were sitting down to dinner. The presence of Julian and Trace had brightened Dominika and she said a few Basque words of blessing over the food in a resonant voice. She ate little, though she sipped more wine than Eden had ever known her to drink.

It seemed to give her strength and ease her breathing to laugh gaily and coquette with Julian as if they were young lovers. Joe sent a puzzled glance at Eden, who could only reply with a slight lift of her shoulder. Maybe all that Dominika needed was to have Julian close by, adding a little gentle excitement.

After supper she proposed *muz*. Her cards were unbeatable and finally she yawned, laughing at them all. "Winning from the lot of you doesn't take much tonight," she said. "Julian, love, give me another glass of wine and then I'll go to sleep."

Joe groaned. "What will you take to come deal for me, *amona*? No one would ever suspect such a sweet lady of being a cardsharp!"

He and Trace both kissed her good-night before she moved off on Julian's arm, casting triumphantly delighted looks back at them. She paused by Eden's picture, still standing on the easel, and gazed at it.

"Why, I'm the tree," she said slowly. Her eyes shone and she embraced Eden. "Good-night, my daughter." They kissed before she moved back to Julian and he took her down the hall.

Eden followed. She was spent from the almost mystical intensity of that day's work and did not want to talk to either Joe or

Trace. Now that Julian was with Dominika, she would leave as soon as she could.

That night Dominika's sleep deepened into death, so peacefully that Julian, who slept beside her, did not know. He simply woke to find her gone.

Eden, roused by his knock, was stunned even though she had been expecting it. Through her numb grief, she was glad that Julian and Trace were there and that Dominika had left them a happy memory of her last day.

When Eden tried to find something to say to Julian, who sat beside his dead wife and held her hand, he said huskily, "She was ripe. It was a good death." His voice choked off. He shook himself. "I can't believe she's really not going to wake up again but—will you call Foss and the doctor and whoever needs to know?"

Nodding, her throat filled with tears, Eden woke Joe and asked him to tell Trace. She went herself to tell Estevannia, who had just entered the kitchen.

The dark woman cried out, said something in Basque and then crossed herself as tears ran down her plump cheeks. "I will light the candles and dress her. She has a nice black outfit."

Eden shook her head. "No. Let's dress her in her festival clothes, those she wore back in her valley."

Estevannia looked scandalized. "But—she's a married woman. Old."

"Today she starts all over." When the housekeeper was still unconvinced, Eden said, "Ask Julian," and began to look for Foss's number in the small book beside the telephone.

"Have you called Joe?" he asked her after a moment's startled quiet.

"He's here."

"Oh? I suppose Julian's been sent for."

"He's here, too."

Foss's laugh sounded like a bark. "Everyone's there but me, right?"

She gripped the phone, determined not to fight with him. "After all, Foss, you are in Washington."

"Was my grandmother sick? Did anyone see this coming?"

Parrying without falsehood, Eden said, "Dominika has been tired but what can you expect? Last night we played *muz* and she beat us all."

"I have a meeting I can't miss but I'll be there tonight. I suppose you'll have to take her to Elko for embalming."

"I don't know. Julian hasn't decided about all that."

"I'll call right before I leave here. See you soon." He hung up.

Eden phoned the doctor and returned to Dominika's room.

Dominika had long ago told Julian that she wished to be buried next to Kattalin in the wrought-iron-fenced ranch cemetery on the side of the mountain. Joe drove Julian, Estevannia and Eden into town behind the hearse while Trace took the camp-tender out to replace Koni so that the long-time herder might attend the funeral.

Hundreds of people came to honor Dominika as she lay in her festival garments, candles burning on four sides, the acorn rosary in her hands. It was only as the mourners spoke their memories that Eden learned how many people Dominika had aided, especially mothers without husbands, women who had to make a living for their children.

At least a score of such women, many now grandmothers, told Julian how Dominika had given them encouragement and funds with which to learn skills that made them self-supporting. She had been godmother to the children of her married herders and to all she had given scholarships or a start in whatever work interested them.

Foss stayed at the funeral home most of the time and though Eden knew he grieved for his grandmother, she also suspected that he was deliberately garnering political benefit from her popularity. After the funeral service, only the family, Koni, Estevannia and Eden followed the hearse to the old cemetery, where the Basque priest said a last blessing.

When they returned to the house, Foss poured a stiff drink, tossed it down and took another, looking from Joe to Trace to Julian. "Who has got a copy of the will?"

Julian stiffened. "Mr. McElroy said he'd be out tomorrow to read it and answer any questions."

"I'm a lawyer myself," Foss snorted. "I sure don't need that hick McElroy to explain a document. Aren't you an executor, Julian?"

"Yes."

"Well, don't you have the will?"

Trace cut in, eyes glinting. "Look here, Foss, if you can't wait for McElroy, you can stop in town and get a copy but don't hassle Julian."

Foss shrugged. "I can wait. Just thought we might start negotiating what you and Joe will want for your shares in the ranch."

"Aren't you assuming a lot?" Trace asked dryly.

Coloring, Foss glanced at Julian. "No offense, Julian, but I'd understood that you told *amona* you didn't want to take charge and that the ranch should go to her blood heirs."

"I didn't say anything about who should get it," Julian said grimly. "Just that it shouldn't be me."

Foss turned up his hands. "Well, then?"

"Well?" shot back Trace.

"Name a price and I'll see what I can do for you."

There was a cutting edge to Trace's laugh. "If *amona* split the ranch in the way you think she did, I need to know what the two of you want for your interests."

Foss sputtered on his drink. Eyes narrowing, he heaved an exasperated sigh. "Can't you get it through your head? This ranch is in the way of the MX."

"With all the Federal land in Nevada, the MX can scrape along."

Foss glowered. "It's an important gesture, to show my belief in the program."

"A gesture?" Trace was on his feet like an uncoiled spring. "You'd wreck this place as a *gesture?*"

Green eyes clashed with gray.

"Fellas!" Joe begged nervously.

Finishing his whisky, Foss said deliberately, "If the ranch's grazing leases are canceled, you couldn't stay in the stock-raising business."

Trace shrugged. "This will surprise the hell out of you but I've never intended to stay in it."

Foss's jaw dropped. "You don't? How will you make a living?"

"By doing what I trained for. Being a range management consultant."

"Then why," demanded Foss as if talking to a madman, "do you want the ranch?"

"To live on. To bring back the grass the way it used to be. I might run just enough mohair goats to keep the grass trimmed."

"I bet you never told *amona* that."

"You bet I did. The land needs a rest. I argued her down to ten thousand sheep but there she stuck."

When Trace started for the door, Foss blocked his way. "We might as well settle some basics right now."

"I've said all I'm going to until we hear the will."

Foss's hands clenched but he moved out of Trace's path. Julian muttered something distractedly and went into Dominika's room. Distressed by the quarrel and intent now on preparing to leave as soon as possible, Eden started down the hall.

"Just a minute," Foss called.

She turned questioningly.

Glancing at Joe, who reddened and looked miserable, Foss strode to her. "Joe tells me that he was asked to come down. Trace went up the mountain after Julian. It sounds to me, my dear, as though you knew damned well my grandmother was on the brink, yet chose to leave me uninformed."

"She asked me to call Joe."

Foss's eyes dilated. "And she didn't ask for me?"

"Foss, for heaven's sake—" Joe began. Foss cut him off with a wave. "Well, Eden?"

"You have to believe that there wasn't any conspiracy. She had been weak but on that last day she actually seemed to be feeling better."

Hard fingers clamped on Eden's wrist. "Still, when she wanted Joe, didn't it occur to you to call me?" When Eden did not answer, his grip tightened painfully. "Did Trace or Julian tell you to skip me? Did they?"

"You've had too much to drink." Eden tried to wrench free.

Foss dragged her back. "I'm going to find out," he grated, "so you might as well tell me."

Angered, Eden blazed, "All right, she didn't want you! She said you were too busy to come but it was clear that she didn't want you bullying her."

He looked ready to hit her but Joe, who had jumped up and come across to them, caught his arm. "Foss! Lay off Eden. She's been wonderful company to *amona* this summer."

A kind of shudder went through Foss. "I'm sorry, Eden. I guess I shouldn't be surprised. But I—I loved her."

He obviously did, yet Eden believed that he would have wrangled with Dominika on her deathbed if it would have cleared the way for his ambitions.

Baffled, yet strangely sorry for him, Eden said awkwardly, "Foss, she loved you, too." Then she went to her room and the task of readying her paintings for shipment.

Next morning Julian asked Eden to go through Dominika's things and decide what, if anything, should be kept. Most of her clothes, he thought, could go to Estevannia's family but Eden was welcome to anything she might want. It turned out to be simple. In the big chest there was a note saying that the bride and baby clothes were to be saved for family keepsakes, along with the old prayerbook, family pictures and Kattalin's festival clothes. Estevannia was to have Dominika's clothing and any personal things that she could use. By noon the sorting was over, the bed was neatly made and Eden had taken the blue bird to her own room.

Robert McElroy, a thin, freckled man with a brick-colored moustache and frizzy hair, arrived in time for lunch, during which he and Foss discussed politics. After the table was cleared, the lawyer moved his chair back a fraction and glanced around the table.

"If you're ready, I'll read Mrs. Matthews' will."

Eden's mind roved away from the legal terminology. She needed to copy the painting she had made on the last day that she had spent with Dominika and send it along with the book. She might as well mail the bulky package from Las Vegas when she drove there to catch a plane. And that reminded her that she had better phone the airlines and see about connections—

". . . to Eden Lowrie," droned McElroy.

She had not heard the sentence but from the way that Foss gasped and Joe stared, it must have been startling. Trace's gray eyes were unreadable and as cold as a frozen lake.

"What did you say?" she faltered.

Foss made a choking sound. Trace gave her a wintry smile. Joe rubbed his ear. McElroy cleared his throat. "I do give and bequeath the property known as Faraway Ranch, including all deeded land and leasing rights, the dwellings and other improvements, to Eden Lowrie."

She put out a hand. "But—that's impossible! I don't—"

The lawyer ignored her. "It is my wish that my grandson, Tracy Steele, remain in charge of ranch management at his present salary. Estevannia Lerua shall be given a home for life and the sum of ten thousand dollars when my estate is settled, with a salary or the sum of twenty-five thousand dollars should she choose to leave upon my death."

Koni was to have the sheep. Joe received an office building in Reno, and Foss and Trace were given assorted bonds and securities. Julian was granted a lifetime right to use the house or build another.

Eden's brain abstractly took in the information but she could not grasp the meaning of the bequest that still electrified the men at the table. They regarded her with amazement; only Julian, after his first shock, was faintly smiling.

"Are there any questions?" McElroy asked when he had finished.

"Maybe later," Foss said. "For now we had better just let it all soak in."

McElroy nodded. "In case it should come up," he said diffidently, "let me state that when Mrs. Matthews made this will, she was in full command of her faculties. I did—uh—go over the implications carefully with her. This is what she wanted."

Rising, he shook hands with the men, bowed to Eden as he favored her with a puzzled stare and was escorted to the door by Julian. As the cousins watched her, Eden felt her face heating.

"I—I'm just as surprised as you are," she blurted.

"I'll bet!" Rasping back his chair, Trace towered over her. "Well, boss lady, you can start looking for a new manager."

"Trace," Julian began but his grandson brushed past him, stalking out the door.

Feeling accused and miserable, Eden said, "I don't want the ranch! Dominika never—"

Julian's hand dropped on her shoulder. "Dominika had her reasons. Don't do anything in a big rush. Just think about it."

Joe chuckled. "*Amona* must have been tired of listening to all of our plans for the ranch. I guess this was her way of showing us."

Foss said nothing but Eden felt his gaze as she stood up and hurried to her room.

X

JULIAN AND TRACE drove out to the camp in the afternoon to tell Koni of his inheritance. Since Joe had gone back to Reno, only Foss and Eden sat down to dinner.

"I'm sorry that I blasted you because *amona* chose not to send for me," he said, giving her a frank smile. "That hurt." He shook his head with rueful amusement. "She was so proud of me when I followed Dad in the Senate. And it wasn't easy. Even though he had blazed the way, there were plenty of my fellow Western congressmen who called me the Basco or the sheepherder senator and liked to ask whether I had any favorite ewes."

"Foss!"

He laughed and raised his wineglass. "Anyway, Eden, forgive my outburst. Congratulations on your inheritance."

"I don't see how you can mean that."

"Oh, I can mean the congratulations though I haven't in the least changed my plans." His eyes held hers. "I still want you but I suppose that even brand-new heiresses are wary of proposals. I'll ask you again after you've decided to accept a handsome sum for the ranch."

As soon as she returned from the Basque country, she was going to transfer the ranch to Trace. She had, that afternoon, written to Earth Heritage's director to explain that Trace's plans for the land would meet with the approval of Heritage and there was no need for the organization to use its resources in managing it. She still did not understand Dominika's will; perhaps she had hoped that leaving Eden the ranch would compel Trace to work with Eden and that gradually that would melt away his distrust.

Yes, that was it. Dominika had thought this a way to ensure herself of great-grandchildren who would inherit both the ranch and the spiritual legacy that she had entrusted to Eden. It had certainly not been her intent to dispossess Trace. She just hadn't realized the depth of his hostility toward women.

Eden could not contend with that sort of mistrust, nor did she mean to discuss with Trace her plan of returning the land to him, convinced that Dominika had actually wished him to have it. Nor did she expect the transfer to bring about an understanding between herself and Trace. Even should he feel briefly apologetic, she was bitterly angry at his assumption that she had influenced Dominika to make the astounding bequest.

Finding a certain balm in Foss's admiration, Eden smiled at him although she shook her head. "Foss, I'm not going to sell the ranch any more than Dominika was."

His eyes darkened. "My dear, you won't have much choice."

"No?"

"No. I've convinced the key people. Hell, all anyone has to do is look at the map! I didn't want to pressure *amona* though the time was coming when I would have had to."

"I suppose you'll try to get the land through eminent domain."

"There's no higher use than national security."

"I call MXs more of a national hazard."

He shrugged. "Nevertheless." His gaze traveled caressingly from her mouth to her throat. "Don't fight me on this, Eden. I'm going to win."

Shock went through her as if he had touched her naked flesh. Her blood seemed thick, heavily weighted. "Sweet Eden," he said in a deeply vibrant tone, "we don't agree on the MX but there are lots of issues that I could help you with, provide entree, work for conservation measures, which, generally, you must know that I do support." He grinned, closing his well-kept hands over hers. "Of course, I want you to love me for my own sake but it can't hurt to point out the fringe benefits."

She managed a cool smile that belied the speeding of her pulse as his fingers gently fondled her hands. "There's not much point to conservation if we're to have nuclear leaks and ra-

diation while targeting Russia with super-missiles the Soviets
will have to react against.''

He released her. His mouth thinned. ''We have to be
armed. I'm convinced that MXs are the way.''

''And I'm convinced that they're disastrous. That doesn't
leave us much meeting ground, does it?''

She rose and so did he. ''There's one meeting ground
where we'd be spectacular,'' he said, his manner charming
again. ''Where's your dedication, darling? Maybe a night with
you would change my mind.''

Urgent magnetism coursed between them. She stepped
back quickly, fearing what might happen should he take her in
his arms. ''I think we both know better,'' she said with a lightness that she didn't feel.

Before he could close the space between them, she escaped
into the kitchen to help Estevannia.

Foss's determination in the matter of the MXs made one
change in her plans. When she phoned next day for reservations, she routed herself to Washington. Right now, before
Foss's scheme went any further, she wanted to serve notice that
the Department of Defense was not going to get the ranch without a public battle and plenty of withering publicity.

She could count on Earth Heritage's Washington staff for
advice and she would talk to Toby, their lobbyist, as well as try
to see the men whom Foss had brought to the Basque Festival—
Donald Selwyn of the Department of Defense and General Bixby
Scott from the Pentagon.

Foss left next morning after telling Eden that he'd be back in
a few weeks to ''work something out.'' She didn't tell him she
was going to Washington and Spain, thinking that the less he
knew about her plans, the better.

It was necessary that she speak to Trace, though. When he
returned from seeing Koni and taking Julian up the mountain,
she expected that he'd come to the house for dinner. But he did
not. After much hesitation Eden nerved herself to go out and
knock on his door.

''Why don't you just barge in?'' he asked truculently as he
eyed her through the screen. ''After all, it's your property.''

She'd be damned if she would fight with him. Remaining on the porch, she said frigidly, "Dominika had something she wanted done back in her home valley. I'm going to take care of it right away. In fact, I'm leaving for Spain tomorrow. I hope that you have enough concern for the ranch to stay here and look after things till I get back."

"When will that be?"

"Oh, ten days maybe. While I'm there, I want to see the cave paintings."

"I guess I can do that."

"Thanks."

She turned to leave, stiff-shouldered. His voice stopped her. "Are you going to turn the place over to your precious Earth Heritage?"

"No. I've already written to the director, telling him that the way in which the place will be managed makes a guardian group unnecessary."

His mouth quirked. "Just can't resist being a big rancher, can you? It's what I've always thought about people like you. You howl about preserving the wilderness and public lands because you don't have any of your own."

Flayed by the contempt in his voice and eyes, she said with poisonous sweetness, "Now that you don't, either, let's see what you do!"

Spinning on her heel, she marched back to the house to pack.

"Does Foss know that you're in town?" Donald Selwyn fidgeted in the big chair beneath the medallion of the Department of Defense, smoothing back his thin gray hair. "Maybe we could have lunch and discuss this in—uh—more relaxed surroundings."

"Your office is just fine," Eden assured him. "After all, my message is short and plain."

His tight smile showed his narrow teeth. "But, Miss Lowrie, Foss is eager to prove his support for the missiles by turning over the old home ranch to accommodate them. That has real drama, patriotism—"

"The ranch is no longer even potentially Foss's to give up."

Eden rose to her feet. "I've seen the Director of Earth Heritage and he already has the promise of several other leading environmental groups to help make this situation a showdown that will receive international publicity. I'll go to jail before I allow a missile to cross that land, and I won't be alone."

"I think we have jails big enough to hold you."

"We'll see about that," Eden said. "Good-day, Mr. Selwyn."

Her next call was on General Bixby Scott, who beamed upon her and reminisced about the festival. His jovial red face congealed when she told him why she was there.

He reached for a phone. "Hold on, just let me call Foss. He hasn't said anything about this."

"I'm saving him the trouble. He may think he can change my mind, General, but I promise you he can't."

Heavy, hair-tufted fingers tapped the polished desk. "Foss is a capable and ambitious man, Miss Lowrie. You can create a stink but he'll win. The country's defense comes before personal concerns."

"Defense? When there's no feasible way of basing MXs so the Soviets can't destroy them?" Eden could not keep the stinging scorn from her voice. "Tell me, General Scott, didn't the Joint Chiefs of Staff publicly oppose the current basing plan?"

"There are a few kinks to work out but we need the MX."

"I think it's the last thing we need."

He sneered. "Since when did artists become weapons experts?"

"No one has to be an expert to see the suicidal folly of upping the nuclear ante. I'm not half as scared of Russia as I am of us."

"You sound like a left-over flower child from the sixties," he said in a bored voice.

"And then we have the people who never learned anything from that decade."

He eyed her with distaste. "All you can do is embarrass Foss and prevent his appointment as Secretary of Defense."

She laughed. "General, I can do better than that."

Dismissing her, he reached for a stack of notes. "I have an appointment," he said without rising.

"Thank you for your time," she said politely.

As she walked to the door, she felt his eyes following her and she knew that this time he was not watching her legs but viewing her as a problem. She was also willing to bet that by now Foss knew that she was in Washington. But she would be out of her hotel and headed for the airport before he could start to track her down.

From Madrid she flew to Bilbao and caught the train to Gernika. On several occasions she had seen Picasso's mural of the city's destruction when the painting had hung in New York's Museum of Modern Art. Strange that since it had been returned to Spain, it hung in the Prado rather than being displayed in the ancient town that it commemorated.

Only part of the trunk was left of the old tree that had shaded Jaun Zuria, de Haro and all the lords and ladies of Vizcaya, including Isabela, unlucky Don Carlos and the first and last president of Euzkadi, who had taken his oath only six months before Fascist planes wrecked the city. Although the ancient oak had miraculously survived the bombing, time had claimed it and now one of its descendants stood proudly before the graceful memorial building.

As she explored the little town, Eden tried to imagine it as it would have been when Dominika last saw it, over eighty years ago. Bicycles and cars had replaced ox-carts and donkeys but many of the older women wore black, and berets were as common as hats. Boys were playing *pelota* and the market square was jammed with booths and carts offering everything for sale from espadrilles to round cheeses.

The owner of the small hotel where she was spending the night had been a herder in Nevada and he knew of Dominika. When he learned that Eden wished to visit Dominika's former village, he said that his nephew lived in the valley, was in town for market and would be glad to take Eden with him when he returned to the village next day. There was a comfortable inn and the nephew could help her find a guide if she needed one.

By the time she had a light meal, it was six in the evening in Gernika but her internal clock insisted that, even by Washington time, it was eleven and she had not really slept on the night flight crossing the Atlantic.

With the innkeeper's assurance that she would be called in plenty of time to leave with his nephew, Eden went upstairs and to bed.

There were mountains, just as in Nevada, but they were luxuriantly green except for the lower slopes, where stone-walled fields made patches of various colors. From Dominika's account Eden had expected to see lots of apple trees. There were some, heavy with ripening fruit, but there were far more compactly grown pine lots.

"Sometimes owners rent out the farm and arable land but put the rough land into pine and get the price of that when it matures," explained Lencho Seseta, a long-headed young man with large, reddish ears that poked out from under his beret. He spoke English, having spent three years in Idaho. When he could not think of a word, he used Spanish. "About the only ones who make a living from a farm now are those who have dairies. Most of the men have jobs at the marble quarry or the sawmills or a factory in town. Women and youngsters do most of the farm work."

"I don't see many sheep."

Lencho sighed as he swung his truck around a faggot-laden donkey. "My grandmother remembers when nearly every household had fifteen or twenty sheep grazing on the commons. Few people keep sheep now. But we fatten pigs and most of us have a few cows. At our farm we have a dairy. I lease the meadows of two neighbors who have moved to town to work but hope to save enough to move back someday." He laughed dourly. "Used to be it was good and proud to be the heir. These days it's often the least capable child who's willing to stay on the farm."

"My friend's farmstead was called Etchahoun," Eden said. "Your uncle thinks that the house was never rebuilt after the bombing."

Lencho shrugged. "There's just a pile of rocks and the corner of a stone tower left. The oldest grandson of Esteban, who was killed there, was in the army at the time. After he came back, he sold the land to the Bigatzis, who farm it now.''

To the family of that Nicolas whom Dominika had refused to marry? ''But the *sepulturie?*'' Eden demanded. ''Don't those go with the farmstead?''

''They're supposed to,'' Lencho frowned. ''But the Bigatzis didn't need it. So now it's just used for anyone whose family has no *sepulturie* of its own. People didn't like the way the whole thing was done. They thought that Esteban's grandson, Koni, who had gone to America, should have been given a chance at the farm, or your friend, Dominika, the daughter of Maria. Esteban wasn't even from this valley. But it was done fast and quiet and you know how that is—what's everyone's business is no one's.''

The valley had widened. A church spire rose above the other buildings. The ball court was still at one side of it but the village now had a town hall, a school, a doctor's clinic and a cluster of shops, an inn, a restaurant and several taverns.

Lencho pulled up in front of the inn and carried in Eden's light canvas bag. Since he refused payment for the ride, she asked him to wait for a minute and she dashed into a wine-seller's, returning with a bottle of Izarra, which he did accept.

''If you need to be driven anywhere, just let me know,'' he said.

Eden thanked him, registered, unpacked and went out to explore the village.

In the cemetery she found Maria's headstone and those of her two husbands. Here were Cristóbal Urdin, Marya and Ruy Narvarte, the aged stone of Engrâce and that of Lael, she who had been rescued from unblessed ground by her *serora* daughter, Kattalin.

Eden intended to burn candles for all of them, as well as for Dominika and her dead daughters, but she wanted first to change from her pants suit to a skirt and find a headcovering in one of the shops. She would do that tomorrow.

The village had sprawled until, at its outskirts, Eden could see a slope covered with a mass of weed-grown rubble and a ruined wall. Her heart pounded as she took the narrow road leading up to it and her scalp prickled as she recognized an over-grown mound beneath an ancient tree stump. Abram's tomb.

She glanced toward the trees that obscured the rocky sides of the mountains. Although Dominika had given her careful directions, it might take considerable exploration to find the right cave. Till now the tradition had seemed like a myth but suddenly it was becoming unbearably real.

For a long time Eden stood beside what had been Etcha-houn, the Good House. In her mind she recreated the big kitchen and hearth, the stairs leading to *sala* and bedrooms, the ox-byre and storage rooms. Wonderingly she touched the an-cient stones, all that was left of the *dorrea* that had been a prison to Lael after the roses and palaces of Cordova.

This was where Dominika had grown up, listening to the birds singing under the house tiles of a morning; where, except for Esteban, she would have raised her family. Instead she had gone to America with only a prayerbook, a rosary and the blue-bird shard for comfort.

Eden wandered to the spring from which generations of women had fetched water, and knelt among the grass and flow-ers to drink thirstily of the clear, sweet water.

Cattle were grazing in the meadows where once a splendid white Arab had pastured. Eden stepped in the timeless though invisible footprints of all those women of whom she had been told, the ancestresses whose hands would speak to her when she found the cave.

Time seemed to waver. She felt that Dominika was with her, not in sadness but in assurance that what remained was ages older than Etchahoun itself and could not be destroyed. When Eden lit her candles, she would burn one for this vanished house as well as for its people.

Then she allowed herself one small thievery. From an apple tree near the spring she took a firm, ripe apple, which she en-joyed right down to the core.

"As any daughter of Eve should do."

Starting guiltily, she whirled toward the voice before she could identify it. With his head on one side, hands in his pockets, Foss stood smiling at her.

XI

HE CHOSE an apple and tasted it as sensuously as if it had been Eden's body. "Some rusty old priest declared centuries ago that the Basque country was deep in apple trees and all the women had eaten of the fruit," he teased. "May I hope that the stolen apple signals a change in your heart?"

She could not tell him that to her it had been a sacrament, an earthy, good-tasting one. "How did you know I was here?"

"Well, of course both Bixby and Selwyn called me the minute you left their offices. When you proved to have checked out of the hotel, all I had to do was phone the ranch. Estevannia told me you were bound for my grandmother's valley in some promised act of piety." He fell in step beside her. "I've always meant to visit this place and I decided that I'd never again have such good company."

"You must be furious about my meetings with your friends."

"I hope you'll see the light, of course."

She stopped. "Foss, there's no use. MXs will never be housed on that land as long as I can do anything about it."

He gave her a searching look, shook his head and said resignedly, "Look, let's forget about that for now and enjoy the next couple of days." His eyes danced. "We could pretend it was a honeymoon, you know. Or even make it a real one."

Puzzled but relieved that he seemed intent on a holiday rather than harassing her, Eden said, "All right. Let's go to the church and burn candles for your family."

"Lunch first," insisted Foss.

He had a broiled lobster. Eden chose an omelette flavored

with red and green peppers and they both had wine. He found a beret in a little shop where she located a black mantilla with which she covered her head after changing into a skirt. They bought several loaves of bread in the bakery before going to the church.

It was so dark inside that it was several minutes before they saw the black-garbed old woman who was mopping the floor. There were long pews on one side of the aisle and on the other cloths were spread on the floor, most of them with two candle-sticks, some with half a dozen or more. Chairs stood at the foot of several of the *sepulturie*.

The old woman stared at Eden's proffered loaves and spoke in Basque. "She says that no one brings bread anymore," Foss said. "Not since bread was rationed during the war."

He talked for a few minutes and then handed the woman an amount of money that made her wrinkled old face broaden in a smile. Briskly she spread a fresh cloth on one of the *sepulturie*, brought six brass candlesticks and set candles in them. Graciously she stepped back, motioning that Eden could put the loaves down if she wished.

Eden gently placed the loaves and lit the candles, kneeling on the stones as Dominika had done before her. Although she had no formal religious background she prayed for Dominika's peace and silently remembered those who were gone and those yet to be born.

At last she rose. Foss had been kneeling in one of the pews. He gave the old woman a number of bills, thanked her and smiled at Eden as they emerged into the daylight.

"She'll light candles at each anniversary of Grandmother's death. Her mother was a girlhood friend of Dominika's." He laughed. "And she will enjoy your bread. That job doesn't pay much."

It was surely a far cry from the time when the *serora* had been considered almost a priestess. Perhaps the wonder was that so much persisted.

They sat on a bench next to one that was occupied by five elderly men and watched the boys play handball, each young-ster doubtless envisioning himself as a future world champion.

Foss had rented a car in Bilbao and now he suggested a drive up the valley. The fields were green, tidy and charming, yet after the American West, the countryside seemed to be modeled on a miniature scale—except for the majestic mountains, some so high they reared into the clouds.

"I wonder if we Basques really are directly descended from the people who did the cave paintings," Foss mused. "Probably we'll never know for sure but it's certain that we were here at the latest by three thousand B.C."

"Oh," Eden teased, "I think you must at the minimum lay claim to speaking the language shared by all peoples before the Tower of Babel."

"The language of Eden?" chuckled Foss. "At least one geneticist thinks that the earliest European race had no blood-type B and a high Rh negative factor. This would tie in with the fact that the Basques have the world's highest occurrence of Rh negative and the lowest of blood-type B."

"You wonder if you date back to the caves," Eden laughed. "I don't even know who my parents were."

"We're both here now, which is what matters." He nodded toward the distance, where the closer ranges faded into purple peaks. "How's about a little exploring tomorrow?"

"I'm not a real climber."

"You're not? You, the great wilderness trekker?"

"It's disgraceful," she admitted, "but heights turn me to jelly. Count me out of anything that calls for ropes or pitons."

"We don't have to get into anything technical. It would just be sort of fun to go up some of the trails that my great-great-greats did when they hustled sheep to summer pasture."

"Maybe we could go to Mari's cave."

He frowned, then apparently remembered and laughed. "Sure. If people trudged there on every Day of the Holy Cross, I reckon we can make it. We'll take lunch and make a day of it."

"Tomorrow?"

He patted back a yawn. "The day after? I want to sleep late tomorrow and whip this jet-lag."

"Fine," said Eden, surprised and pleased that he was proving so amiable. His use of Basque when asking questions had a disarming effect on people and made her feel less an interloper.

She did not delude herself that they wouldn't have an all-out struggle back in the States but for now he offered a truce she was glad to accept.

If only he were Trace.

She steeled herself against a rush of longing. When she returned, together they would have to plan strategy against Foss's MX plans but after that was settled, she would collect her things and leave. She hoped that he would be at least slightly ashamed when he discovered that she had not coveted his home.

Anyway, she would take with her the best painting that she had ever done, where woman and tree merged into one. She had known both Dominika and bristlecones. That was worth some pain.

Foss excused himself shortly after dinner. Eden's sense of time had not adjusted sufficiently to dispose her to stay up much later, and the golden Izarra, redolent of Pyrenean herbs and flowers, made her even drowsier. Her room was fitted with a wash basin and she took a sponge bath rather than use the communal bath down the hall.

If Foss was sleeping in tomorrow, she would start her search for the summer cave. She believed that Dominika would somehow know and be glad when the shard was restored at last to its proper place.

She dreamed of Dominika that night but there was no fear or strangeness in it. A deep communion flowed between them as Dominika told her many wonderful, wise things. *I have to remember all this when I wake up*, Eden thought in her dream. When she woke, she did not remember but she retained a sense of having shared with the old woman she had so loved many lives and many times.

Be with me today, she silently asked Dominika before she dressed and went down to breakfast.

The innkeeper assured her that the forested stretches beyond the fields that reached up the mountain were part of the commons, open to everyone for gathering nuts or the bracken used instead of straw in mangers. She could take any of the roads that led past farmsteads up into the trees and have no fear of trespass.

His wife packed a generous lunch of cheese, bread, quince loaf, salted almonds and a flask of aged cider, which she said was made by the Bigatzis from the apples of Etchahoun. Eden had brought a small daypack into which she tucked the carefully wrapped blue bird, a candle and matches. Her flashlight would have been easier but modern light was unknown in the cave. To use it now would seem impious. Lacing up her light hiking boots, she slipped on her jacket and pack and started out.

The simplest thing was to go by way of Etchahoun, reach the trees and then explore toward the right until she found the grotto, an opening so small that few people would bother to enter. The whole Basque region was full of caves, many known to contain paintings, so it was not remarkable that an insignificant aperture had been ignored.

Eden gently touched the rocks on Abram's grave, sending her thoughts to him through time, drank sparkling water at Etchahoun's spring and followed the rutted tracks that led to the trees. From here she could see scars of limestone-quarrying along the cliffs and her heart sank.

What if the cave had been destroyed?

Only one area had been disturbed, though. Eden wandered along, visualizing the generations of women who had come this way. Long after the painter there must have been priestesses, women who became *seroras* after the Christian faith changed the old shrines into churches. The women before doughty old Engrâce seemed to Eden to melt into antiquity, surviving only as keepers of the secret.

Was this the end of it? Even if there were someday a great-granddaughter of Dominika's blood to know the story, would she care? To a child brought up in a land half a world away, how could the remote cave have a vital meaning, provide sanctuary and retreat?

The first cavern that Eden noticed was too large, the next too shallow. The third could not have been entered by any creature larger than a cat. Eden sighed, halted and searched the face of the overgrown cliff. According to Dominika, it was about a half-hour's walk from the house. Therefore it couldn't be much farther. If she didn't glimpse it soon, she would double back and go over the likely stretches again. A bush or tree might easily hide the entrance.

Scanning the rocks more closely, she went on for ten minutes before deciding that she had gone past the site. She worked her way back, staying close to the base of the gray bluffs and peering behind any sizable shrub or vine mass that might disguise an opening.

Here and there she clambered over rock falls broken off by time and weather. Suppose one of them had sealed the entrance? In a way it would be fitting that Dominika be the last woman in the cave—but Eden fervently wished to return the little bird.

She stripped off her jacket, put it in the pack and took a refreshing drink of cider. The sun was climbing toward noon. Foss should be up by now. He would be curious about what she was doing that morning but "taking a walk" could cover any undertaking. She desperately hoped that she could find the cave today; getting away from him later might be a problem.

Shrugging into the pack, she moved along carefully and then caught her breath as from a side angle she saw a hole that was concealed by low-growing laurels. Hurrying forward, she bent and pushed back the limbs. The opening was round, large enough to admit a crawling body.

It had to be Dominika's cave.

The pack would not fit. She took out her jacket, the bird, the candle and matches and stuffed the pack under the laurels. She put the shard in her jacket pocket along with the matches.

Inside, she was blinded after the sunlight but the smell, although pungent, was not unpleasant. The earth was fine dust on top of rock, cool and silken to her hands. After a moment the passage grew larger, just as Dominika had said it would.

Eden's hands trembled as she rose, struck a match against another and lit the tall white candle. The mellow light showed streaks of black and green on the walls and lit up the entrance lying ahead. Eden took out the shard as if it were her entitlement.

Dominika, be with me now.

Almost holding her breath, she passed into the chamber, where she cried out with wonder as hundreds of earth-red hands flickered, beckoning to her. There was the archaic mother, the smiling child on her lap reaching for the flying birds, the eternally green tree above them. And there was the place from where the blue bird had fallen, who knew in what millenium?

The Cave of Always Summer.

Studying the hands, Eden looked for and found the poignant small hand of Kattalin pressed over Engrâce's big one, with exiled Lael's nearby. She could only guess at the others, only wonder which had been Dominika's. But she felt moved by some spell of the place to set her hand over one of the palmprints and close her eyes, linking herself for an indescribable time with women who now were spirit.

She frowned as she noticed that part of the roof had fallen along one side and other ledges seemed to be split, ready to separate. The entrance might well have been blocked. But it wasn't. The blue bird was home now. All she had to do was put it on the niche beside the mother, close to the baby's hand.

She wedged the candle into a crevice, unwrapped the shard and nestled it in her hands for a moment. It was the most precious thing, by any standard, that she would ever hold again. And she might well be the last person who would ever see it, who would ever behold this place.

Awed, she knelt and put the bright little bird on the rock from which Dominika had taken it eighty years ago.

It was done.

Rising, she was reaching for the candle when a voice said from the opening, "So this was your errand."

Foss stood there, the beam of a powerful flashlight glancing harsh over the hands that seemed to shrink from the assault. Striking mother and child, the beam was an attack—male desecration, unspeakable sacrilege.

"Very pretty," he commented. "*Amona* never mentioned this when she told us stories of Mari and Basa Jaun."

"You should not be here!"

His teeth flashed. "But I am."

There was suddenly a gun in his hand. "It would have been easy for you to slip and fall in the mountains. That was what I had planned. But this is a better tomb for you, Eden."

Numb, she could only stare at him. Her lips seemed to

pucker strangely when at last she forced them to move. "If this is your idea of a joke—"

He shook his head regretfully. He had never been more handsome but the light turned his eyes to a green blaze like those of a cat come upon in darkness.

"I love you but I can't let you sabotage the defense of our country. I can still salvage things if you have an accident. Otherwise—" His voice broke off. "I'm sorry, darling. Very, very sorry."

The gun came up and leveled.

Eden ducked and sprang forward, powered by a volition that did not seem to be her own. She thrust the candle toward his eye as a shot exploded, reverberated, echoing in the labyinths of the cave.

Foss leaped back, shrieking as the hot wax of the candle seared his eye. As he lurched against the fallen rocks, trying to center the gun on Eden by the beam of the flashlight which had rolled across the ground, the sound that Eden had thought an echo of his shot suddenly increased, finally erupting into chaos.

Whether dislodged by the shot, his stumbling against the wall or some nameless inevitability, a ledge was crumbling. Fragments of rock fell around her, one cutting her cheek.

"Eden!" Foss cried, taking a blinded step toward her.

Without thinking, she started to reach out to him. A stone struck down her hand as the whole side of the wall enfolded him, a sharp edge almost severing his head from his body.

Choking, she ran out of the chamber as the internal avalanche gathered momentum, shaking the earth, spewing rock debris after her. She stumbled, lay in the dust for a moment and was trying to scramble up when the tunnel ahead darkened.

Was it blocked, too?

She gasped in dread. Then a light flicked on. It found her but she couldn't see who was behind it till the man was through the narrowing and came to stand erect.

"Trace!"

His breath caught jaggedly as he helped her to her feet. "What the hell are you doing? Blowing up the mountain?"

"Please, let's get out of here first!"

Outside, he tended her scratches while she explained what

had happened without divulging Dominika's secret, now sealed forever. "There's no use in trying to get Foss out," she said, shuddering. "His—his head was almost cut off."

She shook in nervous reaction while Trace sat in brooding silence.

"So he really tried to kill you?" Trace said at last. "He was crazy!"

"He had it pretty cleverly worked out." Eden controlled herself, drank thirstily of the cider and offered it to him. "Why in the world are you here? If you want to murder me too, you'll have to wait for another day."

He pulled her into his arms and kissed her in a way that left no doubt of why he had come, though as soon as he drew back, she touched his cheek and whispered, "Why?"

"Because I love you."

"You needn't sound so grim about it."

"It is grim. I had just about worked myself up to admit it when Grandmother's will hit me between the eyes. How could I propose after that? You'd think I was just trying to get the ranch."

"What changed your mind?"

"I missed you. I had to think of how it would be to never see you again. And I kept looking at that picture—*amona* as tree, tree as *amona*. No one could possibly paint such a magnificent thing and be a gold digger." He caressed her cheek, the curve of her throat and breast. "Marry me, sweetheart. I would like to manage the ranch but if you want to turn it over to that outfit of yours, I guess I can stand it. What I can't stand is not being with you."

"It just so happens that I am looking for a manager," she whispered. And then she was in his arms.

The police went up to the cave to investigate. They took Eden's testimony and then went their way. All the world had to know was that Faustin Uhalde, influential Nevada senator and top choice for the next Secretary of Defense, had been killed by a rockslide while vacationing in his ancestral homeland.

When they were finally alone, Eden and Trace walked slowly up to what remained of Etchahoun. Trace had explained to her that he had flown to Washington, hoping to catch her there, and learned from Foss's secretary that the senator had gone to Spain.

"I'm surprised you came," she thrust. "You must have thought that we were meeting over here."

Trace slipped her hand inside his shirt and held it over his heart. "I did think so. But who could blame you after the way I've acted? I decided to damn well find you, tell you how I felt and let you make up your own mind."

He took her in his arms. They made love beside the old wall in the last golden light of the sun. Their union was so deep, such an irrevocable mingling, that she was startled when Trace raised on one elbow to smooth her hair and ask, "Shall we be married here?"

"In a way we have been." She smiled at him, certain now that Dominika knew. "But let's get married on the mountain at the ranch so Julian can be there."

"That will be good."

They lay together on the sun-warmed earth, healed and peaceful, and as Eden looked past Trace toward the cave, she knew that the spirits there were joyful, giving their ancient blessings to her and her beloved.

GLOSSARY

aitona grandfather

alboka musical instrument made of two horns

almendrados almond cookies

Amerikanuak Basques who had worked in America or who stayed there.

amona grandmother

andrea pl. *andreak* lady or woman

ardiak pl. sheep

artu-emon donation for Masses; when accepted by a bereaved household, the bereaved household was supposed to return the donation when a member of the donor household died.

aur bazkaria infant's meal given by relatives of an *etcheko andrea* who has just had a baby, attended by all mistresses of households in the neighborhood.

Basa Andrea (or Mari) daughter of *Basa Jaun* but usually benevolent. Probably a mother goddess, Christianity changed her into the Queen of the Witches. There are Basques today who say their parents saw her in one guise or another.

Basa Jaun the Wild Man who sometimes joked with shepherds and sometimes ate them.

bertsulari quick-witted singers who often improvise stanzas till one or the other is vanquished.

chahakoa wineskin

chorizos sausages

churros coarse-wooled sheep brought from Spain to the New World; also a finger-length doughnut-type batter fried crisp.

dorrea pl. *dorreak* square stone house of medieval times

eltzekarea a stew, "everything in the pot"

eria the state of a sheep's becoming ill

errezelatu general term for sheep diseases that cause the animal to waste away *etcheko andrea*   mistress of the household and farmstead

etcheko jaun   master of the household and farmstead

etcheko primu   heir to the farmstead

ezpatadantzari pl. *ezpatadantzariak*   carefully trained Basque dancer; some dances are involved and difficult.

fuero   charter of rights granted by Spanish rulers to cities or provinces

Jaun Zuria   the White Lord; semi-legendary first Lord of Vizcaya

jota   Basque form of the Spanish fandango; *jota* is a Spanish term.

Lamiña pl. *Lamiñak*   generally benevolent sort of fairy-goblin, famous as builders, living in caves or beneath rivers. They do house and farm work if well fed.

llurun   earth's living breath

loriua   ground-floor space with a large arched entrance where threshing and such farm chores can be done under a roof.

makhila   shepherd's staff, often beautifully carved

muz   Basque card game

onrak   service for the dead held just before the principal funeral banquet

panash   half beer, half soda often served to women

parrokia   small village

pelota   ancient game of ball, once played with bare hand or a sort of glovelike leather scoop, now with a long curved basket called a *chistera.*

pelotari pl. *pelotariak*   *pelote* player

reata   cowboy's rope, often of braided leather

sala   living room or parlor

sanbenito   garment worn by the accused at an *auto da fé*

Señorío   the lords of Vizcaya

sepulturie   site on floor of church serving same function as a *yarleku;* household members weren't necessarily buried beneath.

serora   woman assistant to the priest and caretaker of the church who combined a sacristan's duties with leading the *etcheko andreak* of the parish in the rituals for the dead. Probably developed from early priestesshood.

yarleku pl. *yarlekuak*   sepulchral stone on floor of church beneath which members of a household used to be buried and where the mistress of that house lit candles and made offerings.

Zazpi Jautziak   a dance, "Seven Jumps," to commemorate the seven Basque provinces

zelauria   in a Basque house, a ground-floor area used to store fodder